the big D

Divorce Thru the Eyes of a Teen

Leaders Guide

Krista Smith

Typeset design by Jane Tokar

This curriculum is not intended to be used as a replacement for psychologists or other healthcare professionals. It is designed to be an additional resource to assist in the healing process. If further help is needed, please refer individuals to a psychologist or healthcare professional.

Printed in the United States of America.

Publishing services by AMFM Press, Arizona. The views expressed or implied in this work do not necessarily reflect those of AMFM Publishing.

ISBN: 978-0-9796620-5-8
LCCN 2010903786

Dedication

It is with great love and appreciation I dedicate this book to:

My Heavenly Father, my true source of healing who made my life complete again. It is only through His forgiveness we are able to look into His eyes and say "Abba Father".

The love of my life, my husband Jon. You held me up when I could not stand. You stick by me through thick and thin. You wipe away my every tear. You know my every thought. You see inside my heart even when my actions don't show it. You are my strength, my joy, my comfort, my leader, but most of all, my best friend. You have restored my faith to trust, taught me to rest in the comfort of your love, and have rekindled my joy to live. Thank you for always loving me and never giving up. It is only through your encouragement that this dream has come true.

My forever pride and joy, my children Brittany and Tyler, who have, because of my shortcomings, had to endure the pain and heartache of divorce. By grace you have loved me throughout and have found it in your hearts to forgive. No other parent could be more proud of the way you have traveled this road with grace and love and through it all kept your eyes upon our Savior. Everyday I thank my Heavenly Father for giving me the greatest treasure of all– YOU!

My enduring step children, Ella and Isaac, for loving and accepting me despite my continual mistakes and shortcomings. I may not have done it all right, but all I've done has been out of love. Thank you for finding room in your hearts and lives to love one more person.

This book was inspired by:

There is no greater pain than the pain of a child but no greater love than the love of a mother. It is through this endless amount of love I have been able to experience this heartache and allow God to truly make something beautiful out of the ashes of my life . This is my prayer for you.

Foreword

When I was asked to write the forward for "The Big D – Divorce Thru the Eyes of a Teen" curriculum, I felt a little overwhelmed; primarily because I thought "what can I add?" The heart and soul of Krista Smith, the author, bleeds forth in every page, every activity, and every idea. Her passion and love for the brokenhearted is demonstrated in each page and she makes it clear throughout the curriculum why "The Big D" is so critical for any young person to experience. This curriculum is another example of Krista's relentless search for meeting the needs and healing the hurts of those in the church and outside of it.

The teenage population is already an awkward stage of trying to find independence while simultaneously seeking belonging. Trust is such a critical piece of a teenager's relationship expectation, and the curriculum provides a format to develop a trusting relationship with the leader by providing fun, interactive times, as well as private times of introspection for a teen to reflect on the Lord's heart for them.

"The Big D" also meets the identity formation needs of a teen by providing a place to belong that is fun, and culturally relevant. There is information, but it is presented in an experiential learning format allowing the teen to independently articulate and process in their own way, the pain, sadness, and other feelings from their parent's divorce. It is easy to overlook the teenage population, sometimes they seem so mature and able to handle the pain, but we, as a church community, need to ensure that the next generation has an opportunity for a successful marriage. We can do this by providing a place and a format, for them to process their experience of the only marriage they have ever seen, that of their parents.

Krista has provided all the key ingredients essential to reaching a teenager experiencing divorce. Her labor of love is divinely inspired and now available for those who share her passion to reach teens. My hope and prayer is that every person who picks this curriculum up will identify with her heart of ministry and emphatically pursue utilizing "The Big D" curriculum in their church or community. The teenagers we reach need hope for a future; this is a great place to start.

In Christ,

Christine Meland MSW, L.G.S.W
Marriage Counselor, Family Educator, and Rule 114 Qualified Neutral

THE SLIPPERY SLOPE
The Grief Cycle of Divorce

THE SLIPPERY SLOPE
The Grief Cycle of Divorce
DENIAL
BARGAINING
ANGER
DEPRESSION
FORGIVENESS
ACCEPTANCE
action
feelings
grace

The Slippery Slope
The Grief Cycle of Divorce
DENIAL
BARGAINING
ANGER
DEPRESSION
FORGIVENESS
ACCEPTANCE
ACTION ADMIT ONE
FEELINGS ADMIT ONE
GRACE ADMIT ONE

THE SLIPPERY SLOPE
The Grief Cycle of Divorce
DENIAL
BARGAINING
ANGER
ACTION
DEPRESSION
THE PIT
FORGIVENESS
ACCEPTANCE
FEELINGS
GRACE

Introduction

"I will never forget when my mom came into my room and told me that dad was moving out. I knew they had not been getting along but I never thought he would actually leave. Now what do I do? What do I say to my friends? Maybe I don't need to say anything because he'll come back. Things will be back to normal again soon."

"Every day I come home from school and get reminded that my parents are split up and I become sick to my stomach. Sometimes I purposely plan things after school just so I don't have to come home and be reminded of it."

"I went to my dad's house last week and we went out to dinner with his new girlfriend. Does he not understand how that makes me feel? I'm the teenager whose starting to date, not my dad! How embarrassing! He's supposed to be with my mom. This is just not right!"

"My dad left me and my brothers when I was younger. Most of the time when it was time for him to come and see us he would not show up. I kept on begging God to make him come. I missed him. Why did he not miss me? As I'm growing up, I am noticing it is very hard for me to trust anyone. I don't let anyone, especially a guy, get close because I'm so afraid he will leave and hurt me. Will I ever be able to get beyond all this pain and learn to trust again?"

"When my dad left my mom she cried all the time. As the years went by, she kept on coming to me with her problems and expected me to always be there for her. It's almost like she needs me to fill some void in her life. I love her and want to help her, but how do I tell her that I have my own life to live? I wish I didn't have to feel so responsible for her emotional well being all the time."

"I have never been the same since my dad left. I long so much to be loved by someone, that I have made a lot of wrong choices with the guys I have dated. I just want someone to love me. There is this emptiness in my heart that I keep hoping someone will fill. Will anyone ever love me for who I am?"

Do you ever have teenagers come up to you and ask you these questions? Do they pour their hearts out to you but leave you feeling hopeless in helping them? When divorce happens to a child, no matter what age, it is probably one of the hardest things they will ever have to endure. Their lives spin out of control and they are forced to accept changes they have no say in. And what about the kids who just hide in the corner because the hurt is so deep they don't even know how to talk about it?

Divorce is not an unforgivable sin that creates broken families. It is not something they have to feel helpless or hopeless about. Divorce however, does change and wound families, but it does not have to destroy the people it involves. Teens need to be taught to walk through the journey of recovery and find hope in the midst of this tragedy. Their parents' divorce does not have to rob them of their future. They can learn to process their feelings and hurts and find themselves healthier on the other side.

I have always felt my calling was to reach out to parents experiencing the tragedy of divorce with the hope that through reaching them, they could make better choices and eliminate some of the pain for these kids. But over the years I have realized that it is the teens that need our help. Divorce rates are climbing faster than ever. I soon realized God was calling me to reach these teens and help them move beyond the devastation of divorce. To help them accept God's healing grace now in hopes of preventing more heartache in their own relationships later. This is why this curriculum was written. We need to reach these youth now, before they carry this baggage into their own future relationships.

My personal passion stems from watching my own children go through this. I was divorced when they were only 5 and 7. Although the divorce was very emotional, and a tragedy to our family, my biggest concern was for them and how it was going to affect their lives and their future relationships. I would have sleepless nights praying that God's grace and protection would surround them and bring them through this awful set of circumstances they were left to deal with. Although I know I did not always make right choices, God has always been there for my children. It is only by His grace that we have all made it this far. My kids are now 17 and 20 and I am so thankful for the passion God has laid on my heart to see them through and to continue to empower them to be victorious in their individual adult lives. If my personal experience can help anyone else, that is my heart's desire.

There are hundreds of books and material for adults recovering from divorce and yet tragically there is only a handful of resources for kids, and very little available for teens. A teenagers life is filled with so many other challenges and decisions, I think it is imperative that we offer something specifically targeted for their recovery process of divorce. This is what The Big D offers. It offers the freedom to explore feelings, challenge behavior patterns, receive the freedom of forgiveness, accept the unacceptable, and find hope for the future.

Along with this 12 week program, I have also created a weekend curriculum. This program has all different information and activities. It is perfect for a group who does not have the resources or possibly leadership to pull off an entire 12 week program. The shortened weekend can also be used as a great way to kick off your 12 week program. For more information or to purchase the weekend curriculum please go directly to www.thebigdinfo.com.

In August of 2009 I created a new ministry tool called *The Slippery Slope*. It is a board game that encourages healing as you continue down the path of the Grief Cycle. *The Slippery Slope* comes in 3 unique versions, one for kids, one for teens and one for adults. These games are a great tool to be used in all Recovery or Care Groups but the kids and teen games are also a great resource for parents to use at home to encourage communication and promote healing within the family. Please check them out at www.sonsetpointministries.com.

With printing costs increasing and looking for a better way of getting The Big D into the lives of more teens, in 2010 The Big D became published by AMFM Publishing. The Big D is now available on Amazon along with many other bookstores. With being published this has forced me into making a few changes. My number one priority continues to be providing you with an excellent product at a reasonable price. At this point through other media outlets you are only able to buy this Leaders Guide as part of the Curriculum Kit. Additional Leaders Guides for your leaders can be purchased individually at my website. In order to get this reduced price you will need to go to my website at www.thebigdinfo.com and order them directly from me. I will also continue to carry the original Big D tote bags for you to purchase there as well. I hope this helps in empowering your leaders.

I invite you to join me in my passion to accept the challenge and reach out to the hearts of these teens who want to heal from the painful effects of divorce and commit to a future filled with hope and promise. There is also a great opportunity built into The Big D, to share the gospel with those who are searching for a new way of life. This gospel message alone can be the first step in speaking hope and truth into a hurting teen's life. By the grace of God, may we all be counted among those who impart that hope.

Krista Smith
The Big D

Sonset Point Ministries

HOW TO USE "THE BIG D"

I am so glad you invested in "The Big D". I know it will be worth the investment for years and years to come. To help you facilitate your group, I have summarized the curriculum for you. I hope this helps set out a path for success as you minister to the hearts and lives of your teens.

The goals of "The Big D" are four fold:

1. *To help teens express and accept their grief and teach them tools to move through the healing process.*
2. *To encourage teens to complete their healing journey so they don't carry their pain with them into future relationships and thus put an end to the generational cycle.*
3. *To create a venue to bring teens to Christ or develop a closer relationship and reliance in Christ, the complete healer of all our pain.*
4. *To equip parents to walk alongside their teen in their healing journey.*

The curriculum is basically divided into six main sections each week.

1. *An opening mixer – a fun way to encourage sharing and build relationships.*
2. *Wheel of Fortune – a fun way to introduce each week's topic.*
3. *Nuggets of Truth – the meat of the curriculum each week.*
4. *Workbook pages – application for each week's topic.*
5. *Taking It Home assignments – homework for the week to go deeper.*
6. *Parent Link—a take home information sheet for the parents (see Appendix).*

We suggest at least an hour and a half time frame each week to get through the curriculum. There is enough material each week to easily stretch it to 2 hours, but probably could not do it in one hour. Depending on your group size and dynamics, you may have to pick and choose activities in some weeks. It will really depend on how many teens you have in your group and how much they are willing to share and participate with the activities and application questions. If you have extra time, weeks 5 & 7 could easily be split into 2 weeks. In whatever situation you find yourself in, I'm confident there will be no lack of material to use.

The Leaders Guide does a good job of laying out the activities and schedule. I highly encourage each leader to have their own Leaders Guide. To purchase them at a reduced price, go to www.thebigdinfo.com. Be sure to open in prayer and close by taking individual prayer requests. It is important for them to see us model our everyday reliance on God for our needs as we bring our requests before His throne of grace.

The goals of every mixer are to promote unity and likeness through a fun activity. It will usually have something to do with the topic and we have found it is a great way to bring the group together and get things started. It is through these mixers that the teens learn they are not alone in their situations and that others are experiencing the same dilemmas they are. This opens the door to awesome opportunities for building friendships and a comfortable atmosphere for everyone to share their lives and individual situations.

Wheel of Fortune was created as an opportunity to introduce the topic. Be sure to come early and prepare by taping the letters to the wall. To get the teens involved, it is fun to allow a different "Vanna" each week. Some other groups have done the same thing by playing Hangman. Both ideas are a great way to get things rolling for the night. "The Big D" is specifically designed to include more teaching material during the first four weeks. It is assumed that by week five the group will take on the role itself as you go through the workbook and activities provided. Be sure to encourage the teens to share, as it is through their sharing that the groups begin to mold and the real healing takes place. Be involved enough to facilitate, but allow the Holy Spirit to move and trust Him to guide you.

At the end of each session there is a Taking It Home section to be completed by the teens on their own during the week. This is their opportunity to go deeper into their healing journey. Every assignment is set up to be three fold:

1. *Towards Yourself: Looking Inward*
2. *Towards Others: Looking Outward*
3. *Towards God: Looking Upward*

When you come back the next week you will be highlighting a few questions from their homework. Please encourage them to take the time during the week to do their homework. It will help pull everything together.

By the end of "The Big D", the ultimate goal is to ensure that your teens have had the opportunity to accept Christ as their Savior and to develop a personal relationship with Him. In Week Five, "Jesus Bags", is specifically designed to help you do this. You will lead the teens into evaluating for themselves their personal spiritual condition of their hearts. We ask that you be prepared during that session to share your personal testimony and be ready to ask and lead your teens to Christ. If you need assistance in doing this, you can walk them through the Salvation Message in their workbook. This session is followed up with Week Six, "Where is God When I Hurt", which is a perfect transition to their understanding of what this relationship means.

By Week Twelve, I am confident the group will have bonded and that healing is well on it's way. This session is designed primarily to take a glimpse into their futures to give them hope and a plan for their lives. This is a great time for a purity talk. It is also a time to encourage them to make goals for themselves and their futures. This is a time for them to let go of the weight of thinking their lives are forever scarred and to allow themselves to dream of the life God has planned for them. It also serves as a great time to celebrate by toasting to their success and their future. You may want to add an extra party night for this reason. I would also suggest if you are adding a week, to invite their parents to attend. It would be a great opportunity for them to show interest and appreciation for their child having completed the program.

If you are looking for additional ideas, please look through the Activity Guide or please go to www.thebigdinfo.com and click on Additional Ideas and you will find a host of options to choose from. There are also sidebars throughout the material with additional ideas to drive home the points. I would also like to provide you with a DVD of video clips of teens sharing their experiences to introduce each week's topic. But because of copyright laws, I am not allowed to include this with the curriculum. Please e-mail me at info@thebigdinfo.com and request a copy or fill out a request on the website under the Contact Us page. I would be happy to send it to you.

I hope you have been as blessed by this curriculum as we have been sharing it with our teens over the years. Thank you for opening your hearts to minister to these hurting teens. The rewards will be worth it!

Sincerely,
Krista Smith

Want Additional Leaders Guides for Your Leaders?

Go to www.thebigdinfo.com for reduced pricing.

Equip your leaders with what they need to prepare each week. Go to THE BIG D website and order more Leaders Guides today.

Welcome to THE BIG D!

I am so glad you chose to follow God's leading and minister to one of the most overlooked groups in our society - teens dealing with their parents' separation or divorce. As divorce continues to wreak havoc in our society, it is our teens that often get left behind. It's easy for us to overlook them. They feel they are too old to cry and share their emotions yet too young to make decisions for themselves.

A teen's basic coping mechanism is to fill their lives so full with friends, school, sports, etc., that they don't give themselves any time to feel, much less take time to share with their parents how they are doing.

More often than not, they won't be able to hide forever from the feelings they are running from. For many teens these feelings reappear later on in life, affecting their futures and their future relationships.

It is my passion, and now yours, to bring them out of this jungle and into the light as they navigate this journey of healing. My prayer is that together we can help them experience the freedom and hope they deserve.

TABLE OF CONTENTS

Stepping Stones to Healing

There Are No Perfect Families

Welcome to week one! It's time to get to know one another and share some ground rules. Our objectives for this session are to let group members know that this is their *Comfort Zone;* for them to share their feelings without fear of judgment or ridicule and to show that there is no such thing as a *perfect family.* And while there is no such thing as a perfect family, we can call upon our heavenly Father who offers His perfect love to each one of us.

PREP TIME

1. Spend time in prayer for:
   a. your heart as you prepare for this lesson
   b. the students who will be attending this week, that God would open their hearts and help them to share their feelings
   c. the other leaders helping with the lesson
2. Read through the lesson and make sure you understand the material and activities
3. Gather supplies for projects
4. Make copies of "Your Own Story" (Attachment A)
5. Go over The Big D Guidelines (Attachment B)
6. Purchase Styrofoam cups (approx. 12 per person)
7. Prepare Wheel of Fortune sheets (Attachment C) and tape them to wall
8. Whiteboard with Guidelines (optional)
9. Workbooks

HIGHLIGHTS

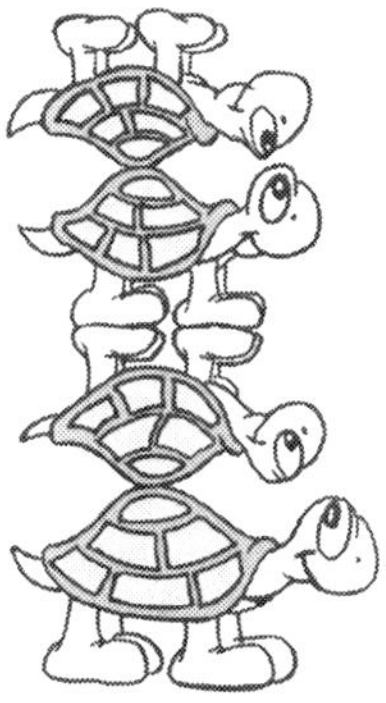

Stepping Stones to Healing

1. "Your Own Story" worksheet
2. Paper Cup Family Structures activity
3. Ground Rules
4. Family Definitions
5. Nugget of Truth: Overview of Stages
6. Attitude Check
7. The Slippery Slope
8. Taking It Home

Lesson One
Week 1

Verse of the week:

There is no fear in love, but perfect love casts out fear. For fear has to do with punishment, and whoever fears has not been perfected in love.

1 John 4:18

Be Blessed!

May the Lord bring you into an ever deeper understanding of the love of God and endurance that comes from Christ.

2 Thessalonians 3:5

WEEK ONE - SESSION ONE

WELCOME: Greet teens as they come in. Hand out "Your Own Story…" (Attachment A) and ask the teens to complete it while you wait for everyone to arrive. Be sure to give each teen time to complete this exercise. Collect the worksheet once you are ready to start. Begin to get to know everyone during this session. Be sure to spend time building connections.

Spend some time this week looking through their completed "Your Own Story…" worksheets. It is important that you understand their family structures and the situations these teens are currently facing.

PAPER CUP FAMILY STRUCTURES

You will need approximately a dozen Styrofoam cups per person and magic markers.

Hand out one Styrofoam cup to every person for every person in their immediate family. Hand out markers and have them draw faces and label each cup to identify each member of their family. Encourage them to be creative.

When done, have each teen introduce their family structures using the cups. For instance, Dad and Mom would be on separate sides. Any step parents would be on their parent's side along with any step siblings. Any birth brother and sisters who travel back and forth with them would be included with their (the teen's) cup. If living with friends or grandparents, they can be included too. Pets can be included if wanted. Have them explain how much time is spent at each home as well.

This is a great opportunity to learn more about their family situations. Allow them to describe and share as much about their families as possible. Be observant on how they draw each family member and their body language as they explain their family dynamics.

After *Paper Cup Families* open in prayer.

COMFORT ZONE

ATTACHMENT B

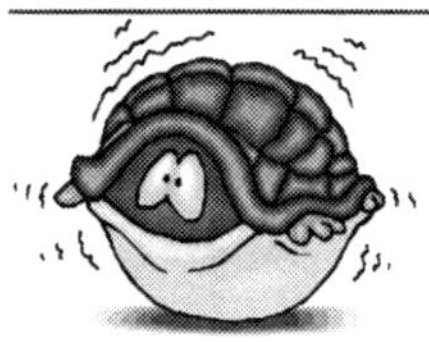

After everyone has explained their family structures, it's time to reinforce the concept of our ***Comfort Zone.***

Hand out workbooks and go over the Guidelines in their workbook.

Be sure to remind everyone that this is our ***Comfort Zone.*** Here they are free to share their feelings without fear of shame, ridicule, or judgment. This is a place where everyone can feel comfortable sharing their hopes, fears, struggles and successes.

WORKBOOK PAGE XI

Mailbox

Prepare a box where they can leave anonymous questions to be answered each week.

Nugget of Truth: What is Divorce?

WORKBOOK PAGE 14 **Divorce Stats**

Divorce is the separation and death of a marriage. Some of your parents have been divorced a long time, for others this is new. And there may be some here whose parents have not yet decided if they are divorcing. Either way this life shattering experience can leave you feeling a deep sense of abandonment and loss. Our goal is to help you through that loss and give you hope for your future.

Not only is divorce devastating, but unfortunately it is also extremely common in America. Consider these facts:

- During your generation, at one time or another, *over half of all teenagers will live in a broken home.
- Currently *67% of all marriages will end in divorce.
- There are now more than *3 million unmarried couples living together in the USA, an 80% increase since 1980. These relationships are proven to have a higher divorce rate.
- Approximately one out of every *4 children in the nation today are growing up without a father in their home.
- Over *13 million kids are currently living in single parent households.

These statistics do not have to define your future. You have the power & opportunity to prevent further heartache. We are here to help you do that. You may feel like you have no control of anything that has happened to you and that may be true, but you DO HAVE control of your future. The best way for you to do this is to take the time and effort necessary now to heal from your parents' divorce. We want to give you hope for your future. This is YOUR future - take charge and make it what you want it to be!! You don't have to be just one of these statistics. You can choose to do the work and change your future!

For I know the plans I have for you says the Lord, they are not to harm you but to prosper you, to give you a future and a hope. Jeremiah 29:11

* Census 2000 statement

WORKBOOK PAGE 15

Family Definitions

In order for us all to understand each other, why don't we go over some common family definitions that we will be using over the next few weeks. Turn in your workbooks and follow along.

Birth or Biological Family -

A family that consists of a birth father, a birth mother, yourself and any biological siblings.

Single Parent Family –

A family where separation or divorce has taken place and your parents live in different homes. You will typically have 2 homes now – one with your mom and one with your dad. The families will consist of your mom, yourself and any other siblings and your dad, yourself, and any other siblings. Variations can take place, like you and your siblings don't have the same schedules between homes, or you may only have one single parent home because the other parent has moved far away, have passed away, or is just out of the picture.

Blended Family or Step Family –

A family where divorce has happened and one or both of your parents have remarried. This is when you add a step dad or mom and any step brothers or sisters to your once single parent home. How this family system works is different for everybody depending on everyone's parenting time schedules. In some cases you may also end up having a half brother or sister if your parent and their spouse, your step parent, decide to have another child.

WHEEL OF FORTUNE

ATTACHMENT C

There Are No Perfect Families

At the beginning of every session, there will be a phrase posted on the wall that they will need to figure out. This activity is played like the Wheel of Fortune game on TV. You will have each letter on a separate sheet of paper and place them with the letter side facing the wall. Make sure to put a space between every word in the phrase. Take turns asking each teen to select a letter and for each letter they pick correctly, you turn the letter(s) over. Every time a person selects a correct letter they get to take a guess at the phrase. If they guess incorrectly, their turn is over and it is the next person's turn.

SUGGESTED RULES:

1. One person can select only one letter at a time. If their letter is correct, they can take a guess at the phrase but they cannot select another letter.
2. Vowels are no different than consonants.
3. Make sure everyone takes turns.
4. Commas, apostrophes, dashes, etc. get revealed before the game begins.
5. They must guess the entire phrase, not one word at a time.
6. If there is more than one of the letters guessed, all of the same letters in the phrase must be turned over.

Nugget of Truth: Overview of the Stages of Grief

Do you have an BAD attitude?
A grief attitude?

Grief? What is grief? Grief is the empty feeling you have when you are hurting inside.

Webster Says: *it is a deep and poignant distress caused by or as if by bereavement; a cause of such suffering; an unfortunate outcome.*

There are many feelings that follow the seperation of your mom and dad. One reason is because it is something you thought you would never have to go through. Another is because you have so much loyalty and love for your parents that it can be hard to understand your own feelings. It is important for you to know all your feelings are normal. Every single person in this room has probably felt the exact same way at one time or another. Do you ever feel like these feelings will last forever? If so, understanding how our body processes through grief will help.

Everyone who experiences a separation or divorce in a family has a grief cycle to go through. This is usually a very difficult time for everyone. However, your attitude about your grief can help you move through it smoother and quicker. It will never be pain free, but you can decide how long it will last and how much pain you want to carry with you. Perhaps you have been taught that expressing grief is a private matter. Or that God only comforts the grieving. Or maybe crying is only for the weak and you need to be strong and appear that nothing is wrong. The truth is everyone needs to grieve. Keep in mind that grieving is different for everyone. Understanding what you think about grief will help you learn how to live through grief.

ATTITUDE CHECK

Let's take an Attitude Check together!

WORKBOOK PAGE 16

Attitude Check

What's your "Grief Attitude"?

Circle True or False for each statement below.

a. People only feel grief when someone dies.

True ~ False

b. If you replace a loss (with a pet, girlfriend etc.), your grief will go away.

True ~ False

c. You have to feel grief in order to heal.

True ~ False

d. Grief eventually ends.

True ~ False

e. Keeping super busy can help you get through grief.

True ~ False

f. You should express grief only in private.

True ~ False

g. When someone is expressing grief, you should leave him/her alone.

True ~ False

h. Grieving usually lasts one year.

True ~ False

i. It is okay to be angry when you are grieving.

True ~ False

Attitude Check Answers:

a. False. We feel grief about all losses. It could be a death but we can also grieve over the changes in our lives. (examples: divorce, memories, being lonely)

b. False. Each relationship is unique. This makes it impossible to replace our losses. By trying to replace the loss you usually delay your healing and cause the hurt to be more painful and last longer.

c. True. Grief will not go away if we ignore it. Instead, it will snowball and affect us in worse ways. We need to keep expressing our feelings in order to be healed from them. This takes time and effort. There is no "quick fix".

d. False. We are never fully unaffected by our losses. Instead, over time, we can learn to live with loss and move on.

e. False. Busying ourselves is a way of denial. It can prevent you from feeling grief and thus prevent you from getting though it.

f. False. We cannot control when and where we feel grief. It is as normal as breathing.

g. False. We need to share our grief with others and receive support to help us move through grief. This is a time when we need friends we can trust, and we need to be a friend to others.

h. False. With grieving there is no beginning and end. It will get better as time goes by and as your healing takes place, but there will always be lingering affects. Grieving is different for everyone and there is no time table. There is no right or wrong way to grieve.

i. True. Anger is a normal reaction to grieving. It is not wrong to be angry. It is what you do with your anger that can be wrong.

Stepping Stones to Healing

After any tragedy or loss, such as a divorce, all people will experience the same stages in healing. We are going to call these steps "The Stepping Stones to Healing".

They are:

Denial,

Anger,

Bargaining,

Depression,

Forgiveness

And finally

Acceptance.

You will probably experience each one of these at some time during and after your parent's divorce. But, don't expect it to be an easy, progressive walk from one stone to the other. It will not be a walk in the park. You will probably not move through the steps in any exact order and you will probably get "bumped around" a bit and even possibly find yourself going backwards a few times. In other words, at some point you might feel emotions that you thought you had already gotten over. When this happens, don't be alarmed. We are emotional beings and different things can trigger unexpected emotions at different times .

For example, you may be bargaining by thinking, "If I do really good in basketball and become a starter, then my dad will show more interest in me and come to my games". So you work really hard to become a starter but nothing changes between you and your dad. All of a sudden you find yourself back into the depths of anger saying, "This is so unfair!! I hate it!!" Sometimes you may even find yourself going way back to denial by saying, "I'm probably just overreacting. Maybe this really isn't as bad as I think. I'm sure he was just too busy at work." Keep in mind that it is very normal to go back and experience feelings you felt before. You may also get stuck in a stage that you can't seem to get out of, as if you're in quicksand and no matter how hard you try, you end up sinking deeper. Sometimes having to face the truth of situations is too hard to accept so it is easier for you to stay in one area longer than what is healthy or you are so angry at one or both of them that you can't seem to get beyond the anger. Take comfort in knowing that there is no quick fix and that it is normal to be stuck sometimes. We need to let our bodies deal with our losses in their own time. It simply means that you're not ready to take the next step. There are many emotions to process. Be sure that you do not rush yourself through them. You won't want to go through this again years later. There is no required timetable for moving through grief. It's not like having to pass Algebra so you can move into Geometry. You will move through grief at your own pace and in your own way. So give yourself a break and let your body heal in its own timing.

Stop here and have teen complete the slippery slope page in their workbooks.

THE SLIPPERY SLOPE

WORKBOOK PAGE 17

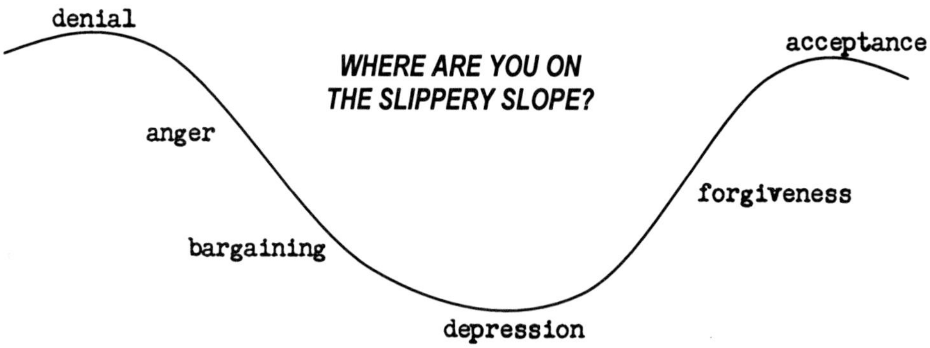

EXPLAIN THE "TAKING IT HOME" ASSIGNMENTS

WORKBOOK PAGE 18-20

Each week they will have a Taking It Home assignment to be completed by the next week. There are three sections called: Towards Yourself, Towards Others, and Towards God. Encourage everyone to take the time and do the assignments as you will be briefly going through them the next week. If you are afraid they will not bring their books back to group with them, you can make photocopies of these pages to send home with them. Or if time permits you can set aside time at the end of each session to do their home work so they can they can leave their workbooks there until the end of the 12 weeks.

CLOSING TIME: Ending the session

Take Prayer Requests

This can be done a variety of ways:

- verbally shared in group setting
- hand out note cards to group members to write out their requests.
- set out a note book that students can write in throughout the session
- put out a Prayer Request Box and Prayer Request Slips
- encourage the group members to come up with other ways to share prayer requests.

Close in prayer

Go or Grow:
Which Will it Be?

You can go through your parents' separation or divorce or you can grow through it. If you choose to deal with it, share your experiences, and learn from others, you can really end up better on the other side. The choice is yours.

Which will you choose?

TAKING IT HOME

WEEK ONE

TOWARDS YOURSELF...A Question to Take to My Heart:

Look into your heart for the answer to these questions. This is introspection time – time to grapple with what drives your thinking and behavior. Be sure to "capture your thoughts".

◈ Write something about your strongest desire regarding your parents or family situation.

◈ Do you ever wonder if, because this has happened to your parents, it might happen to you someday? If so, how does that make you feel?

◈ Are there times when you are too embarrassed or sad to tell your friends that your parents are separated or divorced? What do you say? How can we help make this easier for you to do?

◈ Will you go or grow through this experience?

TOWARDS OTHERS...A Question to Take to Others:

Healing cannot become complete without affecting the lives of those around us as well. Be courageous and go outside your comfort zone to take a risk and work on your relationships with others.

◈ Do you feel like you have some “unfinished business” with either one of your parents? What is it?

◈ Does divorce run in your family? Who? How does that make you feel?

◈ If you have had an attitude at home lately, what can you do this week to “level the playing field”?

◈ What do other people, especially your friends, think about you now that your parents are separated or divorced?

◈ List all the teenagers you know who have parents who are divorced or separated.

TOWARDS GOD...A Question to Take to God:

When you ask God a question, expect His Spirit to respond to your heart. Be careful not to rush it, or manufacture an answer. Don't jot down your idea of the "right answer". Just pose the question to God, and wait on Him to speak personally in a fresh way.

- All God asks is for us to be willing to listen. What do you think He would say to you today if you had lunch together?

- Do you think God is there for you or do you think you are all alone?

- If you were to describe who God is to you right now, how would you describe your relationship?

ATTACHMENT A

Your Own Story

*Name*____

*Age*______________ *Grade*_______________ *School*__________________

*What five-letter word best describes you?*______________________________
(examples: brave, liked, tired, happy, suave, lucky, alien)

What do you often do on Saturday afternoons?

What is your favorite thing to do?

Who do you like to do this with?

How old were you when you first realized your parents were having problems?

Do you live with your mom or your dad more?

How often do you visit the other parent?

If you do, what 3 words best describe these visits? __________ __________ __________

Has your mom or dad remarried? If so, when?

What would you say are the three most important events in your life in the past two years?

1.

2.

3.

"THE BIG D" WEEKLY GUIDELINES

ATTACHMENT B

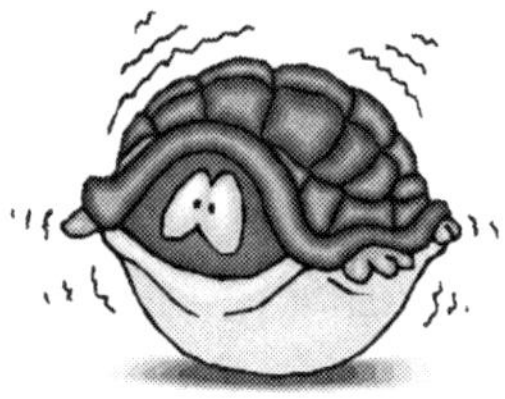

This is our "***COMFORT ZONE***". What is said in this room stays in this room!!

There are no wrong answers and no wrong feelings.

There will be absolutely no making fun of people!

You are free to share any feeling you have.

Everyone will be accepted for who they are and how they feel.

Everyone has a chance to speak and be heard.

When others are sharing, you are listening!

There will be no rough housing allowed.

There will be no PDA (physical display of affection) allowed.

Please refrain from using vulgar or offensive language.

Make time for "Taking It Home" assignments.

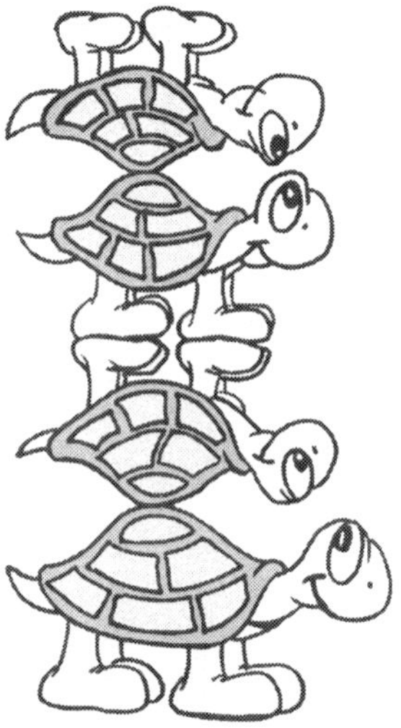

(1) N

(1) O

(1) P

(1) F

(1) M

(2) T

(1) H

(6) E

(3) R

(2) A

For the "Wheel of Fortune" activity you will need to enlarge and copy these letters onto card stock. You will need to make the number of letters indicated on each card (for example two T's, one H, six E's and so on). You will need letters to spell out "There Are No Perfect Families."

I (2)

L (1)

S (1)

C (1)

For the "Wheel of Fortune" activity you will need to enlarge and copy these letters onto card stock. You will need to make the number of letters indicated on each card (for example two T's, one H, six E's and so on). You will need letters to spell out "There Are No Perfect Families."

Step by Step

Denial, Bargaining, Depression

Welcome Back! We hope week one went well. This week we will be exploring the stages of denial, bargaining, and depression. These are three emotions on the "Slippery Slope" worksheet that we introduced at our last session. These can be very difficult emotions for teens to admit they are struggling with, so be sure you reinforce our "Comfort Zone" and let your teens know that these emotions are steps in the healing process that we must go through in order to arrive at a place of true acceptance and healing.

PREP TIME

1. Spend time in prayer for:
    a. your heart as you prepare for this lesson
    b. the students who will be attending this week, that God would open their hearts and help them to share their feelings
    c. the other leaders helping with the lesson
    d. all prayer requests from the students attending the first session
2. Read through the lesson and make sure you understand the material and activities.
3. Gather supplies for projects.
4. Prepare for the Twister Mixer– make sure you have enough mats (Attachment A)
5. Prepare Wheel of Fortune sheets (Attachment B) and tape them to the wall
6. Make copies of the Slippery Slope (Attachment C)
7. Copy Denial statements (Attachment D) on cardstock and cut out
8. Copy Bargaining statements (Attachment E) on cardstock and cut out
9. Copy Depression statements (Attachment F) on cardstock and cut out
10. Workbooks

HIGHLIGHTS

Step by Step

1. Review "Comfort Zone" and Ground Rules
2. Twister Mixer
3. Wheel of Fortune
4. Nugget of Truth: Denial, Bargaining, & Depression
5. Children's Bill of Rights
6. Taking it Home

Lesson Two
Week 2

Verses of the week:

"So be strong and take courage, all you who put your hope in the Lord."

Psalm 31:24

Be Blessed!

"May our Lord Jesus Christ and God our Father, who loved us and in his special favor gave us everlasting comfort and good hope, comfort your hearts and give you strength in every good thing you do and say."

2 Thessalonians 2:16 & 17

This week we are going to dig deeper into Denial, Bargaining and Depression. Make sure to welcome and introduce any new teens to the group. Let's get started right away!

TWISTER MIXER RULES

ATTACHMENT A

1. You will need a Twister mat.
2. Depending on how many teens you have, you may need to tape 2 or 4 twister mats together.
3. Read the situations (Attachment A) and have everyone who pertains to that situation follow what it says.
4. You may mix up the order for variety.
5. You may add any others that you choose.
6. Object of the game:
   - Have fun
   - Get teens to mix and mingle
   - Help them realize they are not the only ones in these situations
   - Help them discover what they have in common

Leaders Note - you may want to divide up the guys and gals for this activity and have a different twister mat for each

After the *Twister Mixer*, bring everyone together and open in prayer.

WHEEL OF FORTUNE

The Slippery Slope

ATTACHMENT B

The title of this week's lesson is "The Slippery Slope". Be sure to print the letters ahead of time and post on a bulletin board or wall before the teens arrive. Take turns like last week asking each teen to select a letter. For each correct letter they select, turn the letter(s) over and give them a chance to solve the puzzle. See **Lesson One** for a complete list of suggested rules.

COMMON GROUND

Last week we briefly outlined all the steps in the grief process, or as we are calling it, "The Slippery Slope". Let's take a look at last weeks **Taking It Home** assignment.

Go over *TAKE HOME* assignment

- How can we help make it easier to tell your friends that your parents are separated or divorced?

- What did you do this last week to help level the playing field in your home?

- All God asks is for us to be willing to listen. What do you think He would say to you today if you had lunch together?

Hand out another copy of "The Slippery Slope" (Attachment C) to everyone. Go around and share where they marked themselves on the Slippery Slope.

This week we are going to look deeper into three of the stepping stones; denial, bargaining, and depression. Although anger comes between denial and bargaining, we are saving Session 3 to work through that one.

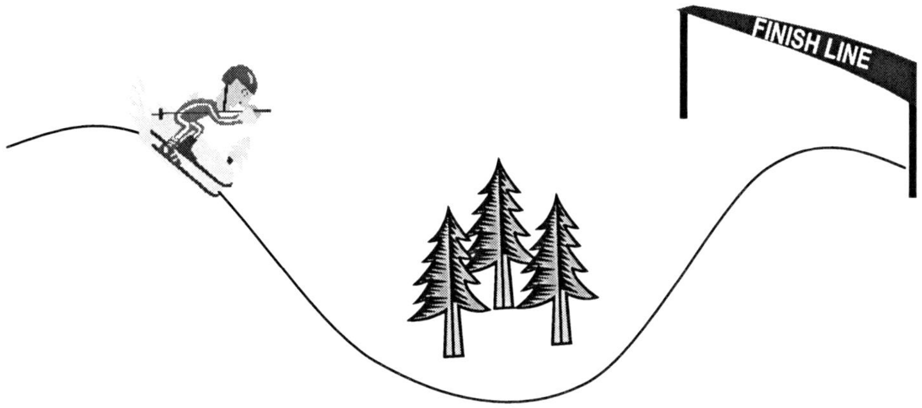

Nugget of Truth: Denial

WORKBOOK PAGE 22

What is Denial?

Hand out a Denial statement (Attachment D) to different teens and have them read them out loud.

These may be things you are saying on the outside but they are just covering up what you are truly feeling inside. On the outside you say things that make it look like you don't care or it's no big deal but in reality on the inside, it's killing you. You're feeling scared, hurt, and angry. The truth is, when you deny that something is happening to you, you are really refusing to believe the truth. This is a very common reaction at first. It is our body's way of dealing with a pain that is too great to feel. It is a numbing reaction that gives our bodies and minds time to adjust and figure out what to do next. Eventually though, you need to face the facts and face your feelings. This is hard to do, but you'll soon find denial is way too painful a place to stay for too long.

What ways can you get help to work through denial?

- Admit that you do have feelings and pain. Ignoring those feelings will only lead to more pain.
- Identify what it is you are really feeling.
- Take time to think and pray. Spend time with God sharing the fears you are too afraid to accept.
- Seek help from a counselor, youth pastor or other pastor.
- Talk with someone that you trust and will help you accept what is happening.
- Understand that no matter what happens, God will still love you and care for you the same. He doesn't change.

Is denial wrong? Absolutely not! It is a natural and necessary first step in the grieving process. It provides you with the time needed to prepare emotionally for what comes next.

Webster Says...

Denial: a negotiation in logic or a refusal to admit the truth or reality.

Denial *is a protective emotion that shields you from pain, just as shoulder pads protect athletes in a football game. It can look different on different people. Denial can simply mean avoiding talking about the divorce, or always keeping busy, never slowing down enough to feel or talk.*

DENIAL

What is DENIAL?

Denial is choosing to ignore our __TRUE____ feelings or circumstances and telling ourselves __LIES_____ to help take away the pain.

Example:	Denial Says:
When my friends didn't invite me to their party ...	"That's o.k. I didn't want to go anyway."
When no one asks me out for a date...	"That's o.k. because I don't have time to date right now."

What Denial says about Divorce

It's okay that mom and dad got a divorce because it is better not to have her around.

So what if my parents got divorced, I'll just be living at home for a few more years.

I don't mind it at all that dad has left us; I get to be the man of the house.

What does denial have to do with divorce?

The trauma and pain that goes along with separation and divorce is not over quickly. The loss is incomplete and the pain is ongoing. Denial can be helpful in dealing with the shock that our emotions take during traumatic experiences. But if we stay in a state of denial, it can become hurtful to us.

How to not get stuck in Denial.

Tell the truth

1. **Be _____HONEST_____ with yourself.** Don't try to cover your pain with denial or try to minimize what has happened. Chances are you have been deeply hurt and you need to deal with that hurt. Denying an emotional problem does not make it go away.
2. **Be _____HONEST_____ with God.** God is not a god of denial. He wants us to be honest with ourselves and our emotions and circumstances and deal with them in His power. Jesus in His life proved that denial was not the way to tackle the tough, painful issues of life. In the Garden of Gethsemane, He realized He was going to face the worst possible pain imaginable at the Cross. Jesus faced His painful emotions head on.

Bargaining:

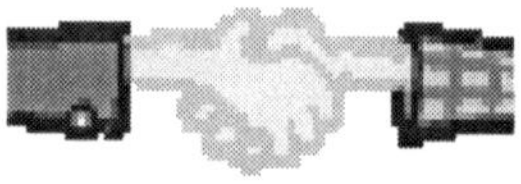

Hand out a Bargaining statement (Attachment E) to different teens and have them read them out loud.

Bargaining is trying to find an easy solution to take the pain away. Maybe it's convincing yourself to get better grades, to be nicer, to be home more, to get a job, etc. thinking that would make a difference. In actuality, it is trying to manipulate the people involved to get what you want. It's believing the lies you tell yourself that the separation or divorce is about something you did or didn't do. And that you can do something to change it. Sometimes it may even involve lying and cheating, but you fall into it believing it's for a good cause. The problem here is that in reality, the problems between your parents were never about you. So all the effort you put into trying to please your parents or manipulate them back together will get you nowhere. You will probably end up reverting back to anger because of all your wasted time and effort and you will end up feeling more frustrated.

Bargaining: What Does It Mean?

WORKBOOK PAGE 24

Webster Says...

Bargaining *is testing whether something is open to negotiation or is reversible.*

Bargaining can include trying to get your parents to see a counselor, attempting to act as a mediator, or even becoming sick or becoming a problem to get your parents to work together. Bargaining doesn't work in divorce because it's your parents' decision not based on anything you do or say.

Depression:

Hand out a Depression statement (Attachment F) to different teens and have them read them out loud.

Depression is when you've given up and you feel that there is no hope. You pull away from everyone and become secluded, not wanting to be around anybody. It hits when you give up and realize that no matter how hard you try to bargain, nothing is going to work.

Depression can come in the form of sleeping too much and not wanting to get out of bed or it can also be indicated by not being able to sleep. Some people eat to try to feel better, some people don't have any appetite at all. It takes on many different forms, most if left unattended for a long period of time, are harmful for you.

Depression is the natural conclusion to denial, anger, and bargaining. This is when you have hit the bottom and feel like giving up. The good news is, there is no where else to go but up. But realize, on your way up, you may slip back down into depression many times before reaching acceptance. It's all a process. You will soon notice that your periods of depression will lessen over time. Keep in mind though that not everyone is the same. Some may be more susceptible to depression and some may breeze right though it.

Helpful Hints for Depressed

1. A prayer journal
2. Exercise
3. Brighten your room (sun, lights)
4. Avoid staying in the house too much
5. Eat a banana each morning and evening
6. Have hope in Christ
7. A one second blast of cold water
8. Everyday achieve a small task
9. Mix up daily responsibilities & routines
10. Dress & look your best
11. Laugh out loud 3 times a day
12. Read personal devotional books or tapes
13. Sing along
14. Accentuate the positive
15. Listen to your favorite music
16. Seek support from your friends & family
17. Volunteer
18. Enjoy your hobby

LEADERS WARNING:

Suicidal feelings sometimes accompany depression. Encourage anyone who has suicidal feelings to get help right away.
See Appendix

This sad and overwhelming feeling may last for awhile. It is important though that you do not stay in the pit too long. To start working your way out you must first want to get better. In the meantime, you need to force yourself to be with your friends, look out for other people's needs, and keep connected to God. It also helps to say something positive about yourself every so often. If you find yourself stuck in this stage too long, it is important to go to a doctor and get checked out. Medication can be given to help you out of this slump. If you think you may need this kind of help, talk to your parents or someone you trust about it.

WORKBOOK PAGE 25 — **What I Can Do When I Am Feeling Blue?**

Webster Says… a state of feeling sad.

Depression shows itself in many ways. You may cry, withdraw, lose interest in fun or work, have lack of energy, think about problems over and over, stop eating or overeat, have trouble sleeping , or sleep all the time. Some people get so busy and active they never slow down and face the problem.

GOD IS NEAR

Why do you weep? Don't you know that even the sun and moon will be darkened, and there will be times when you just can't see? This is one of those seasons. Getting through the valley will take time and effort, but don't worry.

I will provide all the grace you need and I am here with you. Before your feet stumble on the darkening hills, take my hand and hold on tight.

-God

Did You Know That You Have Rights Too?

WORKBOOK PAGE 26 — Children's Bill of Rights

Read through "The Children's Bill of Rights" and remind yourself of them often. If you need to remind your parents sometimes, just let them read them too. Don't forget—you are the teen– they are the adults. Be careful not to allow yourself or others to put you in any adult situations. You will be an adult soon enough.

EXPLAIN THE "TAKING IT HOME" ASSIGNMENTS

WORKBOOK PAGES 27-29

Each week they will have a Taking It Home assignment to be completed by the next week. There are three sections called: Towards Yourself, Towards Others, and Towards God. Encourage them all to take the time and do the assignment as you will be briefly going through them the next week. Remember to photo copy these pages if you are not sending the workbooks home with the students.

CLOSING TIME: Ending the session

Take Prayer Requests

This can be done in a variety of ways:

- verbally shared in group setting
- hand out note cards to group members to write out their requests.
- set out a note book that students can write in throughout the session
- put out a Prayer Request Box with Prayer Request Slips
- encourage the group members to come up with other ways to share prayer requests.

Close in Prayer

BILL OF RIGHTS FOR CHILDREN OF DIVORCE

The right not to be placed in the position of a message carrier.

The right not to be asked to be the family spy.

The right to remain connected to both parents' families.

The right not to be interrogated after a visit with the other parent.

The right to express or not to express his or her own feelings.

The right to a stable, safe environment.

The right to remain a child and not a parental confidant.

The right to be loved unconditionally.

The right to be treated as important human beings, with unique feelings, ideas and desires, and not as a source of argument between parents.

The right to express love and affection for each parent without having to stifle that love because of fear of disapproval by the other parent.

The right to continuing care and guidance from both parents.

The right to honest answers to questions about the changing family relationships.

The right to know and appreciate what is good in each parent without one parent degrading the other.

The right to have both parents not undermine the other parent's time with the children by suggesting tempting alternatives or by threatening to withhold parental contact as a punishment for the children's wrong doing.

The right to experience regular and consistent contact with both parents and to be protected from disputes or disagreements.

Note: These Bill of Rights assume both parents are healthy and safe. If your situation is unsafe in any way, please consider sharing with your leader. Your safety is our primary concern.

WEEK TWO

TOWARDS YOURSELF...A Question to Take to My Heart:

Look into your heart for the answer to these questions. This is introspection time...time to grapple with what drives your thinking and behavior. Be sure to "capture your thoughts".

◈ Denial –

Did you experience denial after your parents split?

_____ Yes
_____ No
_____ I don't know
_____ I think I'm still in denial
_____ No way, not me, I'm fine

What did you deny? (or what are you currently trying to deny?)

_____ That your parents were/are divorcing
_____ That they won't get back together
_____ That one or both of them did something wrong
_____ That you feel bad about it
_____ Other

◈ Bargaining -

How have you tried to bargain?

_____ Tried to get my parents back together
_____ Lied
_____ Promised God to be good if He would change things
_____ Sabotaged a parent's new romance
_____ Other
_____ I haven't tried to bargain

◈ Depression –

Are you feeling depressed right now?

_____ No, I was, but got over it
_____ No, I haven't reached that point yet
_____ No, I think I sailed right past it
_____ Yes, I'm in the pits
_____ Yes, I think I'm stuck in it

How long have you been feeling depressed?

Is this something you should talk to someone about?

How is this depression affecting your life?
(check all that apply)

_____ not sleeping right
_____ not eating right
_____ sick a lot
_____ withdrawing from my friends
_____ other
_____ nothing is fun anymore
_____ lack of concentration
_____ school grades are suffering
_____ have no self-confidence

TOWARDS OTHERS...A Question to Take to Others:

Healing cannot become complete without affecting the lives of those around us as well. Be courageous and go outside your comfort zone to take a risk and work on your relationships with others.

- Have you ever tried to manipulate someone or a situation to get what you wanted?

  Did it work?

  How long did it last?

  How did it make you feel afterwards?

- Has anything happened recently that you tried to pretend didn't happen? What was it?

- Is anyone is your family denying the reality of the divorce?

- How does being in any of these stages affect other people in your life?

- Have any of your relationships changed as a result of the divorce or separation? If so, how?

TOWARDS GOD...A Question to Take to God:

When you ask God a question, expect His Spirit to respond to your heart. Be careful not to rush it, or manufacture an answer. Don't jot down your idea of the "right answer". Just pose the question to God, and wait on Him to speak to you personally in a fresh way.

- Is it easier or harder to have hope right now? Why or why not?

- Have you ever made a promise to God as a way of bargaining?

- Do you blame God for allowing this to happen to your family?

- Ask God, what negative thoughts and behaviors are holding you captive to my depression? Ask Him to help you decide what is reasonable depression given what you're going through and what is harmful depression that needs to be in check?

- Set aside and make time for God on a daily basis about whatever you wish. Try it everyday for at least one week then consider the effect it has on you.

Twister Mixer

1. If your parents are currently separated, place your left hand on blue.
2. If you have a little brother, place your left foot on red.
3. If you have a step mom, place your right foot on green.
4. If you have a little sister, place your right hand on yellow.
5. If you have a big brother, place your left hand on red.
6. If you have a step dad, place your left foot on blue.
7. If your parents are divorced, place your right foot on blue.
8. If your parents have been divorced for over 3 years, put your right hand on red.
9. If you have a step sister, place your left hand on red.
10. If your dad lives out of the state, place your left foot on green.
11. If you had to move because of the divorce, place your right foot on yellow.
12. If you had to change schools because of the divorce, place your right hand on blue.
13. If your parents are still living in the same home, place your left foot on blue.
14. If you have a half brother, place your left foot on yellow.
15. If you live mostly with your mom, place your right foot on red.
16. If you have a step brother, place your right hand on green.
17. If you have a big sister, place your left hand on green.
18. If you have a pet dog, place your left foot on blue.
19. If you have 8 sets of grandparents, place your right foot on yellow.
20. If you have a big sister, place your right hand on blue.
21. If you have a pet cat, place your left hand on yellow.
22. If you have had to move to a different town, place your left foot on green.
23. If you go to your dads every other weekend, place your right foot on red.
24. If you live mostly with your dad, place your right hand on blue.
25. If your mom has moved out of state, place your left hand on red.
26. If you dad lives more than 2 hours away, place your right foot on blue.
27. If you are seeing a counselor, place your right hand on yellow.
28. If your mom has remarried, place your left foot on blue.
29. If your dad has remarried, place your right foot on green.
30. If you have a best friend, place your left hand on blue.
31. If you don't see your dad, place your left foot on red.
32. If you don't see your mom, place your right foot on yellow.
33. If you hate divorce, place your right hand on yellow.
34. If you are angry, place your left hand on green.
35. If you stay with your parents equal time, place your right foot on red.

(1) T

(1) H

(3) E

(2) S

(2) L

(1) I

(3) P

(1) R

(1) Y

(1) O

For the "Wheel of Fortune" activity you will need to enlarge and copy these letters onto card stock. You will need to make the number of letters indicated on each card. You will need letters to spell out "The Slippery Slope."

ATTACHMENT C

The Slippery Slope

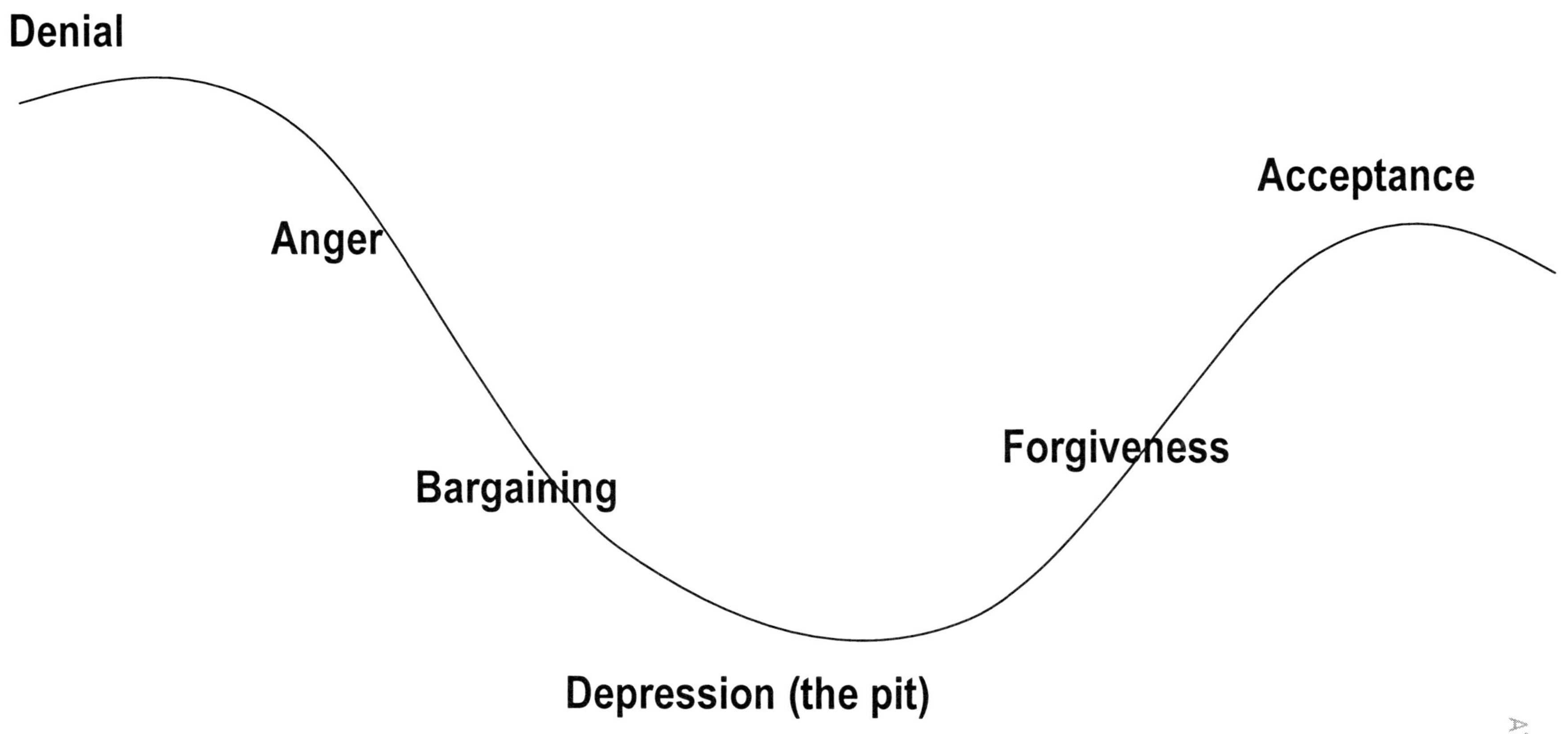

Put an X on the slope where you think you are.

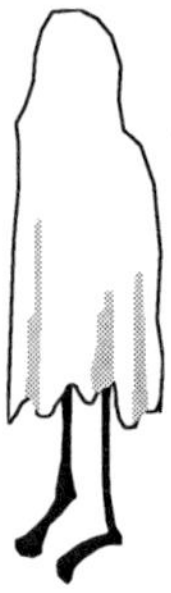

DENIAL STAGE STATEMENTS

"Hey look, I'm okay. It doesn't bother me."

"It's probably best for all of us."

"It's no big deal, they'll get back together."

"This isn't happening to me."

"He will be there for me someday."

ATTACHMENT E

BARGAINING STAGE STATEMENTS

"Hey Mom, Dad was asking about you. I think he is still interested. You should give him a call."

"Dear God, if you get my parents back together, I'll to never ask another thing."

"Hey Dad, if you come pick me up, maybe mom will be there and you can talk to her.

"I promise I'll be a better person if you and Dad get back together

"Once I make the A Squad, Dad will make more time for me.

DEPRESSION STAGE STATEMENTS

"What good is life, anyway? Nothing is fun anymore."

"If it can't be the way it was, then I don't want to be part of it"

"Go away. Leave me alone. Life stinks."

"If they don't want me, nobody will."

"I just don't care about anything anymore"

Getting a Grip

Dealing with Anger

This week we will be examining anger. We all have feelings of anger at times. It is a natural emotion designed by God. However, it can be unhealthy for us to carry around our anger like a pressure cooker ready to explode at any time. We all have to discover ways of dealing with and releasing our anger. In this session, we will discover that it is possible to learn skills to deal with anger in a way that we will feel in control instead of our anger controlling us. Be sure to spend some time asking God to wear down the defenses that our teens may have in place. Learning how to deal with anger can really help open the lines of communication between parents and children. May God richly bless your time together this week. Be sure to appreciate each one of the teens for returning for week three.

PREP TIME

1. Spend time in prayer for:
   a. your heart as you prepare for this lesson
   b. the students who will be attending this week, that God would open their hearts and help them to share their feelings
   c. the other leaders helping with this session
   d. all prayer requests from last week
2. Read through the lesson and make sure you understand the material and activities.
3. Gather supplies for projects.
4. Deck of cards
5. Prepare Wheel of Fortune sheets (Attachment A) and tape to wall
6. Make copies of "Anger Smarts" (Attachment B)
7. Workbooks

HIGHLIGHTS

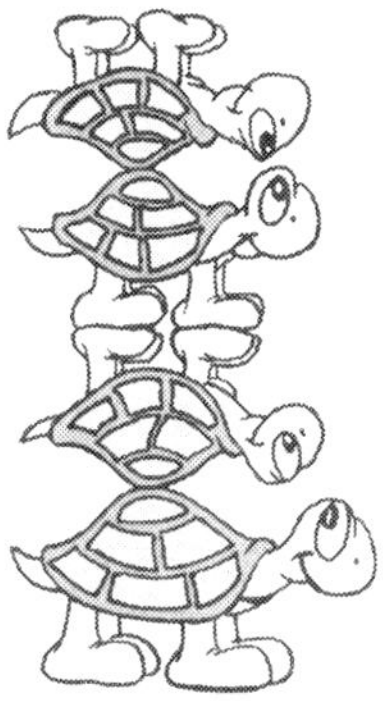

Getting A Grip

1. Playing Card Mixer
2. Wheel of Fortune
3. Nugget of Truth: Anger
4. Taking It Home

Lesson Three
Week 3

Verses of the week:

"My dear brother, take note of this; everyone should be quick to listen, slow to speak, and slow to become angry, for man's anger does not bring about the righteous life that God desires."

James 1:19 & 20

Be Blessed!

"So use every piece of God's armor to resist the enemy whenever he attacks, and when it is all over, you will still be standing up."

Ephesians 6:13
(TLB)

WEEK THREE - SESSION THREE

Lesson Three
Week 3

In week three, we will be exploring the many faces of anger. We will help you to recognize your own feelings of anger. We will discuss how you have handled anger in the past and discover possible warning signs to help control your outbursts. At the end of our time together we will identify healthy coping skills and learn healthy ways to express your anger. Remember anger is not the sin. It's how we choose to respond to anger that causes us problems.

PLAYING CARD MIXER RULES

Take a deck of playing cards and mix them up. As you greet the teens when they come have them pick a card – any card. Using a large deck can add a different dimension.

When it is time to start the evening, go around the room and have everyone say something about themselves they haven't shared yet for every number represented on the card.

For example: if you pull an eight, you need to share eight different new things about you.

or

Say one thing you get angry or frustrated about for every number represented on the card.

Rules: Aces are considered one and Kings, Queens and Jacks are considered ten.

After the *Playing Card Mixer* gather back into a group and open in prayer.

WHEEL OF FORTUNE

Getting a Grip ATTACHMENT A

The title of this week's lesson is "Getting a Grip". Be sure to print the letters ahead of time and post on a bulletin board or wall before the teens arrive. Take turns like last week asking each teen to select a letter. For each correct letter they select, turn letter(s) over and give them a chance to solve the puzzle. See **Lesson One** for a complete list of suggested rules.

COMFORT ZONE

Be sure to remind everyone that this is our ***Comfort Zone.*** Here they are free to share their feelings without fear of shame, ridicule, or judgment. This is a place where everyone can feel comfortable sharing their hopes, fears, struggles and successes.

COMMON GROUND

Last week we discussed three of the Stepping Stones to Healing-Denial, Bargaining and Depression. Let's look at some of the Taking It Home questions that you did over the week.

Go over TAKE HOME assignment

- *Have you ever tried to manipulate someone or a situation to get what you wanted? Explain.*

- *How has being in these stages affected the other people in your life?*

- *How have any of your relationships changed as a result of the separation or divorce?*

- *Is it easier or harder to have hope right now? Why or why not?*

Nugget of Truth: Anger

As your slippery slope shows, anger usually comes after denial but before bargaining. During this session, we are going to take the whole night discussing this stage. Anger is an emotion that people have an easy time falling into but a harder time crawling out of. You can become angry at your parents, angry at yourself, angry at others, angry at God, and pretty much angry at everything and everyone in life. Don't get me wrong, you may have very good reasons to be angry. Being angry isn't necessarily wrong. Many times you have every right to be angry. It's very normal to get angry about the split up from your parents' separation or divorce. It is how you express your anger that can get you into trouble.

Go Ahead,
Be Angry at God

If you sense that your group is struggling with anger towards God, take a look at this page in the appendix. It will offer you some reassurance that it is okay and normal to be angry at God sometimes. After all He already knows.

When your parents split up, many emotions develop. Things that used to not bother you may all of a sudden become a pressure point. You become more sensitive to everything. Sometimes it is easier to hide from these emotions than to deal with them. How do you respond when emotions start to stir in you? Do you tend to get angry? Do you pull back from the world or do you react to the world?

Anger is a natural response to hurt, fear, or not getting your own way. Beneath the anger though is mostly hurt. Maybe you're angry at how one of your parents is treating the other. Perhaps you're angry because your parent is making a boyfriend or girlfriend more of a priority than you. The list of things you could be angry at is endless. For instance, maybe your mom promised to come to your prom, and then didn't show up because she decided to spend time with someone else. Or maybe you are needing to take on a lot more responsibilities and have less time with your friends because your mom and dad have split up. You may even be angry because you feel your parents did not try hard enough to keep the family together. In all these circumstances, it would appear to be unfair and anyone would be angry and hurt.

Anger can actually be a good emotion. It protects us and lets us know when we've been hurt or wronged. It also allows us to stand up for ourselves. The problem comes when we keep it all in until it gets to a point where we can't control our anger or we are so scared of becoming angry that we under react by stuffing our anger and try to convince ourselves that we're not angry. Stuffing your anger can be just as harmful as overreacting. If you are afraid of sharing your feelings because you are afraid of rejection or losing contact with one of your parents, then it will build up until you explode. And you will probably explode on the person you feel the safest with, still carrying that deep down fear of rejection. Let's try to evaluate if you are a person who has a tendency to over-react or under-react.

Anger: 3 ways to deal with anger

1. ***Taking it out on others.***
   This aggressive way of dealing with anger includes hitting, screaming, cussing, accusing others, putting others down, damaging property, etc. It is destructive, tends to hurt others, and resolves very little. Aggressive anger is often directed toward "safe" people, such as younger siblings or friends.

2. ***Holding it in.***
   You can passively bottle your feelings by not talking about them. Anger still comes out in pouting and withdrawing as the person tries to punish others, but it usually hurts the angry person the most.

3. ***Talking it out.***
   This is the assertive way; honestly and openly telling others that you feel mad and why. You can be animated and loud or soft and reasonable. When we talk through our anger, we move through it and don't stay angry too long.

YOUR ANGER GRIP

WORKBOOK PAGE 32

Whether you found out you respond by either over-reacting or under-reacting is really not the issue. It is good to realize what your natural response is when you feel pressure. Anger is one of life's trickier emotions because it can be loud and hurtful or subtle and destructive. But it's important to remember that angry feelings are not wrong or bad. It is what you do when you are angry that can be the problem. It is difficult to know what to do when you feel your whole world is changing and you have no say in it. Not only may your parents be treating you unfairly, but you also may be treating yourself unfairly by holding on to thoughts and beliefs that aren't accurate. What you need to realize is that whether you are an over-reactor or under-reactor, this is the way you are going to respond to any conflict that may come your way. Now that you know whether or not your personality is to blow things out of proportion or to brush things under the rug, it is important for you to understand how you respond to conflict. Conflict is going to happen in life, whether you like it or not. So learning what your natural tendency is a good place to start. When conflict comes, what do you do? Do you put on your shield for battle? Do you spend hours trying to talk it through? Do you pass the blame on others? Is it easy for you to forgive or do you tend to hold grudges? Take a look at this next worksheet and see how you rate.

HOW I RESPOND TO CONFLICT

WORKBOOK PAGES 33 & 34

Since anger is going to come out whether you want it to or not, you need to take charge. Take control of your anger before it takes control of you. The first step is to pay attention to the signs that warn you when you're getting angry (see sidebar on next page). Whatever it may be, you need to treat these signs as warning signs that tell you to stop and think before you react. This is your chance to do something constructive, not destructive with your anger. If you ignore these signs, your anger will only cause you to lose control and you'll likely find yourself in trouble. It also can be helpful to remind yourself what you can and can't do about the situations. Let's look at some ways you can constructively handle your anger.

MANAGING YOUR ANGER

WORKBOOK PAGE 35

Although what comes naturally may be the easiest, it may not be what is best for you right now. This may be a time when you need to exercise some patience, self-control, or courage. What is important is that you learn to do what it takes to keep you from getting stuck in the middle and react in negative angry outbursts. One word of caution though, be aware that sometimes you can't fix things the way you want. You are only one side. It usually always takes two parties who are willing to do whatever it takes to promote a healthy environment. You are only in control of your half. You may need to work together to try to create the best solution possible. In some situations, you may need to get a third party involved. Be sure to find someone you both can respect, trust and will listen to.

Anger Warning Signs

- Heart pounds faster
- Mouth gets dry
- Talk louder
- Start throwing insults
- Clench your teeth
- Clench your fists
- Breathe faster
- Hold your breath
- Start to panic
- Get a headache
- Blood pressure rises
- Get defensive

ANGER HELPS

WORKBOOK PAGE 36

As we finish up on anger tonight lets take some time to go over some alternatives to dealing with our anger. Remember, you will get angry so the question is – what will you do with your anger? Make a commitment this week to respond by using some of the helps that you marked. You will be surprised at the difference it will make inside yourself and with those around you.

ANGER SMARTS

ATTACHMENT B

Even though the compromise may not be exactly what you wanted, keep in mind the important facts on the Anger Smarts worksheet.

EXPLAIN THE "TAKING IT HOME" ASSIGNMENTS

WORKBOOK PAGES 37-39

Each week they will have a Taking It Home assignment to be completed by the next week. There are three sections called: Towards Yourself, Towards Others, and Towards God. Encourage them to take the time and do the assignment as you will be briefly going through them the next week.

CLOSING TIME: Ending the session

Take Prayer Requests

This can be done a variety of ways:

- verbally shared in group setting
- hand out note cards to group members to write out their requests.
- set out a note book that students can write in throughout the session
- put out a Prayer Request Box with Prayer Request Slips.
- encourage the group members to come up with other ways to share prayer requests.

Close in Prayer

TAKING IT HOME

WEEK THREE

TOWARDS YOURSELF...A Question to Take to My Heart:

Look into your heart for the answer to these questions. This is introspection time...time to grapple with what drives your thinking and behavior. Be sure to capture your thoughts.

◈ How would I rate my current level of anger?

1.........2..........3..........4..........5..........6..........7..........8..........9
cool quite warm simmering very hot boiling over

◈ How would I rate my current effectiveness in handling my anger?

1.........2..........3..........4..........5..........6..........7..........8..........9
disastrous ineffective somewhat effective very effective

◈ Which anger helps that I checked have I used this week and how have they worked?

◈ What are some ways I am coping with my pain? In what ways are my current coping skills helping me?

◈ In what ways are my current coping skills keeping me stuck?

◈ What are my warning signs that signal when I am getting angry?

◈ Write about a recent time when you got angry. How did you handle the situation? Do you think your action (or inaction) worked for or against you?

TOWARDS OTHERS...A Question to Take to Others:

Healing cannot become complete without affecting the lives of those around us as well. Be courageous and go outside your comfort zone to take a risk and work on your relationships with others.

◈ Are you angry at your parents right now? If so, what are you angry at them for?

I'm angry at my dad because:

I'm angry at my mom because:

◈ What things would you like to say to either or both parents right now? These are your private thoughts. They will not be shared so make them as honest as possible.

Mom –

Dad -

◈ Take a minute and think about a recent time when you got angry. Did you express it freely? Did you direct it toward the right people? Or did you keep your anger inside? And if you did express it, did you do it appropriately or did you make a scene?

TOWARDS GOD…A Question to Take to God:

When you ask God a question, expect His Spirit to respond to your heart. Be careful not to rush it, or manufacture an answer. Don't jot down your idea of the "right answer". Just pose the question to God, and wait on Him to speak personally in a fresh way.

◈ What questions about God does your family situation cause for you?

◈ Do you need to reach out to Jesus and let Him heal your pain?

◈ Do you believe anger is a sin? Why or why not?

◈ "God, it's not easy to admit that I am angry at You. What do you think of my anger toward You? What would you like to tell me about my anger towards you? I know you know my every thought anyway, so how do you feel about me right now?"

ATTACHMENT A

(3) G

(1) E

(2) T

(2) I

(1) N

(1) A

(1) R

(1) P

For the "Wheel of Fortune" activity you will need to enlarge and copy these letters onto card stock. You will need to make the number of letters indicated on each card. You will need letters to spell out "GETTING A GRIP."

ANGER SMARTS

- ☐ Anger is a normal response to hurt, frustration or fear.
- ☐ It isn't wrong to get angry. It's what you do when you're angry that can create a problem.
- ☐ You control what you do with your anger. It's a choice that only you can make.
- ☐ Expressing anger from time to time can be good for your health. Keeping it bottled in can be harmful to your health.
- ☐ It is easier to express anger in responsible ways when you stop and think first.
- ☐ Anger drains energy that you could apply toward other goals.
- ☐ The more you take control of your anger, the more at peace you will become.
- ☐ When you stay angry at someone, you are giving that person control over you.
- ☐ It is wrong for you to be the target of another's anger. It is also wrong for you to use anger to scare and control others.
- ☐ Forgiveness will help you let go of anger.
- ☐ Anger turns into bitterness that will eat a hole right through you.
- ☐ Learn to recognize your anger signs. When you feel things boiling, walk away before you say or do something you will regret.
- ☐ Be careful not to take your anger out on other people.
- ☐ If anger persists, find someone you trust to talk to; maybe a pastor or a counselor.

Hurts Band-aids Don't Cover

IDENTIFYING THE HURTS

This is a very important session. In this session, we will be stressing that it is not their fault. Make sure they know that there is nothing they could or could not have done to cause or prevent their parents' divorce. We will begin by exploring deeper into their self-esteem and move into a time of reflection as they identify the hurts and disappointments they have experienced. Be sure to hold this week up in your prayers as this is when the real work begins.

Lesson Four
Week 4

Verse of the week:

"Come to Me, all you who labor and are heavy laden, and I will give you rest...the gift of God is eternal life in Christ Jesus our Lord."

Matthew 11:2

PREP TIME

1. Spend time in prayer for:
   a. your heart as you prepare for this lesson
   b. the students who will be attending this week, that God would open their hearts and help them to share their feelings
   c. the other leaders helping with the evening
   d. all student prayer requests from last week
2. Read through the lesson and make sure you understand the material and activities
3. Gather supplies for projects
4. Write feeling words on the back of index cards (Attachment A)
5. Bring double sided tape, pens, and thumb tacks or push pins
6. Prepare Wheel of Fortune sheets (Attachment B) and tape them to wall
7. CD player with soft Christian music
8. Make a large heart on a piece of red poster board and cut a zigzag through it
9. Copy and cut out paper band-aids (Attachment C) (approx. 6 per person)
10. Workbooks

Be Blessed!

"The Lord is a shelter for the oppressed, a refuge in time of trouble. Those who know your name trust in you, for you, O Lord, have never abandoned anyone who searches for you."

Psalms 9:9-10

HIGHLIGHTS

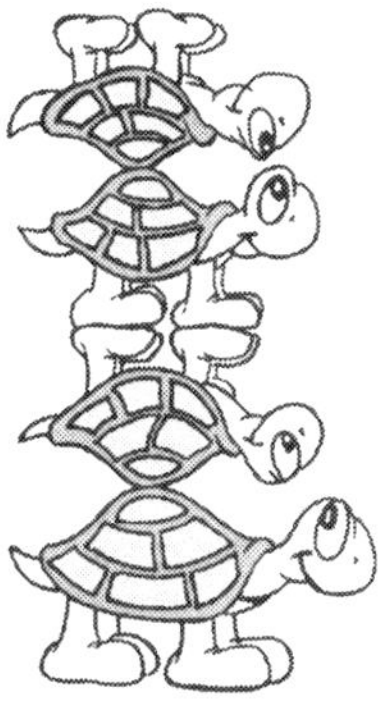

Hurts Band-aids Don't Cover

1. Get Off My Back Mixer
2. Wheel of Fortune
3. Nugget of Truth – Your Self Esteem Temperature
4. Identifying the Hurts
5. Common Worries & Stressors
6. Hurts Band-aids Don't Cover
7. Taking It Home

WEEK FOUR - SESSION FOUR

We are so glad you are here tonight. Going through a divorce can be very hard on your self-esteem. Tonight we are going to take a deeper look into the various hurts and losses you are experiencing. Be sure to quiet yourself and allow your feelings to open up. Remember we are all going through the same things and are experiencing the same pain. Don't forget that this is your comfort zone. You are safe here.

GET OFF MY BACK MIXER

ATTACHMENT A

Write a feeling word (found on Attachment A) on a 3x5 card or label for every teen. Place a piece of double sided tape on the back of each card. As each teen enters put a card or label (that they have not seen) on their back. If the tape does not stick use a pin to attach it to the back of their shirt. Tell them they have to guess what feeling is written on their back by asking other people questions.

Rule: They can only ask "Yes" or "No" questions.

Examples of feelings you could use: Depressed, Lonely, Relieved, Scared, Abandoned, Aching, Aggravated, Alone, Anxious, Conflicted, Bitter, Bruised, Burdened, etc. See Attachment A for more suggestions.
After some time, go around the room and ask everyone what they think their feeling is.

After the *Get Off My Back Mixer* gather back into a group and open in prayer. This would be a good time to check in with the group and see how things are going for them at home.

WHEEL OF FORTUNE

ATTACHMENT B

It's Not My Fault

The title of this week's lesson is "It's Not My Fault". Be sure to print the letters ahead of time and post on a bulletin board or wall before the teens arrive. Take turns like last week asking each teen to select a letter. For each correct letter they select, turn the letter or letters over and give them a chance to solve the puzzle. See **Lesson One** for a complete list of suggested rules.

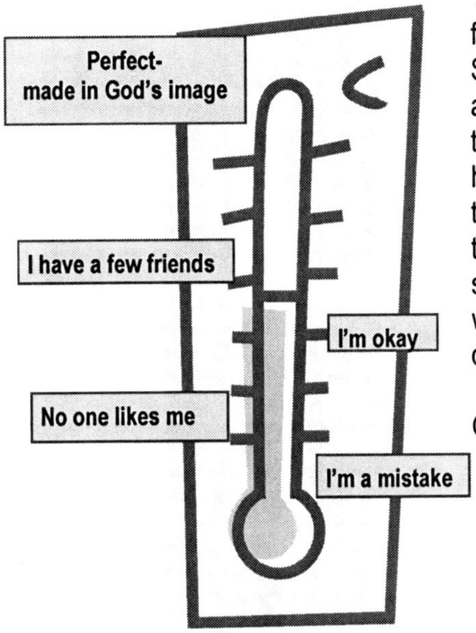

What's your self - esteem temperature?

Take some time to go over the homework assignment from last week. Do not feel pressured to answer the questions teens share for question #4 below. Sometimes it is enough just knowing that it is okay to ask questions about God and/or realize that there are others who struggle with the same type of questions. Sometimes teens can come up with some pretty deep questions, if this happens, don't hesitate to tell them you'll look further into it and get back to them next week. It is okay to respond by saying, "That is a very good question. Can I have some time to consider it before I give you my opinion?" Or sometimes it is best to say to the student, "That is a very thoughtful question, what do you think?" This validates them and also gives them an opportunity to clarify their thoughts, feelings and ideas.

Go over TAKE HOME assignment:

- Which Anger Helps that I checked last week have I used and how have they worked?
- What are the warning signs that signal when you're getting angry?
- Tell us about a recent time when you got angry. How did you handle the situation? Do you think your action (or inaction) worked for or against you?
- What questions about God does your family situation cause for you?

More than a Shadow
(optional activity)

Get an overhead projector and some thin white paper. Have each kid, one at a time, stand between the projector and paper and a leader traces their outline from shoulders up. Then as you're doing that, have everyone list positive comments about the person to be written on the same paper. Write comments in the inside of the shadow.

Nugget of Truth: Your Self-Esteem Temperature

Your self esteem can take quite a beating at a time like this. It is very important that you do not internalize what is happening and beat yourself up. There was nothing you could or could not have done to change what is happening to your family. We need to continue to find people who will build us up and remind us of our good qualities. It is a time to find honest, caring friends. Let's see how you're doing?

HOW YA DOING?

So, If It's Not Your Fault, Whose Is It? WORKBOOK PAGES 42-43

When things go wrong, it is a normal response to want to blame someone. It is human nature, when things go wrong, to think someone else has caused them to happen. It is easy to say someone did something or someone didn't do something to cause the problem. Either way someone is to blame. When divorce happens in a family you feel the same way. We tend to blame ourselves, others, or God. Let's take a look at some scenarios and see who you tend to blame.

BLAME GAME

WORKBOOK PAGES 44-46

Look back at the "Blame Game" workbook page, who do you usually tend to blame? Yourself? God? Others? Or No One? It is very important for you not to blame yourself. Your parents are adults and they made this choice themselves. You could not have done anything to change the situation, no matter how hard you tried.

There is one more important piece to this self-esteem puzzle. No matter how your parents or anyone treats you, you are valuable in God's eyes. Depending on where you are in your faith journey right now, this may be hard for you to accept. But no matter what happens, hang on to this simple truth – You are made in God's image. This means that you are truly good; that you are more special than you can even imagine. You never have to earn God's love; only trust it. Letting God love you will help you love yourself and others again.

Nugget of Truth: Identifying the Hurts

There are so many things that can affect how we feel about ourselves and our lives. One of the major reasons is because we feel our life is out of control. There are many things that are going on around us and we have little idea how to handle them. As life is changing all around you, there are so many questions without any real answers. Sometimes they say only time will tell. But when so much is happening and so much is at stake, it is hard to just wait patiently. What are some common worries and stressors that you may be facing right now? How do these fears, questions, and unknown answers affect your surroundings and your relationships?

TIPS TO REBUILD YOUR SELF-ESTEEM

Surround Yourself with Positive People - Negative people drag you down, positive people motivate others.

Take Risks – Step outside your comfort zone.

Keep an Acknowledgement Journal – Acknowledge your self worth by recognizing your accomplishments.

Make a Commitment to Change – You can choose to feel motivated, or you can choose to feel discouraged about yourself and your life.

Change your Negative Self Talk – If you find yourself talking negatively, find a way to turn it around.

Ask for Support – If you find you cannot make these changes on your own, then ask others for help.

Take Action – Get involved in a physical fitness program.

COMMON WORRIES AND STRESSORS

WORKBOOK PAGE 47-48

Go over the questions that some of the teens are worrying about. Try to encourage them to ask their parents any questions they feel comfortable asking. For the ones there are no answers for, encourage them to keep those in mind over the next few weeks and maybe we can help them discover some peace in those situations. Ask them to lay each fear and stress down at the feet of Jesus over the next week. He is the only one that truly has all the answers and He always knows what's best for them. Help them to find their hope and rest in Him. Knowing that whatever the answers will be, God will always be there for them.

We are now going to move into a very serious, quiet time of reflection and healing. This activity will be one of your most revealing activities. Encourage everyone to calm down and tell them that this is a time to reflect on their lives and their own personal experiences. Try to eliminate any extra talking and help the teens to focus on themselves right now. It may be helpful to put some space between them.

Build Me Up Note Card
(Optional Activity)

Pass around a note card t each teen. Have them write something positive about the person on their left. At the end of the ses sion, take time for them t share their cards with eac other. You can also con- tinue passing the card to the right until you make it around the circle. Give each teen their card at the end of

HURTS BAND-AIDS CAN'T COVER

Have soft music playing in the background. (see Reflective Songs in Activity Guide)

ATTACHMENT C

This activity encourages teens to consider their hurts, worries and fears and gives them an opportunity to share hurts that they have been carrying inside. Beforehand, you need to prepare a large red heart and cut a zigzag through it like a broken heart and put it on the wall. You also need to copy and cut out plenty of the band-aids (Attachment C). Make sure you have plenty of pens, thumb tacks or tape. Place enough band-aids out on the tables so every person has enough for at least six each, but don't specifically hand six to each person. Play some soft soothing Christian music in the background (see Activity Guide for suggestions). Leave at least a half hour for this activity.

Start by saying something like:

We all have many hurts that have affected us by our parent's choice to separate or divorce. Many times these hurts were not caused by us and we have no control over stopping them. The hard thing about these hurts is that there is no quick fix. Whatever it is that has caused pain in your life, it hurts very bad. We were taught when we were young that band-aids cured everything. When we fell and got hurt, we would run to our mom and she would give it a kiss and put a band-aid on it, it was so easy then. But divorce is not a minor scrape that heals quickly. These hurts cannot be healed by simply putting a band-aid on it. These hurts go deep and we may think that we will never be okay again. On every table there are some band-aids. Spend some time reflecting on different hurts, worries or fears that you have experienced. When you do, write them on the band-aids in front of you. When you feel ready you can pin or tape them on the broken heart on the wall.

Follow Up Time

1. Take time this week to send out "Miss You" cards to those who may have only come to one session.
2. Send a note of appreciation to someone in your group who was particularly helpful in your group.
3. Send a note of encouragement to someone in your group who was open or shared a vulnerability.
4. Send an "You're in my prayers" note to someone who shared a prayer request.

There is no need for these to be lengthy notes. Remind them that they are important to the group and important to God.

Leaders Note: To get things going, you can read some of the suggestions in Attachment D. Make sure you also remind them that this is their safe zone and no one else will be seeing what they write.

After you feel they are ready to move on, remind them that the things they have shared will not be seen by anybody else. Then tell them you will be bringing these band-aids back and will be using them in another activity down the road.

Leaders: Take the heart with all the band-aids on it home or place in storage until week # 10.

EXPLAIN THE "TAKING IT HOME" ASSIGNMENTS

WORKBOOK PAGE 49-51

Take time to look over the Taking It Home assignment with your group. Let them know that this assignment is a great way for them to really process what you have covered this week. Encourage them all to take the time and do the assignment as you will be briefly going through them the next week.

CLOSING TIME: Ending the session

Take Prayer Requests

This can be done in a variety of ways:

- verbally shared in group setting
- hand out note cards to group members to write out their requests.
- set out a note book that students can write in throughout the session
- put out a Prayer Request Box with Prayer Request Slips
- encourage the group members to come up with other ways to share prayer requests.

Close in Prayer:

TOWARDS YOURSELF...A Question to Take to My Heart:

Look into your heart for the answer to these questions. This is introspection time – time to grapple with what drives your thinking and behavior. Be sure to capture your thoughts.

- Has your parents' breakup stirred up any negative thoughts and feelings about yourself? If so, what are they?

- Do you or have you ever blamed yourself for your parent's divorce? Why?

- Set a goal for yourself. Make sure it is realistic, specific and measurable and has a deadline. For example: "I'm going to get a job and work at it for at least 2 months, so I can have money to go out with my friends."

- Because your life might be difficult now, that doesn't mean it always will be. Write about how you want your life to be in the future. For example: What career do you want to pursue? Will you marry and have children? Where do you want to live?

TOWARDS OTHERS...A Question to Take to Others:

Healing cannot become complete without affecting the lives of those around us as well. Be courageous and go outside your comfort zone to take a risk and work on your relationships with others.

- What questions do you need to ask your parents that would relieve some unnecessary stress or worry in your life? When will you ask them?

- Ask a close friend or family member what he or she thinks is good about you. Write down what they tell you.

- Who can you put into your life that will feed you with positive things?

- Who do you need to remove from your life because they fill you with too many negative things?

TOWARDS GOD...A Question to Take to God:

When you ask God a question, expect His Spirit to respond to your heart. Be careful not to rush it, or manufacture an answer. Don't jot down your idea of the "right answer". Just pose the question to God, and wait on Him to speak personally in a fresh way.

- You are made in God's image. What does that mean to you? Read Genesis 1:27.
  Does God make mistakes?

- What do you have to do to earn God's love and acceptance?

- Imagine having a conversation with God. Ask how God sees you, and then listen for God's voice in your heart. Write down what you hear God saying.

"GET OFF MY BACK" MIXER

Write each feeling on a 3x5 card or label. Place a piece of double sided tape on the back of each card or label. As each teen enters put a card (that they have not seen) on their back. Tell them they have to guess what feeling is written on their back by asking other people questions for them to answer.

Rule: They can only ask "Yes" or "No" questions.

FEELINGS

GUILT
ANGER
BLAME
FRUSTRATION
JEALOUSY
HURT
FEAR
NUMB
WORRY
UGLY
QUIET
ANXIOUS
SELFISH
RELIEVED
ANNOYED
SILLY
SURPRISED
DISCOURAGED
INSECURE
CALM
HELPLESS
MISERABLE
HOPEFUL
FUNNY
IMPATIENT
MISUNDERSTOOD
EXCITED
NERVOUS
PHONY
NEUTRAL
TERRIBLE
NEEDY
LOVED

STRESSED
TIRED
SAD
DEPRESSED
MAD
REJECTED
EMPTY
ALONE
SCARED
SORRY
NEGLECTED
UNHAPPY
ASHAMED
BITTER
UNAPPRECIATED
UPSET
CONFUSED
BRAVE
EXHAUSTED
HAPPY
LONELY
OVERWHELMED
IRRITATED
PESSIMISTIC
GRATEFUL
INDIFFERENT
RESENTFUL
JUDGED
GLAD
LOYAL
OPTIMISTIC
STRONG
SECURE

ATTACHMENT B

(1) I

(3) T

(1) '

(1) S

(1) O

(1) M

(1) Y

(1) F

For the "Wheel of Fortune" activity you will need to enlarge and copy these letters onto card stock. You will need to make the number of letters indicated on each card. You will need letters to spell out "IT'S NOT MY FAULT."

ATTACHMENT B

A

(1)

U

(1)

L

(1)

N

(1)

For the "Wheel of Fortune" activity you will need to enlarge and copy these letters onto card stock. You will need to make the number of letters indicated on each card. You will need letters to spell out "IT'S NOT MY FAULT."

ATTACHMENT C

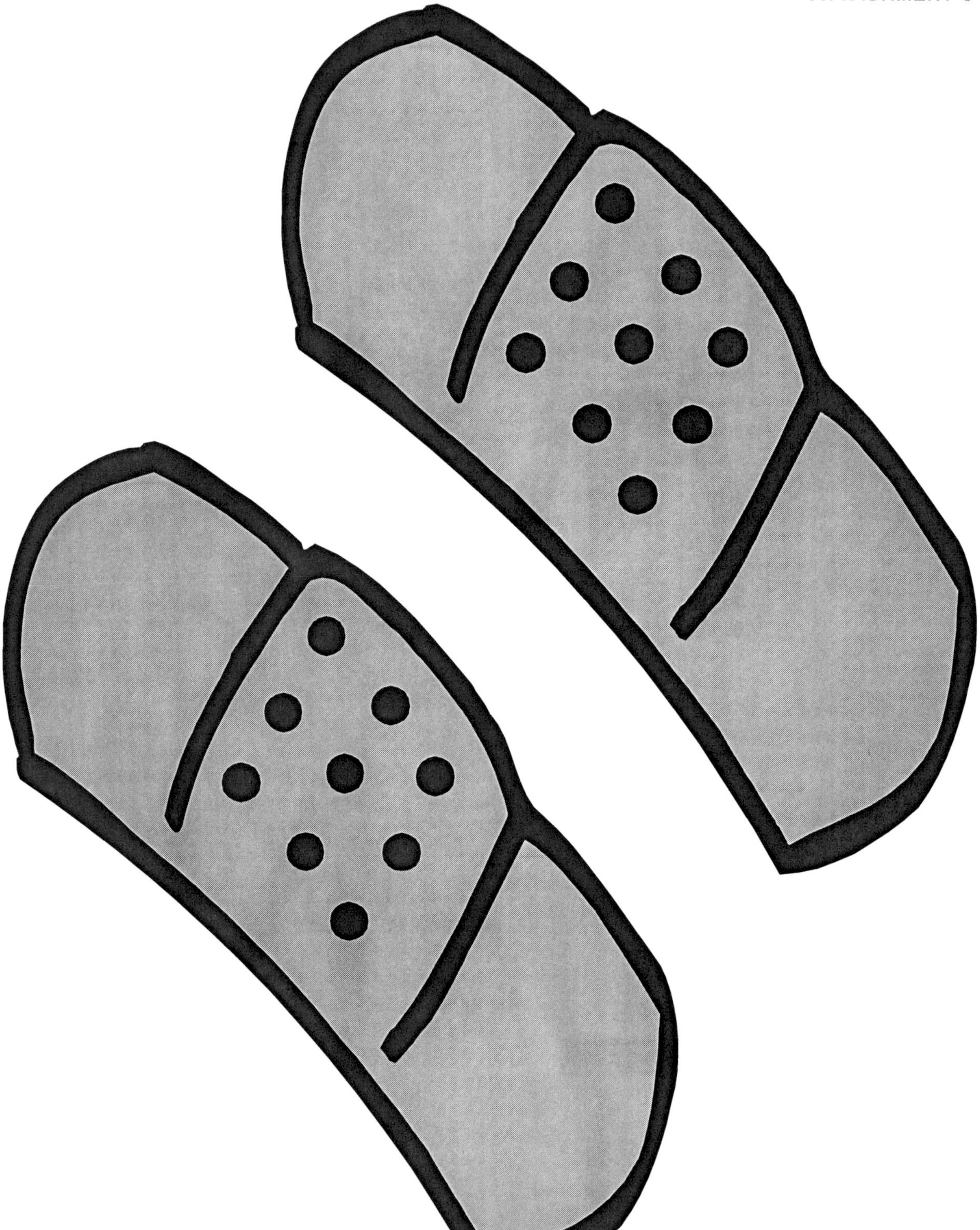

HURTS BAND-AIDS CAN'T COVER

Here are some examples to get things rolling

ATTACHMENT D

⇒ Loss of both parents in the same home

⇒ Feeling rejected by either parent

⇒ Loss of friends

⇒ Loss of home

⇒ Hearing parents fighting

⇒ Feeling like being torn between two homes

⇒ Seeing mom or dad hurting

⇒ Feeling abandoned by a parent

⇒ Loss of grandparents

⇒ Feeling it was your fault (that you did something wrong)

⇒ Blame

⇒ Loneliness

⇒ Questioning why God isn't answering your prayers

⇒ Feeling stuck in the middle

⇒ Mixed loyalties

⇒ Having to move

⇒ Missing your parent not living with you

⇒ Jealous of boyfriend/girlfriend/new spouse or step children who get to live with other parent

⇒ Loss of dreams

⇒ Loss of planned family vacations

⇒ Hurts from overhearing things said between parents in arguments

⇒ Loss of a pet

⇒ Questioning God's love for you

Jesus Bags

Lesson Five
Week 5

Salvation Message

In this session, we will be stressing two main ideas; first, to help them define who they are and second, to help them to accept and understand who they are in Christ. Be prepared to share your salvation story and the gospel message. Be in prayer for those who do not yet know Jesus as their personal Savior; that they will pray to receive Him as a result of this session.

PREP TIME

1. Spend time in prayer for:
   a. your heart as you prepare for this lesson
   b. the students who will be attending this week, that God would open their hearts and help them to share their feelings
   c. the other leaders helping with this session
   d. any prayer requests from the students from last week
2. Read through the lesson and make sure you understand the material and activities
3. Gather supplies for projects.
4. Bring index cards and pens for everyone
5. Prepare Wheel of Fortune sheets (Attachment A) and tape to wall
6. Find items for Pick Two (Attachment B)
7. Copy and cut out Jesus Hearts (Attachment C)
8. Copy on card stock and cut out My Identity in Christ wallet cards (Attachment D) (laminate if possible)
9. CD player with soft Christian music
10. Bring paper lunch bags, markers, and glue
11. Bring old magazines for teens to cut out pictures
12. Workbooks

HIGHLIGHTS

Jesus Bags

1. Review Ground Rules
2. Who Am I Mixer
3. Wheel of Fortune
4. Common Ground
5. Nugget of Truth: I Miss Being Me
6. Jesus Bags
7. Nugget of Truth: Where Is Jesus In Your Life?
8. My Identity in Christ
9. Taking it Home

Verses of the week:

"And have put on the new self, which is being renewed in knowledge in the image of its creator."

Colossians 3:10

Be Blessed!

"I will praise you because I am fearfully and wonderfully made; your works are wonderful, I know that full well."

Psalm 139:14

WEEK FIVE - SESSION FIVE

Lesson Five
Week 5

Tonight we are going to have fun rediscovering who we are. We encourage you to be creative and thoughtful in the process. Sometimes when we go through tough times, we lose sight of who we are or try to become someone we aren't. Be free tonight to explore who you are as we embark on a journey to find ourselves again.

WHO AM I? MIXER

Hand out an index card to everyone as they enter the room. Tell them to write their first name vertically on the card, one letter at a time. When they are done, ask them to come up with a descriptive word or phrase about themselves that starts with that letter of the alphabet. When finished, go around the room and have everyone describe themselves.

EXAMPLES:

B – Basketball player
E – Exhausted
T – Tall
H – Happy

Or

L – Lonely
A – Anxious
U – Unhappy
R – Rambunctious
A – Angry

After the *"Who Am I?"* mixer, gather back into a group and open in prayer.

WHEEL OF FORTUNE

ATTACHMENT A

Who Knows You Baby?

The title of this week's lesson is "Who Knows You Baby?". Be sure to print the letters ahead of time and post on a bulletin board or wall before the teens arrive. Take turns like last week asking each teen to select a letter. For each correct letter they select, turn the letter or letters over and give them a chance to solve the puzzle. See **Lesson One** for a complete list of suggested rules.

How's the Take Home Assignment Going?

Encourage everyone to take some time every week to press on deeper and work through the questions. Remind them that if they ever want to talk to you one on one you are available.

Teens need to feel important and know that you value their friendship.

Last time we discussed common stresses and worries we feel when our family goes through a divorce. In our Taking It Home assignments, we worked on asking our parents the questions we needed answered and then releasing the rest to Christ. Let's review some of your assignments.

Go over *TAKE HOME* assignment:

- Set a goal for yourself. Make sure it is realistic, specific and measurable and has a deadline. For example: I'm going to get a job and work at it for at least 2 months, so I can have money to go out with my friends.
- You are made in God's image. What does that mean to you?
- Because your life might be difficult now, that doesn't mean it always will be. Write about how you want your life to be in the future. For example: What career do you want to pursue? Will you marry and have children? Where do you want to live?

Nugget of Truth: I Miss Being Me

Divorce can really shake up our lives. You may find yourself wondering if you are a different person now compared to who you were before your parents' separation or divorce. It's true, sometimes when our circumstances or surroundings change, it makes us feel like we have changed. But those changes are usually only temporary. You should find yourself back to the "old you" as time goes on.

PICK TWO

ATTACHMENT B

Place your miscellaneous objects out in the middle of the room (see Attachment B for ideas). Go around the room and have each teen pick out one item that reminds them of who they were before the divorce and one item that represents them after the divorce. Each teen then takes a turn sharing why they chose those items or what they thought of when picking those items. It could relate to a situation, a story, a memory, whatever.

Did you find yourself remembering things you haven't thought of in awhile? How did that feel? Hopefully this activity triggered some memories past and present. Let's take a deeper look into who you were before your parents separated and who you are now.

OLD VERSUS NEW

WORKBOOK PAGE 54

Take some time to complete the workbook page Old vs. New. This is a chance for you to look at how you have changed since your parents divorce or separation or how things have changed around you. Examples: carefree, sense of humor, deep thinker, worrier, responsible, cry a lot, home more, home less, patient, impatient, moody, happy, sad, etc. Are you surprised at the difference? Do you miss the old you?

JESUS BAGS

ATTACHMENT C

Play soft music in the background for this activity. (see Reflective Songs in Activity Guide)

We are now going to do an activity that will help each of us concentrate and remember who we are, on the inside and on the outside. It is time to remind yourself what makes you unique. What sports you enjoy, things you like to do in your spare time, people you like to be with, activities you enjoy, foods you like, things that drive you crazy, things that are important to you, what makes you tick, what ticks you off, memories that mean the most to you, school subjects you enjoy, dreams for your future, fears in your life. It can be anything.

The idea of this activity is to get the kids to think about who they are and how they think others see them. Try to get them to think beyond who others say they are and to go deeper into who **they** really are. Things **they** like to do, things **they** feel, things that mean a lot to **them,** people who mean a lot to **them,** not just who others want them to be.

Hand out a lunch size paper bag to everyone and have lots of miscellaneous magazines out on the tables. Tell them to envision the bag representing themselves. Have them go through the magazines and cut out and glue pictures or words onto their bag that illustrate who they are. Ask them to decorate the outside of the bag with things that describe who they are on the outside. Make sure they include their names somewhere as well. Then tell them you want them to look at who they are on the inside as well and as they go through the magazines, cut out things that represent who they are in the inside and place them inside their bag. This could be feelings **they** feel, close relationships **they** have, fears **they** feel, secrets **they** hold, thoughts **they** have, struggles **they** experience, people **they** trust, etc. Give them about 30 minutes to work on this part of the project.

Now is the time to share the salvation story. Be prepared to share your personal salvation message. While they are doing their bags, take some time to explain how God wants to come into their lives and help them through their struggles and pain. Share with them all they have to do is ask Jesus into their hearts and He will heal all those hurts and take away all those fears. By asking Him into their heart, they can receive forgiveness for all those secrets and feelings they try to hide.

At this time, put the Jesus hearts (Attachment C) on the tables and encourage them to decorate their heart how they perceive Jesus in their lives. Then invite those who have Christ in their lives to put their Jesus heart inside their bag. Be careful to not just assume everyone has accepted Christ. Let them know that if they have not accepted Christ, encourage them to come and talk to any of the leaders sometime during the night so that they can be sure that they have Jesus in their life (bag).

After the bags are completed, put the bags aside until the end of this sesson. At that time have everyone go around the room and explain what they put on their bags, in their bags and why. Or if time is short you can do some next week or spread them out over the next few weeks.

Nugget of Truth: Where is Jesus in Your Life?

Although divorce can feel like your whole life has been turned upside down, it is good to remember that the person you were before your parents separated is still the same person you are now. You have the same likes and dislikes. You enjoy the same activities as you did before. Who you are on the inside, the person God created, is the same today as yesterday, as last week, as last year, even as before your parents separated. Maybe priorities or behaviors have seemed to have changed temporarily but the real you will appear again someday.

God has created each of us for a specific purpose. That purpose does not change although things around us may be changing daily; sometimes even minute by minute. This is very exciting for those who have given their lives to Jesus because they know their identity is not based on things that change every time the wind blows. God has made you unique. There is no other person like you in the whole universe! No one else can take your place in this exact situation that you are in. You have a very significant purpose for who you are and what you can do in the circumstances that surround you. If you ever feel you don't belong here and you were just a mistake - remember you do have a purpose and you were born for "such a time as this". How can this purpose be fulfilled today? How about in this specific trial in your life?

WHO I AM IN CHRIST

WORKBOOK PAGE 55

Go over the chart in their workbooks with everyone in order to remind them who they are in Christ. Don't take the time tonight to go over each one. Encourage them to take a closer look at it over the week and spend some time looking up the scriptures.

My Identity In Christ Cards

ATTACHMENT D

Pass out a wallet card to everyone. Realizing that your true identity lies in Christ is a very important part of how you view yourself. You need to remind yourself that you are perfect in His sight. Although others may look at you and remind you of all your faults, remember God doesn't make mistakes and you are a beautiful person inside and out. When you feel as if you are spinning in circles and are being constantly told you are never good enough, take out this card to remind yourself of your unending worth in Christ.

WRAPPING UP THE JESUS BAGS

Take the remainder of the night and have everyone go around the room and explain everything they put on their bags, in their bags, and why. Make sure the atmosphere is full of respect and common courtesy as they share. Depending on the number of teens you have, you may not have enough time to do them all in one night. If not, keep them and finish the next time you meet.

EXPLAIN THE "TAKING IT HOME" ASSIGNMENTS

WORKBOOK PAGES 56-58

Take time to look over the Taking It Home assignment with your group. Let them know that this assignment is a great way for them to really process what you have covered this week. Encourage them all to take the time and do the assignment as you will be briefly going through them the next week.

CLOSING TIME: Ending the session

Take Prayer Requests

This can be done a variety of ways:

- verbally shared in group setting
- hand out note cards to group members to write out their requests
- set out a note book that students can write in throughout the session
- put out a Prayer Request Box with Prayer Request Slips
- encourage the group members to come up with other ways to share prayer requests

Close in Prayer:

TOWARDS YOURSELF...A Question to Take to My Heart:

Look into your heart for the answer to these questions. This is introspection time – time to grapple with what drives your thinking and behavior. Be sure to capture your thoughts.

- Were there things you thought of but were afraid to put on or in your Jesus bag? What were they? Why could you not share them?

- What things on your bag were you proud of? Not proud of?

- After doing your Jesus Bags and seeing others, what things would you like to improve in yourself?

- Do you miss the old you? What are some things you can do to bring that person back?

TOWARDS OTHERS…A Question to Take to Others:

Healing cannot become complete without affecting the lives of those around us as well. Be courageous and go outside your comfort zone to take a risk and work on your relationships with others.

- Are your frustrations and hurts about your current home situation affecting those around you? Your relationships? Your grades? In what way?

- What items did you pick for the "pick two" exercise and why?

- Ask someone you trust what changes they have seen in you since your parents separated. Do you think these are good changes or bad changes?

- Take your "Jesus bag" home with you and share it with one or both of your parents.

TOWARDS GOD...A Question to Take to God:

When you ask God a question, expect His Spirit to respond to your heart. Be careful not to rush it, or manufacture an answer. Don't jot down your idea of the "right answer". Just pose the question to God, and wait on Him to speak personally in a fresh way.

- If you have not previously asked Jesus into you heart, go to your leader, a pastor or another Christian friend and do it right away!!!

- If you asked Jesus into your heart tonight at group, tell someone about it right away. Who did you tell and how did they respond?

- If you are not ready to receive Jesus into your life yet, just ask Jesus to show Himself and His love to you this week.

- As you read the scriptures that prove your worth to Christ, which two meant the most to you?

(1) N

(2) W

(1) S

(1) H

(2) Y

(3) O

(1) U

(1) K

For the "Wheel of Fortune" activity you will need to enlarge and copy these letters onto card stock. You will need to make the number of letters indicated on each card. You will need letters to spell out "WHO KNOWS YOU BABY?."

B

(2)

A

(1)

?

(1)

For the "Wheel of Fortune" activity you will need to enlarge and copy these letters onto card stock. You will need to make the number of letters indicated on each card. You will need letters to spell out "WHO KNOWS YOU BABY?."

Pick Two

Possible items to put out for teens to pick from. Have each teen pick one item that represents who they were before the divorce and one item that represents them after the divorce. When finished, go around the room and share why they picked these items.

An old tennis shoe
A bat
A cookie
Dish soap
Toothbrush
Camera
CD
Photo album
Piece of gum
Watch
Glue
Keys
Lotion
Stapler
Credit card
Picture
Ring
Pen
Spoon
Glove
Cell phone
Hat
Dryer sheet
Lunch box
Candy
Notebook
Battery
Toy
Lego
Deck of cards
Earphones
Coupon
A button
Eraser
Marker
Remote control
A ball
Doll
A box
Movie
Dollar bill
A coin
Refrigerator magnet
Kleenex
Paper clip
Scissor

JESUS BAGS

MY IDENTITY IN CHRIST CARDS

My Identity in Christ

Because of Christ's redemption, I am a new creation of infinite worth.
I am deeply loved, I am completely forgiven,
I am fully pleasing, I am totally accepted by God.
I am absolutely complete in Christ.

When my performance,
Reflects my new identity in Christ,
That reflection is dynamically unique.

There has never been another like me in the history of mankind,
Nor will there ever be.
God has made me an original, One of a kind,
Really somebody!

My Identity in Christ

Because of Christ's redemption, I am a new creation of infinite worth.
I am deeply loved, I am completely forgiven,
I am fully pleasing, I am totally accepted by God.
I am absolutely complete in Christ.

When my performance,
Reflects my new identity in Christ,
That reflection is dynamically unique.

There has never been another like me in the history of mankind,
Nor will there ever be.
God has made me an original, One of a kind,
Really somebody!

My Identity in Christ

Because of Christ's redemption, I am a new creation of infinite worth.
I am deeply loved, I am completely forgiven,
I am fully pleasing, I am totally accepted by God.
I am absolutely complete in Christ.

When my performance,
Reflects my new identity in Christ,
That reflection is dynamically unique.

There has never been another like me in the history of mankind,
Nor will there ever be.
God has made me an original, One of a kind,
Really somebody!

My Identity in Christ

Because of Christ's redemption, I am a new creation of infinite worth.
I am deeply loved, I am completely forgiven,
I am fully pleasing, I am totally accepted by God.
I am absolutely complete in Christ.

When my performance,
Reflects my new identity in Christ,
That reflection is dynamically unique.

There has never been another like me in the history of mankind,
Nor will there ever be.
God has made me an original, One of a kind,
Really somebody!

My Identity in Christ

Because of Christ's redemption, I am a new creation of infinite worth.
I am deeply loved, I am completely forgiven,
I am fully pleasing, I am totally accepted by God.
I am absolutely complete in Christ.

When my performance,
Reflects my new identity in Christ,
That reflection is dynamically unique.

There has never been another like me in the history of mankind,
Nor will there ever be.
God has made me an original, One of a kind,
Really somebody!

My Identity in Christ

Because of Christ's redemption, I am a new creation of infinite worth.
I am deeply loved, I am completely forgiven,
I am fully pleasing, I am totally accepted by God.
I am absolutely complete in Christ.

When my performance,
Reflects my new identity in Christ,
That reflection is dynamically unique.

There has never been another like me in the history of mankind,
Nor will there ever be.
God has made me an original, One of a kind,
Really somebody!

My Identity in Christ

Because of Christ's redemption, I am a new creation of infinite worth.
I am deeply loved, I am completely forgiven,
I am fully pleasing, I am totally accepted by God.
I am absolutely complete in Christ.

When my performance,
Reflects my new identity in Christ,
That reflection is dynamically unique.

There has never been another like me in the history of mankind,
Nor will there ever be.
God has made me an original, One of a kind,
Really somebody!

My Identity in Christ

Because of Christ's redemption, I am a new creation of infinite worth.
I am deeply loved, I am completely forgiven,
I am fully pleasing, I am totally accepted by God.
I am absolutely complete in Christ.

When my performance,
Reflects my new identity in Christ,
That reflection is dynamically unique.

There has never been another like me in the history of mankind,
Nor will there ever be.
God has made me an original, One of a kind,
Really somebody!

My Identity in Christ

Because of Christ's redemption, I am a new creation of infinite worth.
I am deeply loved, I am completely forgiven,
I am fully pleasing, I am totally accepted by God.
I am absolutely complete in Christ.

When my performance,
Reflects my new identity in Christ,
That reflection is dynamically unique.

There has never been another like me in the history of mankind,
Nor will there ever be.
God has made me an original, One of a kind,
Really somebody!

My Identity in Christ

Because of Christ's redemption, I am a new creation of infinite worth.
I am deeply loved, I am completely forgiven,
I am fully pleasing, I am totally accepted by God.
I am absolutely complete in Christ.

When my performance,
Reflects my new identity in Christ,
That reflection is dynamically unique.

There has never been another like me in the history of mankind,
Nor will there ever be.
God has made me an original, One of a kind,
Really somebody!

Where Is God When It Hurts

God is a God of Comfort

God is a God of comfort. In this session, we will read about Job and explore His healing touch through scripture. We will also help them discover their support system. We should constantly be reminding them that they have people who love them, including God. Be sure to be prayed up as many doors may be opened this week.

PREP TIME

1. Spend time in prayer for:
    a. your heart as you prepare for this lesson
    b. the students who will be attending this week, that God would open their hearts and help them to share their feelings
    c. the other leaders helping with this session
    d. all student prayer requests from last week
2. Read through the lesson and make sure you understand the material and activities
3. Gather supplies for projects
4. Bring extra Bibles
5. Copies of Scripture Search Game (Attachment A)
6. Prepare Wheel of Fortune sheets (Attachment B) and tape them to wall
7. Copy & cut the Ask for Help Cards (Attachment C) and put into envelopes
8. Copy and cut Comfort Cards (Attachment D) and put into envelopes
9. Prepare copies of Letter to God (Attachment E)
10. Copy on card stock and cut A Pivotal Prayer When You're in Crisis (Attachment F) (laminate if possible)
11. CD player with Christian music
12. Workbooks

HIGHLIGHTS

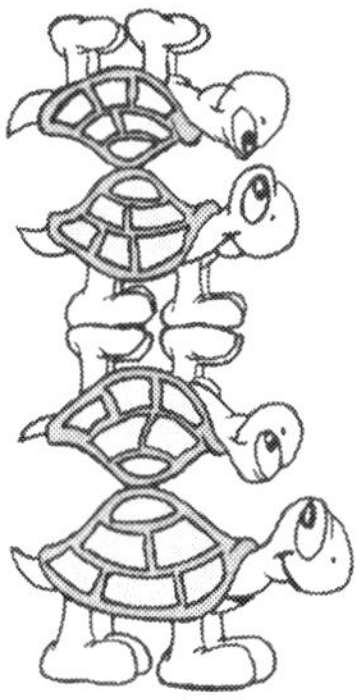

Where Is God When It Hurts

1. Scripture Search Game
2. Wheel of Fortune
3. Common Ground
4. Nugget of Truth– Where Is God
5. Job's Story
6. Nugget of Truth-Your Support System
7. Asking For Help Cards
8. Nugget of Truth– God Will Never Fail Us
9. Comfort Cards
10. Dear God Letter
11. Gently Lord
12. A Pivotal Prayer

Lesson Six
Week 6

Verses of the week:

"Be strong and courageous, do not be afraid or terrified because of them, for the Lord your God goes with you. He will never leave you nor forsake you."

Deuteronomy 31:6

Be Blessed!

"Because he loves me," says the Lord, "I will rescue him; I will protect him, for he acknowledges my name. He will call upon me, and I will answer him; I will be with him in trouble, I will deliver him and honor him. With long life will I satisfy him and show him my salvation."

Psalm 91:14-16

WEEK SIX - SESSION SIX

This session will be a time for you to recognize God's sole desire to comfort you. We will give you the opportunity to pour out your heart to God and allow Him to restore you again. Allow God to speak through His Scriptures and bring comfort to your pain. It won't be easy, but it'll be worth it. It is vital during this time in your life for you to know who you can count on and go to when you need help. God has put many people in our lives to help us through tough times. He never intends on us facing these trials on our own. Sometime the situations seem so overwhelming you cannot seem to bring yourself to ask for help. Remember the most important thing to keep in mind when you need someone, they should be people who you can trust and who will be objective and look out for your best interest.

SCRIPTURE SEARCH GAME

Answers at the end of the chapter.

ATTACHMENT A

Break into teams of two or more on each team. Make sure that each team has a Bible. Hand out a worksheet (Attachment A) to each team. The first team to look up all the scriptures, answer the questions and fill in the blanks to complete the Scripture wins. If time allows read the scriptures they looked up to discover God's true desire to comfort us. NOTE: Use an NIV translation so everyone is on the same page as Attachment A.

After the *Scripture Search Game* gather back into a group and open in prayer.

WHEEL OF FORTUNE

Where Is God When It Hurts?

ATTACHMENT B

The title of this week's lesson is "Where Is God When It Hurts?". Be sure to print the letters ahead of time and post on a bulletin board or wall before the teens arrive. Take turns like last week asking each teen to select a letter. For each correct letter they select, turn letter(s) over and give them a chance to solve the puzzle. If they guess incorrectly, their turn is over and play moves to the next person. See **Lesson One** for a complete list of suggested rules.

CHECK-IN TIME

-How are things going in your relationships with your parents?

-Are there things you are changing in your attitude that are making a difference at home?

-What are any "God Moments" that have happened?

Last week we spent a lot of time getting to know each other better. We learned how important Jesus is in our lives. Let's see how our assignment went.

Go over Take Home assignment:

- Are your frustrations and hurts about your current home situation affecting those around you? Your relationships? Your grades? In what way?

- Did you share your Jesus bag with your parents. How did they respond? How did you feel sharing it?

- As you read the scriptures that prove your worth to Christ which two meant the most to you?

Nugget of Truth: Where Is God?

At times like this, do you ever wonder where God is? Does He know? Does He even care? Are my prayers heard only by the walls that surround me? Is He near, or somewhere distant; only watching? Do you ever wonder if God has forgotten you? Does He hate you? Are you being punished for something you did or didn't do? Do you ever feel like you want to see God and want Him to answer your questions in person? These are good questions and if you hurt enough to ask such questions, you deserve an answer.

There was once a man who did just that. His name was Job. He too had all those questions but he demanded to hear from God himself, and God answered him. The history of this man and his detailed story is found in the book of Job in the Bible.

Job was a blameless and upright man, full of such sincere integrity. If anyone deserved blessings, Job did. Yet one day God allowed him to be tested. Job's life fell to pieces; calamity of every kind descended upon him. Raiders swept his fields, his livestock were captured or destroyed, his servants were put to the sword, and a house collapsed on his sons and daughters and killed them all. Disease struck him, and he was covered with painful sores from the soles of his feet to the top of his head. In all this, he continued to submit patiently to God, only to be mocked by his wife, who told him to "curse God and die!" (Job 2:9) Friends arrived and still he remained patient. For days they sat with him in silence, seeing how greatly he was suffering.

Job's Character

Strengths

- man of faith, patience and endurance
- known to others as a generous and caring person

Weaknesses

- allowed his suffering to overwhelm him and question God

Lessons we can learn from Job

- knowing God is better than knowing answers
- God is not uncaring
- pain is not always a punishment

Finally Job could contain himself no longer. In a torrent of grief and anger, he cries out, wishing he had never lived. He didn't curse God but he cursed the day he was born. The terrible curse he was under demeaned all the previous good in his life; it implied that his joy, his home, his peace, and the lives of his children had never meant a thing, because now they were all gone.

This became too much for Job's friends so they rebuked him also. On and on they lectured him. They told him suffering was a punishment for sin. The greater the sin, the greater the punishment would be. From the pain they saw Job in they assumed he must have done something really terrible to deserve such suffering. Obviously then they accused him of being a hypocrite, saying he was only pretending to be the great man of integrity as his whole life had portrayed. They told him if he would only confess and take his punishment, God would forgive him and relent, but instead, like a fool, he continued to complain. To hear these accusations was too unbearable for Job to stand. He raged in grief, defending himself and denouncing his friends. He even complained more against God and became even more bitter and inconsistent. One moment he wanted God to leave him alone, the next moment he cried out to Him to listen. Doesn't this sound like us today? Cursing God one moment, begging for His help the next.

In the end, Job got his answers. God answered from the heart of the whirlwind he was under. As Job remained faithful, God showed up. Let's look deeper into Job's story.

There are two amazing things about this crisis. The first is that God never explains to Job the reason for his suffering. It wasn't that God fully answered all of Job's questions that Job found his contentment. His contentment lay in feeling His presence and trusting His sovereignty. Secondly, Job was right. He didn't deserve what was happening. Not all suffering is our fault. We do bring some suffering upon ourselves as consequences for bad choices we make. Yet the innocent suffer too. Dreadful things happen, things we don't deserve or things that seem to be senseless.

In His justice though, God understands that this will seem unjust to us. He does not even try to give us the "answers" that we could not understand. Instead, He visits us, as He visited Job. Is He not God? He is a better answer than any "answers" could be. Indeed, He is the only possible answer. Though we find ourselves buried in a deeper dark than night, from the midst of the whirlwind, He will speak.

Nugget of Truth: Your Support System

Just like the solar system works interdependently, we work best when we rely on and work together with our support system. God never intended for us to face pain and loneliness alone. He surrounds us with people who love us and want what is best for us. Who has God put in your life?

Talking to people about our hurts and feelings is very important to do. In order to do this, we need to find people we can trust with our hurts, feelings, fears, and hearts. We need to find safe people who can help us, not hurt us. At a time of divorce or separation you really need to find people who you feel safe sharing with. At this point it may or may not be one of your parents. These people need to listen and act on behalf of your best interests. You must feel safe with them no matter what. These people could be Mom, Dad, siblings, other family members, Grandma or Grandpa, a school counselor, friends, a neighbor, Sunday School teacher, youth pastor, cell group leader, a friend of the family or even a coach. Remember: as events change in your lives this list can change. But right now it is very important you know the people who you can trust with your heart. Here is a little exercise for you to explore who is your support system. In your workbook, you will find a solar system. Write your name in the sun. Inside each planet write the names of people in your support system. As you think of these people, ask yourself these questions;

- who really listens to me
- who makes time for me
- who can I depend on
- is there someone who can be honest with me even when I don't want to hear it
- who has asked me how I am doing, who is always there for me
- if I was ever were in trouble who would I call for help
- is this a healthy and safe relationship

SUPPORT SYSTEM

WORKBOOK PAGE 60

Hand out the envelopes of the "Asking For Help" cards you prepared earlier to everyone. Have them go through them and on the cards asking for names, have them write down people who they could trust for help. Some cards are to be used just as reminders of what to do when they need help. Instruct them to keep these cards in a safe place so that when they are feeling overwhelmed, they can just pull them out and make a call or use them as a reminder of what they should do.

ASKING FOR HELP CARDS

ATTACHMENT C

Nugget of Truth: God Will Never Fail Us

Another hurt you may have is people you have counted on for many years may have disappointed you or failed you in some way. This can be hard to accept and understand. Sometimes it seems it's those around us who are doing all the changing. They don't seem to be the same people we thought they were. This can be very hurtful and confusing. We need to remember that at a time of crisis we all find ourselves a little shaky. It's important we continue to lift them up in prayer that God would help them sort out their issues just as He is helping you sort out yours. We can also reach out to others for comfort right now but keep in mind that people are human and they may fail us. That is why we should reach out to Christ, He will never fail us.

COMFORT CARDS

ATTACHMENT D

Let's look up some scriptures that talk about God's comfort in times of need. These would be great scriptures to memorize or to keep with you wherever you go. Spend some time in the group reading them together out loud. Pass out the envelope of comfort cards to everyone to look through and take home with them.

Do you ever feel that nobody will understand? That you are the only one who feels like you do? That no one else has ever gone through what you are going through? Even if it seems like no one else understands you, God does. He made you. He's watched the things that have hurt you. And He has gone through suffering Himself, just for you. He knows what it is like when people hurt you. He knows what it feels like to be rejected. Sometimes when so many things are up in air and we feel like we have no control over anything, we tend to feel too overwhelmed to bring it all to Christ. But that is exactly what God wants us to do. He is reaching out to you wanting to hold you and comfort you. All we need to do is respond to His calling. He has never promised to take away all your problems but He has promised to be with you through them. God has given each one of us a free will and just as your mom and dad have made choices with their free will, you also are given the same choice. There is no minimum age; everyone has a free will. You are not alone because God is just a prayer away. He offers you strength to get through each day. Just ask Him for it.

DEAR GOD LETTER

ATTACHMENT E

Put on some soft music and have everyone take some time to write a letter to God. Encourage them to pour out their hearts to Him and rest in His peace. After about 10 minutes, read "Gently Lord" together and respond to the questions on the next page.

GENTLY LORD

WORKBOOK PAGE 61-63

Read through the prayer as a group and give everyone a chance to answer the questions individually. If time permits, see if anyone wants to share what they have learned through this exercise.

A PIVITOL PRAYER WHEN YOUR'RE IN CRISIS

ATTACHMENT F

Hand this prayer out to everyone and encourage them to bring it home and put it in their Bible. It may be helpful to laminate this.

EXPLAIN THE "TAKING IT HOME" ASSIGNMENTS

WORKBOOK PAGES 64-66

Take time to look over the Taking It Home assignment with your group. Let them know that this assignment is a great way for them to really process what you have covered this week. Encourage them all to take the time and do the assignment because you will briefly go through them the next week.

CLOSING TIME: Ending the session

Take Prayer Requests

This can be done in a variety of ways:

- verbally shared in group setting
- hand out note cards to group members to write out their requests
- set out a note book that students can write in throughout the session
- put out a Prayer Request Box with Prayer Request Slips
- encourage the group members to come up with other ways to share prayer requests

Close in Prayer: Consider praying the "Pivotal Prayer When You're In Crisis" together out loud as a group.

TAKING IT HOME

WEEK SIX

TOWARDS YOURSELF...A Question to Take to My Heart:

Look into your heart for the answer to these questions. This is introspection time – time to grapple with what drives your thinking and behavior. Be sure to capture your thoughts.

- Take your Comfort Cards home with you and tape them in your room, on your mirror, in the bathroom, in your car, anywhere they can remind you of His care and comfort for you.

- Do you have a full support system around you? Are there other who may be able to help? How can you seek out more help?

- Memorize one of your comfort card verses. Which one did you pick and why?

- Fill out all your "Asking For Help Cards" and keep them by your bed. Remember to look at them in time of need.

TOWARDS OTHERS...A Question to Take to Others:

Healing cannot become complete without affecting the lives of those around us as well. Be courageous and go outside your comfort zone to take a risk and work on your relationships with others.

- Share some of your favorite comfort Scriptures with your mom/dad or siblings. Who did you share them with? How did that make you feel?

- Use one of your "Asking For Help Cards" this week. Which one did you use? Did it work?

- If you were to take one of your siblings aside and tell them something you have learned so far, who would you pick and what would you say? Now, can you actually do that?

- How do you handle it when your parents disappoint you? Can you talk to them about how it made you feel? Can you still trust them?

TOWARDS GOD...A Question to Take to God:

When you ask God a question, expect His Spirit to respond to your heart. Be careful not to rush it, or manufacture an answer. Don't jot down your idea of the "right answer". Just pose the question to God, and wait on Him to speak personally in a fresh way.

- Do you think your parents' separation or divorce is moving you closer or farther away from God? Draw on the scale from 1 to 10 to indicate where you stand in relation to God these days.

  1..........2..........3..........4..........5..........6..........7..........8.........9..........10

- Would you say your feelings about God right now are mostly positive, mostly negative, or a little of both?

- Do you feel God has let you down? Tell God exactly why you feel He has let you down. And then listen to what He says through the Bible, through a Pastor or youth leader, or through that quiet voice inside you. Chances are, He's saying something like, "Here, let me help you. I know it is hard. I'll explain later, just trust me."

- Do you need to reach out to Jesus and hold on tight right now?

- What did you feel when you read the poem "Gently Lord"? Do you believe what it says?

- Have you ever felt like Job's friends; thinking this divorce was a punishment from God for something you did or did not do?

Scripture Search Game

1. Psalms 31:9
   Clue - Another word for me.
2. John 16:20
   Clue – What you create to be sure your things are in order when you die.
3. John 14:27
   Clue – To present
4. Matthew 6:8
   Clue – More than one
5. Isaiah 66:13
   Clue – Another word for distress.
6. Numbers 6:26
   Clue – In addition to
7. John 15:11
   Clue – Opposite of sad.
8. Mark 10:43
   Clue – Word for another option.
9. Psalms 116:5
   Clue – Rhymes with dove.
10. Psalms 119:28
    Clue – Prolonged sadness

________ (1) ________ (2) ________ (3) ________ (4) ________ (5) ________ (6)

________ (7) ________ (8) ________ (9) ________ (10)

Be sure to use the NIV Bible to solve this puzzle.

Scripture Search Game Answers

1. Psalms 31:9
   Clue - Another word for me.
2. John 16:20
   Clue – What you create to be sure your things are in order when you die.
3. John 14:27
   Clue – To present
4. Matthew 6:8
   Clue – More than one
5. Isaiah 66:13
   Clue – Another word for distress.
6. Numbers 6:26
   Clue – In addition to
7. John 15:11
   Clue – Opposite of sad.
8. Mark 10:43
   Clue – Word for another option.
9. Psalms 116:5
   Clue – Rhymes with dove.
10. Psalms 119:28
    Clue – Prolonged sadness

I	will	give	them	comfort	and
(1)	(2)	(3)	(4)	(5)	(6)
	joy	instead	of	sorrow.	
	(7)	(8)	(9)	(10)	

Be sure to use the NIV Bible to solve this puzzle.

(2) I

(2) W

(2) S

(3) H

(1) G

(3) E

(1) O

(2) R

For the "Wheel of Fortune" activity you will need to enlarge and copy these letters onto card stock. You will need to make the number of letters indicated on each card. You will need letters to spell out "WHERE IS GOD WHEN IT HURTS?."

(1) U

(1) D

(1) ?

(1) N

(2) T

For the "Wheel of Fortune" activity you will need to enlarge and copy these letters onto card stock. You will need to make the number of letters indicated on each card. You will need letters to spell out "WHERE IS GOD WHEN IT HURTS?."

I'm angry—What is a healthy way to express it?

I'm tired—I need to slow down. Take a break and regroup.

I'm scared because I need to do something hard. Take it one thing at a time. Don't overwhelm yourself.

I need a friend. Pick up the phone and share with some-one you can trust.

I need to write a letter to tell someone how I feel. Share with someone close to you.

I need God's help!
Time to spend some time in prayer.

I was wrong—I need to apologize.

I'm upset—I need some physi-cal exercise. This is a great way to blow off some steam.

I feel stuck in the middle.
I need to:

Who can help me at work?

Which friend can I trust the most with my feelings?

When I am scared—who can I turn to?

I'm confused. I need to ask some questions.

Who do I feel safest with?

I am feeling lonely—who can I call?

When I am angry who can I trust to help me calm down?

Who can help me in my family?	Who can help me at school?
Who can help me in my neighborhood?	Who can help me at my church?
I'm confused—I need help to understand. Talk it over with someone you can trust.	I'm upset—I need comforting. Reach out to a family or friend. Don't forget to cry out to God.
I feel pressured—I need to say NO!	I'm lonely—I need friends. Who can I call? Remember God is always there.

What the Bible Says About Comfort and the One Who Gives Us Comfort

ATTACHMENT D

Hebrews 13:6a So we say with confidence, "The Lord is my helper; I will not be afraid. What can man do to me?"	Psalm 145:13b,14,18 The Lord is faithful in all He says; He is gracious in all He does. The Lord helps the fallen and lifts up those bent beneath their loads. The Lord is close to all who call on Him, yes, to all who call on Him sincerely.
Psalm 139:2-5 You know everything I do; from far away, You understand all my thoughts. You see me whether I am working or resting; You know all my actions. Even before I speak, you already know what I will say. You are all around me on every side; You protect me with Your power.	John 14:16-17a,18 {Jesus speaking} "I will ask the Father, and He will give you another Comforter, who will never leave you. He is the Holy Spirit, who leads into all truth...I will not abandon you as orphans – I will come to you."
Psalms 46:1 God is our refuge and strength, an ever-present help in trouble.	Psalm 102:17 God will listen to the prayers of the destitute. He will not reject their pleas. The Lord watches over those who fear Him; those who rely on His unfailing love.
Matt. 28:20b Surely I am with you always, to the very end of age.	2 Corinthians 1:3-7 He comforts us in all our troubles so that we can comfort others. When others are troubled, we will be able to give them the same comfort God has given us. You can be sure that the more we suffer for Christ, the more God will shower us with His comfort through Christ.
Isaiah 66:13a As a mother comforts her child, so will I comfort you;	Jeremiah 31:13b I will turn their mourning into gladness; I will give them comfort and joy instead of sorrow.

ATTACHMENT E

Dear God,

A Pivotal Prayer When You're In Crisis

By Tim Elmore and John Hull

God, I cry out to you.
The news that's just hit me is so hard to bear.
I'm close to being in shock right now.
I don't know what to do.
I'm angry, I'm hurt, I'm confused.
So, Lord I call out to You. Please hear my prayer.
Give me strength to get through this mess.
Help me to make wise choices and not to say something
That will just make things worse.
Please, don't let this thing get any worse than it is.
And God, help me not to do anything stupid.
This is going to take a long time to get through; and right now,
I don't feel like I'll ever get on top of it.
So, here it is Lord. A big mess.
Thank you that You're here to show me how to clean it up.
Amen.

A Pivotal Prayer When You're In Crisis

By Tim Elmore and John Hull

God, I cry out to you.
The news that's just hit me is so hard to bear.
I'm close to being in shock right now.
I don't know what to do.
I'm angry, I'm hurt, I'm confused.
So, Lord I call out to You. Please hear my prayer.
Give me strength to get through this mess.
Help me to make wise choices and not to say something
That will just make things worse.
Please, don't let this thing get any worse than it is.
And God, help me not to do anything stupid.
This is going to take a long time to get through; and right now,
I don't feel like I'll ever get on top of it.
So, here it is Lord. A big mess.
Thank you that You're here to show me how to clean it up.
Amen.

A Pivotal Prayer When You're In Crisis

By Tim Elmore and John Hull

God, I cry out to you.
The news that's just hit me is so hard to bear.
I'm close to being in shock right now.
I don't know what to do.
I'm angry, I'm hurt, I'm confused.
So, Lord I call out to You. Please hear my prayer.
Give me strength to get through this mess.
Help me to make wise choices and not to say something
That will just make things worse.
Please, don't let this thing get any worse than it is.
And God, help me not to do anything stupid.
This is going to take a long time to get through; and right now,
I don't feel like I'll ever get on top of it.
So, here it is Lord. A big mess.
Thank you that You're here to show me how to clean it up.
Amen.

A Pivotal Prayer When You're In Crisis

By Tim Elmore and John Hull

God, I cry out to you.
The news that's just hit me is so hard to bear.
I'm close to being in shock right now.
I don't know what to do.
I'm angry, I'm hurt, I'm confused.
So, Lord I call out to You. Please hear my prayer.
Give me strength to get through this mess.
Help me to make wise choices and not to say something
That will just make things worse.
Please, don't let this thing get any worse than it is.
And God, help me not to do anything stupid.
This is going to take a long time to get through; and right now,
I don't feel like I'll ever get on top of it.
So, here it is Lord. A big mess.
Thank you that You're here to show me how to clean it up.
Amen.

Feelings Tune Up

All My Feelings Are Okay

The main emphasis in this session is communication. As you go through this session, try to emphasize using "I" vs. "You" statements. "I" messages usually encourage a more empathic response from others while "You" messages bring about a defensive response. It is also important to remind them that their body language is one of the most expressive ways of communicating. Be sure they are expressing themselves in a positive way and not in a way to promote negative feedback. If they're communicating the right way, but have their finger pointing in someone's face, it will probably not be effective. Make sure you also emphasize how important it is to check their tone as they are speaking. Using the right tone is the most important tool in effective communication.

PREP TIME

1. Spend time in prayer for:
   a. your heart as you prepare for this lesson
   b. the students who will be attending this week, that God would open their hearts and help them to share their feelings
   c. the other leaders helping with this session
   d. all student prayer requests from last week
2. Read through the lesson and make sure you understand the material and activities.
3. Gather supplies for projects
4. Make copies of Feelings Alphabet Race (Attachment A)
5. Get white board and markers
6. Prepare Wheel of Fortune sheets (Attachment B) and tape them to wall
7. Prepare sample Feelings Box Activity (Attachment C)
8. Copy and prepare a Feelings Journal for each person. Make at least 10 copies of Attachment E and form into a booklet.
9. Workbooks

HIGHLIGHTS

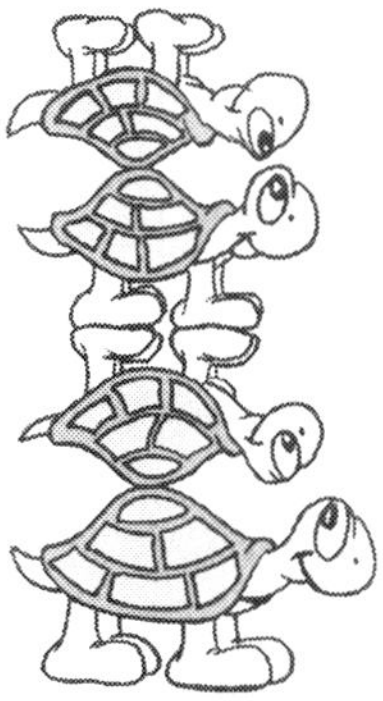

Feelings Tune Up

1. Feelings Alphabet Race
2. Wheel of Fortune
3. Common Ground
4. Nugget of Truth: Caught In The Middle
5. Battle Field Experiences
6. Nugget of Truth: Feelings Are Okay
7. Feelings Activities
8. Taking it Home

Lesson Seven
Week 7

Verse of the week:

"I will go before you and level the mountains; I will break down gates of bronze and cut through the bars of iron. I will give you the treasures of darkness, riches stored in secret places, so that you may know that I am the Lord, the God of Israel who summons you by name."

Isaiah 45:2-3

Be Blessed!

You are my hiding place; you will protect me from trouble and surround me with songs of deliverance.

Psalm 32:7

Welcome back! We are half done with our time together. I hope you have been enjoying your time, learning a lot, and have developed some good friendships along the way. In this session, we are going to have some fun with our feelings. Feelings can be uncomfortable but after this lesson we are hoping you will feel more comfortable acknowledging and expressing them. As situations arise that may put you in the middle of your parents, it will be important for you to discover ways to express yourself clearly and ask for what you need and set appropriate boundaries. There is no one else who knows you better so get comfortable with who you are and what you need.

FEELINGS ALPHABET RACE

ATTACHMENT A

Beforehand place a white board in front of the room labeled A to Z, use this to write the feelings they come up with. This is a fun and easy mixer. Hand out a Feelings Alphabet Race to everyone and tell them to wait for everyone to start together. Explain that you will give them 3 minutes to think of any feeling that starts with that letter of the alphabet. After three minutes go to the white board and have them tell you the feelings they came up with for each letter. Write them beside every letter. This will be a great way to get their minds thinking about different feelings and will be used as a reference point throughout the session.

Rules: 1. No same feeling can be used twice

Option: You can give out a small prize to the person who comes up with the most feelings in 3 minutes.

Leaders Note: Be careful not to spend too much time discussing the feelings. Try to keep this activity to 15 minutes or less.

Additional Note—Attachment A also has an extensive list of feelings in case you get stuck on one letter.

After the *Feelings Alphabet Race* gather back into a group and open in prayer.

WHEEL OF FORTUNE

All My Feelings Are Okay

ATTACHMENT B

The title of this week's lesson is "All My Feelings Are Okay". Be sure to print the letters ahead of time and post on a bulletin board or wall before the teens arrive. Take turns like last week asking each teen to select a letter. For each correct letter they select, turn letter(s) over and give them a chance to solve the puzzle. If they guess incorrectly, their turn is over and play moves to the next person. See **Lesson One** for a complete list of suggested rules.

How's the Take Home Assignment Going?

Encourage everyone to take some time every week to press on deeper and work through the questions. Remind them that if they ever want to talk to you one on one you are available.

Teens need to feel important and know that you value their friendship.

Last week we spent a lot of time searching the scriptures discovering who God is and where He is when we are hurting. I hope you have spent some time going over the scriptures we discovered last week. Let's see how the assignments went this week?

Go over TAKE HOME assignment:

- If you were to take one of your siblings aside and tell them something you have learned so far what would you say? Now did you actually do that? Who did you pick and what did you say?
- Do you think your parents' separation or divorce is moving you closer or farther away from God? Draw on the scale from 1 to 10 to indicate where you stand in relation to God these days.
- Share some of your favorite comfort Scriptures with your mom/dad or siblings. Who did you share them with? How did that make you feel?
- Which one of the Asking For Help Cards did you use this week. Did it help?

This week we are going to discuss feelings. There are many different kinds of feelings as you have already shown us by your list. You did a terrific job on listing all these feelings. As we look over the many different feelings we came up with as a group, are you surprised by why you feel so confused sometimes. We are a very complex creation. Let's go over the list you came up with one more time and decide whether you think the feeling is a negative or positive feeling.

Examples of Positive Feelings	Examples of Negative Feelings
Positive	Enraged
Friendly	Phony
Silly	Smug
Considerate	Trapped
Loving	Humiliated
Alive	Crabby

Leaders Note: Be aware that some feelings can be positive or negative based on it's intent. Be open to discuss how SOME feelings can be negative and positive.

Nugget of Truth: Caught In The Middle

Some feelings are easy to express and others are very hard. There are many feelings that we try to deny because we don't like the way they feel. When we try to hide from our feelings, we are stuffing them and sooner or later they will reveal themselves. Usually, the longer we try to hide them, the more they come out in much more destructive ways. It would have been better to deal with them in the first place.

Have you ever felt like you were going to explode if you didn't tell somebody something? As you keep it inside you bottle up your emotions and this causes more stress and could lead to serious illnesses. Holding our feelings in can cause us headaches or stomach aches and sometimes can lead to more serious health problems, or they can work like volcanoes. Finally, when we can't hold them in anymore, they explode and we end up doing or saying things we don't really mean. We need to look at ourselves and ask: "Who's really in control here? Me or my feelings?"

Kids In the Middle

Parents may put their kids in the middle in 3 ways:

1. As messengers- "Tell your dad...."
2. As spies or detectives- " Tell me about your mom's new boyfriend."
3. As a dumping station- "If you only knew what your dad did to me...."

What things cause you to want to stuff your feelings? (fear, feelings of losing it, fear of rejection, wanting to be in control, denial)

All of our feelings need to be expressed; even the difficult ones. Ignoring our feelings doesn't make them go away. They will come out one way or another, and probably at a time we least expect it or are prepared to deal with it.

Let's "Get a Grip" on our feelings. Go to the Getting a Grip page in your workbook and check the ways you tend to handle your emotions when you're feeling down.

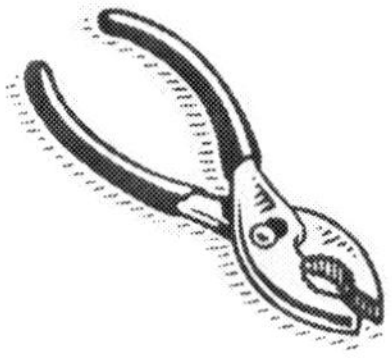

GETTING A GRIP

WORKBOOK PAGE 68

One way I'm sure feelings get stirred up is when you feel like you are caught in the middle between your mom and dad. Your mom and dad don't communicate the way they used to so they can end up putting you in the middle of situations that you should not be in. It's as if you've landed in a Battle Field. When this happens, all kinds of bad things get thrown at you, either intentionally or unintentionally, because your parents are still upset about the separation or divorce and haven't learned a better way to handle their feelings. You may feel like you are playing a game of paintball and you are the target. The difference though, is that this is not fun. In fact, being in the middle of the battle field can really stress you out and make you angry. How do you typically handle these situations?

Know Your Boundaries

1. **Physical** - What is your comfort zone?
2. **Emotional** - How are you feeling?
3. **Intellectual** - What are you thinking?
4. **Spiritual** - Who does your power come from?

ENTERING THE BATTLE FIELD

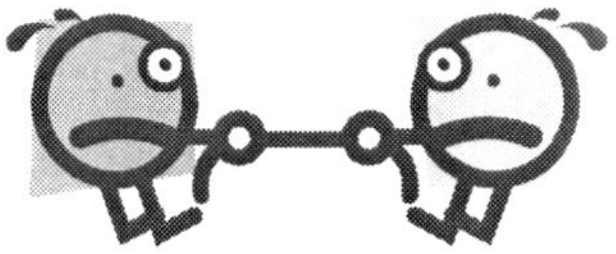

WORKBOOK PAGES 69-72

So how did you check out? How do you usually handle being in the Battle Field? Your particular battle may look somewhat different than another persons battle, but it's a constant battle none the less. How does it make you feel when your parent's bad mouth each other and try to get you to take sides? Or maybe they ask you to deliver messages because they refuse to talk with each other. Or perhaps your parents put you in the battle in more subtle ways, such as by bribing you with money, fun vacations, or clothes to gain your loyalty, or by telling you about ongoing problems with your other parent. When you find yourself in these situations you really have only two choices. You can decide to keep playing the game and get used to getting stuck in the middle or you can talk to your parents and do things to protect yourself. How do your parents put you in the middle?

Review the Children's Bill of Rights from Session #2.

STUCK IN THE MIDDLE

WORKBOOK PAGE 73

If it seems as if war is constantly raging around you, it can be helpful to go "behind enemy lines" to see things from the other side. Your parents probably have a lot of hurt and anger about the separation or divorce just as you do. Maybe one or both are feeling betrayed or abandoned. Sometimes they battle over money, custody or other matters that can take months, if not years to resolve. Maybe they are getting consumed by a desire for revenge against the other, or they may fear feeling the pain of their own choices. Maybe they are struggling with fears of being alone and dealing with all the new responsibilities. As a result they may try to influence you to take sides and help them.

Your parents may not even realize that they're putting you in the middle or how much they're doing it. In addition to all these reasons, they often feel guilty about the separation or divorce. They know it makes life more difficult for you, and they sometimes blame themselves for hurting you.

Understanding your parents' sides won't make the battle go away. However, it may help you look at your parent's actions less personally. When you have a better understanding about the Battle Field, you will be better prepared to protect yourself from getting caught there. Here are some helpful hints on ways to stay off the Battle Field.

"What Did You Say?"
(Optional Activity)

Hand out a 3x5 card to each person. Have them come up with something they have wanted to say to someone but have not been able to. Have them write it down the way they would like to say it and practice it for at least a week. Then when the time comes it should be easier for them to say it.

WHAT TO DO TO STAY OFF THE BATTLE FIELD

WORKBOOK PAGES 74-75

Although what comes naturally may come easiest, it may not be what is best for you right now. This may be a time when you need to exercise some patience, self-control or courage. What is important is that you learn to do what it takes to keep you from getting stuck in the middle and react in negative angry outbursts. One word of caution though; be aware that sometimes you can't always fix things the way you want. You are only one side. It almost always takes two parties who are willing to do what it takes to promote a healthy environment. You are only in control of your half. You may need to work together to try to create the best possible solution, even though that may not be exactly what you wanted.

WHERE'S YOUR BOUNDARY?

Boundaries allow us to be responsible for ourselves and let others be responsible for themselves.

THE REAL DEAL

WORKBOOK PAGE 76

Be sure to read through these as a group. They are important facts for them to remember.

FEELINGS BOX ACTIVITY

ATTACHMENT C

At this time take out the Feelings Box you have prepared for this session. Pass around an item from the box to everyone in the room. When all items are passed out, read the situations on Attachment D and ask the teens to explain how they would use their item to help them process their feelings. On pages 79 and 80 in their workbook it explains how students can make their own Feelings Box at home.

Nugget of Truth: Feelings Are Okay

Now that we have discovered what to do when we feel stuck in the middle, we need to discover how to process our feelings. We can be in control of our feelings by taking the time and examining what we are feeling, why we are feeling it and finally how we can work it out. Let's look at this a little deeper:

Name the feeling

Many times we react to feelings in unhealthy ways because we don't really know what we are feeling. Until we name the feeling, we may be running from it and it will catch up with us one time or another. We need to know what we are feeling so we can go on and figure out what to do about it. We need to ask ourselves: "What am I feeling?"

Stop and Think

When we do things like blow up, shut down, or blame ourselves, we are not thinking clearly. We are letting our feelings take control of us. We need to stop and think about our feelings and ask the question: "What is really going on here?"

Work it out

When we let our feelings control us we usually don't make very good choices. If we know what we are feeling, and stop and think about what's really going on, then we can make a healthy choice about what to do next. At this time, ask yourself this question: "What is the best thing to do right now?"

Alternatives to Conflict

Compromise– one or both parties agrees to some level of sacrifice to prevent a continued conflict.

Agreement—One party decides that the other party's point of view is relevant and they agree to share the same point of view.

Agree to Disagree– Both parties feel that there is no way to agree on the topic and will decide that it is a topic on which they have differing perspectives (and that is okay!).

Seeking guidance from a responsible party– Adults are sought out to help make a decision.

Making a deal-sometimes an agreement can be reached by making a deal.

FEELINGS JOURNAL

Another way to help you process your feelings, is the Feelings Journal. Use this to help you be in control of your feelings by using the three steps we've just gone over. This is a great way to work out your feelings in a positive way. I believe you will feel much more peace when you deal with things this way instead.

ATTACHMENT E

FEELINGS TOOL KIT

Go to your workbooks and pull out your "Feelings Tool Kit". Take a minute and read through some more ideas of what you can do to work out your feelings.

WORKBOOK PAGE 77-78

** If time runs short, have them complete this activity at home.*

EXPLAIN THE "TAKING IT HOME" ASSIGNMENTS

Take time to look over the Taking It Home assignment with your group. Let them know that this assignment is a great way for them to really process what you have covered this week. Encourage them all to take the time and do the assignment as you will be briefly going through them the next week.

WORKBOOK PAGES 81-83

CLOSING TIME: Ending the session

Take Prayer Requests

This can be done a variety of ways:

- verbally shared in group setting
- hand out note cards to group members to write out their requests.
- set out a note book that students can write in throughout the session
- put out a Prayer Request Box with Prayer Request Slips
- encourage the group members to come up with other ways to share prayer requests.

Close in Prayer:

Steps to Conflict Resolution

1. Identifying the Problem

What are we arguing about?

2. Brainstorm Solutions

How can we solve this problem?

3. Choose a solution

Which way seems most reasonable to everyone involved?

4. Make an Agreement

Does everyone agree with the chosen solution?

TOWARDS YOURSELF...A Question to Take to My Heart:

Look into your heart for the answer to these questions. This is introspection time – time to grapple with what drives your thinking and behavior. Be sure to capture your thoughts.

- Choose one of the negative feelings and fill in the following:

  I feel ______________________ when I __________________

  ____
  (describe the situation)

  When I feel ____________________ I _____________________

  ____

  (describe what you do)

- Make yourself a Feelings Box and put it in your room for you to use when you need to release your feelings.

- Do you have a plan for staying out of the middle? Explain your plan. Try it this week and be prepared to share with the group how it went.

- Spend some time filling out your Feelings Journal. Make sure to take some time for prayer.

- If I were to give someone an object that would best describe my feelings right now, the object would be a

  ____

  And I would give it to____

TOWARDS OTHERS...A Question to Take to Others:

Healing cannot become complete without affecting the lives of those around us as well. Be courageous and go outside your comfort zone to take a risk and work on your relationships with others.

- Have either of your parents ever tried to use you as a messenger, informant, or a dumping station? How did that make you feel?

- Is telling your parents how you feel being disrespectful? How do you make sure you come across in a way that is respectful?

- Explain a time you found yourself stuck in the middle this past week. How did it feel & what did you do?

- The Battle Field is an awful place to be. Have you taken steps to protect yourself from ending up there in the future?

TOWARDS GOD...A Question to Take to God:

When you ask God a question, expect His Spirit to respond to your heart. Be careful not to rush it, or manufacture an answer. Don't jot down your idea of the "right answer". Just pose the question to God, and wait on Him to speak personally in a fresh way.

- Write four words or phrases that describe your feelings about God.

    1.

    2.

    3.

    4.

- Read Colossians 1:10-13. How does this passage pertain to your situation.

- Write out your bummed out feelings to God. Leave them with Him and rest in His peace.

Feelings Alphabet Race

A

B

C

D

E

F

G

H

I

J

K

L

M

N

O

P

Q

R

S

T

U

V

W

X

Y

Z

FEELINGS WORDS

Abandoned
Accepted
Accused
Aching
Adventurous
Affectionate
Aggravated
Aggressive
Agony
Agreeable
Alienated
Alive
Alone
Aloof
Alluring
Amazed
Amused
Angry
Anguished
Annoyed
Anxious
Apart
Apologetic
Appreciative
Apprehensive
Approved
Argumentative
Aroused
Astonished
Assertive
Attached
Attacked
Attentive
Attractive
Aware
Awestruck
Badgered
Baited
Battered
Beaten
Beautiful
Belittled
Belligerent
Bereaved
Betrayed
Bitter
Bored
Bothered
Boxed-in
Brave
Breathless
Bristling
Broken-up
Bruised
Bubbly
Bugged
Burdened
Burned
Callous
Calm
Capable
Captivated
Carefree
Careful
Careless
Caring
Carried Away
Cautious
Certain
Chased
Cheated
Cheerful
Choked Up
Close
Cold
Comfortable
Comforted
Competitive
Complacent
Complete
Confident
Conflicted
Confused
Considerate
Consumed
Content
Cool
Coy
Crabby
Cranky
Crappy
Crazy
Critical
Criticized
Crushed
Cuddly
Curious
Cut
Damned
Daring
Deceived
Deceptive
Degraded
Delighted
Demeaned
Demoralized
Dependent
Depressed
Deprived
Deserted
Desirable
Desirous
Despair
Desperate
Destroyed
Different
Dirty
Disappointed
Disconnected
Disgraced
Disgruntled
Disgusted
Distant
Distraught
Distressed
Distrusted
Distrustful
Dominated
Domineering
Doomed
Double-crossed
Down
Dreadful
Eager
Ecstatic
Edgy
Elated
Embarrassed
Empty
Enraged
Enraptured
Enthusiastic
Enticed
Esteemed
Exasperated
Exhilarated
Exposed
Fascinated
Flattered
Foolish
Forced
Forceful
Fortunate
Forward
Friendly
Frightened
Frustrated
Full
Funny
Furious
Generous
Genuine
Giddy
Giving
Grateful
Greedy
Grim
Grouchy
Grumpy
Guarded
Happy-go-lucky
Hard
Hassled
Hateful
Healthy
Helpful
Helpless
Hesitant
High
Hollow
Hopeful
Horrified
Hostile
Humiliated
Hung Up
Hurt
Hyper
Ignorant
Impatient
Impressed
Incompetent
Incomplete
Independent
Innocent
Insecure
Insignificant
Insincere
Inspired
Insulted
Intimate
Intolerant
Involved
Irate
Irked
Irresponsible
Irritated
Jealous
Jittery
Joyous
Left Out
Lively
Lonely
Loose
Lost
Loving
Loved
Low
Lucky
Lustful
Mad

FEELINGS WORDS

Malicious
Mean
Miserable
Misunderstood
Moody
Mystified
Nasty
Nervous
Numb
Obsessed
Offended
Open
Ornery
Out of Control
Overwhelmed
Overjoyed
Pampered
Panicky
Paralyzed
Patient
Peaceful
Peeved
Perceptive
Perturbed
Petrified
Phony
Pleased
Powerless
Pressured
Proud
Pulled Apart
Put-Down
Puzzled
Quarrelsome
Quiet
Ravished
Ravishing
Real
Refreshed
Regretful
Rejected
Rejecting
Relaxed
Relieved
Removed
Repulsed
Repulsive
Resentful
Resistant
Responsible
Responsive
Revengeful
Rotten
Ruined
Safe
Satiated
Satisfied
Scared
Scolded
Scorned
Screwed
Secure
Seduced
Seductive
Self-centered
Self-conscious
Selfish
Separated
Shattered
Shocked
Shot-down
Shy
Sickened
Silly
Sincere
Sinking
Smart
Smothered
Smug
Sneaky
Snowed
Soft
Soothed
Sorry
Spiteful
Spontaneous
Squelched
Starved
Stiff
Stifled
Stimulated
Strangled
Strong
Stubborn
Stunned
Stupid
Subdued
Submissive
Successful
Suffocated
Sure
Sweet
Sympathetic
Tainted
Tender
Tense
Terrific
Terrified
Thrilled
Ticked
Tickled
Tight
Timid
Tired
Tolerant
Tormented
Torn
Tortured
Trapped
Tremendous
Tricked
Trustful
Ugly
Unapproachable
Unaware
Uncertain
Uncomfortable
Under Control
Understanding
Understood
Unfriendly
Unhappy
Unimportant
Unimpressed
Unstable
Upset
Uptight
Useful
Valuable
Valued
Violated
Violent
Vulnerable
Warm
Weak
Whipped
Whole
Wild
Willing
Wiped-out
Withdrawn
Wishful
Wonderful
Worried
Worthy
Wounded
Zapped

ATTACHMENT B

(1) F

(3) A

(3) E

(3) L

(1) I

(1) M

(1) N

(2) Y

For the "Wheel of Fortune" activity you will need to enlarge and copy these letters onto card stock. You will need to make the number of letters indicated on each card. You will need letters to spell out "ALL MY FEELINGS ARE OKAY."

ATTACHMENT B

(1) R

(1) G

(1) O

(1) S

(1) K

For the "Wheel of Fortune" activity you will need to enlarge and copy these letters onto card stock. You will need to make the number of letters indicated on each card. You will need letters to spell out "ALL MY FEELINGS ARE OKAY."

FEELINGS ACTIVITY BOX

Collect as many of the following items as possible and put them into a box. Keep the box in a convenient place so you can use it whenever you are having trouble expressing your feelings. Choose an item or two that will help you get your feelings out in a healthy way.

Pillow: Hit it when you are angry. Cry into it when you are sad. Squeeze it when you need a hug.

Telephone: Call someone you trust and talk about your feelings. Call a friend, a pastor, or a trusted relative.

Notebook and Pen: Journal your feelings. Write a poem. Draw a picture.

Stationery and Envelopes: Write a letter about your feelings and give it to someone you trust. Remember, you don't have to send every letter. Sometimes you just need to get things out on paper.

Drawing Supplies: Drawing or scribbling helps get your feelings out.

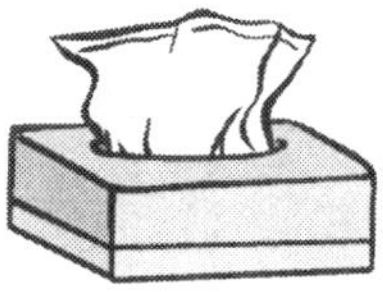

Box of Kleenex: For every time you just need to cry!!

Running Shoes: Doing something physical helps get your feelings out.

Stuffed Animal: Hold it when you feel alone. Squeeze it when you need a hug. Talk to it when you need to talk.

Computer: E-mail a trusted friend or a caring relative. Journal your thoughts.

Large Red Heart: Talk to someone you love about your feelings. Ask for a hug.

Feelings Box Activity

Prepare a Feelings Box as outlined in the workbook. Go through the box one item at a time and as you hand out each item explain how they could be used to help you get your feelings out. When you have emptied the box and everyone has an item from the box read the following scenarios and ask how they could use the items they are holding to deal with the situations in a healthy way.

Scenarios

* Your parents have just told you they are getting a divorce.
* Your dad promises to take you somewhere special and then cancels at the last minute.
* Your mom introduces you to her new boyfriend.
* It's your dad's weekend to have you and he doesn't show up.
* Your step mom says something mean to you.
* You overhear your mom and dad fighting about you.
* Your dad drills you about your mom's life and who she is seeing.
* You want a new outfit or new pair of shoes and your mom says you can't afford them anymore.
* Your mom says you can go to the movies but your step dad says "no" so now you have to stay home.
* Your mom asks you to ask your dad for the child support money or to pay for half a doctor's bill.
* Your dad calls to invite you to the fair this weekend and your mom says "no" because you are with her this weekend.
* You come home from school and you see your mom crying on the couch.
* You have a parents' night for your sporting event and your parents refuse to sit together.
* You invite both of your parents to your concert and your mom tells you she refuses to go if your dad comes.
* You go to your dad's and within an hour of being there, he leaves you to go out on a date.
* Your mom is dating someone you really don't like and is always expecting you to stay home and babysit.
* Your mom has left and abandoned the family.
* Your mom is never home anymore because she has had to get a job.
* You bring your friends home and your mom has been drinking.
* You want to spend more time at your dad's place but your mom won't let you.

ATTACHMENT E

Do not be anxious about anything, but in everything present your requests to God. And the peace of God will guard you hearts and minds in Christ Jesus.

Philippians 4:6 (NIV)

Feelings Prayer Journal

Date__________

Today I feel: ________________

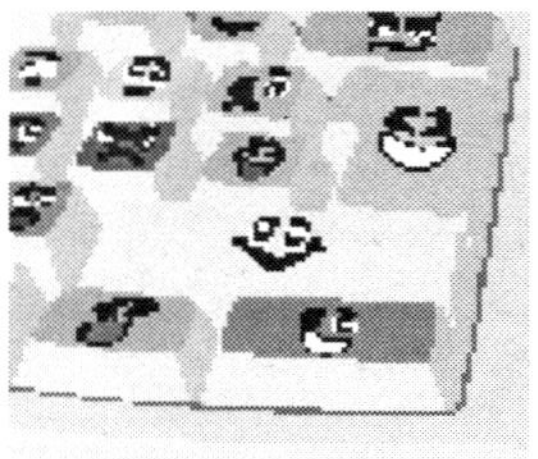

Mad	Confused
Scared	Disappointed
Excited	Hateful
Guilty	Powerful
Afraid	Content
Proud	Left Out
Lovely	Included
Loved	Forgiven
Surprised	Smart
Stupid	

I feel this way because: ________________

I expressed my feelings by: ________________

Dear God,

Right now I feel ________________

I wish that________________

Please help me to________________

Thank you for________________

Amen!

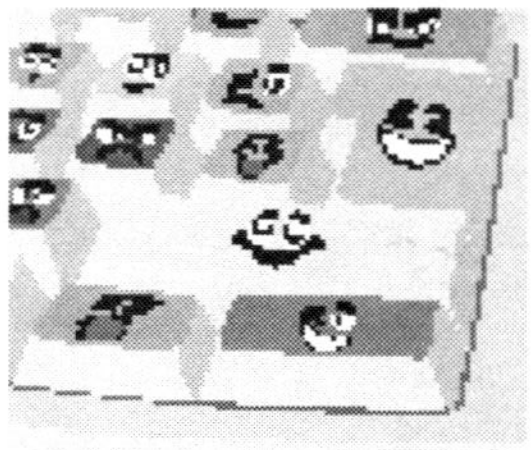

Date__________

Today I feel: ________________

Mad	Confused
Scared	Disappointed
Excited	Hateful
Guilty	Powerful
Afraid	Content
Proud	Left Out
Lovely	Included
Loved	Forgiven
Surprised	Smart
Stupid	

I feel this way because: ________________

I expressed my feelings by: ________________

Dear God,

Right now I feel ________________

I wish that________________

Please help me to________________

Thank you for________________

Amen!

CHANGE– SINGLE PARENT HOMES

Lesson Eight
Week 8

Changes Are Okay

Change is different for everyone. In this session we are going to try to help them begin to see their mom and dad as individual parents rather than one parental unit. We will try to normalize their feelings of fear or uncertainty in the midst of all these changes. At the end of the session, hopefully they will have learned new ways to handle the stress that results from these changes.

PREP TIME

1. Spend time in prayer for:
    a. your heart as you prepare for this lesson
    b. students who will be attending this week, that God would open their-hearts and help them to share their feelings
    c. the other leaders helping with this session
    d. all prayer requests from the students from last week.
2. Read through the lesson and make sure you understand the material and activities
3. Purchase M & M's, Skittles, or similar candy (Attachment A)
4. Gather enough small paper cups for everyone
5. Bring one small bowl per table
6. Prepare Wheel of Fortune sheets (Attachment B)
7. Copy Letters to Mom and Letters to Dad (Attachments C & D)
8. Workbooks

HIGHLIGHTS

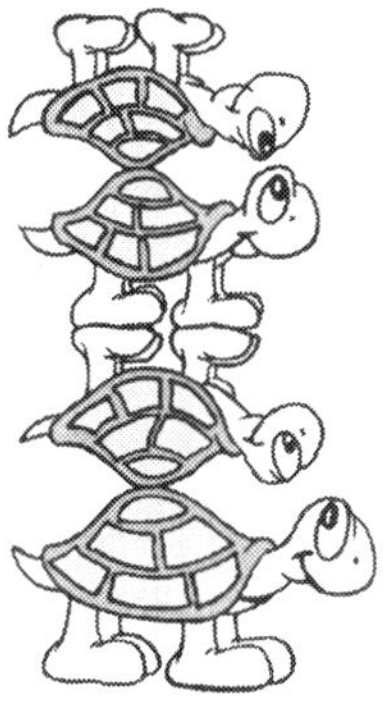

Change—Single Parent Homes

1. Family Change Game
2. Wheel of Fortune: Now What Do I Do?
3. Common Ground
4. Nugget of Truth: Change is Inevitable
5. Changes in My Life
6. Nugget of Truth: Compare the Differences
7. Nugget of Truth: Change is Okay– You'll Make It
8. Letters to Mom & Letters to Dad
9. Taking It Home

Verses of the week:

"When I am afraid, I will trust in you. In God, whose word I praise in God I trust; I will not be afraid."

Psalm 56:3 & 4

Be Blessed!

"My God will meet all your needs according to His glorious riches in Christ Jesus."

Philippians 4:19

WEEK EIGHT - SESSION EIGHT

Change can throw you off balance like if you are standing alongside the road and a big semi drives by. The large gust of wind feels like it could blow you over. Change feels like that sometimes. Everything around you is whirling around and throwing you off balance. These can be difficult times for you. In this session, we will explore the changes you are experiencing and give you tools to adapt to those changes.

FAMILY CHANGE GAME

ATTACHMENT A

Before people arrive, prepare one bowl per table filled with whatever kind of candy you brought. Have enough paper cups for everyone to have one. Once it is time to start, hand out a paper cup to everyone and put a bowl in the center of each table. As you are doing this, ask everyone to go and wash their hands. When everyone is ready, explain to them that they are to start by taking 5 pieces of candy each and put them in their cup. Then as you read the questions, they are to do what you say if that statement applies to them. Continue however long you want. When you are finished, they can eat the candy throughout the night.

> Variation - A prize can be given to the person who ended up with the most candy indicating they are the one who has experienced the most changes and are still hanging in there.

After the *Family Change Game*, gather back into a group and open in prayer.

WHEEL OF FORTUNE

Now What Do I Do?

ATTACHMENT B

The title of this week's lesson is "Now What Do I Do?". Be sure to print the letters ahead of time and post on a bulletin board or wall before the teens arrive. Take turns like last week asking each teen to select a letter. For each correct letter they select, turn letter(s) over and give them a chance to solve the puzzle. If they guess incorrectly, their turn is over and play moves to the next person. See **Lesson One** for a complete list of suggested rules.

CHECK-IN TIME

-How are things going in your relationships with your parents?

-Are there things you are changing in your attitude that are making a difference at home?

-What are any "God Moments" that have been happening?

Last week we spent a lot of time defining our feelings and discussing ways in which we can choose healthy ways to respond to situations that surround us. I hope you have spent some time this week evaluating your reactions and putting some of the suggestions to use that we have talked about. Let's see how the assignments went this week.

Go over TAKE HOME assignment:

- Do you have a plan for staying out of the middle? Explain your plan.
- Is telling your parents how you feel being disrespectful? How do you make sure you come across in a way that is respectful?
- If I were to give someone an object that would best describe my feelings right now, the object would be a

  ____

  And I would give it to__________________________________

Nugget of Truth: Change is Inevitable

This week we are going to talk about change. Our world is constantly changing. Change is around us every day. Change is a normal part of life and we need to learn how to expect and accept it. Whether you realize it or not, throughout your growing years you have already had to experience a variety of changes. If you were to take a moment and look back to when you were a baby, think of all the changes you have already experienced. How about a move into a different home? A new sibling? A new church? A death of a loved one? Riding the bus to school? Starting high school?

TIMELINE OF CHANGES

WORKBOOK PAGE 86

Let's look at this line and have it represent a timeline of your life so far. It starts at your birth and goes until your parents separation. Can you list at least three changes on that time line that you have already had to adapt to?

Were you surprised at how many changes you have already experienced? You see now how change is happening all around us? We are constantly adapting to new situations and new surroundings. Now starting at the time of your parents separation until today, list a few changes that you have had to adapt to due to the divorce or separation of your parents. If you have had any other life changes in that time frame (like a death of a grandparent or something) make sure you write that too. Discuss the amount of changes you have had to adjust to and the amount of time you have had to adjust compared to your whole timeline of changes. What is different and more challenging in this situation is that usually all the changes happen in a very short amount of time, giving you less time to react and less time to adapt. Having to go through so many changes and upsets in life can really add to stress and unrest. Adjusting to new things, new places, new friends takes time. And sometimes letting go of what used to be is the hardest thing of all. Let's look at various changes that divorce can bring into our lives.

CHANGES IN MY LIFE

WORKBOOK PAGE 87

Take some time in the group to answer
the four questions at the bottom of the page:

1. The biggest change I fear most and why:
2. The best change is:
3. The most difficult change for me is:
4. How I feel about this change is:

Out of Your Comfort Zone!

Have everyone fold their arms across their chests. Now tell them to cross their arms the opposite way--with the other arm on top. Help them recognize how uncomfortable it is! Then explain to them that it's the same way we get comfortable with the way we live our lives and when our lives change, it can feel very uncomfortable.

Nugget of Truth : Compare the Differences

All of a sudden you are living in a single parent home and there are a lot of changes to adjust to. You were used to two parents being around and now there is just one. As we look at the different changes living in a single parent home brings, let's take a moment and compare life in a two-parent home. It will also help you to better understand how you feel about being in a single parent home and help you with some tips on how to make the adjustment easier for you and everyone in your family.

WHAT'S THE DIFFERENCE

Suggested answers are at the end of this chapter, page 145. WORKBOOK PAGES 88-89

Nugget of Truth – Change is Okay, You'll Make It

Before your parents separated, you lived with both of your parents. Now they are living in two separate places and there is a good chance that both parents are working. For some of you, that is different because before the separation, maybe one of your parents was able to stay home with you. When there are two separate homes, there is obviously double the expenses for housing and all other living expenses. This can be a very frustrating and unstable time in your life. There may never seem to be enough money to buy the things that you used to buy. Maybe now you are not able to buy "the extras" like music, movies, snacks, clothing, games, etc. There is probably no extra room in the budget for wants and you must now learn how to live on your basic needs. Depending on the situation, this may be the same as it was before, but for some of you this may be a huge difference.

It is bad enough to have a major shake up in your family, but it usually doesn't stop there. Sometimes this means you need to sell your home and move into a smaller home or maybe an apartment. Many times

Stress

Webster says:

A feeling of being overwhelmed that can happen before, during, or after a difficult situation.

Common Signs of Stress

- Hands or body shakes
- Clenched fists
- Clenched teeth
- Tightened muscles
- Feels like you can't do it
- Fatigue
- Irritability
- Scared/worried/ nervous

you may even end up at one of your grandparents' home for awhile. That can be a very hard transition not only for yourself but also for your parent. You may need to have an extra amount of patience and sensitivity for a little while. If you do have to move, that often brings another huge list of changes. Such as a different neighborhood to hang out in, different friends to get to know, possibly even a different school to get used to. Maybe you have been home schooled and now may need to go to public school. These changes are not easy. For teens your age, these changes can bring a lot of anger and frustration. It is hard to understand how it can be fair. Having to deal with these changes can be the most difficult thing to accept when dealing with a divorce.

DIFFICULT CHANGES

WORKBOOK PAGES 90-91

Suggested answers are at the end of this chapter, page 146.

Most of us would rather not have to experience change, but if our life and our world did not change, we would be stuck in the same place and not be given the chance to grow and learn. We need to realize that whether we like it or not, change is always going to happen in our families, and in our lives for the rest of our lives, we can't stop that, but we do have a choice as to how we will deal with the changes that come our way.

It is very sad but true; our family will probably never be the same again. Accepting this loss can be one of the hardest things you may have to do. Many people may never move past that pain. They remain stuck there and it affects them the rest of their lives. This can make us go through our lives looking at other families and falsely believe that families that are still together must have it so easy. At times like this, it is important to look at the whole picture. All families have problems, experience loss and have to adapt to change. Some families experience illness or a death. Some parents lose their jobs and have to move. Other families have their homes destroyed by fires or floods. Some kids don't even know their biological parents. There is no such thing as a perfect family who has everything smooth all the time. We all need to learn how to deal with change. It is

Let Go of Stress!!

1. Find a quiet place where you can escape and enjoy some peace.

2. Close your eyes.

3. Listen to your breathing. Breathe in deeply... full breaths and let them out slowly. Let the stress escape when you breathe out.

4. Breathe in and tighten your leg muscles. Breathe out and relax. Do this for all your muscles-arms, face, stomach etc. Notice how calm you feel as you let them relax.

5. Continue breathing in and out, slowly, releasing more stress with every breath.

6. Imagine being in a favorite place and being very calm and relaxed. Imagine putting your worries in a box on a high shelf.

7. Stay quiet for as long as you need.

how you learn to adapt and accept the changes that come along that will help you throughout your entire life.

"New" can be good and exciting if you choose to look at it that way – or it can be very scary. Of course, you will miss the way it used to be. In order to adjust properly, you need to allow yourself time to mourn the losses that you are experiencing. If you just stuff your feelings, you will not be able to move on and accept the changes that will inevitably come your way. You need to prepare yourself to miss the old house and your two parent home, miss your friends, your school, neighborhood, etc. Then you need to look forward to the new changes and opportunities that are on their way. When you do this you will be able to find happiness and contentment again. Spend some time and go through the next workbook exercise. Learning better ways to deal with Mom and Dad can help you adjust.

DEALING WITH MOM AND DAD

WORKBOOK PAGE 92

Suggested answers are at the end of this chapter, page 147.

One of the most important issues when moving into a single parent home is to work out a visitation schedule with your parents, if possible, that is best for you, your parents, and your siblings. This can be a very hot topic for your parents. Each one is hopefully going to try to do what they feel is best for you. And in most cases, neither one of them are going to want to share you and spend time without you in their lives. If they fight over spending time with you, try to look at it like both your parents love you so much and want to be with you. And if the situation is safe for you, it is very important that you get to spend time with both of your parents. It is very normal to miss whichever parent you are not with at the time. It is a hard thing to learn to balance. It is like you miss them when you are not with them and when you are with them, you miss the other parent. A part of you may never feels whole again. There are no easy answers to these situations. It is something you are going to have to learn to make the best of and not allow what has happened to come between your personal relationships with either of your parents.

In most situations, whom you stay with is not your decision. Whether it is a judge, the lawyers, your parents, or whomever, you need to learn to do your best to work with both your parents to meet everyone's needs. If you could pretend that you are the judge that set up the visitation agreement between you and your parents. Write down the details of what that agreement would look like in your eyes. If you feel safe, show it to your parents. Although this may not change anything because it is not legal, it can be a way to communicate with your parents how you feel about your visitation situation.

VISITATION WISHES

WORKBOOK PAGE 93

LETTERS TO MOM & DAD

ATTACHMENT C & D

Play soft music in the background for this activity.

Communicating with each of your parents is very important. We are going to hand out a letter for your mom and your dad. We will give you a few quiet moments to reflect on what you would like to share with your parents. Maybe you have been angry about the changes that have happened and were making it harder on them than necessary. Maybe you have hurts about how the visitation schedule has been working or not working. Maybe you need to ask for a new start and commit to being part of the family again, whether or not it is the way you want it to be. Maybe you want to give them a copy of your visitation agreement that you came up with. Whatever it is that you feel you need to say to them, take a moment to write them. If you feel safe, we would encourage you to give it to them. But if you don't, it is still important you write it. Maybe now is not a good time to share it, so tuck it away and maybe someday you may feel more able to share it with them. Really put your heart into it. Be honest. If you need more time, you can take the letters home and finish them there.

Custody Definitions

Sole Physical/Legal:

This parent has sole responsibility for you physically and legally.

Sole Physical/Joint Legal:

This parent has sole physical responsibility but share legal custody with the other parent.

Joint Physical/ Joint Legal:

Both parents equally share physical and legal responsibility for you.

What's the Difference?

1. **What are some things that have changed since living in a single parent home compared to your two parent world you were used to?**
(rules, responsibilities, loneliness, chores, money, mom working, etc.)

2. **In what ways are things the same as when you were living in the same home?**
(rules, chores, love, school schedules, eating schedules, free time, friends, etc.)

3. **What do you miss most about your parents not living together anymore?**
(your absent parent, doing things as a family, meal times together, laughter vs. crying, worrying about money, etc.)

4. **How did you respond when you found out or were told that your parents were separating or getting a divorce?**
(sad, confused, angry, scared, empty, rejected, etc.)

5. **How did they tell you?**
(together, just your mom, just your dad, didn't tell me, you asked, your siblings, over heard it, counselor, etc.)

6. **What did your parents do to help you feel better?**
(nothing, held me, took me to counseling, let me talk to a pastor, listened, let you cry, let you get angry, etc.)

7. **Did anybody else do anything to try to make you feel better?**
(Grandparents, brother, sister, friend, pastor, aunt, uncle, cousin, etc.)

8. **Did you cry? Why or why not? Have you cried since? Do you think it helps to cry?**
(answers will vary)

9. **Did you get angry? Who were you angry at and why?**
(answers will vary)

DIFFICULT CHANGES

1. **Have both your parents had to work outside the home? How is this different than before the seperation?**
   (coming home to an empty house, more chores, etc.)

2. **Have you noticed a change in how you spend money in your home since the seperation?**
   (answers may vary)

3. **Are there things that you used to get or do prior to the seperation that you cannot afford anymore? Like what?**
   (answers may vary)

4. **What are some things you have had to accept that your family will not be able to afford right now?**
   (answers may vary)

5. **Have you had to sell anything? If so, what? Was that hard for you?**
   (answers may vary)

6. **Have you had to sell your home because of the divorce?**
   (answers may vary)

7. **Have you had to move into a different place because of the divorce?**
   (an apartment, your grandparents home, a relative's home, another home, not yet, but we probably will very soon)

8. **How did you feel about the move?**
   (angry, happy, frustrated, sad, mad)

9. **If you have moved or are going to be moving soon, do you think the new place will be better than the old one or not as good? Why or why not?**
   (answers may vary)

10. **What is one thing you miss about your old home?**
    (answers may vary)

11. **What is one thing you like or will like about your new home?**
    (answers may vary)

DEALING WITH MOM AND DAD

Note: Depending on which parent is your primary guardian, you many need to substitute your Mom or Dad

Dealing with Mom: (assuming your Mom is your primary caregiver, if not substitute your Dad)

1. **What are some of the changes and conflicts you have experienced with mom as a single parent.**
   (answers may vary but some suggestions are: new responsibilities, less money and less free time, less contact with Dad and perhaps with Mom too if she had to get a new job)

2. **Learning to communicate and compromise with Mom rather than reacting out of anger or giving up is a significant skill to learn. How can you help in communicating?**
   (answers may vary but some suggestions are: think of what you want and feel, make your requests/points clearly and respectfully, be flexible and willing to cooperate, try to see Mom's side of it)

3. **Sometimes your Mom tries to be your best friend. She lets you come and go as you please and doesn't make you do any work around the house. What should you do if this is your Mom?**
   (answers may vary but some suggestions are: tell your Mom you enjoy spending time with her but she also needs some friends her own age)

Dealing with Dad: (assuming your Dad is the non-custodial parent, if not, substitute your Mom)

1. **What are some of the challenges you face in relating to your non-custodial parent.**
   (answers may vary but some suggestions are: forgetting things you need, Not having your own "place", uncomfortable surroundings)

2. **Sometimes the non-custodial parent tries to appease their guilt by constantly showing the kids a good time or buying them things. What should you do if this is a common occurrence?**
   (answers may vary but some suggestions are: tell your Dad you just want some quiet time with him)

3. **Sometimes the parent never really learns how to be a single parent and often expects you to fulfill that role. What should you do if this occurs in your family?**
   (answers may vary but some suggestions are: ask to do chores together.)

You need to make a place of your own at your Dad's and Mom's where you can keep a few personal things that make it feel a little more like home.

FOLLOW UP TIME

1. Take time this week to send out "Miss You" cards to those who may have missed some sessions.
2. Send a note of appreciation to someone in your group who was particularly helpful in your group.
3. Send a note of encouragement to someone in your group who was open or shared a vulnerability.
4. Send an "You're in my prayers" note to someone who shared a prayer request.

There is no need for these to be lengthy notes. Remind them that they are important to the group and important to God.

EXPLAIN THE "TAKING IT HOME" ASSIGNMENTS

WORKBOOK PAGES 94-96

Take time to look over the Taking It Home assignment with your group. Let them know that this assignment is a great way for them to really process what you have covered this week. Encourage them all to take the time and do the assignment as you will be briefly going through them the next week.

CLOSING TIME: Ending the session

Take Prayer Requests

This can be done in a variety of ways:

- verbally shared in group setting
- hand out note cards to group members to write out their requests.
- set out a note book that students can write in throughout the session
- put out a Prayer Request Box with Prayer Request Slips.
- encourage the group members to come up with other ways to share prayer requests.

Close in Prayer

TAKING IT HOME

WEEK EIGHT

TOWARDS YOURSELF…A Question to Take to My Heart:

Look into your heart for the answer to these questions. This is introspection time – time to grapple with what drives your thinking and behavior. Be sure to capture your thoughts.

- Which 5 words would best describe your family right now?

- If you could change one thing about your family what would it be?

- You may feel opposite feelings sometimes – like being really angry at someone and also loving and missing them very much. List some of the opposites that you feel.

- How do you handle different rules at mom's house vs. dad's house?

- Do you share what you do at one parents home with the other parent? Are you supposed to?

- How do you think your parents are going to change as a result of the divorce?

TOWARDS OTHERS...A Question to Take to Others:

Healing cannot become complete without affecting the lives of those around us as well. Be courageous and go outside your comfort zone to take a risk and work on your relationships with others.

- Is it hard to talk to your parents about your feelings concerning your visitation schedule? Why or why not?

- What is one thing you wish you could share with your parents?

- What are the best parts about your relationship with your Mom?

- What are the worst parts about your relationship with your Mom?

- Rate your relationship with your Mom [1 being no relationship at all – 10 being the best possible].

1 2 3 4 5 6 7 8 9 10

- What are the best parts about your relationship with your Dad?

- What are the worst parts about your relationship with your Dad?

- Rate your relationship with your Dad [1 being no relationship at all – 10 being the best possible].

1 2 3 4 5 6 7 8 9 10

TOWARDS GOD...A Question to Take to God:

When you ask God a question, expect His Spirit to respond to your heart. Be careful not to rush it, or manufacture an answer. Don't jot down your idea of the "right answer". Just pose the question to God, and wait on Him to speak personally in a fresh way.

- What things make you feel safe and secure?

- What things make you feel scared?

- What things make you feel alone?

- Read Hebrews 13:5. Who will never leave you or forsake you?

- Read Deuteronomy 31:6 and write it below.

- What changes do you need to lay at the feet of Jesus because you just can't get through them?

FAMILY CHANGE GAME

ATTACHMENT A

Bring in enough M&M's, Skittles, jelly beans or anything like that, depending on how many teens you have attending.

Put out a bowl full of candy on each table, allowing 3 or 4 to share from each bowl. Also hand out one empty bowl or cup to each teen before you start. Be sure to have everyone wash their hands prior to starting this game.

Read the following statements below and for every teen that the statement applies to, they have to do as it says. You can give a prize to the person who ends up with the most candy at the end, indicating they have probably gone through the most changes. After the game, they are free to eat the candy throughout the night or bring it home with them.

FAMILY CHANGE STATEMENTS

If your parents are divorced, take one.
If you had to move into a different home, take two.
If you have a step parent, take one.
If you are still living in the same home prior to the separation, take one.
If you talk disrespectful to either of your parents, put back two.
If you had to change schools, take three.
If you now have a step sibling, take one.
If you had to give away your pet, take three.
If you find yourself purposely trying to stay away from home, put back three.
If you now have to share your room, take two.
If you had to make new friends, take one.
If you've lied in the past 24 hours, put back one.
If you live with your dad, take one.
If you got angry yesterday, put back two.
If your mom had to get a job, take two.
If your parents are only separated and not divorced, take one.
If you see a counselor or school counselor, take two.
If one of your parents has a girlfriend/boyfriend, take two.
If you argue with your parents, put back two.
If your mom changed her last name, take one.
If you have to do more chores now, take one.
If you have skipped school, put back three
If one of your parents has remarried, take two.
If you had to get a job, take one.
If you argue with your sister or brother, put back two.
If you had to move to a different town, take two.
If one of your parents lives out of state, take three.
If you live with your mom, take one.
If you live with another family member (Grandpa & Grandma), take three.
If you were an only child and now you have step siblings, take three.
If both your parents are remarried, take two.

ATTACHMENT B

(1) A

(1) N

(1) T

(3) O

(2) D

(2) W

(1) I

(1) H

For the "Wheel of Fortune" activity you will need to enlarge and copy these letters onto card stock. You will need to make the number of letters indicated on each card. You will need letters to spell out "NOW WHAT DO I DO ?"

LETTER TO MOM

ATTACHMENT C

LETTER TO DAD

Change – Step-Family Homes

Lesson Nine
Week 9

The Bumpy Road

This week could be a little uneasy because we are going to explore the possibility of either or both of their parents dating and eventually remarrying. As hard as it may be, try to have them explore this possibility and what that would feel like. This will help them to be better prepared if and when the time comes. If there are some in the group whose parents have already started to date or are remarried, have them share some stories about how they are handling it. Try to help them to develop a positive attitude about changes in relationships.

PREP TIME

1. Spend time in prayer for:
   a. your heart as you prepare for this lesson.
   b. the students who will be attending this week, that God would open their hearts and help them to share their feelings.
   c. the other leaders helping with this session.
   d. all student prayer requests from last week
2. Read through the lesson and make sure you understand the material and activities.
3. Gather supplies for projects.
4. Arrange a circle of chairs so there is one per person (Attachment A)
5. Prepare the Wheel of Fortune Sheets (Attachment B) and tape to wall
6. Copy Optical Illusions Sheets (Attachment C)
7. Laminate the set of footprints for "In Their Shoes" scenarios or bring a pair of big boots. (Attachment D)
8. Copy and cut the "In Their Shoes" scenarios (Attachment E)

HIGHLIGHTS

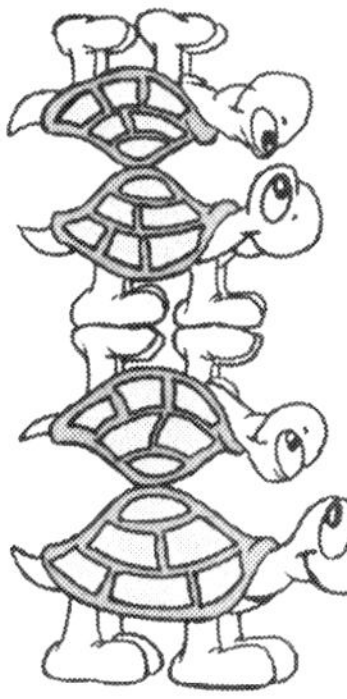

Change-Blended Family Homes

1. Family Chair Game
2. Wheel of Fortune
3. Common Ground
4. Nugget of Truth: Change is Okay
5. My Family & Their Strengths
6. Optical Illusions
7. In Their Shoes
8. Taking It Home

Verses of the week:

"Do not conform any longer to the pattern of this world, but be transformed by the renewing of your mind. Then you will be able to test and approve what God's will is—His good, pleasing and perfect will."

Romans 12:2

Be Blessed!

"...being strengthened with all power according to His glorious might so that you may have great endurance and patience."

Colossians 1:11

The thought of having your parents date is tough. It is even tougher to think about them remarrying and having to add a step mom or step dad to your family. We ask you to put any barriers and fears aside that you may have and open yourselves up to what this may look like. We will help you realize that looking at situations in the other person's shoes can give you a whole new perspective on situations. It is important for us to realize that our perspective, whether negative or positive, can influence our feelings about situations.

FAMILY CHAIR GAME

ATTACHMENT A

Before your teens arrive, set up a circle of chairs, one chair per person. When you are ready to begin, have everyone sit in a chair. Once everyone is seated, remove any extra chairs. Read the statements on Attachment A, one by one. Instruct the students to move the direction and number of chairs read if the statement applies to them. If someone is in that chair, they need to share the chair, sit on a lap, or stand behind that chair. This hopefully will turn into pandemonium as people are stacked 5 high with someone needing to get up from the bottom. The purpose of the game is to be a mixer, have fun, and emphasize that no family is the same. It doesn't matter what your family looks like, families come in various packages. Be creative and add more statements of your own.

After the *Family Chair Game*, gather back into a group and open in prayer.

WHEEL OF FORTUNE

ATTACHMENT B

The Bumpy Road

The title of this week's lesson is "THE BUMPY ROAD". Be sure to print the letters ahead of time and post on a bulletin board or wall before the teens arrive. Take turns like last week asking each teen to select a letter. For each correct letter they select, turn letter(s) over and give them a chance to solve the puzzle. If they guess incorrectly, their turn is over and play moves to the next person. See **Lesson One** for a complete list of suggested rules.

CHANGE

Change often brings new opportunities that will have an impact on your life.

Will this change have a positive or negative impact on you?

You Get To Decide!

Last week we spent time discussing some of the changes you have had to endure. We also discussed what it is like living in a Single Parent Home. I hope you have spent some time this week going through your assignment. Let's see how you did.

Go over TAKE HOME assignment:

- Which 5 words would best describe your family right now?
- I feel opposite feelings sometimes – like being really angry at someone and also loving and missing them very much. List some of the opposites that you feel.
- How do you handle different rules at mom's house vs. dad's house?
- Is it hard to talk to your parents about your feelings concerning visitation schedule? Why or why not?

Nugget of Truth : Change is Okay – It's All About Your Attitude

Once your parents divorce, they become single again. That can be very scary and weird. It is even weirder when they start to date again, sometimes just like you. It seems like once you get used to your single parent families, things start to change again. Just right when you settle in, Mom or Dad start dating. You begin to ask yourself – Who are they? Potential step parents? Just a fling? And what are you supposed to say? What if they remarry? These thoughts and feelings that arise start to bring up a whole new set of questions and uncertainties. What will it be like to have a step parent? Will they try to replace my real parent? What am I suppose to call them? Do I have to obey this person? Or just my biological parent? Will my parent still have enough time for me? What if the step parent has kids of their own? Where will we live? Will I have to move again? Will I have to share my bedroom? What place will I have in the new family? Will my parent have another child?

These questions can go on and on until you drive yourself crazy. These thoughts, fears, and questions can produce a ton of feelings for you. It is very important you recognize these feelings and you talk them through with either your parent or someone you can trust. It can be a very turbulent time. It is of utmost importance that you prepare yourself for the road ahead and not just stuff your feelings. More than likely, these changes will not go away and you will have to learn to accept them.

THE BUMPY ROAD

WORKBOOK PAGE 98

Look back at The SOLAR SYSTEM on page 60 of your workbook and look at your support system. These are people you could talk to about questions or fears you might have.

One of the biggest fears you'll have is wondering if when one of your parents get remarried, are you going to lose your mom or dad. This can be terrifying. You need to remind yourselves that your parents love you very much and it is impossible for them to love you any less. Finding someone special for them to share their lives with actually gives them more, not less, love to give. The love your parents have for you is a very different kind of love. You won't have to compete for it, and it won't fade away the more time he/she spends with their new spouse and their children. While it is true that the new relationship may take up more time in their life, the new relationship could never replace their love for you.

Let's take a look at your new family. If neither of your parents have remarried yet, that is fine, just fill it out as your single parent family.

MY FAMILY

"If you've come for my mom, I'm part of the package."

WORKBOOK PAGES 99-100

Discuss, as a group, the following questions:

The best thing about my new family is:

One thing I would change about my new family is:

I really like it when we:

Healthy families grow when family members work together to make the family strong. What are some things you and your family do that make your family strong?

STEP FAMILY STRENGTHS

WORKBOOK PAGE 101

As your family blends, you may need to make some boundaries to protect yourself from getting too frustrated and help you develop relationships with your new step parent or step siblings. Some things you may want to talk with your parent about are privacy issues, schedules, sharing rooms and personal things, rules, etc. If you are feeling worried at all that your relationship with your parent is going to be different, it is very important that you talk to your mom or dad about that. If you have fears or questions about how your new family will blend, take the time and talk it over with your parent. The more prepared you are, the better the transition will be. Many issues can come up and it will help if you can put yourself in the other persons shoes once in awhile. This transition is not going to be easy on anyone, so try to be patient and understanding as you learn to become a family together. It's important to realize that in any given situation there can be many different views. It is only by seeing things differently that you'll be able to see the whole picture. It's kind of like optical illusions. One picture can be seen many different ways. Is one way more right than the other...or just different?

OPTICAL ILLUSIONS

ATTACHMENT C

Hand out the Optical Illusions and go over each one with the group. Ask them these questions for each picture:

1. Do you see "Optical Illusion"?
2. Can you count the black dots?
3. Are the horizontal lines parallel or do they slope?
4. How many legs does the elephant have?
5. Do you see a rabbit or a duck?
6. Do you see a man playing a horn or a woman's face?
7. Do you see a princess or an old woman?
8. Do you see a two or a three-pronged fork?
9. Stare at the black dot in the center and move your head forward and back.
10. Do you see a rabbit or a duck?

Make sure they recognize there are usually always 2 ways to view a situation, much like these pictures. If you take a negative point of view, there is probably another way to look at the situation to see a different perspective. Try to learn to look at all the different perspectives before reaching a conclusion.

Balloon Balance

(Optional Activity)

Give each teen an inflated balloon. Tell them to try to balance it on one finger. Your finger must have contact with the balloon at all times (you can't tap it to keep it in the air). Who can do it the longest?

It'll be very difficult to keep the balloon balanced on your finger; just like how difficult it is to keep your emotions balanced throughout all these changes. No one expects you to get it right every time– neither does God. But by doing your best, it'll come easier each time.

THINKING ILLUSIONS

WORKBOOK PAGE 102

When given any situation, we all need to consider how we process our information. Do we see things only our way? Do we always push the blame on to others? Do we tend to always think the worst? Let's look at various thinking illusions. Just like when we looked at the optical illusions, at first they looked distorted and then they became clearer. Our thoughts can be distorted or inaccurate too and we may not even realize it. Our thoughts go hand and hand with our emotions and feelings. It is very important to pay attention to both our thoughts and feelings. Your thoughts color and create your emotions and by taking control of your thoughts, you can be in better control of your emotions.

IN THEIR SHOES

ATTACHMENT D AND E

Lay out the set of footprints (Attachment D) on the floor. Copy (Attachment E) and cut into separate cards. Hand out the scenarios to the teens and have the them read the examples out loud and talk about how they would feel in each situation if they were in the other person's shoes. Take a look at each situation from different points of view. Changing your perspective can help you handle difficult situations better and you may discover a more positive aspect that you may not have seen before.

Leaders Note: Option: you can use an old pair of boots or shoes (large enough for teens to slip their foot in and out of) instead of the footprints.

As these changes are taking place, realize that it will take time for everyone to adjust to living under the same roof. It is very important that you get your communication skills back out because you will need to work hard at making this family work for you and not against you.

RESOLVING CONFLICTS

WORKBOOK PAGE 103

Leaders Note: If time is short this worksheet can be done at home

Relax. Take it one step at a time. Remember that new relationships can be good and we can grow as we learn to relate to one another. New relationships provide new opportunities for people to show love and concern for one another and be able to help each other out. It may be scary when you don't know what will happen. And it may take time to get used to new people in your family. But it can be a good experience too.

MOVING ON HELPS

WORKBOOK PAGE 104

As you move on, remember these facts. Be careful not to expect too much too soon. Relationships need time to adjust so allow that time to develop. If you have an open heart and give yourself time, you may be surprised at the outcome.

Party Time?

If you haven't already done so, decide if you are going to add one more night to celebrate their success and toast their future.

If you decide to do this, I suggest you send out an invitation. You could also consider asking the teens if they would like their parents to be invited.

EXPLAIN THE "TAKING IT HOME" ASSIGNMENTS

WORKBOOK PAGES 105-107

Take time to look over the Taking It Home assignment with your group. Let them know that this assignment is a great way for them to really process what you have covered this week. Encourage them all to take the time and do the assignment as you will be briefly going through them the next week.

CLOSING TIME: Ending the session

Take Prayer Requests

This can be done a variety of ways:

- verbally shared in group setting
- hand out note cards to group members to write their requests on.
- set out a notebook that students can write in throughout the session
- put out a Prayer Request box with Prayer Request Slips
- encourage the group members to come up with other ways to share prayer requests.

Close in Prayer

Happiness is knowing how it all fits together.

TAKING IT HOME

WEEK NINE

TOWARDS YOURSELF...A Question to Take to My Heart:

Look into your heart for the answer to these questions. This is introspection time – time to grapple with what drives your thinking and behavior. Be sure to capture your thoughts.

◈ Are you ready for your mom to start dating? What would you say if she asked you if it is okay? If she is, how do you feel about it?

◈ Are you ready for your dad to start dating? What would you say if he asked you if it is okay? If he is, how do you feel about it?

◈ If either or both of your parents are dating, do you like their boyfriend/girlfriend or step-mom or step-dad? List 2 things you like about them.

1. ______________________________

2. ______________________________

◈ If either or both of your parents have remarried, how did you respond when you first heard that they were going to marry someone else?

◈ Which thinking illusion do you struggle with the most? Make a goal on how to clear up your thinking.

TOWARDS OTHERS...A Question to Take to Others:

Healing cannot become complete without affecting the lives of those around us as well. Be courageous and go outside your comfort zone to take a risk and work on your relationships with others.

- Do you think your mom or dad should tell you when and whom they are dating?

- If your parent has remarried, has your relationship with that parent gotten better or worse? In what ways?

- Has your parent gained anything positive from this relationship or do you feel it has all been negative?

- If you are now living in a step family, what things in your family have changed now that your parent has gotten remarried?

- How is your new step family similar to or different from a family with parents who have not divorced or re-married?

- What are some ways your family is still a family? Or, if you can't think of anything, explain why you feel you will never have a real family again.

TOWARDS GOD…A Question to Take to God:

When you ask God a question, expect His Spirit to respond to your heart. Be careful not to rush it, or manufacture an answer. Don't jot down your idea of the "right answer". Just pose the question to God, and wait on Him to speak personally in a fresh way.

- Do you think God will still bless your new family or does He view your family as "different"?

- Does God want you to accept this new family in your life?

- How can God help you deal with the frustrations that creating a new step family can bring?

- What role or example could God be asking you to take on in this new family?

Family Chair Game

ATTACHMENT A

Read each statement one at a time.

If you have an older sister, move one chair to the left.

If you have a dog in your home, move 3 chairs to the right.

If you have 2 grandfathers who are still living, move one chair to the left.

If you have your mom and dad living in the same home, move 2 chairs to the right.

If you have a younger brother, move 3 chairs to the left.

If you have 2 sisters, move 3 chairs to the right.

If you have a step mom, move 2 chairs to the left.

If you have a grandmother who lives in a different state other than ours, move 1 chair to the right.

If your mom and dad are separated and not divorced, move one chair to the left.

If you have a step brother or sister, move 2 chairs to the left.

If your mom and dad live in 2 separate towns ,move 3 chairs to the right.

If you have a half brother or sister, move 2 chairs to the right.

If you have 3 or more siblings (half, whole or step), move 3 chairs to the left.

If you have a step dad, move 2 chairs to the right.

If you have one parent still single and one parent remarried, move 3 chairs to the right.

If you have a grandparent living with you, move 2 chairs to the left.

When you are done, try to get their attention and wrap it up by saying something like:

We all come from different types of families. No two families are alike, but every family has its unique and special qualities. It is important not to compare our family to others and wish it were different. We need to learn to accept our family for who we are and learn to work with it, not against it.

(1)

U

(1)

T

(1)

M

(1)

H

(1)

P

(1)

E

(1)

Y

(1)

B

For the "Wheel of Fortune" activity you will need to enlarge and copy these letters onto card stock. You will need to make the number of letters indicated on each card. You will need letters to spell out "THE BUMPY ROAD"

(1) R

(1) O

(1) A

(1) D

For the "Wheel of Fortune" activity you will need to enlarge and copy these letters onto card stock. You will need to make the number of letters indicated on each card. You will need letters to spell out "THE BUMPY ROAD"

Optical Illusions

You may not see it at first, but the white spaces create the word OPTICAL, while the shadowed landscape spells out ILLUSION.

Can you count the black dots?

Are the horizontal lines parallel, or do they slope?

How many legs does this elephant have?

A rabbit, looking right? Or a duck, looking left?

Man playing a horn? Or woman's face?

Princess or a old woman?

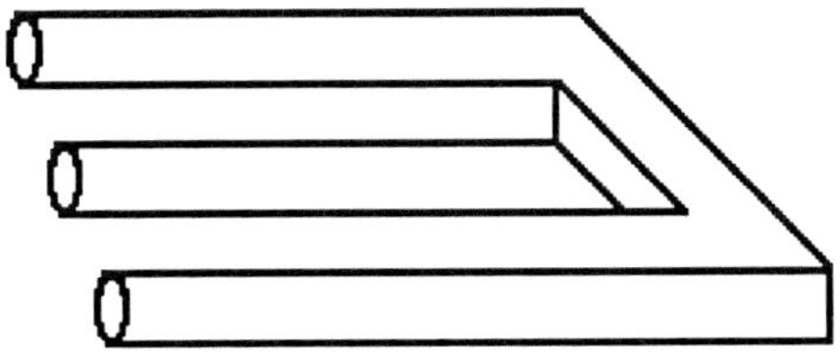

Three prong fork?

Stare at the dark dot in the center for 10 seconds...

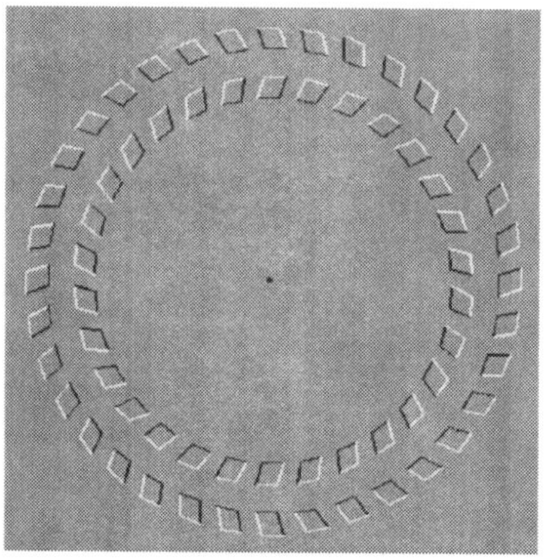

Now move your head forward and backward.
As your head moves closer to the paper
and then back away from your page, the circles
will appear to be spinning.

- - But are they really spinning? Absolutely NOT! - - -

Rabbit or a Duck?

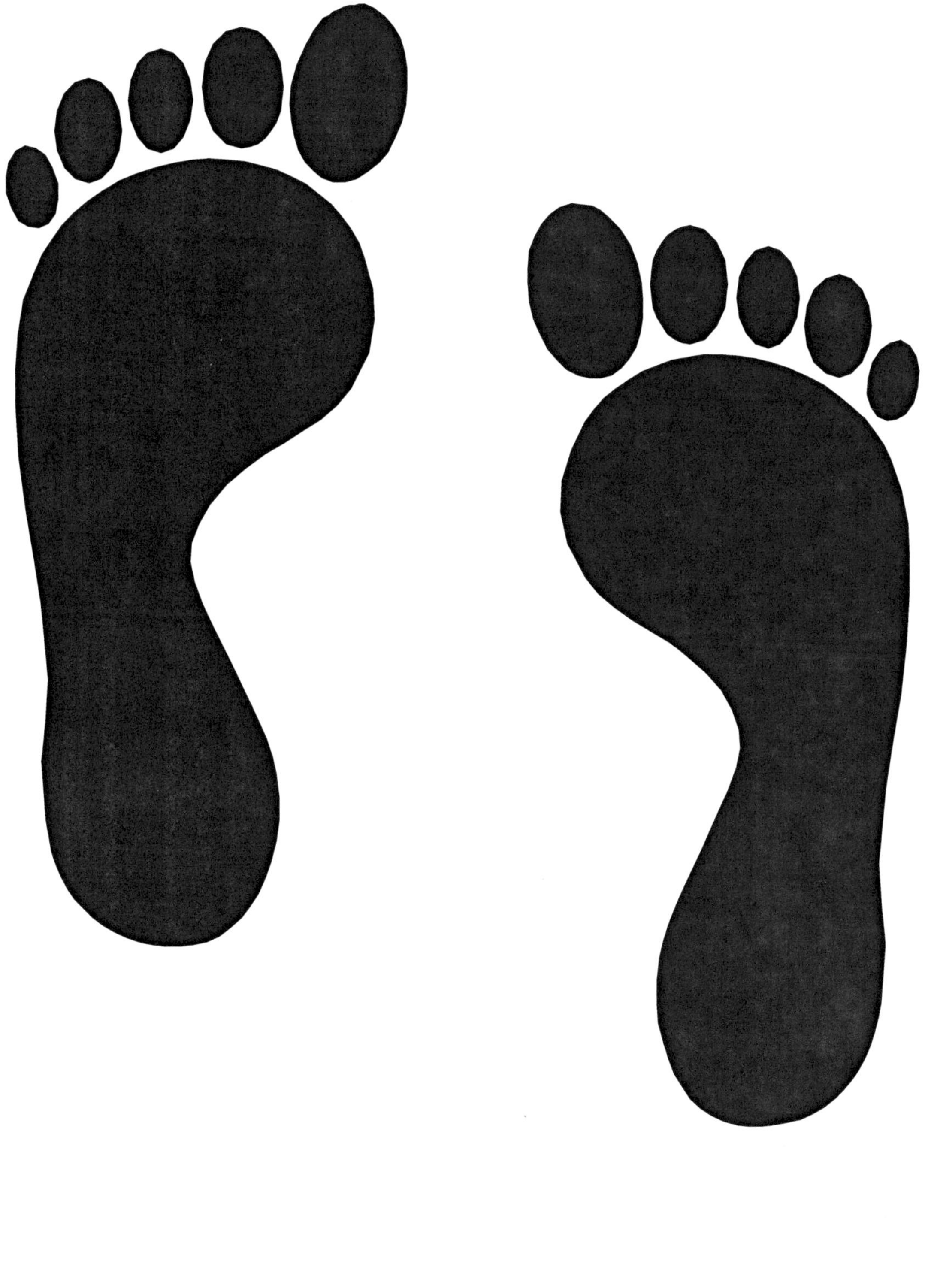

"IN THEIR SHOES"

Julie shares a room with her little sister, Jessica.
Her stepsister, Monica has her own room

After school one day, Julie goes into Monica's room
and starts listening to one of her CD's.
Monica walks in.

How might Monica feel?

How might Julie feel?

"IN THEIR SHOES"

Ben is fishing with his step-dad.
He has been fishing all day with no luck.
Suddenly he catches a big fish. He is so excited!
"I can't wait to tell Dad!" He says.
He shows his step-dad, but his step-dad has no reaction.

What might Ben be feeling?

How about his step-dad?

"IN THEIR SHOES"

Rachel is waiting for her Dad to pick her up from school, so they can go for their Friday "pizza and movie night". Instead Rachel's step-mom comes to pick her up and tells her that her Dad won't be able to go, but she'll be happy to take Rachel. Rachel barely says a word to her step-mom all evening.

How is Rachel feeling?

How might her step-mom be feeling?

"IN THEIR SHOES"

Josh comes home from his Dad's and can't wait to hook up his new video game he got for Christmas. His younger step-brother, Eric, comes in and tells him he wants to try it out too.

How might Josh feel?

How might Eric feel?

"IN THEIR SHOES"

Andy has an X-box. His step-brother, Billy, doesn't have one at his Mom's or Dad's homes.

When Andy gets home from school, he really wants to kick back and play a game. But Billy has some friends over and they are playing a game.

How would Andy handle this situation?

What could Billy be feeling?

"IN THEIR SHOES"

Mark's mom is dropping him off at his dad's house for a visit when he overhears his dad telling his Mom that he will not be able to have him visit during Christmas break this year.

Mark's dad will be going out of town with his wife and stepchildren for the holidays.

How might Mark feel?

How might his dad feel?

"IN THEIR SHOES"

Brittany is in the middle of watching a TV show when her step-brother Eric walks in to watch his favorite show.

Brittany's step-dad, Eric's dad, picks up the remote and changes the channel.

How might Brittany feel?

How about Eric? The step-dad?

"IN THEIR SHOES"

Dan watched an "R" rated movie at his mom's. When he gets back home, he tells his older brother, Steve, what a cool movie it was.
Steve then asks to watch it. Steve's mom said "no" right away because of it's rating.

What is Steve feeling?

Steve's mom?

"IN THEIR SHOES"

Susan wants to go to a movie tonight. Her step-dad says "no" and wants to wait until next weekend when his kids are with him. You have checked and the movie you wanted to see will not be there next week.

How would this make Susan feel?

How might her step-dad be feeling?

"IN THEIR SHOES"

Sarah hurries to set the table for dinner before her step-mom comes home from work.

In her rush, she drops the vase of flowers on the floor, and the step-mom's vase breaks.

How might Sarah feel?

"IN THEIR SHOES"

Joe is in the middle of playing a video game when his step-dad asks him to take out the trash.

He tells his step-dad that he'll do it in a minute. Thirty minutes later, the trash is still there, and Joe's step-dad asks him again to take out the trash. This time, frustration comes out of his voice.

How might Joe feel?

What about his step-dad?

"IN THEIR SHOES"

When Carrie comes home from her dad's, she finds out her mom and step-family all went camping while she was gone. That is all they talked about at supper.

How would Carrie feel?

How about Carrie's mom?

"IN THEIR SHOES"

Jon is 17 and has his driver's license. When he comes to his mom's house, he always has to drive his younger step-sister, Suzie, everywhere. Jon gets tired of being the errand boy.

How would Jon feel week after week?

What about Suzie?

"IN THEIR SHOES"

Jenny goes to her Dad's house every other weekend. Whenever Jenny is at her dad's she has to baby-sit her 4 year old step-sister, Cathy, while Dad takes his new wife out for dinner.

Jenny gets frustrated and says, "Why is it always my responsibility to watch the "little brat" again?

What is Jenny feeling?

How does this make Cathy feel?

"IN THEIR SHOES"

"IN THEIR SHOES"

Forgiveness

Let Go, Let God

As we are nearing the end of our sessions together, we need to spend some time wrestling through forgiveness. This week our goal will be to help the teens better understand what forgiveness is and what it is not. We will also help them reflect on their lives and relationships to see what role forgiveness may play in their personal healing journey. Forgiving themselves and others is often a very difficult thing for teens to do. Pray that they feel God's grace in a way they have never felt before and that they allow Him to open their hearts to be willing to accept and share that grace with others.

PREP TIME

1. Spend time in prayer for:
    a. your heart as you prepare for this lesson
    b. the students who will be attending this week, that God would open their hearts and help them to share their feelings
    c. the other leaders helping with this session
    d. all student prayer requests from last week
2. Read through the lesson and make sure you understand the material and activities
3. Gather supplies for projects.
4. Copy, cut and make a True/False sign for everyone (Attachment A)
5. Prepare Wheel of Fortune sheets (Attachment B) and tape them to wall
6. Bring back the big heart with all the band-aids that you did during Week #4.
7. Make or find a cross of any size and put 3 nails point side out on the sides and bottom
8. CD player with soft Christian music
9. Workbooks

HIGHLIGHTS

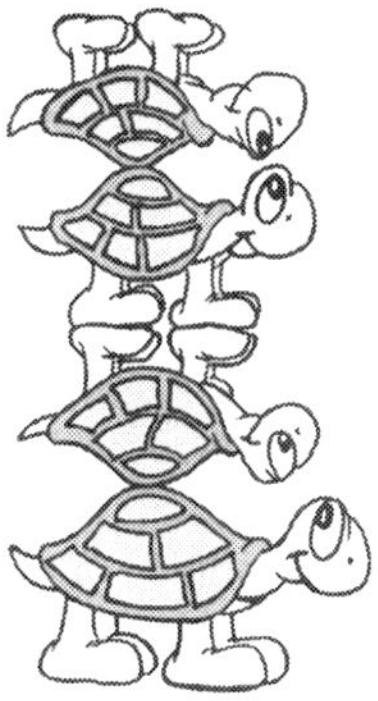

Forgiveness

1. True/False Mixer
2. Wheel of Fortune
3. Common Ground
4. Nugget of Truth: Forgiveness: What It Is and What It Isn't
5. Forgiveness Facts
6. Nugget of Truth: Why Do We Have To Forgive?
7. Forgiveness is Tough
8. Taking it Home

Lesson Ten
Week 10

Verse of the week:

"If we confess our sins, He is faithful and just and will forgive us our sins and purify us from all unrighteousness."

1 John 1:9

Be Blessed!

"Bear with each other and forgive whatever grievances you may have against one another. Forgive as the Lord forgave you.

Colossians 3:13

In order to experience total healing, we need to experience the miracle of forgiveness. In this session we are going to learn what forgiveness is and what it is not. We are going to ask you to think about current relationships that may need your forgiveness. We will also look at situations where you may need to forgive yourself or ask God to forgive you.

TRUE/FALSE MIXER

Ask the questions (on Attachment A) and have everyone hold up their True/False sign as to whether they think it is True or False. Do not make it seem there are "wrong" answers so they don't feel intimidated to play. Make sure after each question you go into the explanation as to whether it was True or False.

ATTACHMENT A

After the *True/False Mixer* gather back into a group and open in prayer.

WHEEL OF FORTUNE

What's The Real Deal?

ATTACHMENT B

The title of this week's lesson is "WHAT'S THE REAL DEAL?". Be sure to print the letters ahead of time and post on a bulletin board or wall before the teens arrive. Take turns like last week asking each teen to select a letter. For each correct letter they select, turn letter(s) over and give them a chance to solve the puzzle. If they guess incorrectly, their turn is over and play moves to the next person. See **Lesson One** for a complete list of suggested rules.

Common Ground

Last week we spent our time talking about the changes that happen when your single parent home turns into a step -family home. This can be a very difficult time for everybody. I hope you have spent some time this week exploring your feelings on this topic. Remember, even if you may not be in a step-family now, the chances of you being in one some day is very possible. Let's see how the assignments went this week?

Go over *TAKE HOME* assignment:

- If either or both of your parents have remarried, how did you respond when you first heard that they were going to marry someone else?

- Do you think your mom or dad should tell you when and whom they are dating?

- If you are now living in a step family, what things in your family have changed now that your parent has gotten married again?

- Which Thinking Illusion do you struggle with the most? Share with the group what goals you made to clear up your thinking.

Nugget of Truth – Forgiveness–What it is and what it isn't

One of the toughest things you may have to do is work through forgiveness. Forgiveness for what you have lost. Forgiveness for why things have happened. Forgiveness for wrong choices people we love make. Forgiveness for our own mistakes. Forgiveness for your thoughts as to why God is allowing these awful things to happen to your family. Forgiveness can go on and on. Many times forgiveness is not just a one time act. It is something we may need to deal with daily as new and old situations keep coming up. It is also important for you to realize sometimes when the wounds are still open, it is difficult to forgive right away. Jesus understands that. All He is looking for is a willing heart. He will allow you time to see it come to pass. With you and Him working together, forgiveness can be an awesome experience. The freedom you feel will be one that you will never regret.

GET OUT OF JAIL

Not forgiving or holding a grudge is like putting someone in a jail inside your heart. Having them in this jail will ensure that you will carry them (and the issue or situation that caused you pain) around forever. Having them in this jail cell in your heart means that you have to attend to and feed them daily, which keeps you attached to them forever. It's your choice to release that person and give them freedom and in doing so you will also be freeing yourself.

FORGIVENESS FACTS

Take time and read through the explanations. This forgiveness concept is very important for them to understand.

WORKBOOK PAGE 110

Suggested answers are listed at the end of this chapter on pages 188 & 189.

Many times we have a tougher time forgiving because we have a wrong understanding of what forgiveness is and what it isn't. Let's take a deeper look at forgiveness.

Nugget of Truth – Why do we have to forgive?

Forgiveness is directly referenced 125 times in the Bible, which leads me to believe it is very important to God. Forgiveness is a marvelous thing! Forgiveness is a promise. Forgiveness is a pledge. Forgiveness is a statement of undeserved, unearned, love that says, "no" matter what you've done, there is no desire for paybacks or punishment. There is nothing we can do on our own. It is only through the grace that God demonstrates to us that gives us the strength to extend the gift to others. Why should we forgive?

- Because Jesus forgave us. (Eph. 4:32, Luke 23:34)
- Because it frees us from bitterness. (Hebrews 12:14-15)
- Because it demonstrates Christ's character. (Colossians 3:12-13)
- Because it will deliver us from Satan's traps. (2nd Cor. 2:9-11)
- Because it delivers us from the discipline from God. (Luke 6:35-37)
- Because if we expect to be forgiven we ourselves need to forgive. (James 2:13)

One sure sign that you need to forgive is when anger has had such a grip on you that it has turned into bitterness. Unsettled anger that lasts and lasts can be very dangerous. You may be thinking "What's wrong with me?" You want to move on but this anger keeps you stuck in the mud. This is a good sign that you have someone you may need to forgive. Who? Maybe your parents for being selfish or stubborn...or for choices they made...it could be for so many things.
Don't be afraid to admit it and now forgive them.

Forgiveness is not a matter of ignoring the wrong that was done. It's facing it head on and saying it is over and you won't hold it against them anymore. It is saying you still love them and you are ready to move on.

If you continue to hang onto your anger you can become bitter. It will not only affect that relationship, but it will affect all your relationships. It is like a poison that robs the joy from your life. The reason we can forgive is that we know and accept that none of us is perfect. God continues to forgive us for our wrongs, so as we have been forgiven, we can extend forgiveness to others who have hurt us.

Forgiveness is not always easy. In fact, most times it is very hard. Maybe you are having trouble forgiving because a parent keeps hurting you over and over again, or maybe a parent has done something so terrible that you don't think he or she deserves to be forgiven. Forgiveness can even seem pointless if your parent doesn't seem to even care about having a relationship with you. Let's take a look at what God says about tough situations like these.

FORGIVENESS IS TOUGH & A CLOSER LOOK

WORKBOOK PAGE 111-113

Forgiving may be one of the toughest jobs that you will ever have to do. Sometimes when it just feels impossible to forgive, it helps to start praying for them. When you pray for someone, God softens your heart toward them. It may even help to remember that they have been hurt too. Opening your heart may mean that you will get hurt again, but it is in opening your heart that makes room for the good stuff to happen – like inner peace and happiness and love. Forgiveness is the ultimate connection – with parents who have hurt you, with yourself, and with God. It's yours for the giving.

LAY IT AT THE CROSS

Get out the Big Red Heart with Band-aids on it from Session 4. Bring out a cross and place it somewhere in the room.

It is now time to bring out the big heart that holds the band-aids that they filled out during week four. Put on some soft music (see Reflective Songs in Activity Guide) and tell them it is time for them to lay their hurts and burdens at the cross and be willing to forgive those who have hurt them. Have the cross setting somewhere in the room and allow time for everyone to come up and collect their band-aids and nail them to the cross.

It is as we lay our hurts and burdens at the feet of Jesus that we are free to forgive those who have hurt us. I'm sure as we reflect on forgiving those around us we will realize our part in the situations. We are now going to take time to ask Jesus to forgive us for our wrongs and to forgive those who have wronged us.

Forgive and Forget?

Forgiving someone does not mean that you necessarily forget. Sometimes it is good to remember the hurt someone else caused you so that you don't set yourself up to be hurt like that again. Forgive, but set up a boundary to protect yourself next time.

"PLEASE FORGIVE ME"

Pour your heart out to God. There is no sin too big for God not to forgive. We all have sinned so don't be afraid to lay it all out to Him. This is a time just between you and God.

WORKBOOK PAGE 114

THOSE I NEED TO FORGIVE

WORKBOOK PAGE 115

Once we have received God's forgiveness, it is time to extend that same gift to others. Look deep inside yourself - what wrongs have you been holding on to and refusing to let go of? When we hold on to hurts and anger, we become bitter. Bitterness burns a hole in our hearts and makes it hard to move forward. When we receive forgiveness as a free gift we don't deserve, we need to extend that gift to others as well. To whom and in what ways do we need to let go of the bitterness that robs our joy and extend forgiveness to? It is in living out this commitment that reminds us that we may need to continuously lay our burdens before the cross daily. Here are a few things we are committing to:

* We are committing not to dwell on the mistakes or the wrongs the other person has done.
* We are committing to not bringing up the situations over and over again and use it as a dart. It is agreeing to leave it in the past and to not hold any more grudges against that person.
* It also commits us to not talk to others about what has happened. We will not necessarily forget about it, but we will choose not to gossip about it anymore either.

These things can be tough to do. That is why forgiveness is such a powerful tool. It can literally change people's lives. Have you ever thought that your forgiveness could be the one thing that changes people's lives forever? Maybe even bring them to Christ?

EXPLAIN THE TAKING IT HOME ASSIGNMENTS

Take time to look over the Taking It Home assignment with your group. Let them know that this assignment is a great way for them to really process what you have covered this week. Encourage them all to take the time and do the assignment as you will be briefly going through them the next week.

WORKBOOK PAGE 116-118

CLOSING TIME: Ending the session

Take Prayer Requests

This can be done in a variety of ways:

- verbally shared in group setting
- hand out note cards to group members to write out their requests.
- set out a notebook that students can write in throughout the session
- put out a Prayer Request box with Prayer Request Slips
- encourage the group members to come up with other ways to share prayer requests.

Close in Prayer

TAKING IT HOME

WEEK TEN

TOWARDS YOURSELF…A Question to Take to My Heart:

Look into your heart for the answer to these questions. This is introspection time – time to grapple with what drives your thinking and behavior. Be sure to capture your thoughts.

◈ What is the hardest thing that has kept you from forgiving? Or still is?

◈ What new truth did you learn about forgiveness this week?

◈ What are some areas in your life that need God's forgiveness right now?

◈ What did it feel like once you forgave?

◈ Sometimes forgiving ourselves is the hardest. Are there things you need to forgive yourself for? If so, what are they?

TOWARDS OTHERS...A Question to Take to Others:

Healing cannot become complete without affecting the lives of those around us as well. Be courageous and go outside your comfort zone to take a risk and work on your relationships with others.

◈ Have you completely forgiven your parents for the divorce or are there things you need to work through? If so, what are they? Are you working towards complete forgiveness?

◈ Are there other things you need to forgive them for since the divorce? Others?

◈ Has your relationship changed since you've extended forgiveness? If so, how?

◈ Once you've forgiven, are you committed to these four things
- not to dwell on the wrongs anymore?
- not to bring them up in conversation anymore?
- not to gossip about them?
- not to hold them against them anymore.

TOWARDS GOD...A Question to Take to God:

When you ask God a question, expect His Spirit to respond to your heart. Be careful not to rush it, or manufacture an answer. Don't jot down your idea of the "right answer". Just pose the question to God, and wait on Him to speak personally in a fresh way.

- Are there still areas in your life which you still need to seek forgiveness from God for yet?

- Describe a time when you have experienced God's forgiveness. How did it feel?

- If you are still holding on to hurts and wrongs, are you willing to start praying for those who have wronged you?

- What is the hardest truth for you to accept about God's forgiveness?

Forgiveness Facts

Check out your perceptions against the answers below. Expanding your understanding of what forgiveness is and isn't can go a long way toward helping you mend your relationship with your parents.

a. **Forgiving someone means you will no longer get angry or have anymore negative feelings toward him or her.**

FALSE – Even when you choose to forgive, it will take some time and you will probably have to work awhile on settling your negative feelings, such as anger or resentment. The feelings often stay around long after the wrong act itself. Forgiveness does not mean everything goes back to normal and behaviors stop happening, but rather you learn to recognize the wrongs for what they are and learn to put up boundaries to protect yourself.

b. **If you forgive, you have to put it all behind you and leave it in the past and become friends to the person who hurt you.**

FALSE – You may want to become close to the person who hurt you (this is called reconciliation), especially when that person is your parent, however, it is not always possible.

c. **You do not have to forgive an immoral person.**

FALSE – It is difficult enough to forgive, let alone forgive someone who trashes good and seems to revel in the bad, however, God wants us to forgive all people. Forgiveness is for everyone, no matter what. God has and continues to forgive us of all our mistakes. Would He not expect us to do the same for others? We all make bad choices, but Jesus came to be our perfect example of what true forgiveness is.

d. **You may want to forgive someone, but, you may not be ready on the inside.**

TRUE – Forgiveness can take a long time to achieve. It may be an effort you need to make over and over again. You will know when you are ready. All God asks of us is to have a willing heart; He will do the rest. Forgiveness is a step by step process.

e. **Forgiving is a necessary part of the healing process and you will not be able to completely heal until you do so.**

TRUE – Forgiveness allows you to find peace both with your parents and yourself. God has intended forgiveness to be a very integral part of the healing process. You will not experience full healing without experiencing true forgiveness.

f. **Forgiveness is based on a feeling you get telling you that are ready to move on. Until then, you are not ready to forgive**

FALSE –Forgiveness is not based on a feeling at all. It is a choice we make in obedience to God's Word and in acceptance of His forgiveness.

g. **You cannot forgive until the offender asks for it or shows that he or she is sorry.**

FALSE – Forgiving someone who does not say or show that he or she is sorry is very hard. However, when you choose to forgive such a person, you are choosing not to let negative feelings consume you, so you can move on with your life. It is your responsibility to forgive; not theirs to ask.

h. **When you forgive others, you believe and accept that God has forgiven you.**

TRUE – Forgiving others is a sign of God's grace for everyone. We all have sinned, but God continues to show us His mercy by extending forgiveness to us every time we humbly come to Him.

i. **If you forgive someone, you have to forget what they've done.**

FALSE – Forgiving doesn't mean forgetting what has happened or excusing the hurts you have felt. God wants us to have realistic expectations of others and to set boundaries with difficult people to protect ourselves. To do this, we need to remember and learn from the past. This helps to prevent us from getting hurt by the same situation over and over again. We need to take control today. Forgetting and putting ourselves back into the same unhealthy situations over and over again only prolongs our pain.
God doesn't want that.

j. **Forgiveness depends on getting a guarantee that someone won't do the same wrong thing again.**

FALSE—Forgiveness does not come with any guarantees. We are all human and are not perfect. We need to be willing to forgive without any promises or expectations. What would we do if Jesus would only forgive us if we guaranteed we would never sin again?

k. **Forgiveness is unconditional.**

TRUE—When we choose to forgive, it is something we do for ourselves and for our relationship with Christ. It has very little to do with the other person. There are no conditions attached. No promises made. It is a free gift we give ourselves.

l. **Forgiveness excuses the other person's sin or wrong doing.**

FALSE—Whether you forgive or not does not mean you have not been wronged or that you are excusing all the pain it caused. The fact remains that you are just choosing to lay your battle weapons aside and are moving on.

TRUE/FALSE MIXER
Questions

Beforehand, make a True/False sign for each person on card stock. Cut them out and glue one on each side of a Popsicle stick.

Hand out a True/False sign to everyone. Ask the questions below one by one and have them answer whether or not they feel the statement is True or False by holding up their sign. When everyone is done holding up their signs, tell them the right answer and share the additional explanation.

Girls have more feelings than guys.

False – we all have feelings. Girls usually just have an easier time showing them.

Big boys don't cry.

False – There is no such thing as boys not crying. God made all of us with emotions and it is okay for everyone to show them and cry.

Everyone has the same feelings.

False – God has made each one of us differently. Although everyone has feelings, they are all different.

Feelings like happy, excited, proud and love are okay to feel.

True – These feelings, as well as other feelings, are great to feel, but feelings are not just limited to positive ones.

Feelings like sad, angry, hate and jealousy are NOT okay to feel.

False – Although these feelings are more difficult, they are still okay to feel. It is very normal to feel these kinds of feelings while you are going through a separation or divorce in your family. It is not wrong to feel these feelings, it is usually how you choose to express them that makes them wrong.

Everyone expresses their feelings in the same way.

False – God has made us all different and you will express your feelings depending on your unique personality.

It's okay to have feelings, but you should never let anyone know what they truly are.

False – Most of your healing will come as you open up and share your feelings with someone you trust. The more you hold them in, the longer it will take to heal.

Only "scaredy cats" and "sissies" are afraid.

False – When your parents are going through a separation or divorce, it is very normal to be afraid. There are a lot of unknowns and you may feel like you have no control over what is going on around you. Everyone feels fear to some degree.

It's okay to be angry as long as you don't hurt anyone or break anything when you are.

True – it is a very normal reaction to be angry. Be very careful how you express your anger though.

Jesus was never angry.

False – In Mark 11 the Bible tells a story when Jesus came into the temple area and they were selling goods. He got angry and overturned the tables and made them leave. This is a great example of it being okay to express your anger when justified, but being careful how you express it.

Teens that can feel all their feelings and express them in good ways are healthier than those who don't express their feelings.

True – One of the healthiest things you can do during this time is to accept and express whatever feelings you are having.

Anger is a sin.

False – It is not a sin to feel angry. It is what you do with your anger that usually turns out to be a sin.

It is possible to have too many emotions.

False – Everyone and every situation is different. No one should be judged according to their own situations. Everyone's situation is different.

Every single feeling is important.

True – There is no feeling that is unimportant and all feelings need to be shared.

It's best to cry when you are alone.

False – It may be easier to cry when you are alone but you should not feel like that is the only time you can cry. Crying is not something that needs be done only in private.

Good kids are always happy.

False – Whether you are happy or not does not determine whether you are good or not.

When you are upset with someone the best thing for you to do is to keep quiet.

False – It is not healthy for you to stuff your feelings. Depending on the situation it may not be best to talk directly to the person you are upset at but it would be good to talk it over with someone you can trust.

Hating something or someone is okay and normal.

False – We are never suppose to hate anything. When you feel hate, you become bitter thus making it very hard to forgive. God has called each one of us to forgive as He has forgiven us.

You always need a reason to be sad or upset.

False – sometimes you don't even know what your reason is. It is through going to groups like this that help you define your reason.

Not talking to someone is a way of solving a problem.

False – By not talking to someone you are ignoring the situation not solving it.

Things would be better if you were perfect.

False – Feeling this way is not reality. We live in a fallen world and no one is perfect. We need to learn to live within our failures and shortcomings in order to learn what God is teaching us.

I am always responsible for my actions.

True – Each one of us are responsible for our actions. Someone else may be responsible for the situation that has made you react but how you react is totally your responsibility.

With enough hard work, I can fix anything.

False – You can fix only that which you have control over. No matter how hard you may try to fix your parents marriage or relationship, you do not have any control over that. What you do have control over is yourself. With hard work you can get through this and take steps to prevent it happening in your life in the future.

My life is my life and no one knows me better than me, so no one can give me advice.

False – although you may think you know yourself better than anybody else, another person who you can trust can often times give you an objective opinion on things in your life that you have never seen before. Getting someone else's opinion is always a good idea, as long as you know that they care about you and you can trust their opinion.

I am considered weak if I ask for help.

False – Everyone needs help every now and then. God has given us the need for others in our lives. We need to allow others to help us when we are in need.

Anger is fine if you can control it.

True – Anger is not a sin, it is what you do with anger that turns it into sin.

God has given each of us an incredible number of feelings. Some of them are fun and we like to feel them, and others are scary and difficult and we will do anything we can to keep from feeling them.

True – As hard as it is to acknowledge your feelings and deal with them, it is only by doing this that you can move on and make changes for your future.

TRUE

TRUE

FALSE

FALSE

ATTACHMENT B

(1) W

(2) H

(3) A

(2) T

(1) ’

(3) S

(3) E

(1) R

For the “Wheel of Fortune” activity you will need to enlarge and copy these letters onto card stock. You will need to make the number of letters indicated on each card. You will need letters to spell out “WHAT’S THE REAL DEAL?”.

ATTACHMENT B

(2) L

(1) D

(1) ?

For the "Wheel of Fortune" activity you will need to enlarge and copy these letters onto card stock. You will need to make the number of letters indicated on each card. You will need letters to spell out "WHAT'S THE REAL DEAL?".

Moving On and Letting Go

Teens of divorce often feel pushed and pulled not really knowing what choices they have in their lives and thereby, what control they have. Identifying the choices they have can be very empowering. In this session we are going to talk about choices. In every situation there is a choice to be made– a good choice or a bad choice. We will also have them write goals for themselves. I recommend you give them an envelope to self address and collect all goals at the end of the session so you can mail them to them in 3 months as a reminder of how they are doing on the goals they set during this session.

PREP TIME

1. Spend time in prayer for:
    a. your heart as you prepare for this lesson
    b. the students who will be attending this week, that God would open their hearts and help them to share their feelings
    c. the other leaders helping with this session
    d. all prayer requests from the students from last week
2. Read through the lesson and make sure you understand the material and activities
3. Purchase small gifts at a dollar store for each teen
4. Prepare Wheel of Fortune sheets (Attachment A) and tape them to wall
5. Bring an envelope for each teen
6. Copy 3 Month Goals (Attachment B)
7. Workbooks

HIGHLIGHTS

Acceptance

1. Hidden Gift Game
2. Wheel of Fortune: Moving On And Letting Go
3. Common Ground
4. Nugget of Truth: Acceptance
5. Growth Goals
6. 3 Month Goals
7. Truths You Can Count On
8. Taking It Home

Lesson Eleven
Week 11

Verses of the week:

The Lord will again delight in you and make you prosperous, just as he delighted in your fathers, if you obey the Lord your God and keep his commands and decrees that are written in this Book of the Law and turn to the Lord your God with all your heart and with all your soul.

Deuteronomy 30:9b-10

Be Blessed!

"All these blessings will come upon you and accompany you if you obey the Lord your God.

Deuteronomy 28:2

Sometimes it is very hard to make the right choice. And then what do you do when you watch your parents making wrong choices? Tonight we are going to help you evaluate your decisions and hopefully encourage you to make wise choices when faced with difficult circumstances. Especially when your parents may not be making the best choices for themselves either. Keep in mind that as you make good choices you will find your way to acceptance and you will begin to notice all those tougher days are behind you. Walk with us as we lead you towards true acceptance.

Hidden Gift Game

This game is like a white elephant gift exchange. During the week purchase a number of gifts ranging in all shapes and sizes. The Dollar Store is a good place to find some good gifts, some silly gifts, and some strange gifts. Wrap the gifts prior to group. Have the kids choose a number from 1 to the number of kids you have present. The teen with the number 1 gets to choose a wrapped gift and sits back in his/her seat. The teen with # 2 may either choose to steal # 1's gift or choose another from the pile. Of course, this is a risk, because # 1's gift is still not revealed. Really emphasize the *choice* in the matter. Say things like, "What will you choose?" "What a difficult choice!" This goes on until the last person chooses a gift. Then everyone can unwrap their gifts. They will find it hilarious when the gift they all fought over was really a bar of soap disguised in a bigger box or a roll of toilet paper or the gift no one wanted is a bag of candy. Wrap up discussion by telling them that sometimes in life the choices you need to make can be scary because you don't know what the outcome will be. Remind them that if they trust in God, they can know that in the end, regardless of their life circumstances, He is always on their side and promises to give them a hope and a future. At the end you can pass out a small gift to everyone (maybe a chocolate hug kiss).

After the *Hidden Gift Game*, gather back into a group and open in prayer.

WHEEL OF FORTUNE

ATTACHMENT A

Moving On and Letting Go

The title of this week's lesson is "MOVING ON AND LETTING GO". Be sure to print the letters ahead of time and post on a bulletin board or wall before the teens arrive. Take turns like last week asking each teen to select a letter. For each correct letter they select, turn letter(s) over and give them a chance to solve the puzzle. If they guess incorrectly, their turn is over and play moves to the next person. See **Lesson One** for a complete list of suggested rules.

Follow Up Time

1. Take time this week to send out "Miss You" cards to those who may have missed last week.
2. Send a note of appreciation to someone in your group who was particularly helpful in your group.
3. Send a note of encouragement to someone in your group who was open or shared a vulnerability.
4. Send an "You're in my prayers" note to someone who shared a prayer request.

There is no need for these to be lengthy notes. Remind them that they are important to the group and important to God.

Last week we looked at one of the most difficult things you may ever have had to do. Forgiveness is a gift God gives to all of us. It is not something we deserve from Him just as it is not always something others deserve from us. But in order to move on to complete wholeness it is something each one of us has to experience. Let's see how the assignments went this week?

Go over *Take Home* assignment:

- What new truth did you learn about forgiveness this week?
- Has your relationship changed since you've extended forgiveness? If so, how?
- Did you feel any differently once you forgave?

Nugget of Truth: Acceptance

You all have done an outstanding job making it this far. We have talked about many difficult things and you have come a long way. We are very proud of you. We are now going to approach the final stage in our Slippery Slope that we talked about many weeks ago. The final stage of Acceptance.

Some people may think with acceptance comes a giddy joy. That is rarely true when it comes to divorce in families. Acceptance does not assume that all problems are solved. It only accepts what has happened and begins to look toward the future. It does not choose to spend all of its time and energy living in the past.

In some cases acceptance comes suddenly. You wake up one morning and say "Hey, I'm going to be alright." But in most cases, it is a slow realization of the great future you still have ahead of you. Sometimes you may even reach a point of acceptance and then slip back into anger and depression. That is why we call it the Slippery Slope. But don't worry, you'll pull through again, and this time the trip will probably be much faster and much less painful.

Acceptance looks like this:

"It happened, it hurt, but I'm okay."

"It may be difficult to put my life back together, but there is nothing I can do to change the past. I can only move forward toward the future."

"With God's help, I will try to make the best of this situation and all the changes that I need to adapt to."

I'm ready for whatever comes my way!"

Acceptance:

Webster Says:

Acceptance is the feeling that we can live with reality and be just fine. We may not necessarily be happy with reality and knowing that their has been a lot of pain, but we can deal with it. We know we can't change it, and we've stopped trying. We start to work on what is left and focus on our future.

Positive Reinforcement

(Optional Activity)

Reinforcement choices by providing two snacks and telling them they have a choice. Remind them that change is all around them and they are going to have to make choices. Which choice will they make? The good choice or the bad choice?

One way we can be sure we stay on the road to change and acceptance is to write up goals for ourselves. We are all human so left to our own doing we will probably fall back into our old patterns. In order to keep our sights set high and focused on everything we have learned we need to refocus ourselves weekly. In your workbook are six weeks worth of Growth Goals. Each week you will come up with a personal growth goal and a family growth goal. We will take a few minutes now to write out some goals for the next week.

GROWTH GOALS

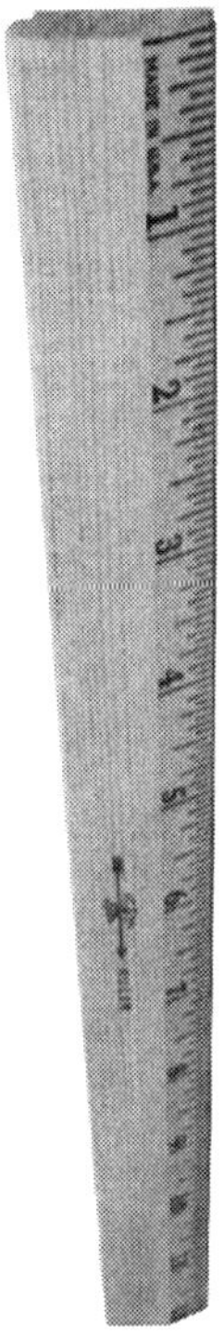

WORKBOOK PAGES 120-125

We have supplied you with 5 Growth Goals to use over the next 5 weeks. Keep these goals somewhere you will remember throughout the week. We will check how you did next week and come up with new goals for the following week.

There will be many times when you thought you were through all the yucky stuff and then all of the sudden, something sneaks up on you again. Don't panic. This happens. You never know when another loss or change will come along. Make sure you remind yourself that slipping down again is a normal part of the healing process. You will discover that every time you slip down, you will jump back quicker.

Just because you have reached this acceptance stage and have done all the hard work to get here, it does not necessarily mean you are automatically past all the other stages and have landed safely at acceptance. It takes most teenagers a long time – years and sometimes decades – before they feel safe and secure in acceptance.

Many things will come your way that will make you question if you have made any progress, but you will notice the time in between will get longer and longer and the pain will seem lesser and lesser. At times like these, seek as much encouragement and support as you can. You may be surprised at the strength you discover in yourself that you never knew you had before. You really have only two choices – one leads to giving up and all your hard work will be for nothing. The other leads to growth and success. When you keep thinking, "Poor me. Life is so unfair. I am powerless." you are giving up. When you choose a healthy attitude and use the information and exercises you have learned in this group you will grow through this and become a much better, stronger person. You will find reason to be hopeful. You will recognize that, although life is tough right now, you do have power. You will realize that your hurts don't have to last forever and you can have a wonderful future of your own. When you go through times like these remind yourself of these truths.

TRUTHS YOU CAN COUNT ON

WORKBOOK PAGE 126

One of the best ways you can find strength to continue is to surround yourself with supportive Christian people. There are four things you need to have in your life:

Join a good youth group that offers you support and encouragement in your personal and spiritual growth.

Read your Bible everyday and get into some sort of devotional routine.

Develop a solid prayer life. Realize prayer is much more than a routine once or twice a day, it is a continual conversation you have with God all day long.

Surround yourself with good solid Christian friends. Your peers shape who you are and how you respond. Be sure to guard yourself by putting a strong fence of good friends around you at all times.

We are now going to set some goals for three months down the road. Next week when we are done it will be so easy for us to slip back into our old habits and past behaviors. To encourage us to stay focused, we are going to set three goals that you would like to accomplish within the next three months.

3 MONTH GOALS

ATTACHMENT B

Pass out Attachment B and have everyone come up with three 3 month goals. They can be anything from spending more time with their Dad, to being kinder to their siblings, or helping out more around the house. They can be to get involved with a youth group or to spend more time in prayer. Whatever it is, make sure it is defined well enough to be attainable in 3 months time.

Now pass out an envelope to everyone. Have them put their goals worksheet inside the envelope, seal it and address it to themselves. When everyone is finished, collect the envelopes and let the students know you will be mailing them their goals in 3 months. They can then look back and see what they have accomplished.

Six Steps to Reach Your Goals

1. Define your values
2. Create goals that reflect your values
3. Brainstorm ways to reach your goals
4. Evaluate your goals– are they practical?
5. Implement your plan
6. Check your progress

EXPLAIN THE "TAKING IT HOME" ASSIGNMENTS

WORKBOOK PAGES 127-129

Take time to look over the Taking It Home assignment with your group. Let them know that this assignment is a great way for them to really process what you have covered this week. Encourage them all to take the time and do the assignment as you will be briefly going through them the next week.

CLOSING TIME: Ending the session

Take Prayer Requests

This can be done a in variety of ways:

- verbally shared in group setting
- hand out note cards to group members to write out their requests.
- set out a note book that students can write in throughout the session
- put out a Prayer Request box with Prayer Request Slips.
- encourage the group members to come up with other ways to share prayer requests.

Close in Prayer

TAKING IT HOME

WEEK ELEVEN

TOWARDS YOURSELF…A Question to Take to My Heart:

Look into your heart for the answer to these questions. This is introspection time – time to grapple with what drives your thinking and behavior. Be sure to capture your thoughts.

- Even though you would never have chosen for your parents to have gone through a divorce, do you think there are some ways in which you are a better person? If so what are they?

- Do you think because of what you have experienced with your parents separation you have learned things that could impact your future?

- Do you think you are closer to either your mom or dad because of the divorce? If so, in what ways?

- How are you doing on your Growth Goals this week?

TOWARDS OTHERS...A Question to Take to Others:

Healing cannot become complete without affecting the lives of those around us as well. Be courageous and go outside your comfort zone to take a risk and work on your relationships with others.

- Do you need to find a group of new Christian friends that support you in this healing process?

- When things get rough again, do you have someone already in mind you can go to? If so, who? If not, who can you think of?

- How does your parents' divorce affect your own personal dating relationships?

- What do you do when you see your parents making bad choices? Can you still respect your parents knowing that they make mistakes?

TOWARDS GOD…A Question to Take to God:

When you ask God a question, expect His Spirit to respond to your heart. Be careful not to rush it, or manufacture an answer. Don't jot down your idea of the "right answer". Just pose the question to God, and wait on Him to speak personally in a fresh way.

- Have you allowed God to help you with your pain or have you been refusing to let God in? If not, what is holding you back?

- Do you have a scheduled devotional time each day? If not, make a commitment to start now.

- How is your prayer life? Do you need to pump it up a bit?

- Is improving your relationship with God one of your goals? If not, consider making one now.

ATTACHMENT A

(1) N

(1) M

(3) G

(3) O

(1) A

(1) V

(1) L

(2) I

For the "Wheel of Fortune" activity you will need to enlarge and copy these letters onto card stock. You will need to make the number of letters indicated on each card. You will need letters to spell out " MOVING ON AND LETTING GO".

ATTACHMENT A

(1) D

(1) E

(2) T

For the "Wheel of Fortune" activity you will need to enlarge and copy these letters onto card stock. You will need to make the number of letters indicated on each card.
You will need letters to spell out " MOVING ON AND LETTING GO".

3 Month Goal Worksheet

ATTACHMENT B

1.

2.

3.

Lesson Twelve
Week 12

Verses of the week:

"I do all this for the sake of the gospel, that I may share in its blessing."

1 Corinthians 9:23

Be Blessed!

For I know the plans I have for you declares the Lord, plans to prosper you and not to harm you, plans to give you a hope and a future.

Jeremiah 29:11

Beauty From Ashes

It is hard to believe this is our last session. It is a great accomplishment these teens stuck with the process over the last 12 weeks. At times I'm sure it was not always easy. I suggest adding an additional night to celebrate their future but if that is not possible, try to leave a little time tonight for celebration. Help them to recognize the journey they have taken during The Big D and the progress they have made. I have purposely left this session shorter in case you need to save some time for your celebration ceremony. If you have decided to add a session 13 for the party just go to the website and you will find all kinds of additional options for you to do.

PREP TIME

1. Spend time in prayer for:
    a. your heart as you prepare for this lesson
    b. the students who will be attending this week, that God would open their hearts and help them to share their feelings
    c. the other leaders helping with this session
    d. pray over student prayer requests from last week
2. Read through the lesson and make sure you understand the material and activities
3. Gather supplies for projects
4. Copy and cut up the Scripture Memory Verse (Attachment A)
5. Prepare Wheel of Fortune sheets (Attachment B) and tape them to wall
6. Cut up pieces of colored paper for Chain of Hope (Attachment C)
7. Make copies of the Light Bulb (Attachment D)
8. Make copies of To My Spouse (Attachment E)
9. Make copies of The Big D Evaluation form (Attachment F)
10. Workbooks

HIGHLIGHTS

Life After Divorce

1. Family Chair Game
2. Wheel of Fortune: Beauty From Ashes
3. Common Ground
4. Nugget of Truth: Looking Up
5. Hope
6. Nugget of Truth: Your Future
7. Evaluation
8. Taking It Home

WEEK TWELVE - SESSION TWELVE

This is our last session. We are so proud of you for completing these steps and joining us on this rocky road we call a journey to healing. We know at times it got difficult but always keep in mind it was for a greater cause. As we complete this session remember God has a plan for your life; one that is not defined by your parents' divorce. If you continue the hard work, it is very possible to move beyond the scars and into a life full of promise. In this session, we will explore your dreams for your future. We will talk about your feelings, your future and the potential to have a healthy relationship. You are not destined to make the same mistakes your parents made.

Scripture Balloon Race

ATTACHMENT A

As you prepare for this session, write out the words from Philippians 4: 6 & 7 (written below) on a small sheet of paper and cut out each word and roll it up. Put the rolled up piece of paper with the word on it inside, a balloon and then blow up the balloon. When the balloons are blown up with the words inside attach a two foot piece of string on each. There will be 38 balloons. If you do not have 38 people you can give each person two, one for each ankle or cut the words in two or more phrases.

Philippians 4: 6 & 7
"Do not be anxious about anything, but in everything, by prayer and petition with thanksgiving, present your requests to God. And the peace of God which transcends all understanding will guard your hearts and minds in Christ Jesus." (NIV)

When you are ready to begin, hand out a balloon (or two) with string to each person and have them tie it around their ankles. When it is time for them to start, they need to chase each other around the room trying to pop each other's balloons and find the pieces of paper. When all the balloons are popped they all need to work together to put the verse together. They can use a Bible if they want to.

WHEEL OF FORTUNE

Beauty From Ashes

ATTACHMENT B

The title of this week's lesson is "BEAUTY FROM ASHES". Be sure to print the letters ahead of time and post on a bulletin board or wall before the teens arrive. Take turns like last week asking each teen to select a letter. For each correct letter they select, turn letters over and give them a chance to solve the puzzle. If they guess incorrectly, their turn is over and play moves to the next person. See **Lesson One** for a complete list of suggested rules.

CHECK-IN TIME

-How are things going in your relationships with your parents?

-Are there things you are changing in your attitude that are making a difference at home?

-What are some "God Things" that have happened?

Last week we looked at the joy that can come once we accept and move on from the pain divorce leaves in our lives. It is assuring to know there is a light at the end of the tunnel and that God will see you through. Let's see how the assignments went this week.

Go over *Take Home* assignment:

- ◈ Even though you would never have chosen for your parents to have gone through a divorce, do you think there are some ways that you are a better person because of it?
- ◈ Do you think you are closer to either your mom or dad because of the divorce? If so, in what ways?
- ◈ How does your parents divorce affect your own personal dating relationships?

Nugget of Truth : Looking Up

For some of you the divorce process is very recent. For others, you may have been dealing with it already for years. When it all comes down to it, we are all the same. Teens trying to make a better life after our parents' divorce. For some, coming to acceptance was easy, but for others it was a struggle all the way. But once you reach this place, there is a real feeling of freedom. When you look back at all you've been through, there is a lot you probably think you could have done without. But when it is all said and done, you went through it for a reason. Although divorce is a very painful experience, you can choose to also see the positive things that come from bad situations. There may be some good things that have happened in your life as a result of the divorce. Why don't you take out this worksheet and change your thinking illusions.

Growth Goals

Take a minute and look at the goals you set last week. How did you do?

Now set goals for this week.

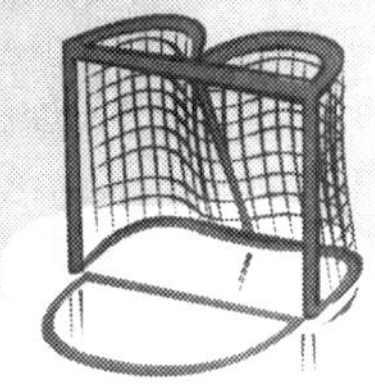

NOT SO BAD...

WORKBOOK PAGE 132

When your vision becomes dark through using your sunglasses vision, remind yourself of these positive results of where you are today. God may not have specifically designed your parents' divorce, but that will not keep Him from using it for your good. Back in our first session, we talked about the losses we have experienced and were encouraged to grieve those losses. We are going to expand that window and look at the whole picture. If you are not able to do that yet, that is fine. Just follow along and see where God leads you. Turn to your workbook and think of certain pluses and minuses that have affected your life over the time period of when your parent left the home until today. I think you will be surprised at how balanced your list becomes. It is an exciting day when we start to realize we are better people today because of the struggles and trials we have had to endure.

PLUSES & MINUSES

WORKBOOK PAGE 133

One of the biggest changes I sure hope we can see is the change in our relationship with Jesus Christ. I know for me my whole understanding of who He is and how He loves me changed my life forever. Take a minute and think about how your relationship with Christ was before and now after the divorce.

ME & GOD BEFORE & AFTER

WORKBOOK PAGE 134

Nugget of truth: Hope

My life is but a weaving
Between the Lord and me.
I do not choose the colors,
But God works steadily.

Often God weaves sorrow,
And I, in foolish pride,
Forget God sees the top
While I the underside.

Not until the loom is silent
And the shuttles cease to fly
Will God unroll the canvas
And explain the reasons why.

But, the dark threads are as needful
In the skillful weaver's hand
As the threads of gold and silver
In the pattern God has planned.

Author unknown

We all need a little more hope in our lives. Hope gives us the promise of a future free from the worries and sins of this world. It is knowing and accepting God has a plan for our lives that is unchanged because of our parents divorce. It is the assurance to know God is in control, even when we feel like no one is. We need to believe there is a plan for our lives. The dark threads (pain and sorrow, trials and tribulations, mistakes and troubles) are mixed in with the threads of gold and silver (our joys, good times, happiness, successes). Both are necessary in order for our lives to be shaped. We don't know what is in store for us down the road, but God does. We question the parts of the weaving that we don't understand, but it is all woven together with care and love. The pain and sorrow are there for a purpose, for us to learn from. And in the end, the picture of our lives will be revealed as a wonderful work of art.

ATTACHMENT C

Hand out a bunch of strips of colored paper. Ask them to write on the strips of paper ways they have changed for the better since their parents' divorce or since attending The Big D. Leaders are encouraged to participate in this activity as well. When everyone has written at least 4 to 6 things, have them make links and chain them together. Then chain all the links together. This will be a great example to themselves of how much these past 12 weeks have made a difference in their lives.

Possible Gains in a Divorce

* better relationship with one or both parents
* peace
* the end of constant conflict or violence
* more self-confidence as a result of having more independence and responsibilities
* learning what makes a marriage work
* closer relationships with siblings
* closer relationship with God

Nugget of truth: Your Future

Ask for a raise of hands of who thinks they will get married one day. Discuss why or why not. Ask them if they think their future (marriage and other parts of the future) will be helped or hurt by their parent's divorce. Drive home the point that their parent's circumstances do not have to define their future, but rather their choices can create their future.

HOPE:

Webster Says:

* an upbeat, positive feeling when we begin to see that in the midst of loss, there can be gain. We see some positive things; some options for happiness ahead. After the dark tunnel of grief, we can see some light.

STORY ABOUT ME

WORKBOOK PAGE 135

Take a moment and write a story about what your life will be like in 10 – 15 years from now. Will you be married? Will you have kids? How will you treat them? What will your marriage be like? Where do you want to live? What do you want to be doing? Where does God fit into your future? Who will be important in your life? We all know our futures can not be foretold, but it is good to dream. For it is because of our dreams that we develop a drive to focus on making them come true. When you are done with your story, tuck it away (maybe in your Bible) and when you come across it in the future, read it as an encouragement and use it to refocus yourself. God wants all your dreams to come true; so if God is for us, who can be against us.

TO MY SPOUSE

ATTACHMENT E

We are now going to write a letter to our future spouse. We want you to share about what you have experienced in your own situation and how it has affected you, what you have learned, and how you want to do things differently in your future relationship. All decisions start with a thought. Take some time and focus on what kind of relationship you want and what it will take to get it there and the commitments it will need to keep it strong. What are some of the characteristics you may be looking for in a relationship someday? It is important to realize this now, so you can prevent your heart from falling in love with the wrong person. Keep your standards high. God wants the best for you – Don't you? You deserve it!

THE BIG D EVALUATION

ATTACHMENT F

As you are wrapping up the night, hand out the Big D Evaluation. Ask everyone to fill it out because their thoughts will matter for future groups. When you collect them, be sure to thank everyone for their honesty.

If you are not planning an additional night for a celebration, make sure you leave at least half an hour of time in your evening to celebrate their individual road to healing. Acknowledge their hard work and make sure they know how proud you are of them.

Light bulb moments

(Optional Activity)

Ask the teens to illustrate with words or pictures inside the light bulb picture (Attachment D).

Have them write down any concept that was learned through The Big D that was like a light bulb going off in your heads. A WOW moment!

Consider Hosting a 6 Month Reunion

EXPLAIN THE "TAKING IT HOME" ASSIGNMENTS

WORKBOOK PAGE 136-138

Take time to look over the Taking It Home assignment with your group. Let them know that this assignment is a great way for them to really process what you have covered this week. Encourage them all to take the time and do the assignment.

CLOSING TIME: Ending the session

Take Prayer Requests

This can be done in a variety of ways:

- verbally shared in group setting
- hand out note cards to group members to write out their requests.
- set out a note book that students can write in throughout the session
- put out a Prayer Request box and Prayer Request Slips
- encourage the group members to come up with other ways to share prayer requests.

Close in Prayer

TOWARDS YOURSELF...A Question to Take to My Heart:

Look into your heart for the answer to these questions. This is introspection time – time to grapple with what drives your thinking and behavior. Be sure to capture your thoughts.

- What are the main reasons people get married? Divorced?

- What are your most important qualities to look for in a wife/husband? Are they the same when looking for a boyfriend/girlfriend?

- What do you think you can do to avoid having your future marriage end in divorce?

- In what ways do you think you will be a better parent?

- What hopes and dreams do you have for your own future?

TOWARDS OTHERS...A Question to Take to Others:

Healing cannot become complete without affecting the lives of those around us as well. Be courageous and go outside your comfort zone to take a risk and work on your relationships with others.

◈ What are some of the positive aspects of your parents' divorce?

◈ What have you learned through this journey?

◈ How do you intend on protecting your future relationships?

◈ Share with your parent(s) three good things that have happened in your life as a result of their divorce.

1. ______________________________

2. ______________________________

3. ______________________________

TOWARDS GOD...A Question to Take to God:

When you ask God a question, expect His Spirit to respond to your heart. Be careful not to rush it, or manufacture an answer. Don't jot down your idea of the "right answer". Just pose the question to God, and wait on Him to speak personally in a fresh way.

- Why do you think God allows divorce to happen?

- What has God taught you through your parents' divorce?

- What role will God have in your future? Your future marriage? Your future family?

- Are you closer to God now or before the separation? How do you plan on continuing to grow spiritually?

ATACHMENT A

Philippians 4: 6 & 7
Do not be anxious about anything,
but in everything, by prayer and
petition with thanksgiving, present
your requests to God. And the
peace of God which transcends all
understanding will guard your hearts
and minds in Christ Jesus. (NIV)

(1) T

(1) B

(1) Y

(2) E

(1) F

(2) A

(1) R

(1) U

For the "Wheel of Fortune" activity you will need to enlarge and copy these letters onto card stock. You will need to make the number of letters indicated on each card. You will need letters to spell out "BEAUTY FROM ASHES".

(1) O

(1) M

(2) S

(1) H

For the "Wheel of Fortune" activity you will need to enlarge and copy these letters onto card stock. You will need to make the number of letters indicated on each card. You will need letters to spell out "BEAUTY FROM ASHES".

Chains of Hope

Cut up 1" x 6" strips of colored paper before the group begins. With this exercise you will end up with a beautiful colorful paper chain sharing things they have changed for the better and learned over the weeks through "The Big D".

Hand out strips of paper with markers and glue to every table. Ask everyone to write on the strips of paper the things they have learned, changed, or benefited from since attending "The Big D". Leaders, you can participate in this activity too. Once everyone has written 5 or 6 things, have them glue their strips together, linking them all together. When everyone is finished making their own links, continue by linking everyone's together. Share with them how exciting it is to see how this chain of links as a true representation of the last few weeks together. We have come together because of a common experience and throughout the past weeks we have learned together, grown together, and developed lasting friendships. Our lives now represent a "Chain of Hope" for the world to see.

Examples of things they could put on their strips:

Grieving is normal and necessary
It is okay to cry
Forgiveness is not excusing the wrong
Nothing can separate us from God's love
I can love both parents equally
I don't have to be put in the middle
It was not my fault
I have a support system that I can trust
I am made in the image of Christ
I am not the only one who feels this way
I can still have a promising future
I have a better relationship with my Mom/Dad now
There is more peace around the house
I'm more accepting of my step dad/mom
I'm more of a help around the house
I now have Jesus living in my heart
God does care about my hurts
My future is not doomed to divorce
Anger is not a sin
I've discovered my anger warning signs
I learned coping skills when I get angry
I do not have to be the messenger between my mom and dad

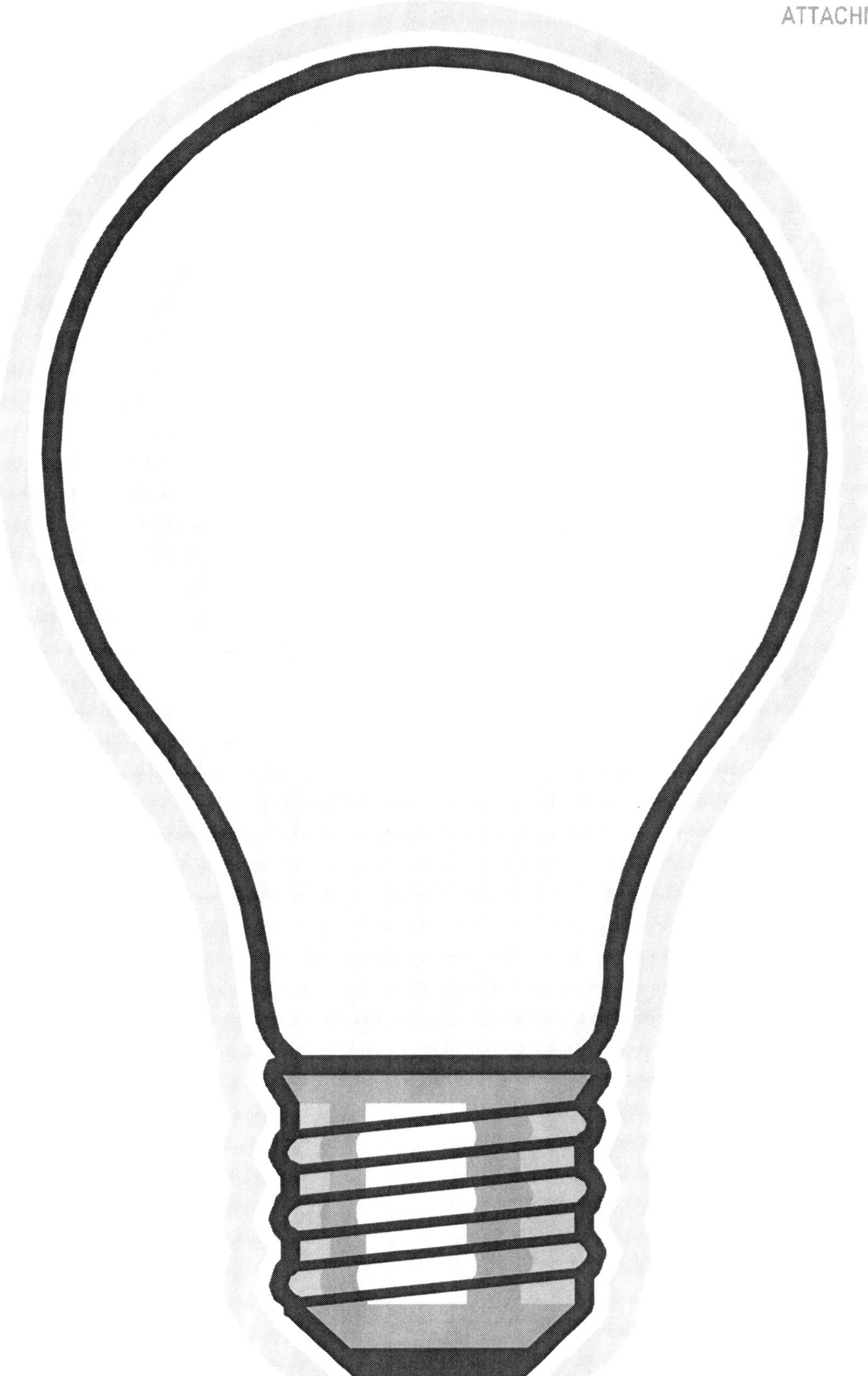

To my future spouse

"The Big D" Evaluation

ATTACHMENT F

What did you think of "The Big D"? ______________________________

What was your favorite part? ______________________________

What was your least favorite part? ______________________________

Did you think "The Big D" was beneficial for your particular situation? ______________

What was your favorite session? ______________ Least favorite? ______________

What was your favorite activity? ______________ Least favorite? ______________

What did you think of the games and mixers? ______________________________

Was there any time when you felt totally uncomfortable? ______________
If so, when? ______________________________

What had the most impact on you? ______________________________

What had the least impact on you? ______________________________

Did you develop a closer relationship with others going through the same situations as you? ______________

Did you develop a closer relationship with Jesus throughout the weeks? ______________

Were the sessions too long or too short? ______________________________

Was the length too long or too short? ______________________________

Would you come back again next time? ______________________________

Would you invite a friend? ______________________________

APPENDIX

Acknowledgements

Special appreciation goes to Jane Tokar, who has encouraged me along this journey and shared her talents to make this dream come true. When she first offered to help, I'm sure she had no idea what she was getting herself into, but then neither did I. Thank you for the endless hours of hard work and for putting up with the millions of e-mails I send you daily. Thank you for being there for me, through all the hours, days and sometimes even into the endless hours of night. Your touch to this ministry is indescribable. "Thank you" does not even come close to convey all you've done. You're the best!! And we could not have done it without the loving support of your hubby and my good friend, Doug. He put up with me in his kitchen night after night and spent many lonely nights in bed. She'll be back holding your hand soon, I promise!! And thanks to the boys, Jordan and Jason, for giving up time with your mom for me. You were very patient and welcomed me at your door every time, even when I'm sure you didn't want to. You've all become more than friends; you're like family

To my parents, Bill and Merrlyn, for their endless supply of love and support. Thank you. It was when my life was at its lowest and I feared your turning away from me that you grabbed on and held on tight. Thank you for your unconditional love and continual prayers throughout my whole life, not to mention the patience at work while I was burning the candle at both ends. I only hope to be as good a parent to my kids as you have been to me. This project is a true reflection of your daily prayers and encouragement over the years.

To my extended family, for always loving, always supporting, and always being there for me. You have been more than family to me and the investment that each one of you have made in Brittany and Tyler's lives through the years has meant the world to me. It is because of this additional love and support that they have always known they are loved and special and could always come to you when they needed someone to talk to. Thank you for loving me enough to take the time to take them under your wings, each in your own special way.

To my best friend, Mar, for loving me like nobody else ever has. When I am at my lowest you come beside me and lift me up. You are the first I want to call to share my joys. Whether good or bad, you never leave my side. You have always been there for me and I could never thank you enough for being the best friend anybody could ever ask for.

To my dear friend, Chris, who has been my friend, counselor, prayer warrior, and ministry partner. I have never been as blessed to have a friend who I can totally lean on to be my supporter and encourager. Our weekly prayer times have been more of a blessing and life support than you'll ever know. It was hard for me to learn to be selfish and let you be there for me and not think I needed to take care of you; a very refreshing and much needed twist. The impact you have had on my life is insurmountable. I don't know what I am going to do when you move!! Love ya, man!!
P.S. – Thanks "big bro" for sharing your wife with me.

To my first husband, Jon, even though we've been divorced since 1995, you have shown me no matter what happens in life, when you keep your eyes on the goal, anything is possible. Thank you for giving me the two greatest gifts of all – our children. Even when our choices have made it difficult, we have been able to focus on what's important and raise exceptional kids. Thank you for the respect and honor you continuously have shown me as a mom. Thank you for never giving up on our kids and being the great dad you are to them.

To Dave and Ann Johnson, thank you for being more than my pastors, but being my friends. Your support in our ministry and our family has meant more to me than you could ever know. Your solid encouragement and spiritual leadership in our lives have changed us forever. You challenge us to be our best, but it is because you believe in us and defend us that we continue to persevere through life's challenges. Thank you for your constant prayers, encouragement and support . Your impact in our lives is immeasurable.

Hosting a 12 week group:

Suggestions for a successful group:

6 to 9 months out:

- Obtain approval from pastor, church leadership or governing committee.
- Establish and approve a budget.
- Choose a starting date for the ministry.
- Fill out order form from website and purchase curriculum.
- Read through entire curriculum and start recruiting volunteers.

3 to 6 months out:

- Start advertising for volunteers.
- Start working with youth leaders in your community to gain their support.
- Put dates on church calendar and finalize rooms needed.

8-12 weeks out:

- Hold informational meeting for potential volunteers.
- Create a promo spot on your website's homepage with on-line registration – if possible. If on-line registration is not possible, include a PDF registration form which can be printed out and mailed in with the payment.
- Set dates for on-site registrations. It is recommended that all registrations be paid in advance. This guarantees a reliable list of attendees, and aids you in planning for the conference.
- Assign a promotions committee. Begin designing posters, bulletin announcements, church and community advertising, newspaper ads, etc.
- Begin working with radio stations to secure promo spots closer to date, if available.
- Send letter from Senior Pastor or Youth Pastor to surrounding area churches (60 mile radius) along with promo information encouraging them to promote this event.
- Start collecting magazines for Jesus Bags.
- Start making announcements to Church Youth Group.

4 to 8 weeks out:

- Have your leadership finalized.
- Begin advertising in local churches, schools, coffee shops, counseling offices etc.
- Place promo posters in prominent places throughout your facility.
- Begin using video clip announcements with verbal endorsement from the pastor on Sunday mornings.
- Mail a letter to students in your Youth Group from Senior Pastor or Youth Pastor endorsing and encouraging parents to register their teens.
- Bulletin and newsletter announcements or inserts.
- Hold a planning meeting.
    - Share vision and passion of "The Big D" to all volunteers.
    - Verify advertising is active.

    - Emphasize the importance of connecting one on one with teens.
    - Review curriculum and nightly format with volunteers.
    - Delegate weekly assignments.
    - Discuss room set up or decorating.

2 to 4 weeks out:

- Do promo spots on local radio stations
- Hold on-site registrations
- Continue with advertising to hosting church, local churches and community.
- Prepare supplies for 1st lesson.
    - Wheel of Fortune cards
    - Have enough workbooks
    - Gather together all activity supplies
    - Type and Copy Big D Quotes to put on walls.
    - Purchase and make Big D Candy
    - Make copies of all attachments needed.
- Purchase supplies for first lesson.
    - Purchase any supplies needed.
    - Purchase any decorating supplies
    - Make sure all refreshments and snacks are purchased
    - Prizes for games (if desire)

2 weeks to before event:

- Work on decorating the room.
- Meet with leaders to finalize agenda and verify all last minute details are covered.
- Keep close watch on Registrations and verify you have enough workbooks.

Suggested volunteers:

- 1 - lead organizer and teacher
- 1 - assistant (your back up)
- 1 - adult volunteer per every 6 teens
- 1 - advertising person
- 1 – person to be in charge of refreshments and snacks
- 1- person to make all copies and purchase weekly supplies for activities

Suggested Weekly Format

Welcome

Mixer Activity

Wheel of Fortune

Review last weeks homework

Teaching and Workbook time

Various Activities

Homework Assignments

Prayer Requests

Closing

The Warning Signs of Suicide

Suicide is rarely a spur-of-the-moment decision. In the days and hours before people kill themselves, there are usually clues and warning signs. The strongest and most disturbing signs are verbal, - "I can't go on." "Nothing matters any more" or even "I'm thinking of ending it all."

Other common warning signs include:

- Becoming depressed or withdrawn
- Behaving recklessly
- Getting affairs in order and giving away valued possessions
- Showing a marked change in behavior, attitudes or appearance
- Abusing alcohol or drugs
- Suffering a major loss or life change

Situations:

- Family history of suicide or violence
- Sexual or physical abuse
- Death of a close friend or family member
- Divorce or separation, ending a relationship
- Failing academic performance, impending exams, exam results
- Job loss, problems at work
- Recent imprisonment or upcoming court date

Behaviors:

- Crying
- Fighting
- Breaking the law
- Impulsiveness
- Self-mutilation
- Writing about death and suicide
- Previous suicidal behavior
- Extremes in behavior
- Changes in behavior

Physical Changes:

- Lack of energy
- Disturbed sleep patterns—sleeping too much or too little
- Loss of appetite
- Sudden weight gain or loss
- Increase in minor illnesses
- Change in sexual interest
- Sudden change in appearance

Thoughts and Emotions:

- Thoughts of suicide
- Loneliness—lack of support from family and friends
- Rejection; feeling marginalized
- Deep sadness or guilt
- Unable to see beyond a narrow focus on their family
- Daydreaming
- Anxiety and stress
- Helplessness
- Loss of self-worth

http://www.befrienders.org
Suicide hotline—800-suicide
(800/784-2433)

Go Ahead, Be Angry at God!

Too often we hear people feel guilty about feeling angry towards God. More often than not, we get angry at God over things we have no control in, like going through a divorce or dealing with an ex-spouse. If we can't control it, God must be able to – after all someone has to be in control!!

So we get angry and since no one else seems to be available to be angry at, we get angry at God.

Then we feel guilty. We feel we shouldn't get angry at God! We worry that God's feelings will be hurt. Or worse yet, God will punish us for our anger and really give us something to be angry about. So we quietly stuff those feelings and keep it all inside.

In times like this, remember these four things –

1. God already knows that we are angry so what are we hiding from? Being all-knowing, God is quite familiar with our anger, even before we are. Our anger will not come as any surprise to God.

2. God knows the source of our anger. God knows the events and experiences that make us angry. God knows our emotions and feelings. God knows all about our situation. Don't be surprised if God doesn't even share in our anger!

3. God knows why we are angry. The feelings of helplessness, fear, confusion, and dismay all lead to our anger. God intimately knows the inner workings of our minds and spirits, and God knows our limitations. We often are angry because we are powerless, and God knows our powerlessness.

4. God can take it. God has faced greater anger than ours and survived! God's shoulders are broad and very powerful. God can certainly deal with our anger.

So, if God already knows about our anger, understands the source of our anger, discerns why we are angry, and can easily handle our anger, why are we reluctant or feel guilty about expressing our anger?

In fact, sometimes expressing our anger can be a good thing for us. It is good to vent a bit. Rather than keeping it inside us, sometimes just letting go and yelling our heads off can be a good thing. Too often we let our anger fester inside us, building up and growing until it seeks escape in destructive and violent ways. Let off some steam – go outside and yell at God. Sit in your room and tell God what you think. Pace your living room and give God a piece of your mind. Remember, He already knows, so nothing will surprise Him!

Then you can go about the business of seeing with a clearer mind if there might be some way for you to do something about the situation. Clear the air with God about your anger, and then sit down with God and try to figure something out, but it is often necessary to get that anger out of the way first. Then you can calmly and clearly consider the problem and find ways to do something constructive about it.

So go ahead; be angry at God. God can take it. There won't be any retribution from God and you might be able to do some clear and constructive thinking about what made you angry after venting your emotions.

By R. Adam DeBaugh

Do you have a personal relationship with Jesus Christ?

Step 1 is to recognize God loves you and longs to have a relationship with you.

God loves you and desires that you experience joy, peace and abundant life. This life is only through God's only Son, Jesus Christ.

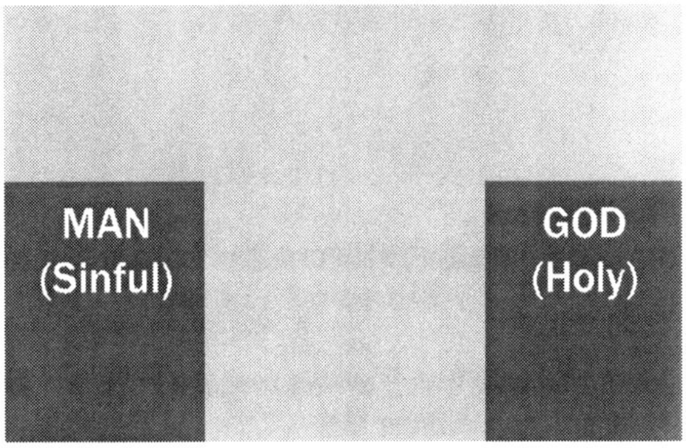

The Bible says...
For God so loved the world, that he gave his only begotten Son, that whosoever believes in him should not perish but have everlasting life.
John 3:16

....I have come that they might have life, and that they might have it more abundantly.
John 10:10

What keeps most people from experiencing the joy, peace and abundant life that God has planned for us?

Step 2 is recognizing man's problem – separation from God.

God created man in His own image but God made us human, capable of making our own decisions. God did not want robots worshiping him but gave us all freedom of choice. Man made the choice to disobey God. Man's separation from God is called sin. Man then is a sinner by will and freedom of choice.

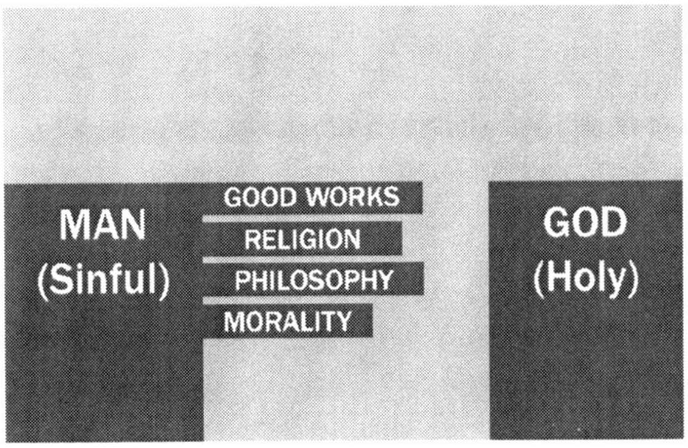

Man willfully chose to disobey God and go his own selfish ways. We all still make this choice today. This results in separation from God and the penalty for that is an eternity in Hell.

The Bible says...
For all have sinned and come short of the Glory of God.
Romans 3:23

For the wages of sin is death; but the gift of God is eternal life through Jesus Christ, our Lord.
Romans 6:23

Men, through the years have tried to bridge this gap without success...

There is only one solution to the problem of separation.

Step 3 is recognizing God's solution – The cross.

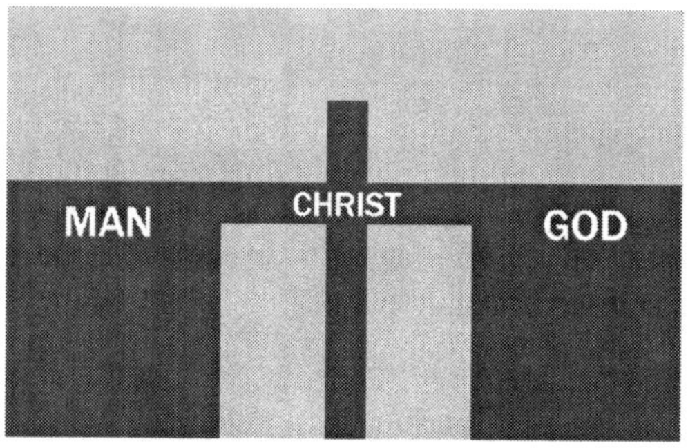

Our Lord Jesus Christ is the only solution to this problem of separation from God. When Jesus died on the cross, He paid the total penalty for all our sins and bridged the gap from God to man.

The Bible says....
But God demonstrates His own love for us in this: while we were still sinners, Christ died for us.
Romans 5:8

Jesus said unto him, "I am the way, the truth, and the life; no man cometh to the Father but by me".
John 14:6

For by grace you are saved through faith; and it is not of yourselves; it is a gift of God: Not of works, lest any man should boast.
Ephesians 2: 8 & 9

God has provided in Jesus Christ the ONLY way of salvation...Man must take the choice to receive God's solution.

Step 4 is recognizing man's response and receive Christ as personal Savior.

We all must trust in the Lord Jesus Christ and receive Him into our hearts by inviting him into our hearts personally.

The Bible says...
Behold I stand at the door and knock; If any man hear my voice, and open the door, I will come in and eat with him, and he with me.
Revelation 3:20

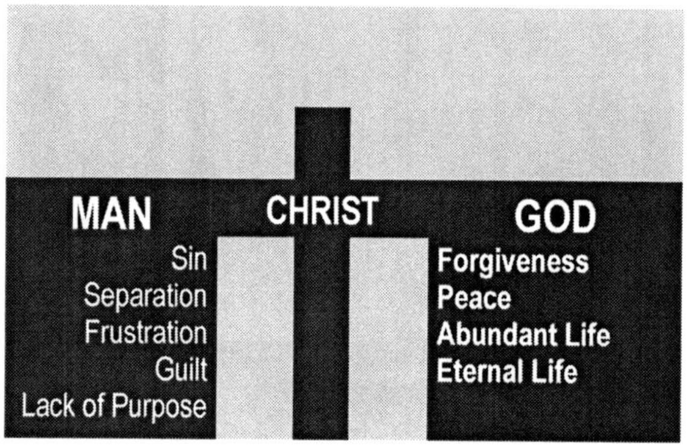

For whosever shall call upon the name of the Lord shall be saved.
Romans 10:13

Is there any good reason why you cannot receive Jesus Christ as your own personal Lord and Savior?

What you must do!

1. Admit your need (I am a Sinner)

2. Be willing to turn from sin (Repent)

3. Believe that Jesus Christ died for you (On the Cross)

4. Through prayer, receive Him as personal Lord and Savior

A Suggested Prayer of Commitment

Dear Father God,
I know that I am a sinner and need your forgiveness.
I believe that your Son, Jesus Christ died in my place, paying the penalty for all my sins.
I am willing to turn away from sin.
I now invite Jesus Christ to come into my heart and life as my own personal Savior.
I am willing by your help, to follow and obey Jesus Christ as the Lord of my life!
Amen

My Personal Decision:
On the ____ day of ____________, 20___, I ________________________
received Jesus Christ as my personal Savior.

What's Next?

1. Pray Daily

2.Read the Bible daily! (Start off with John)

3. Go to a good Bible preaching church where God's Word is preached!

4. Tell others about the decision you made!

5. Tell others about the Good News that Jesus Christ can save them!

MAY GOD RICHLY BLESS YOU!

Blue Fish Video Clips

Session One - (Overview) Divorce Leaves Teen Divided Between Two Parents

Session Two - (The Grief Cycle) Finding Hope: Doug Fields
Struggling With Parents Divorce

Session Three - (Anger) Divorce Leads to Anger and Violence
Angry at God: Doug Fields

Session Four - (Who's to Blame?) Out of Control: A Product of Divorce

Session Five - (Self-Esteem) Finding Your Identity: Chris Hill

Session Six - (Comfort) Bad Home Environment

Session Seven - (Feelings) Caught Between Divorced Parents

Session Eight - (Single Parent Homes) Rebuilding a Family After Divorce

Session Nine - (Step-Family Homes) Honoring Your Parents

Session Ten - (Forgiveness) Betrayed by Your Mother
Forgiving Others: Doug Fields

Session Eleven - (Acceptance) Jennifer Knapp

Session Twelve - (Moving On) Looking to Sex for Love
Filling the Empty Life

Please email info@thebiginfo.com to request your copy

Recommended Resources

Adult

The Slippery Slope—a great tool to use as an icebreaker for your recovery groups.
www.sonsetpointministries.com

DivorceCare weekly support group
Church Initiative
www.divorcecare.org

Healing the Heartbreak of Divorce
Rose Sweet

Starting Over
Thomas Whiteman and Randy Peterson

Healing the Divorced Heart
Rose Sweet

Where is God When it Hurts?
Philip Yancey

Separated and Waiting
Jan Northingon

101 Ways to be a Long Distance Super Dad or Mom Too
George Newman

The Choosing to Forgive Workbook
Less Carter and Frank Minerth

The Anger Workbook
Les Carter and Frank Minerth

When Your Marriage Dies
Laura Petherbridge

Single, Married, Separated, Life After Divorce
Miles Munroe

Father's Love Letter
Barry Adams

Moving Forward After Divorce
David and Lisa Frisbie

When the Vow Breaks
Joseph Warren Kniskern

Healing For Damaged Emotions
David Seamonds

Fresh Start Divorce Recovery Workbook
Thomas Whiteman and Bob Burns

The Complete Divorce Recovery Handbook
John Splinter

The Ex-Factor – Dealing with the Divorced Spouse
Don & Ladean Houck

Parenting Through Divorce
Karen Todd

DivorceCare Devotional
Steve Grissom

Grace & Divorce
Les Carter

Between Two Worlds
Elizabeth Marquardt

Helping Your Kids Survive Your Divorce
Thomas Whiteman

Keeping Your Kids Afloat When it Feels Like You're Sinking
Cindi Lamb-Curry

It's Okay to Cry
H. Norman Wright

Children –

The Slippery Slope –an interactive board game where kids jump from lily pad to lily pad and discover the secrets to overcoming their hurts.
www.sonsetpointministries.com

DC4K – DivorceCare for Kids
Church Initiative
www.dc4k.org

Children and Divorce
Archibald Heart

Innocent Victims
Thomas Whiteman

Your Kids and Divorce
Thomas Whiteman

Kid's Hope
Gary Sprague

I Don't Want to Talk About It
Jeanie Franz

Can Anyone Fix My Broken Heart?
June Thomas Crews

Teens

The Slippery Slope –a board game where teens ride the roller coaster of emotions and feel the thrill of finishing a winner.
www.sonsetpointministries.com

Divorce Recovery for Teenagers
Stephen Murray and Randy Smith

The Divorce Helpbook for Teens
Cynthia MacGregor

Kid's Hope for Teens
Gary Sprague

Longing for Dad
Beth Erickson

Always Daddy's Girl
H. Norman Wright

A Dad-Shaped Hole in My Heart
H. Norman Wright

What in the World Do We Do When Your Parents Divorce?
Kent Winchester

Keeping Your Life Together When Your Parents Pull Apart
Angela Hunt

Parent Link

Submitted by Robyn Besemann

the big D

Divorce Thru the Eyes of a Teen

Parent Link

Stepping Stones to Healing

WEEK ONE

Welcome to the BIG D family! Each week you will receive a Parent Link. This Parent Link will do three things: (1) make you aware of the theme for the week's session, (2) give you tips to create stronger bonds in your single parent/step family home and (3) enhance your parent/teen relationship.

This week's goal: To help teens feel comfortable to share who they are and how they are feeling with this new group of people and recognize they are not alone.

This week in The Big D: We talked about the importance of feeling safe. The teens were told that The Big D is a comfort zone where they can share their feelings without fear of shame, ridicule, or judgment. We want them to share their hopes, fears, struggles and victories. It is our hope that their homes will give them the same sense of security and acceptance.

Slippery Slope—This is a visual to help kids figure out where they are in the grief process concerning the breakup of their family. These stepping stones to healing include: denial, bargaining, anger, depression, forgiveness and acceptance.

Verse of the Week—I John 4:18 *"There is no fear in love, but perfect love casts out fear. For fear has to do with punishment and whoever fears, has not been perfected in love."*

Building family strengths - Try to find a time each week to have a "family meeting". Find a comfortable place, turn electronics off, don't answer the phone/text and allow for at least 1/2 hour of uninterrupted time together. Discuss their day, discuss fears each family member has, and brainstorm ways to overcome these fears. We suggest making a family journal so you can look back and see the progress your family is making. Let the kids do most of the talking and you do most of the listening. Please do not pressure them to talk or share about what happens in the Big D class. <u>They will share when they are ready.</u>

Praying Parents –Please pray as we begin this process that each teen will feel safe to share so they can process through their feelings. Please pray for wisdom for the Big D leaders as we come alongside your teen guiding them toward healing.

the big D

Divorce Thru the Eyes of a Teen

Parent Link

Step By Step -Denial, Bargaining, and Depression

WEEK TWO

This weekly Parent Link will make you aware of the theme for the week's session, give you tips to create stronger bonds in your single parent/step family home and enhance the parent/teen relationship. Please let your teen share when they feel comfortable to and not pressure them.

This week's goal: To help teens understand the beginning stages of the grief cycle...denial, depression and bargaining to take steps forward. They will look at their losses and explore how they deal with them and learned helpful hints to overcome them.

This week in The Big D: We talked about what we do when we would rather deny how we really feel or how we use bargaining as a way to get what we want. Most kids want their parents back together and are willing to do just about anything to help make that happen. We also discussed unhealthy actions they may have considered to make themselves feel better and healthy ways that are better.

Bill of Rights for Children of Divorce—This is a visual to help kids have a sense of what will help them have a healthier life as a teen living through turmoil. This also reinforces the concept that the divorce of their parents is an adult situation/decision.

Verse of the Week—II Thess. 2:16& 17 *"May our Lord Jesus Christ and God our Father, who loved us and in His special favor gave us everlasting comfort and good hope, comfort your hearts and give you strength in every good thing you do and say."*

Building family strengths - Try to find some time to sit quietly with your teen and let them talk about how they really feel about the divorce in your family. Try not to get defensive or try to justify and most importantly, do not put blame on their other parent or speak against them because this puts kids in the middle of your adult battles. Just listen and make sure they understand it is not their fault.

Praying Parents –Please pray that your teen will be able to be honest with themselves, explore their feelings and that they will let God heal their heart. Pray that you see the positives in your child much more than the negative behaviors. Please also pray for our Big D leaders as we walk alongside your teen in this process.

Parent Link

Getting a Grip

WEEK THREE

This weekly Parent Link will make you aware of the theme for the week's session, give you tips to create stronger bonds in your single parent/step family home and enhance the parent/teen relationship. Please let your teen share when they feel comfortable to and not pressure them.

This week's goal: To help teens examine the anger they feel and develop healthier ways of dealing with and releasing it.

This week in The Big D: We talked about how anger is a "cover emotion" for what we truly are feeling (fear, anxiety, hurt, frustration, etc.) We talked about how sometimes we get mad at God and how He knows it and understands. We shared about how anger isn't necessarily wrong, but what we do with it can have negative effects many times. We talked about how teens respond to conflict and how to better manage their anger.

Warning Signs of Anger— Helping teens recognize the signs of anger can help them prevent an outburst or escalating a conflict. We talked about positive ways to react even if someone else is yelling at them and how to resolve conflict in a more mature way.

Verse of the Week—James 1:19 & 20 *"My dear brother, take note of this; everyone should be quick to listen, slow to speak and slow to become angry, for man's anger does not bring about the righteous life that God desires."*

Building family strengths - Think about the conflicts you have had with your teen or in front of them. Teens are at an age of responding better to guidance than control. Conflict between parents and teens can quickly get out of hand and then nothing is accomplished. Ask your teen about the tools we talked about on how to resolve conflict in a healthy and helpful way. Try to support them by listening and then deciding together to try harder at having a more peaceful home.

Praying Parents –Please pray that your home will have a more peaceful and loving environment and that the Lord would heal the anger inside of your teen and maybe even within yourself. We are praying for your family as well.

Parent Link

Hurts Band-aids Can't Cover

WEEK FOUR

This weekly Parent Link will make you aware of the theme for the week's session, give you tips to create stronger bonds in your single parent/step family home and enhance the parent/teen relationship. <u>Please let your teen share when they feel comfortable to and not pressure them.</u>

This week's goal: To help teens identify their level of self-esteem and give them tips to rebuild it. We will also focus on the many deep feelings they have and help them face them and give them to Jesus.

This week in The Big D: We talked about the things that many times lower our self-concept our ourselves. We looked at things that we could be blamed for and things that we could not be blamed for. We talked about how valuable they are in God's eyes. We talked about common worries and stressors and how it is important to share these with their parents.

Hurts Band-aids—This is a visual to help kids bring their hurts to Jesus. The teens write their many, many hurts on lots of big paper band-aids and place them on the broken heart. Jesus' heart is big enough for all those layers of hurts and even bigger than that! A very moving exercise for all of us in class.

Verse of the Week— *Psalms 9:9-10 "The Lord is a shelter for the oppressed, a refuge in time of trouble. Those who know Your name trust in You, for You, O Lord, have never abandoned anyone who searches for You."*

Building family strengths - Take some time to listen to your teen about what they learned in class during this session. Maybe share some of the feelings you have felt, <u>being careful not to weigh your teen down with adult issues or the issues between you and their other parent.</u>

Praying Parents –Please pray that your teen will allow the Lord to release and heal their heart from all the hurt they have been stuffing down inside. Pray for the Lord's healing in your home and in all your family members.

Parent Link

Jesus Bags

WEEK FIVE

This weekly Parent Link will make you aware of the theme for the week's session, give you tips to create stronger bonds in your single parent/step family home and enhance the parent/teen relationship. Please let your teen share when they feel comfortable to and not pressure them.

This week's goal: To help teens define who they are and not allow their family circumstances and issues to define them. Also to accept and understand who they are in Christ.

This week in The Big D: We talked about how divorce can really shake up lives and how teens can feel like they are changing. We looked at who teens were before the divorce in their family and how things may have changed afterwards. We talked about how God made each of us unique and explored and accepted that uniqueness in each of us.

Jesus Bags—This is a visual to help kids explore how others may see in them and how they are in the inside that the world cannot see (feelings, fears, secrets struggles, etc.). A leader shared about how they were before becoming part of God's family and how they have changed.

Verse of the Week—Psalm 139:14 *"I will praise You because I am fearfully and wonderfully made; Your works are wonderful, I know that full well."*

Building family strengths - Take your teen out for a meal, coffee or ice cream and talk to them alone about all the good things you see in them. Try not to just compliment them on what they DO well, but who they ARE. Spend time thanking them.

Praying Parents –Please pray that your teen will see the good in themselves, be able to dream of a positive future and will not define themselves by their family issues. Pray that they will seek God's guidance for their lives and be able to be all that He meant them to be.

the big D

Divorce Thru the Eyes of a Teen

Parent Link

Where Is God When It Hurts!

WEEK SIX

This weekly Parent Link will make you aware of the theme for the week's session, give you tips to create stronger bonds in your single parent/step family home and enhance the parent/teen relationship. Please let your teen share when they feel comfortable to and not pressure them.

This week's goal: To help teens realize that God's sole desire is to comfort them. We also want teens to know how to talk to God and to listen to His voice.

This week in The Big D: We talked about Job in the Bible and how he was going through the worst of times and how God brought him through it. We talked about the support system that each teen has and how important it is to have human beings as well as the Lord supporting and encouraging them through the tough stuff. The teens were able to write a letter to God to help them communicate with Him.

Comfort Cards—These cards help teens know what God's Word says about how He is always there for them and wants the best for them. He is there to comfort them and the cards are there to help them remember that whenever things are getting rough.

Verse of the Week—Deuteronomy 31:6 *"Be strong and courageous, do not be afraid or terrified because of them, for the Lord your God goes with you. He will never leave you nor forsake you."*

Building family strengths - Take some time to talk with your teen about your relationship with God; strong or not. Be honest about your faith and find out how they feel about Him. If you don't go to church on a regular basis, maybe make a commitment to find a church where your family can begin to walk toward God and learn about His love, forgiveness, acceptance and strength.

Praying Parents –Please pray that your teen will not feel like they are all alone in this; that they will find healthy resources in others, in you, but mostly in God, Himself.

Parent Link

Feelings Tune Up!

WEEK SEVEN

This weekly Parent Link will make you aware of the theme for the week's session, give you tips to create stronger bonds in your single parent/step family home and enhance the parent/teen relationship. Please let your teen share when they feel comfortable to and not pressure them.

This week's goal: The main emphasis in this session is communication. We want teens to face their feelings and be able to effectively express them to their parents in a healthy manner.

This week in The Big D: We talked about how many times kids are placed on the battlefield between their parents. We helped them to express what it felt like to be "caught in the middle". We then helped them figure out an effective way of setting boundaries in this area and expressing these to their parents in a respectful way.

Which Animal Best Describes You?—This workbook page helps them to see how they handle conflict between their parents. Are they a lion, a kitty, a snake or a puppy? Then they were given suggestions on how to have a healthier response to the conflict. Interesting insights.

Verse of the Week—Psalm 32:7 *"You are my Hiding Place; You will protect me from trouble and surround me with songs of deliverance."*

Building family strengths - Think about how involved your teen has been in the conflict you have with their other parent. Are they used as a spy, a message carrier, an informant, a referee, or could they feel like they have to take sides? What can you do to take them off the battlefield and just be a kid so you and their other parent can resolve your own adult issues? When you feel you are able, maybe ask your teen how they feel about this issue and try to make the necessary changes so your teen doesn't have to take sides, if this is their issue. Please try not to say, "You shouldn't feel that way." Listen to how they feel with an open heart and a willingness to help.

Praying Parents –Please pray that your teen will be able to step off the battlefield between you and their other parent, so they can have a healthier life. We are praying for you that you will hear the heart of your teen and be able to have better communication with them.

Parent Link

Change - Single Parent Homes

WEEK EIGHT

This weekly Parent Link will make you aware of the theme for the week's session, give you tips to create stronger bonds in your single parent/step family home and enhance the parent/teen relations. Please let your teen share when they feel comfortable to and not pressure them.

This week's goal: To help teens realize that change is different for everyone and changes are okay. We want them to explore the changes that they are experiencing and give them tools to adapt to those changes.

This week in The Big D: We talked about how change is inevitable in life. Our world is constantly changing and we will all see lots of changes in our personal lives. The teens looked at all the changes they have experienced through the breaking up of their families. We looked at the challenges teens experience with their dad and also their mom and some ways that they thought things could improve in each relationship.

Taking it Home/Solo Time—At the end of each lesson there are 3 sections titled: Towards Yourself, Towards Others, and Towards God. These are personal questions about themselves, relationships with others and their relationship with God. It is a way to help them apply what they have learned each week to their own lives. Their answers are not read or shared so that they feel comfortable to be honest with themselves and God.

Verse of the Week—Psalm 56:3 & 4 *"When I am afraid, I will trust in You. In God, whose Word I praise, in God I trust; I will NOT be afraid."*

Building family strengths - Find a time this week to talk with your teen about the many changes you and they have faced with the divorce. Please do not make any negative comments about their other parent, but keep this only about you and your teen. This is not a time for blame or venting or putting your teen back on the battlefield. Discuss possible positive changes since the divorce/separation and maybe talk about possible ways to move past the negative ones.

Praying Parents –Please pray that your teen can see a brighter future ahead and accept the changes that have happened and will happen in their life. We are praying for your families too.

the big D
Divorce Thru the Eyes of a Teen

Parent Link

Change - Step Family Homes

WEEK NINE

This weekly Parent Link will make you aware of the theme for the week's session, give you tips to create stronger bonds in your single parent/step family home and enhance the parent/teen relationship. <u>Please let your teen share when they feel comfortable to and not pressure them.</u>

This week's goal: To help teens explore the possibility that they may someday, if they haven't already, be part of a step-family. We want them to look at the differences between a single parent home and a step-family home.

This week in The Big D: We talked about how hard it may be, or possibly is, to think of you or their other parent dating. We talked with them about looking at situations in the other person's shoes and how it can give them a whole new perspective on situations. We talked about how our attitudes can greatly effect our happiness as well as those around us. We also talked about the different ways we all look at things and how conflict can come from that many times.

Family Strengths—This is a workbook page to help teens see the strengths in their family. The teens write their family strengths on dumbbells. It shows that it takes everyone working toward the same goals to have a strong family.

Verse of the Week—Romans 12:2 *"Do not conform any longer to the pattern of this world, but be transformed by the renewing of your mind. Then you will be able to test and approve what God's will is—His good, pleasing and perfect will."*

Building family strengths - Find a time at the dinner table to talk about the good things about your family. <u>Try not to react when your teen may talk about what is good about their other parent's home or family situation.</u> They may be trying to live peacefully in both family situations and should be able to share that without fear of being put back onto the battlefield. What are some things you and your teen can work on to become a stronger family unit? How do they truly feel about you dating again? How do they feel about someone you may be dating now? Listen.

Praying Parents –Please pray that your teen will be able to accept the endless changes that have and will happen in their life. Pray that you can give them a healthy perspective.

Parent Link

Forgiveness - Let Go, Let God

WEEK TEN

This weekly Parent Link will make you aware of the theme for the week's session, give you tips to create stronger bonds in your single parent/step family home and enhance the parent/teen relationship. Please let your teen share when they feel comfortable to and not pressure them.

This week's goal: To help teens better understand what forgiveness is and what it is not. We will also want to help them reflect on their lives and relationships to see what role forgiveness may play in their personal healing journey.

This week in The Big D: We helped them explore their understanding of what forgiveness is and is not. Interesting discussion. We helped them look at the things they needed to forgive others for and what they felt others need to forgive *them* for. We also looked at the unconditional love and forgiveness of Jesus Christ and how we are to follow His example in that. We talked about how unforgiveness keeps us "on the hook" and takes away our freedom to be all we can be.

Lay It At the Cross—This is a moving exercise as the teens look at the "Hurts Band-aids" they did weeks ago, decide to forgive the people who have caused those hurts and put them on the spikes on a wooden cross. When they do that, they are saying they not only forgive, but lay it before Jesus and will try not to pick it up again. Very personal and very freeing, to say the least!

Verse of the Week—*Col. 3:13 "Bear with each other and forgive whatever grievances you may have against one another. Forgive as the Lord forgave you."*

Building family strengths - Consider if you have been able to forgive your former spouse for the pain they have caused you. Also consider how unforgiveness may have you tied up so you are unable to live in freedom and move on with your life. When a parent can forgive and move on, it makes it much easier for their child to do the same.

Praying Parents –Please pray that forgiveness will take high priority in your family and that each member will be able to live in greater freedom and joy.

Parent Link

Acceptance-Moving On and Letting Go

WEEK ELEVEN

This weekly Parent Link will make you aware of the theme for the week's session, give you tips to create stronger bonds in your single parent/step family home and enhance the parent/teen relationship. Please let your teen share when they feel comfortable to and not pressure them.

This week's goal: To help teens identify the choices they have and realize how empowering making those choices can be. We also want the teens to look toward their future and how they can do their best to make it the best future possible.

This week in The Big D: We talked about how there comes a time when we have to accept the changes in our lives and make a choice to make it a part of our past and move forward. Acceptance is the feeling that we can live with reality and be just fine. We will make it. We looked at growth goals; ways they can make good choices to become a healthier and stronger person.

Three Month Goals—We had the teens write down three goals that they wanted to accomplish in three months. They put these goals in an envelope and we will send that envelope to them in three months to see how they did. Many times, kids are so busy trying to survive the crisis in their families, that they can't even THINK about looking toward their future. This helps begin that process.

Verse of the Week—Deut. 30:9b-10 "The Lord will again delight in you and make you prosperous, just as He delighted in your fathers, if you obey the Lord your God and keep His commands and decrees that are written in this Book of the Law and turn to the Lord Your God with all your heart and with all your soul."

Building family strengths - Take some time and discuss three goals that you and your teen could work on in the next three months to help your family become healthier and stronger (eating healthier, spending a certain amount of time together doing something fun each week, exercising, not yelling at each other, etc.)

Praying Parents –Please pray that our teens will be able to implement all the things they have learned and that their families will become healthier and stronger.

Parent Link

Life After Divorce - Beauty From Ashes

WEEK TWELVE

This weekly Parent Link will make you aware of the theme for the week's session, give you tips to create stronger bonds in your single parent/step family home and enhance the parent/teen relationship. Please let your teen share when they feel comfortable to and not pressure them.

This week's goal: To review what teens have learned, to leave them with hope for their futures, and elevate their relationship with Christ.

This week in The Big D: We talked about the pluses and minuses of their family situations. We looked at the hope we have in Jesus Christ, in His comfort, His unconditional love, His guidance and His grace. We looked at what we learned and how we healed through this process. What a blessing to hear them express that!

To My Spouse—Most of the teens have a difficult time believing that love can last forever, however they want to get married someday. We discussed what they plan to do differently so they don't experience divorce in their own marriage someday. Very important conversation. Then we had them write a letter to their future spouse which we encourage them to give their fiancés before they marry.

Verse of the Week—Jeremiah 29:11 *"For I know the plans I have for you", declares the Lord, "plans to prosper you and not to harm you, plans to give you a hope and a future."*

Building family strengths - The teens will be bringing home their books. We have discussed many things and they have written their personal thoughts in them. Please respect your teen by not pressuring or intruding on them by "sneaking a peak". Hopefully, through this process, you and your teen have developed better communication, so they will feel safer to share their thoughts, hurts, hopes and dreams with you. *Please let your teen share when they are ready to, so they don't feel pressured*.

Praying Parents – Parents, we are praying for you as you move forward in your family. We pray that you will see God's provision, and experience His love, strength, joy, forgiveness and grace. If we can be of further help or encouragement to you, please don't hesitate to call your Big D leader or your church office.

CPSIA information can be obtained at www.ICGtesting.com
Printed in the USA
BVOW05s1225151013

333791BV00002B/5/P

SCHRIFTEN ZUM AGRAR-, UMWELT- UND VERBRAUCHERSCHUTZRECHT

Edited by / publiée par / herausgegeben vom
Institut für Landwirtschaftsrecht, Universität Göttingen

Volume 97

European Council for Agricultural Law/Comité Européen de Droit Rural/Europäisches Komitee für Agrarrecht

edited by Prof. Dr. Roland Norer, General Delegate in the name of European Council for Agricultural Law

Agricultural Law in Times of Crises: Policies and Production Impacts

XXXI European Congress and Colloquium of Rural Law, Cardiff, 6–9 September 2023

XXXIe Congrès et Colloque Européens de Droit Rural, Cardiff, 6–9 septembre 2023

XXXI. Europäischer Agrarrechtskongress mit Kolloquium, Cardiff, 6.–9. September 2023

Comité Européen de Droit Rural
CEDR

Nomos

Die Bände 1 – 52 sowie die Jahrbücher Band I – VI
sind erschienen bei Carl Heymanns Verlag KG, Köln

Die Deutsche Nationalbibliothek verzeichnet diese Publikation in der Deutschen Nationalbibliografie; detaillierte bibliografische Daten sind im Internet über http://dnb.d-nb.de abrufbar.

The Deutsche Nationalbibliothek lists this publication in the Deutsche Nationalbibliografie; detailed bibliographic data are available on the Internet at http://dnb.d-nb.de

ISBN 978-3-7560-3362-1 (Print)
ISBN 978-3-7489-6325-7 (ePDF)

Online Version
Nomos eLibrary

1. Auflage 2025

Contenu - Content - Inhalt

I. Session d'ouverture - Opening - Eröffnung

II. Commission I - Kommission I

V. Colloque – Colloquium – Kolloquium

VI. Rapport de Synthese – Synthesis Report – Synthesebericht

VII. Liste des Rapports nationaux – List of National Reports – Liste der Landesberichte

I.
Session d'ouverture - Opening - Eröffnung

Preface

Prof. Dr. Roland Norer
General Delegate CEDR
University of Lucerne

The XXXI European Congress and Colloquium of Rural Law, held in Cardiff from 6 to 9 september 2023, were organized by the European Council for Rural Law (Comité Européen de Droit Rural; C.E.D.R.) in co-operation with UK's Agricultural Law Association (ALA).

The overlapping theme of the congress was "AGRICULTURAL LAW IN TIMES OF CRISES: POLICIES AND PRODUCTION IMPACTS". The academic work was developed in three separate commissions, national reports provided background information for the discussions within the commissions. All three commissions terminated their academic activities by drawing conclusions and extending recommendations to the competent authorities of the European Union, member and non-member states and international organisations.

The topic for commission I was "MULTIPLE CRISES: RESPONSES IN AGRICULTURAL LAW". This commission dealt among others, with questions referring Ukraine War, COVID, energy crises, disease and climate change as well as safety nets and agricultural reserves, intervention, mandatory stockpiling and insurance.

Commission II chose the topic "CARBON, BIODIVERSITY AND NUTRIENTS: NEW LAND USE CONSIDERATIONS". This commission dealt with the following questions: different models in relation to carbon, biodiversity, nutrient and land use in different jurisdictions, opportunities and threats, especially with regard to pesticides, fertilisers, feeding-stuffs, carbon, nitrates, phosphorus, glyphosate and neonicotinoids (including application and bans on spreading). Further, nutrient trading, land management policies, water protection, authorisation and locus standi of environmental associations.

Commission III tackled the topic "SIGNIFICANT CURRENT DEVELOPMENTS IN RURAL LAW". It dealt with questions such as Nitrate Directive, flood prevention and restoration of water courses, irrigation, climate change and agriculture, action plans and strategies (Green Deal).

Further, integration with food law ("from farm to fork"), support for farmers, implementation of the new CAP, international agreements (such as CETA and TTIP), agricultural registers, wolves and pasture management, labour law (including seasonal workers) and many more.

The topic of the Colloquium was "PUBLIC MONEY FOR PUBLIC GOODS: SUSTAINABLE AGRICULTURE. THE NEW CAP AND THE UK AGRICULTURAL POLICIES".

This publication contains the following parts:

- the opening speeches of Geoff Whittaker, President of the C.E.D.R., Alex Carson-Taylor, President of UK's Agricultural Law Association, Prof. Dave Cowan, Head of the School of Law and Politics of Cardiff University;
- the questionnaires, general reports and conclusions of the three commissions, written by Dr. Alicia Epstein, LL.M., Brandenburg University of Technology (commission I), Catherine Taskis KC, Falcon Chambers (commission II) and Prof. UAM dr hab. Aneta Suchoń, Adam Mickiewicz University Poznań (commission III);
- the Proceedings of the Colloquium, written by Dr. Christian Busse, Federal Ministry of Food and Agriculture, Prof. Dr. Rudolf Mögele, Deputy Director-General for Agriculture and Rural Development at the European Commission and Dr. Ludivine Petetin, Cardiff University;
- the synthesis report of the Delegate General of the C.E.D.R., Prof. Dr. Roland Norer, University of Lucerne; and
- the list of the national and individual reports to the three commissions.

In the spirit of the tradition of the C.E.D.R. I would like to thank UK's Agricultural Law Association for the successful organisation of the congress. The event was inspiring, uniting people and attracted many participants.

Scientific work has been challenging and ambitious. The general reporters of the commissions and the presidents directed it efficiently and productively. Them as well as all national and individual rapporteurs deserve more than a big thank for the excellent contributions to this XXXI European Congress and Colloquium of Rural Law.

Allocution d'ouverture – Opening Adress – Eröffnungsansprache

Geoff Whittaker
President of the CEDR

On behalf of CEDR, I am pleased to introduce this publication of the works of the 31st Congress & Colloquium of agricultural and rural law, held in Cardiff, Wales from the 6th to the 9th of September 2023.

We are especially grateful to the organising committee of the UK Agricultural Law Association, principally CEDR's National Delegate and Deputy National Delegate, namely Dr. Nerys Llewelyn Jones and Dr. Ludivine Petetin, and the UKALA's Secretary and Adviser, Mike Holland, who were assisted by Glain Olwen and Clare Cecil.

Also, our grateful thanks go to the University of Cardiff for providing the facilities for the Congress sessions and to CEDR Delegate-General Prof. Dr. Roland Norer who co-ordinated the working programme, along with the several Commission Presidents and General Rapporteurs credited elsewhere in this book.

The overall title of the Congress – Agriculture in Times of Crisis – more or less presented itself. Our biennial cycle of Congresses had had to be temporarily suspended because of the Covid pandemic; the so-called "special military operation" in eastern Ukraine had generated, apart from the human consequences of warfare, particular issues of supply not only of food and other agricultural products but of oil and fuels and other essential commodities; and the consequential issues affecting supplies and the cost of living presented, and continue to present, difficulties for those sustaining our communities and maintaining the natural environment. Against that background, the discussions on national and international responses were particularly informative.

I will leave the academic summary to Prof. Norer. From my point of view, it suffices to say how satisfying it was to be able once again to resume our programme of Congresses, which had been on hold since 2019. We have been able to conduct our administrative function and continue our academic discussions to a limited extent during the lockdowns imposed by the pandemic by using remote access software, but there is no better means of creating and developing personal relationships with like-minded people than being able to meet in person and to share conversations, whether or not lubricated by food and wine!

Outside the scope of the academic programme, we were given the opportunity to hold our Opening Ceremony in the Pierhead building in Cardiff Bay, formerly the headquarters of Cardiff Railway Company and taken over in 1947 by the Port of Cardiff. Nowadays it sits adjacent to the Senedd (the Welsh Parliament) and is a national history museum.

The Ceremony was embellished with talks from Mick Antoniw, a former student at Cardiff University's School of Law and Politics and now Counsel General and Minister for the Constitution in the Senedd, and Prof. Richard Wyn Jones, Dean of Public Affairs at the University's Welsh Governance Centre.

On the Thursday evening, we were hosted on a visit to Goldsland Farm, a mixed dairy, beef, sheep and arable farm run by the Reader family and home to Abi Reader, who is currently Deputy President of NFU Cymru, the Welsh National Farmers' Union. After a talk about the business of the farm and issues currently affecting it, we were provided with an excellent hog-roast supper which provided another opportunity to relax and enjoy each other's company.

We were also given excellent examples of the deep musical culture of the Principality of Wales. At the Opening Ceremony on Wednesday, Manon Williams, solicitor and partner in Nerys Llewelyn Jones's specialist rural law practice, gave us a recital on the harp, national instrument of Wales since the 11th Century, and Côr Caerdydd (Cardiff Choir), an amateur chorus based in the city, gave an atmospheric aperitif to the traditional Gala Dinner on the final evening of the Congress.

On the Saturday, we were given the opportunity to relax on a tour of St. Fagan's National Museum of History, a fascinating collection of historical buildings which have been dismantled from around Wales and reassembled to create a chronicle of the lifestyle, architecture and culture of the Welsh people.

Over the four days, it was demonstrated once again that we have more in common than separates us and it was encouraging to be able to resume the balance of academic and intellectual discussion with the friendship and camaraderie on which CEDR was founded more than 65 years ago.

On a personal level, it has been an honour, a privilege and a delight for me to have served CEDR in one office or another for almost 20 of those years and I look forward to maintaining my contacts with members through the years to come.

Mot de Bienvenue – Welcome Address – Willkommensansprache

Alex Carson-Taylor
Chair of the Agricultural Law Association

On behalf of the Agricultural Law Association, I am very pleased to welcome you to Cardiff and the 31st CEDR Congress.

The ALA is the principal interdisciplinary organisation in the UK focused on rural law and business. Our circa 1700 members represent a broad range of professions including solicitors, barristers, rural surveyors, accountants, arbitrators, mediators, consultants, other specialists and students.

We operate a network of regional groups covering the UK, run a comprehensive education and continuing professional development programme and a number of annual national events.

The three commission themes for consideration at this Congress are particularly timely given increasing complexity and uncertainty across the international agri-food chain and in broader rural societies.

As practitioners, we are increasingly aware of the impacts resulting from geopolitical events, market volatility, global macroeconomic shifts, rapidly changing legislative and policy agendas, the climate emergency and the relationship the general public has with the food chain.

This Congress presents a unique opportunity to deliberate and better understand these issues, frame thinking, consider the systematic and systemic interconnectivity between elements and engage with the multiple perspectives of our delegates. Outputs from each commission will have an important role in facilitating, enhancing and progressing dialogue within and between CEDR national associations, individuals and relevant institutions.

I should like to thank ALA Vice-Chair, Dr. Nerys Llewelyn Jones, Dr. Ludivine Petetin of the School of Law and Politics at Cardiff University, Glain Olwen from Agri Advisor and, Clare Cecil from the ALA for organising this engaging, diverse programme and the accompanying events showcasing rural Wales and the City of Cardiff.

Discours de Bienvenue – Welcome Speech – Grußwort

Prof. Dave Cowan
Head of the School of Law and Politics of Cardiff University

President, Chair of Congress, distinguished delegates

Bore da pawb a chroeso i Ysgol Gyfraith a Gwleidyddiaeth Caerdydd

A warm welcome to the School of Law and Politics for this important event, which comes at such a critical moment as rural law emerges in a time of inflationary prices, global concerns for the environment, the increasingly questioning nature of state practices and techniques of central planning and delivery, and a sense of crisis in globalism. And, I haven't mentioned what for us is the awful "B" word but that has produced significant concerns about our role in the world and in Europe, as well as, more specifically, our role in the development of rural law.

I am but a humble housing lawyer who also considers homelessness issues. From this perspective, our subjects are what we might call cognate, I am particularly aware of what is sometimes called the rural housing crisis, which forces families away from their rural areas because of the insufficiency and cost of existing housing. For that reason, I particularly welcome your discussions here.

I also want to wish a warm welcome to those delegates who are unable to be here in person. I know that for some of you, it is a question of distance. But, for others, it is a question of necessity. That question of necessity fixes all our minds and provides the critical backdrop to the issues which you will be discussing.

I am grateful that you have chosen our School of Law and Politics as the host of this event, made more important after four years without being able to meet. In the rest of this opening address, I want to set out why this School and the University provides the perfect base for your discussions. And I do not just mean its collegiate environment, its location so close to the centre of government in this jurisdiction, nor this beautiful city, which I hope you will get the chance to explore and enjoy during your visit.

I have only recently arrived at this school. I applied for this job after 28 years at a different institution because, in my view, it is the premier institution for teaching and research in appreciating the contexts of law. It was a pioneer in this respect through its foundation role in the development of what we now call socio-legal studies, the interdisciplinary study of legal phenomena. It is a School which prides itself on its outward facing activities and, more specifically, its impact on policy and policy-makers. In short, we see our roles not just as ivory tower academics – which is an important part of our work – but as partners with policy-makers.

And if we accept, as I say we must, that law works in tandem with policy, then, as a School of Law and Politics, we can produce more insightful, more complete sets of analyses which are not just the handmaidens of policy but actively seek to guide it. Dr. Petetin is in many ways the current embodiment of this interdisciplinary approach, working with colleagues across disciplines as part of our Wales Governance Centre. I commend to you the collection of essays published as The Governance of Agriculture in Post-Brexit UK, as being the perfect example of this analytical blending of law, policy and politics, with a clear direction plotted out for future governance.

Our School also sits in an interdisciplinary environment of a college of arts, humanities and social sciences, and the aim is that we are all free and able to work across those disciplinary boundaries, to understand alternative perspectives and work to better or environment. We have a thriving academic and student community working in this way, interacting through institutes, such as the net zero institute, which is thinking through the issues with which you are also concerned about the environment and sustainability. And, we like to think of ourselves as not just a top University in the UK – a member of the Russell Group – but also a global university, one which you are very much enhancing by your presence and activity here. Our work spans international partnerships and research, and our students who make us what we are come from more than 138 countries. From this perspective, we think your congress is a pivotal event both for our university, our environment, as well as part of our contribution to the resolution of the important issues which you will be discussing.

From this interdisciplinary perspective, and with considerable diffidence as you are indeed the experts to whom we look for guidance, I want to address the theme of crises. In so doing, I want to show the value of this blend of law and politics, and perhaps offer some thoughts on which you might wish to develop in your discussions. The first thing I want to observe is that we use the word "crisis" so much that it devalues the label. As Sylvia Walby describes it, a crisis is a sudden "... event that has the potential to cause a large detrimental change to the social system and in which there is lack of proportionality between cause and consequence" (Walby, 2015: 14), and she argues that it is both real and discursively formed (id: 15-18). Colin Hay talks of crisis as a "moment of decisive intervention". In my amateurish way, I wonder if these political scientists are talking about the same things as yourselves; or, perhaps, you are talking about things that have been a long-time in the making and are continually changing shape. These crises then are splinters from more generalised problems.

In her book, Anti-Crisis, Janet Roitman argues that crises create "moments of truth" through which history is re/formed. The inquiry, then, is to find how crisis is posited as the basis for difference between the past and an imagined future. Such an inquiry relies also on its cognate, critique. As she notes, "The point is to take note of the effects of the claim to crisis, to be attentive to the effects of our very accession to that judgment".

What I am seeking to add, I think, is what no doubt you are aware – that we need to be alive to the ways in which we frame our crisis narratives, and recognise that our framing prescribes the limits to the solutions that we might devise. Those are the lessons from political science which those of us who employ crisis narratives should be thinking about.

I hope that helps and provides an insight as to why our interdisciplinary school provides you with the perfect, most congenial environment for your discussions.

I wish you the very best of luck in those discussions.

Introduction scientifique – Scientific Introduction – Wissenschaftliche Einführung

Prof. Dr. Roland Norer
General Delegate CEDR
University of Lucerne

Dear Mr. President, dear Colleagues, dear Ladies and Gentlemen,

Perhaps you know the children's book series about the beastologist Nathaniel Fludd (or Benjamin Woods in German). Book 3 of the series, "The Wyverns' Treasure", takes us to Wales, the land of dragons. Indeed, these beasts dwell there in huge cave systems and the young hero has his hands full preventing calamity. Now we are in the land of dragons ourselves and it seems to me that the parallels to our conference theme are evident.

The world, including our agricultural law world, is in riot, precisely in times of crisis. Our crisis dragons are called climate change, food security, energy crisis, COVID, Ukraine war and so on. These are extremely difficult to combat, even more so when they occur together. Nathaniel, the teenage hero in the book, manages to negotiate with the dragons. We have only law as an instrument. Whether and how agricultural law can offer answers to the current crises is therefore – quite obviously – this year's congress topic. "Agricultural law in times of crisis: policies and production impacts". As usual, we will devote ourselves to this overall theme in three commissions.

Commission I "Multiple Crises: Responses in Agricultural Law" addresses the individual crises, examines their interrelationships and attempts to provide answers. Prof. Dr. Rudy Gotzen, University of Leuven (Belgium), who as a CEDR veteran was kind enough to take over this office at short notice, acts as President. As General rapporteur, I would like to welcome our Swedish colleague Dr. Alicia Epstein from the Brandenburg University of Technology.

Commission II, "Carbon, biodiversity and nutrients: new land use considerations", is dedicated to the topic of natural capital, including questions of ownership, valuation and incentive systems for its protection. This challenging topic will be chaired by Alex Carson Taylor, President of our host, the UK Agricultural Law Association. As General rapporteur, Catherine Taskis KC will draw her conclusions.

Commission III "Significant current developments in international rural law, in the EU as well as in states and regions" will be particularly detailed this time, as there are four years to consider. Prof. Dr. Franci Avsec from the University of Novo mesto in Slovenia as president and Prof. UAM dr hab. Aneta Suchoň from the Adam Mickiewicz University in Poznań, Poland, where our last congress took place, dedicate themselves to this task.

For the second time, we are again holding a colloquium on Friday evenings. "Public Money for Public Goods: Sustainable Agriculture. The new CAP and the UK agricultural policies" is the topic, which will especially give us mutual EU-UK insights. It will be chaired by Dr. Ludivine Petetin, Dr. Christian Busse and Prof. Dr. Rudolf Mögele.

Ladies and Gentlemen

Dragon fights are tough. They are dangerous. But they are also exciting, fascinating. In this sense: "Pob lwc", which in the language of the land of dragons should mean "Good luck".

II.
Commission I – Kommission I

President:

Prof. Dr. Rudy Gotzen,
Katholieke Universiteit Leuven (Belgium)

General Reporter:

Dr. Alicia Epstein, LL.M.,
Brandenburgische Technische Universität (Germany)

Crises multiples : des réponses en droit agricole

Multiple crises: responses in agricultural law

Multiple Krisen: Antworten im Agrarrecht

Questionnaires - Fragebogen -
Commission I - Kommission I

Version française - French version - Französische Version
Version anglaise - English version - Englische Version
Version allemande - German version - Deutsche Version

Questionnaire de la Commission I – Questionnaire of Commission I – Fragebogen der Kommission I

Questions – Fragen

A. Version française – French version – Französische Version

1. Partie générale

1. Comment la COVID-19 et la reprise-pandémique et post-pandémique ont-elles affecté les secteurs agricoles de votre pays ? Veuillez donner un bref aperçu et envisager, en particulier, les types de mesures juridiques (lois, actes, décrets, etc.) qui ont été introduites pour relever les défis auxquels sont confrontés les secteurs agricoles.
2. Les impacts de la volatilité du marché post-pandémique ont-ils été affectés par d'autres développements, tels que des événements naturels liés au changement climatique ? Si oui, votre pays a-t-il introduit des mesures (législation, lois, décrets, etc.) pour faire face aux défis qui en résultent pour les secteurs agricoles à court et moyen terme ?
3. Quels ont été les principaux impacts de la guerre en Ukraine sur les secteurs agricoles nationaux et votre pays a-t-il publié des documents stratégiques ou introduit des mesures (législation, lois, décrets, etc.) pour relever ces défis ? Si oui, dans quelle mesure ces mesures ont-elles permis de résoudre les problèmes rencontrés par les opérateurs agricoles ?
4. Comment les secteurs agricoles de votre pays ont-ils été affectés par la hausse des coûts des intrants et votre pays a-t-il publié des documents stratégiques ou introduit des mesures (législation, lois, décrets, etc.) pour relever ces défis ? Veuillez notamment examiner le recours à des mesures d'intervention d'urgence et déterminer si celles-ci ont permis de résoudre efficacement les problèmes rencontrés par les secteurs agricoles.
5. Votre pays a-t-il introduit – ou envisagé d'introduire – des mesures juridiques (lois, actes, décrets, etc.) pour limiter l'exportation de pro-

duits agricoles nationaux ? Si oui, ces mesures ont-elles été temporaires et combien de temps ont-elles été appliquées ? Veuillez également indiquer si ces mesures sont compatibles avec les règles de l'OMC.

6. Votre pays a-t-il introduit des mesures (législation, lois, décrets, etc.) pour limiter la spéculation sur le marché des produits agricoles ? Si oui, ces mesures ont-elles atteint les objectifs visés et sont-elles compatibles avec les règles de l'OMC ?
7. Votre pays a-t-il introduit d'autres mesures visant à protéger l'approvisionnement et la production alimentaire nationale ? Si oui, quel a été l'effet de ces mesures sur les producteurs et la production agricole ?
8. Votre pays a-t-il été affecté par des mesures légales introduites par d'autres pays pour protéger leur propre approvisionnement alimentaire national ou limiter les exportations ? Si oui, comment ces actions ont-elles affecté les secteurs agricoles de votre pays et des mesures (législation, lois, décrets, etc.) ont-elles été prises pour faire face à ces impacts ?
9. Votre pays a-t-il introduit des mesures légales pour stimuler la productivité agricole ? Si oui, quel type de mesures ont été adoptées et comment devraient-elles affecter les secteurs et la production agricoles ? En outre, ces mesures visent-elles spécifiquement ou exclusivement à stimuler la production de denrées alimentaires et d'aliments pour animaux ?
10. Votre pays a-t-il introduit des mesures qui permettent aux agriculteurs de déroger aux normes de gestion de l'environnement et des terres, autrement applicables aux producteurs agricoles, afin de maintenir ou d'augmenter les niveaux de production agricole ?
11. Votre pays a-t-il publié des documents stratégiques ou introduit des mesures de contrôle (législation, lois, décrets, etc.) pour s'assurer que les normes environnementales applicables aux agriculteurs ne sont pas compromises par les efforts visant à stimuler la productivité agricole et à faire face à la volatilité des marchés ?

2. Partie spéciale

1. Compte tenu de l'accent mis par les institutions de l'UE sur la stimulation de la productivité, l'approche narrative et stratégique de la sécurité alimentaire a-t-elle changé dans votre pays à la suite des crises récentes et, en particulier, de l'inflation extrême des prix des denrées alimentaires

causée par la guerre en Ukraine ? Si oui, cela a-t-il été reflété dans les documents stratégiques de votre pays ou dans les mesures adoptées (législation, lois, décrets, etc.) et comment cela devrait-il affecter les secteurs agricoles et la production à court et moyen terme ?

2. Compte tenu des préoccupations croissantes en matière d'insécurité alimentaire, les ONG internationales et les universitaires ont mis en garde contre une augmentation de la productivité aux « dépens » de l'environnement, par exemple en suspendant ou en abaissant les normes environnementales destinées à traiter les externalités de l'agriculture. En tenant compte du contexte national, voyez-vous un risque que l'accent mis sur l'augmentation de la productivité puisse saper les normes environnementales applicables aux agriculteurs de votre pays et des mesures (législation, lois, décrets, etc.) ont-elles été introduites à cet effet ?
3. Votre pays a-t-il publié des documents stratégiques ou introduit des mesures (législation, lois, décrets, etc.) pour renforcer la résilience des secteurs agricoles aux futurs chocs liés au changement climatique ? En particulier, veuillez considérer le rôle des régimes d'assurance et des mesures visant à soutenir l'agriculture intelligente face au climat.
4. Considérant que l'instabilité des marchés devrait rester un facteur important pour les producteurs agricoles à court et moyen terme, votre pays a-t-il introduit des mesures (législation, lois, décrets, etc.) ou publié des documents stratégiques dans le but d'améliorer la résilience des secteurs agricoles et leur capacité à répondre efficacement aux crises et à la volatilité futures ? Veuillez notamment prendre en compte l'impact des mesures relatives aux régimes d'intervention et d'assurance agricoles, ainsi qu'aux filets de sécurité et aux politiques de gestion des terres.

3. Pour les Etats Membres de l'UE

1. L'utilisation de la réserve agricole de l'UE en avril 2022 a-t-elle apporté un soutien efficace aux opérateurs agricoles de votre pays pour faire face à la volatilité du marché et aux problèmes d'approvisionnement exacerbés par l'invasion de l'Ukraine ?
2. Comment la décision de l'UE d'autoriser un accès sans entrave au marché européen pour les produits agricoles ukrainiens a-t-elle affecté les secteurs agricoles de votre pays et des mesures (législation, lois, décrets, etc.) ont-elles été introduites pour faire face aux défis potentiels de cette décision ? En particulier, veuillez examiner comment l'accès sans entrave

des produits alimentaires ukrainiens affecte la rentabilité et les décisions de production des agriculteurs de votre pays.
3. Votre pays a-t-il pris des mesures – ou exprimé son intention – de modifier son plan stratégique national de la PAC pour la période de programmation 2023-2027, en réponse aux récentes crises et à la volatilité des marchés ? Si oui, quels sont les objectifs de ces modifications et quelles années de paiement devraient être affectées ? En particulier, veuillez considérer si votre pays a exprimé et a l'intention de suspendre les normes environnementales et de gestion des terres pour les bénéficiaires des paiements directs de la PAC au-delà de 2023.

B. Version anglaise – English version – Englische Version

1. General part

1. How has the COVID-19 and pandemic and post-pandemic recovery affected agricultural sectors in your country? Please give a brief overview and consider, in particular, the types of legal measures (legislation, acts, decrees, etc.) that have been introduced to address the challenges faced by farming sectors.
2. Have the impacts of post-pandemic market volatility been affected by other developments, such as natural events linked to climate change? If yes, has your country introduced measures (legislation, acts, decrees, etc.) to address the resulting challenges faced by agricultural sectors in the short-and-medium term?
3. What have been the main impacts of the war in Ukraine on domestic agricultural sectors and has your country published strategic documents or introduced measures (legislation, acts, decrees, etc.) to address these challenges? If yes, to what extent have such measures been able to address the problems experienced by agricultural operators?
4. How have farming sectors in your country been affected by rising input costs and has your country published strategic documents or introduced measures (legislation, acts, decrees, etc.) to address these challenges? In particular, please consider the use of emergency intervention measures and whether these have been able to effectively address the problems faced by agricultural sectors.
5. Has your country introduced – or considered introducing – legal measures (legislation, acts, decrees, etc.) to limit the export of domestic

agricultural products? If yes, are these measures temporary and how long do they apply for? Also, please consider whether such measures are compatible with WTO rules.

6. Has your country introduced measures (legislation, acts, decrees, etc.) to limit market speculation relating to agricultural commodities? If yes, have these measures attained their intended objectives and are they compatible with WTO rules?
7. Has your country introduced other measures aimed at protecting domestic food supplies and production? If so, what has been the effect of these measures for producers and agricultural output?
8. Has your country been affected by legal measures introduced by other countries to protect their own domestic food supplies or limit exports? If yes, how have such actions affected agricultural sectors in your country and have measures (legislation, acts, decrees, etc.) been taken to address these impacts?
9. Has your country introduced legal measures to boost agricultural productivity? If yes, what type of measures have been adopted and how are they expected to affect agricultural sectors and output? Also, do such measures specifically or exclusively aim to boost the production of food and feed commodities?
10. Has your country introduced measures that allow farmers to derogate from environmental and land management standards, otherwise applicable to agricultural producers, in order to maintain or increase levels of agricultural output?
11. Has your country published strategic documents or introduced control measures (legislation, acts, decrees, etc.) to ensure that environmental standards applicable to farmers are not undermined by efforts to boost agricultural productivity and address market volatility?

2. Special part

1. Considering the focus of EU institutions on boosting productivity, has the narrative and strategic approach to food security shifted in your country as a result of recent crises and, in particular, the extreme food price inflation caused by the war in Ukraine? If yes, has this been reflected in your country's strategic documents or adopted measures (legislation, acts, decrees, etc.) and how is this expected to affect agricultural sectors and output in the short-to-medium term?

2. Given the growing concerns of food insecurity, international NGO's and academic commentators have cautioned that increased productivity should not take place at the 'expense' of the environment, i.e. by suspending or lowering environmental standards intended to address the externalities of farming. Taking into account the national context, do you see any risk that a focus on increased productivity could undermine environmental standards applicable to farmers in your country and have measures (legislation, acts, decrees, etc.) been introduced to this effect?
3. Has your country published strategic documents or introduced measures (legislation, acts, decrees, etc.) to enhance the resilience of agricultural sectors to future shocks linked to climate change? In particular, please consider the role of insurance schemes and measures aimed at supporting climate smart agriculture.
4. Considering that market instability is projected to remain a significant factor for agricultural producers in the short-to-medium term, has your country introduced measures (legislation, acts, decrees, etc.) or published strategic documents with the intention of improving the resilience of agricultural sectors and their ability to effectively respond to future crises and volatility? In particular, please consider the impact of measures relating to agricultural intervention and insurance schemes, as well as safety nets and land management policies.

3. For EU Member States

1. Did the use of the EU's Agricultural Reserve in April of 2022 provide effective support for agricultural operators in your country to cope with the market volatility and supply issues exacerbated by the invasion of Ukraine?
2. How has the EU's decision to allow barrier-free access to the European market for Ukrainian agricultural products affected farming sectors in your country and have measures (legislation, acts, decrees, etc.) been introduced to address the potential challenges of this decision? In particular, please consider how barrier free access for Ukrainian food products is affecting the profitability and production decisions by farmers in your country.
3. Has your country taken steps – or expressed an intent – to modify its CAP National Strategic Plan for the 2023-2027 programming period, in response to recent crises and market volatility? If yes, what are the objec-

tives of these modifications and which payment years are expected to be affected? In particular, please consider if your country has expressed and intention to suspend environmental and land management standards for recipients of CAP direct payments beyond 2023.

C. Version allemande – German version – Deutsche Version

1. Allgemeiner Teil

1. Wie haben sich COVID-19 und die Pandemie sowie die Erholung nach der Pandemie auf den Agrarsektor in Ihrem Land ausgewirkt? Bitte geben Sie einen kurzen Überblick und gehen Sie insbesondere auf die Arten von rechtlichen Maßnahmen (Gesetze, Verordnungen, Erlasse usw.) ein, die eingeführt wurden, um die Herausforderungen für den Agrarsektor zu bewältigen.
2. Wurden die Auswirkungen der Marktvolatilität nach der Pandemie durch andere Entwicklungen, wie Naturereignisse im Zusammenhang mit dem Klimawandel, beeinflusst? Wenn ja, hat Ihr Land Maßnahmen (Gesetze, Verordnungen, Erlasse usw.) ergriffen, um die daraus resultierenden Herausforderungen für den Agrarsektor kurz- und mittelfristig zu bewältigen?
3. Was waren die wichtigsten Auswirkungen des Krieges in der Ukraine auf den heimischen Agrarsektor und hat Ihr Land strategische Dokumente veröffentlicht oder Maßnahmen (Gesetze, Verordnungen, Erlasse usw.) eingeführt, um diese Herausforderungen zu bewältigen? Wenn ja, inwieweit haben diese Maßnahmen die Probleme der landwirtschaftlichen Akteure lösen können?
4. Wie wurden die landwirtschaftlichen Sektoren in Ihrem Land durch die steigenden Inputkosten beeinträchtigt, und hat Ihr Land strategische Dokumente veröffentlicht oder Maßnahmen (Gesetze, Verordnungen, Erlasse usw.) eingeführt, um diese Herausforderungen zu bewältigen? Bitte gehen Sie insbesondere auf den Einsatz von Notfall-Interventionsmaßnahmen ein und prüfen Sie, ob diese die Probleme der landwirtschaftlichen Sektoren wirksam angehen konnten.
5. Hat Ihr Land rechtliche Maßnahmen (Gesetze, Verordnungen, Erlasse usw.) eingeführt oder in Erwägung gezogen, um die Ausfuhr einheimischer landwirtschaftlicher Erzeugnisse zu beschränken? Wenn ja, sind diese Maßnahmen zeitlich befristet und für welchen Zeitraum

gelten sie? Überlegen Sie bitte auch, ob solche Maßnahmen mit den WTO-Regeln vereinbar sind?

6. Hat Ihr Land Maßnahmen (Gesetze, Verordnungen, Erlasse usw.) eingeführt, um die Marktspekulation bei Agrarrohstoffen zu begrenzen? Wenn ja, haben diese Maßnahmen die angestrebten Ziele erreicht und sind sie mit den WTO-Regeln vereinbar
7. Hat Ihr Land weitere Maßnahmen zum Schutz der heimischen Lebensmittelversorgung und -produktion eingeführt? Wenn ja, wie haben sich diese Maßnahmen auf die Erzeuger und die landwirtschaftliche Produktion ausgewirkt?
8. War Ihr Land von rechtlichen Maßnahmen betroffen, die andere Länder eingeführt haben, um ihre eigene Lebensmittelversorgung zu schützen oder die Ausfuhren zu begrenzen? Wenn ja, wie haben sich solche Maßnahmen auf den Agrarsektor Ihres Landes ausgewirkt, und wurden Maßnahmen (Gesetze, Verordnungen, Erlasse usw.) ergriffen, um diesen Auswirkungen zu begegnen?
9. Hat Ihr Land gesetzliche Maßnahmen zur Steigerung der landwirtschaftlichen Produktivität eingeführt? Wenn ja, welche Art von Maßnahmen wurden angenommen und wie werden sie sich voraussichtlich auf die landwirtschaftlichen Sektoren und die Produktion auswirken? Zielen diese Maßnahmen speziell oder ausschließlich auf die Steigerung der Produktion von Nahrungs- und Futtermitteln ab?
10. Hat Ihr Land Maßnahmen eingeführt, die es den Landwirten erlauben, von den ansonsten für landwirtschaftliche Erzeuger geltenden Umwelt- und Bodenbewirtschaftungsnormen abzuweichen, um das Niveau der landwirtschaftlichen Produktion zu halten oder zu steigern?
11. Hat Ihr Land strategische Dokumente veröffentlicht oder Kontrollmaßnahmen eingeführt (Gesetze, Verordnungen, Erlasse usw.), um sicherzustellen, dass die für Landwirte geltenden Umweltstandards nicht durch Bemühungen zur Steigerung der landwirtschaftlichen Produktivität und zur Bewältigung der Marktvolatilität untergraben werden?

2. Besonderer Teil

1. Hat sich angesichts der Tatsache, dass der Fokus der EU-Institutionen auf der Steigerung der Produktivität liegt, der narrative und strategische Ansatz für die Ernährungssicherheit in Ihrem Land infolge der jüngsten Krisen und insbesondere der durch den Krieg in der Ukraine verursach-

ten extremen Lebensmittelpreisinflation geändert? Wenn ja, hat sich dies in den strategischen Dokumenten Ihres Landes oder in den verabschiedeten Maßnahmen (Gesetze, Verordnungen, Erlasse usw.) niedergeschlagen, und wie wird sich dies voraussichtlich kurz- bis mittelfristig auf die Agrarsektoren und die Produktion auswirken?

2. In Anbetracht der zunehmenden Besorgnis über die Ernährungsunsicherheit haben internationale NGOs und akademische Kommentatoren davor gewarnt, dass die Produktivitätssteigerung nicht auf „Kosten" der Umwelt erfolgen sollte, d.h. durch die Aufhebung oder Senkung von Umweltstandards, die die externen Effekte der Landwirtschaft berücksichtigen sollen. Sehen Sie unter Berücksichtigung des nationalen Kontextes die Gefahr, dass die Konzentration auf Produktivitätssteigerungen die für Landwirte in Ihrem Land geltenden Umweltstandards untergraben könnte, und wurden diesbezüglich Maßnahmen (Gesetze, Verordnungen, Erlasse usw.) eingeführt?
3. Hat Ihr Land strategische Dokumente veröffentlicht oder Maßnahmen (Gesetze, Verordnungen, Erlasse usw.) eingeführt, um die Widerstandsfähigkeit des Agrarsektors gegenüber künftigen Schocks im Zusammenhang mit dem Klimawandel zu verbessern? Berücksichtigen Sie bitte insbesondere die Rolle von Versicherungssystemen und Maßnahmen zur Unterstützung einer klimafreundlichen Landwirtschaft.
4. Hat Ihr Land in Anbetracht der Tatsache, dass die Instabilität der Märkte kurz- bis mittelfristig ein wichtiger Faktor für die landwirtschaftlichen Erzeuger bleiben dürfte, Maßnahmen (Gesetze, Verordnungen, Erlasse usw.) eingeführt oder strategische Dokumente veröffentlicht, um die Widerstandsfähigkeit der landwirtschaftlichen Sektoren und ihre Fähigkeit, wirksam auf künftige Krisen und Volatilitäten zu reagieren, zu verbessern? Berücksichtigen Sie bitte insbesondere die Auswirkungen von Maßnahmen in Bezug auf landwirtschaftliche Interventions- und Versicherungssysteme sowie Sicherheitsnetze und Landbewirtschaftungsstrategien.

3. Für EU-Mitgliedstaaten

1. Hat die Inanspruchnahme der EU-Agrarreserve im April 2022 die landwirtschaftlichen Akteure in Ihrem Land bei der Bewältigung der Marktvolatilität und der durch den Einmarsch in die Ukraine verschärften Versorgungsprobleme wirksam unterstützt?

2. Wie hat sich die Entscheidung der EU, ukrainischen Agrarerzeugnissen einen barrierefreien Zugang zum europäischen Markt zu gewähren, auf die Landwirtschaft Ihres Landes ausgewirkt, und wurden Maßnahmen (Gesetze, Verordnungen, Erlasse usw.) eingeführt, um den potenziellen Herausforderungen dieser Entscheidung zu begegnen? Bitte gehen Sie insbesondere darauf ein, wie sich der barrierefreie Zugang für ukrainische Lebensmittel auf die Rentabilität und die Produktionsentscheidungen der Landwirte in Ihrem Land auswirkt.
3. Hat Ihr Land Schritte unternommen – oder die Absicht geäußert – seinen nationalen GAP-Strategieplan für den Programmplanungszeitraum 2023-2027 als Reaktion auf die jüngsten Krisen und die Marktvolatilität zu ändern? Wenn ja, was sind die Ziele dieser Änderungen und welche Zahlungsjahre werden voraussichtlich betroffen sein? Überlegen Sie bitte insbesondere, ob Ihr Land die Absicht geäußert hat, Umwelt- und Landbewirtschaftungsnormen für Empfänger von GAP-Direktzahlungen nach 2023 auszusetzen.

Rapport général de la Commission I –
General Report of Commission I –
Generalbericht der Kommission I

Version française – French version – Französische Version
Version anglaise – English version – Englische Version
Version allemande – German version – Deutsche Version

Rapport général de la Commission I

Version française – French version – Französische Version

Dr. Alicia Epstein, LL.M.
Université technique de Brandebourg

I. Introduction

Au cours des années qui ont suivi le XXXe Congrès européen de droit rural, qui s'est tenu à Poznan en 2019, un certain nombre de crises ont convergé pour exercer une pression sans précédent sur les secteurs agricoles et les chaînes d'approvisionnement. L'apparition de la pandémie de COVID-19 au début de l'année 2020 a eu un impact particulier, les chaînes d'approvisionnement ayant été affectées par une série de facteurs, notamment la pénurie de main-d'œuvre, l'instabilité du marché et la hausse des coûts de production[1]. De même, la reprise après la pandémie a été entravée par les coûts élevés des intrants et les problèmes de la chaîne d'approvisionnement, ainsi que par des phénomènes météorologiques violents liés au changement climatique[2]. Au début de l'année 2022, ces pressions ont été considérablement exacerbées par l'invasion de l'Ukraine par la Russie, qui a déclenché une crise alimentaire mondiale et les plus hauts niveaux d'inflation des prix des denrées alimentaires enregistrés depuis des décennies[3]. L'impact combiné de ces crises a eu des répercussions sur l'ensemble des secteurs agricoles et a suscité une série de réponses juridiques au niveau national et international.

Dans ce contexte, les rapporteurs nationaux ont été invités à rendre compte des impacts spécifiques de ces crises sur les secteurs agricoles ainsi que des réponses juridiques nationales et internationales à ces défis. L'objectif de la Commission I était donc de faire le point sur les événements de ces

---

1 Voir *A. Matthews*, 'EU Food System Strengths and Vulnerabilities during Covid-19' (2020), 19(3) *EuroChoices* 4.

2 *F. Montanari et al*, 'Preliminary impacts of the COVID-19 pandemic on European agriculture: A sector-based analysis of food systems and market resilience' (2021) Parlement européen, Département des politiques structurelles et de cohésion.

3 *S. Jagtap et al*, 'The Russia-Ukraine Conflict: Its Implications for the Global Food Supply Chains' (2022) 11(14) Foods 2098.

dernières années et de mettre en évidence les complexités, les similitudes et les divergences des impacts nationaux de ces crises, ainsi que les réponses juridiques qu'elles ont suscitées. Au total, huit rapports nationaux ont été soumis à la Commission I, dont sept attribuables à des États membres de l'UE (EM)[4] et un soumis en tant que rapport individuel, analysant l'impact des crises récentes sur les secteurs agricoles en Colombie[5]. Ce rapport général est basé sur les rapports nationaux et les travaux scientifiques réalisés au sein de la Commission I sous la présidence de Rudy Gotzen lors du XXXIe Congrès européen de droit rural, qui s'est tenu à Cardiff du 6 au 9 septembre 2023, et vise à refléter les principaux thèmes mis en exergue par les représentants nationaux.

Le rapport est divisé en quatre parties, la première traitant des réponses juridiques à la pandémie de COVID-19 et de leur impact sur les secteurs agricoles. Un thème essentiel identifié par les délégués de la Commission I, à cet égard, concerne l'absence d'un cadre juridique global de l'Union européenne (UE) pour répondre aux crises du marché et relever les défis auxquels sont confrontés les secteurs agricoles d'une manière cohérente. Au lieu de cela, les États membres ont dû combler ces lacunes en s'appuyant sur les instruments juridiques existants ou en en adoptant de nouveaux pour répondre aux besoins et aux défis des secteurs agricoles nationaux. Cela met en évidence un degré élevé de fragmentation juridique entre les États membres dans leurs efforts pour alléger les pressions sur les secteurs agricoles en temps de crise et peut avoir une incidence sur le fonctionnement du marché intérieur. Deuxièmement, le rapport examine la période de reprise post-pandémique, qui a été influencée par un débat croissant sur la résilience du système alimentaire, à la suite de la publication de la stratégie de l'UE « de la ferme à la table » (F2FS) et de la stratégie en matière de biodiversité en 2020. Les objectifs environnementaux fixés par ces stratégies ont notamment suscité un regain d'intérêt pour la sécurité alimentaire et révélé des tensions croissantes entre la politique environnementale de l'UE et les agriculteurs, qui se sont bien organisés pour exprimer leur mécontentement face aux initiatives de l'UE censées avoir un impact sur la productivité et la compétitivité. La troisième partie du rapport se concentre sur les impacts de la guerre en Ukraine sur les secteurs agricoles de l'UE et sur les mesures juridiques prises en réponse à la volatilité significative

4 Autriche, Allemagne, Hongrie, France, Italie, Pologne et Espagne.

5 Le rapport individuel a été rédigé par *Nelson Plazas* (professeur de droit public international, Université Santo Tomás, Colombie).

du marché qui a suivi le déclenchement du conflit. Enfin, la quatrième partie du rapport examine les effets de la crise climatique sur l'agriculture de l'UE et les mesures prises pour relever ces défis aux niveaux national et international.

II. Réponses juridiques à la pandémie de COVID-19 et impacts sur les secteurs agricoles

A. Mesures de l'UE

La pandémie de COVID-19 a posé d'importants défis à l'agriculture européenne et aux systèmes d'approvisionnement alimentaire, nécessitant la mise en œuvre d'une série de mesures juridiques pour assurer la sécurité alimentaire, stabiliser les marchés et soutenir les producteurs agricoles. L'une des premières grandes mesures prises par l'UE en réponse aux problèmes liés à la chaîne d'approvisionnement a donc été l'introduction de l'initiative « voies vertes », en mars 2020, qui visait à assurer le transport ininterrompu des marchandises, y compris des produits agricoles, à travers les États membres en simplifiant les formalités aux frontières et en réduisant les goulets d'étranglement[6]. Cette initiative a permis d'assurer la continuité de la circulation des produits agricoles et a été particulièrement efficace pour réduire les perturbations logistiques dans des États membres tels que la France et l'Allemagne, ce qui était essentiel pour maintenir la sécurité alimentaire pendant les périodes de lockdown[7].

Les mesures de l'UE se sont également concentrées sur la mise en place d'une flexibilité temporaire dans l'application des règles relatives aux aides d'État, permettant aux États membres d'accorder un soutien financier d'urgence aux entreprises, y compris les entreprises agricoles, sans enfreindre les règlements de l'UE en matière d'aides d'État[8]. This allowed for direct

---

6 Commission européenne, Communication de la Commission sur la mise en œuvre des voies vertes dans le cadre des lignes directrices relatives aux mesures de gestion des frontières visant à protéger la santé et à garantir la disponibilité des biens et des services essentiels (2020/C 96 I/01).

7 *S. Liu,* 'Food supply pressure in France and Germany during COVID-19: Causes from manufacturing' (2020) 9(4) Journal of Agriculture, Food Systems, and Community Development 139.

8 Le cadre temporaire pour les aides d'État a été introduit par la Commission européenne en 2020 et adopté en vertu de l'autorité juridique de l'article 107, paragraphe 2,

grants, subsidies, and tax relief to be extended to agricultural producers and helped stabilise agricultural economies and address liquidity issues. Cela a permis d'accorder des aides directes, des subventions et des allègements fiscaux aux producteurs agricoles et a contribué à stabiliser les économies agricoles et à résoudre les problèmes de liquidités. Par exemple, le cadre temporaire a permis à la Hongrie de lancer le programme national de gestion des crises alimentaires[9], tandis que la Pologne a fourni une aide directe aux agriculteurs dans les secteurs vulnérables tels que la production laitière et porcine[10].

En outre, l'UE a autorisé des dérogations temporaires aux obligations en matière de verdissement et a accéléré le versement des paiements directs[11]. Ces changements ont amélioré la liquidité pour les agriculteurs et facilité l'utilisation des terres mises en jachère pour la production, ce dernier point étant particulièrement important pour le maintien de la production en Allemagne et en Espagne. Parmi les autres aides financières, on peut citer l'utilisation de la réserve agricole de l'UE, qui a mis des fonds supplémentaires à la disposition des États membres pour leur permettre d'apporter une aide ciblée aux secteurs les plus touchés par les perturbations du marché[12]. Ces mesures ont permis des interventions sectorielles largement exemptées du droit européen de la concurrence et ont inclus le financement de programmes d'aide au stockage privé pour les produits laitiers, la viande et les denrées périssables.

Ces mesures, guidées par la PAC et d'autres cadres de l'UE, ont joué un rôle essentiel dans l'atténuation des effets immédiats de la crise tout en mettant en évidence les domaines à améliorer à long terme. La pandémie

---

point b), et de l'article 107, paragraphe 3, point b), du traité sur le fonctionnement de l'Union européenne (TFUE).

9 Rapport hongrois, auteurs : *János Ede Szilágyi/Dávid Hojnyák/Nóra Jakab* (ci-après : Rapport hongrois), p. 4.

10 Règlement du ministre de l'agriculture et du développement rural du 24 août 2020 sur les conditions détaillées et la procédure d'octroi et de versement de l'aide financière pour des opérations telles que « Aide aux agriculteurs particulièrement touchés par la crise COVID-19 » dans le cadre de la mesure « Soutien temporaire exceptionnel aux agriculteurs, aux micro-entreprises et aux petites entreprises et moyennes entreprises particulièrement touchées par la crise liée à COVID-19 » couverte par le programme de développement rural pour 2014-2020, (Journal of Laws of 2020, item 1467).

11 Commission européenne, CORONAVIRUS : Réponse d'urgence pour soutenir le secteur agricole et alimentaire, Commission européenne 2020.

12 Pour une liste des règlements de la Commission, voir : Journal officiel de l'Union européenne, L 140, 4 mai 2020.

a notamment mis en évidence l'importance de la coordination au niveau de l'UE pour garantir la sécurité alimentaire et la stabilité du marché. Toutefois, si les mesures juridiques ont permis d'atténuer efficacement les perturbations à court terme, elles ont également révélé des vulnérabilités systémiques, telles que la nécessité d'une plus grande équité dans la distribution de l'aide et le renforcement des stratégies d'adaptation au climat. Par exemple, les petits exploitants agricoles en Pologne ont eu du mal à accéder à l'aide de manière équitable[13], tandis que le rapport espagnol a mis en évidence la nécessité de réformes structurelles pour assurer la résilience climatique à long terme[14]. En outre, le recours à des dérogations temporaires a mis en évidence la nécessité de mettre en place des cadres plus solides pour faire face aux crises futures.

B. Mesures nationales

Les mesures nationales prises par les États membres de l'UE en réponse à la pandémie de COVID-19 ont consisté en une combinaison d'allègements financiers, d'ajustements du marché du travail, de stabilisation du marché et de flexibilité réglementaire. La base juridique de ces mesures était une combinaison de cadres européens (la PAC, les règles relatives aux aides d'État et les dispositions du TFUE), de dispositions constitutionnelles nationales relatives aux situations d'urgence et de la législation agricole et sectorielle existante. Par conséquent, les réponses nationales apportées par les États membres de l'UE pour garantir la sécurité alimentaire, stabiliser les marchés agricoles et soutenir les secteurs vulnérables varient considérablement en fonction de leurs contextes agricoles et de leurs priorités économiques.

Certains États membres, comme l'Autriche, ont pu largement s'appuyer sur les instruments juridiques existants pour relever les défis de la pandémie de COVID-19 dans le secteur agricole, en activant les principaux cadres législatifs qui régissent la gestion des crises et la sécurité de l'approvisionnement en denrées alimentaires[15]. À cet égard, le recours à la Lebens-

13 Rapport polonais, édité par M. *Korzycka/P. Wojciechowski* (ci-après : Rapport polonais), pp. 3-4.

14 Rapport espagnol, auteur : *Teresa Rodríguez-Cachón* (ci-après : Rapport espagnol), p. 2.

15 Bundes-Krisensicherheitsgesetz (B-KGS), BGBl I Nr. 89/2023.

mittelbewirtschaftungsgesetz (loi sur la gestion des denrées alimentaires)[16], qui régit la réglementation des approvisionnements alimentaires en cas de crise et autorise le ministère fédéral de l'agriculture à prendre des décrets spécifiques pour gérer la distribution et le stockage des denrées alimentaires en cas d'urgence, a été déterminant. Pendant la pandémie, cette loi a servi de base à la préparation de plans d'urgence visant à stabiliser les marchés en cas de perturbation de la chaîne d'approvisionnement, bien que l'activation formelle de ces mesures n'ait pas été nécessaire en raison de la conformité volontaire du secteur privé[17]. En outre, la réponse autrichienne s'est appuyée sur la Versorgungssicherungsgesetz (loi sur la sécurité de l'approvisionnement)[18] pour garantir la production et la fourniture ininterrompues de biens essentiels, y compris les produits agricoles, en apportant une aide économique aux producteurs agricoles, en particulier dans des secteurs tels que l'élevage, la production de vin et l'horticulture.

D'autres États membres, y compris la Pologne et la Hongrie, se sont également appuyés sur la législation d'urgence existante et sur les dispositions de la loi fondamentale pour répondre à la pandémie, respectivement. En ce qui concerne la première, par exemple, le gouvernement a invoqué des dispositions d'urgence spéciales pour modifier son programme de développement rural (2014-2020) afin de financer l'aide aux agriculteurs polonais[19]. La Hongrie, quant à elle, a déclaré un « état de danger » en vertu de sa loi fondamentale en 2020, ce qui a permis au gouvernement de suspendre la législation existante et d'introduire des décrets pour le secteur agricole[20]. Des décrets sectoriels ont également été publiés en Italie et en Autriche pour mettre en œuvre des aides financières, des ajustements de main-d'œuvre et des exonérations fiscales. Il s'agit notamment de l'adoption du décret-loi n° 18/2020, qui prévoit des dérogations à la certification COVID-19 pour les transactions agricoles et un financement supplémentaire pour les programmes de distribution de denrées alimentaires en Italie[21]. Dans le cas de l'Autriche, le ministère fédéral de l'agriculture, des forêts, des régions et de la gestion de l'eau (Bundesministerium für Land- und Forstwirtschaft,

16 Lebensmittelbewirtschaftungsgesetz (LMBG 1997), BGBl Nr 789/1996 idF BGBl I Nr 113/2016.

17 Rapport autrichien, auteur : *David Sams* (ci-après : Rapport autrichien), p. 6.

18 Versorgungssicherungsgesetz (VerssG 1992), BGBl Nr 380/1992 idF BGBl I Nr 94/2016.

19 Rapport polonaise, p. 3.

20 Rapport hongrois, p. 3.

21 Rapport italien, Auteur : *Laura Costantino* (ci-après : Rapport italien) p. 1.

Regionen und Wasserwirtschaft - BML) a adopté des décrets sectoriels dans le cadre de ses lois sur la gestion de l'alimentation et de l'énergie afin de sécuriser les chaînes d'approvisionnement alimentaire et de fournir une aide ciblée aux agriculteurs[22].

Bien que ces mesures nationales et bien d'autres puissent être créditées pour maintenir le fonctionnement général des chaînes d'approvisionnement agricole, l'absence de contribution démocratique, par l'utilisation de décrets et d'ordonnances de l'exécutif, a été un thème majeur soulevé dans un certain nombre de rapports nationaux. L'utilisation des pouvoirs exécutifs a été particulièrement controversée dans les cas où ils ont été utilisés pour limiter ou affecter les droits fondamentaux ou constitutionnels. Les rapports nationaux et les travaux scientifiques menés par la Commission I ont mis en évidence la nécessité d'éviter de telles situations à l'avenir en développant des cadres juridiques plus complets pour répondre aux crises, tant au niveau national qu'au niveau de l'UE, y compris l'expansion d'instruments juridiques spécifiques pour fournir un soutien aux opérateurs agricoles et assurer l'approvisionnement alimentaire dans un contexte de volatilité du marché. À cet égard, il convient de noter que l'Autriche a déjà pris des mesures pour développer le cadre juridique existant pour la gestion des crises afin de répondre plus efficacement aux crises futures. Par exemple, la loi fédérale sur la sécurité en cas de crise (Bundes-Krisensicherheitsgesetz) est entrée en vigueur en 2024 et fournit un cadre global pour la déclaration des crises et la coordination des réponses d'urgence intersectorielles[23].

III. Reprise post-pandémie

En mai 2020, la Commission a publié deux communications historiques visant à mettre en œuvre les objectifs du marché vert de l'UE, intitulées « Stratégie de la ferme à la fourchette » (F2F)[24] et « Stratégie de l'UE pour la biodiversité à l'horizon 2030 »[25]. Ces textes incluent les objectifs de

---

22 Rapport autrichien, p. 8.

23 Bundes-Krisensicherheitsgesetz (B-KGS), BGBl I Nr. 89/2023.

24 Commission européenne, Une stratégie « De la ferme à la table » pour un système alimentaire équitable, sain et respectueux de l'environnement COM(2020)381. Bruxelles, CE.

25 Commission européenne, Stratégie de l'UE en faveur de la biodiversité à l'horizon 2030 : remettre la nature au cœur de nos vies, COM(2020) 380 final.

réduction de 50 % de l'utilisation des produits phytopharmaceutiques et de 20 % de l'utilisation des engrais industriels d'ici 2030, ainsi que l'augmentation de l'agriculture biologique à 25 % de la surface agricole européenne. Au moment de la publication, ces communications n'avaient pas encore fait l'objet d'études d'impact et ont été sévèrement critiquées dans des études réalisées par les services de recherche économique du ministère américain de l'agriculture fin 2020[26], et en 2021, par une étude réalisée par le Centre commun de recherche de la Commission européenne[27], ainsi que par des études académiques sous l'angle de la sécurité alimentaire mondiale[28]. Selon ces études, la mise en œuvre des objectifs de la Commission, justifiée par la réduction attendue des émissions de gaz à effet de serre, impliquerait une réduction de la productivité agricole européenne et, par conséquent, une moindre contribution à la sécurité alimentaire mondiale.

Malgré ces critiques, la publication de F2FS et de EU's Biodiversité a eu pour effet de catalyser un débat plus large sur la nécessité d'améliorer la résilience de l'agriculture européenne pour qu'elle puisse faire face aux crises futures, y compris la crise climatique croissante. Au cours de la période de reprise post-pandémique, plusieurs États membres ont donc mis en place des incitations nationales pour renforcer la résilience de leur secteur agricole. Ces mesures étaient principalement concentrées sur l'aide financière, l'investissement dans la durabilité, la stabilisation de la chaîne d'approvisionnement et l'adaptation du marché du travail.

En ce qui concerne le soutien financier au secteur agricole, les États membres ont adopté de nombreux programmes d'aide ainsi que des mesures visant à encourager les investissements pour moderniser les structures agricoles. Par exemple, en 2020, la Hongrie a introduit un programme d'investissement agricole de 80 milliards de HUF (225 millions d'euros) visant à moderniser les secteurs de l'élevage et de l'horticulture[29]. Elle a également lancé de nouvelles lignes de crédit pour les agriculteurs, y compris des prêts

26 *J. Beckman et al*, 'Economic and Food Security Impacts of Agricultural Input Reduction Under the European Union Green Deal's Farm to Fork and Biodiversity Strategies' (Service de recherche économique - Département de l'agriculture des États-Unis 2020) 30.

27 *J. Hurle Barreiro Hurle et al*, Modelling environmental and climate ambition in the agricultural sector with the CAPRI model (Office des publications de l'Union européenne, Luxembourg, 2021).

28 *J. Bremmer et al*, 'Impact Assessment of EC 2030 Green Deal Targets for Sustainable Crop Production' (Recherche économique de Wageningen, 2021) 2021–150.

29 Rapport hongrois, p. 2.

sans intérêt et à faible taux d'intérêt pour soutenir l'investissement dans les nouvelles technologies et a réorienté le programme national de gestion des crises alimentaires, en mettant l'accent sur la résilience à long terme plutôt que sur les secours immédiats en cas de pandémie. De même, la Pologne a accordé des subventions pour la mécanisation agricole et l'agriculture de précision afin de réduire la vulnérabilité aux chocs extérieurs et a alloué un fonds RDP (2014-2020) pour renforcer la liquidité financière des entreprises agricoles[30]. En Italie, l'accent a été mis sur l'encouragement des stratégies de résilience collective par le biais d'une aide financière accrue pour les organisations de producteurs et la mise en œuvre d'un fonds de souveraineté alimentaire, afin de renforcer la production alimentaire nationale et de réduire la dépendance à l'égard des produits importés[31].

Les initiatives visant à renforcer la résilience de l'agriculture se sont de plus en plus concentrées sur la durabilité et la résilience climatique dans le secteur agricole au cours de la période de reprise post-pandémique. En France, une approche à multiples facettes a été élaborée pour renforcer la résilience du système alimentaire et remédier aux vulnérabilités révélées par la pandémie. Des initiatives importantes ont été prises pour renforcer la souveraineté alimentaire et soutenir les transitions agroécologiques. Les mesures françaises se sont concentrées sur l'amélioration de la production alimentaire nationale, la réduction de la dépendance à l'égard des importations et la promotion de pratiques agricoles durables. Il s'agit notamment d'investissements accrus dans la production locale de fruits, de légumes et de volailles – des secteurs qui ont toujours souffert d'une mauvaise balance commerciale et d'une forte dépendance à l'égard des importations - ainsi que de l'augmentation du financement de l'agriculture agroécologique et de la production biologique afin de garantir des approvisionnements alimentaires locaux de haute qualité[32]. Des mesures ont également été prises pour réduire la dépendance à l'égard des intrants agricoles importés (par exemple, les engrais et les aliments pour animaux) en promouvant des alternatives locales et en développant la recherche sur les pratiques agricoles circulaires. En particulier, les initiatives du gouvernement français ont mis l'accent sur la nécessité de développer l'agriculture régénératrice et d'améliorer les infrastructures de gestion de l'eau pour se préparer aux

---

30 Rapport polonais, p. 3.

31 Rapport italien, p. 6. Voir Law No. 197 of 29 December 2022, Article 1, par. 424.

32 Rapport français, auteurs : *Bernard Vallius/ Jean-Baptiste Millard* (ci-après : Rapport français) pp. 15-16.

chocs climatiques tels que les sécheresses. De même, l'Espagne a adapté son plan stratégique de la PAC pour la période de programmation 2023-2027 afin de mettre l'accent sur les stratégies d'atténuation de la sécheresse et l'utilisation durable de l'eau[33], tandis que l'Allemagne a augmenté les subventions pour les pratiques agricoles adaptées au climat, en particulier pour la diversification des cultures et la gestion de la santé des sols[34].

Au cours de la période post-pandémique, certains États membres se sont concentrés sur l'adaptation du marché du travail afin de renforcer leur capacité à faire face aux crises futures. À cet égard, l'Allemagne et la Hongrie ont étendu les mesures de flexibilité du travail post-pandémique, y compris les régimes de travailleurs saisonniers et les incitations financières pour l'emploi agricole domestique[35]. Dans les deux États membres, ces mesures comprenaient l'expansion et le développement de plateformes numériques de recrutement de main-d'œuvre agricole afin de rationaliser la disponibilité de la main-d'œuvre[36]. La nécessité de poursuivre la numérisation et l'adoption de nouvelles technologies dans le secteur agricole a également été un thème central souligné dans les discussions de la Commission I, surtout si l'on considère que les pays ayant un degré élevé de numérisation disposaient d'un outil supplémentaire pour répondre aux crises du marché de la pandémie.

IV. Impacts de la guerre en Ukraine

L'invasion russe de l'Ukraine, en février 2022, a eu un impact profond sur les secteurs agricoles de l'UE, provoquant des perturbations généralisées dans l'approvisionnement en engrais, en aliments pour animaux et dans les importations de céréales[37]. Les prix des denrées alimentaires ont particulièrement augmenté à la suite du blocus russe des exportations de céréales ukrainiennes et de la fermeture des ports de la mer Noire, ce qui a entraîné des pénuries d'approvisionnement et une volatilité des prix sur les marchés

33 Rapport espagnol, p. 6
34 Rapport allemand, auteur : *Anna Kiermeier* (ci-après : Rapport allemand) p. 11.
35 Rapport allemand p. 5; Rapport hongrois p. 6.
36 Rapport allemand p. 8 ; rapport hongrois p. 4.
37 *N. Jia et al*, 'The Russia-Ukraine war reduced food production and exports with a disparate geographical impact worldwide' (2024) 5 Commun Earth Environ 765.

mondiaux[38]. Cette situation a entraîné les plus hauts niveaux d'inflation des prix alimentaires mondiaux depuis des décennies, suscitant des craintes d'insécurité alimentaire généralisée et entraînant des réponses immédiates de la part des organisations et des institutions internationales. En particulier, la ONUAA[39] exhorté à plusieurs reprises les pays exportateurs de denrées alimentaires à éviter l'introduction de mesures protectionnistes telles que les interdictions d'exportation et autres restrictions de marché, afin d'assurer l'approvisionnement continu en produits agricoles des pays importateurs. La Commission européenne l'a également souligné dans sa communication du 23 mars 2022, en insistant sur la nécessité urgente de stabiliser les marchés agricoles et de faire face aux niveaux croissants d'insécurité alimentaire liée à l'accès en Europe et au-delà[40].

A. Réponses de l'UE et des États membres à la volatilité du marché dans le secteur agricole

L'UE a réagi en activant la réserve de crise agricole (ECA) en avril 2022, mettant 500 millions d'euros à la disposition des États membres pour fournir une aide financière directe aux secteurs et aux agriculteurs les plus touchés par la crise, afin de compenser l'augmentation des coûts des intrants[41]. Cette aide a été cruciale pour les États membres de l'UE qui ont pu utiliser les fonds d'urgence pour des interventions ciblées afin d'atténuer les risques immédiats de la crise. En Pologne, par exemple, le gouvernement a alloué des fonds pour aider le secteur de l'élevage, ainsi que les producteurs de céréales et d'oléagineux qui ont été touchés par l'instabilité du marché en raison d'une offre excédentaire d'importations ukrainiennes[42]. Ce soutien financier a aidé les agriculteurs polonais à gérer les excédents de stockage et

---

38 European Parliamentary Research Services, La guerre de la Russie contre l'Ukraine : Implications pour la politique alimentaire de l'UE, Union européenne 2022.

39 ONUAA, Impact du conflit Ukraine-Russie sur la sécurité alimentaire mondiale et les questions connexes relevant du mandat de l'Organisation des Nations Unies pour l'alimentation et l'agriculture (Rome, FAO 2022).

40 Commission européenne, Préserver la sécurité alimentaire et renforcer la résilience des systèmes alimentaires, COM(2022) 133 final.

41 L'ECA, financé par des dotations non utilisées de la PAC, est conçu pour fournir un soutien financier d'urgence en cas de perturbations exceptionnelles du marché et a été officiellement mis en place dans le cadre de la période de programmation 2014-2020.

42 Rapport polonais, pp. 7-8.

à maintenir les liquidités dans un contexte de baisse des prix[43]. De même, l'Espagne a affecté son financement de l'ECA au soutien des éleveurs, en particulier dans les secteurs du lait et de la viande, où l'augmentation des coûts de l'alimentation animale et du carburant a créé une pression financière considérable[44]. L'aide directe a permis aux agriculteurs de poursuivre leur production malgré la hausse des coûts.

En Autriche, un système de paiement à l'hectare a été mis en place pour distribuer l'aide proportionnellement aux terres agricoles touchées, les mesures étant particulièrement destinées à protéger l'horticulture (par exemple, les serres) et la production de volaille de l'augmentation des coûts et des perturbations de la chaîne d'approvisionnement[45]. Le coût élevé des intrants a également été ressenti par les producteurs agricoles en Allemagne, en particulier ceux qui produisent des céréales et des oléagineux, ce qui a incité le gouvernement à donner la priorité à l'aide à ces secteurs et à introduire des mesures permettant aux agriculteurs d'utiliser temporairement des terres mises en jachère pour la production[46]. Parmi les autres utilisations du financement de l'ECA, on peut citer les mesures prises en Hongrie pour stabiliser les coûts des opérations agricoles essentielles, telles que la gestion de l'eau et le transport pour les régions touchées par la sécheresse. En fin de compte, ces actions ont aidé les agriculteurs à couvrir les coûts de transport et à maintenir les niveaux de production malgré les perturbations climatiques et géopolitiques[47].

En réponse à la volatilité du marché causée par la guerre, la Commission européenne a également élargi le cadre de crise temporaire pour les aides d'État, qui avait déjà été mis en place pendant la pandémie et qui permettait aux États membres de soutenir les agriculteurs et les producteurs de denrées alimentaires en détresse financière en raison des prix élevés des intrants. En Italie et en Hongrie, cette flexibilité a été utilisée pour mettre en œuvre des exonérations fiscales et des subventions directes afin de garantir la liquidité des petites et moyennes entreprises agricoles[48], tandis que la Pologne a offert un soutien financier pour le stockage et la vente

43 Rapport polonais, p. 5.
44 Rapport espagnol, p. 4.
45 Rapport autrichien, p. 16.
46 Rapport allemand, p. 11.
47 Rapport hongrois, p. 5.
48 Rapport italien, p. 5 ; Rapport hongrois, p. 2.

des excédents de céréales, à la suite des énormes perturbations causées par l'afflux de céréales ukrainiennes[49].

Une autre mesure clé prise par l'UE en réponse aux perturbations commerciales du début de l'année 2022 concerne l'assouplissement des normes de la PAC en matière d'environnement et de gestion des terres. Plus précisément, la décision d'exécution de la Commission (UE) 2022/484 a donné aux États membres la possibilité d'introduire des dérogations temporaires à l'obligation de maintenir les zones d'intervention écologique (ZIE), c'est-à-dire les terres mises en jachère pour soutenir la biodiversité au titre du règlement UE 1307/2013 pour l'année de paiement 2022. En outre, le règlement d'exécution (UE) 2022/1317 de la Commission prévoyait des dérogations supplémentaires concernant l'application des normes relatives aux bonnes conditions agricoles et environnementales des terres (normes BCAE) 7 et 8 pour l'année de demande 2023. L'objectif de l'adoption de ces mesures était explicitement d'augmenter la production agricole et d'atténuer les pénuries dans l'UE en permettant aux agriculteurs d'utiliser les terres mises en jachère pour la production de denrées alimentaires et d'aliments pour animaux[50]. Un certain nombre d'États membres, dont l'Autriche, l'Allemagne et l'Espagne, ont choisi de le faire en augmentant temporairement la production agricole, en particulier pour les céréales, tandis que la France a été en mesure de maintenir la productivité tout en promouvant des pratiques durables en parallèle.

Alors que l'accent renouvelé sur la sécurité alimentaire, suite à l'invasion de l'Ukraine, a été généralement approuvé par les délégués de la Commission I, l'accent mis par l'UE sur la stimulation de la productivité en suspendant les normes environnementales pour les secteurs agricoles a été accueilli avec beaucoup de scepticisme. En particulier, des inquiétudes ont été exprimées quant à la manière dont l'utilisation des dérogations affecterait la capacité du bloc à atteindre les objectifs de durabilité à long terme dans le cadre de la DG, étant donné que des mesures importantes doivent encore être prises pour atteindre les objectifs fixés par la stratégie F2FS et la stratégie en faveur de la biodiversité. En outre, les discussions au sein de la Commission I ont mis en évidence la nécessité d'examiner la manière dont la mise en œuvre des objectifs de la DG aurait une incidence sur la sécurité alimentaire au niveau mondial. Par exemple, les mesures visant à réduire l'utilisation des pesticides pourraient avoir des

49 Rapport polonais, p. 4.
50 Voir le préambule de la décision d'exécution de la Commission (EU) 2022/484.

conséquences pour les pays exportateurs tels que la Colombie si les normes de l'UE sont imposées aux importations de tiers. En fin de compte, l'UE doit prendre des mesures plus décisives pour garantir que la mise en œuvre de ses objectifs environnementaux à long terme n'affecte pas négativement la sécurité alimentaire mondiale ou n'entrave pas inutilement la capacité des pays en développement exportateurs à accéder au marché intérieur.

B. Implications spécifiques pour les États frontaliers de l'UE

En mai 2022, l'UE a mis en place des « corridors de solidarité » permettant l'importation en franchise de droits des produits agricoles ukrainiens afin de réduire les goulets d'étranglement logistiques causés par les fermetures de ports et de faciliter le transport de ses produits agricoles, en particulier les céréales, vers le marché mondial, dans le cadre d'une stratégie plus large visant à atténuer les risques liés à la sécurité alimentaire mondiale et à soutenir l'économie ukrainienne[51]. Ce mécanisme a permis aux exportations ukrainiennes d'emprunter d'autres itinéraires à travers les États membres de l'UE, par la route, le rail et les voies navigables intérieures, et a contribué à éviter des perturbations catastrophiques sur les marchés céréaliers mondiaux en maintenant les flux commerciaux en provenance d'Ukraine. Toutefois, l'afflux de céréales ukrainiennes par ces corridors de solidarité a créé des déséquilibres sur le marché, en particulier dans les pays voisins tels que la Slovaquie, la Hongrie, la Roumanie et la Pologne, où les céréales ukrainiennes, initialement destinées à l'exportation vers d'autres régions, ont été vendues sur le marché intérieur, ce qui a entraîné une offre excédentaire et une chute importante des prix locaux[52].

Malgré les protestations massives des agriculteurs dans les pays frontaliers et les efforts considérables déployés par leurs gouvernements pour améliorer la situation causée par l'afflux de céréales ukrainiennes bon marché, la Commission européenne s'est montrée peu disposée à modifier le cadre et les conditions d'importation en franchise de droits des céréales ukrainiennes[53]. Cela a finalement conduit à une situation intenable, laissant

51 Commission européenne, Un plan d'action pour la création de corridors de solidarité UE-Ukraine en vue de faciliter les exportations agricoles et les échanges bilatéraux de l'Ukraine avec l'UE, COM(2022) 217 final.

52 Ibid.

53 Rapport hongrois, p. 15.

les États membres, y compris la Pologne et la Hongrie, sans autre choix que d'imposer des interdictions temporaires sur les importations agricoles ukrainiennes en avril 2023, bien que ces produits de base aient continué à transiter par leurs territoires[54]. Par la suite, en mai 2023, l'UE a mis en place des restrictions temporaires permettant à la Pologne, à la Bulgarie, à la Hongrie, à la Roumanie et à la Slovaquie d'interdire les ventes nationales de blé, de maïs, de colza et de graines de tournesol ukrainiens, tout en autorisant le transit vers d'autres marchés[55]. Malgré les tentatives de la Commission pour stabiliser les marchés, la situation a mis en évidence les tensions entre les politiques de solidarité à l'échelle de l'UE et les priorités économiques nationales, les gouvernements devant trouver un équilibre entre le soutien à l'Ukraine et la nécessité de protéger leurs secteurs agricoles nationaux. Pour ce qui est de l'avenir, la poursuite des actions unilatérales risque de compromettre la réponse unifiée de l'UE à la guerre et de conduire à une fragmentation accrue au sein du bloc, ce qui a été soulevé comme un thème majeur par les rapporteurs nationaux de la Commission I.

V. Changement climatique et agriculture

Outre la volatilité du marché causée par la pandémie et la guerre qui a suivi en Ukraine, les États membres de l'UE ont été de plus en plus confrontés à des événements climatiques et météorologiques graves, notamment des sécheresses, des inondations, des tempêtes et des fluctuations extrêmes de température au cours des dernières années. Ces événements ont perturbé la production agricole, réduit les rendements des cultures et provoqué une instabilité économique dans les zones rurales, ce qui a incité les États membres à prendre diverses mesures pour renforcer la résilience et s'adapter aux changements climatiques. En Espagne, par exemple, une sécheresse persistante a affecté une grande partie des terres agricoles du pays, exacerbant des problèmes tels que la désertification et la réduction de la disponibilité de l'eau au cours des dernières années[56]. Cette situation a incité le gouvernement espagnol à intégrer des stratégies d'atténuation de

54 Rapport hongrois, p. 15; Rapport polonais, p. 7.

55 Règlement d'exécution (UE) 2023/903 de la Commission du 2 mai 2023 introduisant des mesures préventives concernant certains produits originaires d'Ukraine.

56 Rapport espagnol, p. 6.

la sécheresse dans son plan stratégique pour la PAC 2023-2027, en mettant l'accent sur la promotion de l'irrigation à l'énergie solaire et des pratiques de gestion durable de l'eau.[57] Les pénuries d'eau ont également gravement affecté les opérations agricoles en Italie, tandis que la Hongrie a connu l'une de ses plus graves sécheresses en 2022, détruisant les cultures de maïs et de blé sur un million d'hectares[58]. Le gouvernement hongrois a réagi en déclarant un état de danger et en mettant en œuvre des mesures telles que des bonifications d'intérêts pour les agriculteurs, un moratoire sur le remboursement des prêts et des subventions pour le transport d'aliments pour animaux[59]. Par la suite, il a également mis en place un système de stabilisation des revenus agricoles afin de protéger les agriculteurs contre les variations extrêmes de revenus dues aux chocs climatiques[60].

De l'autre côté du spectre, plusieurs États membres ont connu des inondations et des tempêtes de grande ampleur, qui ont provoqué l'érosion des sols, détruit les cultures et perturbé les chaînes d'approvisionnement alimentaire. En Autriche, par exemple, le secteur agricole, en particulier dans les régions montagneuses, a subi des dégâts répétés liés aux tempêtes au cours des dernières années, ce qui a conduit à l'adoption de nouvelles mesures d'évaluation des risques pour améliorer la préparation aux catastrophes et à des programmes d'aide financière pour les agriculteurs touchés[61]. De même, les inondations survenues en France ont incité à investir dans l'amélioration des infrastructures de gestion de l'eau et à promouvoir les pratiques agroécologiques afin d'améliorer la résistance des sols et de réduire les risques d'inondation. Le gouvernement a également renforcé les politiques d'adaptation au climat dans le cadre de son plan stratégique pour la PAC.

En outre, les chaleurs extrêmes et les fluctuations de température ont affecté la production végétale et animale, en stressant les cultures et en réduisant les rendements, en particulier dans le sud et le centre de l'Europe. En Italie, la hausse des températures a réduit la productivité de cultures clés telles que le raisin de cuve et les olives, ces dernières entraînant des

57 Pour accéder toutes les modifications du plan stratégique de la PAC espagnole pour la période de programmation 2023-2027, voir: https://n9.cl/ye7p6v.
58 Rapport hongrois, p. 5.
59 Ibid.
60 Ibid. p. 6.
61 Rapport autrichien, p. 21.

hausses de prix significatives pour l'huile d'olive en 2023[62]. Pour soutenir les agriculteurs touchés, le gouvernement italien a introduit des subventions à l'assurance dans le cadre du plan de gestion des risques agricoles, encourageant les agriculteurs à souscrire une assurance contre les phénomènes météorologiques extrêmes[63]. Les phénomènes météorologiques extrêmes ont également entraîné des baisses de rendement importantes dans les cultures céréalières et fourragères en Allemagne. Pour atténuer le stress thermique élevé, qui devrait s'aggraver dans les années à venir, le gouvernement allemand a adopté des mesures visant à promouvoir l'innovation et l'adoption de technologies agricoles numériques[64].

Les rapports nationaux ont mis en évidence le fait qu'un certain nombre d'États membres intègrent de plus en plus la résilience climatique dans les stratégies agricoles à long terme par le biais d'initiatives européennes et nationales. Toutefois, un thème central soulevé par la Commission I concerne la nécessité d'aborder le changement climatique comme une crise permanente et d'aborder les défis croissants d'une manière plus holistique et cohérente. En particulier, les discussions ont mis en évidence la nécessité de développer des liens plus étroits entre les cadres et les objectifs de l'UE, d'une part, et la législation nationale, d'autre part. Il s'agit notamment d'étendre les régimes d'assurance agricole pour qu'ils se concentrent de plus en plus sur la réduction des risques, plutôt que sur leur simple gestion. Le rapport national espagnol, en particulier, souligne le besoin urgent d'améliorer les cadres juridiques des systèmes d'alerte précoce pour les agriculteurs touchés par des catastrophes naturelles ou liées au climat, afin de minimiser les pertes économiques. Alors que les cadres juridiques actuels manquent souvent d'outils et de coordination pour fournir aux agriculteurs des informations vitales qui peuvent être utilisées pour limiter les impacts des catastrophes naturelles, le développement de systèmes d'alerte d'urgence qui intègrent et fournissent des informations aux agriculteurs le plus tôt possible pourrait contribuer à réduire ces risques et à protéger les moyens de subsistance.

62 Eurostat, Le prix de l'huile d'olive a augmenté de 50 % en un an (article de presse du 27 février 2024); https://ec.europa.eu/eurostat/web/products-eurostat-news/w/ddn-20240227-1?utm_source=chatgpt.com.

63 Rapport italien, p. 9. Voir le décret ministériel n° 64591 du 8/2/2023 (modifié par la suite par le décret ministériel n° 31/5/2023).

64 Rapport allemand, p. 16.

General Report of Commission I

Version anglaise – English version – Englische Version

Dr. Alicia Epstein, LL.M.
Brandenburg Technical University

I. Introduction

In the years since the XXXth European Congress on Rural Law, held in Poznan in 2019, a number of crises have converged to put unprecedented pressure on agricultural sectors and supply chains. The outbreak of the COVID-19 pandemic in early 2020 was especially impactful, with supply chains being affected by a range of factors, including labour shortages, market instability and rising production costs[1]. Likewise, the post-pandemic recovery was hampered by high input costs and supply chain issues, as well as severe weather events linked to climate change[2]. In early 2022, these pressures were significantly exacerbated by Russia's invasion of Ukraine, which triggered a global food crisis and the highest levels of food price inflation experienced in decades[3]. The combined impact of these crises has had implications for farming sectors across the board, and has prompted an array of legal responses at both the national and international level.

Against this background, National Reporters were asked to report on the specific impacts of these crises on agricultural sectors as well as the national and international legal responses to these challenges. The focus of Commission I was, therefore, to take stock of the events of recent years and to highlight the complexities, similarities and diverging national impacts of these crises, as well as the legal responses prompted by them. In total, eight National Reports were submitted to Commission I, with seven of

1 See, *A. Matthews*, 'EU Food System Strengths and Vulnerabilities during Covid-19' (2020), 19(3) *EuroChoices* 4.

2 *F. Montanari et al*, 'Preliminary impacts of the COVID-19 pandemic on European agriculture: A sector-based analysis of food systems and market resilience' (2021) European Parliament, Policy Department for Structural and Cohesion Policies.

3 *S. Jagtap et al*, 'The Russia-Ukraine Conflict: Its Implications for the Global Food Supply Chains' (2022) 11(14) Foods 2098.

these attributable to EU Member States (MS)[4] and one submitted as an Individual Report, analysing the impact of the recent crises on agricultural sectors in Colombia[5]. This General Report is based on the National Reports and the scientific work done in Commission I under the Presidency of Rudy Gotzen during the XXXIth European Congress on Rural Law, held in Cardiff from 6-9 September 2023, and aims to reflect the main themes highlighted by the national representatives.

The Report is divided into four parts, with the first part discussing the legal responses to the COVID-19 pandemic and their impact on agricultural sectors. A critical theme identified by Commission I delegates, in this regard, relates to the lack of a comprehensive European Union (EU) legal framework to respond to market crises and address the challenges faced by agricultural sectors in a cohesive manner. Instead, MS have had to fill these gaps by either relying on existing legal instruments or enacting new ones to address the needs and challenges of domestic agricultural sectors. This underscores a high degree of legal fragmentation between MSs in their efforts to alleviate pressures on agricultural sectors in times of crisis and has the potential to impact the functioning of the internal market. Secondly, the report considers the period of post-pandemic recovery, which was influenced by a growing debate around food system resilience, following the publication of the EU's Farm to Fork Strategy (F2FS) and Biodiversity Strategy in 2020. Not least, the environmental targets set by these strategies have prompted a renewed focus on food security and revealed growing tensions between EU environmental policy and farmers, which have been well organised in voicing their dissatisfaction over EU initiatives that are expected to impact productivity and competitiveness. The third part of the report focuses on the impacts of the War in Ukraine on EU agricultural sectors and the legal measures taken in response to the significant market volatility that has ensued following the outbreak of the conflict. Lastly, the fourth part of the report considers the effects of the climate crisis on EU agriculture and the steps taken to address these challenges at the national and international level.

---

4 Austria, Germany, Hungary, France, Italy, Poland and Spain.

5 The Individual Report was authored by *Nelson Plazas* (Professor of International Public Law, University Santo Tomás, Colombia).

II. Legal Responses to the COVID-19 Pandemic and Impacts on Agricultural Sectors

A. EU Measures

The COVID-19 pandemic posed significant challenges to the European agriculture and food supply systems, necessitating the implementation of a range of legal measures to ensure food security, stabilize markets, and support agricultural producers. One of the first major EU measures taken in response to the lock-down related supply chain issues was therefore the introduction of the Green Lanes Initiative, in March 2020, which aimed to ensure the uninterrupted transport of goods, including agricultural products, across MS by simplifying border formalities and minimising bottlenecks[6]. This initiative ensured continuity in the movement of agricultural products and was especially effective in reducing logistical disruptions in MSs such as France and Germany, which was critical for maintaining food security during lockdowns[7].

EU measures also focused on providing temporary flexibility in the application of state aid rules, enabling MSs to grant emergency financial support to businesses, including agricultural enterprises, without breaching EU state aid regulations[8]. This allowed for direct grants, subsidies, and tax relief to be extended to agricultural producers and helped stabilise agricultural economies and address liquidity issues. For example, the temporary framework enabled Hungary to launch the National Food Crisis Management Programme[9], while Poland provided direct aid to farmers in vulnerable sectors such as dairy and pork production[10].

---

6 European Commission, Communication from the Commission on the implementation of the Green Lanes under the Guidelines for border management measures to protect health and ensure the availability of goods and essential services (2020/C 96 I/01).

7 *S. Liu,* 'Food supply pressure in France and Germany during COVID-19: Causes from manufacturing' (2020) 9(4) Journal of Agriculture, Food Systems, and Community Development 139.

8 The Temporary Framework for State Aid was introduced by the European Commission in 2020 and adopted under the legal authority of Articles 107(2)(b) and 107(3)(b) of the Treaty on the Functioning of the European Union (TFEU).

9 Hungarian Report, Authors: *János Ede Szilágyi/Dávid Hojnyák/Nóra Jakab* (hereinafter: Hungarian Report), p.4.

10 Regulation of the Minister of Agriculture and Rural Development of August 24, 2020 on the detailed conditions and procedure for granting and disbursing financial aid for operations such as "Aid to farmers particularly affected by the COVID-19 crisis"

In addition, the EU permitted temporary derogations from greening obligations and accelerated the disbursement of direct payments[11]. These changes enhanced liquidity for farmers and facilitated the use of set-aside land for production, with the latter being especially important for maintaining output in Germany and Spain. Other relevant financial support included the use of the EU's agricultural reserve, which made available additional funding to MSs to enable targeted assistance to those sectors most affected by market disruptions[12]. This allowed for sector-specific interventions that were largely exempt from EU competition law and included the funding of private storage aid schemes for dairy, meat, and perishable.

These measures, guided by the CAP and other EU frameworks, played a critical role in mitigating the immediate effects of the crisis while highlighting areas for long-term improvement. Not least, the pandemic underscored the importance of EU-level coordination for ensuring food security and market stability. However, while the legal measures effectively mitigated short-term disruptions, they also revealed systemic vulnerabilities, such as the need for greater equity in aid distribution and enhanced climate adaptation strategies. For instance, small-scale farmers in Poland faced challenges in accessing aid equitably[13], while the Spanish report highlighted the need for structural reforms to address long-term climate resilience[14]. Furthermore, the reliance on temporary derogations highlighted the need for more robust frameworks to address future crises.

B. National Measures

National measures taken by EU MSs in response to the COVID-19 pandemic reflected a combination of financial relief, labour market adjustments, market stabilization, and regulatory flexibility. The legal basis for such

---

under the measure "Exceptional temporary support for farmers, micro-enterprises and small enterprises and medium-sized enterprises particularly affected by the crisis related to COVID-19" covered by the Rural Development Program for 2014-2020, (Journal of Laws of 2020, item 1467).

11 European Commission, CORONAVIRUS: Emergency response to support the agriculture and food sector, European Commission 2020.

12 For a list of Commission Regulations, see; Official Journal of the European Union, L 140, 4 May 2020.

13 Polish Report, edited by *M. Korzycka/P. Wojciechowski* (hereinafter: Polish Report), pp. 3-4.

14 Spanish Report, Author: *Teresa Rodríguez-Cachón* (hereinafter: Spanish Report), p. 2.

action was a combination of EU-level frameworks (the CAP, state aid rules, and TFEU provisions), national constitutional provisions for emergencies, and existing agricultural and sector-specific legislation. Consequently, national responses by EU MSs to ensure food security, stabilize agricultural markets, and support vulnerable sectors, varied significantly based on their agricultural contexts and economic priorities.

Some MSs, such as Austria, were largely able to rely on existing legal instruments to address the challenges of the COVID-19 pandemic for the agricultural sector, by activating the main legislative frameworks that govern crisis management and food supply security[15]. Key, in this regard, was, for instance, the use of the Lebensmittelbewirtschaftungsgesetz (Food Management Act)[16], which governs the regulation of food supplies during crises and authorizes the Federal Ministry of Agriculture to issue specific decrees for managing food distribution and storage during emergencies. During the pandemic, this law served as the basis for preparing contingency plans to stabilize markets in the case of supply chain disruptions, although the formal activation of these measures was not required due to voluntary compliance by the private sector[17]. In addition, the Austrian response relied on the Versorgungssicherungsgesetz (Supply Security Act)[18] to ensure the uninterrupted production and supply of essential goods, including agricultural products, by providing economic relief to agricultural producers, particularly in sectors like livestock, wine production, and horticulture.

Other MSs, including Poland and Hungary, also relied on existing emergency legislation and fundamental law provisions to respond to the pandemic, respectively. With regards to the former, for instance, the government invoked special emergency provisions to modify its Rural Development Program (2014–2020) in order to finance support for Polish farmers[19]. Hungary, on the other hand, declared a "state of danger" under its Fundamental Law in 2020, which allowed the government to suspend existing legislation and introduce decrees for the agricultural sector[20]. Sector

---

15 Bundes-Krisensicherheitsgesetz (B-KGS), BGBl I Nr. 89/2023.

16 Lebensmittelbewirtschaftungsgesetz (LMBG 1997), BGBl Nr 789/1996 idF BGBl I Nr 113/2016.

17 Austrian Report, Author: *David Sams* (hereinafter: Austrian Report), p. 6.

18 Versorgungssicherungsgesetz (VerssG 1992), BGBl Nr 380/1992 idF BGBl I Nr 94/2016.

19 Polish Report, p. 3.

20 Hungarian Report, p. 3.

specific decrees were also issued in Italy and Austria to implement financial aid, labour adjustments, and tax waivers. This included the Adoption of Decree-Law No. 18/2020, which provided COVID-19 certification waivers for agricultural transactions and additional funding for food distribution programs in Italy[21]. In the case of Austria, the Federal Ministry of Agriculture, Forestry, Regions, and Water Management (Bundesministerium für Land- und Forstwirtschaft, Regionen und Wasserwirtschaft – BML) adopted sectoral decrees under its Food and Energy Management Laws to secure food supply chains and provide targeted aid to farmers[22].

While these and many other national measures may be credited for maintaining the overall functioning of agricultural supply chains, the lack of democratic input, through the use of executive decrees and orders, has been a major theme raised in a number national reports. Not least, the use of executive powers has been especially controversial in cases where these have been used to limit or affect basic or constitutional rights. The national reports and scientific work carried out in Commission I have highlighted the need to avoid such situations in the future by developing more comprehensive legal frameworks to respond to crises, both at the national and EU level, including the expansion of specific legal instruments to provide support for agricultural operators and ensure food supplies amidst market volatility. In this regard, it may be noted that Austria has already taken steps to develop the existing legal framework for crisis management to more effectively respond to future crises. For instance, the Federal Crisis Security Act (Bundes-Krisensicherheitsgesetz) took effect in 2024 and provides a comprehensive framework for declaring crises and coordinating cross-sectoral emergency responses[23].

III. Post-Pandemic Recovery

In May of 2020, the Commission published two landmark communications aimed at implementing the EU's Green Deal (GD) objectives, entitled the

---

21 Italian Report, Author: *Laura Costantino* (hereinafter: Italian Report) p. 1.
22 Austrian Report, p. 8.
23 Bundes-Krisensicherheitsgesetz (B-KGS), BGBl I Nr. 89/2023.

Farm to Fork Strategy (F2FS)[24] and the EU's 2030 Biodiversity Strategy[25]. These texts include the objectives of reducing the use of plant protection products by 50 % and the use of industrial fertilisers by 20 % by 2030, as well as increasing organic farming to 25 % of European agricultural land. At the time of publication, these communications had not yet been the subject of impact studies and were severely criticised in studies carried out by the economic research services of the US Department of Agriculture[26] at the end of 2020, and in 2021, by a study carried out by the EU Commission's Joint Research Centre[27], as well as by academic studies from the angle of global food security[28]. These studies argued that the implementation of the Commission's objectives, justified by the expected reduction in greenhouse gas emissions, would imply a reduction in European agricultural productivity and consequently a lesser contribution to global food security.

Notwithstanding these criticisms, the publication of the F2FS and the EU's Biodiversity had the effect of catalysing a broader discussion around the need to enhance the resilience of EU agriculture to withstand future crises, including the growing climate crisis. During the post-pandemic recovery period several MSs, consequently, introduced national incentives to strengthen the resilience of their agricultural sectors. These measures primarily focused on financial aid, investment in sustainability, supply chain stabilization, and labour market adaptations.

With regards to providing financial support to the farming sector, MSs have adopted numerous aid packages as well as measures aimed at incentivising investment to modernize farming structures. For instance, in 2020 Hungary introduced an HUF 80 billion (€225 million) agricultural investment package aimed at modernising the livestock and horticulture sectors[29]. It also launched new credit lines for farmers, including interest-

---

24 European Commission, A Farm to Fork Strategy for a Fair, Healthy and Environmentally-Friendly Food System COM(2020)381. Brussels, EC.

25 European Commission, EU Biodiversity Strategy for 2030: Bringing nature back into our lives, COM(2020) 380 final.

26 *J. Beckman et al*, 'Economic and Food Security Impacts of Agricultural Input Reduction Under the European Union Green Deal's Farm to Fork and Biodiversity Strategies' (Economic Research Service-United States Department of Agriculture 2020) 30.

27 *J. Hurle Barreiro Hurle et al*, Modelling environmental and climate ambition in the agricultural sector with the CAPRI model (Publications Office of the European Union, Luxembourg, 2021).

28 *J. Bremmer et al*, 'Impact Assessment of EC 2030 Green Deal Targets for Sustainable Crop Production' (Wageningen Economic Research, 2021) 2021-150.

29 Hungarian Report, p. 2.

free and low-interest loans to support investment in new technologies and realigned the National Food Crisis Management Programme, shifting its focus from immediate pandemic relief to long-term resilience. Similarly, Poland provided subsidies for farm mechanization and precision agriculture to reduce vulnerability to external shocks and allocated RDP fund (2014–2020) to strengthen the financial liquidity of agricultural enterprises[30]. In Italy, the focus has been on encouraging collective resilience strategies through increased financial aid for producer organisations and the implementation of a Food Sovereignty Fund, to strengthen national food production and reduce dependency on imported goods[31].

Initiatives to enhance agricultural resilience increasingly focused on sustainability and climate resilience in the agricultural sector during the post-pandemic recovery period. In France, a multi-faceted approach was developed to boost food system resilience and address vulnerabilities exposed by the pandemic. Importantly, significant initiatives were taken to strengthen food sovereignty and support the agroecological transitions, with French measures focused on improving domestic food production, reducing dependence on imports, and promoting sustainable farming practices. This included increased investment in local production of fruits, vegetables, and poultry – sectors that historically suffered from poor trade balances and high dependency on imports – as well as the expansion of funding for agroecological farming and organic production to ensure high-quality local food supplies[32]. Steps were also taken to reduce reliance on imported agricultural inputs (e.g., fertilisers and animal feed) by promoting local alternatives and expanding research into circular farming practices. In particular, French government initiatives have emphasised the need to expand regenerative agriculture and improve water management infrastructure to prepare for climate shocks like droughts. Similarly, Spain adjusted its CAP Strategic Plan for the 2023–2027 programming period to emphasise drought mitigation strategies and sustainable water use[33], while Germany expanded subsidies for climate-adaptive farming practices, particularly for crop diversification and soil health management[34].

---

30 Polish Report, p. 3.

31 Italian Report, p. 6. See, Law No. 197 of 29 December 2022, Article 1, par. 424.

32 French Report, Authors: *Bernard Vallius/ Jean-Baptiste Millard* (hereinafter: French Report) pp. 15-16.

33 Spanish Report, p. 6

34 German Report, Author: *Anna Kiermeier* (hereinafter: German Report) p. 11.

During the post-pandemic period, some MSs focused on labour market adaptations as a means of enhancing their ability to deal with future crises. In this regard, Germany and Hungary extended post-pandemic labour flexibility measures, including seasonal worker schemes and financial incentives for domestic agricultural employment[35]. In both MSs, this included the expansion and development of digitalised agricultural labour recruitment platforms to streamline workforce availability[36]. The need for further digitalisation and the adoption of new technologies in the agricultural sector was also a central theme highlighted in Commission I discussions, especially considering that countries with a high degree of digitalisation, had an additional tool with which to respond to the pandemic market crises.

IV. Impacts of the War in Ukraine

The Russian invasion of Ukraine, in February 2022, had a profound impact on EU agricultural sectors, causing widespread disruptions in the supply of fertilizers, animal feed, and grain imports[37]. Food prices were especially driven up following the Russian blockade of Ukrainian grain exports and closure of Black Sea ports, leading to supply shortages and price volatility across global markets[38]. This resulted in the highest levels of global food price inflation in decades, raising fears of widespread food insecurity and prompting immediate responses by international organisations and institutions. In particular, the FAO[39] repeatedly urged food exporting countries to avoid the introduction of protectionist measures such as export bans and other market restrictions, in order to ensure the continued supply of agricultural commodities for import-reliant countries. This was further highlighted by the EU Commission in its Communication of 23 March 2022, where it stressed the pressing need to stabilise agricultural markets

35 German Report p. 5; Hungarian Report p. 6.

36 German Report p. 8; Hungarian Report p. 4.

37 *N. Jia et al*, 'The Russia-Ukraine war reduced food production and exports with a disparate geographical impact worldwide' (2024) 5 Commun Earth Environ 765.

38 European Parliamentary Research Services, Russia's war on Ukraine: EU food policy implications, European Union 2022.

39 FAO, Impact of the Ukraine-Russia conflict on global food security and related matters under the mandate of the Food and Agriculture Organization of the UN (Rome, FAO 2022).

and address growing levels of access-related food insecurity in Europe and beyond.[40]

A. EU and National Responses to Market Volatility in the Agricultural Sector

The EU responded by activating the Agricultural Crisis Reserve (ACR) in April 2022, making 500 million Euro available to MS to provide direct financial aid to sectors and farmers most affected by the crisis, in order to offset the increased input costs[41]. This provided critical assistance to EU MSs that were able to use the emergency funds for targeted interventions to mitigate the immediate risks of the crisis. In Poland, for instance, the government directed funds to assist the livestock sector, as well as grain and oilseed producers who were affected by market instability due to an oversupply of Ukrainian imports[42]. This financial support helped Polish farmers manage surplus storage and maintain liquidity amidst declining prices[43]. Likewise, Spain allocated their ACR funding to support livestock farmers, particularly in the dairy and meat sectors, where rising costs for animal feed and fuel created considerable financial pressure[44]. The direct aid enabled farmers to continue production despite a surge in costs.

In Austria, a hectare-based payment system was implemented to distribute aid proportionately based on affected farmland, with measures being particularly aimed at protecting horticulture (e.g., greenhouse operations) and poultry production from rising costs and supply chain disruptions[45]. High input costs were also felt by crop producers in Germany, particularly those producing cereals and oilseeds, prompting the Government to prioritize aid for these sectors and introduce measures to temporarily allow farmers to utilize set-aside land for production[46]. Other uses of the ACR funding, include measures taken in Hungary to stabilize the costs

40 EU Commission, Safeguarding food security and reinforcing the resilience of food systems, COM(2022) 133 final.

41 The ACR, funded through unused CAP allocations, is designed to provide emergency financial support during exceptional market disturbances and was formally established under the 2014–2020 programming period.

42 Polish Report, pp. 7-8.

43 Polish Report, p. 5.

44 Spanish Report, p. 4.

45 Austrian Report, p. 16.

46 German Report, p. 11.

of essential agricultural operations, such as water management and transportation for drought-affected regions. Ultimately, these actions helped farmers cover transportation costs and maintain production levels despite climate and geopolitical disruptions[47].

In response to the market volatility caused by the war, the European Commission also expanded the temporary crisis framework for State Aid, which had already been put in place during the pandemic and allowed MSs to support farmers and food producers in financial distress due to high input prices. In Italy and Hungary this flexibility was used to implement tax exemptions and direct subsidies to ensure liquidity for small and medium-sized agricultural enterprises[48], while Poland offered financial support for the storage and sale of surplus grain, following the huge disruptions caused by the influx of Ukrainian grain[49].

Another key measure taken by the EU in response to trade disruptions in early 2022, relates to the easing of CAP environmental and land management standards. More specifically, Commission Implementing Decision (EU) 2022/484 gave MSs the option to introduce temporary derogations from the requirement to maintain Ecological Focus Areas (EFA), i.e. land set aside to support biodiversity under EU Regulation 1307/2013 for the 2022 payment year. Furthermore, Commission Implementing Regulation (EU) 2022/1317 provided for additional derogations regarding application of the standards for good agricultural and environmental conditions of land (GAEC standards) 7 and 8 for claim year 2023. The purpose of adopting these measures was explicitly to increase agricultural output and alleviate shortages in the EU caused by allowing farmers to use set-aside land for the production of food and animal feed[50]. A number of MSs, including Austria, Germany and Spain chose to do so by temporarily expanding agricultural production, particularly for cereals, whereas France was able to maintain productivity while promoting sustainable practices in parallel.

While the renewed emphasis on food security, following the invasion of Ukraine, was generally endorsed by Commission I delegates, the EU's focus on boosting productivity by suspending environmental standards for the farming sectors has been met with considerable scepticism. Not least, concern was expressed over how the use of derogations would impact the Block's ability to attain long-term sustainability goals under the GD, given

47 Hungarian Report, p. 5.
48 Italian Report, p. 5; Hungarian Report, p. 2.
49 Polish Report, p. 4.
50 See Preamble, Commission Implementing Decision (EU) 2022/484.

that significant action still needs to be taken to achieve the targets set by the F2FS and Biodiversity Strategy. Moreover, the discussions in Commission I highlighted the need to consider how implementation of the GD objectives would impact food security at the global level. For instance, measures to reduce pesticide use could have implications for exporting countries such as Colombia if EU standards are imposed on third party imports. Ultimately, there is a need for the EU to take more decisive action to ensure that implementation of its long-term environmental goals do not adversely affect global food security or unnecessarily impede the ability of exporting developing countries to access the internal market.

B. Specific Implications for EU Border States

In May of 2022, the EU introduced so called Solidarity Lanes, allowing tariff-free imports of Ukrainian agricultural commodities to reduce logistical bottlenecks caused by port closures and facilitate the transport of its agricultural goods, particularly grain, to the global market, as part of a broader strategy to alleviate global food security risks and support the Ukrainian economy[51]. The mechanism enabled Ukrainian exports via alternative routes through EU MSs by road, rail, and inland waterways and helped avoid catastrophic disruptions in global grain markets by maintaining trade flows from Ukraine. However, the influx of Ukrainian grain through these solidarity lanes created market imbalances, particularly in bordering countries such as Slovakia, Hungary, Romania and Poland, where Ukrainian grain, initially intended for export to other regions, was being sold domestically, leading to oversupply and a significant drop in local prices[52].

Despite massive farmer protests in border countries and extensive efforts on the part of their governments to alleviate the situation caused by the influx of cheap Ukrainian grain, the European Commission was largely unwilling to alter the framework and conditions concerning tariff-free imports of Ukrainian grain[53]. This eventually led to an untenable situation, leaving MSs including Poland and Hungary with little choice but to im-

51 European Commission, An action plan for EU-Ukraine Solidarity Lanes to facilitate Ukraine's agricultural export and bilateral trade with the EU, COM(2022) 217 final.

52 Ibid.

53 Hungarian Report, p. 15.

pose temporary bans on Ukrainian agricultural imports in April of 2023, though these commodities maintained transit through their territories[54]. Subsequently, in May 2023, the EU implemented temporary restrictions allowing Poland, Bulgaria, Hungary, Romania, and Slovakia to ban domestic sales of Ukrainian wheat, maize, rapeseed, and sunflower seeds, while permitting transit to other markets[55]. Notwithstanding the Commissions attempts to stabilise markets, the situation served to highlight tensions between EU-wide solidarity policies and national economic priorities, as governments had to balance support for Ukraine with the need to protect their domestic agricultural sectors. Looking to the future, continued unilateral actions risks undermining a unified EU response to the war and is likely to lead to further fragmentation within the Block, which was raised as a major theme of the National Reporters in Commission I.

V. Climate Change and Agriculture

In addition to the market volatility caused by the pandemic and the subsequent war in Ukraine, EU MSs have increasingly faced severe climatic and weather events, including droughts, floods, storms, and extreme temperature fluctuations in recent years. These events have disrupted agricultural production, reduced crop yields, and caused economic instability in rural areas, prompting various national measures to build resilience and adapt to climate changes. In Spain, for instance, persistent drought has affected a substantial portion of the country's agricultural land, exacerbating issues like desertification and reduced water availability in recent years[56]. This prompted the Spanish Government to incorporate drought mitigation strategies in its 2023-2027 CAP Strategic Plan, focused on promoting solar-powered irrigation and sustainable water management practices.[57] Water shortages also harshly affected agricultural operations in Italy, while Hungary experienced one of its most severe droughts in 2022, destroying maize and wheat crops across one million hectares[58]. In response, the Hungarian

54 Hungarian Report, p. 15; Polish Report, p. 7.

55 Commission Implementing Regulation (EU) 2023/903 of 2 May 2023 introducing preventive measures concerning certain products originating in Ukraine.

56 Spanish Report, p. 6.

57 To get access to all the modifications of the Spanish CAP Strategic Plan for the 2023-2027 programming period, see: https://n9.cl/ye7p6v.

58 Hungarian Report, p. 5.

government declared a state of danger and implemented measures such as interest rate subsidies for farmers, a loan repayment moratorium, and subsidised feed transport[59]. It has subsequently also introduced an agricultural income stabilisation system to protect farmers from extreme income variability due to climate-related shocks[60].

On the other end of the spectrum, several MS have experienced extensive flooding and storms, which have caused soil erosion, destroyed crops, and disrupted food supply chains. In Austria, for instance, the agricultural sector, especially in mountainous regions, has faced repeated storm-related damage in recent years, leading to the adoption of new risk assessment measures to enhance disaster preparedness and financial support programs for affected farmers[61]. Likewise, flood events in France have prompted investment in improved water management infrastructure and the promotion of agroecological practices to enhance soil resilience and reduce flood risks. The government has also strengthened climate adaptation policies under its CAP Strategic Plan.

Furthermore, extreme heat and temperature fluctuations have affected both crop and animal production, by stressing crops and reducing yields, particularly in Southern and Central Europe. In Italy, rising temperatures have reduced the productivity of key crops such as wine grapes and olives, with the latter causing significant price increases for olive oil in 2023[62]. To support affected farmers, the Italian government introduced insurance subsidies under the Agricultural Risk Management Plan, encouraging farmers to adopt insurance against extreme weather events[63]. Extreme weather events have also caused significant yield reductions in cereal and fodder crops in Germany. To mitigate the high level heat stress, which is projected to increase in the coming years, the German Government adopted measures to promote innovation and digital farming technologies[64].

The National Reports have highlighted that a number of MSs are increasingly integrating climate resilience into long-term agricultural strategies through both EU and national initiatives. However, a central theme raised

59 Ibid.

60 Ibid. p. 6.

61 Austrian Report, p. 21.

62 Eurostat, Price of olive oil up 50 % in one year (news article 27 February 2024); https://ec.europa.eu/eurostat/web/products-eurostat-news/w/ddn-20240227-1?utm_source=chatgpt.com.

63 Italian Report, p. 9. See Ministerial Decree No. 64591 of 8/2/2023 (subsequently amended by Ministerial Decree No. 31/5/2023).

64 German Report, p. 16.

in Commission I relates to the need to tackle climate change as an ongoing crisis and approach the growing challenges in a more holistic and cohesive manner. In particular, discussions highlighted the need to develop closer links between EU frameworks and objectives, on the one hand, and national legislation on the other. This includes, the expansion of agricultural insurance schemes to focus increasingly on reducing risk, rather than just managing it. The Spanish National Report, in particular, stresses the urgent need to improve legal frameworks for early-warning systems for farmers affected by natural or climate-related disasters, in order to minimize economic losses. While current legal frameworks often lack the tools and coordination to provide farmers with vital information that can be used to limit the impacts of natural disasters, developing emergency alert systems and that integrate and provide information to farmers at the earliest possible point could help to reduce these risks and protect livelihoods.

Generalbericht der Kommission I

Version allemande – German version – Deutsche Version

Dr. Alicia Epstein, LL.M.
Brandenburgische Technische Universität

I. Einleitung

In den Jahren seit dem XXX. Europäischen Kongress für Ländliches Recht, der 2019 in Poznań stattfand, sind eine Reihe von Krisen zusammengekommen, die einen noch nie dagewesenen Druck auf den Agrarsektor und die Lieferketten ausgeübt haben. Der Ausbruch der COVID-19-Pandemie Anfang 2020 war besonders einschneidend, wobei die Lieferketten von einer Reihe von Faktoren betroffen waren, darunter Arbeitskräftemangel, Marktinstabilität und steigenden Produktionskosten[1]. Auch die Erholung nach der Pandemie wurde durch hohe Inputkosten und Probleme in der Versorgungskette sowie durch Unwetter im Rahmen des Klimawandels behindert[2]. Anfang 2022 wurde dieser Druck durch die russische Invasion in der Ukraine noch erheblich verschärft, die eine weltweite Nahrungsmittelkrise und die höchste Nahrungsmittelpreisinflation seit Jahrzehnten auslöste[3]. Die kombinierten Auswirkungen dieser Krisen haben sich auf alle landwirtschaftlichen Sektoren ausgewirkt und zu einer Reihe von rechtlichen Maßnahmen auf nationaler und internationaler Ebene geführt.

Vor diesem Hintergrund wurden die nationalen Berichterstatter gebeten, über die spezifischen Auswirkungen dieser Krisen auf den Agrarsektor sowie über die nationalen und internationalen rechtlichen Antworten auf diese Herausforderungen zu berichten. Der Schwerpunkt der Kommission I bestand daher darin, eine Bestandsaufnahme der Ereignisse der letzten Jahre vorzunehmen und die Komplexität, die Ähnlichkeiten und die un-

---

1 Siehe, *A. Matthews*, 'EU Food System Strengths and Vulnerabilities during Covid-19' (2020), 19(3) *EuroChoices* 4.

2 *F. Montanari et al*, 'Preliminary impacts of the COVID-19 pandemic on European agriculture: A sector-based analysis of food systems and market resilience' (2021) Europäisches Parlament, Fachabteilung für Struktur- und Kohäsionspolitik.

3 *S. Jagtap et al*, 'The Russia-Ukraine Conflict: Its Implications for the Global Food Supply Chains' (2022) 11(14) Foods 2098.

terschiedlichen nationalen Auswirkungen dieser Krisen sowie die durch sie ausgelösten rechtlichen Reaktionen aufzuzeigen. Insgesamt wurden der Kommission I acht nationale Berichte vorgelegt, von denen sieben den EU-Mitgliedstaaten (MS) zuzuordnen sind[4] und einer als Einzelbericht vorgelegt wurde, in dem die Auswirkungen der jüngsten Krisen auf den Agrarsektor in Kolumbien analysiert wurde[5]. Dieser Gesamtbericht basiert auf den nationalen Berichten und der wissenschaftlichen Arbeit, die in der Kommission I unter dem Vorsitz von Rudy Gotzen während des XXXI. Europäischen Kongresses für ländliches Recht, der vom 6. bis 9. September 2023 in Cardiff stattfand, geleistet wurde, und soll die von den nationalen Vertretern hervorgehobenen Hauptthemen wiedergeben.

Der Bericht ist in vier Teile gegliedert, wobei der erste Teil die rechtlichen Reaktionen auf die COVID-19-Pandemie und ihre Auswirkungen auf den Agrarsektor erörtert. Ein kritisches Thema, das die Delegierten der Kommission I in diesem Zusammenhang identifiziert haben, ist das Fehlen eines umfassenden Rechtsrahmens der Europäischen Union (EU), um auf Marktkrisen zu reagieren und die Herausforderungen, mit denen die Agrarsektoren konfrontiert sind, auf kohärente Weise anzugehen. Stattdessen mussten die Mitgliedstaaten diese Lücken füllen, indem sie sich entweder auf bestehende Rechtsinstrumente stützten oder neue Instrumente erließen, um den Bedürfnissen und Herausforderungen der heimischen Agrarsektoren gerecht zu werden. Dies unterstreicht die starke rechtliche Zersplitterung zwischen den Mitgliedstaaten bei ihren Bemühungen, den Druck auf den Agrarsektor in Krisenzeiten zu mindern, und kann das Funktionieren des Binnenmarktes beeinträchtigen. Zweitens befasst sich der Bericht mit der Zeit nach der Pandemie, die nach der Veröffentlichung der EU-Strategie „Vom Bauernhof bis zum Teller“ (F2FS) und der Strategie zur Erhaltung der biologischen Vielfalt im Jahr 2020 durch eine wachsende Debatte über die Widerstandsfähigkeit des Lebensmittelsystems beeinflusst wurde. Nicht zuletzt haben die in diesen Strategien festgelegten Umweltziele dazu geführt, dass die Lebensmittelsicherheit wieder stärker in den Mittelpunkt gerückt ist, wobei wachsende Spannungen zwischen der EU-Umweltpolitik und den Landwirten offenbart wurden, die ihren Unmut über EU-Initiativen, die sich voraussichtlich auf die Produktivität und Wettbewerbsfähigkeit auswirken werden, gut organisiert zum Ausdruck gebracht haben. Der

4 Österreich, Deutschland, Ungarn, Frankreich, Italien, Polen und Spanien.

5 Der Einzelbericht wurde von *Nelson Plazas* (Professor für Internationales Öffentliches Recht, Universität Santo Tomás, Kolumbien) verfasst.

dritte Teil des Berichts befasst sich mit den Auswirkungen des Krieges in der Ukraine auf den Agrarsektor der EU und den rechtlichen Maßnahmen, die als Reaktion auf die erhebliche Marktvolatilität nach dem Ausbruch des Konflikts ergriffen wurden. Der vierte Teil des Berichts befasst sich schließlich mit den Auswirkungen der Klimakrise auf die EU-Landwirtschaft und den Maßnahmen, die zur Bewältigung dieser Herausforderungen auf nationaler und internationaler Ebene ergriffen wurden.

II. Rechtliche Reaktionen auf die COVID-19-Pandemie und Auswirkungen auf den Agrarsektor

A. EU-Maßnahmen

Die COVID-19-Pandemie stellte die europäischen Landwirtschafts- und Lebensmittelversorgungssysteme vor erhebliche Herausforderungen und erforderte die Umsetzung einer Reihe von rechtlichen Maßnahmen, um die Lebensmittelsicherheit zu gewährleisten, die Märkte zu stabilisieren und die landwirtschaftlichen Erzeuger zu unterstützen. Eine der ersten wichtigen EU-Maßnahmen, die als Reaktion auf die mit der Pandemie zusammenhängenden Probleme in der Lieferkette ergriffen wurden, war daher die Einführung der „Green-Lanes"-Initiative im März 2020, die darauf abzielt, den ununterbrochenen Transport von Waren, einschließlich landwirtschaftlicher Erzeugnisse, über die Grenzen der Mitgliedstaaten hinweg zu gewährleisten, indem die Grenzformalitäten vereinfacht und Engpässe minimiert werden[6]. Diese Initiative gewährleistete die Kontinuität des Verkehrs mit landwirtschaftlichen Erzeugnissen und trug insbesondere dazu bei, logistische Unterbrechungen in Mitgliedstaaten wie Frankreich und Deutschland zu verringern, was für die Aufrechterhaltung der Lebensmittelsicherheit während der Aussperrungen von entscheidender Bedeutung war[7].

6 Europäische Kommission, Mitteilung der Kommission über die Umsetzung so genannter „Green Lanes" im Rahmen der Leitlinien für Grenzmanagementmaßnahmen zum Schutz der Gesundheit und zur Sicherstellung der Verfügbarkeit von Waren und wesentlichen Dienstleistungen (2020/C 96 I/01).

7 *S. Liu,* 'Food supply pressure in France and Germany during COVID-19: Causes from manufacturing' (2020) 9(4) Journal of Agriculture, Food Systems, and Community Development 139.

Die EU-Maßnahmen konzentrierten sich auch auf eine vorübergehende Flexibilität bei der Anwendung der Vorschriften für staatliche Beihilfen, die es den Mitgliedstaaten ermöglicht, Unternehmen, einschließlich landwirtschaftlicher Betriebe, in Notfällen finanzielle Unterstützung zu gewähren, ohne gegen die EU-Vorschriften für staatliche Beihilfen zu verstoßen[8]. Dies ermöglichte die Gewährung direkter Zuschüsse, Subventionen und Steuererleichterungen für landwirtschaftliche Erzeuger und trug dazu bei, die Agrarwirtschaft zu stabilisieren und Liquiditätsprobleme zu lösen. Der befristete Rahmen ermöglichte es Ungarn beispielsweise, das nationale Programm zur Bewältigung der Nahrungsmittelkrise aufzulegen[9], während Polen Landwirten in gefährdeten Sektoren wie der Milch- und Schweinefleischproduktion direkte Beihilfen gewährte[10].

Darüber hinaus erlaubte die EU vorübergehende Ausnahmen von den Greening-Verpflichtungen und beschleunigte die Auszahlung von Direktzahlungen[11]. Diese Änderungen verbesserten die Liquidität der Landwirte und erleichterten die Nutzung stillgelegter Flächen für die Produktion, wobei letzteres für die Aufrechterhaltung der Produktion in Deutschland und Spanien besonders wichtig war. Eine weitere wichtige finanzielle Unterstützung war die Nutzung der EU-Agrarreserve, die den Mitgliedstaaten zusätzliche Mittel zur Verfügung stellte, um gezielte Hilfe für die von den Marktstörungen am stärksten betroffenen Sektoren zu ermöglichen[12]. Dies ermöglichte sektorspezifische Interventionen, die weitgehend vom EU-Wettbewerbsrecht ausgenommen waren und die Finanzierung von Bei-

---

8 Der Vorübergehende Gemeinschaftsrahmen für staatliche Beihilfen wurde von der Europäischen Kommission im Jahr 2020 eingeführt und auf der Grundlage von Art. 107 Abs. 2 Bst. b und Art. 107 Abs. 3 Bst. b des Vertrags über die Arbeitsweise der Europäischen Union (AEUV) angenommen.

9 Ungarischer Bericht, Autoren: *János Ede Szilágyi/Dávid Hojnyák/Nóra Jakab* (im Folgenden: Ungarischer Bericht), S. 4.

10 Verordnung des Ministers für Landwirtschaft und ländliche Entwicklung vom 24. August 2020 über die detaillierten Bedingungen und das Verfahren für die Gewährung und Auszahlung von Finanzhilfen für Maßnahmen wie „Beihilfen für Landwirte, die von der COVID-19-Krise besonders betroffen sind" im Rahmen der Maßnahme „Befristete Sonderunterstützung für Landwirte, Kleinstunternehmen sowie kleine und mittlere Unternehmen, die von der Krise im Zusammenhang mit COVID-19 besonders betroffen sind", die unter das Programm zur Entwicklung des ländlichen Raums für 2014-2020 fällt, (Journal of Laws of 2020, item 1467).

11 Europäische Kommission, CORONAVIRUS: Notfallmaßnahmen zur Unterstützung des Agrar- und Lebensmittelsektors, Europäische Kommission 2020.

12 Für eine Liste der Verordnungen der Kommission siehe: Amtsblatt der Europäischen Union, L 140 vom 4. Mai 2020.

hilferegelungen für die private Lagerhaltung von Milchprodukten, Fleisch und verderblichen Waren umfassten.

Diese Maßnahmen, die sich an der GAP und anderen EU-Rahmenregelungen orientieren, spielten eine entscheidende Rolle bei der Abmilderung der unmittelbaren Auswirkungen der Krise und zeigten gleichzeitig Bereiche für langfristige Verbesserungen auf. Nicht zuletzt hat die Pandemie gezeigt, wie wichtig eine Koordinierung auf EU-Ebene für die Gewährleistung der Ernährungssicherheit und der Marktstabilität ist. Während die rechtlichen Maßnahmen kurzfristige Störungen wirksam abschwächten, zeigten sie jedoch auch systemische Schwachstellen auf, wie etwa die Notwendigkeit einer gerechteren Verteilung der Hilfe und verbesserter Klimaanpassungsstrategien. So sahen sich beispielsweise Kleinbauern in Polen mit Problemen beim gerechten Zugang zu Beihilfen konfrontiert[13], während der spanische Bericht auf die Notwendigkeit von Strukturreformen hinwies, um die langfristige Klimaresilienz zu verbessern[14]. Darüber hinaus hat der Rückgriff auf befristete Ausnahmeregelungen deutlich gemacht, dass ein robusterer Rahmen für die Bewältigung künftiger Krisen erforderlich ist.

B. Nationale Maßnahmen

Die von den EU-Mitgliedstaaten als Reaktion auf die COVID-19-Pandemie ergriffenen nationalen Maßnahmen waren eine Kombination aus finanzieller Entlastung, Arbeitsmarktanpassungen, Marktstabilisierung und regulatorischer Flexibilität. Die Rechtsgrundlage für diese Maßnahmen war eine Kombination aus EU-Rahmenwerken (GAP, Regeln für staatliche Beihilfen und AEUV-Bestimmungen), nationalen Verfassungsbestimmungen für Notfälle und bestehenden landwirtschaftlichen und sektorspezifischen Rechtsvorschriften. Infolgedessen waren die nationalen Maßnahmen der EU-Mitgliedstaaten zur Gewährleistung der Ernährungssicherheit, zur Stabilisierung der Agrarmärkte und zur Unterstützung gefährdeter Sektoren je nach landwirtschaftlichem Kontext und wirtschaftlichen Prioritäten sehr unterschiedlich.

13 Polnischer Bericht, herausgegeben von *M. Korzycka/P. Wojciechowski* (im Folgenden: Polnischer Bericht), S. 3-4.

14 Spanischer Bericht, Autor: *Teresa Rodríguez-Cachón* (im Folgenden: Spanischer Bericht), S. 2.

Einige Mitgliedstaaten, wie z.B. Österreich, konnten sich weitgehend auf bestehende Rechtsinstrumente stützen, um die Herausforderungen der COVID-19-Pandemie für den Agrarsektor zu bewältigen, indem sie die wichtigsten Rechtsrahmen für das Krisenmanagement und die Lebensmittelversorgungssicherheit aktivierten[15]. Von zentraler Bedeutung war in diesem Zusammenhang beispielsweise die Anwendung des Lebensmittelbewirtschaftungsgesetzes[16], dass die Regulierung der Lebensmittelversorgung in Krisenzeiten regelt und das Bundeslandwirtschaftsministerium ermächtigt, spezifische Verordnungen zur Steuerung der Lebensmittelverteilung und -lagerung in Notfällen zu erlassen. Während der Pandemie diente dieses Gesetz als Grundlage für die Ausarbeitung von Notfallplänen zur Stabilisierung der Märkte im Falle einer Unterbrechung der Versorgungskette, obwohl die formelle Aktivierung dieser Maßnahmen aufgrund der freiwilligen Einhaltung durch den Privatsektor nicht erforderlich war[17]. Darüber hinaus stützte sich die österreichische Reaktion auf das Versorgungssicherungsgesetz[18] um die ununterbrochene Produktion und Versorgung mit lebenswichtigen Gütern, einschließlich landwirtschaftlicher Erzeugnisse, zu gewährleisten, indem den landwirtschaftlichen Erzeugern, insbesondere in Bereichen wie Viehzucht, Weinbau und Gartenbau, wirtschaftliche Erleichterungen gewährt wurden.

Andere Mitgliedstaaten, darunter Polen und Ungarn, stützten sich ebenfalls auf bestehende Notstandsgesetze bzw. Grundgesetzbestimmungen, um auf die Pandemie zu reagieren. Im Falle Polens berief sich die Regierung beispielsweise auf besondere Notstandsbestimmungen, um ihr Programm zur Entwicklung des ländlichen Raums (2014-2020) zu ändern und Unterstützung für polnische Landwirte zu finanzieren[19]. Ungarn hingegen hat im Rahmen seines Grundgesetzes 2020 den „Notstand" ausgerufen, der es der Regierung erlaubt, bestehende Gesetze auszusetzen und Dekrete für den Agrarsektor einzuführen[20]. Auch in Italien und Österreich wurden sektorspezifische Erlasse zur Umsetzung von Finanzhilfen, Arbeitsanpassun-

---

15 Bundes-Krisensicherheitsgesetz (B-KGS), BGBl I Nr. 89/2023.

16 Lebensmittelbewirtschaftungsgesetz (LMBG 1997), BGBl Nr 789/1996 idF BGBl I Nr 113/2016.

17 Österreichischer Bericht, Autor: *David Sams* (im Folgenden: Österreichischer Bericht), S. 6.

18 Versorgungssicherungsgesetz (VerssG 1992), BGBl Nr 380/1992 idF BGBl I Nr 94/2016.

19 Polnischer Bericht, S. 3.

20 Ungarischer Bericht, S. 3.

gen und Steuerbefreiungen erlassen. Dazu gehörte die Verabschiedung des Gesetzesdekrets Nr. 18/2020, das eine Befreiung von der COVID-19-Zertifizierung für landwirtschaftliche Transaktionen und zusätzliche Mittel für Lebensmittelverteilungsprogramme in Italien vorsah[21]. Im Falle Österreichs hat das Bundesministerium für Land- und Forstwirtschaft, Regionen und Wasserwirtschaft (BML) sektorale Verordnungen im Rahmen des Lebensmittel- und des Energiewirtschaftsgesetzes erlassen, um die Lebensmittelversorgungsketten zu sichern und den Landwirten gezielte Beihilfen zu gewähren[22].

Während diese und viele andere nationale Maßnahmen für die Aufrechterhaltung des allgemeinen Funktionierens der landwirtschaftlichen Versorgungsketten verantwortlich gemacht werden können, war der Mangel an demokratischer Mitwirkung durch den Einsatz von Dekreten und Anordnungen der Exekutive ein wichtiges Thema, das in einer Reihe nationaler Berichte angesprochen wurde. Nicht zuletzt war die Ausübung von Exekutivbefugnissen besonders umstritten, wenn diese zur Einschränkung oder Beeinträchtigung grundlegender oder verfassungsmäßiger Rechte genutzt wurden. In den nationalen Berichten und den wissenschaftlichen Arbeiten der Kommission I wurde die Notwendigkeit hervorgehoben, solche Situationen in Zukunft zu vermeiden, indem sowohl auf nationaler als auch auf EU-Ebene umfassendere Rechtsrahmen für die Reaktion auf Krisen entwickelt werden, einschließlich der Ausweitung spezifischer Rechtsinstrumente zur Unterstützung der landwirtschaftlichen Akteure und zur Sicherstellung der Lebensmittelversorgung in Zeiten der Marktvolatilität. In diesem Zusammenhang ist anzumerken, dass Österreich bereits Schritte unternommen hat, um den bestehenden Rechtsrahmen für das Krisenmanagement weiterzuentwickeln, damit auf künftige Krisen wirksamer reagiert werden kann. So trat beispielsweise das Bundes-Krisensicherheitsgesetz 2024 in Kraft und bietet einen umfassenden Rahmen für die Ausrufung von Krisen und die Koordinierung sektorübergreifender Notfallmaßnahmen[23].

---

21 Italienischer Bericht, Autor: *Laura Costantino* (im Folgenden: Italienischer Bericht) S. 1.

22 Österreichischer Bericht, S. 8.

23 Bundes-Krisensicherheitsgesetz (B-KGS), BGBl I Nr. 89/2023.

III. Erholung nach der Pandemie

Im Mai 2020 veröffentlichte die Kommission zwei bahnbrechende Mitteilungen zur Umsetzung der Ziele des europäischen Grünen Deals (GD), die Farm to Fork-Strategie (F2FS)[24] und die Biodiversitätsstrategie 2030 der EU[25]. Diese Texte beinhalten die Ziele, den Einsatz von Pflanzenschutzmitteln bis 2030 um 50 % und den Einsatz von Industriedüngern um 20 % zu reduzieren sowie den ökologischen Landbau auf 25 % der europäischen landwirtschaftlichen Nutzfläche zu erhöhen. Zum Zeitpunkt der Veröffentlichung waren diese Mitteilungen noch nicht Gegenstand von Folgenabschätzungen und wurden in Studien des Wirtschaftsforschungsdienstes des US-Landwirtschaftsministeriums[26] Ende 2020 und 2021, in einer Studie der Gemeinsamen Forschungsstelle der EU-Kommission[27], sowie in akademischen Studien zur globalen Ernährungssicherheit heftig kritisiert[28]. In diesen Studien wird argumentiert, dass die Umsetzung der Ziele der Kommission, die durch die erwartete Verringerung der Treibhausgasemissionen gerechtfertigt sind, eine Verringerung der Produktivität der europäischen Landwirtschaft und folglich einen geringeren Beitrag zur weltweiten Ernährungssicherheit bedeuten würde.

Ungeachtet dieser Kritik hatte die Veröffentlichung des F2FS und der EU-Biodiversitätsstrategie den Effekt, dass sie eine breitere Diskussion über die Notwendigkeit auslöste, die Widerstandsfähigkeit der EU-Landwirtschaft zu verbessern, um künftigen Krisen, einschließlich der zunehmenden Klimakrise, standzuhalten. Während der Erholungsphase nach der Pandemie führten mehrere Mitgliedstaaten nationale Anreize ein, um die Widerstandsfähigkeit ihres Agrarsektors zu stärken. Diese Maßnahmen konzentrierten sich in erster Linie auf Finanzhilfen, Investitionen in die

---

24 Europäische Kommission, „Vom Hof auf den Tisch“ – eine Strategie für ein faires, gesundes und umweltfreundliches Lebensmittelsystem, COM(2020)381. Brüssel, EC.

25 Europäische Kommission, EU-Biodiversitätsstrategie für 2030: Mehr Raum für die Natur in unserem Leben, COM(2020) 380 final.

26 *J. Beckman et al*, ‘Economic and Food Security Impacts of Agricultural Input Reduction Under the European Union Green Deal’s Farm to Fork and Biodiversity Strategies’ (Wirtschaftsforschungsdienst – Landwirtschaftsministerium der Vereinigten Staaten 2020) 30.

27 *J. Hurle Barreiro Hurle et al*, Modelling environmental and climate ambition in the agricultural sector with the CAPRI model (Amt für Veröffentlichungen der Europäischen Union, Luxemburg, 2021).

28 *J. Bremmer et al*, ‘Impact Assessment of EC 2030 Green Deal Targets for Sustainable Crop Production’ (Wirtschaftsforschung Wageningen, 2021) 2021–150.

Nachhaltigkeit, die Stabilisierung der Versorgungskette und Anpassungen auf dem Arbeitsmarkt.

Was die finanzielle Unterstützung des Agrarsektors betrifft, so haben die Mitgliedstaaten zahlreiche Beihilfepakete sowie Maßnahmen zur Förderung von Investitionen zur Modernisierung der landwirtschaftlichen Strukturen verabschiedet. So hat Ungarn im Jahr 2020 ein Agrarinvestitionspaket in Höhe von 80 Mrd. HUF (225 Mio. Euro) zur Modernisierung der Viehzucht und des Gartenbaus eingeführt[29]. Außerdem wurden neue Kreditleitlinien für Landwirte eingeführt, darunter zinslose und zinsgünstige Darlehen zur Förderung von Investitionen in neue Technologien, und das nationale Programm zur Bewältigung von Nahrungsmittelkrisen wurde neu ausgerichtet, wobei der Schwerpunkt von der unmittelbaren Pandemiehilfe auf die langfristige Widerstandsfähigkeit verlagert wurde. In ähnlicher Weise stellte Polen Subventionen für die Mechanisierung der Landwirtschaft und die Präzisionslandwirtschaft bereit, um die Anfälligkeit für externe Schocks zu verringern, sowie Mittel aus dem Entwicklungsprogramm für den ländlichen Raum (2014-2020), um die finanzielle Liquidität der landwirtschaftlichen Betriebe zu stärken[30]. In Italien lag der Schwerpunkt auf der Förderung kollektiver Resilienzstrategien durch eine verstärkte finanzielle Unterstützung von Erzeugerorganisationen und die Einrichtung eines Fonds für Ernährungssouveränität, um die nationale Nahrungsmittelproduktion zu stärken und die Abhängigkeit von Importen zu verringern[31].

Die Initiativen zur Stärkung der Widerstandsfähigkeit der Landwirtschaft konzentrierten sich in der Zeit nach der Pandemie zunehmend auf die Nachhaltigkeit und Klimaresistenz des Agrarsektors. In Frankreich wurde ein vielschichtiger Ansatz entwickelt, um die Widerstandsfähigkeit des Lebensmittelsystems zu stärken und die durch die Pandemie verursachten Schwachstellen zu beseitigen. Vor allem wurden wichtige Initiativen ergriffen, um die Ernährungssouveränität zu stärken und den agrarökologischen Wandel zu unterstützen. Die französischen Maßnahmen konzentrierten sich auf die Verbesserung der einheimischen Nahrungsmittelproduktion, die Verringerung der Importabhängigkeit und die Förderung nachhaltiger landwirtschaftlicher Praktiken. Dazu gehörten verstärkte Investitionen in die lokale Produktion von Obst, Gemüse und Geflügel – Sektoren, die in

29 Ungarischer Bericht, S. 2.

30 Polnischer Bericht, S. 3.

31 Italienischer Bericht, S. 6. Siehe Gesetz Nr. 197 vom 29. Dezember 2022, Art. 1, Abs. 424.

der Vergangenheit unter einer schlechten Handelsbilanz und einer hohen Abhängigkeit von Importen litten – sowie die Ausweitung der Mittel für den agrarökologischen Landbau und die ökologische Produktion, um eine hochwertige lokale Lebensmittelversorgung zu gewährleisten[32]. Es wurden auch Schritte unternommen, um die Abhängigkeit von importierten landwirtschaftlichen Betriebsmitteln (z.B. Düngemittel und Futtermittel) zu verringern, indem lokale Alternativen gefördert und die Forschung im Bereich der Kreislaufwirtschaft ausgebaut wurde. Die französische Regierung hat insbesondere die Notwendigkeit betont, die regenerative Landwirtschaft auszubauen und die Infrastruktur für das Wassermanagement zu verbessern, um auf Klimaschocks wie Dürren vorbereitet zu sein. In ähnlicher Weise hat Spanien seinen GAP-Strategieplan für den Programmplanungszeitraum 2023-2027 angepasst, um Strategien zur Abschwächung von Dürren und eine nachhaltige Wassernutzung in den Vordergrund zu stellen[33], während Deutschland die Subventionen für klimaangepasste landwirtschaftliche Praktiken, insbesondere für die Diversifizierung von Anbaupflanzen und das Bodengesundheitsmanagement, erhöht hat[34].

In der Zeit nach der Pandemie konzentrierten sich einige Mitgliedstaaten auf Arbeitsmarktanpassungen, um ihre Fähigkeit zur Bewältigung künftiger Krisen zu verbessern. In diesem Zusammenhang haben Deutschland und Ungarn nach der Pandemie ihre Maßnahmen zur Flexibilisierung des Arbeitsmarktes ausgeweitet, einschließlich Saisonarbeiterregelungen und finanzieller Anreize für die Beschäftigung in der Landwirtschaft[35]. In beiden Mitgliedstaaten umfasste dies den Ausbau und die Entwicklung digitalisierter Plattformen zur Rekrutierung landwirtschaftlicher Arbeitskräfte, um die Verfügbarkeit von Arbeitskräften zu optimieren[36]. Die Notwendigkeit einer weiteren Digitalisierung und der Einführung neuer Technologien im Agrarsektor war ebenfalls ein zentrales Thema, das in den Diskussionen der Kommission I hervorgehoben wurde, insbesondere in Anbetracht der Tatsache, dass Länder mit einem hohen Digitalisierungsgrad über ein zusätzliches Instrument verfügen, mit dem sie auf die pandemischen Marktkrisen reagieren können.

---

32 Französischer Bericht, Autoren: *Bernard Vallius/ Jean-Baptiste Millard* (im Folgenden: Französischer Bericht) S. 15-16.

33 Spanischer Bericht, S. 6.

34 Deutscher Bericht, Autor: *Anna Kiermeier* (im Folgenden: Deutscher Bericht) S. 11.

35 Deutscher Bericht S. 5; Ungarischer Bericht S. 6.

36 Deutscher Bericht S. 8; Ungarischer Bericht S. 4.

IV. Auswirkungen des Krieges in der Ukraine

Der russische Einmarsch in die Ukraine im Februar 2022 hatte weitreichende Auswirkungen auf den EU-Agrarsektor und verursachte umfangreiche Unterbrechungen bei der Versorgung mit Düngemitteln, Futtermitteln und Getreideeinfuhren[37]. Die Lebensmittelpreise wurden insbesondere durch die russische Blockade der ukrainischen Getreideexporte und die Schließung der Schwarzmeerhäfen in die Höhe getrieben, was zu Versorgungsengpässen und Preisschwankungen auf den Weltmärkten führte[38]. Dies führte zu den höchsten Preissteigerungen bei Lebensmitteln weltweit seit Jahrzehnten, was Befürchtungen über eine weit verbreitete Ernährungsunsicherheit aufkommen ließ und die internationalen Organisationen und Institutionen zu sofortigen Reaktionen veranlasste. Insbesondere die FAO[39] forderte die nahrungsmittelexportierenden Länder wiederholt auf, protektionistische Maßnahmen wie Exportverbote und andere Marktbeschränkungen zu vermeiden, um die kontinuierliche Versorgung der importabhängigen Länder mit Agrarrohstoffen zu gewährleisten. Dies wurde auch von der EU-Kommission in ihrer Mitteilung vom 23. März 2022 hervorgehoben, in der sie auf die dringende Notwendigkeit hinwies, die Agrarmärkte zu stabilisieren und das wachsende Ausmaß an zugangsbedingter Ernährungsunsicherheit in Europa und darüber hinaus anzugehen[40].

A. Reaktionen der EU und der Mitgliedstaaten auf die Marktvolatilität im Agrarsektor

Die EU reagierte darauf, indem sie im April 2022 die Agrarkrisenreserve (ACR) aktivierte und den Mitgliedstaaten 500 Millionen Euro zur Verfügung stellte, um den von der Krise am stärksten betroffenen Sektoren und Landwirten direkte Finanzhilfe zu gewähren, um die gestiegenen Inputkos-

37 *N. Jia et al*, 'The Russia-Ukraine war reduced food production and exports with a disparate geographical impact worldwide' (2024) 5 Commun Earth Environ 765.

38 Europäische Parlamentarische Forschungsdienste, Russlands Krieg gegen die Ukraine: Auswirkungen auf die EU-Lebensmittelpolitik, Europäische Union 2022.

39 Welternährungsorganisation, Auswirkungen des Ukraine-Russland-Konflikts auf die weltweite Ernährungssicherheit und damit zusammenhängende Fragen im Rahmen des Mandats der Ernährungs- und Landwirtschaftsorganisation der Vereinten Nationen (Rom, FAO 2022).

40 Europäische Kommission, Gewährleistung der Ernährungssicherheit und Stärkung der Widerstandsfähigkeit der Lebensmittelsysteme, COM(2022) 133 final.

ten auszugleichen[41]. Damit wurde den EU-Mitgliedstaaten, die die Soforthilfe für gezielte Maßnahmen zur Minderung der unmittelbaren Risiken der Krise nutzen konnten, entscheidende Hilfe geleistet. In Polen beispielsweise leitete die Regierung Mittel zur Unterstützung des Tierhaltungssektors sowie der Getreide- und Ölsaatenerzeuger ein, die von der Marktinstabilität aufgrund eines Überangebots an ukrainischen Importen betroffen waren[42]. Diese finanzielle Unterstützung half den polnischen Landwirten bei der Bewirtschaftung von Überschusslagern und der Aufrechterhaltung der Liquidität in einer Zeit sinkender Preise[43]. Auch Spanien stellte seine ACR-Mittel zur Unterstützung der Viehzüchter zur Verfügung, insbesondere im Milch- und Fleischsektor, wo die steigenden Kosten für Futtermittel und Treibstoff zu einem erheblichen finanziellen Druck führten[44]. Die Direktbeihilfen ermöglichten es den Landwirten, die Produktion trotz des Kostenanstiegs fortzusetzen.

In Österreich wurde ein hektarbezogenes Zahlungssystem eingeführt, um die Beihilfen proportional zu den betroffenen landwirtschaftlichen Flächen zu verteilen, wobei die Maßnahmen insbesondere darauf abzielen, den Gartenbau (z.B. Gewächshausbetriebe) und die Geflügelproduktion vor steigenden Kosten und Unterbrechungen der Lieferkette zu schützen[45]. Die hohen Betriebsmittelkosten machten sich auch bei den Getreide- und Ölsaatenerzeugern in Deutschland bemerkbar, was die Regierung veranlasste, diesen Sektoren vorrangig Beihilfen zu gewähren und Maßnahmen einzuführen, die es den Landwirten vorübergehend ermöglichten, stillgelegte Flächen für die Erzeugung zu nutzen[46]. Zu den weiteren Verwendungszwecken der ACR-Mittel gehören Maßnahmen, die in Ungarn ergriffen wurden, um die Kosten grundlegender landwirtschaftlicher Tätigkeiten zu stabilisieren, z.B. Wassermanagement und Transport für von der Dürre betroffene Regionen. Letztlich halfen diese Maßnahmen den Landwirten, die Transportkosten zu decken und das Produktionsniveau trotz klimatischer und geopolitischer Störungen aufrechtzuerhalten[47].

41 Das ACR, das aus nicht genutzten GAP-Mitteln finanziert wird, soll bei außergewöhnlichen Marktstörungen finanzielle Soforthilfe leisten und wurde offiziell im Programmplanungszeitraum 2014-2020 eingerichtet.

42 Polnischer Bericht, S. 7-8.

43 Polnischer Bericht, S. 5.

44 Spanischer Bericht, S. 4

45 Österreichischer Bericht, S. 16.

46 Deutscher Bericht, S. 11.

47 Ungarischer Bericht, S. 5.

Als Reaktion auf die kriegsbedingte Marktvolatilität erweiterte die Europäische Kommission auch den befristeten Krisenrahmen für staatliche Beihilfen, der bereits während der Pandemie eingeführt worden war und es den Mitgliedstaaten ermöglichte, Landwirte und Lebensmittelproduzenten zu unterstützen, die aufgrund der hohen Inputpreise in finanzielle Schwierigkeiten geraten waren. In Italien und Ungarn wurde diese Flexibilität genutzt, um Steuerbefreiungen und direkte Subventionen zu gewähren, um die Liquidität kleiner und mittlerer landwirtschaftlicher Betriebe zu sichern[48], während Polen finanzielle Unterstützung für die Lagerung und den Verkauf von überschüssigem Getreide anbot, nachdem es durch den Zustrom ukrainischen Getreides zu massiven Störungen gekommen war[49].

Eine weitere wichtige Maßnahme, die die EU als Reaktion auf die Handelsunterbrechungen Anfang 2022 ergriffen hat, betrifft die Lockerung der GAP-Umwelt- und Landmanagementstandards. Konkret wurde den Mitgliedstaaten mit dem Durchführungsbeschluss (EU) 2022/484 der Kommission die Möglichkeit eingeräumt, für das Zahlungsjahr 2022 befristete Ausnahmen von der Verpflichtung zur Erhaltung von ökologischen Schwerpunktflächen (EFA), d.h. von Flächen, die gemäß der Verordnung (EU) 1307/2013 zur Förderung der biologischen Vielfalt stillgelegt wurden, einzuführen. Darüber hinaus sah die Durchführungsverordnung (EU) 2022/1317 der Kommission für das Antragsjahr 2023 zusätzliche Ausnahmen hinsichtlich der Anwendung der Standards für den guten landwirtschaftlichen und ökologischen Zustand der Flächen (GLÖZ-Standards) 7 und 8 vor. Der Zweck dieser Maßnahmen bestand ausdrücklich darin, die landwirtschaftliche Produktion zu steigern und Engpässe in der EU zu lindern, indem den Landwirten gestattet wurde, stillgelegte Flächen für die Erzeugung von Lebens- und Futtermitteln zu nutzen[50]. Einige Mitgliedstaaten, darunter Österreich, Deutschland und Spanien, entschieden sich für eine vorübergehende Ausweitung der landwirtschaftlichen Produktion, insbesondere bei Getreide, während Frankreich in der Lage war, die Produktivität beizubehalten und gleichzeitig nachhaltige Praktiken zu fördern.

Während die erneute Betonung der Ernährungssicherheit nach der Invasion in der Ukraine von den Delegierten der Kommission I allgemein befürwortet wurde, stieß die Konzentration der EU auf die Steigerung der Produktivität durch die Aussetzung von Umweltstandards für den Agrar-

48 Italienischer Bericht, S. 5; Ungarischer Bericht, S. 2.

49 Polnischer Bericht, S. 4.

50 Siehe Präambel, Durchführungsbeschluss (EU) 2022/484 der Kommission.

sektor auf erhebliche Skepsis. Nicht zuletzt wurden Bedenken geäußert, wie sich die Inanspruchnahme von Ausnahmeregelungen auf die Fähigkeit des Blocks auswirken würde, die langfristigen Nachhaltigkeitsziele im Rahmen des GD zu erreichen, da noch erhebliche Maßnahmen ergriffen werden müssen, um die in der F2FS- und Biodiversitätsstrategie festgelegten Ziele zu erreichen. Darüber hinaus wurde in den Diskussionen in der Kommission I die Notwendigkeit hervorgehoben, zu berücksichtigen, wie sich die Umsetzung der GD-Ziele auf die Ernährungssicherheit auf globaler Ebene auswirken würde. So könnten beispielsweise Maßnahmen zur Verringerung des Pestizideinsatzes Auswirkungen auf Exportländer wie Kolumbien haben, wenn EU-Standards für Drittlandimporte vorgeschrieben werden. Letztendlich muss die EU entschlossener handeln, um sicherzustellen, dass die Umsetzung ihrer langfristigen Umweltziele nicht die globale Ernährungssicherheit beeinträchtigt oder die Fähigkeit der exportierenden Entwicklungsländer, Zugang zum Binnenmarkt zu erhalten, unnötig behindert.

B. Spezifische Auswirkungen auf die EU-Grenzstaaten

Im Mai 2022 führte die EU die sog. Solidaritätskorridore ein, die die zollfreie Einfuhr ukrainischer Agrarerzeugnisse ermöglichen, um logistische Engpässe aufgrund von Hafenschließungen zu verringern und den Transport ukrainischer Agrarerzeugnisse, insbesondere von Getreide, auf den Weltmarkt zu erleichtern. Dies ist Teil einer umfassenderen Strategie, die darauf abzielt, die weltweiten Risiken für die Ernährungssicherheit zu verringern und die ukrainische Wirtschaft zu unterstützen[51]. Der Mechanismus ermöglichte ukrainische Exporte über alternative Routen durch die EU-Mitgliedstaaten auf Straße, Schiene und Binnenwasserstraßen und trug dazu bei, katastrophale Störungen auf den globalen Getreidemärkten zu vermeiden, indem die Handelsströme aus der Ukraine aufrechterhalten wurden. Der Zustrom ukrainischen Getreides über diese Solidaritätskorridore führte jedoch zu Marktungleichgewichten, insbesondere in angrenzenden Ländern wie der Slowakei, Ungarn, Rumänien und Polen, wo ukrainisches Getreide, das ursprünglich für den Export in andere Regionen

51 Europäische Kommission, Ein Aktionsplan für Solidaritätskorridore zwischen der EU und der Ukraine zur Erleichterung der Agrarexporte der Ukraine und ihres bilateralen Handels mit der EU, COM(2022) 217 final.

bestimmt war, im Inland verkauft wurde, was zu einem Überangebot und einem erheblichen Rückgang der lokalen Preise führte[52].

Trotz massiver Proteste der Landwirte in den Grenzländern und umfangreicher Bemühungen der dortigen Regierungen, die durch den Zustrom billigen ukrainischen Getreides entstandene Situation zu entschärfen, war die Europäische Kommission kaum bereit, den Rahmen und die Bedingungen für die zollfreie Einfuhr ukrainischen Getreides zu ändern[53]. Dies führte schließlich zu einer unhaltbaren Situation, die den Mitgliedstaaten, darunter Polen und Ungarn, keine andere Wahl ließ, als im April 2023 vorübergehende Einfuhrverbote für ukrainische Agrarerzeugnisse zu verhängen, obwohl diese Waren weiterhin durch ihr Hoheitsgebiet transportiert wurden[54]. Daraufhin führte die EU im Mai 2023 vorübergehende Beschränkungen ein, die es Polen, Bulgarien, Ungarn, Rumänien und der Slowakei erlaubten, den Inlandsverkauf von ukrainischem Weizen, Mais, Raps und Sonnenblumenkernen zu verbieten, während sie die Durchfuhr auf andere Märkte erlaubten[55]. Ungeachtet der Versuche der Kommission, die Märkte zu stabilisieren, machte die Situation die Spannungen zwischen der EU-weiten Solidaritätspolitik und den nationalen wirtschaftlichen Prioritäten deutlich, da die Regierungen die Unterstützung für die Ukraine mit der Notwendigkeit des Schutzes ihres heimischen Agrarsektors in Einklang bringen mussten. Mit Blick auf die Zukunft besteht die Gefahr, dass fortgesetzte unilaterale Maßnahmen eine einheitliche Reaktion der EU auf den Krieg untergraben und wahrscheinlich zu einer weiteren Fragmentierung innerhalb des Blocks führen, was von den nationalen Berichterstattern in Kommission I als wichtiges Thema angesprochen wurde.

V. Klimawandel und Landwirtschaft

Neben der durch die Pandemie und den anschließenden Krieg in der Ukraine verursachten Marktvolatilität waren die EU-Mitgliedstaaten in den letzten Jahren zunehmend mit schweren Klima- und Wetterereignissen konfrontiert, darunter Dürren, Überschwemmungen, Stürme und extreme

52 Ibid.
53 Ungarischer Bericht, S. 15.
54 Ungarischer Bericht, S. 15; Polnischer Bericht, S. 7.
55 Durchführungsverordnung (EU) 2023/903 der Kommission vom 2. Mai 2023 zur Einführung von Präventivmaßnahmen für bestimmte Waren mit Ursprung in der Ukraine.

Temperaturschwankungen. Diese Ereignisse haben die landwirtschaftliche Produktion gestört, die Ernteerträge verringert und zu wirtschaftlicher Instabilität in ländlichen Gebieten geführt. In Spanien zum Beispiel hat die anhaltende Dürre einen großen Teil der landwirtschaftlichen Flächen des Landes in Mitleidenschaft gezogen und damit Probleme wie Wüstenbildung und eine geringere Wasserverfügbarkeit in den letzten Jahren noch verschärft[56]. Dies veranlasste die spanische Regierung, Strategien zur Abschwächung der Dürre in ihren GAP-Strategieplan 2023-2027 aufzunehmen, die sich auf die Förderung solarbetriebener Bewässerung und nachhaltiger Wassermanagementpraktiken konzentrieren[57]. Wasserknappheit beeinträchtigte auch die landwirtschaftlichen Betriebe in Italien, während in Ungarn im Jahr 2022 eine der schwersten Dürren herrschte, die die Mais- und Weizenernte auf einer Million Hektar vernichtete[58]. Daraufhin erklärte die ungarische Regierung den Gefahrenzustand und ergriff Maßnahmen wie Zinszuschüsse für Landwirte, ein Moratorium für die Rückzahlung von Krediten und subventionierte Futtermitteltransporte[59]. In der Folge hat sie auch ein System zur Stabilisierung der landwirtschaftlichen Einkommen eingeführt, um die Landwirte vor extremen Einkommensschwankungen aufgrund von klimabedingten Schocks zu schützen[60].

Am anderen Ende des Spektrums gab es in mehreren Mitgliedstaaten ausgedehnte Überschwemmungen und Stürme, die Bodenerosion verursachten, Ernten zerstörten und die Lebensmittelversorgungsketten unterbrachen. In Österreich beispielsweise war der Agrarsektor, insbesondere in Bergregionen, in den letzten Jahren wiederholt mit sturmbedingten Schäden konfrontiert, was zur Annahme neuer Risikobewertungsmaßnahmen zur Verbesserung der Katastrophenvorsorge und zu finanziellen Unterstützungsprogrammen für betroffene Landwirte führte[61]. Ebenso haben Überschwemmungen in Frankreich zu Investitionen in eine bessere Wasserbewirtschaftungsinfrastruktur und zur Förderung agrarökologischer Praktiken geführt, um die Widerstandsfähigkeit der Böden zu erhöhen und das Überschwemmungsrisiko zu verringern. Die Regierung hat auch die

56 Spanischer Bericht, S. 6.

57 Um Zugang zu allen Änderungen des spanischen GAP-Strategieplans für den Programmplanungszeitraum 2023-2027 zu erhalten, siehe: https://n9.cl/ye7p6v.

58 Ungarischer Bericht, S. 5.

59 Ibid.

60 Ibid. S. 6.

61 Österreichischer Bericht, S. 21.

Maßnahmen zur Klimaanpassung im Rahmen ihres GAP-Strategieplans verstärkt.

Darüber hinaus haben extreme Hitze und Temperaturschwankungen sowohl die pflanzliche als auch die tierische Erzeugung beeinträchtigt, indem sie die Kulturen belasteten und die Erträge verringerten, insbesondere in Süd- und Mitteleuropa. In Italien haben steigende Temperaturen die Produktivität wichtiger Kulturen wie Weintrauben und Oliven verringert, was 2023 zu erheblichen Preissteigerungen bei Olivenöl führen wird[62]. Um die betroffenen Landwirte zu unterstützen, hat die italienische Regierung im Rahmen des Plans zum Risikomanagement in der Landwirtschaft Subventionen für Versicherungen eingeführt, um die Landwirte zu ermutigen, sich gegen extreme Wetterereignisse zu versichern[63]. Extreme Wetterereignisse haben auch zu erheblichen Ertragseinbußen bei Getreide und Futterpflanzen in Deutschland geführt. Um den hohen Hitzestress, der in den kommenden Jahren noch zunehmen dürfte, abzumildern, hat die deutsche Regierung Maßnahmen zur Förderung von Innovationen und der Einführung digitaler Landwirtschaftstechnologien beschlossen[64].

In den nationalen Berichten wurde hervorgehoben, dass eine Reihe von Mitgliedstaaten sowohl durch EU- als auch durch nationale Initiativen die Klimaresilienz zunehmend in die langfristigen Strategien für die Landwirtschaft einbeziehen. Ein zentrales Thema, das in der Kommission I angesprochen wurde, ist jedoch die Notwendigkeit, den Klimawandel als anhaltende Krise anzugehen und die wachsenden Herausforderungen auf ganzheitlichere und kohärentere Weise anzugehen. In den Diskussionen wurde insbesondere die Notwendigkeit hervorgehoben, engere Verbindungen zwischen den EU-Rahmenbedingungen und -Zielen einerseits und den nationalen Rechtsvorschriften andererseits herzustellen. Dazu gehört auch die Ausweitung der landwirtschaftlichen Versicherungssysteme, die sich zunehmend auf die Risikominderung und nicht nur auf das Risikomanagement konzentrieren. Der spanische Nationale Bericht betont insbesondere die dringende Notwendigkeit, die rechtlichen Rahmenbedingungen für Frühwarnsysteme für Landwirte, die von Natur- oder Klimakatastrophen betroffen sind, zu verbessern, um wirtschaftliche Verluste zu mini-

---

62 Eurostat, Preis für Olivenöl innerhalb eines Jahres um 50 % gestiegen (Nachrichtenartikel vom 27. Februar 2024); https://ec.europa.eu/eurostat/web/products-eurostat-news/w/ddn-20240227-1?utm_source=chatgpt.com.

63 Italienischer Bericht, S. 9. Siehe Ministerialerlass Nr. 64591 vom 8.2.2023 (später geändert durch Ministerialerlass Nr. 31.5.2023).

64 Deutscher Bericht, S. 16.

mieren. Während es den derzeitigen rechtlichen Rahmenbedingungen oft an Instrumenten und Koordination fehlt, um Landwirte mit wichtigen Informationen zu versorgen, die zur Begrenzung der Auswirkungen von Naturkatastrophen genutzt werden können, könnte die Entwicklung von Notfallwarnsystemen und die Integration und Bereitstellung von Informationen für Landwirte zum frühestmöglichen Zeitpunkt dazu beitragen, diese Risiken zu verringern und die Existenzgrundlagen zu schützen.

Conclusions de la Commission I –
Conclusions of Commission I –
Schlussfolgerungen der Kommission I

Version française – French version – Französische Version
Version anglaise – English version – Englische Version
Version allemande – German version – Deutsche Version

Conclusions de la Commission I – Conclusions of Commission I – Schlussfolgerungen der Kommission I

A. Version française – French version – Französische Version

Les secteurs agricoles des États membres de l'UE ont été fortement touchés par une convergence de crises, notamment la pandémie de COVID-19, la guerre en Ukraine et des phénomènes climatiques de plus en plus graves. Ces crises ont révélé des vulnérabilités dans les chaînes d'approvisionnement agricole, la disponibilité des intrants et la sécurité alimentaire, suscitant des réponses juridiques et politiques tant au niveau de l'UE qu'au niveau national. Si ces mesures ont apporté un soutien essentiel et une stabilité à court terme, elles ont également mis en évidence des lacunes systémiques et la nécessité de mettre en place des stratégies de résilience globales et à long terme.

La pandémie de COVID-19 a perturbé la disponibilité de la main-d'œuvre, les chaînes d'approvisionnement et l'accès au marché, entraînant une instabilité financière dans les exploitations agricoles. En réponse, l'UE a introduit des mesures telles que l'initiative des « voies vertes », qui a réduit les retards de transport, et le cadre temporaire pour les aides d'État, qui permet aux États membres de fournir un soutien financier d'urgence. Plusieurs États membres, dont la Hongrie et la Pologne, ont lancé des programmes ciblés pour garantir des liquidités aux agriculteurs. Toutefois, ces mesures ont mis en évidence des disparités dans l'accès des petits agriculteurs à l'aide et ont démontré la nécessité de mettre en place des mécanismes de soutien plus équitables et plus souples. En outre, les dérogations temporaires à la PAC ont mis en évidence l'absence d'un cadre juridique unifié permettant de gérer efficacement les crises futures.

Au cours de la période de reprise post-pandémique, les initiatives de l'UE telles que le F2FS et la stratégie en faveur de la biodiversité ont accéléré le passage à la durabilité et à l'adaptation au climat, les États membres adoptant diverses mesures nationales pour renforcer la résilience de leurs secteurs agricoles. Par exemple, la Hongrie a mis en œuvre un programme d'investissement agricole de 225 millions d'euros pour moderniser les infrastructures agricoles, tandis que la France s'est concentrée sur la souveraineté alimentaire en soutenant la production locale et les transitions agroécologiques. Néanmoins, des tensions sont apparues entre les objectifs environnementaux de l'UE et les préoccupations des agriculteurs en matière de productivité et de compétitivité, certaines parties prenantes mettant en garde contre les politiques susceptibles de compromettre la sécurité alimentaire mondiale.

L'invasion de l'Ukraine par la Russie en 2022 a entraîné une volatilité accrue du marché, notamment en raison des perturbations des importations d'engrais, d'aliments pour animaux et de céréales. L'UE a activé l'ECA pour fournir une aide financière directe de 500 millions d'euros aux secteurs touchés. Des pays comme la Pologne, l'Espagne et l'Autriche ont utilisé ces fonds pour soutenir les éleveurs et les producteurs agricoles confrontés à la flambée des coûts des intrants. Cependant, l'introduction par l'UE des « corridors de solidarité », qui permettent aux exportations agricoles ukrainiennes de passer par les pays frontaliers, a entraîné des déséquilibres sur le marché. Les agriculteurs polonais et hongrois ont été confrontés à une offre excédentaire et à une chute des prix, ce qui a entraîné des interdictions nationales temporaires d'importation et a mis en évidence les tensions entre les politiques de solidarité de l'UE et les priorités économiques nationales.

La crise climatique a encore aggravé les défis pour l'agriculture, les États membres connaissant des sécheresses extrêmes, des inondations, des tempêtes et des vagues de chaleur. En Espagne et en Hongrie, une sécheresse persistante a dévasté les rendements agricoles, ce qui a incité à investir dans des stratégies d'atténuation de la sécheresse et des systèmes de stabilisation des revenus agricoles. En Italie et en Allemagne, les gouvernements ont encouragé la diversification des cultures, les subventions aux assurances et les technologies agricoles numériques pour faire face aux effets des conditions météorologiques extrêmes. Toutefois, ces efforts restent fragmentés, et il est de plus en plus admis qu'une coordination à l'échelle de l'UE et une amélioration des cadres juridiques sont nécessaires pour renforcer les systèmes d'alerte précoce et la gestion des risques.

Dans l'ensemble, les crises de ces dernières années ont renforcé la nécessité de mettre en place des cadres nationaux et européens capables d'équilibrer efficacement la productivité, la durabilité et la résilience de l'agriculture. L'extension des mesures d'adaptation au climat, le renforcement des régimes d'assurance agricole et l'amélioration de l'intégration du système alimentaire seront essentiels pour protéger le secteur agricole européen contre les chocs futurs. En outre, l'alignement des objectifs de l'UE sur les priorités nationales, en particulier par le biais de la PAC et des initiatives de développement durable, est essentiel pour garantir la stabilité et la compétitivité à long terme face aux défis mondiaux actuels.

B. Version anglaise - English version - Englische Version

The agricultural sectors of EU Member States have been significantly affected by a convergence of crises, including the COVID-19 pandemic, the war in Ukraine, and increasingly severe climatic events. These crises have revealed vulnerabilities in agricultural supply chains, input availability, and food security, prompting legal and policy responses both at the EU and national levels. While these measures have provided critical support and short-term stability, they have also highlighted systemic gaps and the need for comprehensive, long-term resilience strategies.

The COVID-19 pandemic disrupted labour availability, supply chains, and market access, leading to financial instability in farming operations. In response, the EU introduced measures such as the Green Lanes Initiative, which minimized transport delays, and the temporary state aid framework, enabling MSs to provide emergency financial support. Several MSs, including Hungary and Poland, launched targeted programs to ensure liquidity for farmers. However, these measures underscored disparities in how small-scale farmers accessed aid and demonstrated the need for more equitable and flexible support mechanisms. Additionally, temporary CAP derogations highlighted the lack of a unified legal framework to manage future crises effectively.

In the post-pandemic recovery period, EU initiatives such as the F2FS and Biodiversity Strategy accelerated a shift towards sustainability and climate adaptation, with MSs adopting diverse national measures to strengthen the resilience of their agricultural sectors. For instance, Hungary implemented a €225 million agricultural investment package to modernize farming infrastructure, while France focused on food sovereignty by supporting local production and agroecological transitions. Nevertheless, tensions arose between EU environmental targets and farmers' concerns about productivity and competitiveness, with some stakeholders cautioning against policies that might undermine global food security.

The Russian invasion of Ukraine in 2022 led to heightened market volatility, particularly due to disruptions in fertilizer, feed, and grain imports. The EU activated the ACR to provide 500 million Euro in direct financial aid to affected sectors. Countries like Poland, Spain, and Austria used these funds to support livestock and crop producers facing soaring input costs. However, the EU's introduction of Solidarity Lanes – allowing Ukrainian agricultural exports through bordering countries – resulted in market imbalances. Farmers in Poland and Hungary faced oversupply and price drops, prompting temporary national import bans and exposing tensions between EU-wide solidarity policies and domestic economic priorities.

The climate crisis has further compounded challenges for agriculture, with MSs experiencing extreme droughts, floods, storms, and heatwaves. In Spain and Hungary, persistent drought has devastated crop yields, prompting investments in drought mitigation strategies and agricultural income stabilization systems. In Italy and Germany, governments promoted crop diversification, insurance subsidies, and digital farming technologies to address extreme weather impacts. However, these efforts remain fragmented, with a growing consensus that EU-wide coordination and improved legal frameworks are needed to enhance early-warning systems and risk management.

Overall, the crises of recent years have reinforced the need for both national and EU-level frameworks that can effectively balance productivity, sustainability, and resilience in agriculture. Expanding climate adaptation measures, enhancing agricultural insurance schemes, and improving food system integration will be crucial in safeguarding Europe's agricultural sector against future shocks. Furthermore, the alignment of EU objectives with national priorities, particularly through the CAP and GD initiatives, is essential to ensure long-term stability and competitiveness in the face of ongoing global challenges.

C. Version allemande – German version – Deutsche Version

Die Landwirtschaftssektoren der EU-Mitgliedstaaten wurden durch eine Reihe von Krisen, darunter die COVID-19-Pandemie, der Krieg in der Ukraine und zunehmend schwerwiegende klimatische Ereignisse, erheblich beeinträchtigt. Diese Krisen haben Schwachstellen in den landwirtschaftlichen Versorgungsketten, der Verfügbarkeit von Betriebsmitteln und der Ernährungssicherheit aufgezeigt und rechtliche und politische Maßnahmen sowohl auf EU-Ebene als auch auf nationaler Ebene erforderlich gemacht. Diese Maßnahmen haben zwar wichtige Unterstützung und kurzfristige

Stabilität gebracht, aber auch systemische Lücken und die Notwendigkeit umfassender, langfristiger Resilienzstrategien aufgezeigt.

Durch die COVID-19-Pandemie wurden die Verfügbarkeit von Arbeitskräften, die Lieferketten und der Marktzugang unterbrochen, was zu einer finanziellen Instabilität der landwirtschaftlichen Betriebe führte. Als Reaktion darauf führte die EU Maßnahmen wie die Green-Lanes-Initiative ein, die Transportverzögerungen minimierte, sowie den befristeten Rahmen für staatliche Beihilfen, der es den Mitgliedstaaten ermöglichte, finanzielle Soforthilfe zu leisten. Mehrere Mitgliedstaaten, darunter Ungarn und Polen, legten gezielte Programme auf, um die Liquidität der Landwirte zu sichern. Diese Maßnahmen machten jedoch deutlich, dass Kleinbauern in unterschiedlichem Maße Zugang zu Beihilfen haben und dass gerechtere und flexiblere Unterstützungsmechanismen erforderlich sind. Darüber hinaus machten die vorübergehenden Ausnahmeregelungen für die GAP deutlich, dass ein einheitlicher Rechtsrahmen fehlt, um künftige Krisen wirksam zu bewältigen.

In der Zeit nach der Pandemie beschleunigten EU-Initiativen wie die F2FS- und die Biodiversitätsstrategie den Wandel hin zu Nachhaltigkeit und Klimaanpassung, wobei die Mitgliedstaaten verschiedene nationale Maßnahmen ergriffen, um die Widerstandsfähigkeit ihres Agrarsektors zu stärken. So hat Ungarn beispielsweise ein mit 225 Millionen Euro dotiertes Agrarinvestitionspaket zur Modernisierung der landwirtschaftlichen Infrastruktur umgesetzt, während Frankreich sich auf die Ernährungssouveränität konzentriert, indem es die lokale Produktion und die agrarökologische Umstellung unterstützt. Dennoch kam es zu Spannungen zwischen den Umweltzielen der EU und den Bedenken der Landwirte in Bezug auf Produktivität und Wettbewerbsfähigkeit, wobei einige Interessengruppen vor Maßnahmen warnten, die die globale Ernährungssicherheit untergraben könnten.

Der russische Einmarsch in die Ukraine im Jahr 2022 führte zu einer erhöhten Marktvolatilität, insbesondere aufgrund von Unterbrechungen bei Düngemittel-, Futtermittel- und Getreideimporten. Die EU aktivierte die ACR, um 500 Millionen Euro an direkter Finanzhilfe für die betroffenen Sektoren bereitzustellen. Länder wie Polen, Spanien und Österreich nutzten diese Mittel, um Vieh- und Getreideerzeuger zu unterstützen, die mit steigenden Inputkosten zu kämpfen haben. Die Einführung der Solidaritätskorridore durch die EU – die ukrainische Agrarexporte durch die Nachbarländer ermöglichen – führte jedoch zu Marktungleichgewichten. Die Landwirte in Polen und Ungarn sahen sich mit einem Überangebot und

Preisverfall konfrontiert, was zu vorübergehenden nationalen Einfuhrverboten führte und Spannungen zwischen der EU-weiten Solidaritätspolitik und den Prioritäten der heimischen Wirtschaft offenlegte.

Die Klimakrise hat die Herausforderungen für die Landwirtschaft weiter verschärft, da die Mitgliedstaaten von extremen Dürren, Überschwemmungen, Stürmen und Hitzewellen betroffen sind. In Spanien und Ungarn hat die anhaltende Dürre die Ernteerträge zerstört, was zu Investitionen in Strategien zur Eindämmung der Dürre und in Systeme zur Stabilisierung der landwirtschaftlichen Einkommen führte. In Italien und Deutschland förderten die Regierungen die Diversifizierung von Anbauprodukten, Versicherungssubventionen und digitale Landwirtschaftstechnologien, um den Auswirkungen extremer Wetterbedingungen zu begegnen. Diese Bemühungen sind jedoch nach wie vor fragmentiert, und es besteht ein wachsender Konsens darüber, dass eine EU-weite Koordinierung und ein verbesserter Rechtsrahmen erforderlich sind, um Frühwarnsysteme und Risikomanagement zu verbessern.

Insgesamt haben die Krisen der letzten Jahre die Notwendigkeit sowohl nationaler als auch EU-weiter Rahmenbedingungen verstärkt, die ein effektives Gleichgewicht zwischen Produktivität, Nachhaltigkeit und Widerstandsfähigkeit in der Landwirtschaft herstellen können. Die Ausweitung von Klimaanpassungsmaßnahmen, die Verbesserung von landwirtschaftlichen Versicherungssystemen und die Verbesserung der Integration des Lebensmittelsystems werden entscheidend sein, um den europäischen Agrarsektor vor zukünftigen Schocks zu schützen. Darüber hinaus ist die Angleichung der EU-Ziele an die nationalen Prioritäten, insbesondere durch die GAP und die GD-Initiativen, von entscheidender Bedeutung, um angesichts der aktuellen globalen Herausforderungen langfristige Stabilität und Wettbewerbsfähigkeit zu gewährleisten.

III.
Commission II - Kommission II

President:

Alex Carson-Taylor,
Agricultural Law Association (United Kingdom)

General Reporter:

Catherine Taskis KC,
Falcon Chambers (United Kingdom)

Carbone, biodiversité et nutriments : nouvelles considérations sur l'utilisation des terres

Carbon, biodiversity and nutrients: new land use considerations

Kohlenstoff, Biodiversität und Nährstoffe: neue Überlegungen zur Landnutzung

Questionnaires – Fragebogen – Commission II – Kommission II

Version française – French version – Französische Version
Version anglaise – English version – Englische Version
Version allemande – German version – Deutsche Version

Questionnaire de la Commission II – Questionnaire of Commission II – Fragebogen der Kommission II

Questions – Fragen

A. Version française – French version – Französische Version

1. Caractériser la situation actuelle de votre pays par rapport à l'urgence du changement climatique, y compris les objectifs, les mécanismes et les politiques qui ont été développés dans votre pays pour permettre de faire face à la crise liée au changement climatique, en mettant l'accent sur ceux qui relèvent de l'agriculture. Pensez à inclure :
   - 1.1. Le statut de l'urgence climatique dans la législation et la politique, objectifs et cibles fixés et échéances.
   - 1.2. Les organismes et organisations chargées d'atteindre les objectifs et cibles susmentionnés – quels sont les mécanismes de contrôle et d'application mis en place ? Quelles sont les conséquences de la non-conformité ? Quel est le rôle des différents régulateurs environnementaux de votre pays à cet égard et comment travaillent-ils avec les agriculteurs ?
   - 1.3. Les instruments spéciaux pour la protection et l'amélioration du carbone, de la biodiversité, de l'eau, des sols, etc. Il peut s'agir d'une discussion sur les servitudes, les clauses restrictives ou les restrictions sur les titres de propriété, les contrats ou les accords de gestion.
   - 1.4. Le champ d'application des plans d'occupation des sols (pour l'ensemble du territoire ou seulement certaines zones). Les mécanismes juridiques visant à limiter les changements d'affectation des terres agricoles à des fins non liées à l'agriculture, y compris ceux visant à mettre en œuvre les accords et obligations internationaux tels que la convention-cadre des Nations unies sur les changements climatiques et le protocole de Kyoto, ainsi que les activités du groupe de travail sur l'utilisation des terres, le changement d'affectation des terres et la foresterie (UTCATF).

2. Caractériser la propriété du capital naturel en droit :
   2.1. Qui est propriétaire des actifs de capital naturel liés à la terre ?
   2.2. L'évaluation des instruments adoptés pour la protection du capital naturel à la lumière de la rechercher universitaire nationale.
   2.3. À qui appartient le carbone séquestré sur les terres, le gain net de biodiversité réalisé, la valeur nutritive ?
   2.4. Comment l'occupation de la terre par d'autres personnes, par exemple des locataires ou d'autres utilisateurs de la terre, influe-t-elle sur la situation ?
   2.5. Quels sont les mécanismes dont vous disposez pour résoudre les litiges relatifs à ces questions ?
3. Les aspects financiers : Comment le capital naturel est-il évalué, comment est-il échangé et quelle est la situation fiscale ?
   3.1. Veuillez fournir des détails sur la manière dont le capital naturel est traité à des fins fiscales.
   3.2. Existe-t-il des mécanismes juridiques pour réglementer le commerce des actifs du capital naturel ? Comment fonctionnent-ils ? Quelles sont les exigences en la matière ?
   3.3. Existe-t-il des méthodes reconnues d'évaluation du capital naturel ? Existe-t-il des calculateurs standard ou agréés permettant aux agriculteurs et aux propriétaires fonciers de calculer la valeur de leur capital naturel ? Ces calculateurs sont-ils acceptés par ceux qui souhaitent faire du commerce ?
4. En ce qui concerne les intrants dans les sols et les eaux, quelles sont les préoccupations relatives aux nutriments/engrais/pesticides/herbicides dans les sols et les eaux de votre pays ? Quelles réglementations/méthodes de gestion des terres et des cours d'eau ont été introduites pour répondre à ces préoccupations et sont utilisées dans votre pays ? Commentez en particulier :
   4.1. Quels sont les nutriments/fertilisants/pesticides/herbicides qui suscitent le plus d'inquiétude ?
   4.2. La législation interdit-elle l'utilisation de certains produits sur les terres/cultures ou certaines actions ? Dans l'affirmative, expliquez. Par exemple, quelle est l'approche de votre pays en ce qui concerne le glyphosate et les néonicotinoïdes ?
   4.3. Quelles solutions constructives ont été utilisées pour répondre aux préoccupations concernant les nutriments et comment fonctionnent-elles dans la pratique ?

   4.4. Des objectifs ont-ils été fixés pour les sols et l'eau ? Dans l'affirmative, quels sont ces objectifs et quand doivent-ils être atteints ? Comment ces objectifs sont-ils contrôlés ?
   4.5. Existe-t-il des préoccupations particulières concernant la disponibilité et/ou la qualité de l'eau dans votre pays ?
5. Existe-t-il des mesures incitant les agriculteurs à protéger le capital naturel ? Dans l'affirmative, veuillez les décrire en détail, en tenant compte des points suivants :
   5.1. Les financement/paiements offerts.
   5.2. Quelles sont les exigences/conditions auxquelles les agriculteurs doivent se conformer ?
   5.3. Quels sont les mécanismes d'application mis en place pour garantir le respect de la législation ?

B. Version anglaise – English version – Englische Version

1. Characterise the current position in your country in relation to Climate Change Emergency, including targets, mechanisms and policies that have been developed in your country to enable the crisis in relation to climate change to be addressed with a particular focus on those within agriculture. To include:
   1.1. Status of Climate Change Emergency in law and policy, Objectives and Targets set and timelines.
   1.2. Bodies, organisations that have been tasked with delivering on the above objectives and targets – what monitoring and enforcement mechanisms are in place? What are consequences of non-compliance? What role do various Environmental Regulators in your country have in relation to this and how do these work with farmers?
   1.3. Special instruments for protecting and enhancing carbon, biodiversity, water, soils, etc. These may include discussion of easements/covenants/restrictions on title/contracts/management agreements.
   1.4. Scope of land-use plans (for the whole territory or only certain areas). Mechanisms in law aimed at limiting changes to the intended use of agricultural land for purposes not related to agriculture including those seeking to implement international agreements and obligations such under the United Nations Framework Convention

on Climate Change and the Kyoto Protocol and the activities of the Land Use, Land-Use Change and Forestry (LULUCF) workstream.

2. Characterise the ownership of natural capital assets in law.
   - 2.1. Who owns the natural capital assets related to the land?
   - 2.2. Evaluation of the adopted instruments for the protection of natural capital in the light of national academic literature.
   - 2.3. Who owns any carbon sequestered on the land, biodiversity net gain achieved, nutrient value?
   - 2.4. How is this affected by the occupation of the land by others e.g. tenants, other land users?
   - 2.5. What mechanisms do you have to resolve disputes in relation to such issues?
3. Financial aspects: How is natural capital valued, how is it traded and what is the taxation position?
   - 3.1. Please provide details of how natural capital is treated for taxation purposes.
   - 3.2. Are there legal mechanisms in place to regulate the trading of natural capital assets? How do these work? What requirements are there?
   - 3.3. Are there agreed methods by which natural capital is valued? Are there standard or agreed calculators in place which enable farmers and landowners to calculate the value of their natural capital and are these accepted by those who wish to trade?
4. In terms of inputs on land and water what concerns are there in relation to nutrients/fertilisers/pesticides/herbicides in land and water within your country? What regulations/methods of management of land and water courses have been introduced to respond to those concerns and are being utilized in your country? In particular comment on:
   - 4.1. What nutrients/fertilisers/pesticides/herbicides are causing the most concern?
   - 4.2. Are certain products banned from use on land/crops or certain actions prevented by legislation? If so, explain. What is your country's approach to glyphosate and neonicotinoids for example?
   - 4.3. What constructive solutions have been utilized to overcome concerns about nutrients and how are these working in practice?
   - 4.4. In terms of both soils and water are there targets set in relation to these? If so, what are those targets and by when are they to be achieved? How are these monitored?

4.5. Are there any specific concerns in relation to water availability and/or the quality of water within your country?

5. Are there any incentives provided to farmers to protect natural capital? If so, please detail what those are, taking the following issues into account:
   5.1. Funding/payments offered.
   5.2. What requirements/conditions must farmers adhere to?
   5.3. What enforcement mechanisms are in place to ensure compliance?

C. Version allemande – German version – Deutsche Version

1. Beschreiben Sie die aktuelle Situation in Ihrem Land in Bezug auf den Klimawandel-Notstand, einschließlich der Ziele, Mechanismen und politischen Maßnahmen, die in Ihrem Land entwickelt wurden, um die Krise im Zusammenhang mit dem Klimawandel zu bewältigen, mit besonderem Augenmerk auf diejenigen in der Landwirtschaft. Dazu gehören:
   1.1. Status des Klimawandelnotstands in Gesetz und Politik, festgelegte Ziele und Zeitvorgaben.
   1.2. Gremien, Organisationen, die mit der Umsetzung der oben genannten Ziele und Vorgaben betraut sind – welche Überwachungs- und Durchsetzungsmechanismen gibt es? Welche Folgen hat die Nichteinhaltung? Welche Rolle spielen die verschiedenen Umweltbehörden in Ihrem Land in diesem Zusammenhang und wie arbeiten sie mit den Landwirten zusammen?
   1.3. Spezielle Instrumente zum Schutz und zur Verbesserung von Kohlenstoff, biologischer Vielfalt, Wasser, Böden usw. Dazu kann die Erörterung von Dienstbarkeiten/Vorbehalten/Einschränkungen von Eigentum/Verträgen/Bewirtschaftungsvereinbarungen gehören.
   1.4. Geltungsbereich von Flächennutzungsplänen (für das gesamte Gebiet oder nur für bestimmte Gebiete). Gesetzliche Mechanismen, die darauf abzielen, Änderungen der beabsichtigten Nutzung landwirtschaftlicher Flächen für nicht landwirtschaftliche Zwecke zu begrenzen, einschließlich der Mechanismen, die auf die Umsetzung internationaler Vereinbarungen und Verpflichtungen abzielen, z.B. unter dem Rahmenübereinkommen der Vereinten Nationen über Klimaänderungen und dem Kyoto-Protokolls sowie den Aktivitäten des Arbeitsbereichs Landnutzung, Landnutzungsänderung und Forstwirtschaft (LULUCF).

2. Charakterisierung des Eigentums an Naturkapitalwerten im Recht.
   2.1. Wem gehören die mit dem Land verbundenen Naturkapitalwerte?
   2.2. Bewertung der angenommenen Instrumente für den Schutz des Naturkapitals im Lichte der nationalen wissenschaftlichen Literatur.
   2.3. Wem gehört der auf der Fläche gebundene Kohlenstoff, der erzielte Nettogewinn an biologischer Vielfalt, der Nährstoffwert?
   2.4. Wie wirkt sich die Nutzung des Grundstücks durch andere Personen aus, z.B. durch Pächter oder andere Landnutzerinnen?
   2.5. Welche Mechanismen gibt es zur Beilegung von Streitigkeiten im Zusammenhang mit solchen Fragen?
3. Finanzielle Aspekte: Wie wird das Naturkapital bewertet, wie wird es gehandelt und wie sieht es mit der Besteuerung aus?
   3.1. Bitte geben Sie an, wie Naturkapital steuerlich behandelt wird.
   3.2. Gibt es rechtliche Mechanismen zur Regulierung des Handels mit Naturkapital? Wie funktionieren diese? Welche Anforderungen gibt es?
   3.3. Gibt es vereinbarte Methoden zur Bewertung des Naturkapitals? Gibt es standardisierte oder vereinbarte Berechnungsmethoden, die es Landwirten und Grundeigentümerinnen ermöglichen, den Wert ihres Naturkapitals zu berechnen, und werden diese von denjenigen, die handeln wollen, akzeptiert?
4. Welche Bedenken gibt es in Ihrem Land in Bezug auf den Eintrag von Nährstoffen/Düngemitteln/Pestiziden/Herbiziden in Land und Wasser? Welche Vorschriften/Methoden zur Bewirtschaftung von Böden und Gewässern wurden eingeführt, um auf diese Bedenken zu reagieren, und werden in Ihrem Land angewandt? Nehmen Sie insbesondere Stellung zu:
   4.1. Welche Nährstoffe/Düngemittel/Pestizide/Herbizide geben am meisten Anlass zur Sorge?
   4.2. Ist die Verwendung bestimmter Produkte auf Flächen/Kulturen verboten oder werden bestimmte Handlungen durch Rechtsvorschriften verhindert? Wenn ja, erklären Sie dies. Wie geht Ihr Land z.B. mit Glyphosat und Neonicotinoiden um?
   4.3. Welche konstruktiven Lösungen wurden zur Überwindung von Bedenken hinsichtlich der Nährstoffe eingesetzt und wie funktionieren diese in der Praxis?

4.4. Gibt es für die Bereiche Boden und Wasser Zielvorgaben für diese Bereiche? Wenn ja, wie lauten diese Ziele und bis wann sollen sie erreicht werden? Wie werden sie überwacht?

4.5. Gibt es in Ihrem Land besondere Bedenken in Bezug auf die Verfügbarkeit von Wasser und/oder die Qualität des Wassers?

5. Gibt es Anreize für Landwirte, Naturkapital zu schützen? Wenn ja, geben Sie bitte an, welche das sind, und berücksichtigen Sie dabei die folgenden Punkte:

5.1. angebotene Finanzierungen/Zahlungen.

5.2. Welche Anforderungen/Bedingungen müssen die Landwirtinnen einhalten?

5.3. Welche Durchsetzungsmechanismen gibt es, um die Einhaltung der Vorschriften zu gewährleisten?

Rapport général de la Commission II –
General Report of Commission II –
Generalbericht der Kommission II

Version française – French version – Französische Version
Version anglaise – English version – Englische Version
Version allemande – German version – Deutsche Version

Rapport général de la Commission II

Version française – French version – Französische Version

Catherine Taskis KC
Falcon Chambers

Les rapports nationaux présentés lors du XXXIe Congrès européen de droit rural et les discussions approfondies qui ont suivi ont mis l'accent sur les considérations environnementales nouvelles et émergentes relatives à l'utilisation des terres en ce qui concerne le carbone, la biodiversité et les nutriments. Chacun des rapporteurs nationaux a abordé position actuelle de son pays par rapport au changement climatique et aux mesures environnementales, y compris les politiques, les objectifs et les mécanismes visant à protéger et à améliorer les actifs du capital naturel.

Les travaux de la Commission II se sont appuyés sur les rapports nationaux de la France (Luc Bodiguel), de l'Allemagne (Friederike Heise, Cara von Nolting), de l'Italie (Mario Mauro), de la Norvège (Katrine Broch Hauge), de l'Espagne (Maria José Cazorla González, Fernando del Moral Torres), de la Suisse (Stefanie Hug) et du Royaume-Uni (Mike Holland), ainsi que sur le rapport individuel du professeur Christopher Rodgers.

Les présentations ont été disparates et variées. Voici un bref résumé de certains aspects clés de l'analyse développée par les rapporteurs nationaux.

1. Le consensus de la Commission est que la protection du climat ne peut réussir qu'avec une coopération internationale, efficacement mise en œuvre au niveau national. À l'heure actuelle, les différents niveaux de priorité nationale (influencés par les pressions politiques nationales), la dimension intertemporelle et l'absence de terminologie universelle constituent des obstacles importants à une approche internationale cohérente.

L'importance d'une réponse internationale concertée pour lutter contre le changement climatique a été généralement reconnue. En Allemagne, par exemple, la Cour constitutionnelle fédérale a spécifiquement reconnu en 2021 que le changement climatique était un problème mondial, pour lequel chaque pays a une responsabilité. La protection du climat ne peut réussir qu'au niveau international.

À l'heure actuelle, l'approche de la politique en matière de changement climatique varie considérablement d'un pays à l'autre. Les pays ont des points de vue différents sur l'urgence de la nécessité de traiter les questions environnementales : certains pays (dont l'Espagne) ont identifié un état d'urgence au niveau national, d'autres (comme la Suisse) ne l'ont pas fait. Les pays disposent également de cadres structurels différents pour gérer la protection du climat. L'intention de l'Italie d'être à l'avant-garde de la lutte contre le changement climatique et de la gestion de son capital naturel s'est concrétisée par deux modifications de la constitution, effectuées en 2022 : l'introduction du principe de protection de l'environnement, de la biodiversité et des écosystèmes, et la reconnaissance de la possibilité d'orienter l'activité économique publique et privée vers des objectifs environnementaux. De même, la Constitution fédérale de la Suisse contient un certain nombre de dispositions liées à la protection de l'environnement.

D'un point de vue stratégique, la politique de lutte contre le changement climatique peut être conçue pour protéger directement l'environnement ou s'inscrire dans le cadre de la protection des droits fondamentaux des citoyens du pays. En Italie, les amendements apportés à la constitution ont soutenu la reconstruction de l'environnement en tant que droit fondamental de la personne, distinct du paysage. En Allemagne, les droits subjectifs de la nature ont été critiqués comme étant en contradiction avec la constitution qui protège les citoyens allemands, bien que ces droits subjectifs soient de plus en plus discutés.

Dans certains pays, les mesures climatiques sont explicitement intégrées dans la législation agricole. L'impact des mesures climatiques sur les terres agricoles peut aussi, ou au contraire, être indirect. Ainsi, en Suisse, les restrictions d'émissions, l'aménagement du territoire, le contrôle des terres ou le transfert d'actifs sont des mesures générales qui s'appliquent également aux terres agricoles. Il existe également des mesures mises en œuvre directement dans le droit agricole, notamment celles qui compensent les services publics fournis par les entreprises agricoles. En France, les politiques agricoles et alimentaires visent explicitement à atténuer les effets du changement climatique et à s'y adapter, ce qui est également au cœur du droit français de l'urbanisme. Depuis août 2021, l'intégration directe ou indirecte des questions climatiques dans le droit rural français a été renforcée par la loi n° 2021-1104, qui réaffirme l'engagement de l'État membre à lutter contre le changement climatique et à renforcer la résilience à ses effets : y compris en augmentant la qualité environnementale des produits alimentaires.

En Italie, l'agriculture a toujours été considérée comme un sujet distinct, bénéficiant de règles spéciales. En Norvège, le secteur agricole dispose d'un plan climatique spécifique fonctionnant de manière indépendante. En Allemagne, la loi sur les transactions foncières contient des mesures visant directement à protéger les terres agricoles d'une utilisation non agricole. Au Royaume-Uni, la loi sur l'environnement de 2021 est un élément clé de la législation.

Les États membres ont reconnu le défi que représente la coordination entre les politiques nationales et les choix régionaux. Les mesures climatiques peuvent être conçues et appliquées au niveau national ou régional. En Allemagne, l'urgence du changement climatique est traitée au niveau de l'État, du gouvernement fédéral et des municipalités. En Espagne et en Italie, l'agriculture (et la sylviculture en Italie) est une question régionale, ce qui peut entraîner un manque de cohésion nationale ou un conflit avec les mesures nationales. Cela peut également se traduire (comme en Espagne) par un manque de progrès dans certaines régions. En Norvège, une proposition de mesure visant à imposer une interdiction générale de construire dans toutes les zones humides est actuellement limitée aux seules zones côtières, et même dans ces zones, des dérogations sont possibles, et les municipalités peuvent décider, par le biais de processus politiques, d'autoriser des constructions plus proches de la mer.

Tous les pays sont confrontés et influencés par des pressions internes sur l'élaboration des politiques, qui peuvent résulter de changements dans l'administration, de débats publics et de priorités contradictoires.

Un autre facteur identifié au cours des discussions au sein de la Commission comme un obstacle à une plus grande efficacité internationale est l'utilisation d'un langage différent pour se référer aux différents aspects du capital naturel.

2. Les États membres ont convenu que la politique et la planification nationales en matière de climat devraient tenir compte de la multifonctionnalité du capital naturel, qui entraîne la nécessité d'équilibrer l'exploitation productive des terres (par exemple pour assurer la sécurité alimentaire) et les objectifs de conservation.

Au Royaume-Uni, par exemple, l'obligation faite aux autorités locales (au niveau régional) de désigner des sites à protéger en vertu de la législation SSSI (reconnaissance d'un site d'intérêt scientifique particulier, une désignation officielle de conservation décrivant une zone présentant un intérêt particulier pour la science en raison de la présence d'espèces rares de flore ou de faune ou de caractéristiques géologiques ou physiologiques importantes) est en contradiction avec la concurrence pour l'occupation des sols exercée par des politiques gouvernementales concurrentes (telles que la construction de logements).

Un autre exemple de conflit dans les demandes concurrentes de terres peut être vu dans le défi que représente en Norvège la mise en œuvre de la restriction de la construction sur les zones humides, qui est sujette à des exceptions même dans les zones côtières limitées dans lesquelles l'interdiction s'applique.

Les mêmes pressions s'appliquent à la politique ZAN (zéro artificialisation nette) de la France, mise en œuvre à tous les niveaux locaux, qui vise à interdire la disparition des terres agricoles. Il a été noté que dans ce contexte, la recherche d'un équilibre entre les objectifs de protection des sols et la planification urbaine est particulièrement délicate, non seulement en raison du jeu des acteurs et de la pression sur les décideurs, mais aussi parce qu'il est difficile de définir le champ d'application de cet objectif de neutralité. Différentes mesures ont été mises en œuvre en France pour faciliter cet exercice.

3. L'absence de normes reconnues et objectives pour définir les niveaux de référence et les cibles dans les objectifs environnementaux et les codes de bonne pratique pose des difficultés, tant au niveau national qu'international, pour une réglementation et une mise en œuvre efficaces et cohérentes des mesures relatives au climat.

La Commission a reconnu que l'approche varie d'un pays à l'autre, en fonction de sa situation historique et actuelle. Les niveaux de référence varieront en fonction du moment où ils sont évalués ou testés, et les objectifs en fonction d'un très grand nombre de facteurs, dont la combinaison sera propre à chaque pays à un moment donné. Comme l'indique le rapport national de l'Espagne, il est fréquent que les comptes nationaux n'incluent pas de manière adéquate les services écosystémiques et la valeur du capital naturel.

4. L'adhésion des propriétaires ou des utilisateurs de terres à des accords contractuels volontaires est un moyen essentiel d'atteindre les objectifs de protection du climat. Le succès de ces programmes dépend de l'engagement des acteurs au niveau de la base. Il s'agit d'un aspect culturel et communautaire, en plus d'assurer la viabilité pratique et financière des projets (y compris en fournissant des incitations appropriées et une répartition proportionnelle des responsabilités).

La mise en œuvre des mesures de protection du climat s'appuie sur trois approches principales : l'imposition de contrôles et d'interdictions, les accords contractuels conclus par les acteurs avec l'État et/ou des organismes privés, et l'utilisation de la technologie.

Tous les États membres ont fait état de la législation ou des réglementations mises en œuvre pour imposer des interdictions et/ou des restrictions ou des contrôles sur le comportement en vue de la protection du climat. Ces législations ou réglementations exigent le respect des règles en imposant des sanctions en cas d'infraction. En Espagne, une réglementation supplémentaire figure dans le droit pénal, qui interdit, dans le cadre du code pénal, le pillage et le commerce illégal des biens du patrimoine naturel.

Des exemples de ces restrictions figurent dans les rapports nationaux. Dans la plupart des pays, il s'agit notamment de contrôles de planification. Parmi les autres contrôles plus spécifiques, citons ceux qui s'appliquent à la sylviculture en Italie et la politique française des ZAN, qui vise à éviter toute artificialisation nette des terres d'ici à 2050, avec des objectifs intermédiaires de réduction de la consommation de terres. Cette politique est intégrée dans les documents d'urbanisme régionaux et locaux afin de protéger les zones naturelles, agricoles et forestières de l'étalement urbain.

De tels contrôles nécessitent un suivi et une mise en œuvre. Les États membres se sont inquiétés du fait que la législation ne prévoit souvent pas de structures ou de financements efficaces à cet effet.

Les mesures de protection du climat peuvent être mises en œuvre par le biais d'accords et d'une coopération négociée. Des mesures d'incitation sont mises en place pour obtenir des avantages environnementaux particuliers. Il s'agit par exemple de régimes de paiements directs (PAC dans l'UE ; régimes alternatifs en Norvège, en Suisse et au Royaume-Uni). Dans le cadre de la nouvelle PAC, pour bénéficier de l'aide de base, il est obligatoire de se conformer à des exigences renforcées en matière d'écoconditionnalité, fondées sur l'obtention de bonnes conditions agricoles et environnementales et sur une gestion juridique efficace. En France, les agriculteurs peuvent également recevoir des paiements au titre des services écosystémiques qu'ils produisent ou protègent. En Allemagne, une série d'écosystèmes volontaires ont été mis en place grâce au financement du premier pilier de la PAC, avec des subventions pour (entre autres) l'aménagement de zones destinées à améliorer la biodiversité et le maintien d'une gestion agroforestière. D'autres mesures d'incitation sont prévues en Allemagne par des programmes qui ne sont pas liés à l'UE, comme le modèle de coopération pour la protection de l'eau potable en Basse-Saxe : l'élément central de ce modèle est constitué par des accords volontaires qui comprennent des mesures contractuelles et subventionnées concernant les zones agricoles pour la protection des eaux souterraines, entièrement financées par la redevance sur les prélèvements d'eau. Un autre système d'incitation prévu en Allemagne concerne la protection des sols des landes, qui sont utilisés à des fins agricoles dans l'ensemble du pays.

En Italie, un décret législatif de 2001 prévoit que les organismes publics négocient avec les agriculteurs qui, dans le cadre de leur activité, s'engagent à respecter des obligations spécifiques en matière de protection des ressources naturelles, de la biodiversité et des paysages. En guise de rémunération, les agriculteurs peuvent bénéficier de financements, de concessions et de réductions tarifaires sans avoir à se conformer aux contrats de marchés publics. Ces instruments sont largement utilisés, avec un succès considérable.

Des accords contractuels peuvent également être efficaces, comme dans le domaine de la sylviculture en Italie ou des contrats de séquestration du carbone en France, en vertu desquels l'agriculteur s'engage à réduire les émissions de gaz à effet de serre sur son exploitation selon une méthode approuvée, en recevant une rémunération du bénéficiaire des droits de réduction du carbone ou d'un porteur collectif (association, coopérative agricole, etc.). Au Royaume-Uni, les conventions de conservation sont un moyen pour un propriétaire foncier de conclure un accord par lequel il s'engage à protéger, restaurer ou améliorer les caractéristiques naturelles ou patrimoniales d'un terrain donné. Les accords contractuels peuvent soulever des questions particulières, par exemple lorsque la propriété et l'occupation des terres sont des intérêts distincts ou entre des mains distinctes (par exemple, lorsqu'il y a un locataire sur la terre, comme c'est le cas en France et au Royaume-Uni en particulier).

La Commission a longuement débattu de l'efficacité et de la réussite des accords volontaires, mis en œuvre dans différents pays et portant sur différents aspects environnementaux. Ces systèmes exigent que les acteurs soient directement investis dans le résultat d'un système particulier, ce qui met en jeu l'aspect culturel ou communautaire de la mesure. Comme l'indique le rapport national de la France, l'engagement collectif du secteur agricole, des syndicats et des coopératives en particulier, est essentiel pour créer une dynamique de soutien collectif et d'engagements individuels, ainsi que pour limiter les risques financiers associés.

Un exemple particulier de réussite en matière d'accords volontaires a été donné par la Norvège, dans le domaine de la sylviculture. La Norvège a une forte tradition de propriétaires forestiers qui concluent volontairement des accords de conservation avec le gouvernement. Le propriétaire forestier conserve ses droits de propriété, ainsi que ses droits de chasse, de pêche et de pâturage, et reçoit une compensation non imposable pour la zone protégée (basée sur la valeur de la sylviculture dans la zone) ainsi qu'une assistance gratuite de la part des organisations de propriétaires forestiers tout au long du processus de protection. En près de 20 ans, ce système a contribué à réduire les conflits liés à la protection des forêts, mais il est vulnérable aux changements politiques en raison des besoins de financement.

La conclusion du rapport national de la Suisse est que, dans le cadre actuel de ce pays, l'incitation à protéger le climat par des mesures de soutien financier est faible, et qu'il existe un besoin permanent d'action en ce qui concerne les mesures de protection du climat dans l'agriculture.

5. La politique et la réglementation fiscales peuvent et doivent servir de moteur à l'entrée dans des systèmes contractuels ou volontaires. Elles ne doivent pas constituer une barrière à l'entrée.

En Italie, les universitaires demandent que la législation fiscale environnementale fournisse de nouvelles incitations et un soutien aux mesures de protection du climat, afin de favoriser les entreprises ayant un impact environnemental moindre ou contribuant à l'amélioration de l'environnement. À l'inverse, et sur la base du principe environnemental « le pollueur doit payer », il a été suggéré de taxer davantage les activités ayant des effets négatifs sur l'environnement, afin de les décourager et d'affecter le prélèvement fiscal qui en résulte à des activités compensatoires. En Norvège, où la proposition « le pollueur doit payer » est l'un des principes directeurs de la politique climatique, il existe une incitation fiscale pour encourager et promouvoir la participation à des accords de conservation des forêts.

Les mesures fiscales en Espagne comprennent des mesures relatives aux déchets : elles visent à réduire la production de déchets et à améliorer la gestion des déchets (par un droit d'accise sur les emballages plastiques non réutilisables et une taxe sur la mise en décharge, l'incinération et la co-incinération des déchets).

Lorsque, historiquement, l'activité agricole a été à l'origine d'un allègement fiscal (tel que l'allègement de la propriété agricole (APR) au Royaume-Uni), il peut être nécessaire d'élargir le champ d'application de cette activité pour englober des mesures environnementales en plus de l'activité agricole.

6. L'utilisation de nouvelles technologies et pratiques doit être développée pour améliorer la durabilité de l'environnement, parallèlement à la gestion de l'utilisation des terres par le biais de la réglementation et de systèmes contractuels volontaires. Cela devrait inclure l'examen des structures nécessaires pour explorer et évaluer efficacement les méthodes et pratiques nouvelles ou expérimentales.

La Commission a entendu parler de l'utilisation de la technologie parallèlement à d'autres mesures de protection du climat. En Espagne, par exemple, la technologie est utilisée pour la récupération et la réutilisation de l'eau, dans le cadre de mesures de dessalement. L'édition de gènes est une autre technologie qui peut être appliquée dans le cadre de la protection du climat. Il est important de disposer d'un cadre dans lequel ces technologies peuvent être développées et évaluées rapidement, sur une base scientifique appropriée, afin qu'elles puissent être utilisées de manière optimale. L'Italie a créé un conseil scientifique sur le climat et l'environnement en 2022, afin d'ouvrir un dialogue entre la science et la politique et d'orienter les actions politiques en fonction des avancées scientifiques, mais à ce jour, aucune autre mesure n'a été prise.

Le droit agricole suisse dispose d'un programme de ressources pour l'agriculture qui encourage les innovations organisationnelles, techniques et structurelles et les améliorations dans l'utilisation durable des ressources de production, afin d'améliorer continuellement l'état de l'art dans l'agriculture. Le programme prévoit une approche ascendante : des projets élaborés par des promoteurs privés ou publics régionaux ou sectoriels.

7. Il convient d'examiner si et comment le financement privé et le développement du marché peuvent être intégrés le plus efficacement possible au financement et au soutien de l'État dans la promotion de la durabilité environnementale

Le degré de dépendance à l'égard du financement public et l'implication d'autres parties prenantes et de financements privés varient d'un État membre à l'autre. Au Royaume-Uni, la politique encourage un modèle de financement mixte visant à générer un marché pour les biens et services publics environnementaux. En France, la biodiversité est protégée depuis de nombreuses années par divers systèmes d'étiquetage publics et privés (marques) destinés aux consommateurs, qui sont directement liés aux produits et permettent aux consommateurs de comprendre l'impact des produits qu'ils achètent sur la biodiversité.

Comme l'indique le rapport national de l'Italie, le marché atteint souvent ce que le législateur n'atteint pas. (La Commission a appris qu'en Italie, la demande de produits certifiés obtenus selon des méthodes de production plus respectueuses de l'environnement est élevée). Cette demande pourrait être exploitée plus efficacement dans le cadre d'une transition vers une meilleure utilisation du capital naturel, tant en Italie que dans d'autres États membres.

General Report of Commission II

Version anglaise – English version – Englische Version

Catherine Taskis KC
Falcon Chambers

The focus of Commission II, addressed in the National Reports presented during the XXXI European Congress of Rural Law and in the comprehensive discussions which followed, was new and emerging environmental land use considerations in respect of carbon, biodiversity and nutrients. Each of the National Reporters addressed the current position of their country in relation to climate change and environmental measures, including policies, targets and mechanisms to protect and enhance natural capital assets.

The work of Commission II was based on the National Reports of France (Luc Bodiguel), Germany (Friederike Heise, Cara von Nolting), Italy (Mario Mauro), Norway (Katrine Broch Hauge), Spain (Maria José Cazorla González, Fernando del Moral Torres), Switzerland (Stefanie Hug) and the UK (Mike Holland), as well as the individual report of Professor Christopher Rodgers.

The presentations were disparate and wide-ranging. There follows a short summary of some key aspects of the analysis which was developed by the National Reporters.

1. The consensus of the Commission was that climate protection can only succeed with international cooperation, effectively implemented at a domestic level. At present, different levels of national priority (influenced by domestic political pressures), the intertemporal dimension and the lack of universal terminology are significant obstacles to a coherent international approach.

The importance of a collaborative international response to tackling climate change was generally acknowledged. In Germany, for example, the Federal Constitutional Court had specifically recognized in 2021 that climate change was a global problem, for which every country has a responsibility. Climate protection can only succeed internationally.

At present, the approach to climate change policy varies significantly between nations. Countries have different views of the urgency of the need to deal with environmental issues: some countries (including Spain) have identified a state of emergency at a national level; others (such as Switzerland) have not. Countries also have varying structural frameworks to deal with climate protection. The intention of Italy to be at the forefront of combating climate change and managing its natural capital was embodied in two changes to the constitution, effected in 2022: introducing the principle of protection of the environment, biodiversity and ecosystems, and recognizing the possibility of directing both public and private economic activity for environmental purposes. Similarly, the Federal Constitution of Switzerland contains a number of provisions associated with environmental protection.

Strategically, climate change policy can be framed to protect the environment directly; or it may operate as part of the protection of the fundamental rights of the citizens of the country. In Italy, the amendments introduced to the constitution supported the reconstruction of the environment as a fundamental right of the person, distinct from the landscape. In Germany, subjective rights of nature have been criticized as in contradiction to the constitution that protects German citizens; although such subjective rights are being increasingly discussed.

In some nations climate measures are integrated explicitly into agricultural legislation. The impact of climate measures on agricultural land can also, or alternatively, be affected indirectly. So, in Switzerland restrictions on emissions, land use planning, control of land or asset transfer are broad based measures operating generally, including on agricultural land. There are also measures implemented directly into agricultural law, most relevantly those that compensate for public services provided by agricultural businesses. In France, agricultural and food policies are explicitly aimed at mitigating and adapting to the effects of climate change; which is also at the heart of French urban planning law. Since August 2021 the direct or indirect integration of climate issues into French rural law has been reinforced by law No.2021-1104, which reaffirms the member state's commitment to fight climate change and strengthen resilience to its effect: including by raising the environmental quality of food products.

In Italy, agriculture has always been considered a separate topic, benefitting from special rules. In Norway the agricultural sector has a specific climate plan operating independently; and in Germany the Land Transactions Act contains measures directly aimed at protecting agricultural land from non-agricultural use. In the UK a key piece legislation is the Environment Act 2021.

Member states recognized the challenge of coordination between national policies, and regional choices. Climate measures may be of national or regional conception and application. In Germany the climate change emergency is addressed at state, federal and municipal levels. In Spain and Italy agriculture (and forestry, in Italy) is a regional matter, which may lead to a lack of national cohesion or conflict with national measures. It may also result (as in Spain) in a lack of progress in some regions. In Norway a proposed measure to impose a general building prohibition on all wetlands is presently limited to coastal areas only, and even in those areas dispensations are possible, and municipalities through political processes may decide to allow buildings closer to the sea.

All countries face and are influenced by internal pressures on policy making which may arise from changes in administration, public debate and conflicting priorities.

One further factor identified during discussion in the Commission as a barrier to greater international effectiveness was the use of different language to refer to different aspects of natural capital.

2. Member states agreed that national climate policy and planning should address the multifunctionality of natural capital, which gives rise to the need to balance productive exploitation of land (for example to ensure food security) with conservation goals.

For example in the UK, the duty on local authorities (at regional level) to designate sites for protection under SSSI legislation (recognizing a Site of Special Scientific Interest, a formal conservation designation describing an area of particular interest to science due to rare species of flora or fauna or important geological or physiological features) is at odds with competition for land from competing government policies (such as house building).

A further example of conflict in competing demands on land can be seen in the challenge in Norway in implementing the restriction on building on wetlands, which is subject to exceptions even in the limited coastal areas in which the prohibition operates.

The same pressures apply to the ZAN (zero net artificialization) policy of France, implemented at all local levels, which is aimed at banning the disappearance of agricultural land. It was noted that in this context the search for a balance between soil protection objectives and urban planning is particularly delicate, not only because of the interplay of stakeholders and the pressure on decision-makers, but also because it is difficult to define the scope of this neutrality objective. Various measures have been implemented in France to assist with this exercise.

3. The absence of recognized and objective standards for the purpose of both baselines and targets in environmental objectives and codes of practice presents difficulties at both a domestic and international level for effective and consistent regulation and enforcement of climate measures.

The Commission acknowledged the variations in approach between each country, according to its historic and present position. Baselines will vary according to when these are assessed or tested; and targets according to a huge number of factors, the combination of which will be unique to each country at any particular time. As noted in the National Report from Spain, it is frequently the case that national accounts do not adequately include ecosystem services and the value of natural capital.

4. Entry by land owners or users into voluntary contractual agreements is a crucial means of delivering climate protection goals. The success of these schemes depends on engaging actors at base level. This has a cultural and community aspect, in addition to ensuring schemes are practically and financially viable (including by providing appropriate incentives and proportionate allocation of responsibility).

The delivery of climate protection measures deploys three principal approaches, namely: the imposition of controls and prohibitions; contractual agreements, entered by actors with the state and/or with private bodies; and the use of technology.

Members states all reported on legislation or regulations implemented to impose prohibitions and/or restrictions or controls on behavior in pursuit of climate protection. Such legislation or regulations requires compliance by imposing sanctions for breach. In Spain additional regulation is found in penal law, prohibiting as part of the criminal code the plundering and illegal trade of natural heritage assets.

Examples of such restrictions can be found in the National Reports. In most countries these including planning controls. Other, more specific controls include those operating on forestry in Italy; and France's ZAN policy, which aims to achieve no net land artificialization by 2050, with intermediate targets to reduce land consumption. This policy is integrated into regional and local urban planning documents to protect natural, agricultural, and forested areas from urban sprawl.

Controls such as these require monitoring and enforcement. Member states expressed concern that legislation frequently fails to provide effective structures or funding for this.

Climate protection measures may operate instead by way of agreements and negotiated cooperation. Incentives are provided for delivering particular environmental benefits. Examples include direct payment schemes (CAP in the EU; alternative schemes in Norway, Switzerland and the UK). Under the new CAP, in order to receive basic aid it is compulsory to comply with enhanced cross-compliance requirements, based on achieving good agricultural and environmental conditions and effective legal management. In France farmers can also receive payments resulting from the ecosystem services they produce or protect. In Germany a range of voluntary eco-schemes has been established with funding from the 1st pillar of the CAP, with subsidies for (amongst other things) the provision of areas to improve biodiversity and the maintenance of agroforestry management. Other incentives are provided in Germany by programs that are not linked to the EU, such as the Lower Saxony drinking water protection cooperation model: the central component of this is voluntary agreements that include contractually agreed and subsidized agricultural area measures for groundwater protection, wholly financed through the water abstraction fee. Another incentive scheme intended in Germany is in relation to moorland soil protection, on agriculturally used moorland soils across the country.

In Italy a legislative decree in 2001 provided for public bodies to negotiate with farmers who, in the course of their business, engage in specific obligations to protect natural resources, biodiversity and landscape. As remuneration, farmers can access financing, concessions and tariff reductions without compliance with public procurement contracts. Such instruments are widely used, with considerable success.

Contractual arrangements may also be effective: such as in relation to forestry in Italy, or carbon sequestration contracts in France, under which the farmer undertakes to reduce greenhouse gas emissions on his farm by an approved method, receiving remuneration from the beneficiary of the carbon reduction rights or a collective bearer (association, agricultural cooperative etc.). In the UK conservation covenants are a means by which a landowner may enter an agreement undertaking obligations to protect, restore or enhance the natural or heritage features of specified land. Contractual arrangements may give rise to particular issues, for example where land ownership and occupation are separate interests or in separate hands (such as where there is a tenant on the land: noted in France and UK in particular).

There was considerable discussion in the Commission around the effectiveness and success of voluntary agreements, operated in different countries and in relation to different environmental aspects. These schemes require actors to be directly invested in the outcome of a particular scheme, which brings into play the cultural or community aspect of the measure. As noted in the National Report from France, the collective commitment of the agricultural sector, unions and cooperatives in particular, is essential to create a dynamic of collective support and individual commitments, as well as to limit the associated financial risks.

One particular voluntary agreement success story was given by Norway, in respect of forestry. Norway has a strong tradition of forest owners voluntarily entering conservation agreements with the government. The forest owner retains property rights, as well as hunting, fishing, and grazing rights; and receives tax-free compensation for the protected area (based on the value of forestry in the area) and free assistance from the forest owners' organizations throughout the protection process. In almost 20 years this scheme has contributed to lowering the lever of conflict around protection of forests; although is vulnerable to political changes due to the need for financing.

The conclusion of the National Report from Switzerland was that under the present framework in that country, the incentive to protect the climate through financial support measures is low, and there is a continuing need for action with regard to climate protection measures in agriculture.

5. Tax policy and regulation can and should operate as a driver to entry into contractual or voluntary schemes. It should not operate as a barrier to entry.

In Italy, scholars are asking for environmental tax law to provide new incentives and support for climate protection measures, to favour enterprises with less environmental impact or that contribute to enhancing the environment. Conversely, and based on the environment principle "the polluter should pay", it has been suggested that there should be higher taxation for activities that have negative environmental effects, deterring them and allocating the resulting tax levy to compensatory activities. In Norway, where the "polluters must pay" proposition is one of the guiding principles of climate policy, there is a tax incentive to encourage and promote participation in forest conservation agreements.

Fiscal measures in Spain include measures in relation to waste: to reduce waste generation and improve the management of waste (by an excise duty on non-reusable plastic packaging, and tax on landfilling, incineration and co-incineration of waste).

Where historically agricultural activity has been the trigger for tax relief (such as Agricultural Property Relief (APR) in the UK), the scope of such activity may need to be widened to encompass environmental measures in addition to farming.

6. The use of new technologies and practices needs to be developed to improve environmental sustainability, alongside management of land use by way of regulation, and by voluntary contractual schemes. This should include consideration of structures required to explore and effectively assess new or experimental methods and practices.

The Commission heard about the use of technology alongside other climate protection measures. For example in Spain, technology is used in relation to the recover and re-use of water, in desalination measures. Gene-editing is another technology which can be applied in pursuit of climate protection. It is important for there to be a framework in which such technologies can be developed and assessed rapidly, and on an appropriate scientific basis, in order for these to be utilised to maximum effect. Italy established a Scientific Council on Climate and the Environment in 2022, in order to open a dialogue between science and politics and guide political actions in compliance with scientific advances; but to date, no further steps have been taken.

Agricultural law in Switzerland has a resources program for agriculture which promotes organizational, technical and structural innovations and improvements in the sustainable use of production resources, to continuously improve the state of the art in agriculture. The program provides for a bottom-up approach: projects developed by regional or sector-specific private or public sponsors.

7. Consideration should be given as to whether and how private finance and market development can most effectively be integrated with state funding and support in the promotion of environmental sustainability.

The extent of reliance on state funding, and the involvement of other stakeholders and private finance varies between member states. In the UK, policy encourages a blended finance model aimed at generating a market for environmental public goods and services. In France, biodiversity has for many years been protected by various public and private labelling systems (brands) aimed at consumers relating directly to products by allowing consumers to understand the impact of the products they buy on biodiversity.

As was noted in the National Report from Italy, the market often reaches where the legislature does not. (The Commission heard that in Italy the demand for certified products obtained according to more environmentally friendly production methods is high.) This could be more effectively exploited in a transition to a better use of natural capital, both in Italy and elsewhere across the member states.

Generalbericht der Kommission II

Version allemande – German version – Deutsche Version

Catherine Taskis KC
Falcon Chambers

Der Schwerpunkt der Kommission II, der in den am XXXI. Europäischen Kongress für ländliches Recht vorgelegten nationalen Berichten und in den anschließenden umfassenden Diskussionen behandelt wurde, waren neue und aufkommende ökologische Landnutzungsüberlegungen in Bezug auf Kohlenstoff, Biodiversität und Nährstoffe. Jeder der nationalen Berichterstatter ging auf die aktuelle Position seines Landes in Bezug auf den Klimawandel und Umweltmaßnahmen ein, einschließlich Politiken, Ziele und Mechanismen zum Schutz und zur Verbesserung des Naturkapitals.

Die Arbeit der Kommission II stützte sich auf die nationalen Berichte aus Frankreich (Luc Bodiguel), Deutschland (Friederike Heise, Cara von Nolting), Italien (Mario Mauro), Norwegen (Katrine Broch Hauge), Spanien (Maria José Cazorla González, Fernando del Moral Torres), der Schweiz (Stefanie Hug) und dem Vereinigten Königreich (Mike Holland) sowie auf den Einzelbericht von Professor Christopher Rodgers.

Die Präsentationen waren sehr unterschiedlich und breit gefächert. Es folgt eine kurze Zusammenfassung einiger Schlüsselaspekte der Analyse, die von den nationalen Berichterstattern entwickelt wurde.

1. Die Kommission war sich einig, dass der Klimaschutz nur durch eine internationale Zusammenarbeit gelingen kann, die auf nationaler Ebene wirksam umgesetzt wird. Gegenwärtig sind die unterschiedlichen nationalen Prioritäten (beeinflusst durch innenpolitischen Druck), die intertemporale Dimension und das Fehlen einer allgemeingültigen Terminologie erhebliche Hindernisse für einen kohärenten internationalen Ansatz.

Die Bedeutung einer internationalen Zusammenarbeit bei der Bewältigung des Klimawandels wurde allgemein anerkannt. In Deutschland hatte beispielsweise das Bundesverfassungsgericht im Jahr 2021 ausdrücklich anerkannt, dass der Klimawandel ein globales Problem ist, für das jedes Land Verantwortung trägt. Klimaschutz kann nur international gelingen.

Gegenwärtig ist der Ansatz in der Klimapolitik von Land zu Land sehr unterschiedlich. Die Länder schätzen die Dringlichkeit der Umweltproblematik unterschiedlich ein: Einige Länder (darunter Spanien) haben auf nationaler Ebene einen Notstand ausgerufen, andere (wie die Schweiz) nicht. Die Länder haben auch unterschiedliche strukturelle Rahmenbedingungen für den Klimaschutz. Die Absicht Italiens, bei der Bekämpfung des Klimawandels und der Bewirtschaftung seines Naturkapitals eine Vorreiterrolle einzunehmen, wurde in zwei Verfassungsänderungen im Jahr 2022 verankert mit der Einführung des Grundsatzes des Schutzes der Umwelt, der Biodiversität und der Ökosysteme und der Anerkennung der Möglichkeit, sowohl öffentliche als auch private Wirtschaftstätigkeiten auf Umweltzwecke auszurichten. Auch die Bundesverfassung der Schweiz enthält eine Reihe von Bestimmungen zum Umweltschutz.

Strategisch kann die Klimapolitik so gestaltet werden, dass sie die Umwelt direkt schützt, oder sie kann als Teil des Schutzes der Grundrechte der Bürger eines Landes fungieren. In Italien wurde mit der Verfassungsänderung den Wiederaufbau der Umwelt als Grundrecht des Menschen unterstützt, das sich von dem der Landschaft unterscheidet. In Deutschland wurden subjektive Rechte der Natur als im Widerspruch zum Grundgesetz stehend kritisiert, das die deutschen Bürger schützt, obwohl solche subjektiven Rechte zunehmend diskutiert werden.

In einigen Ländern sind Klimamaßnahmen ausdrücklich in die Agrargesetzgebung integriert. Die Auswirkungen von Klimamaßnahmen auf landwirtschaftliche Flächen können aber auch indirekt erfolgen. So sind in der Schweiz Emissionsbeschränkungen, Flächennutzungsplanung, Kontrolle von Grundstücks- oder Vermögensübertragungen breit angelegte Maßnahmen, die allgemein wirken, auch auf landwirtschaftliche Flächen. Es gibt auch Maßnahmen, die direkt in das Landwirtschaftsgesetz aufgenommen wurden, vor allem solche, die einen Ausgleich für die von den landwirtschaftlichen Betrieben erbrachten öffentlichen Leistungen darstellen. In Frankreich zielt die Landwirtschafts- und Ernährungspolitik ausdrücklich auf die Abschwächung der Auswirkungen des Klimawandels und die Anpassung an diese Auswirkungen ab, was auch im Mittelpunkt des französischen Städtebaurechts steht. Seit August 2021 wird die direkte oder indirekte Integration von Klimafragen in das französische Recht für den ländlichen Raum durch das Gesetz Nr. 2021-1104 gestärkt, dass die Verpflichtung des Mitgliedstaates bekräftigt, den Klimawandel zu bekämpfen und die Widerstandsfähigkeit gegenüber seinen Auswirkungen zu stärken: unter anderem durch die Verbesserung der Umweltqualität von Lebensmitteln.

In Italien wird die Landwirtschaft seit jeher als eigenständiges Thema betrachtet, für das besondere Regelungen gelten. In Norwegen gibt es für den Landwirtschaftssektor einen eigenen, unabhängigen Klimaplan, und in Deutschland enthält das Grundstücksverkehrsgesetz Maßnahmen, die direkt auf den Schutz landwirtschaftlicher Flächen vor nichtlandwirtschaftlicher Nutzung abzielen. Im Vereinigten Königreich ist das Umweltgesetz 2021 ein wichtiger Rechtsakt.

Die Mitgliedstaaten haben die Herausforderung der Koordinierung zwischen nationalen Maßnahmen und regionalen Entscheidungen erkannt. Klimamaßnahmen können auf nationaler oder regionaler Ebene konzipiert und umgesetzt werden. In Deutschland wird der Klimawandel-Notstand auf Landes-, Bundes- und kommunaler Ebene angegangen. In Spanien und Italien ist die Landwirtschaft (und in Italien die Forstwirtschaft) eine regionale Angelegenheit, was zu einem Mangel an nationaler Kohäsion oder zu Konflikten mit nationalen Maßnahmen führen kann. Dies kann auch dazu führen (wie in Spanien), dass in einigen Regionen keine Fortschritte erzielt werden. In Norwegen ist eine vorgeschlagene Maßnahme, die ein allgemeines Bauverbot für alle Feuchtgebiete vorsieht, derzeit nur auf Küstengebiete beschränkt, und selbst in diesen Gebieten sind Ausnahmen möglich, und die Gemeinden können im Rahmen politischer Prozesse beschließen, Gebäude näher am Meer zuzulassen.

Alle Länder sind mit internem Druck auf die Politikgestaltung konfrontiert und werden von diesem beeinflusst, der sich aus Veränderungen in der Verwaltung, öffentlichen Debatten und widersprüchlichen Prioritäten ergeben kann.

Ein weiterer Faktor, der in der Diskussion in der Kommission als Hindernis für eine größere internationale Wirksamkeit identifiziert wurde, ist die Verwendung unterschiedlicher Begriffe für die verschiedenen Aspekte des Naturkapitals.

2. Die Mitgliedstaaten waren sich einig, dass die nationale Klimapolitik und -planung die Multifunktionalität des Naturkapitals berücksichtigen sollte, die ein Gleichgewicht zwischen der produktiven Nutzung des Bodens (z.B. zur Gewährleistung der Ernährungssicherheit) und den Zielen des Naturschutzes erforderlich macht.

Im Vereinigten Königreich beispielsweise steht die Pflicht der lokalen Behörden (auf regionaler Ebene), Gebiete zum Schutz im Rahmen der SSSI-Gesetzgebung auszuweisen (Anerkennung eines Gebiets von besonderem wissenschaftlichem Interesse, einer formellen Schutzausweisung, die ein

Gebiet von besonderem wissenschaftlichem Interesse aufgrund von seltenen Tier- oder Pflanzenarten oder wichtigen geologischen oder physiologischen Merkmalen beschreibt), im Widerspruch zum Wettbewerb um Land durch konkurrierende Regierungspolitiken (wie den Wohnungsbau).

Ein weiteres Beispiel für den Konflikt zwischen konkurrierenden Ansprüchen an den Boden ist die Herausforderung, die sich in Norwegen bei der Umsetzung des Verbots der Bebauung von Feuchtgebieten stellt, das selbst in den begrenzten Küstengebieten, in denen das Verbot gilt, Ausnahmen vorsieht.

Der gleiche Druck gilt für die ZAN-Politik (Zero Net Artificialization) Frankreichs, die auf allen lokalen Ebenen umgesetzt wird und darauf abzielt, das Verschwinden von landwirtschaftlichen Flächen zu verhindern. Es wurde festgestellt, dass in diesem Zusammenhang die Suche nach einem Gleichgewicht zwischen den Zielen des Bodenschutzes und der Stadtplanung besonders heikel ist, nicht nur wegen des Zusammenspiels der Akteure und des Drucks auf die Entscheidungsträger, sondern auch, weil es schwierig ist, die Reichweite dieses Neutralitätsziels zu definieren. In Frankreich wurden verschiedene Maßnahmen ergriffen, um diese Aufgabe zu erleichtern.

3. Das Fehlen anerkannter und objektiver Standards für die Zwecke von Basis- und Zielwerten in Umweltzielen und Verhaltenskodizes führt sowohl auf nationaler als auch auf internationaler Ebene zu Schwierigkeiten bei der wirksamen und einheitlichen Regulierung und Durchsetzung von Klimamaßnahmen.

Die Kommission räumte ein, dass die einzelnen Länder je nach ihrer historischen und aktuellen Lage unterschiedliche Ansätze verfolgen. Die Ausgangswerte variieren je nachdem, wann sie bewertet oder getestet werden, und die Ziele hängen von einer Vielzahl von Faktoren ab, deren Kombination für jedes Land zu einem bestimmten Zeitpunkt einzigartig sein wird. Wie im nationalen Bericht Spaniens festgestellt wird, werden in den volkswirtschaftlichen Gesamtrechnungen die Ökosystemleistungen und der Wert des Naturkapitals häufig nicht angemessen berücksichtigt.

4. Der Beitritt von Landbesitzern oder -nutzern zu freiwilligen vertraglichen Vereinbarungen ist ein entscheidendes Mittel zur Erreichung von Klimaschutzzielen. Der Erfolg dieser Systeme hängt davon ab, dass die Akteure an der Basis einbezogen werden. Dies hat einen kulturellen und gemeinschaftlichen Aspekt, zusätzlich zu der Gewährleistung, dass die Systeme praktisch und finanziell tragfähig sind (einschließlich der Schaffung geeigneter Anreize und einer angemessenen Zuweisung der Verantwortung).

Bei der Umsetzung von Klimaschutzmaßnahmen kommen im Wesentlichen drei Ansätze zum Tragen: das Verhängen von Kontrollen und Verboten, vertragliche Vereinbarungen zwischen Akteuren und dem Staat und/oder privaten Einrichtungen sowie der Einsatz von Technologien.

Alle Mitgliedsstaaten berichteten über Gesetze oder Verordnungen, die eingeführt wurden, um Verbote und/oder Beschränkungen oder Kontrollen für das Verhalten zum Zwecke des Klimaschutzes aufzuerlegen. Solche Gesetze oder Verordnungen verlangen die Einhaltung durch die Verhängung von Sanktionen bei Verstößen. In Spanien findet sich eine zusätzliche Regelung im Strafrecht, die als Teil des Strafgesetzbuches die Plünderung und den illegalen Handel mit Naturgütern verbietet.

Beispiele für solche Beschränkungen sind in den Nationalen Berichten zu finden. In den meisten Ländern gehören dazu auch Planungskontrollen. Zu den anderen, spezifischeren Kontrollen gehören die für die Forstwirtschaft in Italien und die ZAN-Politik Frankreichs, die darauf abzielt, bis 2050 keine künstlichen Flächen zu schaffen, mit Zwischenzielen zur Reduzierung des Flächenverbrauchs. Diese Politik ist in regionale und lokale Stadtplanungsdokumente integriert, um natürliche, landwirtschaftliche und bewaldete Gebiete vor Zersiedelung zu schützen.

Kontrollen wie diese erfordern Überwachung und Durchsetzung. Die Mitgliedstaaten äußerten sich besorgt darüber, dass die Gesetzgebung häufig keine wirksamen Strukturen oder Finanzmittel dafür vorsieht.

Klimaschutzmaßnahmen können stattdessen durch Vereinbarungen und ausgehandelte Zusammenarbeit erfolgen. Anreize werden für die Erbringung bestimmter Umweltleistungen geboten. Beispiele hierfür sind Direktzahlungssysteme (GAP in der EU; alternative Systeme in Norwegen, der Schweiz und dem Vereinigten Königreich). Im Rahmen der neuen GAP ist es für den Erhalt von Basisbeihilfen verpflichtend, erweiterte Cross-Compliance-Anforderungen zu erfüllen, die auf der Erreichung guter landwirtschaftlicher und ökologischer Bedingungen und einem wirksamen rechtlichen Management beruhen. In Frankreich können Landwirte auch Zahlungen erhalten, die sich aus den von ihnen produzierten oder geschützten

Ökosystemleistungen ergeben. In Deutschland wurde mit Mitteln aus der ersten Säule der GAP eine Reihe von freiwilligen Ökosystemen eingerichtet, die unter anderem die Bereitstellung von Flächen zur Verbesserung der biologischen Vielfalt und die Aufrechterhaltung der agroforstlichen Bewirtschaftung fördern. Weitere Anreize setzen in Deutschland Programme, die nicht an die EU gekoppelt sind, wie z.B. das niedersächsische Kooperationsmodell zum Trinkwasserschutz: Zentraler Bestandteil sind freiwillige Vereinbarungen, die vertraglich vereinbarte und bezuschusste landwirtschaftliche Flächenmaßnahmen zum Grundwasserschutz beinhalten, die vollständig über das Wasserentnahmeentgelt finanziert werden. Ein weiteres in Deutschland vorgesehenes Anreizsystem betrifft den Moorbodenschutz auf landwirtschaftlich genutzten Moorböden im gesamten Bundesgebiet.

In Italien sieht ein Gesetzesdekret aus dem Jahr 2001 vor, dass öffentliche Einrichtungen mit Landwirten verhandeln können, die im Rahmen ihrer Tätigkeit bestimmte Verpflichtungen zum Schutz der natürlichen Ressourcen, der biologischen Vielfalt und der Landschaft eingehen. Als Gegenleistung können die Landwirte Finanzmittel, Konzessionen und Tarifermäßigungen in Anspruch nehmen, ohne sich an öffentliche Aufträge halten zu müssen. Solche Instrumente werden weithin und mit beträchtlichem Erfolg eingesetzt.

Auch vertragliche Vereinbarungen können wirksam sein: z.B. im Zusammenhang mit der Forstwirtschaft in Italien oder mit Verträgen über die Kohlenstoffbindung in Frankreich, in denen sich der Landwirt verpflichtet, die Treibhausgasemissionen in seinem Betrieb nach einer genehmigten Methode zu reduzieren und dafür eine Vergütung vom Begünstigten der Kohlenstoffreduktionsrechte oder einem kollektiven Träger (Verband, landwirtschaftliche Genossenschaft usw.) erhält. Im Vereinigten Königreich kann sich ein Landeigentümer in einer Vereinbarung verpflichten, die Natur oder das Kulturerbe eines bestimmten Grundstücks zu schützen, wiederherzustellen oder zu verbessern. Vertragliche Vereinbarungen können zu besonderen Problemen führen, beispielsweise wenn Landeigentum und -nutzung getrennte Interessen sind oder sich in verschiedenen Händen befinden (z.B. wenn ein Pächter auf dem Land ist: dies ist insbesondere in Frankreich und im Vereinigten Königreich der Fall).

In der Kommission wurde viel über die Wirksamkeit und den Erfolg von freiwilligen Vereinbarungen diskutiert, die in verschiedenen Ländern und in Bezug auf verschiedene Umweltaspekte durchgeführt werden. Diese Systeme setzen voraus, dass die Akteure direkt in das Ergebnis eines bestimmten Systems investieren, was den kulturellen oder gemeinschaftlichen Aspekt der Maßnahme ins Spiel bringt. Wie im nationalen Bericht Frankreichs festgestellt wird, ist das kollektive Engagement des Agrarsektors, insbesondere der Gewerkschaften und Genossenschaften, von wesentlicher Bedeutung, um eine Dynamik der kollektiven Unterstützung und des individuellen Engagements zu schaffen und die damit verbundenen finanziellen Risiken zu begrenzen.

Eine besondere Erfolgsgeschichte freiwilliger Vereinbarungen wurde von Norwegen im Bereich der Forstwirtschaft berichtet. In Norwegen ist es Tradition, dass Waldbesitzer freiwillig Schutzvereinbarungen mit der Regierung abschließen. Der Waldeigentümer behält seine Eigentumsrechte sowie Jagd-, Fischerei- und Weiderechte und erhält eine steuerfreie Entschädigung für das Schutzgebiet (auf der Grundlage des Wertes der Forstwirtschaft in dem Gebiet) sowie kostenlose Unterstützung durch die Organisationen der Waldeigentümer während des gesamten Schutzprozesses. In fast 20 Jahren hat dieses System dazu beigetragen, den Konflikt im Zusammenhang mit dem Schutz der Wälder zu verringern, obwohl es aufgrund des Finanzierungsbedarfs anfällig für politische Veränderungen ist.

Das Fazit des Länderberichts aus der Schweiz lautete, dass unter den derzeitigen Rahmenbedingungen in diesem Land der Anreiz zum Klimaschutz durch finanzielle Fördermaßnahmen gering ist und weiterhin Handlungsbedarf bei Klimaschutzmaßnahmen in der Landwirtschaft besteht.

5. Steuerpolitik und -vorschriften können und sollten als Anreiz für den Eintritt in vertragliche oder freiwillige Systeme dienen. Sie sollten nicht als Hindernis für den Beitritt fungieren.

In Italien fordern Wissenschaftler, dass das Umweltsteuerrecht neue Anreize und Unterstützung für Klimaschutzmaßnahmen bieten sollte, um Unternehmen zu begünstigen, die die Umwelt weniger belasten oder die zur Verbesserung der Umwelt beitragen. Umgekehrt wurde auf der Grundlage des Umweltprinzips „der Verursacher soll zahlen" vorgeschlagen, Aktivitäten, die negative Umweltauswirkungen haben, höher zu besteuern, um sie abzuschrecken und die daraus resultierenden Steuereinnahmen für Ausgleichsmaßnahmen zu verwenden. In Norwegen, wo das Verursacherprinzip eines der Leitprinzipien der Klimapolitik ist, gibt es einen steuerlichen Anreiz, um die Teilnahme an Waldschutzvereinbarungen zu fördern.

Zu den steuerlichen Maßnahmen in Spanien gehören auch Maßnahmen im Bereich Abfall: Verringerung des Abfallaufkommens und Verbesserung der Abfallbewirtschaftung (durch eine Verbrauchssteuer auf nicht wiederverwendbare Kunststoffverpackungen und eine Steuer auf die Deponierung, Verbrennung und Mitverbrennung von Abfall).

In den Fällen, in denen die landwirtschaftliche Tätigkeit in der Vergangenheit der Auslöser für Steuererleichterungen war (wie z.B. der Agricultural Property Relief (APR) im Vereinigten Königreich), muss der Anwendungsbereich einer solchen Tätigkeit möglicherweise erweitert werden, um neben der Landwirtschaft auch Umweltmaßnahmen einzubeziehen.

6. Der Einsatz neuer Technologien und Praktiken muss entwickelt werden, um die ökologische Nachhaltigkeit zu verbessern, und zwar neben der Verwaltung der Flächennutzung im Wege von Vorschriften und freiwilligen vertraglichen Regelungen. Dabei sollten auch die Strukturen berücksichtigt werden, die zur Erforschung und effektiven Bewertung neuer oder experimenteller Methoden und Praktiken erforderlich sind.

Die Kommission hörte von der Nutzung von Technologien neben anderen Klimaschutzmaßnahmen. In Spanien zum Beispiel wird Technologie im Zusammenhang mit der Rückgewinnung und Wiederverwendung von Wasser, bei Entsalzungsmaßnahmen, eingesetzt. Auch die Genmanipulation ist eine Technologie, die im Sinne des Klimaschutzes eingesetzt werden kann. Es ist wichtig, dass es einen Rahmen gibt, in dem solche Technologien schnell und auf einer angemessenen wissenschaftlichen Grundlage entwickelt und bewertet werden können, damit sie optimal genutzt werden können. Italien hat im Jahr 2022 einen wissenschaftlichen Rat für Klima und Umwelt eingerichtet, um einen Dialog zwischen Wissenschaft und Politik zu eröffnen und das politische Handeln an den wissenschaftlichen Fortschritten auszurichten; weitere Schritte wurden bisher jedoch nicht unternommen.

Das schweizerische Landwirtschaftsrecht verfügt über ein Ressourcenprogramm für die Landwirtschaft, das organisatorische, technische und strukturelle Innovationen und Verbesserungen bei der nachhaltigen Nutzung von Produktionsmitteln fördert, um den Stand der Technik in der Landwirtschaft kontinuierlich zu verbessern. Das Programm sieht einen Bottom-up-Ansatz vor: Projekte, die von regionalen oder sektorspezifischen privaten oder öffentlichen Trägern entwickelt werden.

7. Es sollte geprüft werden, ob und wie private Finanzierung und Marktentwicklung am wirksamsten mit staatlicher Finanzierung und Unterstützung bei der Förderung der ökologischen Nachhaltigkeit kombiniert werden können

Das Ausmaß der Abhängigkeit von staatlicher Finanzierung und die Einbeziehung anderer Interessengruppen und privater Finanzmittel ist von Mitgliedstaat zu Mitgliedstaat unterschiedlich. Im Vereinigten Königreich fördert die Politik ein gemischtes Finanzierungsmodell, das darauf abzielt, einen Markt für öffentliche Umweltgüter und -dienstleistungen zu schaffen. In Frankreich wird die Biodiversität seit vielen Jahren durch verschiedene öffentliche und private Kennzeichnungssysteme (Marken) geschützt, die sich direkt an die Verbraucher richten und es ihnen ermöglichen, die Auswirkungen der von ihnen gekauften Produkte auf die Biodiversität zu verstehen.

Wie im nationalen Bericht aus Italien festgestellt wurde, kommt der Markt oft dorthin, wo der Gesetzgeber nicht hinkommt. (Die Kommission hörte, dass in Italien die Nachfrage nach zertifizierten Produkten, die nach umweltfreundlicheren Produktionsmethoden hergestellt wurden, hoch ist.) Dies könnte bei einem Übergang zu einer besseren Nutzung des Naturkapitals sowohl in Italien als auch in anderen Mitgliedstaaten effektiver genutzt werden.

Conclusions de la Commission II –
Conclusions of Commission II –
Schlussfolgerungen der Kommission II

Version française – French version – Französische Version
Version anglaise – English version – Englische Version
Version allemande – German version – Deutsche Version

Conclusions de la Commission II – Conclusions of Commission II – Schlussfolgerungen der Kommission II

A. Version française – French version – Französische Version

La Commission II, dont les travaux ont été présentés dans les rapports nationaux présentés lors du XXXIe Congrès européen de droit rural, s'est concentrée sur les nouvelles considérations environnementales émergentes en matière d'utilisation des terres en ce qui concerne le carbone, la biodiversité et les nutriments. Chacun des rapporteurs nationaux a abordé la position actuelle de son pays en matière de changement climatique et de mesures environnementales, y compris les politiques, les objectifs et les mécanismes visant à protéger et à améliorer les actifs naturels.

Un résumé des conclusions de la Commission II est présenté ci-dessous.

1. La Commission a convenu que la protection du climat ne peut réussir qu'avec une coopération internationale, mise en œuvre efficacement au niveau national. Une réponse internationale collaborative est essentielle. À l'heure actuelle, les différents niveaux de priorité nationale (influencés par les pressions politiques nationales, en particulier les changements d'administration et les priorités contradictoires), la dimension intertemporelle et le manque de terminologie universelle constituent des obstacles importants à une approche internationale cohérente.
2. Les États membres ont convenu que la politique et la planification nationales en matière de climat devraient tenir compte de la multifonctionnalité du capital naturel, ce qui implique la nécessité de trouver un équilibre entre l'exploitation productive des terres (par exemple pour assurer la sécurité alimentaire) et les objectifs de conservation.
3. L'absence de normes reconnues et objectives pour les niveaux de référence et les résultats visés dans les objectifs environnementaux et les codes de bonnes pratiques rend difficile, tant au niveau national qu'international, la réglementation et l'application efficaces et cohérentes des mesures climatiques. Les niveaux de référence varient en fonction du moment où ils sont évalués ou testés, et les résultats visés en fonction d'un grand nombre de facteurs qui seront propres à chaque pays à un moment donné.

4. La mise en œuvre de mesures de protection du climat repose sur trois approches principales, à savoir : l'imposition de contrôles et d'interdictions ; les accords contractuels, conclus par les acteurs avec l'État et/ou avec des organismes privés ; et l'utilisation de la technologie. La législation est largement utilisée ; mais les contrôles ainsi imposés nécessitent un suivi et une application cohérents, et les États membres ont exprimé leur inquiétude quant au manque fréquent de structures ou de financements efficaces à cet effet. L'entrée des propriétaires ou des utilisateurs de terres dans des accords contractuels volontaires est un autre moyen essentiel d'atteindre les objectifs de protection du climat. Le succès de ces programmes dépend de l'engagement des acteurs à la base. Cela a un aspect culturel et communautaire, en plus de garantir la viabilité pratique et financière des programmes (notamment en fournissant des incitations appropriées et une répartition proportionnelle des responsabilités).
5. La politique et la réglementation fiscales peuvent et doivent servir de moteur à l'entrée dans des programmes contractuels ou volontaires. Elle ne doit pas constituer un obstacle à l'entrée.
6. L'utilisation de nouvelles technologies et pratiques doit être développée pour améliorer la durabilité environnementale, parallèlement à la gestion de l'utilisation des terres par le biais de la réglementation et de programmes contractuels volontaires. Il convient d'envisager les structures nécessaires pour explorer et évaluer efficacement les méthodes et pratiques nouvelles ou expérimentales.
7. Il convient d'examiner si et comment le financement privé et le développement du marché peuvent être intégrés le plus efficacement possible au financement et au soutien de l'État dans la promotion de la durabilité environnementale.

B. Version anglaise – English version – Englische Version

The focus of Commission II, addressed in the National Reports presented during the XXXI European Congress of Rural Law, was new and emerging environmental land use considerations in respect of carbon, biodiversity and nutrients. Each of the National Reporters addressed the current position of their country in relation to climate change and environmental measures, including policies, targets and mechanisms to protect and enhance natural capital assets.

A summary of the conclusions of Commission II is set out below.

1. The consensus of the Commission was that climate protection can only succeed with international cooperation, effectively implemented at a domestic level. A collaborative international response is essential. At present, different levels of national priority (influenced by domestic political pressures, in particular from changes in administration and conflicting priorities), the intertemporal dimension and the lack of universal terminology are significant obstacles to a coherent international approach.
2. Member states agreed that national climate policy and planning should address the multifunctionality of natural capital, which gives rise to the need to balance productive exploitation of land (for example to ensure food security) with conservation goals.
3. The absence of recognised and objective standards for the purpose of both baselines and targets in environmental objectives and codes of practice presents difficulties at both a domestic and international level for effective and consistent regulation and enforcement of climate measures. Baselines will vary according to when these are assessed or tested; and targets according to a large number of factors which will be unique to each country at any moment in time.
4. The delivery of climate protection measures deploys three principal approaches, namely: the imposition of controls and prohibitions; contractual agreements, entered by actors with the state and/or with private bodies; and the use of technology. Legislation is widely used; but the controls imposed in this way require consistent monitoring and enforcement, and member states expressed concern that effective structures or funding for this is often lacking. Alternatively, entry by land owners or users into voluntary contractual agreements is a crucial means of delivering climate protection goals. The success of these schemes depends on engaging actors at base level. This has a cultural and community aspect, in addition to ensuring schemes are practically and financially viable (including by providing appropriate incentives and proportionate allocation of responsibility).
5. Tax policy and regulation can and should operate as a driver to entry into contractual or voluntary schemes. It should not operate as a barrier to entry.
6. The use of new technologies and practices needs to be developed to improve environmental sustainability, alongside management of land use by way of regulation, and by voluntary contractual schemes. This should

include consideration of structures required to explore and effectively assess new or experimental methods and practices.

7. Consideration should be given as to whether and how private finance and market development can most effectively be integrated with state funding and support in the promotion of environmental sustainability.

C. Version allemande – German version – Deutsche Version

Der Schwerpunkt der Kommission II, der in den Nationalen Berichten behandelt wurde, die während des XXXI. Europäischen Agrarrechtskongresses vorgestellt wurden, lag auf neuen und aufkommenden Überlegungen zur ökologischen Landnutzung in Bezug auf Kohlenstoff, Biodiversität und Nährstoffe. Alle nationalen Berichterstattenden gingen auf die aktuelle Position ihres Landes in Bezug auf den Klimawandel und Umweltmaßnahmen ein, einschließlich Richtlinien, Ziele und Mechanismen zum Schutz und zur Verbesserung des Naturkapitals.

Eine Zusammenfassung der Schlussfolgerungen der Kommission II ist unten aufgeführt.

1. Die Kommission war sich einig, dass Klimaschutz nur durch internationale Zusammenarbeit gelingen kann, die auf nationaler Ebene effektiv umgesetzt wird. Eine gemeinsame internationale Vorgehensweise ist unerlässlich. Derzeit stellen unterschiedliche nationale Prioritätsebenen (beeinflusst durch innenpolitischen Druck, insbesondere durch Regierungswechsel und widersprüchliche Prioritäten), die intertemporale Dimension und das Fehlen einer universellen Terminologie erhebliche Hindernisse für einen kohärenten internationalen Ansatz dar.
2. Die Mitgliedstaaten waren sich einig, dass die nationale Klimapolitik und -planung die Multifunktionalität des Naturkapitals berücksichtigen sollte, was dazu führen wird, dass die produktive Nutzung von Land (z.B. zur Gewährleistung der Ernährungssicherheit) mit den Zielen des Naturschutzes in Einklang gebracht werden muss.
3. Das Fehlen anerkannter und objektiver Standards für die Festlegung von Ausgangswerten und Zielen in Umweltzielen und Verhaltenskodizes erschwert sowohl auf nationaler als auch auf internationaler Ebene eine wirksame und einheitliche Regulierung und Durchsetzung von Klimaschutzmaßnahmen. Ausgangswerte variieren je nachdem, wann sie bewertet oder getestet werden; und Ziele hängen von einer Vielzahl von Faktoren ab, die für jedes Land zu jedem Zeitpunkt einzigartig sind.

4. Bei der Umsetzung von Klimaschutzmaßnahmen werden drei Hauptansätze verfolgt: die Auferlegung von Kontrollen und Verboten, vertragliche Vereinbarungen zwischen Akteuren und dem Staat und/oder privaten Einrichtungen und der Einsatz von Technologie. Rechtsvorschriften sind weit verbreitet, aber die auf diese Weise auferlegten Kontrollen erfordern eine konsequente Überwachung und Durchsetzung, und die Mitgliedstaaten äußerten Bedenken, dass es hierfür oft an wirksamen Strukturen oder Finanzmitteln mangelt. Alternativ dazu sind freiwillige vertragliche Vereinbarungen zwischen Landbesitzern oder -nutzern ein entscheidendes Mittel zur Erreichung der Klimaschutzziele. Der Erfolg dieser Programme hängt von der Einbeziehung der Akteure auf der Basisebene ab. Dies hat einen kulturellen und gemeinschaftlichen Aspekt und stellt außerdem sicher, dass die Programme praktisch und finanziell tragfähig sind (unter anderem durch die Bereitstellung angemessener Anreize und eine verhältnismäßige Aufteilung der Verantwortung).
5. Steuerpolitik und -regulierung können und sollten als Antrieb für den Beitritt zu vertraglichen oder freiwilligen Programmen dienen. Sie sollten nicht als Eintrittsbarriere fungieren.
6. Der Einsatz neuer Technologien und Praktiken muss weiterentwickelt werden, um die ökologische Nachhaltigkeit zu verbessern, und zwar neben der Steuerung der Landnutzung durch Regulierung und durch freiwillige vertragliche Regelungen. Dabei sollten auch die Strukturen berücksichtigt werden, die erforderlich sind, um neue oder experimentelle Methoden und Praktiken zu erforschen und effektiv zu bewerten.
7. Dabei sollte auch geprüft werden, ob und wie private Finanzierungen und Marktentwicklungen am effektivsten mit staatlichen Finanzierungen zur Förderung der ökologischen Nachhaltigkeit kombiniert werden können.

IV.
Commission III - Kommission III

President:

Prof. Dr. Franci Avsec,
University of Novo mesto (Slovenia)

General Reporter:

Prof. UAM dr hab. Aneta Suchoń,
Adam Mickiewicz University Poznań (Poland)

Les évolutions récentes et significatives du droit rural

Significant current developments in rural law

Bedeutende aktuelle Entwicklungen im Recht des ländlichen Raums

Questionnaires – Fragebogen –
Commission III – Kommission III

Version française – French version – Französische Version
Version anglaise – English version – Englische Version
Version allemande – German version – Deutsche Version

Questionnaire de la Commission III – Questionnaire of Commission III – Fragebogen der Kommission III

Questions – Fragen

A. Version française – French version – Französische Version

1. Organisation et conduite de l'activité agricole dans une exploitation.
   1.1. Quels sont les changements récents dans les réglementations légales concernant les principales définitions, les sujets, l'enregistrement et d'autres aspects de l'activité agricole en général, et quelles sont les raisons de ces changements ? De nouvelles réglementations nationales ont-elles été publiées concernant l'enregistrement de l'activité agricole et d'autres registres relatifs à l'activité agricole et aux activités connexes (par exemple, l'agrotourisme, les activités de transformation) ? Les réglementations relatives à la fiscalité ont-elles changé (par exemple, l'impôt sur le revenu des personnes physiques, l'impôt sur le revenu des sociétés, la TVA, les droits d'acquis sur les carburants dans l'agriculture) ?
   1.2. Existe-t-il de nouvelles réglementations nationales concernant la transmission des propriétés agricoles, que ce soit par transfert de propriété ou par bail ? La réglementation a-t-elle changé en ce qui concerne, par exemple, la transmission des terres agricoles d'une génération à l'autre en cas de décès ou entre vifs, les plans de zonage affectant les terres agricoles, la division des biens immobiliers ou l'abolition de la copropriété des exploitations agricoles ?
   1.3. De nouvelles réglementations nationales sur l'emploi dans l'agriculture ont-elles été publiées pour répondre aux défis spécifiques liés aux relations de travail dans l'agriculture (contrats de travail, contrat de mandat et d'aide dans une exploitation, protection des travailleurs saisonniers), aux réglementations sur l'assurance retraite, à l'obtention de retraite par les agriculteurs, à l'assurance sociale ou à l'assurance des biens, à l'assurance responsabilité civile et à l'assurance des récoltes et du bétail ? Le travail est-il effectué par

l'agriculteur et sa famille ou est-il sous-traité à des entrepreneurs qui fournissent des services agricoles ?

1.4. De quelle manière les femmes participent-elles aux activités agricoles ? Les femmes sont-elles davantage impliquées dans les activités agricoles ? Existe-t-il des instruments nationaux soutenant les femmes dans cette activité ?

1.5. Quels sont les exemples d'aides de minimis agricoles existant dans la réglementation nationale et les dispositions ont-elles été modifiées ? De nouveaux exemples d'activités ont-ils été couverts par les aides de minimis agricoles ?

1.6. De nouvelles réglementations nationales ont-elles été adoptées en matière de production végétale et animale, notamment en ce qui concerne l'utilisation de pesticides et d'herbicides (nocifs) sur les terres agricoles ou la production de bétail (générant du méthane)

 1.6.1. Quelles sont les principales évolutions juridiques dans le domaine de la production végétale ? Par exemple, comment le règlement (UE) 2016/2031 sur la législation phytosanitaire est-il mis en œuvre ? Les pays ont-ils publié des réglementations juridiques supplémentaires ?

 1.6.2. Quelles sont les principales évolutions juridiques dans le domaine de la production animale ? Par exemple, comment le règlement (UE) 2016/429 sur la santé animale est-il mis en œuvre ? Les pays ont-ils publié des réglementations juridiques supplémentaires ?

 1.6.3. Quelles sont les principales évolutions juridiques dans le domaine de l'élevage animal ? Par exemple, comment le règlement (UE) 2016/1012 relatif à l'élevage d'animaux est-il mis en œuvre ? Les États membres ont-ils adopté des réglementations concernant la conservation des ressources génétiques des animaux d'élevage, l'évaluation de leur valeur d'utilité et l'évaluation génétique, la tenue des livres généalogiques, des registres d'élevage et des registres, ainsi que le contrôle de l'élevage et de la reproduction de ces animaux ?

 1.6.4. La peste porcine africaine (PPA) pose-t-elle un problème dans votre pays ?

1.7. Quels sont les principaux développements juridiques dans le domaine du droit de la chasse, par exemple en ce qui concerne la protection contre les dommages causés par la chasse aux cultures et aux exploitations agricoles et l'effet des loups sur la gestion des pâturages ?

2. Position des agriculteurs dans la chaîne de valeur, coopératives, organisations, contrats et droit agroalimentaire.
   2.1. Quelles sont les principales évolutions juridiques concernant la position des agriculteurs dans la chaîne de valeur, en particulier dans le cadre de la directive (UE) 2019/633 sur les pratiques commerciales déloyales dans les relations interentreprises au sein de la chaîne d'approvisionnement agricole et alimentaire (le délai de mise en œuvre ayant expiré le 1er mai 2021) ?
   2.2. Quelles sont les principales associations légales de producteurs agricoles, par exemple les coopératives, les groupes de producteurs agricoles ? De nouvelles réglementations ont-elles été publiées concernant la création d'organisations de producteurs agricoles visées par les règlements de l'UE ? Les dispositions légales relatives aux contrats liés à l'agriculture ou à la production agricole ont-elles été modifiées ?
   2.3. Des modifications ont-elles été apportées aux dispositions concernant (i) la vente directe de produits agricoles non transformés et transformés et (ii) le commerce de détail de produits agricoles ?
3. Les zones rurales.
   3.1. Quels sont les principaux développements juridiques en droit national concernant la mise en œuvre des défis identifiés dans la communication de la Commission du 30 juin 2021, intitulée « Une vision à long terme pour les zones rurales de l'UE – Vers des zones rurales plus fortes, connectées, résilientes et prospères à l'horizon 2040 » ?
   3.2. Des dispositions légales ont-elles été adoptées concernant le développement des zones rurales, par exemple en ce qui concerne les activités commerciales non agricoles, le développement régional et les groupes de personnes vivant dans les zones rurales, par exemple les femmes et leurs organisations, les travailleurs isolés, à la suite de la pandémie de COVID-19 ?
4. Un Pacte Vert pour l'Europe (Green Deal), protection de l'environnement dans les exploitations agricoles, lutte contre le changement climatique, y compris l'agriculture biologique, les énergies renouvelables, la législation sur l'eau et le bien-être des animaux.
   4.1. Comment la politique de l'UE exprimée dans le Pacte Vert pour l'Europe influence-t-elle les réglementations nationales ? Quelles

sont les menaces et les difficultés liées au Green Deal européen, compte tenu de la situation et de la spécificité de chaque État membre ? De nouvelles réglementations juridiques ont-elles été émises ou adoptées ?

4.2. Stratégie « de la ferme à la table » : Quels sont les principaux développements juridiques concernant la mise en œuvre des défis identifiés dans la communication de la Commission du 20 mai 2020, intitulée « Une stratégie ‚De la ferme à la table' pour un système alimentaire équitable, sain et respectueux de l'environnement » ?

4.3. Objectif climatique : Quels sont les principaux développements juridiques concernant la mise en œuvre des défis identifiés dans la communication de la Commission du 14 juillet 2021, intitulée « ‚Ajustement à l'objectif 55': atteindre l'objectif climatique de l'UE à l'horizon 2030 sur la voie de la neutralité climatique » ?

4.4. Agriculture biologique : Quels sont les principaux développements juridiques concernant la mise en œuvre des défis identifiés dans la communication de la Commission du 19 avril 2021, intitulée « Plan d'action en faveur du développement de la production biologique » ? Dans le cadre du règlement (UE) 2018/848 relatif à la production biologique, de nouvelles réglementations nationales sur l'agriculture biologique ont-elles été adoptées ? Existe-t-il des instruments internes soutenant le développement de l'agriculture biologique ?

4.5. Stratégie pour les sols : Quels sont les principaux développements juridiques concernant la mise en œuvre des défis identifiés dans la communication de la Commission du 17 novembre 2021, intitulée « Stratégie de l'UE pour la protection des sols à l'horizon 2030. Récolter les fruits de sols en bonne santé pour les êtres humains, l'alimentation, la nature et le climat » ? De nouvelles réglementations concernant la protection qualitative des terres agricoles ont-elles été publiées et introduites ? Quels sont les instruments juridiques actuels pour la protection des terres et sont-ils efficaces ? Ces réglementations s'appliquent-elles à l'ensemble du pays ou les régions peuvent-elles adopter des réglementations tenant compte de leurs besoins spécifiques ?

4.6. Loi sur l'eau : Quels changements ont été apportés à la législation sur l'eau, par exemple en ce qui concerne la pollution par les nitrates d'origine agricole et la prévention de toute nouvelle pollution ? De nouvelles dispositions légales ont-elles été publiées concernant la législation sur l'eau en relation avec les exploitations agricoles et les zones rurales, par exemple en ce qui concerne les nitrates, l'utilisation des eaux usées dans les activités agricoles, l'irrigation, la construction d'installations hydrauliques et l'amélioration des sols dans l'agriculture ?

5. Plans stratégiques de la PAC dans les États membres de l'UE et autres documents stratégiques concernant l'agriculture dans les pays extérieurs à l'Union européenne. Nouvelles règles juridiques pour la politique agricole commune 2023-2027.
   - 5.1. Quelles sont les orientations les plus importantes pour le développement de l'agriculture et des zones rurales de votre pays dans le plan stratégique de la PAC ? Quelles sont les règles applicables aux paiements directs et aux autres paiements au titre du premier pilier ? Quel type d'éco-régimes (*ecoschemes*) votre pays a-t-il choisi ?
   - 5.2. Existe-t-il des initiatives juridiques dans le cadre du premier pilier concernant les paiements directs découplés et couplés (ou des aides comparables), leur plafonnement et leur dégressivité ?
   - 5.3. Quels sont les programmes relevant du deuxième pilier ? Quels sont les programmes consacrés aux jeunes agriculteurs, à la protection de l'environnement dans les exploitations ou à la modernisation des exploitations ? Quelles définitions ont été introduites concernant les agriculteurs actifs, l'activité agricole, etc.
   - 5.4. La politique agricole commune 2023-2027 a-t-elle fait l'objet d'une réglementation nationale ? Les fonds de l'UE sont-ils octroyés dans votre pays sous la forme d'une décision administrative ou d'un accord de droit civil ? Quelles sont, selon vous, les principales dispositions juridiques de la nouvelle PAC ?
   - 5.5. Dans le cas des pays extérieurs à l'UE, quelles sont les modalités de soutien à l'agriculture et sont-elles similaires à celles des premiers et deuxièmes piliers de l'UE ?
6. Relations extérieures avec les pays tiers.
   - 6.1. Votre pays a-t-il signé de nouveaux accords internationaux sur l'agriculture et l'alimentation ? Quels accords ont été conclus avec le Royaume-Uni/l'UE après le Brexit ? À quoi ressemblent l'exportation et l'importation de produits agricoles et d'aliments transformés dans votre pays ? Existe-t-il des réglementations légales concernant la promotion des produits agricoles à l'étranger, et dans quelle mesure ? Les dispositions de l'OMC et de l'UE ont-elles

des répercussions sur l'agriculture de l'UE et des différents États membres ?

6.2. Le paquet final sur l'agriculture de la Conférence ministérielle qui s'est tenue à Genève du 12 au 17 juin 2022 comprenait une déclaration ministérielle sur la réponse d'urgence à l'insécurité alimentaire (WT/MIN(22)/28) et une décision ministérielle visant à exempter les achats de produits alimentaires à des fins humanitaires dans le cadre du Programme alimentaire mondial (PAM) d'interdictions ou de restrictions (WT/MIN(22)/29). Ces deux éléments répondent aux demandes de la communauté internationale qui souhaite que les membres de l'OMC prennent des mesures immédiates pour relever les défis actuels en matière de sécurité alimentaire. Quelles sont les mesures prises par les pays dans le domaine de la sécurité alimentaire mondiale ?

B. Version anglaise – English version – Englische Version

1. Organisation and conduct of agricultural activity on a farm.

1.1. What are the recent changes in legal regulations on the main definitions, subject matters, registration and other aspects of agricultural activity in general, and what are the reasons for these changes? Have any new national regulations been issued regarding the registration of agricultural activity and in respect of other registers concerning agricultural activity and related activities (e.g. Agrotourism, processing activities)? Have the regulations concerning taxation changed (e.g. personal income tax, corporate income tax, VAT, excise duty in agriculture for fuel)?

1.2. Are there any new national regulations regarding the conveyance of agricultural property, whether by transfer of ownership or by lease? Have the regulations changed regarding e.g. the devolution of agricultural land from one generation to the next on death or inter vivos, zoning plans affecting agricultural land, the division of real estate or the abolition of co-ownership of farms?

1.3. Have new national regulations on employment in agriculture been issued to address specific challenges associated with employment relations in agriculture (employment contracts, contract of mandate and helpers on a farm, protection for seasonal workers), regulations on pension insurance, obtaining pensions by farmers, social or property insurance, third party liability insurance and crop and livestock insurance? Is the work done by the farmer and his family or is it outsourced to entrepreneurs who provide agricultural services?

1.4. In what ways do women participate in agricultural activity? Is there a greater involvement of women in agricultural activities? Are there national instruments supporting women in this activity?

1.5. What examples of agricultural de minimis aid exist in national regulation and have provisions been changed? Have new examples of activity been covered by de minimis aid in agriculture?

1.6. Have any new national regulations on plant and animal production been issued, including the use of (harmful) pesticides and herbicides on farmland, or livestock production (generating methane)?

   1.6.1. What are the main legal developments in the field of plant production? For example, how is Plant Health Law Regulation (EU) 2016/2031 implemented? Have countries issued additional legal regulations?

   1.6.2. What are the main legal developments in the field of animal production? For example, how is Animal Health Law Regulation (EU) 2016/429 implemented? Have countries issued additional legal regulations ?

   1.6.3. What are the main legal developments in the field of animal breeding? For example, how is Animal Breeding Regulation (EU) 2016/1012 implemented? Have Member States adopted regulations regarding the conservation of the genetic resources of farm animals, the evaluation of their utility value and genetic evaluation, the keeping of herd books, breeding registers and registers, as well as control over the breeding and reproduction of these animals?

   1.6.4. Is there a problem with African Swine Fever (ASF) in your country?

1.7. What are the main legal developments in the field of hunting law, e.g. concerning protection against hunting damages caused to agricultural crops and farms and the effect of wolves on pasture management?

2. Position of farmers in the value chain, cooperatives, organisations, contracts and agri-food law.

   2.1. What are the main legal developments regarding the position of farmers in the value chain, especially under Directive (EU)

2019/633 on unfair trading practices in business-to-business relationships in the agricultural and food supply chain (the deadline for implementation having expired on 1 May 2021)?

2.2. What are the main legal associations of agricultural producers, e.g. cooperatives, groups of agricultural producers? Have new regulations been issued regarding the establishment of agricultural producer organisations referred to in EU regulations? Have the legal regulations on contracts related to agriculture or agricultural production been changed?

2.3. Have there been changes to provisions on (i) the direct sale of unprocessed and processed agricultural products; and (ii) retail trade in agricultural products?

3. Rural areas.

3.1. What are the main legal developments in national law regarding the implementation of the challenges identified in the Communication from the Commission of 30 June 2021, entitled "A long-term Vision for the EU's Rural Areas – Towards stronger, connected, resilient and prosperous rural areas by 2040"?

3.2. Have any legal regulations been issued regarding the development of rural areas in relation to e.g. undertaking non-agricultural business activity, regional development and groups of people living in rural areas, e.g. women and their organisations, remote workers in the wake of the COVID-19 pandemic?

4. European Green Deal, environmental protection on farms, counteracting climate change, including organic farming, renewable energy, water law and animal welfare.

4.1. How does EU policy expressed in the European Green Deal influence national regulations? What threats and difficulties are raised in connection with the European Green Deal, taking into account the situation and specificity of each Member State? Have new legal regulations been issued or passed?

4.2. Farm to fork strategy: What are the main legal developments regarding the implementation of the challenges identified in the Communication from the Commission of 20 May 2020, entitled "'Farm to fork' strategy for a fair, healthy and environmentally friendly food system"?

4.3. Climate target: What are the main legal developments regarding the implementation of the challenges identified in the Communication from the Commission of 14 July 2021, entitled "'Fit for 55':

delivering the EU's 2030 Climate Target on the way to climate neutrality"?

4.4. Organic farming: What are the main legal developments regarding the implementation of the challenges identified in the Communication from the Commission of 19 April 2021, entitled "Action Plan for the Development of Organic Production"? In connection with the Organic production Regulation (EU) 2018/848 have new national regulations on organic farming been adopted? Are there internal instruments supporting the development of organic farming?

4.5. Soil Strategy: What are the main legal developments regarding the implementation of the challenges identified in the Communication from the Commission of 17 November 2021, entitled "EU Soil Strategy for 2030. Reaping the benefits of healthy soils for people, food, nature and climate"? Have new regulations concerning the qualitative protection of agricultural land been issued and introduced? What are the current legal instruments for land protection and are they effective? Are these regulations for the whole country or can regions issue regulations taking into account their specific needs?

4.6. Water Law: What changes have been made to water law, e.g. addressing nitrate pollution from agricultural sources and the prevention of further pollution? Have new legal regulations been issued regarding water law in relation to farms and rural areas, e.g. regarding nitrates, the use of sewage in agricultural activities, irrigation, construction of water facilities and soil improvement in agriculture?

5. CAP Strategic Plans in EU Member States and other strategic documents concerning agriculture in countries outside the European Union. New legal regulations for the Common Agricultural Policy 2023-2027.

5.1. What are the most important directions for the development of agriculture and rural areas of your country in the CAP Strategic Plan? What are the rules for direct and other payments under the first pillar? What kind of Ecoschemes has your country chosen?

5.2. Are there legal initiatives in the first pillar regarding decoupled and coupled direct payments (or comparable support), their capping and degressivity?

5.3. Which programmes are in the second pillar? What programmes are dedicated to young farmers, on-farm environmental protection or modernisation of farms? What definitions were introduced concerning active farmers, agricultural activity etc.?

5.4. Have national regulations been issued regarding the Common Agricultural Policy 2023-2027? Are EU funds granted in your country in the form of an administrative decision or a civil agreement? What in your opinion are the most important legal regulations in the new CAP?

5.5. In the case of countries outside the EU, what are the arrangements for farm support and are they similar to the first and second pillar of the EU?

6. External relations with third countries of the world.

6.1. Has your country signed any new international agreements on agriculture and food? What deals were made with the UK/EU after Brexit? What does the export and import of agricultural products and processed food look like in your country? Are there any legal regulations concerning the promotion of agricultural products abroad, and to what extent? Are there impacts of WTO and EU provisions on the agriculture of the EU and individual Member States?

6.2. The Agriculture Final Package in the Ministerial Conference in Geneva on 12-17 June 2022 consisted of a Ministerial Declaration on Emergency Response to Food Insecurity (WT/MIN(22)/28) and a Ministerial Decision to exempt purchases of food for humanitarian purposes under the World Food Program (WFP) from bans or restrictions (WT/MIN(22)/29). Both of these elements respond to the demands of the international community for immediate action by WTO members to address the current food security challenges. What actions have been taken by countries in the field of global food security?

C. Version allemande – German version – Deutsche Version

1. Organisation und Durchführung der landwirtschaftlichen Tätigkeit in einem Betrieb.

1.1. Wie lauten die jüngsten Änderungen der gesetzlichen Bestimmungen zu den wichtigsten Definitionen, Themen, der Registrierung und anderen Aspekten der landwirtschaftlichen Tätigkeit im Allgemeinen, und was sind die Gründe für diese Änderungen? Wurden neue nationale Vorschriften zur Registrierung landwirtschaftlicher Tätigkeit und zu anderen Registern für die landwirtschaftliche Tätigkeit und damit verbundene Tätigkeiten (z.B. Agrotourismus, Verarbeitungstätigkeiten) erlassen? Haben sich die Steuervorschriften geändert (z.B. Einkommenssteuer, Körperschaftssteuer, Mehrwertsteuer, Verbrauchssteuer in der Landwirtschaft für Kraftstoffe)?

1.2. Gibt es neue nationale Vorschriften für die Übertragung von landwirtschaftlichem Eigentum, entweder durch Eigentumsübertragung oder durch Verpachtung? Haben sich die Vorschriften geändert, zum Beispiel in Bezug auf die Übertragung landwirtschaftlicher Flächen von einer Generation auf die nächste im Todesfall oder unter Lebenden, in Bezug auf landwirtschaftliche Flächen betreffende Flächennutzungspläne, in Bezug auf die Aufteilung von Grundstücken oder die Auflösung von Miteigentum an landwirtschaftlichen Betrieben?

1.3. Wurden neue nationale Vorschriften über die Beschäftigung in der Landwirtschaft erlassen, um die besonderen Herausforderungen im Zusammenhang mit den Beschäftigungsverhältnissen in der Landwirtschaft zu bewältigen (Arbeitsverträge, Hilfsarbeiter in einem landwirtschaftlichen Betrieb, Schutz für Saisonarbeiter), Vorschriften über die Rentenversicherung, den Bezug von Renten durch Landwirte, Sozial- oder Sachversicherungen, Haftpflichtversicherungen und Ernte- und Viehversicherungen? Wird die Arbeit vom Landwirt und seiner Familie erledigt oder ist sie an Unternehmer ausgelagert, die landwirtschaftliche Dienstleistungen erbringen?

1.4. Auf welche Weise beteiligen sich Frauen an der landwirtschaftlichen Tätigkeit? Gibt es eine stärkere Beteiligung von Frauen an landwirtschaftlichen Tätigkeiten? Gibt es nationale Instrumente zur Unterstützung von Frauen bei dieser Tätigkeit?

1.5. Welche Beispiele für De-minimis-Beihilfen in der Landwirtschaft gibt es in den nationalen Vorschriften, und wurden die Bestimmungen geändert? Gibt es neue Beispiele für Tätigkeiten, die unter De-minimis-Beihilfen in der Landwirtschaft fallen?

1.6. Wurden neue nationale Vorschriften für die Pflanzen- und Tierproduktion erlassen, einschließlich der Verwendung von (schädlichen) Pestiziden und Herbiziden auf landwirtschaftlichen Flächen oder der Viehzucht (Erzeugung von Methan)?

1.6.1. Was sind die wichtigsten rechtlichen Entwicklungen auf dem Gebiet der Pflanzenproduktion? Wie wird z.B. die Verordnung (EU) 2016/2031 zum Pflanzengesundheitsrecht umgesetzt? Haben die Länder zusätzliche gesetzliche Regelungen erlassen?

1.6.2. Was sind die wichtigsten rechtlichen Entwicklungen im Bereich der Tierproduktion? Wie wird z.B. die Verordnung (EU) 2016/429 zum Tiergesundheitsrecht umgesetzt? Haben die Länder zusätzliche gesetzliche Regelungen erlassen?

1.6.3. Was sind die wichtigsten rechtlichen Entwicklungen auf dem Gebiet der Tierzucht? Wie wird z.B. die Tierzuchtverordnung (EU) 2016/1012 umgesetzt? Haben die Mitgliedstaaten Vorschriften über die Erhaltung der genetischen Ressourcen landwirtschaftlicher Nutztiere, die Bewertung ihres Nutzwertes und die genetische Bewertung, das Führen von Herdbüchern, Zuchtbüchern und Registern sowie die Kontrolle der Zucht und Vermehrung dieser Tiere erlassen?

1.6.4. Gibt es in Ihrem Land ein Problem mit der Afrikanischen Schweinepest (ASP)?

1.7. Was sind die wichtigsten rechtlichen Entwicklungen im Bereich des Jagdrechts, z.B. in Bezug auf den Schutz vor Jagdschäden an landwirtschaftlichen Kulturen und Betrieben und die Auswirkungen von Wölfen auf die Weidewirtschaft?

2. Stellung der Landwirte in der Wertschöpfungskette, Genossenschaften, Organisationen, Verträge und Agrar- und Lebensmittelrecht.

2.1. Welches sind die wichtigsten rechtlichen Entwicklungen in Bezug auf die Stellung der Landwirte in der Wertschöpfungskette, insbesondere im Rahmen der Richtlinie (EU) 2019/633 über unlautere Handelspraktiken in den Geschäftsbeziehungen zwischen Unternehmen in der Agrar- und Lebensmittelversorgungskette (die Umsetzungsfrist ist am 1. Mai 2021 abgelaufen)?

2.2. Welches sind die wichtigsten rechtlichen Zusammenschlüsse von landwirtschaftlichen Erzeugern, z.B. Genossenschaften, Erzeugerorganisationen? Wurden neue Vorschriften für die Gründung von landwirtschaftlichen Erzeugerorganisationen im Sinne der EU-Vorschriften erlassen? Wurden die gesetzlichen Bestimmungen über Verträge im Zusammenhang mit der Landwirtschaft oder der landwirtschaftlichen Produktion geändert?

2.3. Wurden die Bestimmungen über (i) den Direktverkauf von unverarbeiteten und verarbeiteten landwirtschaftlichen Erzeugnissen und (ii) den Einzelhandel mit landwirtschaftlichen Erzeugnissen geändert?

3. Ländliche Gebiete.

3.1. Welches sind die wichtigsten rechtlichen Entwicklungen im nationalen Recht im Hinblick auf die Umsetzung der in der Mitteilung der Kommission vom 30. Juni 2021 mit dem Titel „Eine langfristige Vision für die ländlichen Gebiete der EU – Für stärkere, vernetzte, resiliente und florierende ländliche Gebiete bis 2040" genannten Herausforderungen?

3.2. Gibt es gesetzliche Regelungen für die Entwicklung des ländlichen Raums in Bezug auf z.B. die Ausübung einer nichtlandwirtschaftlichen Tätigkeit, die regionale Entwicklung und die in ländlichen Gebieten lebenden Personengruppen, z.B. Frauen und ihre Organisationen, Fernarbeiter im Zuge der COVID-19-Pandemie?

4. Europäischer Grüner Deal (Green Deal), Umweltschutz in landwirtschaftlichen Betrieben, Bekämpfung des Klimawandels, einschließlich ökologischen Landbaues, erneuerbare Energien, Wasserrecht und Tierschutz.

4.1. Wie beeinflusst die EU-Politik, die im Europäischen Green Deal zum Ausdruck kommt, die nationalen Regelungen? Welche Bedrohungen und Schwierigkeiten ergeben sich im Zusammenhang mit dem Europäischen Green Deal, unter Berücksichtigung von Situation und Besonderheiten der einzelnen Mitgliedstaaten? Wurden neue gesetzliche Regelungen erlassen oder verabschiedet?

4.2. Strategie „Vom Hof auf den Tisch (Farm to fork)": Welches sind die wichtigsten rechtlichen Entwicklungen im Hinblick auf die Umsetzung der in der Mitteilung der Kommission vom 20. Mai 2020 mit dem Titel „‚Vom Hof auf den Tisch' – eine Strategie für ein faires, gesundes und umweltfreundliches Lebensmittelsystem" genannten Herausforderungen?

4.3. Klimaziel: Welches sind die wichtigsten rechtlichen Entwicklungen in Bezug auf die Umsetzung der in der Mitteilung der Kommission vom 14. Juli 2021 mit dem Titel „‚Fit für 55': Erreichung des EU-Klimaziels für 2030 auf dem Weg zur Klimaneutralität" genannten Herausforderungen?

4.4. Ökologischer Landbau: Was sind die wichtigsten rechtlichen Entwicklungen in Bezug auf die Umsetzung der in der Mitteilung der Kommission vom 19. April 2021 mit dem Titel „Aktionsplan zur Förderung der ökologischen/biologischen Produktion“ genannten Herausforderungen? Wurden im Zusammenhang mit der Verordnung (EU) 2018/848 über die ökologische/biologische Produktion neue nationale Verordnungen zum Biolandbau erlassen? Gibt es interne Instrumente zur Unterstützung der Entwicklung des Biolandbaus?

4.5. Bodenstrategie: Welches sind die wichtigsten rechtlichen Entwicklungen in Bezug auf die Umsetzung der Herausforderungen, die in der Mitteilung der Kommission vom 17. November 2021 mit dem Titel „EU-Bodenstrategie für 2030 Die Vorteile gesunder Böden für Menschen, Lebensmittel, Natur und Klima nutzen“? Wurden neue Verordnungen zum qualitativen Schutz von landwirtschaftlichen Flächen erlassen und eingeführt? Welches sind die derzeitigen rechtlichen Instrumente zum Bodenschutz und sind sie wirksam? Gelten diese Regelungen für das gesamte Land oder können die Regionen Regelungen erlassen, die ihren spezifischen Bedürfnissen Rechnung tragen?

4.6. Wasserrecht: Welche Änderungen wurden im Wasserrecht vorgenommen, z.B. in Bezug auf die Nitratverschmutzung aus landwirtschaftlichen Quellen und die Verhinderung weiterer Verschmutzung? Wurden neue gesetzliche Regelungen zum Wasserrecht in Bezug auf landwirtschaftliche Betriebe und ländliche Gebiete erlassen, z.B. in Bezug auf Nitrat, die Verwendung von Abwasser in der Landwirtschaft, Bewässerung, Bau von Wasseranlagen und Bodenverbesserung in der Landwirtschaft?

5. GAP-Strategiepläne in den EU-Mitgliedstaaten und andere strategische Dokumente zur Landwirtschaft in Ländern außerhalb der Europäischen Union. Neue gesetzliche Regelungen für die Gemeinsame Agrarpolitik 2023-2027.

5.1. Welches sind die wichtigsten Vorgaben für die Entwicklung der Landwirtschaft und des ländlichen Raums in Ihrem Land im Rahmen des GAP-Strategieplans? Wie sehen die Regeln für Direktzahlungen und andere Zahlungen im Rahmen der ersten Säule aus? Für welche Art von Ökoregelungen (Ecoschemes) hat sich Ihr Land entschieden?

5.2. Gibt es rechtliche Initiativen im Rahmen der ersten Säule in Bezug auf entkoppelte und gekoppelte Direktzahlungen (oder vergleichbare Beihilfen), deren Kappung und Degressivität?

5.3. Welche Programme gehören zur zweiten Säule? Welche Programme sind für Junglandwirte, den betrieblichen Umweltschutz oder die Modernisierung von Betrieben vorgesehen? Welche Definitionen wurden für aktive Landwirte, landwirtschaftliche Tätigkeit usw. eingeführt?

5.4. Wurden nationale Vorschriften betreffend die Gemeinsame Agrarpolitik 2023-2027 erlassen? Werden EU-Mittel in Ihrem Land in Form eines Verwaltungsakts oder einer zivilrechtlichen Vereinbarung gewährt? Welche sind Ihrer Meinung nach die wichtigsten rechtlichen Regelungen in der neuen GAP?

5.5. Wie sehen die Regelungen für die Agrarförderung in Ländern außerhalb der EU aus, und sind sie mit der ersten und zweiten Säule der EU vergleichbar?

6. Außenbeziehungen zu Drittländern.

6.1. Hat Ihr Land neue internationale Abkommen über Landwirtschaft und Lebensmittel unterzeichnet? Welche Vereinbarungen wurden mit dem Vereinigten Königreich/der EU nach dem Brexit getroffen? Wie sehen der Export und Import von landwirtschaftlichen Produkten und verarbeiteten Lebensmitteln in Ihrem Land aus? Gibt es gesetzliche Regelungen zur Förderung von Agrarprodukten im Ausland und in welchem Umfang? Gibt es Auswirkungen von WTO- und EU-Bestimmungen auf die Landwirtschaft der EU und einzelner Mitgliedstaaten?

6.2. Das abschließende Paket zur Landwirtschaft auf der Ministerkonferenz in Genf vom 12. bis 17. Juni 2022 bestand aus einer Ministererklärung zur Soforthilfe bei Ernährungsunsicherheit (WT/MIN(22)/28) und einem Ministerbeschluss, den Kauf von Nahrungsmitteln für humanitäre Zwecke im Rahmen des Welternährungsprogramms (WFP) von Verboten oder Beschränkungen auszunehmen (WT/MIN(22)/29). Beide Beschlüsse entsprechen den Forderungen der internationalen Gemeinschaft nach sofortigen Maßnahmen der WTO-Mitglieder zur Bewältigung der aktuellen Herausforderungen im Bereich der Ernährungssicherheit. Welche Maßnahmen haben die Länder im Bereich der globalen Ernährungssicherheit ergriffen?

Rapport général de la Commission III –
General Report of Commission III –
Generalbericht der Kommission III

Version française – French version – Französische Version
Version anglaise – English version – Englische Version
Version allemande – German version – Deutsche Version

Rapport général de la Commission III

Version française – French version – Französische Version

Prof. UAM dr hab. Aneta Suchoń
Adam Mickiewicz University

Présenter le rapport de fond du Comité III n'est pas une tâche facile en raison des limites quantitatives des publications et de l'étendue des questions qui ont été discutées. Des rapports ont été préparés par les pays suivants : France, Allemagne, Hongrie, Italie, Pays-Bas, Pologne, Slovénie, Espagne, Suisse, Royaume-Uni et États-Unis. Une connexion en ligne a également été établie avec un chercheur ukrainien. La structure des rapports nationaux suivait généralement les questions indiquées dans le questionnaire. Depuis le dernier congrès (Poznań, septembre 2019), de nombreux changements réglementaires ont été apportés à la législation nationale et européenne.

Il convient de rappeler les principales questions identifiées dans le formulaire, notamment les suivantes : Quels sont les principaux changements dans la législation relative aux activités agricoles depuis le dernier Congrès de 2019 ?

- Organisation et conduite de l'activité agricole dans une exploitation.
- La position des agriculteurs dans la chaîne de valeur, les coopératives, les organisations, les contrats et le droit agroalimentaire.
- Zones rurales.
- Pacte vert pour l'Europe, protection de l'environnement dans les exploitations agricoles, lutte contre le changement climatique, y compris l'agriculture biologique, les énergies renouvelables, la législation sur l'eau et le bien-être des animaux.
- Plans stratégiques de la politique agricole commune (PAC) dans les États membres de l'UE et autres documents stratégiques concernant l'agriculture dans les pays extérieurs à l'Union européenne. Nouvelles règles juridiques pour la politique agricole commune 2023-2027.
- Relations extérieures avec les pays tiers du monde.

Une attention particulière a été accordée aux tendances les plus récentes, aux développements et aux solutions distinctes dans les pays étudiés. Au cours de la session, les rapports des États membres de l'UE et d'autres pays européens, ainsi que des États-Unis et de l'Ukraine, ont été présentés et discutés. La principale conclusion des rapports nationaux et des discussions est que de nombreuses nouvelles réglementations ont été adoptées (sont entrées en vigueur) dans les différents pays, tandis que les changements législatifs dans les pays de l'UE sont, dans une large mesure, liés aux nouveaux instruments juridiques dans le domaine de la politique agricole commune (PAC).

Il est donc impossible de mentionner tous les nouveaux aspects importants et intéressants de la législation, de la jurisprudence et des pratiques dans les rapports nationaux. Le catalogue de la législation relative à l'organisation et au fonctionnement des activités agricoles devient de plus en plus vaste, car il doit répondre aux défis des crises qui sont apparues ou se sont aggravées ces dernières années : COVID-19, le changement climatique (y compris la sécheresse), la guerre en Ukraine qui ont un impact significatif sur les activités agricoles.

Il ne fait aucun doute que la plupart des changements apportés à la législation agricole de l'UE et aux réglementations nationales sont liés à l'actuel Cadre financier pluriannuel.

En décembre 2021, trois règlements de base de l'UE ont été adoptés : Règlements du Parlement européen et du Conseil du 2 décembre 2021 n° (UE) 2021/2115[1] ; 2021/2116[2], et 2021/2117.[3]

Les États membres de l'UE ont préparé des plans stratégiques pour la PAC et adopté des règlements nationaux d'application conformément aux nouveaux instruments juridiques.

---

1 Règlement (UE) 2021/2115 du Parlement européen et du Conseil du 2 décembre 2021 établissant des règles relatives au soutien aux plans stratégiques à élaborer par les États membres dans le cadre de la politique agricole commune (plans stratégiques PAC) et financés par le Fonds européen agricole de garantie (FEAGA) et par le Fonds européen agricole pour le développement rural (FEADER) et abrogeant les règlements (UE) n° 1305/2013 et (UE) n° 1307/2013 (Règlement sur les plans stratégiques PAC).

2 Règlement (UE) 2021/2116 du Parlement européen et du Conseil du 2 décembre 2021 relatif au financement, à la gestion et au suivi de la politique agricole commune et abrogeant le règlement (UE) n° 1306/2013 (Règlement horizontal de la PAC).

3 Règlement (UE) 2021/2117 du Parlement européen et du Conseil du 2 décembre 2021 modifiant les règlements (UE) n° 1308/2013 portant organisation commune des marchés des produits agricoles, (UE) n° 1151/2012 relatif aux régimes de qualité applicables aux produits agricoles et aux denrées alimentaires, (UE) n° 251/2014 concernant la définition, la désignation, la présentation, l'étiquetage et la protection des indications géographiques des produits vitivinicoles aromatisés et (UE) n° 228/2013 portant mesures spécifiques dans le domaine de l'agriculture en faveur des régions ultrapériphériques de l'Union (règlement OCM).

Les changements dans la législation agricole des pays déclarants sont également liés à la réglementation des relations dans la chaîne d'approvisionnement agricole et alimentaire (par exemple, le délai de mise en œuvre de la directive (UE) 2019/663 a expiré le 1er mai 2021). L'agriculture et la chaîne d'approvisionnement alimentaire dans son ensemble ont été affectées par le COVID-19 et la guerre en Ukraine (ces questions ont été principalement discutées au sein du Comité I).

I. Organisation et conduite de l'activité agricole dans une exploitation

Les rapports nationaux contenaient des observations et des commentaires sur les développements juridiques importants liés aux questions environnementales de l'agriculture, par exemple, le Pacte vert pour l'Europe, la protection de l'environnement dans les exploitations agricoles, la lutte contre le changement climatique, y compris l'agriculture biologique, les énergies renouvelables, la législation sur l'eau et le bien-être des animaux. La commission III s'est d'abord penchée sur les règles de l'agriculture. Des modifications et des innovations ont été apportées dans ce domaine. Dans certains pays, il y a eu des changements ou des innovations dans la définition principale du droit agricole, à savoir l'agriculteur, l'exploitation agricole ou l'activité agricole.

Il convient de noter que le catalogue des activités liées à l'agriculture s'élargit dans certains pays. Des modifications ont également été apportées à certaines dispositions relatives aux registres, par exemple l'inscription au registre des producteurs agricoles ou au registre des producteurs de vin, de lait ou d'autres produits agricoles, ainsi que l'enregistrement des animaux. Les inscriptions sont généralement nécessaires pour obtenir des fonds de l'UE. La plupart d'entre elles sont effectuées sous forme électronique et les producteurs agricoles peuvent, et parfois doivent, saisir les données par voie électronique. Bien que cela permette d'accélérer le processus et de réduire les délais, certains problèmes persistent.

La numérisation dans le domaine des activités agricoles devient de plus en plus importante. Les applications et les inscriptions au registre sont de plus en plus populaires et il convient de souligner, entre autres, leur impact sur l'agriculture de précision. Il y a également eu des changements dans les taxes agricoles, qui sont liés à l'élargissement de la définition de base des activités agricoles et qui sont associés à la conduite des activités agricoles.

a) Exemples

Des amendements à la loi agricole slovène de mars 2022 ont aligné la définition d'un agriculteur et d'une exploitation agricole sur les plans stratégiques de la PAC (Règlement (UE) 2021/2115) (rapport slovène).

La loi française n° 2022-172 du 14 février 2022 en faveur des activités professionnelles indépendantes,[4] mérite une attention particulière en raison de ses dispositions essentielles. Tout d'abord, la loi introduit la dualité des biens de l'entrepreneur individuel, en distinguant les biens professionnels et les biens personnels. Les biens meubles et immeubles, les droits, les obligations et les titres détenus par un entrepreneur individuel et utilisés pour une ou plusieurs activités professionnelles indépendantes constituent le patrimoine professionnel de l'entrepreneur individuel. L'entrepreneur individuel est, en principe, responsable des obligations découlant de son activité professionnelle uniquement avec ses biens professionnels, ce qui garantit la protection de son patrimoine personnel. La loi réglemente également la transmission universelle des biens professionnels, assurant ainsi la clarté et la sécurité juridique de ces transactions.

En outre, le rapport français met en évidence la définition des paiements verts en tant que revenus agricoles sous certaines conditions ou restrictions dans les réglementations fiscales. Cette disposition est particulièrement importante car elle a un impact direct sur le traitement fiscal des revenus provenant d'activités écologiques, ce qui souligne l'importance croissante des considérations environnementales dans le droit agricole.

En Allemagne, suite à l'amendement de la loi sur la taxe sur les ventes du 21 décembre 2021, le taux forfaitaire de la taxe sur les ventes pour l'agriculture et la sylviculture a changé à partir du 1er janvier 2022.

Le système français d'assurance récolte a été récemment réformé par la loi n° 2022-298, publiée le 2 mars 2022, qui a amélioré la diffusion de l'assurance récolte dans l'agriculture et adapté les outils de gestion des risques aux défis du changement climatique. Un nouveau système basé sur la solidarité nationale et le partage des risques entre l'État, les agriculteurs et les assureurs a été créé, reflétant l'évolution des besoins du secteur (Rapport français).

En Pologne, la législation relative au système national des registres de producteurs, des registres d'exploitations et des registres de demandes de

4 LOI No 2022-172 du 14 février 2022 en faveur de l'activité professionnelle indépendante, JORF No0038 du 15 février 2022.

paiement a été modifiée en 2022. En outre, le ministre de l'agriculture et du développement rural a adopté des règlements spécifiant les exigences détaillées pour les demandes d'inscription dans les registres des producteurs. En raison de l'utilisation de plus en plus répandue de la numérisation et de l'informatisation dans l'agriculture, les amendements législatifs de 2022 permettent aux entités autorisées de soumettre des demandes d'inscription au registre des producteurs non seulement sur papier, mais aussi par voie électronique. La même année, le Parlement polonais a adopté une nouvelle législation sur l'identification et l'enregistrement des animaux, l'alignant sur les instruments juridiques de l'UE, tels que le règlement (UE) n° 2016/429 du Parlement européen et du Conseil du 9 mars 2016 relatif aux maladies animales transmissibles, qui modifie et abroge également certains actes dans le domaine de la santé animale.

En Espagne, un système d'information des exploitations agricoles (SIEX) a été mis en place, qui est techniquement et systématiquement interopérable avec les registres d'exploitation agricole des communautés autonomes, les carnets numériques d'exploitation agricole et d'autres registres publics.

En 2023, la Pologne a modifié les dispositions statutaires relatives à la gestion des biens immobiliers agricoles du Trésor public et d'autres lois, notamment la loi sur l'organisation du système agricole. Les modifications concernant la gestion du stock de propriété agricole du Trésor comprennent, entre autres, des questions liées aux baux et au transfert de biens immobiliers aux gouvernements locaux pour des besoins d'infrastructure et de construction. Les définitions de concepts clés tels que l'exploitation familiale, le parent, la personne ayant des qualifications agricoles et la gestion personnelle d'une exploitation agricole, tels que mentionnés dans la loi sur l'organisation du système agricole, ont été ajoutées ou modifiées. Cette référence directe doit être évaluée positivement

Dans le cadre de l'amendement du 13 juillet 2023, les dispositions relatives aux appels d'offres restreints ont été précisées. Selon les nouvelles dispositions, le Centre national peut stipuler que seuls certains groupes de personnes peuvent participer à l'appel d'offres. Il peut s'agir, par exemple, d'agriculteurs individuels qui ont l'intention d'agrandir leur exploitation familiale.

La loi modifiée sur la formation du système agricole (UKUR, Ustawa z dnia 11 kwietnia 2003 r. o kształtowaniu ustroju rolnego) précise que ses dispositions ne s'appliquent pas aux propriétés agricoles dont la surface agricole est inférieure à 0,3 ha. La modification aura un impact positif sur le développement rural à des fins de logement.

La législation modifiée étend certaines exceptions aux obligations prévues pour les acquéreurs de biens immobiliers agricoles. Il s'agit notamment des biens pour lesquels, après l'achat, un plan d'aménagement local a été adopté, prévoyant leur utilisation à des fins autres qu'agricoles. Il convient de noter que le débat en cours depuis quelques années sur l'impact que les modifications des plans d'aménagement auront sur les obligations des acquéreurs de terres agricoles. La décision du législateur de réglementer cette question est un pas dans la bonne direction, car elle élimine les ambiguïtés juridiques antérieures. Néanmoins, elle peut conduire à un affaiblissement de la protection des terres agricoles dans le cadre de leur préservation quantitative.

L'amendement visait également à clarifier et à rationaliser la mise en œuvre des dispositions relatives au commerce des biens immobiliers agricoles sur le marché privé spécifiées dans la loi sur l'organisation du système agricole. Le développement rural repose non seulement sur le développement des activités agricoles, mais aussi sur la construction d'infrastructures. La modification de la loi sur la gestion des biens agricoles du Trésor public a permis au Centre national de transférer gratuitement des biens aux collectivités locales. Cela s'applique aux terrains destinés à la construction de routes municipales, de district et provinciales, ainsi qu'à ceux qui sont déjà utilisés comme routes. En outre, le Centre national a également la possibilité de transférer d'autres terrains à ces fins, pour autant qu'ils soient conformes aux plans d'aménagement, de régénération ou de reconstruction locaux.

Dans le cadre de l'enquête sur la structure agraire de 2023, l'Allemagne a adapté sa législation sur les statistiques agricoles et les denrées alimentaires à la législation de l'UE (par exemple, le règlement d'exécution (UE) n° 2021/2286 de la Commission) et à l'évolution du secteur agroalimentaire (Rapport allemand).

Le Comité III a également discuté des règles juridiques pour l'agriculture au Royaume-Uni après le Brexit. Le Farm Bill 2019-21 (Farm Bill 2020) a adopté une nouvelle approche des paiements agricoles et de la gestion des terres. En Angleterre, les agriculteurs seront payés pour produire des « biens publics » tels que des améliorations en matière d'environnement ou de bien-être animal. En outre, le gouvernement écossais a présenté une législation agricole en novembre 2019 (Rapport du Royaume-Uni).

Aux États-Unis, les lois fédérales sur l'agriculture (Federal Farm Bills) établissent d'importantes mesures de politique agricole et alimentaire qui régissent de nombreux aspects de la législation rurale. Le Congrès américain adopte généralement une loi agricole tous les cinq ans. La loi agricole la plus récente a été adoptée en 2018 et son successeur était prévu pour la fin de l'année 2023 ou le début de l'année 2024. Toutefois, en 2025, il reste à savoir si une nouvelle loi agricole a été pleinement adoptée ou si les discussions sont toujours en cours (Rapport des Etats-Unis). Les lois agricoles sont des textes législatifs complexes et de grande portée.

Le recensement agricole de 2017 (Census of Agriculture), publié en 2019, fournit des informations détaillées sur les exploitations et les terres agricoles aux États-Unis. Il y avait 2,042 millions d'exploitations agricoles aux États-Unis, couvrant environ 900 millions d'acres, dont 396 millions d'acres de terres cultivées. La taille moyenne des exploitations était de 441 acres, et la plupart des exploitations étaient petites, tant en termes de taille que de valeur des ventes.

Bien qu'environ 60 % des terres agricoles aux États-Unis soient gérées par leur propriétaire, le bail-à-ferme joue un rôle important dans l'agriculture américaine, en particulier dans la production de céréales. Près de 40 % des terres agricoles aux États-Unis sont louées, avec des pourcentages encore plus élevés dans certains États. En 2017, les propriétaires à part entière exploitaient 69 % des fermes, avec une taille moyenne de 220 acres, tandis que les bailleurs exploitaient généralement des fermes plus grandes.

La propriété de terres agricoles par certaines sociétés a des implications significatives pour d'importants États agricoles. Le recensement de l'agriculture de 2017 a révélé que 5,7 % des exploitations agricoles américaines étaient des sociétés, mais que seulement 0,6 % d'entre elles étaient des sociétés non-familiales. Pour répondre aux préoccupations concernant la propriété des sociétés et protéger les exploitations familiales, plusieurs États ont mis en œuvre des mesures visant à limiter la propriété des terres agricoles par les sociétés.

Le ministère américain de l'agriculture (USDA) publie des rapports annuels sur la propriété étrangère des terres agricoles, sur la base des données collectées dans le cadre de la loi sur la divulgation des investissements étrangers dans l'agriculture (Agricultural Foreign Investment Disclosure Act - AFIDA). Le rapport le plus récent analyse la propriété étrangère jusqu'en décembre 2021. Cette année-là, les propriétés étrangères de toutes les terres agricoles aux États-Unis totalisaient environ 40 millions d'acres, soit 1,8 % de toutes les terres américaines et 3,1 % des terres agricoles privées. Entre 2020 et 2021, la superficie des terres agricoles détenues par des entités étrangères a augmenté d'environ 2,4 millions d'acres.

La propriété étrangère est concentrée dans quelques pays clés. Les Canadiens possèdent 31 % des terres agricoles appartenant à des étrangers, suivis par les Pays-Bas (12 %), l'Italie (7 %), l'Allemagne et le Royaume-Uni (6 % chacun). (Rapport des États-Unis).

II. Le rôle des femmes dans l'agriculture

Le rôle des femmes dans l'agriculture a été discuté au sein de la commission. Les femmes participent activement à l'agriculture. Dans certains pays, le modèle traditionnel d'activités agricoles essentiellement dirigées par des hommes est encore très présent, tandis que dans d'autres, en raison de la baisse des revenus agricoles, de la réduction des surfaces agricoles et de l'accroissement des responsabilités, on constate que les hommes sont moins intéressés par la gestion d'entreprises.

Certains pays ont mis en place des réglementations et des programmes visant à encourager l'implication des femmes dans l'agriculture et leur participation à la gestion de l'exploitation et à la prise de décision. Par exemple, en Espagne, le nombre de femmes impliquées dans l'agriculture a augmenté de manière significative ces dernières années. Le recensement agricole de 2020 indique que les femmes représentent désormais 29 % des chefs d'exploitation (261 634 femmes, soit une augmentation de 22 %).

En outre, le nombre d'exploitations agricoles gérées par des femmes n'a cessé d'augmenter. En 2010, il y avait 2 827 exploitations gérées par des femmes, alors qu'en 2020, ce nombre passera à 3 323 exploitations. Cette croissance reflète l'impact positif d'initiatives telles que le IIIe plan stratégique pour l'égalité effective des sexes 2022-2025 (PEIHM), qui vise à promouvoir l'égalité des sexes dans les zones rurales et dans l'agriculture. Ce plan soutient également les agricultrices en leur proposant des formations, des conseils et des possibilités de financement, afin de les aider à surmonter les difficultés et à réussir dans leur entreprise (Rapport espagnol).

Les femmes participent à l'agriculture espagnole de diverses manières : certaines possèdent leur propre exploitation, tandis que d'autres travaillent dans des exploitations appartenant à des parents ou à des employeurs. Elles jouent également un rôle important dans la chaîne de valeur agricole, en contribuant à la production, à la transformation et à la distribution des denrées alimentaires.

Le nombre de femmes travaillant dans l'agriculture en Espagne a augmenté ces dernières années. Selon le recensement agricole de 2020, par rapport aux données de 2009, les femmes représentent désormais 29 % des chefs d'exploitation. Toutefois, elles sont plus susceptibles de gérer des exploitations de petite taille économique. Par exemple, 56,2 % des exploitations dirigées par des femmes génèrent moins de 8 000 euros de production brute standard (PBS), contre 46,3 % des exploitations dirigées par des hommes.

Ces changements sont influencés par plusieurs facteurs, notamment le vieillissement de la population agricole, l'abandon des exploitations par les hommes et l'intégration croissante des femmes dans les activités agricoles.

Aux États-Unis, en 2017, 36 % (1,2 million) des 3,4 millions de producteurs étaient des femmes. Le recensement de l'agriculture définit un producteur comme une personne « impliquée dans la prise de décisions concernant les opérations agricoles », et les exploitations agricoles ont souvent plus d'un producteur. Près de 56 % des exploitations agricoles comptaient une ou plusieurs productrices, tandis que 91 % des exploitations agricoles comptaient un ou plusieurs producteurs.

Le terme « producteur » est utilisé de deux manières distinctes dans le recensement. Moins de femmes (798 500) se sont identifiées comme exploitantes principales - celles qui sont considérées comme les principales décisionnaires sur l'exploitation agricole. Un nombre encore plus faible de femmes (489 000) se sont identifiées comme productrices primaires, c'est-à-dire des personnes qui prennent la majorité des décisions concernant l'exploitation agricole.

La plupart des productrices vivent dans les exploitations qu'elles dirigent et participent activement aux activités quotidiennes, ainsi qu'à la prise de décisions concernant l'utilisation des terres et des cultures, le bétail, la gestion financière et la planification de la succession. Toutefois, pour 66 % des productrices et plus de 60 % des productrices primaires, l'agriculture n'était pas leur activité principale (Rapport des États-Unis).

En Suisse, environ 54 300 femmes étaient employées dans des exploitations agricoles en 2020, dont 6 % en tant que chefs d'exploitation. Le nombre d'exploitations dirigées par des femmes et le nombre total d'exploitations ont tous deux légèrement diminué au cours de l'année sous revue. Toutefois, la diminution du nombre d'exploitations gérées par des femmes a été, en moyenne, légèrement supérieure à la diminution globale du nombre total d'exploitations.

Par rapport à l'évolution globale des exploitations agricoles, le nombre d'exploitations de plus de 30 hectares gérées par des femmes a connu une évolution relativement différente, ce qui suggère des changements dans la structure des exploitations agricoles (Rapport suisse).

III. Bien-être des animaux, santé des plantes

Les rapports nationaux soulignent que les questions de bien-être animal et d'élevage, y compris le traitement des animaux, sont des domaines importants dans lesquels des changements législatifs ont été observés. Les règles d'élevage influencent à la fois la qualité de la viande et l'environnement. Les États membres de l'UE ont adapté leurs dispositions pour se conformer aux instruments juridiques de l'UE, qui ont principalement pris la forme de règlements directement applicables remplaçant des directives antérieures (par exemple, le règlement (UE) 2016/429 sur la santé animale et le règlement (UE) 2016/1012 sur l'élevage).

En Pologne, le règlement relatif aux mesures de protection contre les organismes nuisibles aux végétaux (UE) 2016/2031 a été mis en œuvre principalement par la loi du 13 février 2020 sur la protection des plantes contre les agrophages. Cette loi conserve les dispositions du site qui attribuent toutes les tâches phytosanitaires aux autorités de la protection des végétaux et de l'inspection des semences de l'État. En outre, elle introduit la possibilité de désigner des zones exemptes de certains agrophages, qui peuvent jouer un rôle essentiel pour faciliter l'exportation de marchandises vers des pays tiers. L'inspecteur en chef de la protection des végétaux et de l'inspection des semences est l'autorité compétente pour la désignation des stations de quarantaine et des installations d'isolement.

Pour mettre en œuvre le règlement (UE) 2016/1012 relatif à l'élevage d'animaux en Pologne, la loi du 10 décembre 2020 sur l'organisation de l'élevage et de la reproduction des animaux de ferme a été promulguée. Cette loi réglemente l'élevage et la protection des ressources génétiques du bétail, les évaluations de la valeur fonctionnelle, les évaluations génétiques, la tenue des livres généalogiques, les registres, les dossiers d'élevage et le contrôle des activités d'élevage et de reproduction des animaux de ferme. En outre, la loi définit les autorités et les institutions qui auront les pouvoirs et les compétences énoncés dans le règlement (UE) 2016/1012 sur le territoire de la République de Pologne.

En conséquence, le ministre de l'agriculture s'est vu confier l'autorité de:

- reconnaître les organisations d'élevage ou autres entités demandant la tenue de livres généalogiques et de registres d'élevage pour les bovins,

les porcins, les ovins, les caprins et les équidés en tant qu'associations d'éleveurs et entreprises d'élevage
- approuver les programmes de sélection mis en œuvre par ces associations d'éleveurs ou entreprises de sélection,
- imposer et abroger les mesures prévues par le règlement (UE) 2016/1012 au cas où les entités contrôlées enfreindraient les dispositions de ce règlement.

Le Centre national de l'élevage est chargé d'effectuer des contrôles officiels pour garantir le respect du règlement (Rapport polonais).

Le Comité III s'est également penché sur la question de la peste porcine africaine (ASF). En juillet 2023, la situation épidémiologique concernant cette menace dans l'Union européenne a été mise à jour par le règlement d'exécution (UE) 2023/1485 de la Commission du 18 juillet 2023, qui a modifié les annexes I et II du règlement d'exécution (UE) 2021/605, établissant des mesures spécifiques de lutte contre la peste porcine africaine.

En Pologne, des foyers d'ASF ont été confirmés en juillet 2023, y compris plusieurs nouveaux cas dans les voïvodies de Wielkopolskie et de Mazowieckie, avec des foyers supplémentaires signalés dans des zones restreintes des voïvodies de Podkarpackie et de Lubelskie. Il s'agit d'une amélioration significative par rapport aux plusieurs milliers de foyers précédemment signalés à la Commission européenne. En Pologne, les mesures spécifiques de lutte contre l'ASF sont décrites dans le règlement du ministre de l'agriculture et du développement rural du 10 août 2021 sur les mesures à prendre en cas d'apparition de l'ASF. Ce règlement a été modifié en mai 2023 par l'ordonnance du ministre de l'agriculture et du développement rural, qui met à jour les mesures à mettre en œuvre en réponse aux foyers de peste porcine africaine.

En Allemagne, une nouvelle loi sur la médecine vétérinaire est entrée en vigueur le 28 janvier 2022, abordant les questions au niveau national (fédéral) qui n'étaient pas couvertes par les dispositions directement applicables du règlement (UE) 2019/6 relatifs aux médicaments vétérinaires, qui a abrogé la directive 2001/82/CE. La nouvelle loi consolide systématiquement toutes les dispositions concernant le secteur vétérinaire qui étaient auparavant dispersées dans plusieurs textes législatifs. Cette loi met en œuvre le règlement (UE) 2019/6 du Parlement européen et du Conseil du 11 décembre 2018 relatif aux médicaments vétérinaires et abrogeant la directive 2001/82/CE (JO L 4, 7.1.2019, p. 43 ; L 163, 20 juin 2019, p. 112 ; L 326, 8 octobre 2020, p. 15 ; L 241, 8 juillet 2021, p. 17) (Rapport allemand).

En Suisse, les modifications de l'ordonnance sur l'élevage du 31 octobre 2012, apportées le 2 novembre 2022 et le 5 avril 2023, renforcent les dispositions relatives à la préservation des races suisses et étendent les contributions financières pour leur protection. Ces modifications se fondent sur la « Stratégie de sélection animale à l'horizon 2030 » et sur des propositions parlementaires pertinentes (Rapport suisse).

En mai 2023, la Cour suprême des États-Unis a confirmé la loi californienne sur le bien-être animal (California Animal Welfare Act), qui affectera la production et la vente de viande de porc, de veau et d'œufs tout en imposant des contraintes spécifiques aux éleveurs de bétail à travers les États-Unis (Rapport des Etats-Unis).

L'Agence américaine de protection de l'environnement (EPA) réglemente les plantes génétiquement modifiées (GM) qui contiennent des substances pesticides, connues sous le nom de biopesticides (plant-incorporated protectants en anglais (PIP)). L'EPA exige que certains biopesticides soient enregistrés en vertu de la loi fédérale sur les insecticides, les fongicides et les rodenticides (Federal Insecticide, Fungicide, and Rodenticide Act (FIFRA)) et qu'ils fassent l'objet d'une tolérance ou d'une exemption pour les résidus alimentaires en vertu de la loi fédérale sur les aliments, les médicaments et les cosmétiques (Federal Food, Drug, and Cosmetic Act (FDCA)).

Pour répondre aux développements de la biotechnologie, l'EPA a publié en mai 2023 une règle exemptant certains biopesticides des exigences d'enregistrement de la FIFRA et de tolérance alimentaire de la FDCA. Cette exemption s'applique aux biopesticides qui « ne présentent pas plus de risques que les biopesticides dont l'EPA a déjà déterminé qu'ils répondent aux exigences de sécurité et qui auraient pu être créés par le biais d'une sélection conventionnelle ». Plus précisément, la règle exempte les biopesticides « créés par génie génétique à partir d'une plante sexuellement compatible » et les biopesticides « à perte de fonction ».

Aux États-Unis, certains aspects du bien-être des animaux sont régis par des lois fédérales et des lois d'État. Les lois et réglementations fédérales se concentrent sur la prévention de la cruauté et la garantie d'un abattage sans cruauté ; toutefois, peu de normes fédérales traitent spécifiquement des pratiques de production animale.

IV. Emploi agricole

L'un des défis actuels de l'agriculture est l'emploi. Dans certains pays, une législation nationale sur l'emploi agricole a été introduite pour relever les défis spécifiques liés aux relations de travail dans l'agriculture. Ce sujet a également été abordé au sein de la Commission III, avec des exemples de plusieurs pays illustrant diverses approches pour aborder ces questions.

En Italie, le taux élevé d'emplois irréguliers dans l'agriculture (24,1 % en 2019, soit une augmentation de 3,4 points de pourcentage depuis 2010) constitue un obstacle important à la durabilité du secteur agricole. Pour résoudre ce problème, l'Italie a mis en œuvre les dispositions relatives à la conditionnalité sociale établies par le règlement (UE) n° 2115 de 2021, article 1453. Le décret ministériel du 28 décembre 2022, qui a pris effet le 1er janvier 2023, a introduit un mécanisme d'échange de données entre l'inspection nationale du travail, l'autorité nationale des incendies et les autorités sanitaires locales afin d'améliorer la conformité et l'application des directives de l'UE dans le cadre de la conditionnalité sociale (Rapport italien).

De même, en Espagne, une importante réforme du droit du travail a été adoptée en 2021 pour encourager les contrats de travail à long terme dans le secteur agricole. La réforme limite les circonstances dans lesquelles les contrats à durée déterminée ou temporaires peuvent être utilisés, en donnant la priorité aux contrats à durée indéterminée. Bien que l'agriculture ait traditionnellement recours à des contrats temporaires, la réforme reconnaît les besoins stables et cycliques du secteur en matière de main-d'œuvre tout au long de l'année (Rapport espagnol).

En Suisse, il n'existe pas de législation nationale spécifique régissant les contrats de travail agricoles. Cependant, le droit général des contrats de travail ne s'applique pas non plus aux travailleurs agricoles. En revanche, les cantons sont tenus d'édicter des contrats-types de travail qui règlent des aspects essentiels tels que la durée du travail, le temps de repos et les conditions de travail, en particulier pour les femmes et les jeunes travailleurs (al. 2).

La réglementation du canton de Berne, le plus grand canton agricole de Suisse, est particulièrement intéressante. Son contrat-type de travail date de 2007 et a été modifié en 2012. La réglementation la plus récente vient du canton de Lucerne, le troisième plus grand canton agricole, qui a publié son contrat-type de travail à la fin de 2022 (Rapport suisse).

En ce qui concerne les conditions de travail, la Loi fédérale sur les allocations familiales dans l'agriculture (LFA) prévoit des prestations familiales pour les travailleurs agricoles. En vertu de cette loi, les membres de la famille du chef d'exploitation qui travaillent sur l'exploitation ont également droit à des allocations familiales (Article 1a). Ces allocations comprennent une allocation de ménage et des allocations pour enfants et pour la formation (Article 2, alinéa 1). En outre, les agriculteurs indépendants et les exploiteurs d'alpages ont également droit à des allocations familiales (Article 5).

En Pologne, l'introduction du « contrat d'aide à la récolte » en 2023 a marqué une évolution importante de la législation relative à l'assurance sociale des agriculteurs. En vertu de cette nouvelle disposition, un « aide-agriculteur » accepte d'aider à la récolte des produits agricoles à un endroit précis de la propriété de l'agriculteur pendant une période déterminée. En contrepartie, l'agriculteur accepte de payer la rémunération convenue pour l'aide fournie.

Une fois ce contrat conclu, l'aide-agriculteur est partiellement couvert par l'assurance sociale agricole. Le système polonais d'assurance agricole se distingue par sa séparation du système général d'assurance sociale. Il est géré par le Fonds d'assurance sociale agricole et fonctionne avec un ensemble unique de prestations et des cotisations relativement faibles.

V. Le problème des terres agricoles (diminution de la superficie des terres agricoles) et les conflits d'intérêts, le changement de génération

La Commission III a discuté de la question des terres agricoles, en se concentrant sur la diminution de la disponibilité des terres agricoles et sur les conflits d'intérêts. Le nombre d'exploitations agricoles et la superficie totale des terres agricoles diminuent dans de nombreux pays, ce qui suscite des inquiétudes quant à l'avenir du modèle agricole, en particulier en Europe. La conversion des terres agricoles à des fins de construction et d'investissement est une tendance particulièrement néfaste, qui affecte les terres agricoles de haute qualité et limite considérablement les possibilités d'exploitation.

Le changement de génération est un autre défi pressant qui pourrait s'aggraver à l'avenir. De moins en moins de jeunes sont prêts à reprendre des exploitations agricoles, une tendance liée aux exigences inhérentes à la profession en matière de responsabilité professionnelle et aux risques importants liés aux conditions météorologiques, aux catastrophes naturelles et à la volatilité du marché. Dans ce contexte, la surveillance et le contrôle des activités des producteurs, ainsi que l'obligation de rendre des comptes et les sanctions sont des questions cruciales qui sont abordées à la fois au niveau de l'UE et dans les différents pays.

Pour soutenir les jeunes agriculteurs, l'UE a alloué des fonds supplémentaires dans le cadre des premier et deuxième pilier de la politique agricole commune (PAC). Ces mesures sont étroitement liées à la transmission des exploitations agricoles, un domaine dans lequel plusieurs pays ont récemment introduit des modifications législatives visant à restreindre la transmission des terres agricoles.

Dans certains pays, le marché de l'immobilier agricole est ouvert, ce qui accroît le risque de conversion ou d'exclusion des terres agricoles à des fins de construction ou d'investissement. Dans le même temps, le bail de terres agricoles devient de plus en plus important, certains pays mettant en œuvre des changements législatifs pour répondre à cette tendance et d'autres prévoyant des actions similaires.

Par exemple, 93,5 % des exploitations agricoles italiennes sont des exploitations individuelles ou familiales, ce qui montre que le modèle de l'exploitation familiale continue de dominer. Toutefois, ce modèle est également en déclin. Les plus petites exploitations familiales, en particulier celles du centre et du sud de l'Italie, quittent le secteur à un rythme élevé (-51,2 % des exploitations de moins d'un hectare). En revanche, on assiste à une augmentation des exploitations en partenariat et, surtout, des sociétés à responsabilité limitée.

En outre, la pratique de bail-à-ferme devient de plus en plus importante, remplaçant progressivement le modèle traditionnel de la propriété individuelle (Rapport italien).

En Slovénie, les terres agricoles utilisées ne représentent que 23,7 % de la superficie totale du pays. Les terres agricoles de haute qualité sont limitées en Slovénie, ce qui rend leur protection extrêmement importante. Selon la loi sur l'agriculture, les mesures de politique agricole doivent être principalement orientées vers le développement d'une agriculture durable qui maintient la biodiversité des espèces animales et végétales et préserve la fertilité des sols tout en protégeant les conditions de vie naturelles du sol, de l'eau et de l'air (Article 15) (Rapport slovène).

Le 13 juillet 2023, le Parlement polonais a adopté une loi modifiant la loi sur la formation du système agricole, qui a introduit de nouvelles dispositions pour le contrôle de droit public de la circulation des terres agricoles.

Une nouvelle législation en France, introduite par la loi n° 2021-1756 du 23 décembre 2021, réglemente l'accès au foncier agricole par le biais de structures sociétaires. Ce régime unique vise à contrôler l'achat de parts de sociétés agricoles afin de lutter contre l'accumulation et la concentration excessive de terres agricoles par le biais de structures sociétaires (accaparement des terres) et d'améliorer la souveraineté alimentaire.

En vertu de cette loi, toute entité souhaitant acquérir le contrôle d'une société qui possède ou utilise des biens immobiliers agricoles pour une activité agricole doit obtenir un permis du préfet du département si les biens immobiliers agricoles possédés ou utilisés par la société, combinés aux biens immobiliers agricoles déjà possédés ou utilisés par la même entité, dépassent un certain nombre de biens immobiliers.

En Suisse, l'acquisition de terres agricoles et d'exploitations est, en principe, réservée aux agriculteurs indépendants. Cette limitation découle de la loi fédérale sur le droit foncier agricole (LDFR), qui impose des règles strictes en matière de transfert juridique de terres et d'entreprises agricoles. En cas d'héritage, une entreprise agricole ne peut être reprise que par un héritier ayant la qualité d'agriculteur individuel et jugé apte (Article 11, alinéa 1, de la LDFR).

Au Royaume-Uni, le bail-à-ferme agricole devient de plus en plus populaire. Selon le Rock Review, les exploitations en fermage – qu'elles soient totales ou partielles – occupent 64 % de la superficie agricole totale (8,9 millions d'hectares) en Angleterre, tandis que les exploitations en fermage représentent 45 % de l'ensemble des exploitations agricoles dans le pays. La Commission DEFRA a entrepris une étude sur le fermage en Angleterre. L'étude Rock a formulé plus de 70 recommandations visant à rendre le secteur des fermages plus résilient, afin de garantir une production alimentaire durable, de relever les défis du changement climatique et d'améliorer et de renforcer la biodiversité (Rapport britannique).

VI. La position des agriculteurs dans la chaîne de valeur

La position des agriculteurs dans la chaîne d'approvisionnement alimentaire reste faible. Bien que les pays de l'UE aient mis en œuvre la directive (UE) 2019/633 relative aux pratiques commerciales déloyales entre entreprises dans la chaîne d'approvisionnement agricole et alimentaire, des événements récents, tels que l'agression de la Russie contre l'Ukraine, ont eu un impact négatif sur les marchés agricoles et ont affaibli la position de négociation des producteurs agricoles. Ces défis découlent de la hausse des prix des intrants (carburant, énergie, engrais et produits phytosanitaires) et de la levée des droits de douane sur certains produits agricoles ukrainiens par l'Union européenne, ce qui a rendu la concurrence plus difficile pour les produits agricoles nationaux.

Voici quelques exemples de mise en œuvre nationale et de mesures connexes :

En Slovénie, les modifications apportées en 2021 à la loi sur l'agriculture ont élargi le concept de chaîne d'approvisionnement alimentaire pour y inclure la chaîne d'approvisionnement en produits agricoles et alimentaires et ont introduit le concept de pouvoir de marché significatif (PMS). Le volume des ventes des fournisseurs et des acheteurs est désormais comparé strictement selon l'échelle prévue par la directive (UE) 2019/633. En outre, une nouvelle institution, le médiateur pour les relations dans la chaîne agroalimentaire, a été créée pour superviser ces questions, et de nouvelles règles obligatoires sur les pratiques déloyales interdites ont été introduites (Rapport slovène).

En Italie, le Fonds complémentaire a alloué 1,2 milliard d'euros à la chaîne d'approvisionnement et aux contrats de district dans le secteur agroalimentaire, couvrant l'agriculture, la pêche, la sylviculture, la floriculture et les pépinières. Sur ce montant, 25 % sont réservés à l'agriculture biologique. Le régime d'aides d'État pour les contrats de chaîne d'approvisionnement et de district, couvrant la période de 2021 à 2027, a été notifié à la Commission européenne, qui a confirmé sa compatibilité avec le marché intérieur en vertu de l'article 107, paragraphe 3(c) TFUE. Le régime a été mis en œuvre par le décret ministériel du 22 décembre 2021 (Rapport italien).

En Pologne, la directive (UE) 2019/633 a été transposée en droit national par la loi du 17 novembre 2021 sur la lutte contre l'exploitation déloyale des avantages contractuels dans le commerce des produits agricoles et alimentaires (rapport polonais).

En Espagne, le « contrat agroalimentaire type » a été initialement réglementé par la loi 12/2013 sur les mesures visant à améliorer le fonctionnement de la chaîne alimentaire. Des amendements ultérieurs, notamment en 2020 et en décembre 2021, ont complété la transposition de la directive (UE) 2019/633. Le législateur espagnol a souligné la nécessité de protéger le maillon le plus faible de la chaîne alimentaire, à savoir le secteur de la production primaire, qui se compose essentiellement de petites et moyennes exploitations familiales. Ces exploitations produisent souvent des biens de grande qualité mais ne sont pas rémunérées équitablement par le marché. Les futures réglementations doivent garantir une protection complète contre les pratiques commerciales déloyales, couvrant toutes les étapes des contrats agroalimentaires, y compris les phases préliminaires, précontractuelles et de négociation. Ces mesures devraient viser à fournir une protection équitable au secteur de la production primaire (Rapport espagnol).

VII. Association de producteurs agricoles

Les participants de la Commission III ont discuté de l'association des producteurs agricoles (coopératives et autres organisations). Il s'agit de l'un des principaux instruments permettant d'améliorer la position des producteurs agricoles dans la chaîne d'approvisionnement alimentaire. Conformément aux dispositions de la Politique Agricole Commune (PAC) de l'UE, les organisations de producteurs sont tenues de contribuer à l'autonomisation des agriculteurs dans la chaîne d'approvisionnement alimentaire, au développement des exploitations et aux marchés agricoles.

Les organisations de producteurs et les associations d'agriculteurs, telles que les coopératives, jouent un rôle crucial dans plusieurs domaines. Il s'agit notamment de concentrer l'offre, d'améliorer la commercialisation, de planifier et d'adapter la production à la demande, d'optimiser les coûts de production, de stabiliser les prix à la production, de mener des recherches, de promouvoir les meilleures pratiques, de fournir une assistance technique, de gérer les sous-produits et d'offrir des outils de gestion des risques à leurs membres. Collectivement, ces efforts contribuent de manière significative à renforcer la position des producteurs dans la chaîne d'approvisionnement alimentaire. Le développement de telles entités a été observé dans plusieurs pays.

Il a été souligné que la coopération est essentielle à différents stades de l'agriculture, depuis l'achat d'intrants et l'utilisation de machines agricoles jusqu'au transport des récoltes, en passant par la fourniture de services de conseil, la transformation et la vente des produits. Les producteurs associés sont mieux équipés pour produire des produits agricoles avec une utilisation réduite de pesticides, élever des animaux avec moins de médicaments vétérinaires et s'engager dans une transformation qui permet d'obtenir des produits agroalimentaires non altérés, sains et abordables pour les consommateurs. En outre, ils peuvent jouer un rôle important dans les initiatives en matière d'énergie renouvelable.

La Stratégie « de la ferme à la table » a été présentée comme un élément clé du « Pacte vert » de l'UE. Cette stratégie promeut une croissance durable et inclusive, visant à stimuler l'économie, à améliorer la santé publique et la qualité de vie, et à protéger l'environnement. Certaines associations de producteurs participent activement à des activités environnementales, telles que la protection des zones Natura 2000 (par exemple, aux Pays-Bas). La popularité croissante des coopératives énergétiques a également été soulignée.

Les participants au comité ont souligné la nécessité de renforcer la position juridique et le rôle des coopératives d'agriculteurs, des organisations de producteurs et des associations similaires afin de soutenir le développement de l'agriculture, de l'industrie agroalimentaire et des zones rurales. Dans certains pays, d'autres changements juridiques concernant les organisations de producteurs, les coopératives et les entités apparentées sont nécessaires pour favoriser leur développement et leur efficacité.

VIII. Pacte vert pour l'Europe, protection de l'environnement dans les exploitations agricoles, lutte contre le changement climatique, y compris l'agriculture biologique, les énergies renouvelables, la législation sur l'eau et le bien-être des animaux

La Commission III s'est également penchée sur la question du changement climatique, qui constitue une menace importante pour l'ensemble de la planète. Le réchauffement de la planète affecte de plus en plus le régime des pluies, les océans et les systèmes éoliens. Ces changements devraient rendre l'agriculture plus difficile dans tous les pays. Les problèmes identifiés sont abordés dans le cadre du « Pacte vert pour l'Europe », présenté le 11 décembre 2019 par la Commission européenne. Ces dernières années, les États membres ont adopté de nouvelles réglementations et stratégies liées au Pacte vert.

Divers aspects de la protection de l'environnement, du changement climatique, de la gestion de l'eau et de la conservation de la nature font de plus en plus souvent l'objet de décisions judiciaires. Certains pays ont également signalé l'introduction d'une nouvelle législation en matière d'environnement ou d'aménagement du territoire.

La décision du premier Sénat de la Cour constitutionnelle fédérale allemande du 24 mars 2021, qui reconnaît la protection du climat comme un droit de l'homme, est un exemple notable de la prise en compte des questions climatiques par les tribunaux. La Cour a déclaré ce qui suit :

« Le devoir de protection imposé à l'État par l'article 2, alinéa 2, 1re phrase de la Loi fondamentale inclut le devoir de protéger la vie et la santé humaines contre les dangers émanant du changement climatique. Il peut donner lieu à un devoir de protection objectif même envers des générations futures... »[5]

Cet arrêt souligne l'évolution de la reconnaissance juridique de la protection du climat en tant qu'obligation fondamentale de l'État, qui étend ses responsabilités à la sauvegarde des générations futures.

La Cour a également souligné la nécessité d'une répartition proportionnelle de la liberté et des opportunités entre les générations : « Sous certaines conditions, la Loi fondamentale exige une préservation dans le temps de la liberté garantie par les droits fondamentaux et une répartition proportionnée des opportunités de liberté entre les générations. Dans leur dimension subjective, les droits fondamentaux – en tant que garanties intertemporelles de liberté – protègent contre un report unilatéral vers l'avenir de la charge imposée par l'article 20a de la Loi fondamentale de réduire les émissions de gaz à effet de serre ».[6]

Décision du Premier Sénat du 24 mars 2021 - 1 BvR 2656/18 - 1 BvR 78/20 - 1 BvR 96/20 - 1 BvR 288/20 - L'obligation de protection visée à l'article 2, paragraphe 2, première phrase, de la Loi fondamentale comprend le devoir de protéger la vie et la santé contre les dangers du changement climatique. Elle peut en outre constituer la base d'une obligation objective de protéger les générations futures.

La Cour a souligné que l'article 20a de la loi fondamentale a une dimension internationale. Le fait qu'aucun État ne puisse résoudre seul les problèmes liés au changement climatique en raison de la nature mondiale du climat et du réchauffement de la planète n'invalide pas l'obligation nationale de prendre des mesures pour lutter contre le changement climatique. En vertu de cette obligation, l'État est contraint de s'engager dans une action internationale pour lutter contre le changement climatique au niveau mondial et est tenu de promouvoir l'action climatique dans un cadre international.

---

5 Bundesverfassungsgericht, Ordonnance du Premier Sénat du 24 mars 2021, affaires 1 BvR 2656/18, 1 BvR 78/20, 1 BvR 96/20, 1 BvR 288/20. La traduction française du verdict est disponible sur le site de la Cour constitutionnelle allemande: https://www.bundesverfassungsgericht.de/SharedDocs/Entscheidungen/FR/2021/03/rs20210324_1bvr265618fr.html.

6 Ibidem.

Un État ne peut se soustraire à sa responsabilité en mettant en avant les émissions de gaz à effet de serre d'autres États. « Sous certaines conditions, la Loi fondamentale exige une préservation dans le temps de la liberté garantie par les droits fondamentaux et une répartition proportionnée des opportunités de liberté entre les générations. Dans leur dimension subjective, les droits fondamentaux – en tant que garanties intertemporelles de liberté – protègent contre un report unilatéral vers l'avenir de la charge imposée par l'article 20a de la Loi fondamentale de réduire les émissions de gaz à effet de serre (...) »

La décision de la Cour souligne l'obligation constitutionnelle de l'État allemand de protéger la vie et la santé, non seulement pour la population actuelle, mais aussi pour les générations futures. Cette obligation implique un engagement actif dans des mesures nationales et dans la coopération internationale pour lutter contre le changement climatique de manière globale.

Voici quelques exemples de développements législatifs et politiques influencés par les objectifs en matière d'environnement et de développement durable :

Aux Pays-Bas, la loi sur l'environnement et la planification, introduite le 1er janvier 2024, représente la révision statutaire la plus complète du droit de l'environnement au cours des dernières décennies. Remplaçant 26 lois, 60 décrets gouvernementaux et 75 arrêtés ministériels, la loi vise à consolider les réglementations relatives à la construction, à l'environnement, à l'eau, à l'urbanisme et à la nature. Son objectif est de simplifier les règles régissant les projets spatiaux et le cadre de vie, avec des implications notables pour le secteur agricole.

En Italie, la Constitution a été récemment modifiée pour inclure explicitement la protection de l'environnement, des écosystèmes et de la biodiversité comme principes et critères fondamentaux pour limiter l'activité économique (loi constitutionnelle n° 1 de 2022). Le Plan national pour la reconstruction et la résilience (Piano Nazionale di Ripresa e Resilienza, PNRR) a été publié conformément au règlement (UE) n° 241 de 2021 en tant que réponse de l'Italie au Pacte vert pour l'Europe et à l'initiative Next Generation de l'UE (Rapport italien).

En Espagne, une nouvelle législation a été adoptée pour soutenir la mise en œuvre de la Stratégie européenne « de la ferme à la table ». Cette législation comprend des mesures visant à réduire les émissions de gaz à effet de serre, à promouvoir les énergies renouvelables, à améliorer l'efficacité énergétique, à aider les agriculteurs à adopter des pratiques agricoles plus durables et à réduire la pollution par les nitrates provenant de sources agricoles (Rapport espagnol).

En Allemagne, la loi fédérale sur la protection du climat (Klimaschutzgesetz (KSG)) du 12 décembre 2019 établit un cadre pour la mise en œuvre des objectifs nationaux de protection du climat et le respect des objectifs climatiques européens. Ancrée dans les engagements de l'Accord de Paris sur le climat, la KSG vise à limiter l'augmentation de la température mondiale bien en dessous de 2°C et, si possible, à 1,5°C au-dessus des niveaux préindustriels (§ 1 phrase 2 KSG).

En Hongrie, la mission principale de la gestion de l'eau est d'améliorer la rétention et le stockage de l'eau. La gestion de l'eau basée sur le paysage représente une adaptation hongroise unique du concept de gestion adaptative de l'eau dans le cadre plus large de la gestion intégrée de l'eau (Rapport hongrois).

Le Pacte vert de l'Europe continue d'avoir un impact significatif sur les réglementations nationales des États membres de l'UE, façonnant les politiques environnementales et de développement durable dans divers secteurs.

En Espagne, le Pacte vert de l'Europe a conduit à l'approbation d'une nouvelle législation et de plans stratégiques visant à lutter contre le changement climatique et à promouvoir la durabilité. La loi espagnole sur le changement climatique et la transition énergétique, qui vise à atteindre la neutralité climatique en Espagne d'ici 2050, en est un exemple. Une autre initiative clé est le plan national intégré pour l'énergie et le climat 2021-2030, qui présente des mesures spécifiques pour atteindre les objectifs de la loi sur le changement climatique et la transition énergétique.

Le plan stratégique de la PAC espagnole (CAPSP) établit des lignes d'action pour soutenir les agriculteurs dans leur transition vers des pratiques agricoles plus durables. En outre, l'approbation d'un autre document de programmation, le Projet stratégique agroalimentaire pour la relance et la transformation (ASPERT), a introduit un paquet de soutien spécial pour l'industrie agroalimentaire. Ce paquet vise à encourager l'innovation, la résilience et la durabilité au sein du secteur.

Le projet stratégique agroalimentaire pour la relance et la transformation (ASPERT) vise à améliorer les processus de production, à renforcer la compétitivité, à promouvoir la durabilité et à assurer la traçabilité de la production alimentaire. Il comprend également des mesures visant à soutenir l'adaptation numérique du secteur agroalimentaire. Le projet englobe tous les acteurs de la chaîne de valeur alimentaire, y compris les agriculteurs, les producteurs, les coopératives et les petites et moyennes entreprises impliquées dans la production, la transformation et le commerce.

Un élément clé du projet est son troisième axe, qui se concentre sur des mesures spécifiques de soutien à l'innovation et à la recherche, dans le but de parvenir à un secteur agroalimentaire compétitif à travers tous les maillons de la chaîne.

En outre, il convient de mentionner le plan d'action pour la mise en œuvre de l'Agenda 2030 : vers une stratégie espagnole de développement durable. Ce plan établit divers objectifs et mesures visant à faire progresser le développement rural en Espagne (Rapport espagnol).

IX. Les énergies renouvelables dans l'agriculture

L'augmentation du coût des affaires et la préoccupation croissante pour la protection de l'environnement ont accéléré les investissements dans les énergies renouvelables. Simultanément, l'utilisation des terres pour la production d'aliments et d'énergie, par exemple au moyen d'installations photovoltaïques, est devenue une tendance importante. Par conséquent, l'application de l'agrophotovoltaïque, qui permet l'utilisation agricole simultanée des terres et la récolte d'énergie, s'est développée. Pour les générations futures, les énergies renouvelables revêtent une importance de plus en plus grande. L'impact combiné de l'invasion de l'Ukraine par la Russie et du changement climatique a renforcé les préoccupations en matière de sécurité énergétique. Ces évolutions soulignent l'urgence de réduire la dépendance à l'égard des combustibles fossiles et d'éliminer la dépendance à l'égard des ressources énergétiques fournies par la Russie.

a) Exemple

En Pologne, il n'existe actuellement aucun contrat de fourniture de gaz avec la Russie. La loi du 13 juillet 2023 établit des règles et des procédures détaillées pour la préparation et la mise en œuvre des investissements dans les usines de biogaz agricoles. La loi précise le cadre procédural pour l'émission de décisions sur la construction d'usines de biogaz agricoles, dans le but de faciliter et d'accélérer la préparation et la réalisation de ces investissements. Elle définit également les conditions d'exploitation des installations de biogaz agricole, dans le but de promouvoir des solutions énergétiques durables dans le secteur agricole.

En 2021, les énergies renouvelables représentaient 19,3 % de la consommation finale brute d'énergie en France. La loi française énergie-climat, adoptée en 2019, vise à atteindre un objectif de consommation de 33 % d'énergies renouvelables d'ici 2030. En outre, les États membres de l'Union européenne ont récemment convenu d'un objectif collectif de 42,5 % de consommation d'énergie renouvelable d'ici 2030.

Pour atteindre ces objectifs ambitieux, la France a adopté la loi n° 2023-175 du 10 mars 2023, qui vise à accélérer la production d'énergie renouvelable. Cette législation apporte des modifications importantes au cadre énergétique du pays afin de s'aligner sur les objectifs nationaux et européens (Rapport français).

X. *Politique agricole commune 2023-2027, développement rural et environnement*

La Commission III a débattu de la Politique Agricole Commune (PAC). Il ne fait aucun doute que dans chaque État membre de l'Union européenne, des règlements ont été publiés pour financer la PAC pour la période 2023-2027. La préparation des plans stratégiques de la PAC pour cette période a constitué un défi majeur. Dans chaque pays, l'instrument de base du soutien est constitué par les paiements directs, tandis que chaque État membre a actuellement choisi différents éco-régimes.

Dans le cadre du pilier II de la PAC, il convient de saluer la plus grande liberté accordée aux États membres pour prendre en compte les besoins nationaux lors du choix des programmes et des mesures. En conséquence, les États membres de l'UE ont opté pour différentes mesures de développement rural. Les programmes continuent d'inclure l'aide aux jeunes agriculteurs, la modernisation des exploitations et l'association des producteurs agricoles. Les questions environnementales, y compris les énergies renouvelables, prennent de plus en plus d'importance. L'aide est accordée sous la forme d'une décision administrative ou d'un contrat.

Les paiements directs aux producteurs agricoles existent également dans des pays extérieurs à l'Union européenne. Dans certains pays, les producteurs se plaignent que les règles sont trop compliquées et doivent être simplifiées. Dans certains pays, de telles simplifications ont déjà été introduites.

Un nouvel aspect important concerne les éco-régimes. Selon la loi polonaise du 8 février 2023 sur le plan stratégique pour la politique agricole commune 2023-2027, les paiements au titre des éco-régimes sont accordés à l'agriculteur sous la forme de paiements : 1) pour les zones avec des plantes mellifères, 2) pour l'agriculture du carbone et la gestion des nutriments, 3) pour la production végétale intégrée, 4) pour la protection biologique des cultures, 5) pour la rétention d'eau sur les prairies permanentes, 5a) pour les terres exclues de la production, et 6) pour le bien-être des animaux.

Exemples : Eco-schémas selon les plans stratégiques de la PAC de quatre Etats membres de l'UE

Espagne	**Pologne**	**Allemagne**	**Italie**
Type de surface : Pâturages permanents et prairies permanentes. • Pratiques. Pâturage extensif (P1). • Pratiques. Fauche durable et création d'îlots de biodiversité (P2). • Création d'îlots de biodiversité (P2A). • Semis durable (P2B). Types de surface : Terres arables. • Pratiques. Rotation des cultures avec des espèces améliorantes (P3). • Pratiques. Semis direct (P4). Types de surfaces: Terres arables et cultures permanentes , y compris les cultures ligneuses.	Les paiements au titre des éco-régimes sont accordés aux agriculteurs sous la forme de paiements pour les zones de production de miel, de paiements pour la gestion du carbone et des nutriments dans l'agriculture, de paiements pour la production végétale intégrée, de paiements pour la protection biologique des cultures, de paiements pour la rétention de l'eau dans les prairies permanentes et de paiements pour le bien-être des animaux.	Il existe des éco-schémas: • ÖR 1 : Zones supplémentaires pour la biodiversité (jachères/ bandes fleuries/ bandes de vieilles herbes). • ÖR 2 : Cultures diversifiées dans les terres arables avec au moins 5 cultures principales dont 10 % de légumineuses. • ÖR 3 : Maintien de l'agroforesterie sur les terres arables et les prairies permanentes. • ÖR 4 : Extension de l'ensemble des prairies permanentes de l'entreprise. • ÖR 5 : Gestion extensive de surfaces individuelles de prairies permanentes avec preuve d'au moins 4 caracté-	Introduction de cinq éco-régimes: • ECO-1 Amélioration du bien-être des animaux et lutte contre la antimicrobiens • ECO-2 Enherbement des cultures arboricoles (17,8 % des ressources) ; • ECO-3 Sauvegarde des oliviers ayant une valeur paysagère particulière (17,2 %) ; • ECO-4 Systèmes fourragers extensifs, visant à promouvoir l'introduction de légumineuses et de cultures fourragères en rotation, ainsi que de cultures de renouvellement avec un engagement en faveur de la gestion des résidus du point de vue du puits de

• Pratiques. Mise en place d'espaces de biodiversité ou gestion durable de la nappe phréatique (P5). Types de surfaces : Cultures permanentes. • Pratiques. Couverture végétale spontanée ou semée (P6). • Pratiques. Couverture de végétation inerte (P7).		ristiques régionales. • ÖR 6 : Éviter l'utilisation de pesticides chimiques de synthèse sur les terres arables et dans les cultures permanentes. • ÖR 7 : Gestion axée sur les objectifs de conservation dans les zones Natura 2000	carbone (18,6 %) ; • ECO-5 Mesures spécifiques pour les pollinisateurs dans les cultures herbacées et arboricoles (5 %).

Source : Rapports nationaux pour l'Espagne, la Pologne, l'Allemagne et l'Italie en vue du congrès de la CEDR à Cardiff en 2023.

Selon les plans stratégiques de la PAC 2023-2027, l'Espagne a déjà augmenté son soutien à l'innovation, au transfert de connaissances et à la numérisation. Ce soutien est géré par les administrations régionales, bien que les conditions d'octroi de ce soutien soient généralement uniformes d'une région à l'autre. Les mesures espagnoles au titre du pilier II comprennent l'aide aux jeunes agriculteurs et aux nouveaux agriculteurs pour l'établissement d'entreprises rurales (sous-mesure 6.1), l'investissement dans les exploitations agricoles (sous-mesure 4.1), les initiatives de coopération (LEADER) au titre de la mesure 19, ainsi que le partage des connaissances et la diffusion de l'information.

En Suisse, les agriculteurs reçoivent des paiements directs en compensation des services publics qu'ils fournissent. Ces paiements comprennent des subventions pour les terres agricoles, la garantie de l'approvisionnement, la biodiversité, la qualité du paysage, les systèmes de production, l'efficacité des ressources et les passerelles (Rapport suisse).

Au Royaume-Uni, les aides financières accordées aux agriculteurs sont également liées au respect d'obligations environnementales. Toutefois, ce soutien est appelé à diminuer dans les années à venir.

XI. Guerre en Ukraine

Les questions relatives à l'Ukraine ont été largement débattues au sein de la Commission 1.

Certaines questions juridiques liées à la situation en Ukraine ont été discutées lors d'une connexion en ligne avec des scientifiques ukrainiens. Malgré les défis et les conséquences des hostilités en cours, le parlement et le gouvernement ukrainiens ont mis en œuvre diverses mesures visant à faciliter les activités agricoles.

Le Rapport polonais présente des aspects tels que les réglementations légales qui ont été introduites pour aider les producteurs agricoles polonais touchés par l'impact négatif de la guerre en Ukraine et les réglementations qui aident les citoyens ukrainiens vivant en Pologne, par exemple la loi du 12 mars 2022 sur l'assistance aux citoyens de l'Ukraine dans le cadre du conflit armé sur le territoire de ce pays.

General Report of Commission III

Version anglaise – English version – Englische Version

Prof. UAM Dr. hab. Aneta Suchoń
Adam Mickiewicz University

Presenting the substantive report of Commission III is not an easy task due to the quantitative limitations of the publications and the broad scope of issues that were discussed. Reports were prepared from the following countries: France, Germany, Hungary, Italy, the Netherlands, Poland, Slovenia, Spain, Switzerland, the UK, and the USA. There was also an online connection with a researcher from Ukraine. The structure of the country reports generally followed the questions indicated in the questionnaire. Since the last Congress (Poznań, September 2019), there have been numerous regulatory changes in both national and EU legislation.

It is worth recalling the key issues identified in the form, including the following: What are the main changes in the law relating to agricultural activities since the last Congress in 2019?

- Organisation and conduct of agricultural activity on a farm.
- The position of farmers in the value chain, cooperatives, organisations, contracts and agri-food law.
- Rural areas.
- European Green Deal, environmental protection on farms, counteracting climate change, including organic farming, renewable energy, water law and animal welfare.
- Common Agricultural Policy (CAP) Strategic Plans in EU Member States and other strategic documents concerning agriculture in countries outside the European Union. New legal regulations for the Common Agricultural Policy 2023-2027.
- External relations with third countries of the world.

Special attention was paid to the most recent trends, developments, and distinct solutions in the countries studied. During the session, the reports from EU member states and other European countries, as well as from the US and Ukraine, were presented and discussed. The basic finding from the country reports and discussions is that many new regulations have been adopted (entered into force) in individual countries, whereby legislative changes in the EU countries are, to a great extent, related to the new legal instruments in the field the Common Agricultural Policy (CAP).

Therefore, it is impossible to mention all the important and interesting novel aspects in legislation, case law and practices from the country reports. The catalogue of legislation on the organisation and operation of agricultural activities is becoming more and more extensive since it must respond to challenges of crises that have arisen or deepened in recent years: COVID-19, climate change (including drought), the war in Ukraine which have a significant impact on agricultural activities.

There is no doubt that most changes in terms of EU agricultural law and national regulations are related to the current Multiannual Financial Framework.

In December 2021, three basic EU regulations were adopted: Regulations of the European Parliament and of the Council of 2 December 2021 no (EU) 2021/2115[1]; 2021/2116[2], and 2021/2117.[3]

EU member states prepared CAP strategic plans and adopted national implementing regulations in accordance with the new legal instruments.

Changes in the agricultural legislation of reporting countries are also related to regulating the relations in the agricultural and food supply chain (for example, the deadline for implementing the Directive (EU) 2019/663 expired on May 1, 2021). Agriculture and the food supply chain as a whole have been affected by COVID-19 and the war in Ukraine (these issues were mainly discussed in Commission I).

---

1 Regulation (EU) 2021/2115 of the European Parliament and of the Council of 2 December 2021 establishing rules on support for strategic plans to be drawn up by member states under the Common Agricultural Policy (CAP Strategic Plans) and financed by the European Agricultural Guarantee Fund (EAGF) and by the European Agricultural Fund for Rural Development (EAFRD) and repealing Regulations (EU) No 1305/2013 and (EU) No 1307/2013 (CAP SP Regulation).

2 Regulation (EU) 2021/2116 of the European Parliament and of the Council of 2 December 2021 on the financing, management and monitoring of the common agricultural policy and repealing Regulation (EU) No 1306/2013 (CAP Horizontal Regulation).

3 Regulation (EU) 2021/2117 of the European Parliament and of the Council of 2 December 2021 amending Regulations (EU) No 1308/2013 establishing a common organisation of the markets in agricultural products, (EU) No 1151/2012 on quality schemes for agricultural products and foodstuffs, (EU) No 251/2014 on the definition, description, presentation, labelling and the protection of geographical indications of aromatised wine products and (EU) No 228/2013 laying down specific measures for agriculture in the outermost regions of the Union (CMO Regulation).

I. Organisation and conduct of agricultural activity on a farm

The country reports contained observations and comments on important legal developments related to environmental issues of agriculture, for instance, the European Green Deal, on-farm environmental protection, the fight against climate change, including organic farming, renewable energy, water law and animal welfare. Commission III first discussed the rules of farming. There were modifications and innovations in this area. In some countries, there have been changes or innovations in the main definition of agricultural law, i.e. farmer, farm or agricultural activity.

It is worth noting that the catalogue of agriculture-related activities is expanding in some countries. Changes have also been made to certain provisions on registers, e.g., entries in the register of agricultural producers or the register of producers of wine, milk, or other agricultural products, as well as the registration of animals. Entries are generally necessary for obtaining EU funds. Most of them are made in electronic form, and agricultural producers can, and sometimes must, enter data electronically. While this accelerates the process and reduces time, certain challenges persist.

Digitalisation in the field of agricultural activities is becoming increasingly important. Applications and registry entries are growing in popularity, and among other things, their impact on precision farming should be highlighted. There have also been changes in agricultural taxes, which are related to the expansion of the basic definition of agricultural activities and are associated with the conduct of agricultural activities.

a) Examples

Amendments to the Slovenian Agricultural Act of March 2022 aligned the definition of a farmer and an agricultural holding with the CAP Strategic Plans (Regulation (EU) 2021/2115) (Slovenian Report).

The French Act No 2022-172 of 14 February 2022, in favor of independent professional activities,[4] deserves particular attention due to its key provisions. First, the Act introduces the duality of the property of individual entrepreneurs, distinguishing between business and personal property. Movables and immovables, rights, obligations, and securities held by an individual entrepreneur that are used for one or more independent profes-

4 LOI No 2022-172 du 14 février 2022 en faveur de l'activité professionnelle indépendante, JORF No0038 du 15 février 2022.

sional activities constitute the professional property of the individual entrepreneur. Individual entrepreneurs are, in principle, liable for obligations arising from their professional activity solely with their business property, ensuring the protection of personal assets. The Act also regulates the universal transfer of business property, providing clarity and legal certainty in such transactions.

Moreover, the French report highlights the definition of ecological payments as income from agriculture under certain conditions or restrictions in tax regulations. This provision is particularly significant as it directly impacts the fiscal treatment of income derived from ecological activities, emphasizing the growing importance of environmental considerations in agricultural law.

In Germany, due to the amendment to the Sales Tax Act of 21 December 2021, the flat sales tax rate for agriculture and forestry changed as of 1 January 2022.

The French crop insurance system was recently reformed by Law No. 2022-298, published on 2 March 2022, which improved the spread of crop insurance in agriculture and adapted risk management tools to the challenges of climate change. A new system based on national solidarity and risk-sharing between the state, farmers and insurers has been created, reflecting the changing needs of the industry (France Country Report).

In Poland, the legislation on the national system of producer registers, farm registers, and payment application registers was amended in 2022. Additionally, the Minister of Agriculture and Rural Development adopted regulations specifying the detailed requirements for applications for entry in the producer registers. Due to the increasingly widespread use of digitisation and computerisation in agriculture, the 2022 legislative amendments enable authorised entities to submit applications for entry into the producer register not only in paper form but also electronically. In the same year, the Polish Parliament adopted new legislation on animal identification and registration, aligning it with EU legal instruments, such as Regulation (EU) No 2016/429 of the European Parliament and of the Council of 9 March 2016 on transmissible animal diseases, which also amends and repeals certain acts in the field of animal health.

In Spain, a Farm Information System (SIEX) has been established, which is technically and systematically interoperable with the Autonomous Communities' Agricultural Exploitation Registers, the Digital Farm Exploitation Notebooks, and other public registers.

In 2023, Poland amended statutory provisions on the management of agricultural real estate of the State Treasury and other acts, including the Act on Shaping the Agricultural System. Amendments concerning management of the Treasury Agricultural Property Stock included, inter alia, issues related to leases, and transfer of real property to local governments for infrastructure and construction needs. The definitions of key concepts such as family farm, relative, person with agricultural qualifications, and personal management of an agricultural holding, as referred to in the Act on Shaping the Agricultural System, were added or modified. This direct reference should be assessed positively.

As part of the amendment of 13 July 2023, the provisions on restricted tenders have been clarified. According to the new provisions, the National Centre may stipulate that only certain groups of persons may participate in the tender. For example, these may include individual farmers who intend to expand their family farm.

The amended Act on Formation of the Agricultural System (UKUR, Ustawa z dnia 11 kwietnia 2003 r. o kształtowaniu ustroju rolnego) specifies that its provisions do not apply to agricultural properties where the agricultural area covers less than 0.3 ha. The modification will have a positive impact on rural development for housing purposes.

The amended legislation extends certain exceptions from the obligations laid down for purchasers of agricultural real estate. In particular, this applies to properties for which, after purchase, a local development plan has been adopted, providing for their use for purposes other than agricultural. It is worth noting that the ongoing debate over the last few years regarding the impact that development plans changes will have on the obligations of purchasers of agricultural land. The legislator's decision to regulate this issue is a step in the right direction, eliminating the previous legal ambiguities. Nevertheless, it may lead to a weakening of the protection of agricultural land in the context of its quantitative preservation.

The amendment was also intended to clarify and streamline the implementation of the provisions related to agricultural real estate trade on the private market specified in the Act on Shaping the Agricultural System. Rural development is based not only on the development of agricultural activities, but also on the construction of infrastructure. The amendment to the Act on the Management of Agricultural Property of the State Treasury has opened the door for the National Centre to transfer property to local government units free of charge. This applies to land earmarked for municipal, district, and provincial roads, as well as those already actually used as roads. Additionally, The National Centre also has the option of transferring other land for these purposes, as long as this is in line with local development, regeneration or reconstruction plans.

In connection with the 2023 agrarian structure survey, Germany adjusted its legislation on agricultural statistics and food to EU law (for instance, Commission Implementing Regulation (EU) No 2021/2286) and developments in the agro-food sector (Country Report: Germany).

Commission III also discussed the legal rules for farming in the UK after Brexit. The Farm Bill 2019-21 (Farm Bill 2020) adopted new approach to agricultural payments and land management. In England, farmers will be paid for producing 'public goods' such as environmental or animal welfare improvements. Additionally, the Scottish Government introduced agricultural legislation in November 2019 (UK Report).

In the US, the Federal Farm Bills establish important agricultural and food policy measures that regulate many aspects of rural law. The US Congress typically enacts an agricultural law every five years. The most recent Farm Bill was enacted in 2018, and its successor was anticipated by the end of 2023 or early 2024. However, as of 2025, it remains to be seen whether a new Farm Bill has been fully enacted or if discussions are still ongoing (USA Report). Agricultural laws are complex and far-reaching pieces of legislation.

The 2017 Census of Agriculture, published in 2019, provides detailed information on US farms and farmland. There were 2.042 million farms in the US, covering approximately 900 million acres of land, including 396 million acres of cropland. The average farm size was 441 acres, and most farms were small in both size and sales value.

Although approximately 60 % of farmland in the US is owner-managed, renting plays a significant role in US agriculture, particularly in grain production. Nearly 40 % of agricultural land in the US is rented, with even higher percentages in certain states. In 2017, full owners operated 69 % of farms, with an average size of 220 acres, while renters typically operated larger farms.

Ownership of agricultural land by some corporations has significant implications for important agricultural states. The 2017 Census of Agriculture revealed that 5.7 % of US farms were corporations, but only 0.6 % were non-family corporations. To address concerns about corporate ownership and to protect family farms, several states have implemented measures to limit corporate ownership of farmland.

The US Department of Agriculture (USDA) publishes annual reports on foreign ownership of agricultural land, based on data collected under the Agricultural Foreign Investment Disclosure Act (AFIDA). The most recent report analysed foreign ownership through December 2021. As of that year, foreign holdings of all agricultural land in the US totalled approximately 40 million acres—representing 1.8 % of all land in the US and 3.1 % of private agricultural land. Between 2020 and 2021, the amount of agricultural land owned by foreign entities increased by about 2.4 million acres.

Foreign ownership is concentrated among a few key countries. Canadians own 31 % of foreign-owned agricultural land, followed by the Netherlands (12 %), Italy (7 %), and Germany and the UK (6 % each). (US Country Report).

II. The role of women in agriculture

The role of women in agriculture was discussed in the Commission. Women actively participate in agriculture. In some countries, a traditional model of predominantly male-led agricultural activities is still strongly present, while in others, due to lower agricultural incomes, smaller agricultural areas, and more responsibilities, it is noticeable that men are less interested in running businesses.

Some countries have introduced regulations and programmes to encourage women's involvement in agriculture and their participation in farm management and decision-making. For example, in Spain, the number of women involved in agriculture has increased significantly in recent years. The 2020 agricultural census indicates that women now represent 29 % of farm managers (261,634 women, an increase of 22 %).

In addition, the number of farms managed by women has grown steadily. In 2010, there were 2,827 farms managed by women, while in 2020, this number increased to 3,323 farms. This growth reflects the positive impact of initiatives like the III Strategic Plan for Effective Gender Equality 2022–2025, which aims to promote gender equality in rural areas and agriculture. This plan also supports women farmers by providing training, counselling, and financing opportunities, helping them overcome challenges and succeed in their businesses (Spanish report).

Women participate in Spanish agriculture in various ways: some own their own farms, while others work on farms owned by relatives or employers. They also play a significant role in the agricultural value chain, contributing to food production, processing, and distribution.

The number of women involved in agriculture in Spain has increased in recent years. According to the 2020 agricultural census, compared to data from 2009, women now represent 29 % of farm managers. However, they are more likely to manage farms of smaller economic size. For example, 56.2 % of women-run farms generate less than €8,000 in total standard production (TSP), compared to 46.3 % of farms managed by men.

These changes are influenced by several factors, including the ageing of the agricultural population, the abandonment of farms by men, and the increasing inclusion of women in agricultural activities.

As regards the US, in 2017, 36 % (1.2 million) of the 3.4 million producers were women. The Census of Agriculture defines a producer as a person "involved in making decisions about farm operations," and farms often have more than one producer. Nearly 56 % of farms had one or more female producers, while 91 % of farms had one or more male producers.

The term "producer" is used in two distinct ways in the census. Fewer women (798,500) identified themselves as primary operators – those considered the principal decision-makers on the farm. An even smaller number of women (489,000) identified as primary producers-individuals who made the majority of decisions concerning farm operations.

Most women producers lived on the farms they ran and were actively involved in daily operations, as well as in decision-making related to land and crop use, livestock, financial management, and succession planning. However, for 66 % of women producers and more than 60 % of female primary producers, farming was not their main occupation (US Country Report).

In Switzerland, approximately 54,300 women were employed on farms in 2020, with 6 % employed as farm managers. Both the number of farms managed by women and the total number of farms declined slightly in the reporting year. However, the decrease in the number of farms managed by women was, on average, slightly higher than the overall decline in the total number of farms.

Compared to the overall development of farms, the number of farms over 30 hectares managed by women showed a relatively different trend, suggesting shifts in the structure of agricultural operations (Swiss Report).

III. Animal welfare, plant health

Country reports highlight animal welfare and breeding issues, including the treatment of animals, as significant areas where legislative changes have been observed. Breeding rules influence both meat quality and the environment. EU Member States have adapted their provisions to comply with EU legal instruments, which have predominantly taken the form of directly applicable regulations replacing earlier directives (e.g., Regulation (EU) 2016/429 on animal health and Regulation (EU) 2016/1012 on animal husbandry).

In Poland, the Plant Health Regulation (EU) 2016/2031 was implemented primarily through the Act of 13 February 2020 on the protection of plants against agrophages. This Act retains the provisions that assign all plant health tasks to the authorities of the State Plant Protection and Seed Inspection. Additionally, it introduced the possibility of designating areas free of certain agrophages, which may play a critical role in facilitating the export of goods to third countries. The Chief Inspector of Plant Protection and Seed Inspection serves as the competent authority for the designation of quarantine stations and isolation facilities.

To implement the Animal Breeding Regulation (EU) 2016/1012 in Poland, the Act of 10 December 2020 on the organisation of breeding and reproduction of farm animals was enacted. This Act regulates the breeding and protection of livestock genetic resources, functional value assessments, genetic evaluations, herd book maintenance, registers, breeding records, and the control of breeding and reproduction activities for farm animals. In addition, the Act defines the authorities and institutions that will have the powers and competences set out in Regulation (EU) 2016/1012 on the territory of the Republic of Poland.

Accordingly, the Minister of Agriculture has been granted the authority to:

- recognise breeding organisations or other entities applying for the keeping of herd books and breeding registers for cattle, pigs, sheep, goats and equines as breeders' associations and breeding enterprises,
- approve breeding programmes carried out by these breeders' associations or breeding enterprises,
- impose and repeal the measures set out in Regulation (EU) 2016/1012 in the event that the controlled entities infringe the provisions of that Regulation.

The National Animal Breeding Centre is tasked with carrying out official controls to ensure compliance with the Regulation (Polish report).

Commission III also addressed the issue of African swine fever (ASF). In July 2023, the epidemiological status concerning this threat in the European Union was updated by the Commission Implementing Regulation (EU) 2023/1485 of 18 July 2023, which amended Annexes I and II to Implementing Regulation (EU) 2021/605, laying down specific measures for the control of ASF.

In Poland, ASF outbreaks were confirmed in July 2023, including several new cases in the Wielkopolskie and Mazowieckie Voivodeships, with additional outbreaks reported in restricted areas of the Podkarpackie and Lubelskie Voivodeships. This represents a significant improvement compared to the several thousand outbreaks previously reported to the European Commission. In Poland, specific measures to address ASF are outlined in the Regulation of the Minister of Agriculture and Rural Development of 10 August 2021 on actions to be taken in relation to the occurrence of ASF. This was further amended in May 2023 by the Ordinance of the Minister of Agriculture and Rural Development, updating the measures to be implemented in response to ASF outbreaks.

In Germany, a new Veterinary Medicine Act entered into force on 28 January 2022, addressing issues at the national (federal) level that were not covered by directly applicable provisions of Regulation (EU) 2019/6 on veterinary medicinal products, which repealed Directive 2001/82/EC. The new Act systematically consolidates all provisions concerning the veterinary sector that were previously scattered across multiple pieces of legislation. This law implements Regulation (EU) 2019/6 of the European Parliament and of the Council of 11 December 2018 on veterinary medicinal products and repealing Directive 2001/82/EC (OJ L 4, 7.1.2019, p. 43; L 163, 20 June 2019, p. 112; L 326, 8 October 2020, p. 15; L 241, 8 July 2021, p. 17) (German Country Report).

In Switzerland, amendments to the Animal Breeding Ordinance of 31 October 2012, made on 2 November 2022 and 5 April 2023, strengthened provisions for the preservation of Swiss breeds and extended the financial contributions for their protection. These amendments are based on the "Animal Breeding Strategy 2030" and relevant parliamentary proposals (Swiss Report).

In May 2023, the US Supreme Court upheld the California Animal Welfare Act, which will affect the production and sale of pork, veal, and eggs while imposing specific burdens on livestock producers across the United States (USA Report).

The US Environmental Protection Agency (EPA) regulates genetically modified (GM) plants that contain pesticidal substances, known as plant-incorporated protectants (PIPs). The EPA requires certain PIPs to be registered under the Federal Insecticide, Fungicide, and Rodenticide Act (FIFRA) and subject to food residue tolerance or exemption under the Federal Food, Drug, and Cosmetic Act (FDCA).

To address developments in biotechnology, the EPA issued a rule in May 2023 exempting certain genetically engineered plant-incorporated protectants (PIPs) from FIFRA registration and FDCA food tolerance requirements. This exemption applies to PIPs that "pose no greater risk than PIPs that the EPA has already determined meet safety requirements and that could otherwise have been created through conventional breeding." Specifically, the rule exempts PIPs "created through genetic engineering from a sexually compatible plant" and "loss-of-function" PIPs.

In the United States, aspects of animal welfare are regulated by both federal and state laws. Federal laws and regulations focus on preventing cruelty and ensuring humane slaughter; however, few federal standards specifically address animal production practices.

IV. Agricultural employment

One of the current challenges in agriculture is employment. In some countries, national agricultural employment legislation has been introduced to address specific challenges related to agricultural labor relations. This topic was also discussed in Commission III, with examples from several countries illustrating diverse approaches to tackling these issues.

In Italy, the high rate of irregular employment in agriculture (24.1 % in 2019, a +3.4-percentage point increase since 2010) poses a significant obstacle to the sustainability of the agricultural sector. To address this issue, Italy has implemented the social conditionality provisions established by Regulation (EU) No. 2115 of 2021, Article 1453. The Ministerial Decree of 28 December 2022, which took effect on 1 January 2023, introduced a mechanism for data exchange between the National Labor Inspectorate, National Fire Authority, and local health authorities to enhance compliance and enforcement of EU directives under social conditionality (Italian Report).

Similarly, in Spain, an important labor law reform was enacted in 2021 to encourage long-term employment contracts in the agricultural sector. The reform limits the circumstances under which fixed-term or temporary contracts can be used, prioritizing indefinite-term contracts. Although agriculture has traditionally relied on temporary contracts, the reform acknowledges the sector's stable and cyclical labor needs throughout the year (Spanish Report).

In Switzerland, there is no specific national legislation governing agricultural employment contracts. However, the general law of employment contracts does not apply to agricultural workers either. Instead, the cantons are required to enact standard employment contracts that regulate key aspects such as working hours, rest times, and working conditions, particularly for women and young workers (para. 2).

Of particular interest is the regulation in the canton of Bern, the largest agricultural canton in Switzerland. Its standard employment contract dates back to 2007 and was amended in 2012. The most recent regulation comes from the canton of Lucerne, the third-largest agricultural canton, which issued its standard employment contract at the end of 2022 (Swiss Report).

Regarding working conditions, the Federal Law on Family Allowances in Agriculture (FLG) provides family benefits to agricultural workers. Under this law, family members of the farm manager who work on the farm are also entitled to family allowances (Article 1a). These allowances include a household allowance and allowances for children and education (Article 2(1)). Furthermore, self-employed farmers and alpine farmers are also eligible for family allowances (Article 5).

In Poland, the introduction of the 'harvest assistance contract' in 2023 marked a significant development in legislation related to social insurance for farmers. Under this new provision, a 'farmer's helper' agrees to assist in harvesting agricultural products at a specific location on the farmer's property for a specified period. In return, the farmer agrees to pay the agreed remuneration for the assistance provided.

Once this contract is concluded, the farmer's helper becomes partially covered by agricultural social insurance. A distinctive feature of the Polish agricultural insurance system is its separation from the general social insurance system. It is managed by the Agricultural Social Insurance Fund and operates with a unique set of benefits and comparatively low contributions.

V. The problem of agricultural land (decreasing amount of agricultural land) and conflict of interest, generational change

Commission III discussed the issue of agricultural land, focusing on the declining availability of agricultural land and conflicts of interest. The number of farms and the total area of agricultural land are decreasing in many countries, raising concerns about the future of the agricultural model, particularly in Europe. The conversion of agricultural land for building and investment purposes is a particularly damaging trend, affecting high-quality farmland and significantly limiting farming opportunities.

Generational change is another pressing challenge that may become increasingly serious in the future. Fewer young people are willing to take over farms, a trend linked to the profession's inherent demands for greater professional liability and the substantial risks associated with weather conditions, natural disasters, and market volatility. In this context, monitoring and controlling the activities of producers, along with ensuring accountability and penalties, are critical issues being addressed at both the EU level and within individual countries.

To support young farmers, the EU has allocated additional funding through both the first and second pillars of the Common Agricultural Policy (CAP). These measures are closely tied to the transfer of agricultural holdings, an area where several countries have recently introduced legislative changes aimed at restricting the transfer of agricultural land.

Some countries operate an open market for agricultural real estate, which poses a greater risk of farmland being converted or excluded for construction or investment purposes. At the same time, the leasing of agricultural land is becoming increasingly significant, with some countries implementing legislative changes to address this trend and others planning similar actions.

For example, 93.5 % of Italy's farms are individual or family farms, highlighting the continued dominance of the family farm model. However, this model is also in decline. The smallest family farms, particularly those in central and southern Italy, are leaving the sector at a significant rate (-51.2 % of farms smaller than one hectare). In contrast, there has been an increase in farming by partnerships and, most notably, limited liability companies.

Additionally, the practice of land renting is becoming increasingly important, gradually replacing the traditional model of sole ownership (Italian Report).

In Slovenia, utilised agricultural land accounts for only 23.7 % of the country's total area. High-quality agricultural land in Slovenia is limited, making its protection critically important. According to the Agriculture Act, agricultural policy measures must be directed primarily towards the development of sustainable agriculture that maintains the biodiversity of animal and plant species and preserves soil fertility while protecting the natural living conditions of soil, water, and air (Article 15) (Slovenian Report).

On 13 July 2023, the Polish Parliament passed a law amending the Act on the Formation of the Agricultural System, which introduced new arrangements for public law control of the circulation of agricultural land.

New legislation in France, introduced by Law No. 2021-1756 of 23 December 2021, regulates access to agricultural land through corporate structures. This unique regime aims to control the purchase of shares in agricultural companies to combat the accumulation and excessive concentration of agricultural land through corporate structures (land grabbing) and to improve food sovereignty.

Under this law, any entity seeking to acquire control of a company that owns or uses agricultural real estate for agricultural activity must obtain a permit from the departmental prefect if the agricultural real estate owned or used by the company, when combined with agricultural real estate already owned or used by the same entity, exceeds an amount of real estates.

In Switzerland, the acquisition of agricultural land and farms is, in principle, restricted to self-employed farmers. This limitation arises from the Swiss Federal Act Governing Agricultural Land (BGBB), which imposes strict rules on the legal transfer of agricultural land and businesses. In cases of inheritance, an agricultural enterprise can only be taken over by an heir who qualifies as an individual farmer and is deemed suitable (Article 11(1) BGBB).

In the UK, the tenancy of agricultural land is becoming increasingly popular. According to the Rock Review, tenant holdings – whether whole or partial – occupy 64 % of the total farmable area (8.9 million hectares) in England, while tenant holdings account for 45 % of all agricultural holdings in the country. The DEFRA Commission has undertaken a review of tenant farming in England. The Rock Review made over 70 recommendations to deliver a more resilient tenant sector, aiming to ensure sustainable food production, address the challenges of climate change, and improve and enhance biodiversity (UK presentations).

VI. The position of farmers in the value chain

The position of farmers in the food supply chain remains weak. Although EU countries have implemented Directive (EU) 2019/633 on unfair business-to-business commercial practices in the agricultural and food supply chain, recent developments – such as Russia's aggression against Ukraine – have negatively impacted agricultural markets and weakened the bargaining position of agricultural producers. These challenges stem from rising input prices (fuel, energy, fertilizers, and plant protection products) and the lifting of tariffs on certain Ukrainian agricultural products by the European Union, which has made it more difficult for domestic agricultural products to compete.

Examples of national implementation and related measures include the following:

In Slovenia, the 2021 amendments to the Agricultural Act expanded the concept of the food supply chain to include the agricultural and food product supply chain and introduced the concept of significant market power (SMP). The sales volume of suppliers and buyers is now compared strictly according to the scale provided for in Directive (EU) 2019/633. Additionally, a new institution, the Ombudsman for Relations in the Agri-Food Chain, was established to oversee these matters, and new mandatory rules on prohibited unfair practices were introduced (Slovenian Report).

In Italy, the Supplementary Fund allocated €1.2 billion for supply chain and district contracts in the agri-food sector, covering agriculture, fisheries, forestry, floriculture, and plant nurseries. Of this amount, 25 % is reserved for organic farming. The state aid scheme for supply chain and district contracts, covering the period from 2021 to 2027, was notified to the European Commission, which confirmed its compatibility with the internal market under Article 107 para. 3(c) TFEU. The scheme was implemented by Ministerial Decree of 22 December 2021 (Italian Report).

In Poland, Directive (EU) 2019/633 was transposed into national law through the Act of 17 November 2021 on counteracting the unfair exploitation of contractual advantage in trade in agricultural and food products (Polish Report).

In Spain, the "standard agri-food contract" was initially regulated by Law 12/2013 on measures to improve the functioning of the food chain. Subsequent amendments, notably in 2020 and December 2021, completed the transposition of Directive (EU) 2019/633. The Spanish legislator emphasized the need to protect the weakest link in the food chain – the primary production sector, which is predominantly composed of small and medium-sized family-run farms. These farms often produce high-quality goods but are not fairly compensated by the market. Future regulations must guarantee comprehensive protection against unfair trading practices, covering all stages of agri-food contracting, including preliminary, pre-contractual, and negotiation phases. Such measures should aim to provide equitable protection for the primary production sector (Spanish Report).

VII. Association of agricultural producers

The participants of Commission III discussed the association of agricultural producers (cooperatives and other organizations). This is one of the main instruments for increasing the position of agricultural producers in the food supply chain. Under the provisions of the EU Common Agricultural Policy (CAP), producer organizations are obliged to contribute to the empowerment of farmers in the food supply chain, farm development and agricultural markets.

Producer organizations and farmer associations, such as cooperatives, play a crucial role in several areas. These include concentrating supply, improving marketing, planning and adapting production to demand, optimizing production costs, stabilizing producer prices, conducting research, promoting best practices, providing technical assistance, managing by-products, and offering risk management tools to their members. Collectively, these efforts contribute significantly to strengthening the position of producers in the food supply chain. The development of such entities has been observed in several countries.

It was emphasized that cooperation is essential at various stages of farming, from the purchase of inputs and the use of agricultural machinery to the transport of crops, provision of advisory services, and processing and sale of produce. Associated producers are better equipped to produce agricultural products with reduced pesticide use, raise animals with fewer veterinary drugs, and engage in processing that yields unadulterated, healthy, and affordable agri-food products for consumers. Additionally, they can play a significant role in renewable energy initiatives.

The Farm-to-Fork Strategy was highlighted as a key component of the EU Green Deal. This strategy promotes sustainable and inclusive growth, aiming to boost the economy, improve public health and quality of life, and protect the environment. Some producer associations are actively involved in environmental activities, such as protecting Natura 2000 areas (e.g., in the Netherlands). The growing popularity of energy cooperatives was also noted. Commission participants stressed the need to strengthen the legal position and role of farmers' cooperatives, producer organizations, and similar associations to support the development of agriculture, the agri-food industry, and rural areas. In some countries, further legal changes concerning producer organizations, cooperatives, and related entities are necessary to foster their development and effectiveness.

VIII. European Green Deal: on-farm environmental protection, climate change mitigation, organic farming, renewable energy, water law, and animal welfare

Commission III also discussed the issue of climate change, which poses a significant threat to the entire planet. Global warming is increasingly affecting rainfall patterns, oceans, and wind systems. These changes are expected to make farming more challenging across all countries. The problems identified are addressed in the European Green Deal, presented on 11 December 2019 by the European Commission. In recent years, Member States have adopted new regulations and strategies related to the Green Deal.

Various aspects of environmental protection, climate change, water management, and nature conservation are increasingly becoming the focus of judicial decisions. Some countries have also reported the introduction of new environmental or spatial planning legislation.

A notable example of climate issues being addressed in court is the Decision of the First Senate of the German Federal Constitutional Court from 24 March 2021, which recognized climate protection as a human right. The Court stated:

"The state's duty of protection arising from Art. 2(2) first sentence of the Basic Law also encompasses the duty to protect life and health against the risks posed by climate change. It can furthermore give rise to an objective duty to protect future generations..."[5]

This ruling underscore the evolving legal recognition of climate protection as a fundamental obligation of the state, extending its responsibilities to include safeguarding future generations.

The Court also emphasized the need for proportional provision of freedom and opportunities across generations, stating: "Under certain conditions, the Basic Law imposes an obligation to safeguard fundamental freedom over time and to spread the opportunities associated with freedom proportionately across generations. In their subjective dimension, fundamental rights – as intertemporal guarantees of freedom – afford protection

---

5 Bundesverfassungsgericht, Order of the First Senate of 24 March 2021, Cases 1 BvR 2656/18, 1 BvR 78/20, 1 BvR 96/20, 1 BvR 288/20. English translation of the verdict is available on the German Constitutional Court's website: https://www.bundesverfassungsgericht.de/SharedDocs/Entscheidungen/EN/2021/03/rs20210324_1bvr265618en.html.

against the greenhouse gas reduction burdens imposed by Art. 20a of the Basic Law being unilaterally offloaded onto the future."[6]

Decision of the First Senate of 24 March 2021 - 1 BvR 2656/18 - 1 BvR 78/20 - 1 BvR 96/20 - 1 BvR 288/20 - Obligation to protect under Article 2 para. 2 first sentence of the Basic Law includes the duty to protect life and health from the dangers of climate change. It can furthermore form the basis for an objective obligation to protect future generations.

The Court highlighted that Article 20a of the Basic Law has an international dimension. The fact that no state can solve climate change problems on its own due to the global nature of climate and global warming does not invalidate the national obligation to take climate action. According to this obligation, the state is compelled to engage in international action to address climate change at the global level and is obliged to promote climate action within an international framework. A state cannot evade its responsibility by pointing to the greenhouse gas emissions of other states. "4. Under certain conditions, the Basic Law imposes an obligation to safeguard fundamental freedom over time and to spread the opportunities associated with freedom proportionately across generations. In their subjective dimension, fundamental rights – as intertemporal guarantees of freedom – afford protection against the greenhouse gas reduction burdens imposed by Art. 20a of the Basic Law being unilaterally offloaded onto the future. (...)"

The Court's decision underscores the constitutional obligation of the German state to protect life and health, not only for the current population but also for future generations. This duty includes active engagement in both national measures and international cooperation to address climate change comprehensively.

Examples of legislative and policy developments influenced by environmental and sustainability goals include the following:

In the Netherlands, the Environment and Planning Act, introduced on 1 January 2024, represents the most comprehensive statutory revision of environmental law in recent decades. Replacing 26 laws, 60 government decrees, and 75 ministerial decrees, the Act aims to consolidate regulations related to construction, the environment, water, urban planning, and nature. Its goal is to simplify the rules governing spatial projects and the living environment, with notable implications for the agricultural sector.

6 Ibidem.

In Italy, the Constitution was recently amended to explicitly include the protection of the environment, ecosystems, and biodiversity as fundamental principles and criteria for limiting economic activity (Constitutional Law No. 1 of 2022). The National Plan for Reconstruction and Resilience (Piano Nazionale di Ripresa e Resilienza, PNRR) was issued in accordance with Regulation (EU) No. 241 of 2021 as Italy's response to the EU Green Deal and the Next Generation EU initiative (Italian Report).

In Spain, new legislation has been enacted to support the implementation of the EU farm-to-table strategy. This legislation includes measures to reduce greenhouse gas emissions, promote renewable energy, improve energy efficiency, support farmers transitioning to more sustainable agricultural practices, and reduce nitrate pollution from agricultural sources (Spanish Report).

In Germany, the Federal Climate Protection Act (KSG) of 12 December 2019 establishes a framework for implementing national climate protection targets and ensuring compliance with European climate objectives. Rooted in the commitments of the Paris Climate Agreement, the KSG aims to limit the global temperature increase to well below 2°C and, if possible, to 1.5°C above pre-industrial levels (§ 1 sentence 2 KSG).

In Hungary, the core mission of water management is to improve water retention and storage. Landscape-based water management represents a unique Hungarian adaptation of the concept of adaptive water management within the broader framework of integrated water management (Hungarian Report).

The European Green Deal continues to have a significant impact on the national regulations of EU Member States, shaping environmental and sustainability policies across diverse sectors.

In Spain, the European Green Deal has led to the approval of new legislation and strategic plans aimed at addressing climate change and promoting sustainability. An example is the Spanish Climate Change and Energy Transition Act, which aims to achieve climate neutrality in Spain by 2050. Another key initiative is the National Integrated Energy and Climate Plan 2021-2030, which outlines specific measures to achieve the objectives of the Climate Change and Energy Transition Act.

The Spanish CAP Strategic Plan (CAPSP) establishes lines of action to support farmers in their transition to more sustainable agricultural practices. Additionally, the approval of another programming document, the Strategic Agri-Food Project for Recovery and Transformation (ASPERT), has introduced a special support package for the agri-food industry.

This package aims to foster innovation, resilience, and sustainability within the sector

The Strategic Agri-Food Project for Recovery and Transformation (AS-PERT) aims to improve production processes, enhance competitiveness, promote sustainability, and ensure the traceability of food production. It also includes measures to support the digital adaptation of the agri-food sector. The project encompasses all actors within the food value chain, including farmers, growers, cooperatives, and small and medium-sized enterprises involved in production, processing, and trading.

A key component of the project is its third axis, which focuses on specific measures to support innovation and research, with the goal of achieving a competitive agri-food sector across all links of the chain.

Additionally, mention should be made of the Action Plan for the implementation of Agenda 2030: Towards a Spanish Strategy for Sustainable Development. This plan establishes various objectives and measures aimed at advancing rural development in Spain (National Report Spain).

IX. Renewable energy in agriculture

Rising costs of doing business and increasing concern for environmental protection have accelerated investment in renewable energy. Simultaneously, the use of land for both food and energy production, such as through photovoltaic installations, has become a significant trend. As a result, the application of agrophotovoltaics, which enables simultaneous agricultural use of land and energy harvesting, has been growing. For future generations, renewable energy is assuming ever greater importance. The combined impact of Russia's invasion of Ukraine and climate change has heightened concerns about energy security. These developments underscore the urgency of reducing dependency on fossil fuels and eliminating reliance on energy resources supplied by Russia.

a) Example

In Poland, there are currently no gas supply contracts with Russia. The Act of 13 July 2023 establishes detailed rules and procedures for the preparation and implementation of investments in agricultural biogas plants. The Act specifies the procedural framework for issuing decisions on the construction of agricultural biogas plants, with the objective of facilitating and expediting the preparation and realization of such investments. It also sets forth the operational conditions for agricultural biogas plants, aiming to promote sustainable energy solutions within the agricultural sector.

In 2021, renewable energy accounted for 19.3 % of gross final energy consumption in France. The French Energy and Climate Law, adopted in 2019, aims to achieve a consumption target of 33 % renewable energy by 2030. Additionally, European Union member states have recently agreed to a collective target of 42.5 % renewable energy consumption by 2030.

To meet these ambitious goals, France adopted Law No. 2023-175 of 10 March 2023, which aims to accelerate the production of renewable energy. This legislation introduces significant amendments to the country's energy framework to align with national and EU targets (French Report).

X. Common agricultural policy 2023-2027, rural development and environment

Commission III discussed the Common Agricultural Policy (CAP). There is no doubt that in each European Union Member State, regulations have been issued to finance the CAP for the period 2023–2027. A major challenge was the preparation of the Strategic Plans of the CAP for this period. In each country, the basic instrument of support is direct payments, while each Member State has currently chosen different eco-schemes.

Within Pillar II of the CAP, the greater freedom granted to Member States to take into account national needs while choosing programs and measures is to be welcomed. As a result, EU Member States have opted for different rural development measures. Programs continue to include aid for young farmers, the modernization of farms, and the association of agricultural producers. Environmental issues, including renewable energy, are becoming increasingly important. Support is granted in the form of an administrative decision or contract.

Direct payments to agricultural producers also exist in countries outside the European Union. In some countries, producers complain that the rules are too complicated and need to be simplified. In certain countries, such simplifications have already been introduced.

An important new aspect concerns eco-schemes. According to the Polish Act of 8 February 2023 on the Strategic Plan for the Common Agricultural Policy 2023–2027, payments under eco-schemes are granted to the farmer in the form of payments: 1) for areas with honeydew plants, 2) for carbon farming and nutrient management, 3) for integrated plant production, 4) for biological crop protection, 5) for water retention on permanent grassland, 5a) for land excluded from production, and 6) for animal welfare.

Examples: Eco-schemes according to the CAP Strategic Plans of four EU member states.

Spain	**Poland**	**Germany**	**Italy**
Type of surface: Permanent pastures and permanent grasslands. • Practices. Extensive grazing (P1). • Practices. Sustainable mowing and the establishment of biodiversity isles (P2). • Establishment of islands of biodiversity (P2A). • Sustainable sowing (P2B). Surface types: Arable land. • Practices. Crop rotation with improver species (P3). • Practices. Direct sowing (P4). Types of surfaces: Arable land and permanent crops, including woody crops. • Practices. Establishment of biodiversity spaces or sustainable	Payments under eco-schemes are granted to farmers in the form of payments for areas with honey-producing plants, payments for carbon and nutrient management in agriculture, payments for integrated plant production, payments for biological crop protection, payments for water retention in permanent grasslands, and animal welfare payments.	There are eco-schemes: • ÖR 1: Additional areas for biodiversity (set aside/ flower strips/old grass strips). • ÖR 2: Diverse crops in arable farming with at least 5 main crops including 10 % legumes. • ÖR 3: Retention of agroforestry on arable land and permanent grassland. • ÖR 4: Extensification of the entire permanent grassland of the company. • ÖR 5: Extensive management of individual permanent grassland areas with evidence of at least 4 regional characteristics. • ÖR 6: Avoidance of chemical-synthetic pesticides on arable land	Introduced five eco-schemes: • ECO-1 Improved animal welfare and fight against antimicrobial resistance • ECO-2 Grassing of tree crops (17.8 % of the resources); • ECO-3 Safeguarding olive trees of particular landscape value (17.2 %); • ECO-4 Extensive forage systems, aimed at promoting the introduction of leguminous and forage crops in rotation, as well as renewal crops with a commitment to the management of residues from a carbon sink perspective (18.6 %); • ECO-5 Specific measures for pollinators on both herbaceous and tree crops (5 %).

management of the sheet of water (P5). Types of surfaces: Permanent crops. • Practices. Spontaneous or sowed vegetation cover (P6). • Practices. Inert Vegetation cover (P7).		and in permanent crops. • ÖR 7: Conservation goal-oriented management in Natura 2000 areas.	

Source: Country reports for Spain, Poland, Germany and Italy for CEDR Congress in Cardiff 2023.

According to the CAP Strategic Plans 2023–2027, Spain has already increased its support for innovation, knowledge transfer, and digitalization. This support is administered by regional administrations, although the requirements for granting such support are typically uniform across regions. Spanish measures under Pillar II include support for young farmers and new farmers in establishing rural enterprises (Sub-measure 6.1), investment in agricultural holdings (Sub-measure 4.1), cooperation initiatives (LEADER) under Measure 19, and knowledge sharing and information dissemination.

In Switzerland, farmers receive direct payments as compensation for the public services they provide. These payments include subsidies for farmland, supply assurance, biodiversity, landscape quality, production systems, resource efficiency, and bridging (Swiss Report).

In the UK, financial support for farmers is also tied to meeting environmental obligations. However, this support is set to decrease in the coming years.

XI. War in Ukraine

Issues relating to Ukraine were discussed extensively in Commission I.

Some legal issues related to the situation in Ukraine were discussed during an online connection with scientists from Ukraine. Despite the challenges and consequences of the ongoing hostilities, the Ukrainian parliament and government have implemented various measures aimed at facilitating agricultural activities.

The report from Poland presented such aspects as legal regulations that were introduced to help Polish agricultural producers affected by the negative impact of the war in Ukraine and regulations that help Ukrainian citizens living in Poland, e.g. the Act of 12 March 2022 on assistance to citizens of Ukraine in connection with the armed conflict on the territory of that country.

Generalbericht der Kommission III

Version allemande – German version – Deutsche Version

Prof. UAM Dr. hab. Aneta Suchoń
Adam Mickiewicz University

Die Darstellung des Sachberichts der Kommission III ist aufgrund der quantitativen Begrenztheit der Veröffentlichungen und des breiten Spektrums der behandelten Themen keine leichte Aufgabe. Aus den folgenden Ländern wurden Berichte erstellt: Frankreich, Deutschland, Ungarn, Italien, die Niederlande, Polen, Slowenien, Spanien, die Schweiz, das Vereinigte Königreich und die USA. Außerdem gab es eine Online-Verbindung mit einem Forscher aus der Ukraine. Die Struktur der Länderberichte folgte im Allgemeinen den im Fragebogen angegebenen Fragen. Seit dem letzten Kongress (Poznań, September 2019) hat es zahlreiche regulatorische Änderungen sowohl in der nationalen als auch in der EU-Gesetzgebung gegeben.

Es lohnt sich, die in dem Formular identifizierten Schlüsselfragen in Erinnerung zu rufen, darunter die folgenden: Welches sind die wichtigsten gesetzlichen Änderungen im Bereich der landwirtschaftlichen Tätigkeiten seit dem letzten Kongress im Jahr 2019?

- Organisation und Durchführung der landwirtschaftlichen Tätigkeit in einem Betrieb.
- Stellung der Landwirte in der Wertschöpfungskette, Genossenschaften, Organisationen, Verträge und Agrar- und Lebensmittelrecht.
- Ländliche Gebiete.
- Europäischer Grüner Deal, Umweltschutz in landwirtschaftlichen Betrieben, Bekämpfung des Klimawandels, einschließlich ökologischer Landbau, erneuerbare Energien, Wasserrecht und Tierschutz.
- Strategische Pläne der Gemeinsamen Agrarpolitik (GAP) in den EU-Mitgliedstaaten und andere strategische Dokumente zur Landwirtschaft in Ländern außerhalb der Europäischen Union. Neue gesetzliche Regelungen für die Gemeinsame Agrarpolitik 2023-2027.
- Außenbeziehungen zu Drittländern der Welt.

Besonderes Augenmerk wurde auf die jüngsten Trends, Entwicklungen und unterschiedlichen Lösungen in den untersuchten Ländern gelegt. Während der Sitzung wurden die Berichte aus den EU-Mitgliedstaaten und anderen europäischen Ländern sowie aus den USA und der Ukraine vorgestellt und diskutiert. Die grundlegende Erkenntnis aus den Länderberichten und Diskussionen ist, dass in den einzelnen Ländern viele neue Verordnungen verabschiedet wurden (in Kraft getreten sind), wobei die Gesetzesänderungen in den EU-Ländern zu einem großen Teil mit den neuen Rechtsinstrumenten im Bereich der Gemeinsamen Agrarpolitik (GAP) zusammenhängen

Daher ist es unmöglich, alle wichtigen und interessanten neuen Aspekte in der Gesetzgebung, Rechtsprechung und Praxis in den Länderberichten zu erwähnen. Der Katalog der Rechtsvorschriften für die Organisation und Durchführung landwirtschaftlicher Tätigkeiten wird immer umfangreicher, da er auf die Herausforderungen der Krisen reagieren muss, die in den letzten Jahren entstanden sind oder sich verschärft haben: COVID-19, Klimawandel (einschließlich Dürre), der Krieg in der Ukraine, die erhebliche Auswirkungen auf die landwirtschaftlichen Tätigkeiten haben.

Es besteht kein Zweifel daran, dass die meisten Änderungen im EU-Agrarrecht und in den nationalen Vorschriften mit dem aktuellen mehrjährigen Finanzrahmen zusammenhängen.

Im Dezember 2021 wurden drei grundlegende EU-Verordnungen verabschiedet: Verordnungen des Europäischen Parlaments und des Rates vom 2. Dezember 2021 Nr. (EU) 2021/2115[1]; 2021/2116[2] und 2021/2117.[3]

---

1 Verordnung (EU) 2021/2115 des Europäischen Parlaments und des Rates vom 2. Dezember 2021 mit Vorschriften für die Unterstützung von Strategieplänen, die von den Mitgliedstaaten im Rahmen der Gemeinsamen Agrarpolitik (GAP-Strategiepläne) aufgestellt und aus dem Europäischen Garantiefonds für die Landwirtschaft (EGFL) und dem Europäischen Landwirtschaftsfonds für die Entwicklung des ländlichen Raums (ELER) finanziert werden, und zur Aufhebung der Verordnungen (EU) Nr. 1305/2013 und (EU) Nr. 1307/2013 (GAP-SP-Verordnung).

2 Verordnung (EU) 2021/2116 des Europäischen Parlaments und des Rates vom 2. Dezember 2021 über die Finanzierung, Verwaltung und Überwachung der Gemeinsamen Agrarpolitik und zur Aufhebung der Verordnung (EU) Nr. 1306/2013 (Horizontale GAP-Verordnung).

3 Verordnung (EU) 2021/2117 des Europäischen Parlaments und des Rates vom 2. Dezember 2021 zur Änderung der Verordnung (EU) Nr. 1308/2013 über eine gemeinsame Marktorganisation für landwirtschaftliche Erzeugnisse, der Verordnung (EU) Nr. 1151/2012 über Qualitätsregelungen für Agrarerzeugnisse und Lebensmittel, der Verordnung (EU) Nr. 251/2014 über die Begriffsbestimmung, Bezeichnung, Aufmachung und Etikettierung von aromatisierten Weinerzeugnissen sowie zum Schutz geografischer Angaben für aromatisierte Weinerzeugnisse und der Verordnung (EU)

Die EU-Mitgliedstaaten haben strategische GAP-Pläne ausgearbeitet und nationale Durchführungsverordnungen im Einklang mit den neuen Rechtsinstrumenten erlassen.

Änderungen in der Agrargesetzgebung der berichterstattenden Länder stehen auch im Zusammenhang mit der Regulierung der Beziehungen in der Agrar- und Lebensmittelversorgungskette (zum Beispiel ist die Frist für die Umsetzung der Richtlinie (EU) 2019/663 am 1. Mai 2021 abgelaufen). Die Landwirtschaft und die Lebensmittelversorgungskette als Ganzes waren von COVID-19 und dem Krieg in der Ukraine betroffen (diese Themen wurden hauptsächlich im Kommission I erörtert).

I. Organisation und Durchführung der landwirtschaftlichen Tätigkeit in einem Betrieb

Die Länderberichte enthielten Bemerkungen und Kommentare zu wichtigen rechtlichen Entwicklungen im Zusammenhang mit Umweltfragen in der Landwirtschaft, z.B. Europäischen Grünen Deal, zum betrieblichen Umweltschutz, zum Kampf gegen den Klimawandel, einschließlich des ökologischen Landbaus, zu erneuerbaren Energien, zum Wasserrecht und zum Tierschutz. Die Kommission III befasste sich zunächst mit den Vorschriften für die Landwirtschaft. In diesem Bereich gab es Änderungen und Neuerungen. In einigen Ländern gab es Änderungen oder Neuerungen in der Hauptdefinition des Agrarrechts, d.h. Landwirt, landwirtschaftlicher Betrieb oder landwirtschaftliche Tätigkeit.

Es ist erwähnenswert, dass der Katalog der landwirtschaftlichen Tätigkeiten in einigen Ländern erweitert wird. Geändert wurden auch einige Bestimmungen zu Registern, z.B. Einträge in das Register der landwirtschaftlichen Erzeuger oder das Register der Erzeuger von Wein, Milch oder anderen landwirtschaftlichen Erzeugnissen sowie die Registrierung von Tieren. Die Eintragungen sind in der Regel erforderlich, um EU-Mittel zu erhalten. Die meisten dieser Einträge erfolgen in elektronischer Form, und die landwirtschaftlichen Erzeuger können und müssen manchmal auch Daten elektronisch eingeben. Dies beschleunigt zwar den Prozess und verkürzt die Zeit, aber es gibt noch einige Herausforderungen.

Die Digitalisierung im Bereich der landwirtschaftlichen Tätigkeiten gewinnt zunehmend an Bedeutung. Anwendungen und Registereinträge

---

Nr. 228/2013 über Sondermaßnahmen im Bereich der Landwirtschaft zugunsten der Regionen in äußerster Randlage der Union (GMO-Verordnung).

werden immer beliebter, und ihre Auswirkungen auf die Präzisionslandwirtschaft sollten unter anderem hervorgehoben werden. Auch bei den Agrarabgaben gibt es Veränderungen, die mit der Ausweitung der grundlegenden Definition der landwirtschaftlichen Tätigkeit zusammenhängen und mit der Ausübung der landwirtschaftlichen Tätigkeit verbunden sind.

a) Beispiele

Durch Änderungen des slowenischen Landwirtschaftsgesetzes vom März 2022 wurde die Definition eines Landwirts und eines landwirtschaftlichen Betriebs an die GAP-Strategiepläne (Verordnung (EU) 2021/2115) angepasst (Slowenischer Bericht).

Das französische Gesetz Nr. 2022-172 vom 14. Februar 2022 zugunsten der freien Berufe[4] verdient aufgrund seiner wichtigsten Bestimmungen besondere Aufmerksamkeit. Erstens führt das Gesetz die Dualität des Eigentums von Einzelunternehmern ein und unterscheidet zwischen geschäftlichem und persönlichem Eigentum. Bewegliche und unbewegliche Sachen, Rechte, Verpflichtungen und Wertpapiere eines Einzelunternehmers, die für eine oder mehrere selbständige berufliche Tätigkeiten genutzt werden, bilden das berufliche Vermögen des Einzelunternehmers. Der Einzelunternehmer haftet für Verbindlichkeiten aus seiner beruflichen Tätigkeit grundsätzlich nur mit seinem Geschäftsvermögen, wodurch der Schutz des Privatvermögens gewährleistet ist. Das Gesetz regelt auch die universelle Übertragung von Unternehmensvermögen und sorgt für Klarheit und Rechtssicherheit bei solchen Transaktionen.

Darüber hinaus hebt der französische Bericht die Definition von ökologischen Zahlungen als Einkommen aus der Landwirtschaft unter bestimmten Bedingungen oder Einschränkungen in den Steuervorschriften hervor. Diese Bestimmung ist besonders wichtig, da sie sich direkt auf die steuerliche Behandlung von Einkommen aus ökologischen Tätigkeiten auswirkt und die wachsende Bedeutung von Umweltaspekten im Agrarrecht unterstreicht.

In Deutschland hat sich durch die Änderung des Umsatzsteuergesetzes vom 21. Dezember 2021 der pauschale Umsatzsteuersatz für die Land- und Forstwirtschaft ab dem 1. Januar 2022 geändert.

4 LOI No 2022-172 du 14 février 2022 en faveur de l'activité professionnelle indépendante, JORF No0038 du 15 février 2022.

Das französische Ernteversicherungssystem wurde kürzlich durch das am 2. März 2022 veröffentlichte Gesetz Nr. 2022-298 reformiert, es hat dazu geführt, dass die Verbreitung der Ernteversicherung in der Landwirtschaft verbessert wurde und die Risikomanagementinstrumente an die Herausforderungen des Klimawandels angepasst wurden. Es wurde ein neues System geschaffen, das auf nationaler Solidarität und Risikoteilung zwischen dem Staat, den Landwirten und den Versicherern beruht und das den sich ändernden Bedürfnissen der Branche Rechnung trägt (Nationaler Bericht Frankreich).

In Polen wurden die Rechtsvorschriften über das nationale System der Erzeugerregister, der Betriebsregister und der Register der Zahlungsanträge im Jahr 2022 geändert. Außerdem hat der Minister für Landwirtschaft und ländliche Entwicklung Verordnungen erlassen, in denen die detaillierten Anforderungen für Anträge auf Eintragung in die Erzeugerregister festgelegt sind. Aufgrund der zunehmenden Digitalisierung und Informatisierung in der Landwirtschaft ermöglichen die Gesetzesänderungen von 2022 den befugten Stellen, Anträge auf Eintragung in das Erzeugerregister nicht nur in Papierform, sondern auch elektronisch einzureichen. Im selben Jahr verabschiedete das polnische Parlament neue Rechtsvorschriften zur Tierkennzeichnung und -registrierung und passte sie an EU-Rechtsinstrumente an, wie die Verordnung (EU) Nr. 2016/429 des Europäischen Parlaments und des Rates vom 9. März 2016 über übertragbare Tierseuchen, mit der auch bestimmte Rechtsakte im Bereich der Tiergesundheit geändert und aufgehoben werden.

In Spanien wurde ein landwirtschaftliches Informationssystem (SIEX) eingerichtet, das technisch und systematisch mit den landwirtschaftlichen Betriebsregistern der Autonomen Gemeinschaften, den digitalen Betriebsbüchern und anderen öffentlichen Registern interoperabel ist.

Im Jahr 2023 änderte Polen die gesetzlichen Bestimmungen über die Verwaltung des landwirtschaftlichen Grundbesitzes des Staatsschatzes und andere Gesetze, einschließlich des Gesetzes über die Gestaltung des Agrarsystems. Die Änderungen, die die Verwaltung des Bestandes an landwirtschaftlichem Eigentum des Staatsschatzes betrafen, umfassten unter anderem Fragen im Zusammenhang mit Pachtverträgen und der Übertragung von Immobilien an die lokalen Behörden für Infrastruktur- und Bauzwecke. Die Definitionen von Schlüsselbegriffen wie Familienbetrieb, Verwandter, Person mit landwirtschaftlicher Qualifikation und persönliche Leitung eines landwirtschaftlichen Betriebs, auf die im Gesetz zur Gestaltung des

Agrarsystems Bezug genommen wird, wurden hinzugefügt oder geändert. Dieser direkte Bezug ist positiv zu bewerten.

Im Rahmen der Änderung vom 13. Juli 2023 wurden die Bestimmungen über beschränkte Ausschreibungen präzisiert. Nach den neuen Bestimmungen kann das nationale Zentrum festlegen, dass nur bestimmte Personengruppen an der Ausschreibung teilnehmen können. Dazu können zum Beispiel einzelne Landwirte gehören, die ihren Familienbetrieb erweitern wollen.

Das geänderte Gesetz über die Gestaltung des Agrarsystems (UKUR, Ustawa z dnia 11 kwietnia 2003 r. o kształtowaniu ustroju rolnego) legt fest, dass seine Bestimmungen nicht für landwirtschaftliche Grundstücke gelten, deren landwirtschaftliche Fläche weniger als 0,3 ha beträgt. Die Änderung wird sich positiv auf die ländliche Entwicklung zu Wohnzwecken auswirken.

Mit den geänderten Rechtsvorschriften werden bestimmte Ausnahmen von Verpflichtungen für Erwerber von landwirtschaftlichen Grundstücken erweitert. Dies gilt insbesondere für Grundstücke, für die nach dem Erwerb ein örtlicher Bebauungsplan erlassen wurde, der eine andere als die landwirtschaftliche Nutzung vorsieht. Es sei darauf hingewiesen, dass die in den letzten Jahren geführte Debatte über die Auswirkungen der Änderung von Bebauungsplänen auf die Verpflichtungen von Käufern landwirtschaftlicher Grundstücke zu beachten ist. Die Entscheidung des Gesetzgebers, diese Frage zu regeln, ist ein Schritt in die richtige Richtung und beseitigt die bisherigen rechtlichen Unklarheiten. Sie kann jedoch zu einer Schwächung des Schutzes der landwirtschaftlichen Flächen im Rahmen ihrer quantitativen Erhaltung führen.

Mit der Änderung sollte auch die Umsetzung der im Gesetz über die Gestaltung des Agrarsystems festgelegten Bestimmungen über den Handel mit landwirtschaftlichen Immobilien auf dem privaten Markt klarer und einfacher gestaltet werden. Die Entwicklung des ländlichen Raums beruht nicht nur auf der Entwicklung der landwirtschaftlichen Tätigkeit, sondern auch auf dem Aufbau der Infrastruktur. Die Änderung des Gesetzes über die Verwaltung des landwirtschaftlichen Vermögens des Staatsschatzes hat dem Nationalen Zentrum die Möglichkeit eröffnet, den lokalen Gebietskörperschaften unentgeltlich Eigentum zu übertragen. Dies gilt sowohl für Grundstücke, die für Gemeinde-, Kreis- und Provinzstraßen vorgesehen sind, als auch für solche, die bereits tatsächlich als Straßen genutzt werden. Darüber hinaus hat das Nationale Zentrum auch die Möglichkeit, andere

Grundstücke für diese Zwecke zu übertragen, sofern dies mit lokalen Entwicklungs-, Sanierungs- oder Wiederaufbauplänen in Einklang steht.

Im Zusammenhang mit der Agrarstrukturerhebung 2023 hat Deutschland seine Rechtsvorschriften zur Agrarstatistik und zur Ernährung an das EU-Recht (z.B. Durchführungsverordnung (EU) Nr. 2021/2286 der Kommission) und an die Entwicklungen Agrar- und Ernährungssektor angepasst (Nationaler Bericht Deutschland).

Die Kommission III erörterte auch die rechtlichen Regelungen für die Landwirtschaft im Vereinigten Königreich nach dem Brexit. Mit der Farm Bill 2019-21 (Farm Bill 2020) wurde ein neuer Ansatz für landwirtschaftliche Zahlungen und Landmanagement verabschiedet. In England werden die Landwirte für die Produktion „öffentlicher Güter" wie Umwelt- oder Tierschutzverbesserungen bezahlt. Darüber hinaus hat die schottische Regierung im November 2019 ein Agrargesetz eingeführt (Nationaler Bericht des Vereinigten Königreichs).

In den USA werden mit den Federal Farm Bills wichtige agrar- und ernährungspolitische Maßnahmen festgelegt, die viele Aspekte des ländlichen Rechts regeln. Der US-Kongress erlässt in der Regel alle fünf Jahre ein Agrargesetz. Das letzte Farm Bill wurde 2018 verabschiedet, und sein Nachfolger wurde für Ende 2023 oder Anfang 2024 erwartet. Bis zum Jahr 2025 bleibt jedoch abzuwarten, ob ein neues Agrargesetz vollständig verabschiedet wurde oder ob die Diskussionen noch andauern (Nationaler Bericht USA). Agrargesetze sind komplexe und weitreichende Rechtsakte.

Die Landwirtschaftszählung 2017, die 2019 veröffentlicht wurde, liefert detaillierte Informationen über landwirtschaftliche Betriebe und landwirtschaftliche Flächen in den USA. In den USA gab es 2,042 Millionen landwirtschaftliche Betriebe, die rund 900 Millionen Acres Land bewirtschafteten, darunter 396 Millionen Acres Ackerland. Die durchschnittliche Betriebsgröße betrug 441 Acres, und die meisten Betriebe waren sowohl von der Größe als auch vom Verkaufswert her klein.

Obwohl etwa 60 % der landwirtschaftlichen Flächen in den USA von Eigentümern bewirtschaftet werden, spielt die Verpachtung in der US-Landwirtschaft eine wichtige Rolle, insbesondere in der Getreideproduktion. Nahezu 40 % der landwirtschaftlichen Flächen in den USA sind gepachtet, wobei der Anteil in einigen Bundesstaaten noch höher ist. Im Jahr 2017 wurden 69 % der landwirtschaftlichen Betriebe mit einer durchschnittlichen Größe von 220 Acres von Volleigentümern betrieben, während Pächter in der Regel größere Betriebe bewirtschafteten.

Der Besitz von landwirtschaftlichen Flächen durch einige Unternehmen hat erhebliche Auswirkungen auf wichtige Agrarstaaten. Die Landwirtschaftszählung 2017 ergab, dass 5,7 % der US-Farmen Unternehmen waren, aber nur 0,6 % waren Nicht-Familienunternehmen. Um Bedenken hinsichtlich des Eigentums von Unternehmen auszuräumen und Familienbetriebe zu schützen, haben mehrere Bundesstaaten Maßnahmen zur Begrenzung des Eigentums von Unternehmen an landwirtschaftlichen Flächen eingeführt.

Das US-Landwirtschaftsministerium (USDA) veröffentlicht jährliche Berichte über ausländisches Eigentum an landwirtschaftlichen Flächen, die auf Daten beruhen, die im Rahmen des Agricultural Foreign Investment Disclosure Act (AFIDA) erhoben werden. Im jüngsten Bericht wurde der ausländische Besitz bis Dezember 2021 analysiert. In diesem Jahr belief sich der ausländische Besitz an landwirtschaftlichen Flächen in den USA auf insgesamt etwa 40 Millionen Hektar, was 1,8 % aller Flächen in den USA und 3,1 % der privaten landwirtschaftlichen Flächen entspricht. Zwischen 2020 und 2021 stieg die Zahl der landwirtschaftlichen Flächen in ausländischem Besitz um etwa 2,4 Millionen Acres.

Ausländischer Besitz konzentriert sich auf einige wenige Schlüsselländer. Kanadier besitzen 31 % der landwirtschaftlichen Flächen in ausländischem Besitz, gefolgt von den Niederlanden (12 %), Italien (7 %) sowie Deutschland und dem Vereinigten Königreich (jeweils 6 %). (Nationaler Bericht USA).

II. Rolle der Frauen in der Landwirtschaft

Die Rolle der Frauen in der Landwirtschaft wurde in der Kommission diskutiert. Frauen beteiligen sich aktiv an der Landwirtschaft. In einigen Ländern ist das traditionelle Modell der überwiegend von Männern geführten landwirtschaftlichen Tätigkeiten immer noch stark ausgeprägt, während in anderen Ländern aufgrund geringerer landwirtschaftlicher Einkommen, kleinerer landwirtschaftlicher Flächen und größerer Verantwortung ein geringeres Interesse der Männer an der Führung von Betrieben festzustellen ist.

Einige Länder haben Regelungen und Programme eingeführt, um das Engagement von Frauen in der Landwirtschaft und ihre Beteiligung an der Betriebsführung und Entscheidungsfindung zu fördern. In Spanien zum Beispiel ist die Zahl der in der Landwirtschaft tätigen Frauen in den letzten Jahren deutlich gestiegen. Aus der Landwirtschaftszählung 2020 geht hervor, dass der Anteil der Frauen an den Betriebsleitern auf 29 % gestiegen ist (261.634 Frauen, d.h. ein Anstieg um 22 %).

Darüber hinaus ist die Zahl der von Frauen geführten landwirtschaftlichen Betriebe stetig gestiegen. Im Jahr 2010 gab es 2.827 landwirtschaftliche Betriebe, die von Frauen geführt wurden, während diese Zahl im Jahr 2020 auf 3.323 Betriebe anstieg. Dieses Wachstum spiegelt die positiven Auswirkungen von Initiativen wie dem III. Strategischen Plan für eine wirksame Gleichstellung der Geschlechter 2022-2025 wider, der die Gleichstellung der Geschlechter in ländlichen Gebieten und in der Landwirtschaft fördern soll. Dieser Plan unterstützt auch Landwirtinnen durch Schulungen, Beratung und Finanzierungsmöglichkeiten und hilft ihnen, Herausforderungen zu überwinden und in ihren Betrieben erfolgreich zu sein (Nationaler Bericht Spanien).

Frauen sind auf unterschiedliche Weise an der spanischen Landwirtschaft beteiligt: Einige besitzen ihre eigenen Betriebe, andere arbeiten in Betrieben von Verwandten oder Arbeitgebern. Sie spielen auch eine wichtige Rolle in der landwirtschaftlichen Wertschöpfungskette, indem sie an der Produktion, der Verarbeitung und dem Vertrieb von Lebensmitteln mitwirken.

Die Zahl der in der spanischen Landwirtschaft tätigen Frauen ist in den letzten Jahren gestiegen. Laut der Landwirtschaftszählung 2020 machen Frauen im Vergleich zu 2009 nun 29 % der Betriebsleiter aus. Allerdings leiten sie eher Betriebe mit geringerer wirtschaftlicher Größe. So erwirtschaften 56,2 % der von Frauen geführten Betriebe weniger als 8 000 Euro an Standard-Gesamtproduktion (TSP), verglichen mit 46,3 % der von Männern geführten Betriebe.

Diese Veränderungen werden von mehreren Faktoren beeinflusst, darunter die Überalterung der landwirtschaftlichen Bevölkerung, die Aufgabe von landwirtschaftlichen Betrieben durch Männer und die zunehmende Einbeziehung von Frauen in landwirtschaftliche Tätigkeiten.

In den USA waren im Jahr 2017 36 % (1,2 Millionen) der 3,4 Millionen Erzeuger Frauen. Der Census of Agriculture definiert einen Erzeuger als eine Person, „die an Entscheidungen über landwirtschaftliche Tätigkeiten beteiligt ist", und Betriebe haben oft mehr als einen Erzeuger. Fast 56 % der Betriebe hatten einen oder mehrere weibliche Erzeuger, während 91 % der Betriebe einen oder mehrere männliche Erzeuger hatten.

Der Begriff „Erzeuger" wird in der Volkszählung auf zwei verschiedene Arten verwendet. Weniger Frauen (798.500) bezeichneten sich selbst als

Hauptbetreiberinnen, d.h. als die Hauptentscheidungsträgerinnen im Betrieb. Eine noch geringere Zahl von Frauen (489.000) bezeichnete sich als Haupterzeugerinnen, d.h. als Personen, die die meisten Entscheidungen in Bezug auf den landwirtschaftlichen Betrieb treffen.

Die meisten Erzeugerinnen lebten auf den von ihnen geführten Betrieben und waren aktiv in den täglichen Betrieb sowie in die Entscheidungsfindung in Bezug auf Land- und Erntenutzung, Viehbestand, Finanzmanagement und Nachfolgeplanung eingebunden. Für 66 % der Erzeugerinnen und mehr als 60 % der Primärerzeugerinnen war die Landwirtschaft jedoch nicht ihr Hauptberuf (Nationaler Bericht USA).

In der Schweiz waren im Jahr 2020 rund 54'300 Frauen in landwirtschaftlichen Betrieben beschäftigt, davon 6 % als Betriebsleiterinnen. Sowohl die Zahl der von Frauen geführten Betriebe als auch die Gesamtzahl der Betriebe ist im Berichtsjahr leicht zurückgegangen. Allerdings war der Rückgang der von Frauen geführten Betriebe im Durchschnitt etwas stärker als der Rückgang der Gesamtzahl der Betriebe.

Im Vergleich zur Gesamtentwicklung der landwirtschaftlichen Betriebe entwickelte sich die Zahl der von Frauen geführten Betriebe über 30 Hektar relativ anders, was auf Verschiebungen in der Struktur der landwirtschaftlichen Betriebe hinweist (Nationaler Bericht Schweiz).

III. Tierschutz, Pflanzengesundheit

In den Länderberichten werden Tierschutz- und Zuchtfragen, einschließlich der Behandlung von Tieren, als wichtige Bereiche hervorgehoben, in denen Gesetzesänderungen zu beobachten sind. Die Zuchtvorschriften wirken sich sowohl auf die Fleischqualität als auch auf die Umwelt aus. Die EU-Mitgliedstaaten haben ihre Vorschriften angepasst, um den EU-Rechtsinstrumenten zu entsprechen, die überwiegend die Form von direkt anwendbaren Verordnungen angenommen haben, die frühere Richtlinien ersetzen (z.B. die Verordnung (EU) 2016/429 über Tierseuchen und die Verordnung (EU) 2016/1012 über Tierzucht- und Abstammungsbestimmungen).

In Polen wurde die Pflanzenschutzverordnung (EU) 2016/2031 vor allem durch das Gesetz vom 13. Februar 2020 über den Schutz von Pflanzen gegen Agrophagen umgesetzt. Dieses Gesetz behält die Bestimmungen von bei, die alle Aufgaben im Bereich der Pflanzengesundheit den Behörden des staatlichen Pflanzenschutzes und der Saatgutinspektion zuweisen. Darüber hinaus wurde die Möglichkeit eingeführt, Gebiete zu benennen, die frei von bestimmten Agrophagen sind, was bei der Erleichterung der Ausfuhr von Waren in Drittländer eine entscheidende Rolle spielen kann. Der Chefinspektor für Pflanzenschutz und Saatgutinspektion ist die zuständige Behörde für die Ausweisung von Quarantänestationen und Isoliereinrichtungen.

Zur Umsetzung der Tierzuchtverordnung (EU) 2016/1012 in Polen wurde das Gesetz vom 10. Dezember 2020 über die Organisation der Zucht und Vermehrung von Nutztieren erlassen. Dieses Gesetz regelt die Zucht und den Schutz der genetischen Ressourcen von Nutztieren, die Bewertung des funktionalen Wertes, die genetische Bewertung, die Führung von Zuchtbüchern, Registern und Zuchtaufzeichnungen sowie die Kontrolle der Zucht- und Reproduktionstätigkeiten für Nutztiere und definiert die Behörden und Institutionen, die auf dem Gebiet der Republik Polen die in der Verordnung (EU) 2016/1012 festgelegten Befugnisse und Kompetenzen haben.

Dementsprechend ist der Landwirtschaftsminister ermächtigt worden:

- Zuchtorganisationen oder andere Einrichtungen, die das Führen von Zuchtbüchern und Zuchtregistern für Rinder, Schweine, Schafe, Ziegen und Equiden beantragen, als Züchtervereinigungen und Zuchtunternehmen anzuerkennen
- die von diesen Züchtervereinigungen oder Zuchtunternehmen durchgeführten Zuchtprogramme zu genehmigen,
- die in der Verordnung (EU) 2016/1012 festgelegten Maßnahmen zu verhängen und aufzuheben, falls die kontrollierten Einrichtungen gegen die Bestimmungen der genannten Verordnung verstoßen.

Das Nationale Tierzuchtzentrum ist mit der Durchführung amtlicher Kontrollen beauftragt, um die Einhaltung der Verordnung zu gewährleisten (Nationaler Bericht Polen).

Die Kommission III befasste sich auch mit dem Thema Afrikanische Schweinepest (ASP). Im Juli 2023 wurde der epidemiologische Status dieser Bedrohung in der Europäischen Union durch die Durchführungsverordnung (EU) 2023/1485 der Kommission vom 18. Juli 2023 aktualisiert, mit der die Anhänge I und II der Durchführungsverordnung (EU) 2021/605 geändert wurden, in denen spezifische Maßnahmen zur Bekämpfung der ASP festgelegt sind.

In Polen wurden im Juli 2023 Ausbrüche der ASP bestätigt, darunter mehrere neue Fälle in den Woiwodschaften Wielkopolskie und Mazowieckie, wobei weitere Ausbrüche in begrenzten Gebieten der Woiwodschaften Podkarpackie und Lubelskie gemeldet wurden. Dies stellt eine erhebliche Verbesserung gegenüber den mehreren tausend Ausbrüchen dar, die der Europäischen Kommission zuvor gemeldet wurden. In Polen sind die spezifischen Maßnahmen zur Bekämpfung der ASP in der Verordnung des Ministers für Landwirtschaft und ländliche Entwicklung vom 10. August 2021 über Maßnahmen im Zusammenhang mit dem Auftreten der ASP festgelegt. Diese wurde im Mai 2023 durch die Verordnung des Ministers für Landwirtschaft und ländliche Entwicklung geändert, mit der die Maßnahmen, die als Reaktion auf ASP-Ausbrüche durchzuführen sind, aktualisiert wurden.

In Deutschland ist am 28. Januar 2022 ein neues Tierarzneimittelgesetz in Kraft getreten, das auf nationaler (Bundes-)Ebene Fragen regelt, die nicht durch die unmittelbar geltenden Bestimmungen der Verordnung (EU) 2019/6 über Tierarzneimittel abgedeckt sind, mit der die Richtlinie 2001/82/EG aufgehoben wurde. Das neue Gesetz konsolidiert systematisch alle Bestimmungen zum Tierarzneimittelsektor, die zuvor über mehrere Rechtsakte verstreut waren. Das Gesetz dient der Umsetzung der Verordnung (EU) 2019/6 des Europäischen Parlaments und des Rates vom 11. Dezember 2018 über Tierarzneimittel und zur Aufhebung der Richtlinie 2001/82/EG (ABl. L 4 vom 7.1.2019, S. 43; L 163 vom 20. Juni 2019, S. 112; L 326 vom 8. Oktober 2020, S. 15; L 241 vom 8. Juli 2021, S. 17) (Nationaler Bericht Deutschland).

In der Schweiz wurden mit den Änderungen der Tierzuchtverordnung vom 31. Oktober 2012, die am 2. November 2022 und am 5. April 2023 in Kraft traten, die Bestimmungen zur Erhaltung der Schweizer Rassen gestärkt und die finanziellen Beiträge zu deren Schutz verlängert. Diese Änderungen stützen sich auf die „Strategie Tierschutz 2030" und entsprechende parlamentarische Vorstösse (Nationaler Bericht Schweiz).

Im Mai 2023 bestätigte der Oberste Gerichtshof der USA das kalifornische Tierschutzgesetz (California Animal Welfare Act), das sich auf die Produktion und den Verkauf von Schweinefleisch, Kalbfleisch und Eiern auswirkt und den Viehzüchtern in den gesamten Vereinigten Staaten besondere Belastungen auferlegt (Nationaler Bericht USA).

Die US-Umweltschutzbehörde (EPA) reguliert gentechnisch veränderte Pflanzen, die pestizide Substanzen, so genannte Biopestizide (plant-incorporated protectants (PIPs)), enthalten. Die EPA verlangt, dass bestimmte Biopestizide gemäß dem Federal Insecticide, Fungicide, and Rodenticide Act (FIFRA) registriert werden und gemäß dem Federal Food, Drug, and

Cosmetic Act (FDCA) einer Toleranz oder Ausnahme für Lebensmittelrückstände unterliegen.

Um den Entwicklungen in der Biotechnologie Rechnung zu tragen, hat die EPA im Mai 2023 eine Vorschrift erlassen, die bestimmte gentechnisch hergestellte Biopestizide von der FIFRA-Registrierung und den FDCA-Toleranzanforderungen für Lebensmittel ausnimmt. Diese Ausnahme gilt für Biopestizide, die „kein größeres Risiko darstellen als Biopestizide, bei denen die EPA bereits festgestellt hat, dass sie die Sicherheitsanforderungen erfüllen, und die andernfalls durch konventionelle Züchtung hätten erzeugt werden können". Insbesondere werden Biopestizide ausgenommen, die durch Gentechnik aus einer sexuell kompatiblen Pflanze entstanden sind, sowie Biopestizide mit Funktionsverlust.

In den Vereinigten Staaten werden Aspekte des Tierschutzes sowohl durch Bundes- als auch durch Landesgesetze geregelt. Die Bundesgesetze und -verordnungen konzentrieren sich auf die Verhinderung von Grausamkeiten und die Gewährleistung einer humanen Schlachtung; es gibt jedoch nur wenige Bundesnormen, die sich speziell auf Tierproduktionspraktiken beziehen.

IV. Beschäftigung in der Landwirtschaft

Eine der aktuellen Herausforderungen in der Landwirtschaft ist die Beschäftigung. In einigen Ländern wurde eine nationale Gesetzgebung zur Beschäftigung in der Landwirtschaft eingeführt, um spezifische Herausforderungen im Zusammenhang mit den Arbeitsbeziehungen in der Landwirtschaft anzugehen. Dieses Thema wurde auch der Kommission III erörtert, wobei Beispiele aus mehreren Ländern die verschiedenen Ansätze zur Bewältigung dieser Probleme veranschaulichten.

In Italien stellt die hohe Quote der irregulären Beschäftigung in der Landwirtschaft (24,1 % im Jahr 2019, ein Anstieg um 3,4 Prozentpunkte seit 2010) ein erhebliches Hindernis für die Nachhaltigkeit des Agrarsektors dar. Um dieses Problem anzugehen, hat Italien die Bestimmungen zur sozialen Konditionalität gemäß Artikel 1453 der Verordnung (EU) Nr. 2115 von 2021 umgesetzt. Mit dem Ministerialerlass vom 28. Dezember 2022, der am 1. Januar 2023 in Kraft trat, wurde ein Mechanismus für den Datenaustausch zwischen der nationalen Arbeitsaufsichtsbehörde, der nationalen Brandschutzbehörde und den lokalen Gesundheitsbehörden eingeführt, um die Einhaltung und Durchsetzung der EU-Richtlinien im Rahmen der sozialen Konditionalität zu verbessern (Nationaler Bericht Italien).

Auch in Spanien wurde im Jahr 2021 eine wichtige Arbeitsrechtsreform verabschiedet, um langfristige Arbeitsverträge im Agrarsektor zu fördern. Die Reform schränkt die Umstände ein, unter denen befristete oder temporäre Verträge verwendet werden können, und gibt unbefristeten Verträgen den Vorzug. Obwohl die Landwirtschaft traditionell auf befristete Verträge angewiesen ist, trägt die Reform dem stabilen und zyklischen Bedarf des Sektors an Arbeitskräften während des gesamten Jahres Rechnung (Nationaler Bericht Spanien).

In der Schweiz gibt es keine spezifischen nationalen Rechtsvorschriften für landwirtschaftliche Arbeitsverträge. Aber auch das allgemeine Arbeitsvertragsrecht gilt nicht für landwirtschaftliche Arbeitnehmer. Stattdessen sind die Kantone verpflichtet, Normalarbeitsverträge zu erlassen, die wichtige Aspekte wie Arbeits- und Ruhezeiten sowie Arbeitsbedingungen, insbesondere für Frauen und junge Arbeitnehmer, regeln (Abs. 2).

Von besonderem Interesse ist die Regelung im Kanton Bern, dem größten Landwirtschaftskanton der Schweiz. Sein Normalarbeitsvertrag stammt aus dem Jahr 2007 und wurde 2012 geändert. Die jüngste Regelung stammt aus dem Kanton Luzern, dem drittgrössten Landwirtschaftskanton, der seinen Normalarbeitsvertrag Ende 2022 herausgegeben hat (National Bericht Schweiz).

Was die Arbeitsbedingungen betrifft, so sieht das Bundesgesetz über Familienzulagen in der Landwirtschaft (FLG) Familienleistungen für landwirtschaftliche Arbeitnehmer vor. Nach diesem Gesetz haben auch die im Betrieb mitarbeitenden Familienangehörigen des Betriebsleiters Anspruch auf Familienzulagen (Artikel 1a). Diese Leistungen umfassen eine Haushaltszulage sowie Kinder- und Ausbildungszulagen (Artikel 2 Absatz 1). Darüber hinaus haben auch Selbständigerwerbende Landwirte und Älpler Anspruch auf Familienbeihilfen (Artikel 5).

In Polen stellte die Einführung des „Erntehelfervertrags" im Jahr 2023 eine bedeutende Entwicklung in der Gesetzgebung im Zusammenhang mit der Sozialversicherung für Landwirte dar. Nach dieser neuen Bestimmung erklärt sich ein „Helfer des Landwirts" bereit, für einen bestimmten Zeitraum an einem bestimmten Ort auf dem Grundstück des Landwirts bei der Ernte von landwirtschaftlichen Erzeugnissen zu helfen. Im Gegenzug verpflichtet sich der Landwirt, die vereinbarte Vergütung für die geleistete Hilfe zu zahlen.

Sobald dieser Vertrag abgeschlossen ist, wird der Helfer des Landwirts teilweise in die landwirtschaftliche Sozialversicherung einbezogen. Eine Besonderheit des polnischen Agrarversicherungssystems ist seine Trennung vom allgemeinen Sozialversicherungssystem. Es wird vom landwirtschaftlichen Sozialversicherungsfonds verwaltet und arbeitet mit einem einzigartigen Leistungspaket und vergleichsweise niedrigen Beiträgen.

V. Problem der landwirtschaftlichen Flächen (abnehmender Umfang der landwirtschaftlichen Flächen) und Interessenkonflikte, Generationswechsel

Die Kommission III erörterte die Frage der landwirtschaftlichen Flächen, wobei er sich auf die abnehmende Verfügbarkeit von landwirtschaftlichen Flächen und Interessenkonflikte konzentrierte. Die Zahl der landwirtschaftlichen Betriebe und die Gesamtfläche der landwirtschaftlichen Nutzfläche nehmen in vielen Ländern ab, was insbesondere in Europa Anlass zur Sorge über die Zukunft des Agrarmodells gibt. Die Umwandlung landwirtschaftlicher Flächen für Bau- und Investitionszwecke ist ein besonders schädlicher Trend, der hochwertiges Ackerland beeinträchtigt und die landwirtschaftlichen Möglichkeiten erheblich einschränkt.

Der Generationswechsel ist eine weitere dringende Herausforderung, die sich in Zukunft noch verschärfen könnte. Immer weniger junge Menschen sind bereit, landwirtschaftliche Betriebe zu übernehmen, ein Trend, der mit den berufsbedingten Anforderungen an die Berufshaftpflicht und den erheblichen Risiken im Zusammenhang mit Wetterbedingungen, Naturkatastrophen und Marktschwankungen zusammenhängt. In diesem Zusammenhang sind die Überwachung und Kontrolle der Tätigkeiten der Erzeuger sowie die Gewährleistung von Rechenschaftspflicht und Sanktionen wichtige Themen, die sowohl auf EU-Ebene als auch in den einzelnen Ländern behandelt werden.

Zur Unterstützung von Junglandwirten hat die EU sowohl im Rahmen der ersten als auch der zweiten Säule der Gemeinsamen Agrarpolitik (GAP) zusätzliche Mittel bereitgestellt. Diese Maßnahmen stehen in engem Zusammenhang mit der Übertragung von landwirtschaftlichen Betrieben, einem Bereich, in dem mehrere Länder kürzlich Gesetzesänderungen eingeführt haben, die die Übertragung von landwirtschaftlichen Flächen einschränken sollen.

In einigen Ländern gibt es einen offenen Markt für landwirtschaftliche Grundstücke, was ein größeres Risiko birgt, dass landwirtschaftliche Flächen für Bau- oder Investitionszwecke umgewandelt oder ausgeschlossen werden. Gleichzeitig gewinnt die Verpachtung von landwirtschaftlichen Flächen zunehmend an Bedeutung. Einige Länder haben gesetzliche Änderungen vorgenommen, um diesem Trend entgegenzuwirken, andere planen ähnliche Maßnahmen.

So sind beispielsweise 93,5 % der landwirtschaftlichen Betriebe in Italien Einzel- oder Familienbetriebe, was die anhaltende Dominanz des Familienbetriebsmodells verdeutlicht. Allerdings ist auch dieses Modell im Niedergang begriffen. Die kleinsten Familienbetriebe, vor allem in Mittel- und Süditalien, verlassen den Sektor in erheblichem Maße (-51,2 % der Betriebe unter einem Hektar). Demgegenüber ist eine Zunahme der landwirtschaftlichen Betriebe in Form von Personengesellschaften und vor allem von Gesellschaften mit beschränkter Haftung zu verzeichnen.

Darüber hinaus gewinnt die Praxis der Landverpachtung zunehmend an Bedeutung und ersetzt allmählich das traditionelle Modell des Alleineigentums (Nationaler Bericht Italien).

In Slowenien machen die landwirtschaftlich genutzten Flächen nur 23,7 % der Gesamtfläche des Landes aus. Hochwertige landwirtschaftliche Flächen sind in Slowenien begrenzt, weshalb ihr Schutz von entscheidender Bedeutung ist. Nach dem Landwirtschaftsgesetz müssen agrarpolitische Maßnahmen in erster Linie auf die Entwicklung einer nachhaltigen Landwirtschaft ausgerichtet sein, die die biologische Vielfalt der Tier- und Pflanzenarten und die Bodenfruchtbarkeit erhält und die natürlichen Lebensbedingungen von Boden, Wasser und Luft schützt (Artikel 15) (Nationaler Bericht Slowenien).

Am 13. Juli 2023 verabschiedete das polnische Parlament ein Gesetz zur Änderung des Gesetzes über die Gestaltung des Agrarsystems, mit dem neue Regelungen für die öffentlich-rechtliche Kontrolle des Verkehrs mit landwirtschaftlichen Flächen eingeführt wurden.

Eine neue Gesetzgebung in Frankreich, die durch das Gesetz Nr. 2021-1756 vom 23. Dezember 2021 eingeführt wurde, regelt den Zugang zu landwirtschaftlichen Flächen durch Unternehmensstrukturen. Diese einzigartige Regelung zielt darauf ab, den Erwerb von Anteilen an landwirtschaftlichen Unternehmen zu kontrollieren, um die Anhäufung und übermäßige Konzentration von landwirtschaftlichen Flächen durch Unternehmensstrukturen (Land Grabbing) zu bekämpfen und die Ernährungssouveränität zu verbessern.

Nach diesem Gesetz muss jedes Unternehmen, das die Kontrolle über ein Unternehmen erwerben möchte, das landwirtschaftliche Grundstücke besitzt oder für landwirtschaftliche Tätigkeiten nutzt, eine Genehmigung des Präfekten des Departements einholen, wenn die landwirtschaftlichen Grundstücke, die das Unternehmen besitzt oder nutzt, zusammen mit den landwirtschaftlichen Grundstücken, die dasselbe Unternehmen bereits besitzt oder nutzt, eine bestimmte Anzahl von Grundstücken überschreiten.

In der Schweiz ist der Erwerb von landwirtschaftlichen Flächen und Betrieben im Prinzip auf selbständige Landwirte beschränkt. Diese Beschränkung ergibt sich aus dem Bundesgesetz über die landwirtschaftlichen Grundstücke (BGBB), das strenge Regeln für die rechtliche Übertragung von landwirtschaftlichen Grundstücken und Betrieben aufstellt. Im Erbfall kann ein landwirtschaftlicher Betrieb nur von einem Erben übernommen werden, der als selbstständiger Landwirt geeignet ist (Artikel 11 Absatz 1 BGBB).

Im Vereinigten Königreich wird die Verpachtung von landwirtschaftlichen Flächen immer beliebter. Dem Rock Review zufolge nehmen Pachtbetriebe – ganz oder teilweise – 64 % der gesamten landwirtschaftlich nutzbaren Fläche (8,9 Millionen Hektar) in England ein, während Pachtbetriebe 45 % aller landwirtschaftlichen Betriebe des Landes ausmachen. Die DEFRA-Kommission hat eine Überprüfung der Pachtlandwirtschaft in England vorgenommen. Der Rock Review enthält über 70 Empfehlungen für einen widerstandsfähigeren Pachtsektor, der eine nachhaltige Nahrungsmittelproduktion gewährleisten, die Herausforderungen des Klimawandels bewältigen und die biologische Vielfalt verbessern und fördern soll (Nationaler Bericht Vereinigter Königreich).

VI. Stellung der Landwirte in der Wertschöpfungskette

Die Position der Landwirte in der Lebensmittelversorgungskette ist nach wie vor schwach. Obwohl die EU-Länder die Richtlinie (EU) 2019/633 über unlautere Handelspraktiken in den Geschäftsbeziehungen zwischen Unternehmen in der Agrar- und Lebensmittelversorgungskette umgesetzt haben, haben sich die jüngsten Entwicklungen – wie die Aggression Russlands gegen die Ukraine – negativ auf die Agrarmärkte ausgewirkt und die Verhandlungsposition der landwirtschaftlichen Erzeuger geschwächt. Diese Herausforderungen ergeben sich aus den steigenden Preisen für Betriebsmittel (Kraftstoff, Energie, Düngemittel und Pflanzenschutzmittel) und der Aufhebung der Zölle auf bestimmte ukrainische Agrarerzeugnisse durch die Europäische Union, was die Wettbewerbsfähigkeit einheimischer Agrarerzeugnisse erschwert hat.

Beispiele für die Umsetzung auf nationaler Ebene und damit zusammenhängende Maßnahmen sind die folgenden:

In Slowenien wurde mit den Änderungen des Landwirtschaftsgesetzes von 2021 der Begriff der Lebensmittelversorgungskette auf die Lieferkette für landwirtschaftliche Erzeugnisse und Lebensmittel ausgeweitet und das Konzept der beträchtlichen Marktmacht (SMP) eingeführt. Das Verkaufsvolumen von Lieferanten und Käufern wird nun streng nach der in der Richtlinie (EU) 2019/633 vorgesehenen Skala verglichen. Darüber hinaus wurde eine neue Institution, der Ombudsmann für die Beziehungen in der Agrar- und Lebensmittelkette, eingerichtet, um diese Angelegenheiten zu überwachen, und es wurden neue verbindliche Regeln für verbotene unlautere Praktiken eingeführt (Nationaler Bericht Slowenien).

In Italien wurden aus dem Ergänzungsfonds 1,2 Mrd. Euro für Lieferketten- und Bezirksverträge im Agrar- und Ernährungssektor bereitgestellt, die die Bereiche Landwirtschaft, Fischerei, Forstwirtschaft, Blumenzucht und Baumschulen abdecken. Von diesem Betrag sind 25 % für den ökologischen Landbau reserviert. Die staatliche Beihilferegelung für Lieferketten- und Distriktverträge für den Zeitraum von 2021 bis 2027 wurde bei der Europäischen Kommission angemeldet, die ihre Vereinbarkeit mit dem Binnenmarkt gemäß Artikel 107 Absatz 3(c) AEUV bestätigte. Die Regelung wurde durch einen Ministerialerlass vom 22. Dezember 2021 umgesetzt (Nationaler Bericht Italien).

In Polen wurde die Richtlinie (EU) 2019/633 durch das Gesetz vom 17. November 2021 zur Bekämpfung der unlauteren Ausnutzung vertraglicher Vorteile im Handel mit landwirtschaftlichen Erzeugnissen und Lebensmitteln (Nationaler Bericht Polen) in nationales Recht umgesetzt.

In Spanien wurde der „Standard-Lebensmittelvertrag“ zunächst durch das Gesetz 12/2013 über Maßnahmen zur Verbesserung der Funktionsweise der Lebensmittelkette geregelt. Spätere Änderungen, vor allem im Jahr 2020 und im Dezember 2021, vervollständigten die Umsetzung der Richtlinie (EU) 2019/633. Der spanische Gesetzgeber betonte die Notwendigkeit, das schwächste Glied in der Lebensmittelkette zu schützen – den Sektor der Primärproduktion, der sich überwiegend aus kleinen und mittleren Familienbetrieben zusammensetzt. Diese Betriebe produzieren oft qualitativ hochwertige Waren, werden aber vom Markt nicht gerecht entschädigt. Künftige Regelungen müssen einen umfassenden Schutz gegen unfaire Handelspraktiken gewährleisten, der alle Phasen der Auftragsvergabe im Agrar- und Lebensmittelsektor abdeckt, einschließlich der vorvertraglichen und der Verhandlungsphase. Solche Maßnahmen sollten darauf abzielen, einen gerechten Schutz für den Sektor der Primärproduktion zu gewährleisten (Nationaler Bericht Spanien).

VII. Verband der landwirtschaftlichen Erzeuger

Die Teilnehmer der Kommission III diskutierten über den Zusammenschluss von landwirtschaftlichen Erzeugern (Genossenschaften und andere Organisationen). Dies ist eines der wichtigsten Instrumente zur Stärkung der Position der landwirtschaftlichen Erzeuger in der Lebensmittelversorgungskette. Nach den Bestimmungen der Gemeinsamen Agrarpolitik der EU (GAP) sind die Erzeugerorganisationen verpflichtet, zur Stärkung der Rolle der Landwirte in der Lebensmittelversorgungskette, der Entwicklung der landwirtschaftlichen Betriebe und der Agrarmärkte beizutragen.

Erzeugerorganisationen und Bauernverbände, wie z.B. Genossenschaften, spielen in mehreren Bereichen eine entscheidende Rolle. Dazu gehören die Konzentration des Angebots, die Verbesserung der Vermarktung, die Planung und Anpassung der Produktion an die Nachfrage, die Optimierung der Produktionskosten, die Stabilisierung der Erzeugerpreise, die Durchführung von Forschungsarbeiten, die Förderung bewährter Verfahren, die Bereitstellung technischer Hilfe, die Verwaltung von Nebenprodukten und die Bereitstellung von Risikomanagementinstrumenten für ihre Mitglieder. Zusammengenommen tragen diese Bemühungen erheblich zur Stärkung der Position der Erzeuger in der Lebensmittelversorgungskette bei. Die Entwicklung solcher Einrichtungen ist in mehreren Ländern zu beobachten.

Es wurde hervorgehoben, dass die Zusammenarbeit in den verschiedenen Phasen der Landwirtschaft von entscheidender Bedeutung ist, angefangen beim Kauf von Betriebsmitteln und dem Einsatz von Landmaschinen bis hin zum Transport der Ernte, der Bereitstellung von Beratungsdiensten sowie der Verarbeitung und dem Verkauf der Erzeugnisse. Zusammengeschlossene Erzeuger sind besser in der Lage, landwirtschaftliche Produkte mit geringerem Pestizideinsatz zu produzieren, Tiere mit weniger Tierarzneimitteln zu züchten und eine Verarbeitung vorzunehmen, die unverfälschte, gesunde und für den Verbraucher erschwingliche Agrar- und Lebensmittelprodukte hervorbringt. Außerdem können sie eine wichtige Rolle bei Initiativen für erneuerbare Energien spielen.

Die „Vom Hof auf den Tisch"-Strategie wurde als eine Schlüsselkomponente des EU-Grünen-Deals hervorgehoben. Diese Strategie fördert nachhaltiges und integratives Wachstum und zielt darauf ab, die Wirtschaft anzukurbeln, die öffentliche Gesundheit und Lebensqualität zu verbessern und die Umwelt zu schützen. Einige Erzeugergemeinschaften engagieren sich aktiv für den Umweltschutz, etwa beim Schutz von Natura-2000-Gebieten (z.B. in den Niederlanden). Auch die wachsende Beliebtheit von Energiegenossenschaften wurde festgestellt.

Die Teilnehmer des Ausschusses betonten, dass die rechtliche Stellung und die Rolle von landwirtschaftlichen Genossenschaften, Erzeugerorganisationen und ähnlichen Vereinigungen gestärkt werden müssen, um die Entwicklung der Landwirtschaft, der Agrar- und Ernährungsindustrie und der ländlichen Gebiete zu fördern. In einigen Ländern sind weitere rechtliche Änderungen in Bezug auf Erzeugerorganisationen, Genossenschaften und ähnliche Einrichtungen erforderlich, um deren Entwicklung und Effizienz zu fördern.

VIII. Europäischer Grüner Deal: Umweltschutz in landwirtschaftlichen Betrieben, Eindämmung des Klimawandels, ökologischer Landbau, erneuerbare Energien, Wasserrecht und Tierschutz

Die Kommission III befasste sich auch mit der Frage des Klimawandels, der eine erhebliche Bedrohung für den gesamten Planeten darstellt. Die globale Erwärmung wirkt sich zunehmend auf die Niederschlagsmuster, die Ozeane und die Windsysteme aus. Es wird erwartet, dass diese Veränderungen die Landwirtschaft in allen Ländern vor größere Herausforderungen stellen werden. Die ermittelten Probleme werden im Europäischen Grünen Deal behandelt, der am 11. Dezember 2019 von der Europäischen Kommission vorgestellt wurde. In den letzten Jahren haben die Mitgliedstaaten neue Verordnungen und Strategien im Zusammenhang mit dem Grünen Deal verabschiedet.

Verschiedene Aspekte des Umweltschutzes, des Klimawandels, der Wasserwirtschaft und des Naturschutzes rücken zunehmend in den Mittelpunkt gerichtlicher Entscheidungen. Einige Länder haben auch über die Einführung neuer Umwelt- oder Raumplanungsgesetze berichtet.

Ein bemerkenswertes Beispiel für die gerichtliche Behandlung von Klimafragen ist die Entscheidung des Ersten Senats des Bundesverfassungsgerichts vom 24. März 2021, in der der Klimaschutz als Menschenrecht anerkannt wurde. Das Gericht stellte fest:

„Die aus Art. 2 Abs. 2 Satz 1 GG folgende Schutzpflicht des Staates umfasst auch die Verpflichtung, Leben und Gesundheit vor den Gefahren des Klimawandels zu schützen. Sie kann eine objektivrechtliche Schutzverpflichtung auch in Bezug auf künftige Generationen begründen..."[5]

Dieses Urteil unterstreicht die zunehmende rechtliche Anerkennung des Klimaschutzes als eine grundlegende Verpflichtung des Staates, die auch den Schutz künftiger Generationen einschließt.

Der Gerichtshof betonte auch die Notwendigkeit einer verhältnismäßigen Gewährung von Freiheit und Chancen über die Generationen hinweg und stellte fest „Das Grundgesetz verpflichtet unter bestimmten Voraussetzungen zur Sicherung grundrechtsgeschützter Freiheit über die Zeit und zur verhältnismäßigen Verteilung von Freiheitschancen über die Generationen. Subjektivrechtlich schützen die Grundrechte als intertemporale Freiheitssicherung vor einer einseitigen Verlagerung der durch Art. 20a GG aufgegebenen Treibhausgasminderungslast in die Zukunft."[6]

Beschluss des Ersten Senats vom 24. März 2021 - 1 BvR 2656/18 - 1 BvR 78/20 - 1 BvR 96/20 - 1 BvR 288/20 - Die Schutzpflicht aus Art. 2 Abs. 2 Satz 1 GG umfasst die Pflicht, Leben und Gesundheit vor den Gefahren des Klimawandels zu schützen. Sie kann darüber hinaus die Grundlage für eine objektive Schutzpflicht gegenüber künftigen Generationen bilden.

Das Gericht betonte, dass Artikel 20a des Grundgesetzes eine internationale Dimension hat. Die Tatsache, dass kein Staat die Probleme des Klimawandels aufgrund des globalen Charakters des Klimas und der globalen Erwärmung allein lösen kann, entbindet nicht von der nationalen Verpflichtung, Klimaschutzmaßnahmen zu ergreifen. Gemäß dieser Verpflichtung ist der Staat gezwungen, sich an internationalen Maßnahmen zu beteiligen, um den Klimawandel auf globaler Ebene anzugehen, und er ist verpflichtet, Klimaschutzmaßnahmen in einem internationalen Rahmen zu fördern. Ein Staat kann sich seiner Verantwortung nicht entziehen, indem er auf die Treibhausgasemissionen anderer Staaten verweist. „Das Grundgesetz verpflichtet unter bestimmten Voraussetzungen zur Sicherung grundrechtsgeschützter Freiheit über die Zeit und zur verhältnismäßigen Verteilung von Freiheitschancen über die Generationen. Subjektivrechtlich

5 Bundesverfassungsgericht, Beschluss des Ersten Senats vom 24. März 2021, Az. 1 BvR 2656/18, 1 BvR 78/20, 1 BvR 96/20, 1 BvR 288/20. Die englische Übersetzung des Urteils ist auf der Website des Bundesverfassungsgerichts verfügbar: https://www.bundesverfassungsgericht.de/SharedDocs/Entscheidungen/EN/2021/03/rs20210324_1bvr265618en.html.

6 Ebenda.

schützen die Grundrechte als intertemporale Freiheitssicherung vor einer einseitigen Verlagerung der durch Art. 20a GG aufgegebenen Treibhausgasminderungslast in die Zukunft. (...)".

Die Entscheidung des Gerichts unterstreicht die verfassungsrechtliche Verpflichtung des deutschen Staates, Leben und Gesundheit nicht nur für die heutige Bevölkerung, sondern auch für künftige Generationen zu schützen. Diese Pflicht beinhaltet ein aktives Engagement sowohl bei nationalen Maßnahmen als auch bei der internationalen Zusammenarbeit, um dem Klimawandel umfassend zu begegnen.

Beispiele für gesetzgeberische und politische Entwicklungen, die von Umwelt- und Nachhaltigkeitszielen beeinflusst wurden, sind folgende:

In den Niederlanden stellt das am 1. Januar 2024 in Kraft getretene Umwelt- und Planungsgesetz die umfassendste gesetzliche Überarbeitung des Umweltrechts der letzten Jahrzehnte dar. Das Gesetz, das 26 Gesetze, 60 Regierungsverordnungen und 75 Ministerialerlasse ersetzt, zielt darauf ab, die Vorschriften in den Bereichen Bau, Umwelt, Wasser, Stadtplanung und Natur zu konsolidieren. Ziel ist die Vereinfachung der Vorschriften für Raumordnungsprojekte und den Lebensraum, was sich insbesondere auf den Agrarsektor auswirkt.

In Italien wurde die Verfassung kürzlich geändert, um den Schutz der Umwelt, der Ökosysteme und der biologischen Vielfalt ausdrücklich als grundlegende Prinzipien und Kriterien für die Begrenzung der Wirtschaftstätigkeit aufzunehmen (Verfassungsgesetz Nr. 1 von 2022). Der Nationale Plan für Wiederaufbau und Resilienz (Piano Nazionale di Ripresa e Resilienza, PNRR) wurde gemäß der Verordnung (EU) Nr. 241 aus dem Jahr 2021 als Italiens Antwort auf den Grünen Deal der EU und die EU-Initiative der nächsten Generation veröffentlicht (Nationaler Bericht Italien).

In Spanien wurden neue Rechtsvorschriften erlassen, um die Umsetzung der EU-Strategie „vom Erzeuger zum Verbraucher" zu unterstützen. Diese Rechtsvorschriften umfassen Maßnahmen zur Verringerung der Treibhausgasemissionen, zur Förderung erneuerbarer Energien, zur Verbesserung der Energieeffizienz, zur Unterstützung der Landwirte bei der Umstellung auf nachhaltigere landwirtschaftliche Praktiken und zur Verringerung der Nitratverschmutzung aus landwirtschaftlichen Quellen (Spanischer Bericht).

In Deutschland wird mit dem Bundesklimaschutzgesetz (KSG) vom 12. Dezember 2019 ein Rahmen für die Umsetzung der nationalen Klimaschutzziele und die Einhaltung der europäischen Klimaziele geschaffen. Verwurzelt in den Verpflichtungen des Pariser Klimaabkommens zielt das KSG darauf ab, den globalen Temperaturanstieg auf deutlich unter 2°C und möglichst auf 1,5°C über dem vorindustriellen Niveau zu begrenzen (§ 1 Satz 2 KSG).

In Ungarn besteht die Hauptaufgabe der Wasserbewirtschaftung darin, die Wasserrückhaltung und -speicherung zu verbessern. Die landschaftsbasierte Wasserbewirtschaftung stellt eine einzigartige ungarische Anpassung des Konzepts der adaptiven Wasserbewirtschaftung innerhalb des breiteren Rahmens der integrierten Wasserbewirtschaftung dar (Ungarischer Bericht).

Der Europäische Green Deal hat weiterhin einen erheblichen Einfluss auf die nationalen Vorschriften der EU-Mitgliedstaaten und prägt die Umwelt- und Nachhaltigkeitspolitik in verschiedenen Sektoren.

In Spanien hat der Europäische Grüne Deal zur Verabschiedung neuer Gesetze und strategischer Pläne geführt, die auf die Bekämpfung des Klimawandels und die Förderung der Nachhaltigkeit abzielen. Ein Beispiel ist das spanische Gesetz zum Klimawandel und zur Energiewende, das darauf abzielt, Spanien bis 2050 klimaneutral zu machen. Eine weitere wichtige Initiative ist der Nationale Integrierte Energie- und Klimaplan 2021-2030, der spezifische Maßnahmen zur Erreichung der Ziele des Gesetzes zum Klimawandel und zur Energiewende vorsieht.

Der spanische GAP-Strategieplan (CAPSP) legt Aktionslinien fest, um Landwirte bei der Umstellung auf nachhaltigere landwirtschaftliche Praktiken zu unterstützen. Darüber hinaus wurde mit der Genehmigung eines weiteren Programmplanungsdokuments, des Strategischen Agrar- und Lebensmittelprojekts für Wiederaufbau und Transformation (ASPERT), ein spezielles Unterstützungspaket für die Agrar- und Lebensmittelindustrie eingeführt. Dieses Paket zielt auf die Förderung von Innovation, Widerstandsfähigkeit und Nachhaltigkeit in diesem ab.

Das Strategic Agri-Food Project for Recovery and Transformation (ASPERT) zielt darauf ab, die Produktionsprozesse zu verbessern, die Wettbewerbsfähigkeit zu steigern, die Nachhaltigkeit zu fördern und die Rückverfolgbarkeit der Lebensmittelproduktion zu gewährleisten. Es umfasst auch Maßnahmen zur Unterstützung der digitalen Anpassung des Agrar- und Lebensmittelsektors. Das Projekt umfasst alle Akteure innerhalb der Lebensmittelwertschöpfungskette, einschließlich Landwirte, Erzeuger, Genossenschaften sowie kleine und mittlere Unternehmen, die an der Produktion, der Verarbeitung und dem Handel beteiligt sind.

Eine Schlüsselkomponente des Projekts ist sein dritter Schwerpunkt, der sich auf spezifische Maßnahmen zur Unterstützung von Innovation und

Forschung konzentriert, mit dem Ziel, einen wettbewerbsfähigen Agrar- und Ernährungssektor über alle Glieder der Kette hinweg zu erreichen.

Darüber hinaus ist der Aktionsplan zur Umsetzung der Agenda 2030: Auf dem Weg zu einer spanischen Strategie für nachhaltige Entwicklung zu erwähnen. Dieser Plan legt verschiedene Ziele und Maßnahmen zur Förderung der ländlichen Entwicklung in Spanien fest (Nationaler Bericht Spanien).

IX. Erneuerbare Energien in der Landwirtschaft

Steigende Geschäftskosten und zunehmende Sorge um den Umweltschutz haben die Investitionen in erneuerbare Energien beschleunigt. Gleichzeitig ist die Nutzung von Land für die Nahrungsmittel- und Energieerzeugung, z.B. durch Photovoltaikanlagen, zu einem wichtigen Trend geworden. Infolgedessen hat die Anwendung der Agrophotovoltaik, die eine gleichzeitige landwirtschaftliche Nutzung von Flächen und Energiegewinnung ermöglicht, zugenommen. Für künftige Generationen gewinnen erneuerbare Energien immer mehr an Bedeutung. Die kombinierten Auswirkungen der russischen Invasion in der Ukraine und des Klimawandels haben die Sorge um die Energiesicherheit verstärkt. Diese Entwicklungen unterstreichen die Dringlichkeit, die Abhängigkeit von fossilen Brennstoffen zu verringern und die Abhängigkeit von Energieressourcen, die von Russland geliefert werden, zu beenden.

a) Beispiele

In Polen gibt es derzeit keine Gaslieferverträge mit Russland. Das Gesetz vom 13. Juli 2023 legt detaillierte Regeln und Verfahren für die Vorbereitung und Durchführung von Investitionen in landwirtschaftliche Biogasanlagen fest. Das Gesetz legt den Verfahrensrahmen für den Erlass von Entscheidungen über den Bau von landwirtschaftlichen Biogasanlagen fest, um die Vorbereitung und Durchführung solcher Investitionen zu erleichtern und zu beschleunigen. Es legt auch die Betriebsbedingungen für landwirtschaftliche Biogasanlagen fest, um nachhaltige Energielösungen im landwirtschaftlichen Sektor zu fördern.

Im Jahr 2021 lag der Anteil der erneuerbaren Energien am Bruttoendenergieverbrauch in Frankreich bei 19,3 %. Das französische Energie- und Klimagesetz, das 2019 verabschiedet wurde, zielt darauf ab, bis 2030 einen Anteil von 33 % erneuerbarer Energien am Verbrauch zu erreichen. Darüber hinaus haben sich die Mitgliedstaaten der Europäischen Union kürzlich auf ein kollektives Ziel von 42,5 % für den Verbrauch erneuerbarer Energien bis 2030 geeinigt.

Um diese ehrgeizigen Ziele zu erreichen, hat Frankreich das Gesetz Nr. 2023-175 vom 10. März 2023 verabschiedet, mit dem die Erzeugung erneuerbarer Energien beschleunigt werden soll. Mit diesem Gesetz werden wichtige Änderungen am Energierahmen des Landes eingeführt, um die nationalen und EU-Ziele zu erreichen (Nationaler Bericht Frankreich).

X. Gemeinsame Agrarpolitik 2023-2027, ländliche Entwicklung und Umwelt

Die Kommission III befasste sich mit der Gemeinsamen Agrarpolitik (GAP). Es besteht kein Zweifel daran, dass in jedem Mitgliedstaat der Europäischen Union Verordnungen zur Finanzierung der GAP für den Zeitraum 2023-2027 erlassen worden sind. Eine große Herausforderung war die Ausarbeitung der strategischen Pläne der GAP für diesen Zeitraum. In jedem Land sind die Direktzahlungen das grundlegende Instrument der Unterstützung, während jeder Mitgliedstaat derzeit verschiedene Ökoregelungen gewählt hat.

Im Rahmen der zweiten Säule der GAP ist die größere Freiheit zu begrüßen, die den Mitgliedstaaten eingeräumt wird, um bei der Wahl der Programme und Maßnahmen den nationalen Bedürfnissen Rechnung zu tragen. Infolgedessen haben sich die EU-Mitgliedstaaten für unterschiedliche Maßnahmen zur Entwicklung des ländlichen Raums entschieden. Zu den Programmen gehören weiterhin die Förderung von Junglandwirten, die Modernisierung von landwirtschaftlichen Betrieben und die Vereinigung von landwirtschaftlichen Erzeugern. Umweltfragen, einschließlich erneuerbarer Energien, gewinnen zunehmend an Bedeutung. Die Unterstützung wird in Form einer Verwaltungsentscheidung oder eines Vertrags gewährt.

Direktzahlungen an landwirtschaftliche Erzeuger gibt es auch in Ländern außerhalb der Europäischen Union. In einigen Ländern beklagen die Erzeuger, dass die Vorschriften zu kompliziert sind und vereinfacht werden müssen. In einigen Ländern sind solche Vereinfachungen bereits eingeführt worden.

Ein wichtiger neuer Aspekt betrifft die Öko-Regelungen. Gemäß dem polnischen Gesetz vom 8. Februar 2023 über den Strategieplan für die

Gemeinsame Agrarpolitik 2023-2027 werden Zahlungen im Rahmen von Öko-Regelungen an den Landwirt in Form von Zahlungen gewährt: 1) für Flächen mit Honigtaupflanzen, 2) für Kohlenstoffanbau und Nährstoffmanagement, 3) für integrierten Pflanzenbau, 4) für biologischen Pflanzenschutz, 5) für Wasserrückhaltung auf Dauergrünland, 5a) für aus der Produktion genommene Flächen und 6) für Tierschutz.

Beispiele: Öko-Regelungen gemäß den GAP-Strategieplänen von vier EU-Mitgliedstaaten

Spanien	**Polen**	**Deutschland**	**Italien**
Art der Oberfläche: Dauerweiden und Dauergrünland. • Praktiken. Extensive Beweidung (P1). • Praktiken. Nachhaltiges Mähen und die Einrichtung von Biodiversitätsinseln (P2). • Schaffung von Inseln der biologischen Vielfalt (P2A). • Nachhaltige Aussaat (P2B). Oberflächenarten: Ackerland. • Praktiken. Fruchtfolge mit Verbesserungsarten (P3). • Praktiken. Direktsaat (P4). Arten von Flächen: Ackerland und Dauerkulturen ( ), einschließlich Holzkulturen.	Zahlungen im Rahmen von Öko-Regelungen werden Landwirten in Form von Zahlungen für Flächen mit honigproduzierenden Pflanzen, Zahlungen für die Kohlenstoff- und Nährstoff-bewirtschaftung in der Landwirtschaft, Zahlungen für den integrierten Pflanzenbau, Zahlungen für den biologischen Pflanzenschutz, Zahlungen für die Wasserrückhaltung in Dauergrünland und Tierschutzzahlungen gewährt.	Es gibt Öko-Regelungen: • ÖR 1: Zusätzliche Flächen für die biologische Vielfalt (Brachflächen/Blühstreifen/Altgrasstreifen). • ÖR 2: Vielfältige Kulturen im Ackerbau mit mindestens 5 Hauptkulturen, davon 10 % Leguminosen • ÖR 3: Beibehaltung der Agroforstwirtschaft auf Ackerland und Dauergrünland. • ÖR 4: Extensivier-ung des gesamten Dauergrünlandes des Unternehmens. • ÖR 5: Extensive Bewirtschaftung von einzelnen Dauergrünlandflächen mit Nachweis von mindestens 4 re-	Einführung von fünf Öko-Regelungen: • ECO-1 Verbesserter Tierschutz und Kampf gegen Antibiotikaresistenz • ECO-2 Begrünung von Baumkulturen (17,8 % der Mittel); • ECO-3 Schutz von Olivenbäumen mit besonderem Landschaftswert (17,2 %); • ECO-4 Extensive Futtersysteme zur Förderung der Einführung von Leguminosen und Futterpflanzen in der Fruchtfolge sowie von nachwachsenden Rohstoffen mit der Verpflichtung zur Bewirtschaftung von Rückständen unter dem Ge-

• Praktiken. Einrichtung von Biodiversitätsräumen oder nachhaltige Bewirtschaftung der Wasserflächen (P5). Arten von Flächen: Dauerkulturen. • Praktiken. Spontane oder gesäte Vegetationsdecke (P6). • Praktiken. Inerte Vegetationsdecke (P7).		gionalen Merkmalen. • ÖR 6: Verzicht auf chemischsynthetische Pestizide auf Ackerflächen und in Dauerkulturen. • ÖR 7: Erhaltungszielorientiertes Management in Natura 2000-Gebieten	sichtspunkt der Kohlenstoffsenke (18,6 %); • ECO-5 Spezifische Maßnahmen für Bestäuber sowohl bei krautigen als auch bei baumartigen Kulturen (5 %).

Quelle: Nationale Berichte für Spanien, Polen, Deutschland und Italien für den CEDR-Kongress in Cardiff 2023.

Gemäß den GAP-Strategieplänen 2023-2027 hat Spanien seine Unterstützung für Innovation, Wissenstransfer und Digitalisierung bereits erhöht. Diese Unterstützung wird von den regionalen Verwaltungen verwaltet, obwohl die Anforderungen für die Gewährung einer solchen Unterstützung in der Regel in allen Regionen einheitlich sind. Zu den spanischen Maßnahmen im Rahmen der zweiten Säule gehören die Unterstützung von Junglandwirten und neuen Landwirten bei der Gründung ländlicher Unternehmen (Untermaßnahme 6.1), Investitionen in landwirtschaftliche Betriebe (Untermaßnahme 4.1), Kooperationsinitiativen (LEADER) im Rahmen der Maßnahme 19 sowie Wissensaustausch und Informationsverbreitung.

In der Schweiz erhalten die Landwirte Direktzahlungen als Ausgleich für die von ihnen erbrachten öffentlichen Leistungen. Diese Zahlungen umfassen Subventionen für Kulturlandschaft, Versorgungssicherheit, Biodiversität, Landschaftsqualität, Produktionssysteme, Ressourcen-effizienz und Übergang (Nationaler Bericht Schweiz).

Im Vereinigten Königreich ist die finanzielle Unterstützung der Landwirte auch an die Erfüllung von Umweltauflagen gebunden. Diese Unterstützung wird jedoch in den kommenden Jahren abnehmen.

XI. Krieg in der Ukraine

Fragen im Zusammenhang mit der Ukraine wurden in der Kommission I ausführlich erörtert.

Einige rechtliche Fragen im Zusammenhang mit der Situation in der Ukraine wurden während einer Online-Verbindung mit Wissenschaftlern aus der Ukraine erörtert. Trotz der Herausforderungen und Folgen der anhaltenden Feindseligkeiten haben das ukrainische Parlament und die Regierung verschiedene Maßnahmen zur Erleichterung der landwirtschaftlichen Tätigkeiten ergriffen.

Im Bericht Polens wurden u.a. gesetzliche Regelungen zur Unterstützung polnischer landwirtschaftlicher Erzeuger, die von den negativen Auswirkungen des Krieges in der Ukraine betroffen sind, sowie Regelungen zur Unterstützung ukrainischer Bürger, die in Polen leben, vorgestellt, z.B. das Gesetz vom 12. März 2022 über die Unterstützung ukrainischer Bürger im Zusammenhang mit dem bewaffneten Konflikt im Hoheitsgebiet der Ukraine.

Conclusions de la Commission III –
Conclusions of Commission III –
Schlussfolgerungen der Kommission III

Version française – French version – Französische Version
Version anglaise – English version – Englische Version
Version allemande – German version – Deutsche Version

Conclusions de la Commission III – Conclusions of Commission III – Schlussfolgerungen der Kommission III

A. Version française – French version – Französische Version

Entre le dernier congrès de la CEDR à Poznań en 2019 et le congrès de la CEDR au Royaume-Uni en 2023, un certain nombre de nouveaux règlements ont été publiés. Ceux-ci étaient liés à Covid-19 et à la guerre en Ukraine (ces questions ont été principalement discutées au sein de la Commission I).

La Commission III s'est principalement occupée de la législation agricole dans les pays européens et aux États-Unis. Les changements dans le cadre législatif de la politique agricole ont fait l'objet d'une attention particulière. Les participants des États membres de l'UE ont rendu compte des méthodes et des bases juridiques pour la mise en œuvre des plans stratégiques de la PAC conformément aux instruments juridiques de base de l'UE pour la période 2023-2027. Le Royaume-Uni a élaboré sa propre politique agricole à la suite du Brexit, tandis qu'une nouvelle Farm Bill était en cours de préparation aux États-Unis. D'autres pays, comme la Suisse, ont également révisé leur législation et leur politique agricole entre les deux congrès.

Les rapports nationaux ont mis en évidence des évolutions significatives dans la législation nationale concernant la définition des activités agricoles et autres, le statut juridique et fiscal des producteurs agricoles et l'accès à la propriété et à l'utilisation des terres agricoles. Les réglementations agricoles abordent de plus en plus les questions sociales, notamment l'égalité de statut des femmes, les droits des travailleurs agricoles et le renouvellement des générations dans les exploitations. Elles se concentrent également sur les défis environnementaux, tels que les méthodes de production durables, l'adaptation au changement climatique, la conservation de la biodiversité, la gestion de l'eau et la promotion des sources d'énergie renouvelables.

Seule une rédaction et un suivi attentifs des réglementations légales peuvent garantir un juste équilibre entre la viabilité économique, l'équité sociale et les exigences environnementales, favorisant ainsi le développement durable.

Il ne fait aucun doute que l'adoption de nouveaux règlements de l'UE pour la politique agricole commune (PAC) 2023-2027 et la publication des règlements nationaux correspondants étaient d'une importance capitale. Il convient de noter que la PAC 2023-2027 met de plus en plus l'accent sur le soutien et le renforcement de la protection de l'environnement, y compris la biodiversité et l'action pour le climat, et sur la contribution aux objectifs environnementaux et climatiques de l'Union européenne, en particulier ses engagements dans le cadre de l'Accord de Paris. L'agriculteur n'est plus seulement un producteur de denrées alimentaires, mais porte également une responsabilité environnementale importante. Ce double rôle entraîne des coûts de production plus élevés et une plus grande responsabilité.

La protection des exploitations et des producteurs agricoles est essentielle pour garantir la continuité de l'approvisionnement alimentaire et préserver les générations futures. Le concept de chaîne agroalimentaire durable, qui intègre les aspects économiques, sociaux et environnementaux, gagne en importance. Cependant, de nouveaux défis aux niveaux mondial, européen et national mettent en évidence les limites des instruments juridiques prévus dans le cadre de la PAC 2023-2027 pour protéger et améliorer suffisamment la situation des producteurs agricoles en Pologne, par exemple.

D'autre part, les règlements juridiques pour le financement de l'UE dans le cadre du plan stratégique de la PAC 2023-2027, en particulier ceux qui visent les investissements dans les sources d'énergie renouvelables (SER) dans les exploitations agricoles, constituent une évolution positive. L'un des principaux défis reste la réduction des coûts de production agricole, et les investissements dans les SER peuvent contribuer à la réalisation de cet objectif. La situation des producteurs agricoles peut encore être améliorée par des solutions innovantes, des avancées technologiques, la numérisation et la promotion de la coopération entre les producteurs agricoles, par exemple par la construction conjointe d'installations de biogaz.

Les activités liées à l'agriculture se développent à la fois dans les pays de l'UE et dans les pays tiers, englobant un large éventail de fonctions supplémentaires au-delà de l'agriculture traditionnelle. En Suisse, par exemple, ces activités comprennent l'agrotourisme, les services sociaux (green care), la sylviculture et les services environnementaux ou municipaux. En outre, l'agriculture offre un potentiel important pour la production d'énergie renouvelable, y compris l'utilisation des déchets organiques ainsi que de l'énergie solaire et éolienne. Toutefois, il convient de souligner que la production d'énergie ne doit pas se faire au détriment de la production alimentaire. Malgré les efforts des législateurs européens et des gouvernements nationaux, il subsiste un déséquilibre dans la chaîne d'approvisionnement alimentaire. Ce déséquilibre résulte de la disparité du pouvoir économique entre les agriculteurs et les transformateurs ou les détaillants.

B. Version anglaise – English version – Englische Version

Between the last CEDR Congress in Poznań in 2019 and the CEDR Congress in the UK in 2023, a number of new regulations were issued. These were related to Covid-19 and the war in Ukraine (these issues were primarily discussed in Commission I).

Commission III primarily dealt with agricultural legislation in European countries and the USA. Significant attention was dedicated to changes in the legislative framework of agricultural policy. Participants from EU Member States reported on the methods and legal bases for the implementation of CAP Strategic Plans in accordance with the basic legal instruments of the EU for the period 2023–2027. The United Kingdom developed its own agricultural policy following Brexit, while a new Farm Bill was being prepared in the USA. Other countries, such as Switzerland, also revised their legislation and agricultural policy during the period between the two congresses.

The country reports highlighted significant developments in national legislation concerning the definition of agricultural and other activities, the legal and tax status of agricultural producers, and access to ownership and use of agricultural land. Agricultural regulations are increasingly addressing social issues, including the equal status of women, the rights of agricultural workers, and generational renewal on farms. They also focus on environmental challenges, such as sustainable production methods, adaptation to climate change, conservation of biodiversity, water management, and the promotion of renewable energy sources.

Only careful drafting and monitoring of legal regulations can ensure the right balance between economic viability, social equity, and environmental requirements, ultimately fostering sustainable development.

There is no doubt that the adoption of new EU regulations for the Common Agricultural Policy (CAP) 2023–2027 and the issuance of corresponding national regulations were of critical importance. It should be noted that the CAP 2023–2027 increasingly emphasizes supporting and strengthening environmental protection, including biodiversity and climate action, and contributing to the European Union's environmental and climate objectives, particularly its commitments under the Paris Agreement. The farmer is no longer solely a food producer but also bears significant environmental responsibility. This dual role entails higher production costs and increased accountability.

Protecting farms and agricultural producers is vital for ensuring the continuity of food supply and safeguarding future generations. The concept of a sustainable agri-food chain, which integrates economic, social, and environmental aspects, is gaining importance. However, new challenges at the global, European, and national levels highlight the limitations of the legal instruments provided under the CAP 2023–2027 in sufficiently protecting and improving the situation of agricultural producers in Poland, for example.

On the other hand, the legal regulations for EU funding under the CAP Strategic Plan 2023–2027, particularly those aimed at on-farm investments in renewable energy sources (RES), are a positive development. One key challenge remains reducing the cost of agricultural production, and investments in RES have the potential to contribute to this objective. The situation of agricultural producers can be further improved through innovative solutions, technological advancements, digitalization, and fostering cooperation among agricultural producers, such as through the joint construction of biogas plants.

Farm-related activities are expanding in both EU and non-EU countries, encompassing a wide range of additional functions beyond traditional farming. In Switzerland, for instance, these activities include agrotourism, social services (green care), forestry, and environmental or municipal services. Moreover, agriculture holds significant potential for renewable energy production, including the utilization of organic waste as well as solar and wind energy. However, it should be emphasized that energy production must not come at the expense of food production. Despite efforts by both EU legislators and national governments, there remains an imbalance in the food supply chain. This imbalance arises from the disparity in economic power between farmers and processors or retailers.

C. Version allemande – German version – Deutsche Version

Zwischen dem letzten CEDR-Kongress in Poznań im Jahr 2019 und dem CEDR-Kongress im Vereinigten Königreich im Jahr 2023 wurde eine Reihe neuer Verordnungen erlassen. Diese stehen im Zusammenhang mit Covid-19 und dem Krieg in der Ukraine (diese Themen wurden hauptsächlich in der Kommission I diskutiert).

Der Ausschuss III befasste sich hauptsächlich mit der Agrargesetzgebung in den europäischen Ländern und den USA. Große Aufmerksamkeit wurde den Änderungen des rechtlichen Rahmens der Agrarpolitik gewidmet. Die Teilnehmer aus den EU-Mitgliedstaaten berichteten über die Methoden und Rechtsgrundlagen für die Umsetzung der GAP-Strategiepläne im Einklang mit den grundlegenden Rechtsinstrumenten der EU für den Zeitraum 2023-2027. Das Vereinigte Königreich entwickelte seine eigene Agrarpolitik nach dem Brexit, während in den USA eine neue Farm Bill vorbereitet wurde. Andere Länder, wie die Schweiz, überarbeiteten in der Zeit zwischen den beiden Kongressen ebenfalls ihre Gesetzgebung und Agrarpolitik.

In den Länderberichten wurde auf wichtige Entwicklungen in der nationalen Gesetzgebung hingewiesen, die die Definition von landwirtschaftlichen und anderen Tätigkeiten, den rechtlichen und steuerlichen Status von landwirtschaftlichen Erzeugern sowie den Zugang zu Eigentum und Nutzung von landwirtschaftlichen Flächen betreffen. In den landwirtschaftlichen Vorschriften werden zunehmend soziale Fragen behandelt, darunter die Gleichstellung von Frauen, die Rechte von Landarbeitern und die Erneuerung der Generationen in den Betrieben. Sie konzentrieren sich auch auf ökologische Herausforderungen wie nachhaltige Produktionsmethoden, Anpassung an den Klimawandel, Erhaltung der biologischen Vielfalt, Wassermanagement und die Förderung erneuerbarer Energiequellen.

Nur eine sorgfältige Ausarbeitung und Überwachung von Rechtsvorschriften kann das richtige Gleichgewicht zwischen wirtschaftlicher Rentabilität, sozialer Gerechtigkeit und Umweltanforderungen gewährleisten und letztlich eine nachhaltige Entwicklung fördern.

Es besteht kein Zweifel, dass die Verabschiedung der neuen EU-Verordnungen für die Gemeinsame Agrarpolitik (GAP) 2023-2027 und der Erlass der entsprechenden nationalen Verordnungen von entscheidender Bedeutung waren. Es ist anzumerken, dass die GAP 2023-2027 zunehmend den Schwerpunkt auf die Unterstützung und Stärkung des Umweltschutzes, einschließlich der biologischen Vielfalt und des Klimaschutzes, legt und einen Beitrag zu den Umwelt- und Klimazielen der Europäischen Union leistet, insbesondere zu ihren Verpflichtungen im Rahmen des Pariser Abkommens. Der Landwirt ist nicht mehr nur Lebensmittelproduzent, sondern trägt auch eine große Verantwortung für die Umwelt. Diese Doppelrolle bringt höhere Produktionskosten und eine größere Verantwortung mit sich.

Der Schutz der landwirtschaftlichen Betriebe und der landwirtschaftlichen Erzeuger ist von entscheidender Bedeutung für die Kontinuität der Lebensmittelversorgung und den Schutz künftiger Generationen. Das Konzept einer nachhaltigen Agrar- und Lebensmittelkette, das wirtschaftliche, soziale und ökologische Aspekte integriert, gewinnt zunehmend an Bedeutung. Neue Herausforderungen auf globaler, europäischer und nationaler Ebene machen jedoch deutlich, dass die im Rahmen der GAP 2023-2027 vorgesehenen Rechtsinstrumente nicht ausreichen, um die Situation der landwirtschaftlichen Erzeuger beispielsweise in Polen ausreichend zu schützen und zu verbessern.

Andererseits sind die gesetzlichen Regelungen für die EU-Finanzierung im Rahmen des GAP-Strategieplans 2023-2027, insbesondere die für Investitionen in erneuerbare Energiequellen (EE) in landwirtschaftlichen Betrieben, eine positive Entwicklung. Eine zentrale Herausforderung ist nach wie vor die Senkung der Kosten für die landwirtschaftliche Produktion, und Investitionen in erneuerbare Energien haben das Potenzial, zu diesem Ziel beizutragen. Die Situation der landwirtschaftlichen Erzeuger kann durch innovative Lösungen, technologische Fortschritte, Digitalisierung und die Förderung der Zusammenarbeit zwischen landwirtschaftlichen Erzeugern, z.B. durch den gemeinsamen Bau von Biogasanlagen, weiter verbessert werden.

Sowohl in den EU- als auch in den Nicht-EU-Ländern nehmen die mit der Landwirtschaft verbundenen Tätigkeiten zu und umfassen ein breites Spektrum an zusätzlichen Funktionen, die über die traditionelle Landwirtschaft hinausgehen. In der Schweiz beispielsweise umfassen diese Aktivitäten Agrotourismus, soziale Dienstleistungen (Green Care), Forstwirtschaft und Umwelt- oder kommunale Dienstleistungen. Darüber hinaus birgt die Landwirtschaft ein erhebliches Potenzial für die Erzeugung erneuerbarer Energien, einschließlich der Nutzung von organischen Abfällen sowie von Sonnen- und Windenergie. Es sollte jedoch betont werden, dass die Energieerzeugung nicht auf Kosten der Nahrungsmittelproduktion gehen darf. Trotz der Bemühungen sowohl der EU-Gesetzgeber als auch der nationalen Regierungen besteht nach wie vor ein Ungleichgewicht in der Lebensmittelversorgungskette. Dieses Ungleichgewicht ergibt sich aus dem wirtschaftlichen Machtgefälle zwischen Landwirten und Verarbeitern oder Einzelhändlern.

V.
Colloque - Colloquium - Kolloquium

“Public money for public goods” as a model for supporting agriculture?

Proceedings

Introduction

As part of the XXXI European Agricultural Law Congress of the Comité Européen de Droit Rural (CEDR), which took place from 6 to 9 September 2023 in Cardiff, United Kingdom, a colloquium was held on the topic of "*Public money for public goods*". As part of the XXX. European Agricultural Law Congress in 2019, the CEDR revived the colloquium format, which had not been used for a long time, with an event on the latest CAP reform. The colloquium, which took place on 8 September 2023 from 16:00 to 18:15 h, followed on from the deliberations of the three commissions and provided an opportunity to discuss a specific topic in detail.

The chosen topic lent itself for two reasons. Firstly, the organisation of the next CAP funding period is already being discussed. Secondly, in connection with Brexit, the United Kingdom has announced that it no longer wishes to align its agricultural policy with the CAP, but with the guiding principle of "*public money for public goods*". The reorganisation of agricultural policy in the UK has not yet been completed. In terms of competences, it is primarily the responsibility of the four "*devolved nations*", i.e. England, Northern Ireland, Scotland and Wales. Four different agricultural policies will therefore apply in future. While England and Wales have already passed the relevant legislation, it is still in preparation in Northern Ireland and Scotland. Scotland wants to keep it as close as possible to the CAP in order to be prepared for potential accession to the EU.

The United Kingdom therefore currently offers concise illustrative material on the meaningfulness and practicability of the concept of "*public money for public goods*". It can already be seen that, contrary to what was originally announced, the concept is not being applied in its pure form. After introductory remarks, the colloquium first focused on the situation in the United Kingdom (overview; England; Wales; Scotland; Northern Ireland) in five short presentations, followed by two short presentations on the situation in the EU (EU; Netherlands). There was also time for discussion. At the end there were brief conclusions.

The colloquium was jointly prepared and chaired by Dr. Christian Busse, Prof. Dr. Rudolf Mögele and Dr. Ludivine Petetin, Cardiff University, who also played a key role in organising the entire congress. The colloquium was held exclusively in English, which is why it is only included in English in these conference proceedings. The short presentations on Wales, Scotland and Northern Ireland were not submitted for the conference proceedings and could therefore unfortunately not be reproduced. Some of the short presentations that have been included have been expanded and supplemented with footnotes, but without substantially altering the content. The contributions exclusively reflect the personal views of the authors involved. The three short presentations by the organisers and the joint conclusions have been pre-printed in the journal "Agrar- und Umweltrecht" (AUR), the organ of the German Society for Agricultural Law, in agreement with the CEDR (AUR 2024, 2-10). The explanatory introduction by Busse, which has been slightly adapted here, can also be found there.

A. Opening remarks

Roland Norer

For the second time since 2019, the new colloquium format will be held at a CEDR congress. As a congress within a congress, as it were, it offers the opportunity to address a current topic in plenary session. The aim is to focus on a strategic point of view that takes us beyond day-to-day business and opens up new perspectives.

This time, the topic "Public money for public goods" more than fulfils this requirement. A new Common Agricultural Policy is just around the corner and, since Brexit, the United Kingdom has had to develop and implement a national agricultural policy in all of its nations, which should provide exciting insights, comparisons and discussions.

I would like to sincerely thank Christian Busse, Rudolf Mögele and Ludivine Petetin for organising and preparing this colloquium. My thanks also go to all the other contributors: Michael Cardwell (England), Victoria Jones (Wales), Peter Hall (Scotland), James McCluggage (Northern Ireland) and especially Jeroen Rheinfeld for the perspective of a member state.

To be continued!

B. Preliminary reflections

Christian Busse

This is the second edition of the revived Colloquium format. After some decades of absence, the format was filled with life again at our latest congress 2019 in Poland. We are very grateful to Roman Budzinowski, host of the congress in Poznań, that he supported the revival of the Colloquium idea right up from the beginning. In Poznań, the Colloquium was dedicated to the latest reform of the Common Agricultural Policy of the European Union (CAP), at that time in the midterm of negotiations in Brussels.[1] And, of course, in 2019, the United Kingdom (UK) was still a member of the European Union (EU), struggling with the Brexit negotiations. Nowadays, Brexit is reality, and the reform of the CAP has entered into force at the beginning of this year.

In the last months, first signs of the next reform of the CAP, covering the period from 2028 to 2034, have been flagged. Hence, it seems to be the right moment to look at concepts for the upcoming reform, thereby taking into account the thoughts and experiences of States outside the EU. One important concept discussed is the notion of "public money for public goods". To be realized or not to be realized, that is the question with this concept, and hopefully, our Colloquium helps us to find some answers.

As incentive and, at the same time, framework for our Colloquium, I would like to present some preliminary reflections on the concept "public money for public goods". That concept is not limited to agriculture, because it may apply to all situations, in which public money is spent. But in latest times, it has developed into a catchphrase especially used in agricultural policies.

At the beginning of my reflections, I do not want to hide, that I am skeptical regarding the one-to-one transfer of the concept to the agricultural sphere. To explain this skepticism, I would like to look closer into the elements of the concept. There is no need to discuss here the term "public money", although in some cases, it might be doubtful, if financial means

---

1 Cf. for the proceedings of that Colloquium: CEDR (ed.), Food sovereignty, food security and the contribution of agricultural law – XXX European Congress and Colloquium of Rural Law, Poznań, 18-21 September 2019 (2023), pp. 375-430.

are public or private money. That belongs to the sphere of state aid law, which should not bother us at our Colloquium. Generally speaking, all money spent either directly or indirectly by the state may be judged as public money, mostly raised in the way of taxes from citizens and private undertakings.

I. "Public goods" versus "public interest"

If we look at "public goods" as the second element of the concept, the difficulties of how to define them are well known. Within the concept, "goods" are not to be understood in a verbatim way as something, which is physical and can be traded, but in a more metaphoric sense. To pick up a wide-spread definition, a "public good" has to be non-excludable and non-rivalrous. Everybody should have access to it and may use it. It exists to such an extent, that no rival comes up. Such "public goods" are rare, and therefore called "pure public goods". For example, the air or free public broadcast are such "pure public goods", but not drinking water, because access can be limited and rival situations may arise. Hence, a second category has been created, named "impure public goods". Examples are a public road or a nature reserve area, which can only be entered after paying a fee.

It is obvious that, from this angle, "public goods" may differ from country to country. In some countries, public broadcast is free of charge, in others, a basic fee has to be paid to finance the broadcasting companies. Often, the access to a beach is open to everybody, but in some countries, the beach is private property.

In my mind, the term "public goods", as part of the catchphrase used in agricultural policies, does not match entirely the described general definition of 'public goods'. The reason is, that identifying which "goods" fulfill the given definition runs into a range of problems. Either, some important aspects of, especially, environmental protection will fall out of the concept, or the "public goods" remain so vague, that they are of no use for the implementation in agricultural policy. For illustration, an intact environment can be judged as a "public good", but, with-out concretization, it seems not suitable for justifying a certain subsidy. Also, it is not clear, if only existing "public goods" are meant, or also "public goods" which have to be achieved first. For example, the access to clean drinking water is, even in Europe, not in all countries guaran-teed. In addition, there exists different levels of "public goods", to name local, national, European and worldwide "public goods".

Looking at these difficulties the notion "public goods" seems for me to be, in our context, rather a synonym for "public interest". For each cent spent by the state in the agricultural sector, the beneficiary should provide action that serves the public interest. That matches the overall principle in democracies that public funds have to be used in the public interest. In Germany, we know the term "Gemeinwohlleistungen", which may be translated as "performance which benefit the public interest".[2]

II. Four aspects of detail

Leaving that general level of discussion, I would like to highlight four aspects of detail which fit the notion 'public goods' as well as the notion "public interest". At first, purely private interests are excluded. Consequently, a connection between the used public funds and a certain public interest has to exist to prove that not only private interests are at stake. Of course, in many cases, the public interest cannot be separated from a private interest. If, for example, public money is spent to prevent the pollution of a creek by pesticides, and the beneficiary intends to use the then cleaner water of the creek to wash his cultivated fruits, both interest spheres are involved. On a case-by-case basis, it may be judged, which interest prevails. But often, that is too laborious. Hence, it seems more useful to exclude only categories of situations in which the private interests clearly dominate. As conclusion, private interests may be generally involved.

At second, all relevant aspects of public interest have to be evaluated in order to determine a corresponding amount of money. In quite some cases, the concrete value of the contribution of the beneficiary for the public

2 As striking parallel, it may be hinted to the long-lasting debate in which way aspects of public interest should be taken into account in competition law, especially in cartel law; cf. as important milestone in Germany *P. Kirchhof* (ed.), Gemeinwohl and Wettbewerb (2005). As agricultural law, competition law follows certain principles and ideas. In its center is the free competition as guarantor for public welfare, and in particular consumer welfare. For some years, it has been intensively discussed, how sustainability can be integrated into that concept. On a smaller scale, EU agricultural law is a pioneer of such integration, as, in December 2021, Article 210a Regulation (EU) No 1308/2013 (CMO Regulation – CMO) entered into force, allowing sustainability initiatives to form a cartel, agreeing, inter alia, on prices and margins; cf. in detail the upcoming commentary on Article 210a CMO of *C. Busse*, in: C. *Busse/A. Gayk* (ed.), Law on the agricultural organisations and the food supply chain, which also takes into account the – until now limited – legal literature in Germany on Article 210a CMO.

interest is not measurable, for example, the value of abstaining from certain pesticides on twenty hectares to improve the population of bees. Therefore, the additional costs for the beneficiary are usually the benchmark[3]. In my example, that would be the costs for alternative pesticides. Or, if no other pesticides are used or the alternative pesticides are less effective, it may be the deficit in the production, as well as expenses for changing the production method. Reduced costs for pesticides, and for storage and bringing out of pesticides, have to be subtracted.

At third, it has to be decided, if measures can be financed, which are taken to follow mandatory law. The first reaction is often to deny such a possibility, although the observance of, for example, the prohibition of the use of certain pesticides contributes to the public interest of protecting the environment. But sometimes, it might be useful to finance such measures, especially, when restrictions are newly introduced. Under certain circumstances, it can be even legally unavoidable to give financial help, because, otherwise, property rights or the principle of legitimate interests may be infringed.

At fourth, normally, the burden of proof, that public funds are used for activities in the public interest is vested with the beneficiaries. That follows the normal path that the correct spending of public money has to be proved and verified. Regarding the achievement of the public interest, it is important to note, that, again, for the single subsidy, it has often to be referred to the concrete action taken, and not to the benefit for the public interest in general. Hence, whether, in my example, the population of bees has been improved, is no part of the verification process of the correct use of the single subsidy. The beneficiary has only to show, that he or she has not applied the pesticides in question. The benefit for the public interest is then to be looked at as part of the evaluation of the whole scheme. Of course, there exist exceptions, in which a concrete result is part of the single payment. As example, I would like to mention the re-opening of a lost creek

3 In any case, an economic equivalent has to be determined, thereby usually creating a market value. This fact implies that to exclude per se actions which have a market value, seems to be a questionable approach (for such an approach cf.: Welsh Parliament/Senedd Research, Sustainable Farming Scheme – Research Briefing [August 2022], p. 2: "[A]s food has a market value it should not be classed as a public good, and so should not be directly funded by the state"; at the same time, p. 2, "sustainable food production" is classified as a public good, thereby implying, that sustainable-produced food has no special market value, which contradicts, e.g., the existing market for organic food).

to improve water supply or the elimination of a pollution source like an old diesel aggregate.

III. How to select the aspects of public interest

After these four aspects of detail – the private interest problem, the calculation problem, the mandatory law problem and the verification problem –, I would like to mention as last point the most crucial and controversial one: how to select the aspects of public interest, which ought to be supported by public means. That, basically, remains a question of political choice, influenced, inter alia, by scientific evidence, the scope of the public funds available, economic, social and legal aspects, and the public opinion. It may differ from country to country, or even from region to region.

The CAP contains in Article 39 TFEU a set of goals, which, in my mind, all serve the public interest. That includes the goal "to ensure a fair standard of living for the agricultural community", which is closely connected to the goal "to ensure that supplies reach the consumers to reasonable prices". If there exists no appropriate income, farmers will, as we have seen in the past, give up. That may endanger the food supply in the given country. The agricultural products and food in question then will be imported. In the light of environmental protection, such imports contradict the necessity to shorten transport by processing and consuming local products. In addition, farmers, who struggle for their living, will have less energy and possibilities to support the protection of the environment. Also, in many rural areas, the farms are the backbone of the local communities. Hence, the vanishing of farms endangers the social life in question. Nowadays, it is acknowledged that the goal of sustainability is to be split into three dimensions: environmental, social and economic. These three dimensions have to go hand in hand.[4]

Taken that perspective, the instrument of a basic support for farmers is not as outdated as it is quite often stated[5]. The key point seems to be the creation of a concrete link between the need for basic support and the sub-

---

4 Cf. the grim – and sarcastic un-ecological – remark of *R. Norer* in his synthesis report of the Poznań Congress in: CEDR (fn. 1), p. 474: '[T]he core aim is to kill what feels like 7 x 1000 flies at one stroke with rules on sustainable land management, from the ecological to the eco-nomic to the social dimension.'

5 Cf. already as part of the findings of the Poznań Colloquium C. Busse, Conclusion, in: CEDR (fn. 1), p. 429.

sidy. In comparison with schemes which intend to generally provide basic support for each and every farmer, the state has to identify the agricultural sectors which are not capable to satisfy the public interest at stake by their own means. Regarding food security, for example, governments then would have to analyze which sectors either do not produce enough to meet the basic demand of the population, or will, without public support, reduce the production needed. A parallel approach might be taken to keep rural areas or disadvantaged regions alive. That is, of course, not an easy undertaking. On the whole, the implementation of the concept "public money for public goods" seems tending to be quite complex.

IV. A more holistic approach

Despite that, the concept might help to develop a more holistic approach, bringing together all three dimensions of sustainability and, in addition, other public interest at stake. One could draw the picture of a farming system, which provides for the basic needs of the population, using as much as possible environmental friendly production methods, contributes to other aspects of public interest such as sustainable energy production, and helps to maintain the social structure in rural areas. Therefore, the farming system has to be resilient against economic, environmental and social ruptures. To invest the public means for agriculture in such a sense is a huge, but important task.

To summarize my thoughts, the notion of "public money for public goods" is by far not self-explanatory. It is covered by quite some terminological fog. I propose to read "public goods" in the context of agricultural policy as "public interest", because the acknowledged general definition of "public goods" seems not to fit all the goals which should be achieved in the context of agricultural policy. The main task is to identify a range of objectives, subsidies in the agricultural sector should be aiming at. As we are living more and more in a world of crisis, resilience seems to be of overall importance. For each subsidy, one or more concrete aspects of public interest ought to be determined, and the result of the subsidized measure should be verified. The latest reform of the CAP already took up that idea to a certain extent, looking at now primarily outputs of the subsidy schemes.

I am now happy to learn more from our respected colleagues about the situation in the UK and in particular in the four nations of the UK. Ludivine Petetin from Cardiff University will introduce and moderate this first part of our Colloquium. She has published together with Mary Dobbs last year the extensive book "Brexit and Agriculture", which gives a profound analysis of the attempt to rebuild agriculture after Brexit with the help of the notion of "public money for public goods".[6] Hence, the first part of the Colloquium will present a country-wide living experiment. The second part of the Colloquium deals with the situation in the EU. That part is guided by Rudi Mögele, our well-known expert and insider with European agricultural policies. I sincerely hope that, in the seaside town of Cardiff, we are able to lift the fog at least to some extent.

6 *L. Petetin/M. Dobbs*, Brexit and Agriculture, 2022. These preliminary reflections owe that study helpful impetus, especially regarding the aspect of resilience, which constantly runs through the monograph. To note just one point, the British Agricultural Act of 2020 does not mention the notion "public money for public goods" at all (in the study shortly noted, p. 183: 'not expressly stated as such'). The ten "purposes" listed in Part 1 Chapter 1(1)(1) for giving "financial assistance" to English farmers cannot each be attributed directly to a certain concrete "public good", e.g. litera (d), which talks of "mitigating or adapting to climate change". In addition, Part 1 Chapter 1(1)(2)(a) foresees "financial assistance" for "starting, or improving the productivity of, an agricultural ... activity", which reminds of Article 39(1)(a) TFEU. The study indicates that in the other three devolved nations similar considerations exist (Wales, p. 84: "a stable income for farmers"; Northern Ireland, p. 88: "increased productivity"; Scotland, p. 95: "productivity"), final decisions at that time pending. Whether, p. 126, the "economic viability of farms" could be judged as a "public good", is not clearly stated in the study. It mentions, p. 127, that goal besides "public goods", and remarks: "suitable for public support". Furthermore, the study raises the difficult question, pp. 103-108, how the concept of "public money for public goods" fits into the three WTO boxes. The definition of "public goods" seems to be, again, crucial.

C. The concept across the United Kingdom

Ludivine Petetin

Following such interesting remarks on the concept of "public money for public goods", I will take a look at the outline of the concept underlying the new agricultural policies across the UK.

When thinking about "public money for public goods", it is important to remember that agriculture generates both negative and positive environmental and social externalities: it can cause environmental damage (e.g. water pollution, soil erosion); conversely, it can help to maintain environmental and/or social assets (e.g. pollination, rural vitality). In economic terms, these externalities are often poorly assessed and accounted for – making it difficult for governments to design policies[1]. The application of the theory of "public goods" to the agricultural sector provides a more recent source of legitimacy for public intervention due to the environmental and social benefits that farmers can create[2]. For example, in the UK, the concept public money for "public goods" first underpinned a 2005 policy document to reform the CAP[3]. For the purpose of this Colloquium, with "public goods" we are focusing on the positive externalities of agriculture.

In terms of terminology, I agree with Christian Busse that there are other, better terms to de-scribe "public goods". It is key to mention that "public goods" are not constrained to goods but can include services, described around attributes of 'publicness'[4]. To this extent, the term "public good"

1 *J. M. Harris/B. Roach*, Environmental and Natural Resource Economics: A Contemporary Approach, 2017.

2 For more see: *I. Hodge*, Agri-environment Policy in an Era of Lower Government Expenditure: CAP Reform and Conservation Payments, Journal of Environmental Planning and Management 56 (2013), p. 254; *M. Lefebvre et al.*, Agricultural Landscapes as Multi-scale Public Good and the Role of the Common Agricultural Policy, Journal of Environmental Planning and Management 58 (2015), p. 2088.

3 HM Treasury/DEFRA, A Vision for the Common Agricultural Policy, December 2005.

4 *T. Cooper/K. Hart/D. Baldock*, Provision of Public Goods through Agriculture in the European Union, Institute for European Environmental Policy, Report Prepared for DG Agriculture and Rural Development, Contract No 30-CE-0233091/00-28, 2009, p. VI.

means that actions are taken for the common good or in the public interest, i.e. the collective or institutional choices.

Another term that would be more suitable in agricultural policy is social-ecological services. Social-ecological services can be defined as the "non-material benefits obtained from ecosystems through spiritual enrichment, cognitive development, reflection, aesthetic experience and include things like social relations, aesthetic values and human well-being"[5]. The term highlights the relationship between humans and ecosystems and a move towards a more suitable holistic, resilient framework assessing human and social interactions with the environment[6]. Social-ecological services bring an additional dimension that reflects a more accurate picture of farming activities that moves beyond environmental economic resources and the production of food, fuel and fibre by combining social and biophysical aspects alongside the wellbeing of citizens strengthening the resilience of agriculture.

Now, I am going to consider briefly the constitutional framework of the UK as this plays a crucial role in understanding the development of agricultural policies. So for those of you less familiar with the UK constitutional structure, the UK is constituted of four nations: England, Wales, Scotland and Northern Ireland and each have their own powers or competences to develop their own policies and regulate agriculture accordingly (for as long as it does not interfere with reserved or central powers such as trade)[7]. This process is called devolution and mostly started in 1998 when the UK was an EU Member. When leaving the EU, the four UK nations left the policies and regulatory frameworks of the EU and had to create their own ways of functioning together without the umbrella of the EU or the CAP. This repatriation of power has been rather complicated and resulted in important tensions between the three de-volved nations of Wales, Scotland and Northern Ireland and the central UK Government[8].

5 *J. Dwyer et al.*, Public Goods and Ecosystem Services from Agriculture and Forestry – A Conceptual Approach, 2015, p. 11; see also *T. Plieninger/C. Bieling* (ed.), Resilience and the Cultural Landscape: Understanding and Managing Change in Human-shaped Environments, 2012.

6 *L. Petetin/M. Dobbs* (Chapter B. fn. 6), p. 111.

7 See the Devolved Settlements, which include the Northern Ireland Act 1998, the Scotland Act 1998 and the Government of Wales Acts 1998 and 2006.

8 *V. Gravey/L. Petetin/M. Dobbs*, Quitter la PAC, Comment et Pour Quoi Faire ? La (Re)Construction des Politiques Agricoles Britanniques au Cœur des Turbulences du Brexit, Politique Européenne 73 (2021), p. 150; J. Hunt, Subsidiarity, Competence and the UK Territorial Constitution, in: *O. Doyle/A. McHarg/J. Murkens* (ed.), The Brexit

All four nations are now developing their own and theoretically separate policies with the idea of simplifying[9] their future systems and breaking away from the CAP's red tape, complexity and regulatory burdens (rhetoric which played a huge role in the Brexit referendum campaign)[10].

In early iterations of the policies, the main objective was for farmers to be financially supported by "public money" only if they deliver "public goods" – bringing an end to payments directly supporting farmers' income – a central plank of the CAP. The emphasis was on payments by outcomes or results with the goal of strengthening agri-environment schemes as they exist-ed under the previous CAP reform. The level of direct payments given to farmers would gradually diminish to fund new schemes mainly based on "public money for public goods" away from the CAP. Another aim was not to pay farmers to fulfil the minimal regulatory (especially environmental) baseline but to go beyond it in order to apply the polluter pays principle.

Across the UK, there exist visions for agricultural policy: a "Green Brexit" for England and the UK[11]; "Sustainable Land Management" for Wales[12]; "Sustainable and Regenerative Farming" for Scotland[13]; and "Environmental Sustainability" for Northern Ireland[14] . And two acts are now in place: for England the Agriculture Act 2020 and the Agriculture (Wales) Act 2023. Agricultural transition periods are under way across the four nations with

Challenge for Ireland and the United Kingdom Constitutions Under Pressure, 2021; *L. Petetin*, Setting the Path for UK and Devolved Agriculture, p. 40, in: *I. Antonopoulos/A. Čavoški/M. Bell/L. Petetin*, The Governance of Agriculture in Post-Brexit UK, 2022, p. 40 et seq.

9 *DEFRA*, Farm Inspection and Regulation Review, 2018 (available on: https://www.gov.uk/government/publications/farm-inspection-and-regulation-review).

10 *I. Antonopoulos/A. Čavoški, M. Bell/L. Petetin* (fn. 14); *L. Petetin/V. Gravey/B. Moore*, Setting the Bar for a Green Brexit in Food and Farming, 2019.

11 *M. Gove*, Green Brexit: A New Era for Farming, Fishing and the Environment, 2018 (available on: https://www.gov.uk/government/speeches/green-brexit-a-new-era-for-farming-fishing-and-the-environment).

12 The Agriculture (Wales) Act 2023.

13 Scottish Government, The Next Step in Delivering our Vision for Scotland as a Leader in Sustainable and Regenerative Farming, 2022 (available on: https://www.gov.scot/publications/next-step-delivering-vision-scotland-leader-sustainable-regenerative-farming/documents/).

14 DAERA, Northern Ireland Future Agricultural Policy Framework: Stakeholder Engagement, 2018 (available on: https://www.daera-ni.gov.uk/sites/default/files/consultations/daera/NI%20Future%20Agricultural%20Policy%20Framework%20-%20Stakeholder%20Engagement%20-%20FINAL_0.pdf); *M. Dobbs*, Northern Ireland's Agricultural Quagmire: How to Develop a Sustainable Agricultural Policy?, in: I. Antonopoulos, *A. Čavoški/M. Bell/L. Petetin* (fn. 14), p. 177 et. seq.

testing and pilot schemes already taking place or about to start. They are aimed at giving time to farmers to adapt to the emerging mechanisms and structures.

However, in England the diversity of schemes available provides farmers with small pots of funds, which means that farmers have to keep abreast of the numerous requirements and the various deadlines for each scheme. This new approach complicates the system for farmers to receive financial support.

In practice these new policies tend to generally do more of the same (in comparison to what existed under the CAP before EU exit) and not effectively aiming at public money for "public goods" in various ways:

1. Focus mostly on economic aspects, especially economic resilience;
2. Narrow definitions of the environment;
3. Very little emphasis on social aspects (apart from Scotland with rural development);
4. A "return" to payments for actions, i.e. 'does and don'ts' rather than payments for out-comes. For example, with England's main scheme Sustainable Farming Incentive[15] and the Sustainable Farming Scheme in Wales[16];
5. Scotland and Northern Ireland keep some direct payments;
6. When looking at the requirements of the Sustainable Farming Incentive in England and the Sustainable Farming Scheme in Wales, the existing requirements are very similar to the existing regulatory baselines, thereby not raising the bar; and,
7. There is little in the policies on regenerative farming (apart from Scotland) or achieving net zero.

Why this U-turn? As Christian Busse mentioned, measuring and assessing "public goods" is problematic. This matter has become a key issue and led the four governments to effectively back track on the initial push for "public money for public goods".[17] Further, payments by results-based schemes can be quite technical and intricate to negotiate and often demand high set-up costs (both for the farmer and responsible agencies).[18] Another reason

15 DEFRA, Sustainable Farming Incentive Guidance, 2023 (available on: https://www.gov.uk/government/collections/sustainable-farming-incentive-guidance).
16 Welsh Government, Sustainable Farming Scheme, 2023 (available on: https://www.gov.wales/sustainable-farming-scheme-guide).
17 *L. Petetin/M. Dobbs* (Chapter B. fn. 6), p. 259.
18 *L. Petetin/M. Dobbs* (Chapter B. fn. 6), p. 131.

is that not sup-porting farmers for their actions could lead to negative consequences for the environment, the wider countryside and rural communities.

Therefore, the visions discussed straight after EU exit were rather innovative but, due to the various hurdles mentioned above, the implementation and practice of newly established schemes are not forward looking enough and generally lack ambition. I will now turn to the situation across the four nations starting in England with Professor Michael Cardwell, then Wales with Victoria Jones, followed by Scotland with Peter Hall and last but not least Northern Ireland with James McCluggage.

D. England

Michael Cardwell

In England, Brexit was seen as offering an opportunity to put into practice a move away from direct payments, with the new agricultural policy instead "to be underpinned by payment of public money for the provision of public goods"[1]. And Michael Gove, the Environment Secretary and an enthusiastic supporter of this model[2], was clear that the most important "public good" was "environmental protection and enhancement"[3]. To ensure robustness of implementation, it was also proposed that there should be a "clear distinction, and coherent relationship, between the basic requirements farmers are obliged to meet by law, and scheme standards where they are paid to go beyond this minimum"[4], with the aim of ensuring that the public received value for their financial commitment.

Particular attention may be directed to two aspects. First, there continues in England (and elsewhere) to be debate as to what constitutes a "public good", with specific reference to food production and food security following the global pandemic and Ukraine War. And, secondly, as already observed by Ludivine Petetin, concerns have been expressed as to the extent that ongoing revisions to the proposed support regime has seen a

1 DEFRA, Health and Harmony: the Future for Food, Farming and the Environment in a Green Brexit (Health and Harmony), February 2018, Cm 9577, p. 32; see also, for example, *M. Cardwell/F. Smith*, 'Charting a new course for the United Kingdom agri-food sector – Health and Harmony: The Future for Food, Farming and the Environment in a Green Brexit', (2018) 89(3) Political Quarterly 497.

2 See generally, for example, *H. Kam/H. Smith/C. Potter*, 'Public money for public goods: the role of ideas in driving agriculture policy in the EU and post-Brexit UK', (2023) 129 Land Use Policy 106618.

3 *M. Gove*, 'A Brighter Future for Farming', 20.2.2018 (available at: https://www.gov.uk/government/speeches/a-brighter-future-for-farming).

4 DEFRA, The Path to Sustainable Farming: An Agricultural Transition Plan 2021 to 2024 (The Path to Sustainable Farming), November 2020, p. 15 (available at: https://assets.publishing.service.gov.uk/government/uploads/system/uploads/attachment_data/file/954283/agricultural-transition-plan.pdf).

retreat from the "public goods" model, notwithstanding assurance form Government that "we remain as ambitious as ever"[5].

I. What constitutes a "public good" for the purposes of agriculture in England?

As indicated, in England there has been steady focus on the 'public good' of environmental protection and enhancement, arguably reflecting the strength of environmental non-governmental organisations[6]; and, importantly, it features prominently in the list of practices which may benefit from financial assistance under the Agriculture Act 2020[7]. In particular, Section 1 provides that the Secretary of State may give such assistance for or in connection with, inter alia:

A. managing land or water in a way that protects or improves the environment;
B. supporting public access to and enjoyment of the countryside, farmland or woodland and better understanding of the environment;
C. managing land or water in a way that maintains, restores or enhances cultural or natural heritage;
D. managing land, water or livestock in a way that mitigates or adapts to climate change;
E. managing land or water in a way that prevents, reduces or protects from environmental hazards;
F. protecting or improving the health of plants;
G. conserving plants grown or used in carrying on an agricultural, horticultural or forestry activity, their wild relatives or genetic resources relating to any such plant;
H. protecting or improving the quality of soil.'

Financial assistance is not, however, confined to the arena of the environment: for example, under Section 1(f) it may also be given to "protecting or improving the health or welfare of livestock", which is likewise gener-

---

5 *T. Coffey*, 'Environment Secretary speech at CLA Business Conference', 1.12.2022 (available at: https://www.gov.uk/government/speeches/environment-secretary-speech-at-cla-business-conference).

6 *H. Kam/H. Smith/C. Potter* (fn. 2).

7 The financial assistance provisions in the Agriculture Act 2020 are applicable only in England: Section 1(3).

ally accepted to be a "public good"[8]. Moreover, under Section 1(2) the grant of financial assistance may further extend to starting or improving productivity of an agricultural, horticultural or forestry activity[9], not in itself generally accepted as a "public good": according to the analysis of Cooper/Hart/Baldock, "the case for public intervention in relation to food production per se is small".[10] That said, the position would seem less clear with regard to food security as more broadly construed, it being described by Cooper/Hart/Baldock as "an example of a public good with distinct private characteristics".[11]

And such debate as to whether food security does indeed qualify as a 'public good' has been reinvigorated in light of the pressure on food supply chains consequent upon the global pandemic and Ukraine War. Notably, the National Farmers' Union (NFU) has again advanced argument that, if the adopted approach is to be the payment of public money for public goods, then sustainable food production and environmental delivery should work in tandem.[12] While, however, the Agriculture Act 2020 does in this way provide support for productivity, no mention is made of financial assistance for matters of nutrition and public health[13] , an exclusion which has attracted considerable criticism. In the words of the non-governmental organisation Sustain, "recognition of public health as a public good could

8 For a comprehensive study of "public goods" in EU agriculture, see *T. Cooper/K. Hart/D. Baldock*, Provision of Public Goods Through Agriculture in the European Union, 2009.

9 See, for example, *L. Petetin/M. Dobbs* (Chapter B. fn. 6), pp. 8-80 and 122-127.

10 *T. Cooper/K. Hart/D. Baldock* (fn. 8), p. 15.

11 Ibid. See also A. Burrell, Evaluating Policies for Delivering Agri-environmental Public Goods, in: Evaluation of Agri-environmental Policies: Selected Methodological Issues and Case Studies, 2012, pp. 49-68.

12 See, for example, NFU, NFU Responds to Latest Environmental Land Management Announcement, 6.1.2022 (available at: https://www.nfuonline.com/media-centre/releases/nfu-responds-to-latest-environmental-land-management-announcement-1/); and, for earlier articulation, see, for example, NFU, Delivering a Bold and Ambitious Future for Farming: Domestic Agricultural Policy – a Framework for Success, October 2017.

13 It is, however, provided that the Secretary of State must at least once every three years prepare and lay before Parliament a report containing an analysis of statistical data relating to food security in the United Kingdom – and that this report may include data on, inter alia: household expenditure on food (including in comparison to expenditure on other items); and food safety and consumer confidence in food: Section 19.

help pave the way for beneficial improvements to farming standards, investment of public money and publicly supported research and development"[14].

II. Revisions to the payment regime

The flagship programme for the delivery of financial assistance to farmers in England is the Environmental Land Management Scheme, consistent with the focus on the "public good" of environmental protection and enhancement. When the initial payment regime was sketched out in February 2020, three "tiers" were proposed, with increasing levels of ambition.[15] And these three "tiers" were subsequently replaced by three "components", namely the Sustainable Farming Incentive, Local Nature Recovery and Landscape Recovery, with it being stated that "[f]rom 2024, we will introduce in full new schemes to reward farmers for producing public goods".[16] Importantly, the new approach would include greater focus on outcomes (as op-posed to payment for actions);[17] and there was also early affirmation that farmers would only be paid for exceeding a strong regulatory baseline, consistent with the polluter-pays principle.[18]

Later revisions to the proposed payment regime have arguably seen a retreat from the "public goods" model; and three such shifts may be highlighted. First, as noted, a greater focus on outcomes was understood to promote the delivery of "public goods",[19] but there is now evident an increasing return to payment for prescribed actions. While this is most apparent in the case of the Sustainable Farming Incentive,[20] it may also be mentioned that the second component of the Environmental Land

14 House of Commons Environment, Food and Rural Affairs Committee, The Future for Food, Farming and the Environment, Sixth Report of Session 2017-19, HC 870, para. 69; see also *L. Petetin/M. Dobbs* (Chapter B. fn. 6), p. 131 et seq.

15 DEFRA, Farming for the Future: Policy and Progress Update, February 2020, p. 10.

16 DEFRA (fn. 4), p. 11.

17 DEFRA (fn. 4), p. 31.

18 DEFRA (fn. 1), p. 50.

19 On results-based agri-environmental schemes generally, see, for example, *M. Cardwell*, Results-based agri-environmental scheme design: legal implications, Environmental Law Review, (2023) 25(4) 260.

20 DEFRA, Environmental Land Management Update: How Government will Pay for Land-based Environment and Climate Goods and Services, January 2023, p. 8 et seq. (available at: https://assets.publishing.service.gov.uk/government/uploads/system/uploads/attachment_data/file/1136855/Environmental-Land-Management-Update-January-2023-Accessible-Final.pdf).

Management Scheme, Local Nature Recovery, has been replaced by an enhanced Countryside Stewardship Scheme which will see expansion and refinement to include payment "for a wider range of targeted, specific actions at the right level of ambition to contribute to our environment and climate goals"[21]. Emphasis on outcomes would now therefore appear largely to be confined to the Landscape Recovery component, where the aim continues to be implementation of bespoke longer-term and larger-scale projects to enhance the natural environment (such as woodland planting and peatland restoration), these projects most naturally falling within the "public goods" model.

Secondly, as details have emerged of the prescribed actions to be undertaken to unlock payment under the Sustainable Farming Incentive, questions arise as to the extent that they exceed a strong regulatory baseline and "raise the bar". In particular, they are described by Government as "intended to be universal and straightforward for farmers to undertake in the course of their farming activities".[22] And, by way of illustration, standards for 2023 vary from establishing and maintaining legumes (under the nutrient management standard) and establishing and maintaining a 4m to 12m buffer strip on arable and horticultural land (under the arable and horticultural land standard). Against this background, concerns have developed that the Sustainable Farming Incentive is not so much a vehicle to deliver "public goods" as a source of funds to secure the financial viability of farmers as direct payments are phased out in England post-Brexit, it being noteworthy that the NFU has expressly stated that it must be "profitable".[23]

Thirdly, although it was originally envisaged that by 2028 there would an even allocation of funding across farm-level, locally tailored, and landscape-scale investment[24], the strong indications are now that the majority of expenditure will be devoted to the Sustainable Farming Incentive. Indeed,

21 DEFRA (fn. 20), p. 11.

22 DEFRA (fn. 20), p. 8.

23 *C. Marshall/M. Prior*, Government Review of ELMS Farming Subsidies Stokes Anger, BBC, 26.9.2022 (available at: https://www.bbc.com/news/science-environment-63029266). For the challenges faced by farmers consequent upon the removal of direct payments, see, for example, *D. Arnott et al*, Vulnerability of British farms to post-Brexit subsidy removal, and implications for intensification, extensification and land sparing, (2021) 107 Land Use Policy 104154.

24 DEFRA, Agricultural Transition Plan: June 2021 Progress Update (available at: https://www.gov.uk/government/publications/agricultural-transition-plan-june-2021-progress-update/agricultural-transition-plan-june-2021-progress-update).

the budget for Landscape Recovery is not projected to exceed £50 million over the three-year period from 2022. This may be compared with a total of £286 million spent on agri-environmental schemes in England in 2022[25] (although that sum would include, for example, Countryside Stewardship payments).[26] And it has also been pointed out by Aglionby as Chair of the Uplands Alliance, that the restoration target of 300,000 hectares of wildlife habitat by 2042 amounts to less than 3 per cent of the land mass of England.[27]

III. Conclusion

The "public goods" model has bulked large in the development of agricultural policy in England post-Brexit, promoted originally by an enthusiastic Environment Secretary and also throughout by environmental non-governmental organisations. Notwithstanding significant headwinds, the environment remains at the heart of financial assistance to farmers from Government, by virtue of the flagship Environmental Land Management Scheme. The strength of those headwinds has, however, arguably increased over recent years as the global pandemic and Ukraine War have put pressure on food supply chains, prompting demands for food security to be prioritised as a "public good". Further, the Sustainable Farming Incentive, with its focus on actions as opposed to outcomes, relatively light regulatory burden and expanding budget may increasingly be regarded as a "broad but shallow" measure, with at least as great an ability to transfer resources to farmers as to deliver "narrow but deep" dividends in the form of "public goods". That said, Landscape Recovery offers a pattern for long-term and large-scale projects which have the capacity to be transformational; and further encouragement may be derived from its evident popularity, there having been 51 applications for the 15 places available in its first round.[28]

---

25 DEFRA, How We're Making Sure All Farm Businesses can Fairly Access Money Released from Basic Payments, 6.6.2022 (available at https://defrafarming.blog.gov.uk/2022/06/06/how-were-making-sure-all-farm-businesses-can-fairly-access-money-released-from-basic-payments/).

26 DEFRA et al., Agriculture in the United Kingdom 2022, 2023, Table 10.2.

27 *J. Evans*, Farm Subsidy Reform in England Aiming to Return Land to Nature, Financial Times, 6.1.2022.

28 DEFRA, Landscape Recovery: Round Two, 18.5.2023 (available at: https://www.gov.uk/government/publications/landscape-recovery-more-information-on-how-the-scheme-will-work/landscape-recovery-round-2).

E. The concept across the European Union

Rudolf Mögele

In the discussions about further reform of the CAP, the slogan "public money for public goods" has become a widely used code for calling for the abolition of direct income support in its present form and its replacement with schemes that reward farmers for delivering environ-mental, climate and animal welfare services to society.[1] The purpose of these reflections is to examine a number of legal issues in EU and WTO law arising from the concept of "public goods".

I. What are "public goods"?

While the meaning of the term "public goods" may seem clear at first glance, it is worth examining it in more detail to avoid misunderstandings. In economics, "the main characteristics of public goods are non-excludability and non-rivalry. A good is public when if it is available to one person, others cannot be excluded from the benefits it confers (non-excludable); at the same time, if a public good is consumed by one person it does not reduce the amount available to others (non-rival)."[2] "Public goods" in this sense are e.g. a healthy environment, clean air and water, biodiversity, etc.

In the context of agricultural policy, the concept of "public goods" has gained ground over the last decade.[3] Here, it concerns goods and services of public interest, such as related to environment and climate, or food security. The specification of what is pursued by the CAP is being determined by the legislator. For the purposes of this analysis, it makes good sense to follow the policy-related interpretation according to which "public money for public goods" should be understood to mean that agricultural funds

1 *R. Mögele*, The Integration of Environmental and Climate Protection into the Common Agri-cultural Policy – Legal Concepts and Developments, EurUP 2018, p. 405 (414).

2 *F. Vanni*, Agriculture and Public Goods, 2013, p. 1.

3 *H. Kam/H. Smith/C. Potter* (fn. 26), p. 5; *C.S. Vogeler*, The integration of environmental objectives in the common agricultural policy – partisan politics in the European Parliament, Z Vgl Polit Wiss (2022), p. 551 (553).

should only be paid for the provision of goods and services that are in the public interest and which cannot be purchased individually on markets. This will also allow us to capture the debate in its entirety.

As an example, one could refer to Section 1 subsection (1) of the UK Agriculture Act 2020 which reflects the UK legislator's post-Brexit intention to reserve agricultural support to "public goods" provision.[4] According to this provision, "public goods" are i.a. about sound environment, accessible and enjoyable countryside, farmland or woodland or well-kept cultural or natural heritage. It is interesting to note that the UK Agriculture Act also caters for the improvement of productivity which is a rather traditional agricultural good.

Another option would be to refer to the eco-schemes which were introduced by the 2021 CAP reform, the logic of which follows the concept of "public money for public goods". The "goods" set out in Article 31(3) Regulation (EU) 2021/2115 resemble to a large extent those just quoted from the UK Agriculture Act: climate, clean water, good soil, biodiversity etc.

II. Would "public money for public goods" be a novelty under the CAP?

The answer is a clear "no". "Public goods" have long been the subject of CAP support, even before the term has come up in the CAP discussion.[5] So far, however, "public goods" were to be delivered by means of specific requirements linked with the granting of income support.[6] This was the idea:

- 1992 when agri-environmental measures were introduced by the MacSharry reform,[7]
- 2003 at the Fischler reform with the introduction of cross compliance which made CAP support dependant on compliance with a series of regulatory requirements in areas such as environment and public health,[8]

4 *H. Kam/H. Smith/C. Potter* (Chapter D. fn. 2), p. 7.
5 See e.g. *A. Greer*, The Common Agricultural Policy and the EU budget: statis or change?, EJGE 2 (2013), p. 119 (128).
6 *R. Mögele* (fn. 1), p. 410 et seq.
7 Regulation (EEC) No 2078/92 on agricultural production methods compatible with the requirements of the protection of the environment and the maintenance of the countryside.
8 Article 3 et seq. Regulation (EC) No 1782/2003.

- 2013 with the greening scheme in the context of the Ciolos reform and lately[9]
- 2021 when the greening and cross-compliance schemes were replaced by a new conditionality mechanism.[10]

In addition, the new eco-schemes, which are separate from the basic payments and voluntary for farmers, can be seen as an entry to the concept of "public money for public goods".[11]

Against this background, it is fair to say that while the provision of 'public goods' has always been part of the CAP's mission, it has never been its sole or primary purpose. This was reflect-ed, in particular, in the concept of multifunctionality of the CAP, a term which was at the heart of the CAP policy debate for a long time in the 1990 and 2000 years: "Multifunctionality highlights both the benefits of agriculture as well as the costs and promoted a shift of CAP's primary objective from productivity, to the incorporation of concerns for the environment, trade and food safety."[12]

Nowadays, the concept of "public money for public goods" is mainly advocated by environ-mental and climate NGOs and Member States with green agendas[13] and has also become the "mantra" of post-Brexit agricultural policies in the UK.[14] As the Institute for Government put it in September 2021: "In 2018, DEFRA – the Department for Environment, Food and Rural Affairs of UK Government – announced its intention to adopt the principle of 'public money for public goods', whereby farmers and other land managers will be paid for delivering (primarily) environmental benefits rather than the amount of land they farm." and: "The Agriculture Act, passed in November 2020, sets out a legislative framework for the new subsidy regime

9 *R. Mögele* (fn. 1), p. 411 et seq.

10 See e.g. *R. Mögele* (fn. 1), p. 403 et seq.

11 *R. Mögele* (fn. 1), p. 405.

12 *H. Kam/H. Smith/C. Potter* (Chapter D. fn. 2), p. 5.

13 See e.g. the agreement of the German "traffic light coalition", p. 45 (available on: https://www.spd.de/koalitionsvertrag2021/); see *J. Martinez/A. Kiermeier*, Die Grüne Architektur der Gemeinsamen Agrarpolitik (GAP) 2023 – ein Zwischenschritt, EurUP 2023, p. 130 (140 et seq.).

14 *A. Shirley/K. Frank*, The Agriculture Act – What it means for landowners and farmers, The Intelligence Lab Global property market insight, 15.11.2020 (available on: https://www.knightfrank.com/research/article/2020-11-15-the-agriculture-act-what-it-means-for-landowners-and-farmers).

in England, including the list of 'public goods' for which subsidies may be paid."[15]

III. What is the scope of support under the "public money for public goods" approach?

The classic scope of support for such measures includes compensation for additional costs and loss of income, as is already the case with agri-environment and climate measures (AECM) in pillar 2, plus transaction costs.[16] Largely the same approach applies to the eco-schemes as part of the 2021 reform regulation,[17] with one notable exception. Instead of compensating farmers "*for all or part of the additional costs incurred and income foregone as a result of the commitments*",[18] Member States may choose to make "*payments additional to the basic income support*".[19] In the eco-schemes the "public goods"-compensation takes the form of a per hectare flat rate top-up to direct payments, i.e. it does not reflect additional cost and income loss.

For many years, for the agri-environmental payments in the second pillar, there have been strong political demands to provide for an income-generating component to create an incentive effect and, more recently, to enable farmers to earn money with their environmental and cli-mate activities. This is the position i.a. of the German government, Agora Agriculture Germany and COPA-COGECA, and it has also played a role in the post-Brexit discussions on the new UK and devolved farm policy.

15 Institute for Government, Agriculture subsidies after Brexit, 2.9.2021 (available on: https://www.instituteforgovernment.org.uk/article/explainer/agriculture-subsidies-after-brexit).

16 Article 70(4) Regulation (EU) 2021/2115 'made on the basis of the additional costs incurred and income foregone resulting from the commitments made'.

17 Article 31 Regulation (EU) 2021/2115.

18 Article 70(7)(b) Regulation (EU) 2021/2115.

19 Article 70(7)(a) Regulation (EU) 2021/2115.

IV. Would the implementation of "public money for public goods" lead to WTO compatibility issues?

The compatibility of "public money for public goods"-payments with the WTO Agreement on Agriculture (AoA) is not at stake as such. Under the agreement's rules on domestic support[20] the EU's only "hard" commitment is to not exceed its current AMS (Aggregate Measurement of Support), which currently stands at 72 billion Euro per year.[21] This amount is high enough to cover the entire current CAP budget. Even if "public goods" payments were fully notified as trade-distorting domestic support falling within the Amber Box, there would be no problem under WTO law provided that future financing of the CAP remained the same.

A. Green box

However, it is expected that the EU, as a staunch defender of a rules-based international trading system, will stick to its practice of bringing as many support programes as possible under the Green Box in order to keep them out of its current AMS system. In this context, it should be examined whether and under which conditions a "public money for public goods" scheme would comply with the Green Box criteria in Annex 2 AoA and, in particular, those referred to in para. 12 and para. 5 and 6 thereof. However, the interpretation of these provisions is inevitably subject to a certain degree of uncertainty due to the lack of relevant case law from the WTO Dispute Settlement Body.[22]

Para. 12 sets out the Green Box criteria for environmental measures.[23] To qualify for green box status a measure must be

---

20 Article 6 and 7 AoA.

21 See the Commission's notification for marketing year 2019/20, WTO G/AG/N/EU/79 of 7.7.2022.

22 *L. Brink/D. Orden*, Agricultural Domestic Support under the WTO, 2023, p. 177 et seq.

23 12. Payments under environmental programmes

(a) Eligibility for such payments shall be determined as part of a clearly-defined government environmental or conservation programme and be dependent on the fulfilment of specific conditions under the government programme, including conditions related to production methods or inputs.

(b) The amount of payment shall be limited to the extra costs or loss of income involved in complying with the government programme.

- "part of a clearly-defined government environmental or conservation programme and be dependent on the fulfilment of specific conditions under the government programme, including conditions related to production methods or inputs." and
- it must be "be limited to the extra costs or loss of income involved in complying with the government programme"

Whilst the first condition is pretty straightforward, the limitation to additional cost or income loss is far from being trivial, for it matters whether at least some sort of incentive is possible or any payment going beyond compensating losses is strictly forbidden.

Annex 2(6) sets out the Green Box criteria for "Decoupled Income Support". Without going into too much detail, the provision provides that payments may not be linked to the current quantity or type of production, to current prices and to current factors of production used.

In addition, Annex 2(1) of Annex 2 AoA specifies in the form of an overarching chapeau clause, that green box support

- shall have no, or at most minimal, trade-distorting effects or effects on production, and
- may neither involve transfers from consumers
- nor have the effect of providing price support to producers.

In its WTO notification of 8 February 2017 for the 2013 reform the Commission[24]

- qualified 2nd pillar payments for AECM, organic farming, Natura 2000 and the Water Framework Directive, for areas with national constraints and animal welfare measures as "green" under para. 12 of Annex 2 AoA, and
- 'greening' support (30 % top-up to basic payments) as "green" under para. 6 of Annex 2 AoA (decoupled income support).[25]

---

24 WTO G/AG/N/EU/35 of 8.2.2017.

25 6. Decoupled income support
(a) Eligibility for such payments shall be determined by clearly-defined criteria such as in-come, status as a producer or landowner, factor use or production level in a defined and fixed base period.
(b) The amount of such payments in any given year shall not be related to, or based on, the type or volume of production (including livestock units) undertaken by the producer in any year after the base period.

In this notification the Commission argued that "*The greening payment is a payment granted with no requirement to produce. It is a decoupled income support and not related to price support. Payments under the greening measure comply with paragraph 1 of Annex 2 to the Agreement on Agriculture as well as with the relevant criteria of paragraph 6.*"[26]

As regards the "eco schemes" introduced by the 2021 reform, Member States are explicitly required to shape them in line with the green box criteria.[27] On 7.8.2023 the Commission submitted its WTO notification,[28] in which it made a distinction according to the two types of eco schemes that are provided for in Article 31 Regulation (EU) 2021/2115.

- If they are granted as a top-up to the basic income payment "for and remunerating the pro-vision of public goods by agricultural practices beneficial to the environment and climate", the Commission considers that they comply with para. 5 or 6 of Annex 2 AoA, depending on whether the basic payment scheme works with or without payments entitlements.
- However, if they are "granted as compensation for carrying out practices beneficial to the environment and climate [they] comply with paragraph 1 of Annex 2 to the Agreement on Agriculture as well as with the relevant criteria of paragraph 12".[29]

B. Principles of green box compatibility

Which are the main principles that can be inferred from the AoA, the Commission's WTO notification and the observations made by the Commission

---

(c) The amount of such payments in any given year shall not be related to, or based on, the prices, domestic or international, applying to any production undertaken in any year after the base period.
(d) The amount of such payments in any given year shall not be related to, or based on, the factors of production employed in any year after the base period.
(e) No production shall be required in order to receive such payments.

26 WTO G/AG/N/EU/35 (fn. 24), p. 4.

27 Article 10 Regulation (EU) 2021/2115.

28 WTO G/AG/N/EU/88 of 7.8.2023, p. 5.

29 WTO G/AG/N/EU/88 (fn. 28), p. 5.

during the CAP reform negotiation process in a number of working documents?[30]

- If a "public goods"-payment only compensates for "the extra costs or loss of income involved in complying with the [environmental] government programme", it is a priori consistent with para. 12 of Annex 2 AoA. In this context it should not be overlooked that, un-der Union law, compensation for additional costs and income foregone is possible, whereas para. 12 expressly provides for an "or" instead of the "and" generally used in EU provisions.
- However, the uptake of agri-environmental payments essentially depends on incentivising farmers to make a contribution to improving the agri-environmental situation. In practice, the calculation of compensation is based on aggregate costs determined for an entire programme area, rather than for each individual farm or hectare. An individualised calculation would be administratively unmanageable and is not required by the wording of Annex 2(12) AoA. Accordingly, farmers could be expected to join the programme up to the one whose individual costs equals the payment level, economically referred to as the "marginal provider". All other participants would have individual cost lower than the payment level, which is an incentive to participate.

Thus, whereas the cost-based payment calculation strictly follows the need to achieve the pro-gramme's environmental objective, participating farmers, except the "marginal provider", enjoy an income benefit. For this reason, farms that operate below the cost level which was used to calculate the compensation, necessarily benefit from incentive and income effects. So far, this approach has not led to disputes at WTO level, and is unlikely to do so in the future. It is in a certain way inherent to the functioning of agri-environmental support.

If, however, the compensation were to include a specific additional income component, be it calculated e.g. as a percentage above the actual cost level or flat rate, they are very likely to be incompatible with para. 12 of Annex 2 AoA. Such arrangements would overstretch the ordinary meaning of the text of para. 12(2) AoA. However, as stressed by the Commission in its latest WTO-notification, such payments could qualify under para.

30 See Questions and Answers Eco-Schemes Article 28 of the SPR Proposal and related provisions, V3 Expert Group for Direct Payments, 20.7.2021.

5 or 6 of Annex 2 as decoupled income support, provided the measure specification does not incentivize higher levels of production.

Should eco-scheme measures target a specific land use or production type, the Commission has clarified that they cannot be implemented as top-up payments classified under paragraphs 5 or 6. In the light of the Appellate Body's findings in the Upland Cotton case,[31] measures related to a production factor and/or a specific type of production cannot not be taken under para-graphs 5 or 6. In these cases only the compensation mechanism as referred to in Annex 2(12) AoA can be used to justify their green box status.[32]

While the focus has so far been on payments for "public goods" for environmental, climate or animal welfare services, the question also arises as to the classification of payments to ensure food security, a "public good" that farmers' associations in particular are invoking.[33] Regardless of their specific form as coupled or decoupled payments, they would in many cases aim to counteract a decline in production or promote its increase. Because of their production-promoting effect, such payments could therefore hardly be brought into line with Annex 2, whose paragraph 1 expressly excludes "effects on production". However, it would be conceivable to keep them out of the current AMS e.g. by setting Blue Box compatible maximum numbers in accordance with Article 6(4) AoA. Furthermore, payments aimed at achieving food security by increasing production should be distinguished from measures aimed solely at improving agricultural productivity[34], for the latter are mainly of a structural nature.[35]

C. SCM

Notwithstanding their compatibility with the rules of the Agreement on Agriculture, "public goods"-payments may conflict with the Agreement on Subsidies and Countervailing Duties (SCM). Although the relationship

31 Appelate Body Report, WT/DS267/AB/R, US-Upland Cotton, para. 324 and 329.

32 *A. Matthews*, Are WTO rules an unreasonable constraint on the design of EU agri-environmental-climate policy?, CULTIVAR – Cadernos de Análise e Prospetiva No. 23 – Impactos agroambientais: metodologias de quantificação e valorização económica, Agosto de 2021.

33 J. *Martinez/A. Kiermeier* (fn. 13), p. 141.

34 *L. Brink/D. Orden* (fn. 22), p. 202.

35 In this respect see para. 13 of Annex 2.

between the two agreements under Article 21 AoA may not have been fully clarified yet,[36] both the Appellate Body report in US Upland cotton[37] and the Panel report in the EU table olives case[38] point in that direction.[39] Therefore, if a "public goods"-payment qualifies as a specific subsidy under Articles 1 and 2 SCM and it adversely affects the interests of another WTO member, it could be actionable under Article 5 SCM. There are substantial arguments that green box payments, by their very nature, cannot be treat-ed as actionable subsidies.[40] Nevertheless, it cannot be ruled out that, for example, agri-environmental measures within the meaning of Annex 2(12) AoA which turn out to be product-specific can come into the focus of the SCM. However, we may expect "public goods"-payments to reduce agricultural production, which will make it unlikely for them to adversely affect interests of other WTO members.

V. Would a strict "public money for public goods"-approach be compatible with the CAP treaty rules?

Could a regime that focuses on a "*repurposing of current agricultural subsidies*"[41] by implementing a pure concept of "public money for public goods" still fall under the CAP legal base in Article 43(2) TFEU? Given that Article 43(2) TFEU serves to realise the agricultural and rural objectives set out in Article 39 TFEU the question arises whether "public goods"-payments would still be covered by one of these objectives. This is at least questionable should only "public goods" in the areas of environment and climate be targeted.

In this case, there would also be doubts as to whether the environmental clause in Article 11 TFEU would be sufficient to justify the application of Article 43(2) TFEU, since this cross-cutting provision only serves to justify

36 *L. Brink/D. Orden* (fn. 22), p. 43 and 48 et seq.

37 Appelate Body Report (fn. 31), para. 229 et seq.

38 Panel Report, WT/DS577/R, EU-Anti-Dumping and Countervailing Duties on Ripe Olives from Spain of 19.11.2021.

39 *L. Brink/D. Orden* (fn. 22), p. 43 et seq.

40 *R. Mögele/R. Möhler*, in: H.G. *Krenzler/Ch. Herrmann/M. Niestedt* (ed.), EU-Außenwirtschafts- und Zollrecht, Nr. 40 Landwirtschaft, Section 115, Date: April 2020.

41 E. *Régnier/N. Bolduc/P.-M. Aubert*, Greening the agrifood system through the EU budget: can we repurpose agricultural subsidies?, IDDRI IssueBrief No. 5, June 2023, p. 2 (available on: https://www.iddri.org/en/publications-and-events/issue-brief/greening-agrifood-system-through-eu-budget-can-we-repurpose).

the pursuit of environmental concerns within the CAP. As regards the relationship between the CAP and the EU's environmental policy the ECJ underlined as a matter of principle that the latter does not take precedence over other EU policies such as the CAP so that a measure does not fall under Article 192(1) TFEU merely because it takes account of environmental concerns.[42] However, one may reasonably conclude that measures intended to tackle general environmental problems such as water or air pollution or the preservation of nature should be based on Article 192(1) TFEU. The same would apply where, as stated above, a measure is only vaguely linked with the CAP objectives set out in Article 39(1) TFEU.[43] Against this background, given the criteria developed by the ECJ for delimiting EU competences, there are good reasons to assume that such a pure system of "public money for public goods" would have rather to be based on the environmental legal basis in Article 192 (1) TFEU rather than on Article 43 (2) TFEU.[44]

Should Artilce 192(1) TFEU be actually applicable, also the EAGF, which is based on Article 40(3) TFEU would need to be transformed into an environment policy instrument, i.e. the "public goods"-payments would need to be financed through a new land management fund outside the CAP[45] which would be about financing environmental measures in the agricultural sector. It is unlikely, however, that such a change will actually take place for several reasons. Under ECJ case law, the agricultural legislator has large discretion with regard to applying Article 39 TFEU and the objectives therein. Income and market support is likely to remain a substantial part of the CAP, and agri-specific rural development measures other than AECM and animal welfare support will certainly be maintained.

Finally, while the concept of "public money for public goods" will certainly continue to gain weight, it appears questionable that all or the lion's share of CAP money be exclusively spent on climate, environmental and animal welfare measures. First, in light of the Ukraine war and its impact on agricultural markets, a food security argument is building up that is essentially about strengthening the productivity and therefore the viability of the EU agricultural sector. Secondly, the share of direct income support

42 *R. Mögele* (fn. 1), p. 408.

43 *R. Mögele* (fn. 1), p. 408.

44 The delimitation is to be based on objective, judicially verifiable criteria that are based on the content and objectives of the measure. For the relation between Article 43(2) and Article 192 TFEU see R. Mögele (fn. 1), p. 407 et seq.

45 *E. Régnier/N. Bolduc/P.-M. Aubert* (fn. 41), p. 1.

in agricultural factor income is still 24 % on aver-age in the EU[46], so foregoing income support would have serious economic consequences for many farms. Both aspects are likely to have considerable weight in the political process and play an important role in the decision making of both the AgriFish Council's and the Committee for Agriculture in the EP (COMAGRI).

VI. What would actually change in the CAP should "public money for public goods" be implemented?

Under the "public money for public goods"-approach traditional income support (direct payments) would be phased out and replaced progressively by "public goods"-payments. In this case a number of policy options would have to be taken into consideration by the CAP legislator. Of course, each of the following considerations is subject to the budgetary decisions in the next MFF for the period after 2027.

- Both the eco-schemes (first pillar) and the AECM (second pillar) are, by their nature, "public goods"-payments and thus "public money for public goods"-precursors.[47] Therefore, it would make sense to consider, when introducing the "public money for public goods"-approach, whether to merge them into a single "public money for public goods"-tool as both pursue largely the same objectives. By reducing the number of CAP schemes, this would al-so contribute to policy simplification.
- With the "public money for public goods"-approach the distinction between Pillars 1 and 2 would become even fuzzier, as is already the case in the current CAP. By introducing a single type of support, implemented through national strategic CAP plans, there would be little justification for maintaining two pillars. However, Member States may well be reluctant to abandon the pillar structure as, similar to the past, they may continue to view Pillar 1 as the political and financial core of the CAP, which is essential to ensuring sufficient CAP funding in the next MFF.

46 European Commission, Common Agricultural Policy: Key graphs & figures, Graph 4, October 2022.

47 *J. Martinez/A. Kiermeier* (fn. 13), p. 140, speak of an intermediate step towards a complete system change away from a primarily competition-oriented towards a common good-oriented system.

- It is an open question whether the legislator would convert the entire funding of "public goods" into a multiannual system with differentiated appropriations,[48] as is currently the case for rural development (EFRD).[49] On the one hand, it is argued that a multi-year peri-od for environmental and climate measures is more effective. On the other hand, however, experience shows that differentiated appropriations tend to lead to a further increase in the RAL ("reste à liquider"),[50] which would make budget management more difficult.
- In this context, the question would arise as to whether co-financing, which currently only applies to funding in the second pillar,[51] should be extended to the new commons instrument, i.e. to all direct CAP support. This could be an option, although many Member States are likely to reject such a change due to limited national budgets.
- The concept of "public money for public goods" would be ideally implemented on a performance basis instead of having recourse to abstract eligibility criteria as is currently the case with eco-schemes.[52] This would mean linking eligibility to receive EU funds to results not only at Member State level, as provided for in Regulation (EU) 2021/2115, but also at beneficiary level. Since such an approach aims to assess whether the relevant "public good" has been provided, it would be significantly more demanding in its practical and legal ap-plication, as a reliable baseline must first be established before assessing the actual impact of the rewarded measure.
- The future of conditionality (former cross compliance)[53] would also have to be sorted out. Given that conditionality pertains to legal baseline requirements whilst "public goods"-payments would be subject to respecting environmental and climate targets going beyond legal obligations, both schemes could well coexist.

48 Article 7(2) Regulation (EU) 2018/1046 (Financial Regulation); European Commission, European Union, Public Finance, 5th ed., 2014, p. 153 et seq.

49 Article 113(1) Regulation (EU) 2018/1046.

50 European Commission, Reste à liquider, a natural phenomenon, not financial debt, April 2019 (available on: https://op.europa.eu/en/publication-detail/-/publication/b3ea5d9a-e4c2-11e9-9c4e-01aa75ed71a1/language-en).

51 Article 6 Regulation (EU) 2021/2116 in conjunction with Article 90 et seq. Regulation (EU) 2021/2115.

52 Article 31 Regulation (EU) 2021/2115.

53 Article 12 f. Regulation (EU) 2021/2115.

- Finally, it should be noted that the introduction of "public goods"-payments would reduce the overall coverage of agricultural support for two reasons: First, direct support which is currently available to virtually all farmers would be focused on farms concentrating their activities on sustainability objectives and delivering ecological services.[54] Accordingly, there would be no longer a general self standing income support tool. Second, "public goods"-payments would be significantly higher than current hectare payments, and would, there-fore, absorb high shares of the available CAP funds. As a result, "public money for public goods"-payments could only be made to a limited number of beneficiaries.

54 *R. Mögele* (fn. 1), p. 414.

F. The Netherlands – The new CAP from a Dutch perspective

Jeroen Rheinfeld

Today I get to speak to you about the new CAP from a Dutch perspective. When I look at the introduction of the new CAP in the Netherlands and make an analysis of it, a clear distinction should be made between "process" on the one hand and "content" on the other. Furthermore, I want to make some brief remarks about the control and enforcement aspects and I will end this short overview with some tax aspects of the new CAP.

I. Process

Let me start with the "process". To be brief and to the point; the introduction of the new CAP policy in the Netherlands has been rather bumpy.

- The Implementing regulation CAP 2023 (the regulation whereby the Netherlands gives sub-stance to the new CAP at the national level) was published in the Staatscourant on November 1, 2022 and subsequently amended several times.
- The simulation tool for experimenting with the cropping plan and which eco-activities fit was only realized around February 1, 2023.
- The application of the Combined Declaration regularly showed malfunctions or slow in use when adapting parcels/locks/landscape elements.
- Farmers and their advisors need much more time in 2023 to complete the Combined Decla-ration, which is why the deadline for submission has been moved from May 15 to June 15, 2023. For both farmers and advisor, the regulations (also in relation to manure policy) are complex.
- Much uncertainty about the regulations concerning the Combined Declaration by farmer, advisor and RVO.
- Technical error in the Combined Declaration due to which thousands of farmers had to check the Combined Declaration again in June 2023, error in calculating points and value of eco-schemes. Consequence could be that farmers did not end up in the right category after all (bronze, silver or gold). Farmers did not always have the opportunity to adjust the building plan, as it was already June 2023.

- In view of the above, the minister appointed 2023 as a learning and transition year.

II. Content

Next, the "content". The regulations show that, as in the previous CAP-regulations, active farmers may be eligible for the following grants:

- Basic premium plus additional subsidy. Agricultural entrepreneurs who own or use land will receive, subject to conditions, a basic premium of approximately 220 Euro per hectare plus an additional subsidy of approximately 54 Euro for the first 40 hectares of land.
- Additional payment young farmers. Young farmers can receive an additional subsidy of 2,800 Euro per year for up to five years.
- ANLb subsidy (agricultural nature management) for agricultural partnerships. The cooperatives eligible for subsidy are the collectives that are committed to landscape management.
- Agricultural businesses that want to innovate in agriculture can receive a subsidy to modernize or make the business more sustainable.
- Agricultural businesses can participate in the eco-scheme, for which they can receive a subsidy if they meet the conditions.

What is new in the Dutch CAP is that landscape elements (ditches, groups of trees, hedges and hedgerows) will be added to eligible arable land. This is to promote the conservation of landscape elements. Of the approximately 55,000 combined declarations submitted, approximately 45,000 farms requested basic income support. Approximately 35,000 farms applied for the eco-schemes.

The Netherlands has chosen 22 eco-activities through which farmers can earn the eco premium in the bronze, silver or gold category. Organic farms automatically score gold. About 80 % of the farms have signed up for the eco-activities, my estimation is that this is a nice score.

You can see that in the public eye, many farmers are agitating against "doing more for less money", but in the end, entrepreneurs are still working individually to see what eco-activities can still be incorporated into the business operations to score the highest possible category. For example, in the period from 2020 to 2023, the protein crop field beans grew from a sowing of 1,100 to 2,500 hectares. Side note with this is that firstly it is not known what category (bronze, silver or gold) these farms score and secondly the eco-activities must of course still be actually implemented in 2023.

III. Control and enforcement

When the new CAP in terms of control and enforcement aspects is juxtaposed with the old one, it appears that while not very much has changed in broad terms very much has changed, but new emphases have been added. There are more rules that the farmer must meet in order to qualify for support eligibility (conditionality). In addition, the eco-activities de facto simply brings additional obligations with it. None of this makes the CAP easier and it increases the likelihood of lumps.

To illustrate, I have now heard from several advisors, independently, that they expect to spend to spend two to three times as much time filling out a combined statement than before, and farmers who have hitherto always done it themselves decide en masse to outsource it. It becomes a specialist work. On the other hand, the changed application procedure lowers the risk of facing penalties, because one only makes the application at the end of the crop year. With regard to enforcement, the Minister of Agriculture, Nature and Food Quality has indicated that he views the first year (2023) as a transitional and learning year in which, in principle, a warning will be given for violations of new conditions. As of 2024, a sanction will be imposed for violations.

IV. Tax aspects

Finally, a brief comment on the tax aspects of the new CAP. The fact that the new CAP no longer refers to property rights, but to an annual entitlement to one or more subsidies for active farmers who meet the set conditions, does not mean that tax question points regarding the CAP have decreased as a result. Subsidies received under the CAP fall under the fiscal income concept and as such are taxed with income tax. An exception to this is the subsidy received by active farmers when their farm is not a source of income in the tax sense. In this circumstance, the agricultural land is included in the box 3 assets and taxed as investment assets on the basis of a fixed return.

V. Conclusion

In conclusion: the new CAP aims to reward future-proof farmers more strongly. With the introduction of the eco-schemes, farmers who want to go the extra mile in making the farm more sustainable will be supported with CAP public funds. It can be established that, at least for the first year, the new CAP is perceived as extremely complex in Dutch agricultural practice. Practice will show how the new CAP has actually landed in the sector.

G. Concluding remarks

Christian Busse, Rudolf Mögele, Ludivine Petetin

Throughout this Colloquium, we have seen that that the notion of "public money for public goods" is a rather vague concept. A preferable term instead of "public goods" seems to be "public interest". "Public interest" covers all facets of the three dimensions of sustainability (ecological, social and economic) as well as other aspects of public interest, for example, food security and food quality. As a more specific term, "social-ecological services" might be an alternative choice. It emphasizes two dimensions of sustainability which ought to be more in the focus than in the past.

To circumscribe the term as concrete as possible is important to prevent confusion, because different meanings of "public money for public goods" are already in existence, being an obstacle to the legal and interdisciplinary debate. In order to balance the proposed wide under-standing of the term, causality between a given subsidy and a certain public interest is indispensable. It has to be established and verified, that the subsidy unfolds a positive effect on the public interest at stake.

In which way to measure the positive effect and how to calculate the amount of the subsidy in relation to the intended effect are aspects to be further discussed, as well as how to design the burden of proof. Also a point of relevance is, that the involvement of private interests does not exclude per se fundings. It seems to be a question of assessment, in which situations private interests may be acceptable.

In relation to the UK, there are three characteristics of note: first, EU red tape has been re-placed with UK or devolved red tape with the establishment of numerous schemes and their respective deadlines. Second, there are discrepancies between the vision of "public money for public goods" and the reality and practice with payments for actions. Third, the emphasis of the schemes is placed on economic aspects in particular with business resilience whilst environmental protection is narrowly defined and social components, like rural development (apart from Scotland) are neglected. The English example shows in detail, how the approach of the newly introduced schemes alter the idea of "public money for public goods" in different ways.

For the CAP, "public money for public goods" is not a new approach. So far, it has been enshrined in the concept of multifunctional European agriculture where income and market support is supplemented by environmental, climate and animal welfare requirements. Since more recently it has been advocated namely by NGOs as a means to abandon area based direct in-come support and replace it by concentrating support on the provision of services which are in the public interest.

"Public goods"-payments as such would not conflict with WTO rules as there is enough room under the EU's current AMS. However, if such payments were to be brought under the green box, they would need to comply with Annex 2 of AoA, in particular the para. 12 and 5 or 6 thereof. The main issue here is that "public goods"-payments do not only compensate for additional cost and/or income forgone but also contain an income-generating component. This is in line with para. 12 of Annex 2 as long as the incentive amount is only the result of the calculation of the compensation. Specific additional financial components could only be justified under para. 5 or 6, provided that they are not linked with production. In addition, there is a risk that in particular payments driving production could become actionable under the SCM even though they fall under para. 12 of Annex 2.

A pure "public money for public goods"-approach would raise questions as to using Article 43(2) TFEU as a legal basis. Instead Article 192 TFEU might be more pertinent. However, this would probably not be the case if the new system continued to comprise a tangible income and rural development element.

The Dutch experience which is related to the implementation of the 2021 CAP reform shows that switching to "public goods"-support tends to make the CAP more complex, requiring farmers to shoulder a higher administrative burden. On the other hand, the concept of "public money for public goods" can be shaped so as to make payments economically interesting and incentivizing farmers to participate in such schemes.

The UK part as well as the EU part of the Colloquium illustrate the various difficulties of the notion "public money for public goods". That indicates the conceptional and practical obstacles to implement such a notion. But, at the same time, it shows that some agricultural programs are already heading towards that notion.

VI.
Rapport de Synthese – Synthesis Report – Synthesebericht

Prof. Dr. Roland Norer

General Delegate CEDR,
Universität Luzern (Switzerland)

Version française – French version – Französische Version
Version anglaise – English version – Englische Version
Version allemande – German version – Deutsche Version

Rapport de Synthese

Version française – French version – Französische Version

Prof. Dr. Roland Norer
Délégué général du CEDR,
Université de Lucerne

I. Introduction et remerciements

Monsieur le Président,
Mesdames et Messieurs
chers collègues,[1]

En tant que délégué général, j'ai l'honneur d'assumer la dernière partie académique à la fin du XXXIe Congrès européen de droit rural. Le début a été marqué par la crise – les reports successifs dus au COVID, l'attente et l'angoisse, les questions relatives à une organisation hybride – tout cela a mis nos nerfs à rude épreuve. Nous sommes d'autant plus heureux que le congrès ait pu avoir lieu en 2023 et qu'une rencontre personnelle ait été à nouveau possible après une pause forcée de quatre ans.

Je tiens à remercier tout particulièrement le Dr *Nerys Llewelyn Jones* et le Dr *Ludivine Petetin*, qui étaient déjà prêts il y a deux ans et qui ont organisé ce congrès dans des circonstances différentes (y compris sur le plan personnel) et dans un délai extrêmement court. Un grand merci à eux ! Mes remerciements vont également à *Alex Carson-Taylor*, président et *Mike Holland*, secrétaire général et conseiller de l'Association britannique de droit agricole (ALA), ainsi qu'à tous les collègues de notre plus grande association nationale. Le fait que vous restiez fidèles au CEDR à l'heure du Brexit et que vous organisiez même un congrès européen mérite notre plus grand respect. L'engagement dans l'organisation ici, dans les locaux de l'Université de Cardiff, a été impressionnant. Vous avez tous contribué, par votre hospitalité et votre professionnalisme, à ce que nous puissions vivre ici des journées inoubliables.

1 Version élargie et complétée par l'appareil de notes de bas de page, le style de présentation a été conservé.

Je tiens également à remercier les rapporteurs généraux et les présidents des commissions pour leur excellent travail. Ils ont dirigé les travaux des commissions de manière souveraine et coordonnée. Pour la Commission I, il s'agissait du professeur Dr *Rudy Gotzen* (merci pour ton remplacement de dernière minute) et du Dr *Alicia Epstein*, pour la Commission II, *d'Alex Carson Taylor* et *de Catherine Taskis* KC, et pour la Commission III, du professeur Dr *Franci Avsec* et du professeur UAM dr hab. *Aneta Suchoń*.

En outre, tous les rapporteurs nationaux et individuels méritent un grand merci. Au total, 26 rapports nationaux et 4 rapports individuels ont été soumis.

Je tiens également à féliciter l'équipe qui a organisé ce colloque pour la deuxième fois, le Prof. Dr *Rudolf Mögele*, le Dr *Christian Busse* et le Dr *Ludivine Petetin*.

Enfin, je voudrais également vous remercier, chers participants. Par votre participation active, vos contributions écrites et orales, vous avez apporté une contribution importante au succès de ce Congrès européen du droit agraire.

Dans l'analyse scientifique de ce XXXIe Congrès et colloque européen de droit rural, il s'agit maintenant, comme le veut la tradition, de faire un tour d'horizon des trois commissions et du colloque dans le rapport de synthèse. J'essaierai de ne pas procéder selon la devise bien connue « tout a déjà été dit, mais pas encore par tout le monde », mais de faire quelques réflexions générales qui me semblent particulièrement importantes.

II. Thèmes

Le dernier congrès de Poznań 2019 a déjà repris un élément important de la thématique de cette année avec les thèmes « food sovereignity » et « food security ». A l'époque, le rapport de synthèse avait désigné ce sujet comme l'un des problèmes les plus urgents de notre époque, à côté du changement climatique, de la perte de biodiversité et des dommages environnementaux.[2] Depuis, la crise COVID et la crise ukrainienne sont venues s'ajouter à la liste.

Comme le Job biblique, ils sont assis là, se conditionnent mutuellement, se réfèrent les uns aux autres et se mettent en réseau pour former une

2 *Norer*, Rapport de synthèse, in : CEDR (éd.), Food sovereignty, food security and the contribution of agricultural law (2023), p. 434.

alliance contre nature. Quoi de plus naturel donc que de se consacrer cette fois-ci aux crises multiples ? « Le droit agricole en temps de crise : Impacts politiques et production », tel est le thème général. Celui-ci aborde des problèmes globaux et concerne aussi bien les États membres de l'UE que les pays tiers – comme notre hôte.

Naturellement, ce thème n'a pas encore fait l'objet de congrès antérieurs. Certes, certains aspects, notamment la régulation du marché[3] et l'influence de la législation environnementale sur la production agricole[4] , ont été traités à plusieurs reprises par le passé, mais toujours dans toute leur ampleur et moins axés sur le mode de crise. Le dernier congrès de Poznań en 2019[5] est plus ou moins le seul point de départ.

Nous avons formulé l'objet des délibérations de la Commission I de manière peut-être un peu vague : « Crises multiples : des réponses en droit agricole ». Mais le choix des thèmes à traiter se lisait effectivement comme une horde de cavaliers apocalyptiques : guerre en Ukraine, COVID, crises énergétiques, maladies et changement climatique. Les contre-stratégies possibles en matière de droit agricole, telles que les filets de sécurité et les réserves agricoles, les interventions, la constitution de réserves obligatoires ou les assurances, semblaient en revanche discrètes et techniques. 8 rapports nationaux et 2 rapports individuels se sont penchés sur la question de savoir si cela était vraiment le cas.

La Commission II, intitulée « Carbone, biodiversité et nutriments : nouvelles considérations sur l'utilisation des terres », les discussions ont porté sur le capital naturel, qui constitue le fondement de notre vie à tous. L'examen de différents modèles relatifs au carbone, à la biodiversité, aux nutriments et à l'utilisation des terres dans différents systèmes juridiques, ainsi que des opportunités et des menaces, a permis d'analyser un domaine

3 Notamment XIVe Congrès, Commission II « Old and new legal techniques for market regulation », Salzbourg 1987 ; XXe Congrès, Commission I « AGENDA 2000 - Market and price policy », Amsterdam 1999 ; XXIe Congrès, Commission I « Legal instruments of the agricultural products market », Helsinki 2001.

4 Notamment XIVe Congrès, Commission I « The law of agriculture and forestry and environmental problems », Salzbourg 1987 ; XVIIIe Congrès, Commission I « The penetration of environmental law in the field of rural law », Oxford 1995 ; XXVIIIe Congrès, Commission II « Legal framework of environmental law for agricultural production » Lucerne 2013. Voir aussi IIIe Symposium « Environmental pollution and agriculture », Plymouth 1986.

5 XXXe Congrès, Commission I « Souveraineté alimentaire et sécurité alimentaire : concepts et cadre juridique », Commission II « Protection des terres cultivées : droit de l'aménagement rural et droit de la propriété agricole et de l'immobilier », Poznań 2019.

important, mais généralement négligé, du moins sur le plan juridique. Les pesticides, les engrais et les aliments pour animaux ainsi que l'utilisation du carbone, des nitrates, du phosphore, du glyphosate et des néonicotinoïdes, y compris les règles d'épandage et les interdictions d'épandage, font actuellement l'objet de critiques, mais peuvent contribuer à une agriculture et donc à une production alimentaire plus résistantes aux crises. Des thèmes tels que le commerce des éléments nutritifs, la politique de gestion des terres et la protection des eaux s'offraient tout autant que les régimes d'autorisation et le correctif des droits de recours des associations environnementales. Dans ce domaine, 7 rapports nationaux et 1 rapport individuel ont été rédigés.

La Commission III s'est penchée sur le thème des « Développements actuels importants du droit rural international, dans l'UE ainsi que dans les états et les régions », comme c'est le cas depuis le Congrès de Cambridge de 2009. Il s'agissait d'évoquer les développements juridiques nationaux remarquables dans les différents pays des rapporteurs, mais aussi les liens avec le droit européen et la mise en œuvre de celui-ci, ainsi que les tendances générales. Les thèmes proposés dans le questionnaire, tels que la directive sur les nitrates, la protection contre les inondations et la renaturation, l'irrigation, le changement climatique et l'agriculture, ont à nouveau servi de points de référence, qui pouvaient être complétés et élargis à volonté. Du point de vue du droit européen, l'accent pouvait être mis sur les nombreux plans d'action et stratégies dans le cadre du Green Deal, tout comme sur la mise en œuvre de la nouvelle PAC dans le droit national ou sur l'intégration à observer avec le droit alimentaire (« farm to fork »). Enfin, le champ thématique a pu être élargi aux accords internationaux (notamment CETA, TTIP), aux cadastres agricoles, au droit du travail (travailleurs saisonniers) ou au problème urgent des loups et de la gestion des pâturages dans de nombreux États. 11 rapports nationaux et 1 rapport individuel ont été soumis ici.

Les questionnaires, élaborés par les rapporteurs généraux en concertation avec le délégué général, ont constitué la base des rapports nationaux et donc du travail de la commission. En même temps, il y avait suffisamment de liberté pour suivre ses propres priorités et structures tout en garantissant la comparabilité. Les débats ont ensuite été intégrés dans les rapports généraux et les conclusions des différentes commissions.

Le colloque « Public Money for Public Goods : L'agriculture durable. La nouvelle PAC et les politiques agricoles au Royaume-Uni » a été spécialement conçu pour l'organisateur et s'est penché, outre sur la nouvelle politique agricole commune de l'UE, en particulier sur la future politique agricole de l'Angleterre, du Pays de Galles, de l'Écosse et de l'Irlande du Nord post-Brexit. Un aperçu des concepts et de leur mise en œuvre, notamment dans l'UE dans les plans stratégiques nationaux et dans le UK « Four Nations » in Agriculture Act 2020 et Agriculture (Wales) Bill 2022, promettait un élargissement intéressant de l'horizon. Pour les États membres de l'UE, il s'agissait soit d'une source d'inspiration pour la conception d'une politique agricole européenne renationalisée, soit d'un encouragement à rester « unis ».[6] Ce n'est que la deuxième fois[7] qu'un tel bloc thématique, auquel tous les participants ont assisté ensemble hors programme, a été organisé sur et a une nouvelle fois fait ses preuves. Ce format devrait donc s'établir définitivement comme complément au travail de la Commission.

III. Commission I

Les crises multiples évoquées dans le questionnaire de la Commission sont une réalité et nous posent des défis particuliers. Le thème à traiter ici visait à cet égard des réponses possibles. Mais y en a-t-il vraiment, notamment en droit agricole ?

A. Sécurité alimentaire

Dans sa communication du 23 mars 2022 intitulée « Garantir la sécurité alimentaire et renforcer la résilience des systèmes alimentaires »[8], mentionnée

---

6 Voir *Bianchi*, Y a-t-il encore quelque chose de « commun » dans la nouvelle Politique agricole commune ?, RTDE 2005, p. 623 ss ; *Gilsdorf*, Der Grundsatz der Subsidiarität und die gemeinsame Agrarpolitik, GS Grabitz (1995), p. 77 ss ; *Priebe*, Wie « subsidiär » kann die Gemeinsame Agrarpolitik sein ? EuZW 1993, p. 425 ; *le même*, Differenzierung und Dezentralisierung in der gemeinsamen Agrarpolitik, FS Steinberger (2002), p. 1347 ; *Seidel*, Rückführung der Landwirtschaftspolitik in die Verantwortung der Mitgliedstaaten ? – Rechts- und Verfassungsfragen des Gemeinschaftsrechts, AgrarR 2000, p. 381.

7 Voir le colloque « La réforme de la PAC » au Congrès de Poznań en 2019 ; voir CEDR (éd.), Food sovereignty, food security and the contribution of agricultural law (2023), p. 375 ss.

8 Communication de la Commission au Parlement européen, au Conseil européen, au Conseil, au Comité économique et social européen et au Comité des régions, « Préserver la sécurité alimentaire et renforcer les systèmes alimentaires » du 23 mars 2022, COM(2022) 133 final.

dans le questionnaire, la Commission européenne constate que l'invasion de l'Ukraine déstabilise davantage des marchés agricoles déjà fragiles. En raison de la pandémie de COVID-19 et du changement climatique, l'agriculture mondiale est sous pression. La sécurité alimentaire est déjà menacée par les sécheresses, les inondations et les vagues de chaleur ainsi que par l'élévation du niveau de la mer, et ces menaces ne feront qu'augmenter en raison du réchauffement de la planète et toucheront particulièrement les régions vulnérables. Même si l'approvisionnement alimentaire de l'UE n'est pas menacé pour l'instant, l'invasion de l'Ukraine et une explosion mondiale des prix des matières premières feraient grimper les prix sur les marchés des produits agricoles et marins et mettraient en évidence les faiblesses du système alimentaire, à savoir la dépendance vis-à-vis, entre autres, des importations d'énergie, d'engrais et d'aliments pour animaux. Une certaine désolation se dégage de ces explications, mais l'angle agronomique qui relie toutes les plaintes est également clair : une fois de plus, le droit agricole concerne la sécurité alimentaire et l'approvisionnement en denrées alimentaires. Et les réponses – internationales, supranationales et nationales – qui ont été présentées et discutées au sein de la Commission I sont principalement de nature économique.

B. Instruments

Les instruments cités, tels que la réglementation de la main-d'œuvre, les aides COVID, la garantie des liquidités, les restrictions à l'exportation, la limitation des opérations spéculatives, le recours à la réserve agricole de l'UE et bien d'autres[9] sont nombreux, parfois très différenciés et probablement plus ou moins efficaces. Il semble donc que tout un ensemble d'instruments revienne par ce biais, que l'on ne peut décrire que de manière impropre par le terme de régulation du marché. Des mots clés comme filets de sécurité et réserves agricoles, intervention, réserves obligatoires et solutions d'assurance sonnent comme une époque pré-libérale perdue (sans nécessité).

L'une de ces crises les plus longues et les plus puissantes est toutefois le changement climatique et la perte de biodiversité. Ces thèmes, qui faisaient à l'origine l'objet du droit de la protection du climat et de l'environ-

9 Rapport national Allemagne (Commission I).

nement, ont été intégrés depuis longtemps dans le droit agricole,[10] avec une accentuation considérable lors de la récente réforme de la PAC. Il est intéressant d'observer comment, en mode de crise, les conflits d'intérêts ont été résolus par une suspension temporaire de ces réglementations en faveur de la production alimentaire.[11] On peut inévitablement se demander si les réglementations agroenvironnementales et de protection de la nature ne se sont pas révélées trop ambitieuses et pas assez équilibrées. Il convient de remettre en question la primauté de la politique environnementale dans la politique agricole, qui ne tient pas suffisamment compte de l'objectif de la sécurité alimentaire, pourtant de même importance. Les discussions sur la loi européenne sur la restauration de la nature (EU Nature Restoration Law) au Parlement européen l'ont récemment montré de manière exemplaire.

Les législateurs nationaux n'ont guère de marge de manœuvre à cet égard. En Allemagne, le secteur agroalimentaire a certes été reconnu comme une infrastructure d'importance systémique, mais les effets juridiques qui en découlent devraient être limités.[12] En outre, la « garantie d'une agriculture performante » fait partie des intérêts publics reconnus par la Constitution.[13] Les rapports nationaux font référence à des actes législatifs de droit commun tels que les lois sur la sécurité en cas de crise, les lois sur la gestion des denrées alimentaires et la sécurité de l'approvisionnement, ainsi qu'à des aides financières pour faire face aux crises.[14] Mais les prestations de

---

10 *Mögele*, The Integration of Environmental and Climate Protection into the Common Agricultural Policy - Legal Concepts and Developments, EurUP 4/2018, p. 405 ss ; *Norer*, Saving the world under agricultural law or overtaxing it ? - On the methodology of integration non-agricultural claims into European agricultural law, CEDR-JRL 1/2022, p. 28 ss.

11 Par exemple, Décision d'exécution (UE) 2022/484 prévoyant des dérogations au règlement (UE) no 1307/2013 du Parlement européen et du Conseil et au règlement délégué (UE) no 639/2014 de la Commission en ce qui concerne la mise en œuvre de certaines conditions relatives au paiement en faveur du verdissement pour l'année de demande 2022, JO L 98/105 ; Règlement d'exécution (UE) 2022/1317 prévoyant des dérogations au règlement (UE) 2021/2115 en ce qui concerne l'application des normes relatives aux bonnes conditions agricoles et environnementales des terres (normes BCAE) 7 et 8 pour l'année de demande 2023, JO L 199/1. L'objectif est de permettre l'utilisation des terres disponibles pour la production de denrées alimentaires et d'aliments pour animaux dans toute la mesure du possible.

12 Rapport national Allemagne (Commission I).

13 Rapport national Allemagne (Commission I).

14 Rapport national Autriche (Commission I) ; Rapport national Allemagne (Commission I) ; Rapport national Pologne (Commission I), Aide à la production d'engrais minéraux ; Rapport national Espagne (Commission I).

l'État aux assurances récolte et aux fonds de solidarité[15] ou le vissage des tarifs douaniers[16] sont également un sujet de discussion. En France et en Italie, la dénomination des ministères a même été modifiée,[17] en Italie, un nouveau Fonds de souveraineté alimentaire a été créé,[18] en Pologne, il existe de nombreuses réglementations liées à l'Ukraine[19] et en Espagne, le plan stratégique national de la PAC a été adapté.[20] On pourrait multiplier les exemples.

Dans la lutte pour l'équilibre des intérêts, la situation de départ est parfois précaire. Les intérêts liés au climat et à la protection de l'environnement s'expriment aussi bien dans la législation sur le climat et la protection de l'environnement que – sous une forme thématiquement ciblée – dans la législation sur la PAC. En revanche, les intérêts de la sécurité d'approvisionnement sont presque exclusivement ancrés dans le droit agricole. Même si les deux intérêts doivent être jugés formellement sur un pied d'égalité, ce qui est même le cas dans le droit primaire avec les articles 39 et 191 du TFUE, le processus d'écologisation du droit agricole, déjà observable depuis des décennies, s'est encore nettement accentué ces derniers temps. D'un point de vue systématique, la pression au détriment de la production vient donc doublement, de l'extérieur (droit de l'environnement) et de l'intérieur (droit agricole), tandis que les intérêts de l'approvisionnement ne sont soutenus que simplement (droit agricole).

Dans l'ensemble, et les travaux de la Commission I l'ont à mon avis clairement montré, il ne semble pas y avoir de concept juridique global face aux multiples crises qui s'influencent mutuellement. Une petite boîte à outils de droit économique, allant jusqu'à la suspension temporaire (mais sans préjudice par ailleurs) des réglementations agricoles écologiques, peut permettre d'apporter des réponses à court terme, mais ne semble pas suffisamment appropriée pour s'armer de manière adéquate contre les crises

15 Rapport national Autriche (Commission I) ; Rapport national Italie (Commission I) ; Rapport national Pologne (Commission I).

16 Rapport individuel Plazas (Commission I) ; rapport national France (Commission I).

17 En France depuis 2022 « Ministère de l'Agriculture et de la Souveraineté Alimentaire » ; Rapport national France (Commission I). Voir également l'initiative « Food and Agriculture Resilience Mission (FARM) ». En Italie, depuis 2022, « Ministry of Agriculture, Food Sovereignty and Forests » ; rapport national Italie (Commission III).

18 Rapport national Italie (Commission I).

19 Rapport national Pologne (Commission I).

20 Rapport national Espagne (Commission I).

futures. Le plus grand défi sera de coordonner les activités au niveau de l'UE, en tenant compte des différences économiques, sociales et législatives entre les différents pays.[21]

C. Résumé

Comme on pouvait s'y attendre, les réponses possibles du droit agricole aux crises multiples actuelles sont multiples et fragmentées. Ici, on suspend temporairement une norme environnementale, ici on parle d'une aide de trésorerie et là on promeut une aide d'assurance. Ce qui manque, c'est un concept global et systématisé ayant pour objectif de garantir la sécurité alimentaire et la résilience dans le secteur agroalimentaire et de l'imposer, si nécessaire contre des intérêts (environnementaux) contraires.

IV. Commission II

Les réflexions sur une nouvelle utilisation des terres en termes de carbone, de biodiversité et de nutriments, abordées dans la Commission II, sont fondamentales. Comme indiqué dans le questionnaire, 38 % de l'utilisation des sols dans le monde se fait sur des terres agricoles, ce qui place ces dernières, et donc la politique agricole commune et la législation de la PAC, sous les feux de la rampe en ce qui concerne la gestion du capital naturel. La problématique la plus évidente, et donc la plus souvent abordée, est celle de l'utilisation des produits phytosanitaires et des engrais.

A. Titre juridique

Le mérite de cette commission particulièrement exigeante est de se pencher aussi une fois du côté des utilisateurs, c'est-à-dire de s'interroger notamment sur les titres juridiques des utilisateurs ainsi que sur l'évaluation, le commerce et la fiscalité.

---

21 Rapport national Pologne (Commission I).

- En ce qui concerne les titres d'occupation, il convient de distinguer toutes les formes de propriété[22] – unique ou partagée, privée et publique[23] – et, habituellement, le bail. Il s'agit là d'un domaine juridique traditionnellement national, qui se manifeste par des droits de propriété constitutionnels et leurs restrictions[24] ainsi que par divers droits de location de terres.[25] Il s'agit souvent de droits très anciens, comme c'est le cas ici au Royaume-Uni, ou il suffit de penser aux commons,[26] qui peuvent peut-être fournir des indications sur des formes d'exploitation plus durables. Cela devrait toutefois faire l'objet d'un prochain congrès de droit agraire.
- En ce qui concerne l'évaluation, le commerce et la fiscalité, les différents systèmes juridiques nationaux présentent une image différenciée.[27] Les prescriptions en matière de bonus, le trafic de terrains (verts), les droits d'utilisation de l'eau et du bois ainsi que le droit fiscal font bien la distinction entre les sols, les eaux et les forêts. Jusqu'à présent, leur influence sur la thématique est restée nettement en retrait par rapport à celle des réglementations écologiques et mérite d'être étudiée plus en détail.

---

22 Voir la proposition d'une nouvelle catégorie de « biens publics » en Italie ; Rapport national Italie (Commission II). Une définition pourrait être trouvée dans la proposition de loi élaborée par la Commission Rodotà, les biens communs se référant aux « choses qui expriment des utilités fonctionnelles pour l'exercice des droits fondamentaux ainsi que des libertés des êtres humains » (*Rodota*, Verso i beni comuni, Riv. Crit. Dir. Priv. 2017, p. 495 ss). Là aussi sur la spécificité de ce que l'on appelle les banques de terres.

23 Rapport national Espagne (Commission II).

24 En ce qui concerne plus particulièrement la problématique du cumul des interventions sur la propriété foncière agricole, voir *Kreuzer*, Mehrfachverplanung von landwirtschaftlichen Nutzflächen, AgrarR 1979, p. 183 et 185 ; *Schulze-Hagen*, Ausgleich von Mehrfachbelastungen von hoher Hand - DGAR-Ausschuss « Enteignungsrecht » zu Mehrfachbelastungen, AgrarR 1991, p. 188 ; *Norer*, Land- und forstwirtschaftliches Eigentum - Aktuelle Rechtsfragen, in : Norer/Reinl (éd.), Land- und forstwirtschaftliches Eigentum - aktuelle Rechtsfragen (2004), p. 52 ss ; dernièrement *Holzer/Lienbacher*, Agrarisches Eigentum und seine Beschränkungen (2024), p. 73 ss.

25 Notamment le rapport national Royaume-Uni (Commission II).

26 *Ostrom*, Governing the commons : The evolution of institutions for collective action (1990) ; *Elliott/Boland*, Handbook of Research on Cooperatives and Mutuals (2023). Voir par exemple *Haller/Liechti/Stuber/Viallon/Wunderli*, Balancing the Commons in Switzerland (2021).

27 Cf. uniquement le rapport national Allemagne (Commission II) ; rapport national Italie (Commission II) ; rapport national Espagne (Commission II).

B. Apports de substances

C'est dans le domaine des produits phytosanitaires et des engrais que la problématique des sujets traités par la Commission II est la plus évidente. Les discussions sur le glyphosate et les néonicotinoïdes, en particulier, sont passionnées et ont donné lieu à des résultats législatifs remarquables.

En Allemagne, par exemple, l'utilisation de produits phytosanitaires a été interdite dans les zones importantes pour la protection de la nature et le long des cours d'eau, et le glyphosate a été interdit dans les jardins familiaux et sur les surfaces utilisées par le grand public.[28] Le législateur autrichien a fait preuve de plus de créativité en interdisant la mise sur le marché de produits phytosanitaires contenant du glyphosate sur les terrains de sport et de loisirs accessibles au public, après qu'une interdiction générale déjà décidée au Parlement ait été rejetée par la Commission européenne comme étant formellement inadmissible,[29] les piscines, les établissements de garde d'enfants, les établissements d'enseignement, les aires de jeux pour enfants, les parcs et jardins, les cimetières, les établissements d'aide aux personnes handicapées, les établissements d'aide aux personnes âgées, et les établissements de santé et de soins, pour les jardins familiaux et les jardins d'agrément, ainsi que pour les usages non professionnels, sauf si un certificat de compétence est disponible.[30] En Suisse, le sujet a réveillé l'esprit de démocratie directe, deux initiatives populaires ayant été nettement rejetées dans les urnes en 2021. Ainsi, l'initiative dite « pour une eau potable propre »[31] exigeait que seules les exploitations agricoles qui

---

28 §§ 4, 4a Verordnung über Anwendungsverbote für Pflanzenschutzmittel (Pflanzenschutz-Anwendungsverordnung) du 10 novembre 1992 (BGBl. I S. 1887). Dans le rapport national allemand, également pour la désignation de « zones rouges » (pollution par les nitrates) et de « zones jaunes » (pollution par le phosphore) conformément au règlement sur les eaux souterraines.

29 Sur ce point, *Holzer*, Glyphosatverbot im Spannungsfeld von Unionsrecht und nationalem Recht, in : Norer/ders. (éd.), Agrarrecht Jahrbuch 2020 (2020), p. 246 ss.

30 Art. 3 al. 4 de la loi sur les produits phytosanitaires 2011, BGBl. I 2011/10.

31 L'initiative « *Pour une eau potable propre et une alimentation saine - Pas de subventions pour l'utilisation de pesticides et l'utilisation d'antibiotiques à titre prophylactique* » de l'association pour « Une eau propre pour tous » visait à modifier l'art. 104 Cst. sur l'agriculture de manière à garantir un approvisionnement sûr de la population en denrées alimentaires saines et en eau potable propre. Cet objectif devait être atteint en ne soutenant par des paiements directs ou des subventions que les exploitations agricoles qui n'utilisent pas de pesticides, ne pratiquent pas l'utilisation prophylactique d'antibiotiques dans leur élevage et n'élèvent que le nombre d'animaux qu'elles peuvent nourrir sans importer de fourrage. Le Parlement fédéral a

n'utilisent pas de pesticides, entre autres, puissent bénéficier de paiements directs ou de subventions. L'initiative sur les pesticides[32] visait à interdire de manière générale l'utilisation de pesticides synthétiques dans la production agricole, la transformation de produits agricoles et l'entretien des sols et des paysages, ainsi que l'importation de denrées alimentaires contenant des pesticides synthétiques ou produites à l'aide de ceux-ci. Mais d'autres rapports nationaux décrivent également l'utilisation – légalement autorisée – de certaines substances actives comme étant controversée.[33]

C. Incitations

Outre le droit réglementaire,[34] des incitations financières sont souvent mises en place pour protéger le capital naturel dans l'agriculture, principalement par le biais de financements proposés dans le cadre du premier et du deuxième pilier de la PAC dans l'UE[35] ou dans des pays tiers par le biais de subventions nationales.[36]

---

recommandé le rejet de l'initiative. L'initiative a finalement été rejetée par une nette majorité du peuple et des cantons lors de la votation du 13 juin 2021.

32 L'initiative populaire fédérale « *Pour une Suisse sans pesticides de synthèse* » allait dans le même sens. Cette initiative demandait une adaptation de l'art. 74 Cst. relatif à la protection de l'environnement, selon laquelle l'utilisation de pesticides de synthèse dans la production agricole, la transformation de produits agricoles et l'entretien du sol et du paysage, ainsi que l'importation de denrées alimentaires contenant des pesticides de synthèse ou produites à l'aide de ceux-ci, devaient être interdites de manière générale. L'initiative et le contre-projet présenté par la Commission devaient être traités en même temps que la nouvelle politique agricole (PA22+). En raison de la suspension de la PA22+, l'initiative a toutefois été soumise au vote le 13 juin 2021 déjà. Le peuple et les cantons ont suivi la recommandation de l'Assemblée fédérale et ont clairement rejeté l'initiative.

33 Rapport national Italie (Commission II) ; rapport national Espagne (Commission II), y compris sur la mise en œuvre de la directive 91/676/CEE concernant la protection des eaux contre la pollution par les nitrates à partir de sources agricoles, JO L 375/1.

34 Voir en particulier la « voie de la baisse » inscrite dans la loi en Suisse ; Rapport national Suisse (Commission II).

35 Rapport national France (Commission II), y compris sur la labélisation ; Rapport national Allemagne (Commission II) ; Rapport national Italie (Commission II), y compris sur les obstacles à la mise en œuvre nationale des *paiements pour services écosystémiques (PSE)* ; Rapport national Espagne (Commission II).

36 Rapport national Suisse (Commission II).

Actuellement, ce sont surtout les paiements directs qui font office de porte d'entrée.[37] Ceux-ci se prêtent directement aux objectifs étudiés ici et sont tout à fait idéaux du point de vue de la protection de l'environnement, car la perception de paiements directs

- est de facto indispensable pour les agriculteurs ;
- s'effectue en grande partie sur l'ensemble du territoire, ce qui permet d'obtenir rapidement un large impact sur le terrain ;
- peut être renforcée dans une large mesure sans problème sur le plan juridique (étant donné qu'en règle générale, aucun problème de droit de propriété ne se pose) ;
- soit contrôlée par une exécution efficace de la promotion agricole (contrairement à l'exécution parfois peu efficace du droit de l'environnement) ;
- se fait sur le budget agricole.

On retrouve ici une fois de plus la tendance, déjà observée à plusieurs reprises, de la mise en œuvre du droit de l'environnement par le droit agricole,[38] étendue désormais au droit de la protection du climat ainsi qu'au droit du travail et au droit social avec la conditionnalité sociale.[39]

D. Droits procéduraux

Les droits procéduraux jouent également un rôle important dans ce contexte, car le droit évolue actuellement sur deux voies différentes. D'une part, dans le droit procédural classique et – par extension – dans la question de la justiciabilité des valeurs du capital naturel. D'autre part, et en amont, dans le débat sur les droits subjectifs de la nature.

---

37 Ainsi *Norer*, Gewässerschutz und Landwirtschaft im Recht: Nutztierhaltung, Produktionsmittel und Verunreinigungsverbot, in : ders. (éd.), Landwirtschaft und Wasser – Gewäserreinhaltung, Gewässerräume und Bewässerung in rechtlicher Perspektive (2023), p. 32 s.

38 C'est déjà le cas de *Hofer*, Das neue Landwirtschaftsgesetz und dessen Entstehung, BlAR 2/1996, p. 71 ; critique de *Norer*, Lebendiges Agrarrecht. Lignes de développement et perspectives du droit dans l'espace rural (2005), p. 348.

39 Art. 14 du règlement (UE) 2021/2115 établissant les règles applicables au soutien des plans stratégiques à élaborer par les États membres dans le cadre de la politique agricole commune et à financer par le Fonds européen agricole de garantie (FEAGA) et le Fonds européen agricole pour le développement rural (Feader) (plans stratégiques de la PAC), JO L 435/1.

- En ce qui concerne le droit procédural classique, il convient de mentionner à titre d'exemple la jurisprudence européenne et nationale relative au droit de recours des associations dans le cadre de l'autorisation des produits phytosanitaires. Ainsi, au niveau supranational, les tribunaux européens ont à plusieurs reprises classé les documents sur lesquels se fondent les procédures d'autorisation des produits phytosanitaires comme informations environnementales et ont confirmé les droits d'accès des ONG à ces informations.[40] En Suisse, à titre d'exemple d'État non membre de l'UE, les plus hautes juridictions ont admis le droit de recours des associations dans la procédure de l'Office fédéral de l'agriculture pour le contrôle ciblé des produits phytosanitaires autorisés.[41] Ces deux jurisprudences sont liées à la Convention d'Aarhus[42] qui, d'une part, prescrit l'accès aux procédures administratives pour pouvoir contester les actes de particuliers et d'autorités publiques qui enfreignent les dispositions relatives à l'environnement (art. 9, al. 3) et, d'autre part, exige que les autorités publiques mettent à la disposition du public des informations environnementales (art. 4, al. 1).

  Un deuxième exemple, plus connu, est celui des nombreuses plaintes relatives au climat.[43] Alors que tous les regards sont actuellement tournés vers la CEDH, parmi les jugements nationaux, la décision de la Cour constitutionnelle allemande sur le climat[44] a particulièrement fait parler d'elle. Bien qu'elle rejette la possibilité pour les associations de protection de l'environnement de déposer des recours constitutionnels et qu'elle ne

40 Affaire C-442/14 de la CJUE du 23 novembre 2016 ; mais affaire C-673/13 P du 23 novembre 2016. Affaire T-545/11 RENV de la TPICE du 21 novembre 2018 ; affaire T-716/14 du 7 mars 2019 ; affaire T-329/17 du 7 mars 2019, mais affaire T -725/15 du 14 décembre 2018. Voir également Buonsante/Friel, What is Information Relating to Emissions into the Environment ?, EJRR 2017, p. 453 ss.

41 Tribunal fédéral : TF 1C_312/2017 du 12 février 2018. Voir aussi *Thurnherr*, Anmerkung der Redaktion, URP 2018, p. 214 ss.
Tribunal administratif fédéral : TAF, arrêt B-64/2016 du 25 avril 2017 ; arrêts B-662/2016, B-663/2016, B-665/2016 et B-666/2016 du 3 avril 2019 ; arrêts B-532/2019, B-535/2019 et B-556/2019 du 25 octobre 2019. Voir également *Seferovic*, Ideelle Verbandsbeschwerde im Zulassungsverfahren für Pflanzenschutzmittel ? – Ein Beitrag zum Begriff der Bundesaufgabe nach Art. 2 NHG, URP 2017, p. 418 ss.

42 Convention sur l'accès à l'information, la participation du public au processus décisionnel et l'accès à la justice en matière d'environnement (Convention d'Aarhus) du 25 juin 1998.

43 Rapport national Allemagne (Commission II).

44 BVerfG, décision du premier sénat du 24 mars 2021 - 1 BvR 2656/18. Voir le rapport national Allemagne (Commissions II et III).

reconnaisse pas la violation de la garantie de la propriété, elle affirme que l'État a un devoir fondamental de protection de la propriété en ce qui concerne les dangers du changement climatique.

- En ce qui concerne les droits subjectifs de la nature, ces questions font l'objet de discussions depuis des décennies, sans pour autant – c'est du moins mon impression – que des progrès significatifs aient été réalisés.[45] Malgré les demandes d'une large prise en compte des entités naturelles et donc aussi des forêts ou des eaux (il suffit de penser à la lagune d'eau salée Mar Menor en Espagne),[46] la discussion se concentre actuellement sur les droits des animaux et donc aussi sur la critique de l'élevage agricole.[47] Un changement de notre système juridique, en fin de compte anthropocentrique, vers un modèle écocentrique fait l'objet de discussions parfois controversées dans la science et la philosophie du droit.[48]

E. Résumé

Les réflexions sur les nouvelles formes d'utilisation des terres et notamment les questions d'évaluation, de commerce et de taxation du capital naturel sont rarement posées de manière fondamentale. D'un point de vue juridique, les réglementations supranationales et nationales s'entremêlent parfois de manière particulièrement étroite, créant une compilation peu propice et désagréable à l'application du droit. La gamme des moyens de production agricole s'élargit considérablement dans certains domaines en raison des progrès scientifiques, il suffit de penser aux nouvelles techniques

45 Rapport national Allemagne (Commission II) concernant l'initiative bavaroise « Droits de la nature », qui souhaite introduire un art. 101 dans la constitution bavaroise par le biais d'un référendum.

46 Rapport national Espagne (Commission II). Concernant les actions en nature, notamment « *Seehunde in der Nordsee* », VG Hamburg, décision du 22.09.1988 - 7 VG 2499/88 ; « *Massentötung von Rindern* », VG Frankfurt a.M., décision du 01.03. 2001 - 1 G 429/01 ; « *Kivalina* », Native Village of Kivalina v. ExxonMobil Corp.d 849 (2012) ; « *Ganges et Yamuna* », Haute Cour de l'Uttarakhand à Nainital, 126/2014, Ordre du 20.03.2017 - Cour suprême de l'Inde, 07.07.2017 ; « *Urgenda* », The Hague District Court C/09/456689/HA ZA 13-1396 (2015), Urgenda Foundation v. The State of the Netherlands ; « Huaraz », OLG Hamm, procédure d'appel pendante depuis 2018 I-5 U 15/17, Saúl Luciano Lliuya/RWE.

47 Au lieu de nombreux *Stucki*, Grundrechte für Tiere: Eine Kritik des geltenden Tierschutzrechts und rechtstheoretische Grundlegung von Tierrechten im Rahmen einer Neupositionierung des Tieres als Rechtsubjekt (2018).

48 Rapport national Allemagne (Commission II) avec références.

génomiques pour la sélection végétale (NGT), mais le cadre juridique, lui, se rétrécit de plus en plus. Les petites guerres juridiques entre le droit européen et le droit national, comme on l'a vu avec le glyphosate, n'apportent pas grand-chose et rendent difficile la prise de conscience du fait que l'agriculture moderne, même technicisée, dépend des engrais, des fourrages, des produits phytosanitaires et des semences pour garantir la sécurité alimentaire. Il en va de même si l'on interprète la Convention d'Aarhus de manière large ou si l'on attribue des droits subjectifs aux entités naturelles.

V. Commission III

Le questionnaire relatif à la Commission III a été particulièrement détaillé cette fois-ci, car les questions portaient sur des thèmes importants et étaient assez exhaustives. Il n'est donc pas surprenant que les réponses soient parfois très complètes. J'ai été très impressionné par les rapports nationaux, qui dépassent parfois les 60 pages.[49] Il est impossible de rendre compte ici, même approximativement, de l'ampleur des informations présentées. C'est pourquoi je me contenterai de citer quelques points.

A. Des stratégies plutôt que des normes

Comme on le sait, la Commission européenne et les législateurs européens en général disposent des formes d'action de l'art. 289 du TFUE, c'est-à-dire des règlements, des directives, des décisions, etc. En revanche, les plans d'action et les stratégies n'y figurent pas. Pourtant, nous sommes actuellement submergés par une multitude de déclarations d'intention juridiquement non contraignantes : Green Deal, stratégie Farm to Fork, stratégie de biodiversité, agriculture biologique, espace rural, stratégie des sols ou « Fit for 55 ». Les visions sont suivies de stratégies et de plans d'action, les stratégies et les plans d'action sont suivis de lignes directrices et les lignes directrices sont suivies de propositions législatives. Cela ne veut pas dire qu'il ne peut pas y avoir de réglementations « dures », comme l'a prouvé par exemple la loi européenne sur la restauration de la nature déjà mentionnée. Néanmoins, on a l'impression que la mise en œuvre de ces domaines

49 Cf. rapport national Pologne (Commission III) en tant qu'œuvre commune.

thématiques donnera lieu à un vaste et confus mélange de nouvelles réglementations supranationales et nationales.[50] La Pologne a même déposé une plainte auprès de la Cour de justice européenne.[51]

Le contre-programme semble exister aux États-Unis, où les Farm Bills centraux établissent d'importantes mesures de politique agricole et alimentaire qui régissent de nombreux aspects du droit rural aux États-Unis.[52]

B. Mise en œuvre de la PAC

Les réponses des rapports nationaux sur le thème de la mise en œuvre des nouveaux plans stratégiques de la PAC révèlent de manière impressionnante la renationalisation de la politique agricole prétendument « commune » qui en découle. Les marges de décision sont utilisées dans toute leur ampleur et la profusion d'offres différentes au niveau national semble déconcertante. Il en va de même pour l'activité normative des États membres qui en résulte et qui suit l'approbation des différents plans stratégiques.[53] Celle-ci se fait généralement de manière très détaillée.[54]

Il est inévitable que des problèmes de mise en œuvre se posent. Ils vont de la question pas si simple de la nature juridique des plans stratégiques[55] aux questions de contenu.[56]

50 Cf. rapport individuel Perteguer Prieto (Commission III) en ce qui concerne les registres fonciers espagnols.

51 En ce qui concerne « Fit for 55 » ; Rapport national Pologne (Commission III).

52 Rapport national États-Unis (Commission III).

53 Rapport national France (Commission III) ; rapport national Allemagne (Commission III) au niveau fédéral et régional ; rapport national Slovénie (Commission III) ; rapport national Espagne (Commission III).

54 Voir par exemple les nombreuses définitions dans les actes de transposition allemands ; Rapport national Allemagne (Commission III). En Italie, le plan stratégique national compte déjà plus de 4000 pages ; Rapport national Italie (Commission III).

55 Voir *Holzer*, Grundsätzliches zur Umsetzung der GAP-Reform 2023-2027 in Österreich, in: Norer/ders. (éd.), Agrarrecht Jahrbuch 2023 (2023), p. 173 ss. Cette question revêt une grande importance en raison de la mise en œuvre de la PAC en Autriche telle qu'elle a été pratiquée jusqu'à présent, tant en droit public qu'en droit privé.

56 Rapport national Allemagne (Commission III).

C. Chaîne de valeur

En ce qui concerne le renforcement de la position des agriculteurs dans la chaîne de valeur, plusieurs États membres ont adopté des actes législatifs nationaux à cet effet, en application de la directive UTP[57].[58] Les États non membres de l'UE, comme la Suisse, ne disposent pas de réglementations comparables.[59]

C'est le cas de l'Allemagne avec une loi visant à renforcer les organisations et les chaînes d'approvisionnement dans le secteur agricole, qui réglemente la reconnaissance et l'exemption des organisations agricoles en matière de droit des cartels et l'interdiction des pratiques commerciales déloyales.[60] En Pologne, en Slovénie et en Espagne, une réglementation nationale existante a été adaptée en conséquence.[61] D'autres pays misent en outre sur des allégements fiscaux[62] ou des subventions en capital et des prêts à taux réduit aux entreprises du secteur agroalimentaire.[63]

D. Plus de devoirs ou de droits ?

Globalement, à la lecture des rapports et des discussions au sein de la Commission III, on pourrait se demander si, en fin de compte, on a créé plus de devoirs ou plus de droits pour les agriculteurs.

57 Directive (UE) 2019/sur les pratiques commerciales déloyales dans les relations interentreprises au sein de la chaîne d'approvisionnement agricole et alimentaire, JO L 111/59.

58 Voir *Paredis/Keirsbilck/Terryn/Verdonk*, Unfair Trading Practices in the Agricultural and Food Supply Chain. Implementation of Directive (EU) 2019/663 in the EU-27 (2024) ; *Mögele/Sitar*, in : Montag/Säcker/Bien/Meier-Beck, Münchener Kommentar zum Wettbewerbsrecht, 4e édition (2022), C. Agriculture, Rn. 482 ss ; *Daskalova*, Regulating Unfair Trading Practices in the EU Food Supply Chain, in : Lianos/Ivanov/Davis, Global Food Value Chains and Competition Law (2022), p. 373 ss.

59 Rapport national Suisse (Commission III).

60 Loi sur les organisations agricoles et la chaîne d'approvisionnement (AgrarOLkG) du 24 août 2021 (BGBl. I p. 4036) ; Rapport national Allemagne (Commission III). Voir également le rapport national italien (Commission III).

61 Rapport national Pologne (Commission III) ; Rapport national Slovénie (Commission III), voir le soi-disant Food Supply Chain Relationships Ombudsman ; Rapport national Espagne (Commission III), voir les soi-disant standard agri-food contracts.

62 Rapport national France (Commission III) ; Rapport national Pologne (Commission III).

63 Ainsi nommé Supply Chain Contracts and District ; rapport national Italie (Commission III).

Hormis le projet à long terme de simplification de la PAC,[64] il n'y a pas de réponse claire à cette question. D'une part, on trouve des évaluations, en particulier dans le domaine de l'organisation et de la mise en œuvre de l'activité agricole, selon lesquelles les exploitations sont confrontées à des charges accrues dues à la législation.[65] Ces obligations accrues ne peuvent toutefois pas être imputées uniquement au droit européen, mais résultent souvent aussi de la législation ou de la jurisprudence nationales.[66] D'un autre côté, il est possible d'identifier – timidement, mais tout de même – des allègements ou du moins des tentatives d'allègement. Ainsi, les Pays-Bas ont adopté une nouvelle loi sur l'environnement et la planification qui remplace 26 lois, 60 décrets gouvernementaux et 75 arrêtés ministériels.[67] Le simple maintien de réglementations qui ont fait leurs preuves peut peut-être aussi en faire partie.[68]

E. Résumé

Le résumé de cette commission lors du dernier congrès[69] peut être repris tel quel, même s'il date de quatre ans. Compte tenu de la similitude des problèmes et du fait que la PAC est le point commun de la plupart des rapports, la diversité des thèmes, des accents et des formes rapportés ne cesse

64 Voir *Norer/Bloch*, G. Agrarrecht, in : Dauses (éd.), Handbuch des EU-Wirtschaftsrechts, Bd. 1 (29e livraison complémentaire 2011), Rz. 268 ss avec d'autres références. Voir également Simplification de la politique agricole commune de l'UE (PAC), https://www.consilium.europa.eu/en/policies/cap-simplification/.

65 Rapport national Allemagne (Commission III).

66 Par exemple, en Allemagne, à la législation nationale (modifications des statistiques agricoles, forfaits pour la taxe sur le chiffre d'affaires et exigences en matière d'enregistrement pour les éleveurs, prescriptions plus strictes en matière de protection des plantes et des insectes dans la loi fédérale sur la protection de la nature) et à la jurisprudence (prescriptions du tribunal administratif fédéral concernant l'interdiction des poussins de poules mâles) ; rapport national Allemagne (Commission III).

67 L'objectif de cette loi est de combiner différentes lois et réglementations relatives à la construction, à l'environnement, à l'eau, à l'aménagement du territoire et à la nature, afin de simplifier les règles applicables aux projets territoriaux et au cadre de vie. Le secteur agricole et les avocats spécialisés dans le droit agricole sont également concernés par cette loi, car elle comprend des réglementations relatives à la propriété foncière et à l'utilisation des terres dans la zone périphérique ; Rapport national Pays-Bas (Commission III).

68 Rapport national Suisse (Commission III).

69 *Norer*, Rapport de synthèse, in : CEDR (éd.), Food sovereignty, food security and the contribution of agricultural law (2023), p. 451.

d'étonner. Si l'on peut dénier à l'UE, dans la frénésie créative du Green Deal, une main ordonnatrice parmi toutes les visions, stratégies, plans d'action et propositions législatives, il en va de même pour les législateurs nationaux. Ils s'efforcent de transposer les directives européennes, de les intégrer le mieux possible dans le paysage juridique national existant et, comme si cela ne suffisait pas, de les enrichir d'extensions nationales (Gold-plating[70]). Cela ne contribuera que très rarement à une réduction des obligations et des charges administratives des agriculteurs en activité.

VI. Colloque[71]

Enfin, le colloque montre qu'il y a beaucoup à perdre. Il s'agit précisément des prestations fournies par l'agriculture dans le cadre du concept multifonctionnel qui a fait ses preuves. Celles-ci sont liées à l'agriculture – soit directement, parce qu'elles sont en quelque sorte un sous-produit dans le « sillage » de l'exploitation agricole[72] (ou de la non-exploitation dans le cas des surfaces de compensation écologique), soit indirectement, parce qu'il s'agit de prestations qui se sont éloignées de l'activité agricole classique. La tentative de définir de telles prestations multifonctionnelles et de les valoriser au moyen de l'internalisation des coûts externes a parfois occupé intensivement le droit agricole.[73]

D'une certaine manière, le débat actuel sur le « Public money for public goods » rappelle ces développements bien connus. Dans un premier temps, il faut trouver et définir un tel « bien public »,[74] dans un deuxième temps, il faut que quelqu'un – en l'occurrence le monde politique, peut-être même l'opinion publique – reconnaisse cette prestation comme un bien public et soit prêt à utiliser des fonds publics à cet effet. La seule différence avec le concept de multifonctionnalité, comme l'a souligné *Mögele* dans sa décla-

---

70 https://en.wikipedia.org/wiki/Gold-plating_(EU_law).

71 Voir également *Busse/Mögele/Petetin*, Das Kolloquium « Public money for public goods » im Rahmen des XXXI. Europäischen Agrarrechtskongresses des CEDR in Cardiff, AUR 2024, p. 2 ss.

72 La « théorie du sillage », qui n'est plus défendue aujourd'hui, affirme que la plupart des fonctions utiles à la société suivent gratuitement la production agricole et forestière dans le sillage de celle-ci. Cf. *Glück*, Das Elend der Kielwassertheorie, Internationaler Holzmarkt 5/1982, p. 15 ss.

73 Cf. *Norer* (éd.), Agrarische Diversifikation – rechtliche Aspekte von Agrotourismus bis Energieerzeugung (2013).

74 Fondamental *Vanni*, Agriculture and Public Goods. The Role of Collective Action (2014).

ration, réside probablement dans le fait que ces prestations indemnisables étaient jusqu'à présent considérées comme des « prestations accessoires » à l'agriculture – il s'agit tout de même ici de politique agricole –, alors que dans le concept « Public money for public goods », ces prestations accessoires menacent de devenir autonomes et de s'ériger en prestation principale, ce qui semble toutefois, à mon avis, les faire sortir définitivement de la PAC, déjà très généreuse en termes de droit des compétences.

De nombreux exemples ont été cités. Les biens publics relevant du droit de l'environnement, de la nature et du climat sont connus de tous, la protection du paysage ou la protection contre les risques naturels doivent être discutées, tout comme la sécurité de l'approvisionnement et l'occupation des régions périphériques. Peu importe comment on positionne théoriquement les biens publics – et il y a beaucoup à dire pour les assimiler à des « intérêts publics » – il est utile que le législateur les ait déjà normalisés comme étant d'intérêt public ou comme un bien juridique.

Pour donner un exemple : Dans le contexte de la problématique du loup et de son impact sur le pastoralisme dans les Alpes, j'ai dû me pencher sur les intérêts publics qui plaident en faveur de l'exploitation des alpages. La présence d'animaux d'élevage pendant les mois d'été entraîne un nombre surprenant d'effets qui sont tous en soi d'intérêt public. Sans entrer dans les détails : La gestion des alpages

1. maintient le paysage ouvert (sinon, les prairies de montagne dégagées seraient peu à peu envahies par la végétation), ce qui est particulièrement important pour le tourisme ;
2. préserve la biodiversité alpine (la richesse des espèces est plusieurs fois supérieure dans les prairies de fauche de montagne entretenues que dans les surfaces non entretenues ou recouvertes de végétation) ;
3. protège contre les risques naturels (notamment protection contre l'érosion et les avalanches) ;
4. préserve les formes d'exploitation traditionnelles et entretient le patrimoine culturel ;
5. soulage les exploitations agricoles de l'achat d'aliments pour animaux (importés) dans les exploitations de plaine ;
6. améliore la qualité des produits agricoles et peut générer une plus grande valeur ajoutée grâce à un étiquetage approprié (« étiquetage des alpages ») ;

etc.

Ce qui est surprenant, c'est que presque tous ces effets multifonctionnels sont également ancrés dans des normes correspondantes comme étant d'intérêt public. Dans cet exemple, dans le droit international (Convention de l'UNESCO pour la sauvegarde du patrimoine culturel immatériel, Convention alpine), dans le droit européen (2e pilier de la PAC avec mesures agro-environnementales, directive FFH) ou dans le droit national au niveau fédéral (par exemple au niveau constitutionnel en Autriche, la sécurité d'approvisionnement dans la BVG Nachhaltigkeit[75]) ou au niveau régional et local (par exemple en Autriche, les lois sur la protection des alpages de différents Länder).

Nous devons donc nous focaliser sur d'autres domaines que le droit agraire et mettre en discussion ou créer de tels ancrages normatifs pour la question de la reconnaissance et de la valorisation de certains biens publics. Ils deviennent ainsi des intérêts visibles, ancrés normativement, qui ne peuvent pas être ignorés sans autre lors de la négociation sociale des « public goods ».[76]

VII. Conclusion

Pour finir, un petit bilan de ce congrès. 11 heures de travail en commission, 2 heures de colloque, 9 heures de repas. J'adore les biscuits gallois. Je pense qu'à l'avenir, on ne pourra plus déguster de hog roast que dans des rangées de haies galloises. Le whisky gallois est génial. Apprendre le gallois est probablement moins compliqué que de comprendre la vision de la politique agricole des quatre nations du Royaume-Uni. À l'avenir, je ne taillerai plus la haie de mon jardin qu'avec une bétaillère. Vous serez peut-être d'accord avec certaines de mes impressions.

Les Commissions I et II ont résisté aux crises et ont montré qu'il était notamment nécessaire de mettre en place une législation agroenvironnementale plus résistante aux crises, qui tienne également suffisamment compte de la sécurité alimentaire. En outre, les nouvelles formes d'utilisation des terres doivent être basées sur des réflexions globales qui ne se

75 Loi constitutionnelle fédérale sur la durabilité, la protection des animaux, la protection globale de l'environnement, la garantie de l'approvisionnement en eau et en denrées alimentaires et la recherche, BGBl. I 2013/111.

76 Cela permet de préparer le terrain pour la question importante, mais non plus juridique, de l'évaluation monétaire de ces services. En ce qui concerne les services écosystémiques, j'ai l'impression que l'on en est déjà très loin, alors que l'évaluation des paysages ou des effets récréatifs, par exemple, n'est qu'à l'état de projet.

limitent pas à l'apport de substances, mais qui intègrent également les conditions générales de l'utilisation, du commerce et de la fiscalité.

Face à la « stratégie » de Bruxelles qui fait rage actuellement et à une nouvelle PAC plus renationalisée, la Commission III a ouvert une plus grande marge de manœuvre au législateur national, qui ne devrait pas, si possible, entraîner plus d'obligations pour les agriculteurs.

Enfin, le colloque a mis en évidence la négociation de l'approche « public money for public goods » et a démontré l'importance d'un ancrage juridique des intérêts originaux du droit agricole et alimentaire.

Cependant, il y aura toujours un vide dans la succession biennale de nos congrès, 2017 Lille, 2019 Poznań, 2023 Cardiff. 2021 ? C'était peut-être le congrès intime avec nous-mêmes et la lutte contre les crises. Le congrès qui n'a eu lieu que dans nos pensées et nos cœurs, chacun pour nous dans un lieu différent, à des moments différents et sur des thèmes différents. Notre travail ici a prouvé que le droit agricole est capable d'apporter une contribution significative à la gestion de crises multiples et diverses. Nous devons continuer dans cette voie. Car nous ne voulons pas d'une nouvelle lacune dans l'agenda. Nous voulons nous retrouver en 2025, où nous espérons que certaines crises auront été maîtrisées ou du moins endiguées. Peut-être justement à cause de la législation agricole. Pour boucler la boucle : Espérons que nous aurons appris à dompter nos dragons.

Merci de votre attention !

Synthesis Report

Version anglaise – English version – Englische Version

Prof. Dr. Roland Norer
General Delegate CEDR,
University of Lucerne

I. Introduction and thanks

Dear Mr. President,
Ladies and Gentlemen,
Dear colleagues,[1]

As General Delegate, I have the honor of taking on the last academic part at the end of the XXXI European Congress of Rural Law. The start was crisis-ridden – the repeated COVID-related postponements, the waiting and worrying, the questions of a hybrid implementation – all this put a strain on our nerves. We are all the more pleased that the congress could now be held in 2023 and that a face-to-face meeting was possible again after a four-year break.

I would like to thank Dr. *Nerys Llewelyn Jones* and Dr. *Ludivine Petetin* in particular, who were ready two years ago and have now organized this congress with an extremely short preparation time under (also personally) changed circumstances. Thank you very much! My thanks also go to *Alex Carson-Taylor*, Chair, and *Mike Holland*, Secretary & Adviser, of the British Agricultural Law Association (ALA) and to all colleagues of our largest national association. The fact that you remain loyal to the CEDR in the wake of Brexit and even hold a European Congress deserves our respect. The commitment to the organization here at Cardiff University was impressive. With your hospitality and professionalism, you have all contributed to the fact that we have been able to experience unforgettable days here.

I would also like to thank the general rapporteurs and presidents of the committees for their excellent work. They led the work of the commissions in a confident and coordinated manner. For Commission I, these were Prof. Dr. *Rudy Gotzen* (thank you for stepping in at short notice) and Dr. *Alicia*

1 Expanded version with footnotes, the style of presentation has been retained.

Epstein, for Commission II *Alex Carson Taylor* and *Catherine Taskis* KC, and for Commission III Prof. Dr. *Franci Avsec* and Prof. UAM dr. hab. *Aneta Suchoń*.

In addition, a big thank you is due to all national and individual reporters. A total of 26 national reports and 4 individual reports were submitted.

My appreciation also goes to the team of the colloquium, which was held for the second time, Prof. Dr. *Rudolf Mögele*, Dr. *Christian Busse* and Dr. *Ludivine Petetin*.

Finally, I would also like to thank you, dear participants. Through your active participation, your written and oral contributions, you have made an important contribution to the success of this European Agricultural Law Congress.

Following tradition, the scientific analysis of this XXXI European Congress and Colloquium of Rural Law will now take the form of a summary report covering all three commissions and the colloquium. In doing so, I am not trying to proceed according to the well-known motto "everything has already been said, but not yet by everyone", but rather to make a few general observations that seem particularly important to me.

II. Topics

The last congress in Poznań in 2019 already included an important element of this year's theme with the topics of "food sovereignty" and "food security". At that time, these themes were described in the synthesis report as one of the most pressing problems of our time, alongside climate change, biodiversity loss and environmental damage.[2] The COVID and Ukraine crises have since been added to the list.

Like the biblical Job, they sit there, dependent on each other, refer to each other and form an unholy alliance. So what could be more obvious than to devote ourselves to the multiple crises this time? "Agricultural law in times of crisis: policies and production impacts" is the general theme. This addresses global problems and affects EU member states and third countries – such as our host – in equal measure.

---

2 *Norer*, Synthesis Report, in: CEDR (ed.), Food sovereignty, food security and the contribution of agricultural law (2023), p. 456.

Naturally, this topic has not been the subject of previous congresses. Aspects of market regulation in particular[3] and the influence of environmental legislation on agricultural production[4] have been discussed repeatedly in the past, but always in its entirety and less focused on crisis mode. The actual starting point is more or less only the last congress in Poznań in 2019[5].

In Commission I, "Multiple crises: responses in agricultural law", we perhaps worded it somewhat uncertainly. But the selection of topics to be dealt with did indeed read like a horde of apocalyptic horsemen: Ukraine war, COVID, energy crises, diseases and climate change. Possible agricultural counter-strategies such as safety nets and agricultural reserves, interventions, compulsory stockpiling or insurance sounded inconspicuous and technical in comparison. 8 national reports and 2 individual reports examined whether this was really the case.

In Commission II, the focus was on "Carbon, biodiversity and nutrients: new land use considerations", the discussions focused on natural capital, the basis of life for all of us. The discussion of various models relating to carbon, biodiversity, nutrients and land use in different legal systems, as well as opportunities and risks, provided an chance to analyse an important but, at least from a legal perspective, largely neglected topic. Pesticides, fertilizers and animal feed as well as the use of carbon, nitrate, phosphorus, glyphosate and neonicotinoids including application regulations and application bans are currently under criticism but can contribute to a more crisis-resistant agriculture and thus food production. Topics such as nutrient trading, land management policy and water protection were just as relevant as the approval regimes and the corrective effect of environmental

3 In particular XIV Congress, Commission II "Old and new legal techniques for market regulation", Salzburg 1987; XX Congress, Commission I "AGENDA 2000 - Market and price policy", Amsterdam 1999; XXI Congress, Commission I "Legal instruments of the agricultural products market", Helsinki 2001.

4 In particular XIV Congress, Commission I "The law of agriculture and forestry and environmental problems", Salzburg 1987; XVIII Congress, Commission I "The penetration of environmental law in the field of rural law", Oxford 1995; XXVIII Congress, Commission II "Legal framework of environmental law for agricultural production" Lucerne 2013. See also III Symposium "Environmental pollution and agriculture", Plymouth 1986.

5 XXX Congress, Commission I "Food Sovereignty and food security: concepts and legal framework", Commission II "Protection of Cultivated Land: Rural Planning Law and Agricultural property and Real Estate Law", Poznań 2019.

associations' rights of appeal. 7 national reports and 1 individual report were submitted.

As has been customary since the 2009 Cambridge Congress, Commission III was dedicated to the topic of "Significant current developments in international rural law, in the EU as well as in states and regions". The focus was on noteworthy national legal developments in the individual countries of the rapporteurs, but also on the reference to and implementation of European law as well as general trends. The topics proposed in the questionnaire, such as the Nitrates Directive, flood protection and renaturation, irrigation, climate change and agriculture, were again used as reference points, which could be supplemented and expanded as required. In terms of EU law, it was possible to focus on the numerous action plans and strategies under the Green Deal as well as the implementation of the new CAP in national law or the integration to be observed with food law ("farm to fork"). Finally, the range of topics was extended to include international agreements (in particular CETA, TTIP), agricultural land registers, labor law (seasonal workers) and the pressing problem of wolves and pasture management in many countries. 11 national reports and 1 individual report were submitted here.

The questionnaires, which had been drawn up by the general rapporteurs in consultation with the general delegate, formed the basis of the country reports and therefore the Commission's work. At the same time, there was sufficient freedom to follow one's own priorities and structures while still ensuring comparability. The debates were then also incorporated into the general reports and conclusions of the individual commissions.

The colloquium "Public Money for Public Goods: Sustainable Agriculture. The new CAP and the UK agricultural policies" was specially tailored to the organiser and, in addition to the EU's new Common Agricultural Policy, dealt in particular with the future agricultural policy of England, Wales, Scotland and Northern Ireland post-Brexit. An insight into the concepts and their implementation, especially in the EU in the national strategy plans and in the UK "Four Nations" in Agriculture Act 2020 and Agriculture (Wales) Bill 2022, promised an interesting broadening of horizons. For the EU member states, this was either as inspiration for how a renationalized European agricultural policy could be designed, or as encouragement to stick to the "common" approach.[6] This was only the second

6 Cf. *Bianchi*, Y a-t-il encore quelque chose de "commun" dans la nouvelle Politique agricole commune?, RTDE 2005, pp. 623 ff.; *Gilsdorf*, Der Grundsatz der Subsidiarität

time[7] that such a thematic block, which was attended by all participants outside of the program, was held and it once again proved to be a great success. The format is therefore likely to have finally established itself as a supplement to the Commission's work.

III. Commission I

The multiple crises mentioned in the Commission's questionnaire are a reality and present us with particular challenges. The topic to be dealt with here was aimed at possible answers. But are there any, especially in agricultural law?

A. Food security

In its communication of 23 March 2022 on ensuring food security and strengthening the resilience of food systems[8], which was mentioned in the questionnaire, the European Commission notes that the invasion of Ukraine has further destabilised the already fragile agricultural markets. Agriculture is under pressure worldwide due to the COVID-19 pandemic and climate change. Food security is already threatened by droughts, floods and heatwaves as well as rising sea levels, and these threats will increase further due to global warming and affect vulnerable regions in particular. Even if food supplies in the EU are not currently at risk, the invasion of Ukraine and a global explosion in commodity prices would drive up prices on the markets for agricultural and marine products and highlight the vulnerabilities of the food system, namely the dependence on imports of

---

und die gemeinsame Agrarpolitik, GS Grabitz (1995), pp. 77 ff.; *Priebe*, Wie "subsidiär" kann die Gemeinsame Agrarpolitik sein? EuZW 1993, p. 425; *Priebe*, Differenzierung und Dezentralisierung in der gemeinsamen Agrarpolitik, FS Steinberger (2002), p. 1347; *Seidel*, Rückführung der Landwirtschaftspolitik in die Verantwortung der Mitgliedstaaten? - Rechts- und Verfassungsfragen des Gemeinschaftsrechts, AgrarR 2000, p. 381.

7 Cf. the colloquium "The reform of the CAP" at the congress in Poznań 2019; see CEDR (ed.), Food sovereignty, food security and the contribution of agricultural law (2023), pp. 375 ff.

8 Communication from the Commission to the European Parliament, the European Council, the Council, the European Economic and Social Committee and the Committee of the Regions, "Safeguarding food security and reinforcing the resilience of food systems" of 23 March 2022, COM(2022) 133 final.

energy, fertilizers and animal feed, among other things. A certain bleakness can be felt in these statements, but the agricultural perspective that links all the complaints also becomes clear: once again, agricultural law is about food security and food supply. And the answers – international, supranational and national – that were presented and discussed in Commission I are primarily of an economic law nature.

B. Instruments

The instruments mentioned, such as labor regulations, COVID aid, liquidity protection, export restrictions, limits on speculative transactions, use of the EU agricultural reserve and many more[9] are numerous, in some cases very differentiated and presumably with varying degrees of success. As a result, a whole range of instruments seems to be returning, which can only be inaccurately described as market regulation. Buzzwords such as safety nets and agricultural reserves, intervention, compulsory share storage and insurance solutions sound like a lost pre-liberal era (without necessity).

However, one of the longest and most powerful crises is climate change and biodiversity loss. These issues, originally the subject of climate protection and environmental law, have long since been integrated into agricultural law[10], and have been significantly accentuated by the latest CAP reform. Interestingly, in crisis mode, it has now been possible to observe how conflicts of interest have been countered by temporarily suspending such regulations in favor of food production.[11] Inevitably, the question must be allowed as to whether the agri-environmental and agri-nature conservation

9 Country Report Germany (Commission I).

10 A.o. *Mögele*, The Integration of Environmental and Climate Protection into the Common Agricultural Policy – Legal Concepts and Developments, EurUP 4/2018, pp. 405 ff.; *Norer*, Saving the world under agricultural law or overtaxing it? – On the methodology of integration non-agricultural claims into European agricultural law, CEDR-JRL 1/2022, pp. 28 ff.

11 E.g. Implementing Decision (EU) 2022/484 providing for derogations from Regulation (EU) No 1307/2013 and from Delegated Regulation (EU) No 639/2014 as regards the implementation of certain conditions relating to the greening payment for claim year 2022, OJ L 98/105; Implementing Regulation (EU) 2022/1317 granting derogations from Regulation (EU) 2021/2115 as regards the application of the standards of good agricultural and environmental condition. L 98/105; Implementing Regulation (EU) 2022/1317 allowing derogations from Regulation (EU) 2021/2115 as regards the application of the standards for good agricultural and environmental condition (GAEC standards) 7 and 8 for the claim year 2023, OJ L 199/1. This is

regulations have proven to be too ambitious and not balanced enough. The primacy of environmental policy in agricultural policy, which does not take sufficient account of the equally important goal of food security, must be questioned. This was recently exemplified by the discussions on the EU Nature Restoration Law in the European Parliament.

National legislators have little room for manoeuvre here. In Germany, for example, the agricultural and food industry has been recognized as systemically relevant infrastructure, although the associated legal effects are likely to be manageable.[12] In addition, the "guarantee of an efficient agricultural sector" is one of the recognized public interests under constitutional law.[13] The state reports contain references to simple legislative acts such as crisis security laws, food management and supply security laws as well as financial support for crisis management.[14] However, government payments to crop insurance and solidarity funds[15] or the tightening of customs tariffs[16] are also an issue. In France and Italy, the name of the ministry has even been changed[17], in Italy a new Food Sovereignty Fund has been created[18], in Poland there are numerous regulations relating to Ukraine[19] and in Spain the national CAP strategic plan has been adapted[20]. The examples could go on and on.

In the struggle for a balance of interests, the starting position is sometimes precarious. Climate and environmental protection interests are expressed both in climate and environmental protection law and – in a thematically focused form – in CAP law. In contrast, the interests of security of supply are almost exclusively anchored in agricultural law. Even if both

intended to allow available land to be used as far as possible for the production of food and feed.

12 Country Report Germany (Commission I).

13 Country Report Germany (Commission I).

14 Country Report Austria (Commission I); Country Report Germany (Commission I); Country Report Poland (Commission I), support for the production of mineral fertilizers; Country Report Spain (Commission I).

15 Country Report Austria (Commission I); Country Report Italy (Commission I); Country Report Poland (Commission I).

16 Individual Report Plazas (Commission I); Country Report France (Commission I).

17 In France since 2022 "Ministère de l'Agriculture et de la Souveraineté Alimentaire"; Country Report France (Commission I). See also the "Food and Agriculture Resilience Mission (FARM)" initiative. In Italy since 2022 "Ministry of Agriculture, Food Sovereignty and Forests"; Country Report Italy (Commission III).

18 Country Report Italy (Commission I).

19 Country Report Poland (Commission I).

20 Country Report Spain (Commission I).

interests are formally to be assessed as equally important, which is even the case in primary law with Art. 39 and Art. 191 TFEU, the process of greening agricultural law, which has been observed for decades, has recently become even more accentuated. From a systematic point of view, the pressure to the detriment of production is therefore twofold, coming from outside (environmental law) and inside (agricultural law), while supply interests are only supported once (agricultural law).

Overall, and in my opinion the work in Commission I has clearly shown this, that there is no legal framework to address the multiple crises that are influencing each other in various ways. A small-scale toolbox of economic law, including the temporary suspension (but otherwise unchallenged) of environmental regulations under agricultural law, may provide short-term answers, but does not seem to be sufficiently suitable for future crises. The greatest challenge will be to coordinate activities at EU level, taking into account the economic, social and legislative differences in the various countries.[21]

C. Summary

As expected, the possible responses of agricultural law to the current multiple crises are diverse and fragmented. An environmental standard is temporarily suspended, liquidity support is provided here and insurance support is propagated there. What is missing is an overarching and systematized overall concept with the aim of holistically ensuring food security and resilience in the agricultural and food sector and its implementation, if necessary even against conflicting (environmental) interests.

IV. Commission II

The considerations on new land use in terms of carbon, biodiversity and nutrients discussed in Commission II are of fundamental importance. As stated in the questionnaire, as much as 38 % of global land use takes place on agricultural land, which puts the focus on this and thus on the Common Agricultural Policy and CAP legislation and its handling of natural capital. The most obvious and therefore most frequently addressed issue is the handling of pesticides and fertilizers.

21 Country Report Poland (Commission I).

A. Legal title

The merit of this particularly demanding commission is, among other things, to devote itself for once to the user side, i.e. to ask in particular about the legal titles of the users as well as valuation, trade and taxation.

- As far as usage titles are concerned, a distinction must be made between all forms of ownership[22] – sole or shared, private and public[23] – and usually leasehold. This refers to a traditionally national area of law, which manifests itself in constitutional property rights and their restrictions[24] as well as various land lease rights[25]. These are often very old rights, such as here in the United Kingdom, or one need only think of the commons[26], which may offer clues to more sustainable forms of use. However, this would have to be the subject of a forthcoming congress on agricultural law.
- As far as valuation, trade and taxation are concerned, the individual national legal systems present a differentiated picture.[27] Valuation requirements, green land use, water and timber use rights as well as tax law differentiate between soil, water and forest. Their influence on the topic has so far clearly taken a back seat to that of ecological regulations and is worth examining in more detail.

---

22 Cf. the proposal for a new category of "public goods" in Italy; Country Report Italy (Commission II). A definition could be found in the law proposal drafted by the Rodotà Commission, common goods refer to "things that express functional utilities for the exercise of fundamental rights as well as the freedoms of the human beings" (*Rodota*, Verso i beni comuni, Riv. Crit. Dir. Priv. 2017, pp. 495 ff.). There also on the specifics of the so-called land banks.

23 Country Report Spain (Commission II).

24 In particular on the problem of the accumulation of property interventions in agricultural land ownership, see *Kreuzer*, Mehrfachverplanung von landwirtschaftlichen Nutzflächen, AgrarR 1979, pp. 183 and 185; *Schulze-Hagen*, Ausgleich von Mehrfachbelastungen von hoher Hand – DGAR-Ausschuss „Enteignungsrecht" zu Mehrfachbelastungen, AgrarR 1991, p. 188; *Norer*, Land- und forstwirtschaftliches Eigentum – Aktuelle Rechtsfragen, in: Norer/Reinl (eds.), Land- und forstwirtschaftliches Eigentum – aktuelle Rechtsfragen (2004), pp. 52 ff.; most recently *Holzer/Lienbacher*, Agrarisches Eigentum und seine Beschränkungen (2024), pp. 73 ff.

25 In particular Country Report United Kingdom (Commission II).

26 *Ostrom*, Governing the commons: The evolution of institutions for collective action (1990); *Elliott/Boland*, Handbook of Research on Cooperatives and Mutuals (2023). See, for example, *Haller/Liechti/Stuber/Viallon/Wunderli*, Balancing the Commons in Switzerland (2021).

27 Cf. only Country Report Germany (Commission II); Country Report Italy (Commission II); Country Report Spain (Commission II).

B. Substance inputs

The issues addressed in Commission II are most evident in the handling of pesticides and fertilizers. The discussions surrounding glyphosate and neonicotinoids in particular are being passionately debated by the public and have also led to remarkable legislative results.

In Germany, for example, the use of plant protection products was banned in areas important for nature conservation and along bodies of water, and glyphosate in particular was banned in domestic and allotment gardens and on land used by the general public.[28] The Austrian legislator proved to be more creative in this respect: after a general ban that had already been passed in parliament was rejected by the European Commission as formally inadmissible,[29] the marketing of plant protection products containing the active ingredient glyphosate was banned for publicly accessible sports and leisure areas, swimming pools, childcare facilities, educational facilities, children's playgrounds, parks and gardens, cemeteries, facilities for the disabled, care facilities for the elderly, health and care facilities, for the home and allotment garden sector and for non-professional use, unless proof of expertise is available.[30] In Switzerland, the issue aroused the spirit of direct democracy, with two popular initiatives being clearly rejected at the ballot box in 2021. The so-called drinking water initiative[31] called for only those farms that do not use pesticides, among other things, to be supported with direct payments or subsidies. The so-called pesticide

28 §§ 4, 4a Ordinance on Prohibitions on the Use of Plant Protection Products (Plant Protection Application Ordinance) of 10 November 1992 (BGBl. I S. 1887). In the Country Report Germany also on the designation of "red areas" (nitrate pollution) and "yellow areas" (phosphorus pollution) in accordance with the Groundwater Ordinance.

29 *Holzer*, Glyphosatverbot im Spannungsfeld von Unionsrecht und nationalem Recht, in: Norer/ders. (eds.), Agrarrecht Jahrbuch 2020 (2020), pp. 246 ff.

30 Art. 3 para. 4 Plant Protection Products Act 2011, BGBl. I 2011/10.

31 The initiative "*For clean drinking water and healthy food – no subsidies for the use of pesticides and prophylactic antibiotics*" by the association "Clean water for all" intended to use Art. 104 of the Federal Constitution to modify the agriculture article of the Federal Constitution in such a way that the safe supply of healthy food and clean drinking water to the population should be ensured. This was to be achieved by only supporting farms with direct payments or subsidies that do not use pesticides, do not use antibiotics prophylactically in their livestock farming and only keep as many animals as they can feed without importing feed. The federal parliament recommended that the initiative be rejected. The initiative was ultimately rejected by a clear majority of the people and the cantons in the vote on 13 June 2021.

initiative[32] wanted to ban the use of synthetic pesticides in agricultural production, in the processing of agricultural products and in soil and landscape conservation, as well as the import of foodstuffs containing or produced with synthetic pesticides. However, other national reports also describe the – legally permissible – use of certain active substances as controversial.[33]

C. Incentives

In addition to regulatory law,[34] financial incentives are often provided to protect natural capital in agriculture, primarily through funding offered under the first and second pillars of the CAP in the EU[35] or in third countries through national subsidies.[36]

Currently, direct payments are particularly visible as a gateway.[37] These lend themselves directly to the purposes examined here and are ideal from an environmental protection perspective because the receipt of direct payments

32 The federal popular initiative "*For a Switzerland without synthetic pesticides*" took the same line. This initiative called for an amendment to Art. 74 of the Federal Constitution regarding environmental protection, according to which the use of synthetic pesticides in agricultural production, in the processing of agricultural products and in soil and landscape conservation, as well as the import of foodstuffs containing or produced with the aid of synthetic pesticides, should be generally prohibited. The initiative and the counter-proposal submitted by the Commission should actually be dealt with together with the new agricultural policy (AP22+). However, due to the suspension of AP22+, the initiative was already put to the vote on 13 June 2021. The people and cantons followed the recommendation of the Federal Assembly and clearly rejected the initiative.

33 Country Report Italy (Commission II); Country Report Spain (Commission II), there also on the implementation of the Nitrates Directive 91/676/EEC concerning the protection of waters against pollution caused by nitrates from agricultural sources, OJ L 375/1.

34 See in particular the legally anchored so-called reduction path in Switzerland; Country Report Switzerland (Commission II).

35 Country report France (Commission II), also on labelling; Country Report Germany (Commission II); Country Report Italy (Commission II), also on the obstacles to national implementation of *payments for ecosystem services (PES)*; Country Report Spain (Commission II).

36 Country Report Switzerland (Commission II).

37 *Norer*, Gewässerschutz und Landwirtschaft im Recht: Nutztierhaltung, Produktionsmittel und Verunreinigungsverbot, in: ders. (ed.), Landwirtschaft und Wasser - Gewässerreinhaltung, Gewässerräume und Bewässerung in rechtlicher Perspektive (2023), pp. 32 f.

- is de facto indispensable for farmers;
- will ensure that the project is largely implemented across the board and can therefore quickly achieve a broad impact;
- can be tightened up without any legal problems (as there are generally no ownership issues);
- is controlled by efficient enforcement of agricultural subsidies (in contrast to the sometimes less efficient enforcement of environmental law);
- is funded from the agricultural budget.

This once again demonstrates the frequently observed tendency for environmental law to be enforced by agricultural law,[38] now also extended to climate protection law and, with social conditionality,[39] to labour and social law.

D. Procedural rights

An important point here is also procedural law, where legal developments are currently taking place on two different tracks. Firstly, in traditional procedural law and – extended – in the question of the justiciability of natural capital values. On the other hand, and provided for in the discussion about subjective rights of nature.

- As far as traditional procedural law is concerned, the European and national case law on the right of associations to lodge complaints about the authorization of plant protection products is a good example. At supranational level, the European courts have repeatedly classified the documents underlying the authorisation procedures for plant protection products as environmental information and affirmed the associated access rights of NGOs.[40] As an example for a non-EU member state, the Federal Supreme Court of Switzerland, for example, has approved the

38 *Hofer*, Das neue Landwirtschaftsgesetz und dessen Entstehung, BlAR 2/1996, p. 71; critically *Norer*, Lebendiges Agrarrecht. Entwicklungslinien und Perspektiven des Rechts im ländlichen Raum (2005), p. 348.

39 Art. 14 Regulation (EU) 2021/2115 establishing rules on support for strategic plans to be drawn up by Member States under the common agricultural policy (CAP Strategic Plans) and financed by the European Agricultural Guarantee Fund (EAGF) and by the European Agricultural Fund for Rural Development (EAFRD), OJ L 435/1.

40 ECJ Case C-442/14 of 23 November 2016; but Case C-673/13 P of 23 November 2016. EGC Case T-545/11 RENV of 21 November 2018; Case T-716/14 of 7 March 2019; Case T-329/17 of 7 March 2019, but Case T-725/15 of 14 December 2018. See also

right of associations to lodge complaints in proceedings conducted by the Federal Office for Agriculture for the targeted review of approved plant protection products.[41] Both jurisdictions are related to the Aarhus Convention,[42] which on the one hand prescribes access to administrative proceedings in order to be able to challenge actions taken by private individuals and public authorities that violate environmental regulations (Art. 9 para. 3), and on the other hand requires public authorities to make environmental information available to the public (Art. 4 para. 1).
A second and more well-known example are the numerous climate lawsuits.[43] While all eyes are currently on the ECHR, the climate ruling by the German Federal Constitutional Court[44] has caused a particular stir among national judgments. Although it rejects the right of environmental associations to lodge constitutional complaints and denies a violation of the guarantee of property rights, it does affirm the state's fundamental duty to protect property with regard to the dangers of climate change.

- As far as subjective rights of nature are concerned, these questions have been discussed for decades without – at least in my opinion – any significant progress having been made.[45] Despite calls for the extensive inclusion of natural entities, including forests and bodies of water (just think of the Mar Menor saltwater lagoon in Spain)[46], the discussion is

---

Buonsante/Friel, What is Information Relating to Emissions into the Environment?, EJRR 2017, pp. 453 ff.

41 Federal Supreme Court: BGer 1C_312/2017 of 12 February 2018. See also *Thurnherr*, Anmerkung der Redaktion, URP 2018, pp. 214 ff.
Federal Administrative Court: FAC, judgment B-64/2016 of 25 April 2017; judgments B-662/2016, B-663/2016, B-665/2016 and B-666/2016 of 3 April 2019; judgments B-532/2019, B-535/2019 and B-556/2019 of 25 October 2019. See also *Seferovic*, Ideelle Verbandsbeschwerde im Zulassungsverfahren für Pflanzenschutzmittel? – Ein Beitrag zum Begriff der Bundesaufgabe nach Art. 2 NHG, URP 2017, pp. 418 ff.

42 Convention on Access to Information, Public Participation in Decision-making and Access to Justice in Environmental Matters (Aarhus Convention) of 25 June 1998.

43 Country Report Germany (Commission II).

44 BVerfG, Decision of the First Senate of March 24, 2021 - 1 BvR 2656/18. See Country Report Germany (Commission II and III).

45 Country Report Germany (Commission II) concerning the Bavarian initiative "Rights of Nature", which would like to include Art. 101 in the Bavarian constitution by means of a referendum.

46 Country Report Spain (Commission II). On the nature claims, in particular "*Seals in the North Sea*", VG Hamburg, order of 22.09.1988 - 7 VG 2499/88; "*Mass killing of cattle*", VG Frankfurt a.M., order of 01.03. 2001 - 1 G 429/01; "*Kivalina*", Native Village of Kivalina v. ExxonMobil Corp., 696 F.3d 849 (2012); "*Ganges and Yamuna*", High Court of Uttarakhand at Nainital, 126/2014, Order of 20.03.2017 - Supreme Court of

currently focused on animal rights and therefore also on criticism of agricultural livestock farming.[47] A change in our ultimately anthropocentric legal system towards an ecocentric model is being hotly debated in jurisprudence and legal philosophy.[48]

E. Summary

Considerations of new forms of land use and, in particular, questions of valuation, trade and taxation of natural capital are rarely addressed at a fundamental level. From a legal point of view, supranational and national regulations are sometimes particularly closely intertwined, resulting in a compilation that is not very conducive to the application of the law and is unpleasant. The range of agricultural means of production is expanding significantly in some areas due to scientific progress, for example new plant breeding (NGT), while the legal framework is becoming ever narrower. Legal battles between EU law and national law, as seen with glyphosate, are of little use and make it more difficult to understand that even mechanised modern agriculture is dependent on fertilizers, animal feed, pesticides and seeds if it is to guarantee food security. This also applies if one interprets the Aarhus Convention broadly or assigns subjective rights to natural entities.

V. Commission III

The questionnaire for Commission III was particularly detailed this time, as it covered relevant topics in a fairly comprehensive manner. It is therefore not surprising that some of the answers were very detailed. I was very impressed by the country reports, some of which were more than 60 pages long.[49] It is impossible to even come close to doing justice to the breadth of

India, 07.07.2017; "*Urgenda*", The Hague District Court C/09/456689/HA ZA 13-1396 (2015), Urgenda Foundation v. The State of the Netherlands; "Huaraz", OLG Hamm, since 2018 pending appeal proceedings I-5 U 15/17, Saúl Luciano Lliuya/RWE.

47 Instead of many *Stucki*, Grundrechte für Tiere: Eine Kritik des geltenden Tierschutzrechts und rechtstheoretische Grundlegung von Tierrechten im Rahmen einer Neupositionierung des Tieres als Rechtssubjekt (2018).

48 Country Report Germany (Commission II) with further references.

49 Cf. Country Report Poland (Commission III) as a joint work.

information presented here. For this reason, I would like to highlight just a few points here.

A. Strategies instead of standards

As is well known, the European Commission and European legislators in general have the forms of action provided for in Art. 289 TFEU at their disposal, i.e. regulations, directives, decisions etc. Action plans and strategies, on the other hand, are not listed there. Nevertheless, we are currently inundated with a multitude of such legally non-binding declarations of intent: Green Deal, Farm to Fork Strategy, Biodiversity Strategy, Organic Farming, Rural Areas, Soil Strategy or "Fit for 55". Visions are followed by strategies and action plans, strategies and action plans are followed by guidelines and guidelines are followed by legislative proposals. This does not mean that "hard" regulations cannot follow, as the aforementioned EU Nature Restoration Law has shown. Nevertheless, the impression is that the implementation of these issues will result in a broad and confusing mix of new supranational and national regulations.[50] Poland has even lodged a complaint with the ECJ.[51]

The counterpart program appears to exist in the United States, where Federal agricultural statutes (Farm Bills) establish important agricultural and food policy measures that govern many aspects of rural law in the United States.[52]

B. CAP implementation

The responses to the national reports on the implementation of the new CAP strategic plans impressively demonstrate the associated renationalization of the ostensibly "common" agricultural policy. The scope for decision-making is used across the board and the abundance of nationally differing offers seems confusing. The same applies to the resulting standard-setting

50 Cf. Individual Report Perteguer Prieto (Commission III) in relation to the Spanish land registers.

51 In relation to "Fit for 55"; Country Report Poland (Commission III).

52 Country Report USA (Commission III).

activities of the Member States, which follow the approval of the individual strategic plans.[53] These are usually very detailed.[54]

It is inevitable that implementation problems will arise. These range from the not-so-simple question of the legal nature of the strategic plans[55] to questions of content.[56]

C. Value chain

As far as strengthening the position of farmers in the value chain is concerned, various Member States have adopted national legislative acts to implement the UTP Directive[57].[58] Non-EU Member States such as Switzerland have no comparable regulations.[59]

Germany, for example, passed a law to strengthen organizations and supply chains in the agricultural sector, which regulates the recognition and antitrust exemption of agricultural organizations and prohibits unfair trading practices.[60] In Poland, Slovenia and Spain, existing national regulations

---

53 Country Report France (Commission III); Country Report Germany (Commission III) at federal and state level; Country Report Slovenia (Commission III); Country Report Spain (Commission III).

54 See, for example, the numerous definitions in the German implementation files; Country Report Germany (Commission III). In Italy, the National Strategic Plan already comprises more than 4000 pages; Country Report Italy (Commission III).

55 See *Holzer*, Grundsätzliches zur Umsetzung der GAP-Reform 2023-2027 in Österreich, in: Norer/ders. (eds.), Agrarrecht Jahrbuch 2023 (2023), pp. 173 ff. This question is of great importance due to the implementation of the CAP in Austria to date, both in public and private law.

56 Country Report Germany (Commission III).

57 Directive (EU) 2019/633 on unfair trading practices in business-to-business relationships in the agricultural and food supply chain, OJ L 111/59.

58 See *Paredis/Keirsbilck/Terryn/Verdonk*, Unfair Trading Practices in the Agricultural and Food Supply Chain. Implementation of Directive (EU) 2019/663 in the EU-27 (2024); *Mögele/Sitar*, in: Montag/Säcker/Bien/Meier-Beck, Münchener Kommentar zum Wettbewerbsrecht, 4th ed. (2022), C. Landwirtschaft, para. 482 ff.; *Daskalova*, Regulating Unfair Trading Practices in the EU Food Supply Chain, in: Lianos/Ivanov/Davis, Global Food Value Chains and Competition Law (2022), pp. 373 ff.

59 Country Report Switzerland (Commission III).

60 Agrarorganisationen-und-Lieferketten-Gesetz (AgrarOLkG) vom 24. August 2021 (BGBl. I S. 4036); Country Report Germany (Commission III). See also Country Report Italy (Commission III).

have been adapted accordingly.[61] Other countries also rely on tax relief[62] or capital grants and subsidized loans are allocated to agri-food enterprises.[63]

D. More duties or rights?

Overall, after reading the reports and the discussions in Commission III, the question could be asked as to whether, on balance, more obligations or more rights have been created for farmers.

Apart from the long-term project to simplify the CAP,[64] there is probably no clear answer to this question. On the one hand, there are evaluations, particularly in the area of organization and implementation of agricultural activities, according to which a legislatively induced increased effort at the expense of the farms is identified.[65] However, these increased obligations can probably not only be blamed on European law, but are often also due to national legislation or case law.[66] On the other hand, it is also possible to identify - delicately, but nevertheless - something like relief or at least attempted relief. In the Netherlands, for example, a new Environment and Planning Act was passed, which replaces 26 laws, 60 governmental decrees and 75 ministerial regulations.[67] The mere retention of tried and tested regulations can perhaps also be counted as such.[68]

---

61 Country Report Poland (Commission III); Country Report Slovenia (Commission III), see the so-called Food Supply Chain Relationships Ombudsman; Country Report Spain (Commission III), see the so-called standard agri-food contracts.

62 Country Report France (Commission III); Country Report Poland (Commission III).

63 So-called Supply Chain Contracts and District; Country Report Italy (Commission III).

64 See *Norer/Bloch*, G. Agrarrecht, in: Dauses (ed.), Handbuch des EU-Wirtschaftsrechts, vol. 1 (29. Ergänzungslieferung 2011), para. 268 ff. with further references. Cf. also Simplification of the EU's Common Agricultural Policy (CAP), https://www.consilium.europa.eu/en/policies/cap-simplification/.

65 Country Report Germany (Commission III).

66 For example, in Germany to national legislation (changes to agricultural statistics, flat-rate VAT and record-keeping requirements for livestock farmers, stricter requirements for plant protection and protection of insects in the Federal Nature Conservation Act) and to case law (requirements of the Federal Administrative Court regarding the ban on male chicken chicks); Country Report Germany (Commission III).

67 The purpose of this law is to combine various laws and regulations related to construction, environment, water, spatial planning and nature in order to simplify the rules for spatial projects and the living environment. The agricultural sector and lawyers specializing in agricultural law are also affected by this law, as it includes

E. Summary

The summary of this commission from the last congress[69] can be adopted without hesitation, even though it was four years ago. In view of comparable problem situations and the unifying bracket of the CAP for most reports, the diversity of reported topics, accents and forms is always astonishing. If the EU can be denied an organizing hand in the creative frenzy of the Green Deal among all the visions, strategies, action plans and legislative proposals, this must also apply to the national legislators. They are busily working on implementing the European legal requirements, fitting them as ideally as possible into the existing national legal landscape and, as if that were not enough, adding national extensions (gold-plating[70]). In very few cases will this contribute to a reduction in obligations and administrative burdens for practising farmers.

VI. Colloquium[71]

Ultimately, the colloquium shows that there is a lot to lose. It is also about the services that agriculture provides in the tried and tested multifunctional concept. These are linked to agriculture – either directly, because they occur as a by-product in the "wake"[72] of agricultural management (or non-management in the case of ecological compensation areas), or indirectly, because they are services that have moved away from traditional agricultural activity. The attempt to define such multifunctional services and to put a

---

regulations related to land ownership and land use in the outlying area; Country Report Netherlands (Commission III).

68 Country Report Switzerland (Commission III).

69 *Norer*, Synthesis Report, in: CEDR (ed.), Food sovereignty, food security and the contribution of agricultural law (2023), p. 472.

70 https://en.wikipedia.org/wiki/Gold-plating_(EU_law).

71 See also *Busse/Mögele/Petetin*, Das Kolloquium „Public money for public goods“ im Rahmen des XXXI. Europäischen Agrarrechtskongresses des CEDR in Cardiff, AUR 2024, pp. 2 ff.

72 The "wake theory", which is no longer supported today, states that most socially useful functions follow in the wake of agricultural and forestry production free of charge. Cf. *Glück*, Das Elend der Kielwassertheorie, Internationaler Holzmarkt 5/1982, pp. 15 ff.

value on them by internalizing external costs has been the subject of intense debate in agricultural law.[73]

Somehow, the current debate about "public money for public goods" is reminiscent of these well-known developments. In a first step, such a "public good" must be found and defined,[74] in a second step, someone – here probably politics, perhaps even reflecting public opinion – must also recognize this service as a public good and be prepared to use public money for it. The only difference to the multifunctionality concept, as *Mögele* pointed out in his statement, is probably that these compensable services were previously understood as "ancillary services" to agriculture – after all, this is agricultural policy – whereas in the "public money for public goods" concept, these ancillary services threaten to take on a life of their own and want to become the main service, which in my opinion seems to mean that they are finally leaving the CAP, which is very generous in terms of competence anyway.

Many examples were mentioned. The public goods under environmental, nature and climate protection law are generally known, landscape protection or protection against natural hazards must be discussed, as must security of supply and the settlement of peripheral areas. Regardless of how public goods are positioned in theory – and there is much to be said for treating them as "public interests" – it helps if the legislator has already enshrined them in law as being of public interest or as a legal good.

To give an example: In connection with the wolf problem and its impact on grazing in the Alps, I had to deal with the public interests that speak in favor of alpine pasture management. Stocking livestock during the summer months has a surprising number of effects, all of which are of public interest in their own right. Without going into too much detail: Alpine pasture management

1. keeps the landscape open (otherwise the open mountain meadows would gradually become overgrown), which is particularly important for tourism;
2. preserves alpine biodiversity (species richness is many times higher on cultivated mountain meadows than on uncultivated or overgrown areas);

---

73 Cf. *Norer* (ed.), Agrarische Diversifikation – rechtliche Aspekte von Agrotourismus bis Energieerzeugung (2013).

74 Fundamental *Vanni*, Agriculture and Public Goods. The Role of Collective Action (2014).

3. protects against natural hazards (in particular protection against erosion and avalanches);
4. preserves traditional forms of farming and maintains the cultural heritage;
5. relieves farms of the need to purchase (imported) animal feed in the valleys;
6. increases the quality of agricultural products and can achieve more added value with appropriate labeling ("Alp labelling");
   etc.

What is surprising is that almost all of these multifunctional effects are also enshrined in corresponding standards as being of public interest. In this example, for example, in international law (UNESCO Convention for the Conservation of the Intangible Cultural Heritage, Alpine Convention), in European law (2nd pillar of the CAP with agri-environmental measures, Habitats Directive) or in national law at federal level (e.g. at constitutional level in Austria the security of supply in the Federal Act on the Sustainability[75]) or at regional and local level (e.g. in Austria the mountain pasture protection laws of various Länder).

We must, of course, shift our focus beyond agricultural law and bring such normative anchors into the discussion or create them for the question of the recognition and valorization of certain public goods. In this way, they become visible, normatively anchored interests that cannot simply be overlooked in the social negotiation of public goods.[76]

VII. Conclusion

Finally, a brief summary of this congress. 11 hours commission work, 2 hours colloquium, 9 hours of eating. I love Welsh cakes. I think Hog Roast can only be enjoyed in Welsh hedgerows in the future. Welsh whiskey is great. Learning Welsh is probably less complicated than understanding the agricultural policy visions of the 4 UK nations. I will only cut my garden

75 Federal Constitutional Act on Sustainability, Animal Welfare, Comprehensive Environmental Protection, Safeguarding the Water and Food Supply and Research, BGBl. I 2013/111.

76 This can prepare the ground for the important, but no longer legal, question of the monetary valuation of such services. As far as ecosystem services are concerned, I think we are already very far advanced, whereas the valuation of landscape or recreational effects, for example, has only just been considered.

hedge with a cattle truck in the future. Maybe you can agree with some of my impressions.

Commissions I and II have defied the crises and demonstrated the need for a more crisis-resistant agri-environmental law in particular, which also takes food security sufficiently into account. Moreover, new forms of land use must be based on comprehensive considerations that include not only the input of substances but also the framework conditions of use, trade and taxation.

In view of the currently rampant Brussels "strategy" and a more renationalised new CAP, Commission III has opened up increased scope for national legislators, which should not lead to more obligations for farmers if possible.

Finally, the Colloquium revealed the negotiation of the "public money for public goods" approach and proved the importance of a legal anchoring of original agricultural and food law interests.

Ultimately, however, there will always be a gap in the two-year sequence of our congresses, 2017 Lille, 2019 Poznań, 2023 Cardiff. 2021? That was perhaps the intimate congress with ourselves and the fight against the crises. The congress that took place only in our minds and hearts, each of us in a different place, at different times and on different topics. Our work here has proven that agricultural law is capable of making a significant contribution to overcoming multiple, mutiple crises. We must continue to do so. Because we don't want another gap in the agenda. We want to meet again in 2025, when hopefully some of the crises will have been overcome or at least contained. Perhaps also precisely because of agricultural law. To close the circle: Hopefully we have learned, how to train our dragons.

Thank you for your attention!

Synthesebericht

Version allemande – German version – Deutsche Version

Prof. Dr. Roland Norer
Generaldelegierter des CEDR,
Universität Luzern

I. Einleitung und Dank

Sehr geehrter Herr Präsident,
sehr geehrte Damen und Herren,
liebe Kolleginnen und Kollegen,[1]

Als Generaldelegierter habe ich die Ehre am Ende des XXXI Europäischen Agrarrechtskongresses den letzten akademischen Part zu übernehmen. Der Start war krisenhaft – die mehrmalige COVID-bedingte Verschiebung, das Warten und Bangen, die Fragen einer hybriden Durchführung – all das hat unsere Nerven gehörig strapaziert. Umso mehr sind wir froh, dass der Kongress nun 2023 durchgeführt werden konnte und ein persönliches Treffen nach vier Jahren Zwangspause wieder möglich war.

Bei meiner Danksagung darf ich speziell Dr. *Nerys Llewelyn Jones* und Dr. *Ludivine Petetin* erwähnen, die ja schon vor zwei Jahren bereit waren und nun unter (auch persönlich) geänderten Umständen diesen Kongress mit extrem kurzer Vorbereitungszeit organisiert haben. Vielen Dank! Mein Dank geht weiter an *Alex Carson-Taylor*, Präsident, and *Mike Holland*, Generalsekretär, der britischen Agricultural Law Association (ALA) und an alle Kolleginnen und Kollegen dieser unserer größten nationalen Gesellschaft. Dass Sie im Zeichen von Brexit dem CEDR die Treue halten und sogar einen Europäischen Kongress durchführen verdient unseren höchsten Respekt. Das Engagement bei der Organisation hier in den Räumen der Universität Cardiff war beeindruckend. Sie alle haben mit Ihrer Gastfreundschaft und Professonalität dazu beigetragen, dass wir hier unvergessliche Tage erleben durften und dürfen.

---

1 Erweiterte und um den Fußnotenapparat ergänzte Fassung, der Vortragsstil wurde beibehalten.

Ich möchte auch den Generalberichterstattern und Präsidenten der Kommissionen für ihre hervorragende Arbeit danken. Sie haben die Kommissionsarbeiten souverän und koordiniert geleitet. Für die Kommission I waren dies Prof. Dr. *Rudy Gotzen* (danke für Dein kurzfristiges Einspringen) und Dr. *Alicia Epstein*, für die Kommission II *Alex Carson Taylor* und *Catherine Taskis* KC sowie für die Kommission III Prof. Dr. *Franci Avsec* und Prof. UAM dr. hab. *Aneta Suchoń*.

Darüber hinaus gebührt allen National- und Einzelberichterstattern ein großes Dankeschön. Insgesamt wurden 26 Landesberichte und 4 individuelle Berichte eingereicht.

Meine Anerkennung gilt auch dem Team des bereits zum zweiten Mal durchgeführten Kolloquiums, Prof. Dr. *Rudolf Mögele*, Dr. *Christian Busse* und Dr. *Ludivine Petetin*.

Schließlich möchte ich mich auch bei Ihnen, liebe Teilnehmerinnen und Teilnehmer, bedanken. Durch Ihre aktive Teilnahme, ihre schriftlichen und mündlichen Beiträge haben Sie einen wichtigen Beitrag zum Erfolg dieses Europäischen Agrarrechtskongresses geleistet.

In der wissenschaftlichen Analyse dieses XXXI. Europäischen Agrarrechtskongresses mit Kolloquium soll nun traditionsgemäß im Synthesebericht ein Bogen über alle drei Kommissionen und Kolloquium geschlagen werden. Dabei versuche ich nicht nach dem bekannten Motto „es wurde schon alles gesagt, aber noch nicht von jedem“ vorzugehen, sondern ein paar allgemeine Betrachtungen anzustellen, die mir besonders wichtig erscheinen.

II. Themen

Der letzte Kongress in Poznań 2019 hat mit den Themen „food sovereignty“ und „food security“ bereits ein wichtiges Element der heurigen Themenstellung aufgenommen. Damals wurde dies im Synthesebericht als eines der drängendsten Probleme unserer Zeit bezeichnet, neben Klimawandel, Biodiversitätsverlust und Umweltschäden.[2] Inzwischen haben sich noch COVID- und Ukraine-Krise dazugesellt.

Wie der biblische Hiob sitzen sie da, bedingen einander, nehmen aufeinander Bezug und vernetzen sich zu einer unheiligen Allianz. Was lag

2 *Norer*, Synthesebericht, in: CEDR (Hrsg.), Food sovereignty, food security and the contribution of agricultural law (2023), S. 476.

also näher als sich diesmal den multiplen Krisen zu widmen? „Agrarrecht in Zeiten der Krise: Auswirkungen auf Politik und Produktion" so das Generalthema. Dieses spricht globale Probleme an und betrifft die EU-Mitgliedstaten und die Drittstaaten – wie unseren Gastgeber – gleichermaßen.

Naturgemäß war dieses Thema bisher nicht Gegenstand früherer Kongresse. Zwar wurden Aspekte insbesondere der Marktregulierung[3] und des Einflusses der Umweltgesetzgebung auf die landwirtschaftliche Produktion[4] in der Vergangenheit wiederholt verhandelt, allerdings stets in seiner ganzen Breite und weniger auf den Krisenmodus ausgerichtet. Eigentlicher Anknüpfungspunkt ist mehr oder weniger allein der letzte Kongress in Poznań 2019[5].

Den Beratungsgegenstand von Kommission I formulierten wir mit „Multiple Krisen: Antworten im Agrarrecht" vielleicht etwas unsicher. Aber die Auswahl an zu bearbeitenden Themen las sich tatsächlich wie eine Horde apokalyptischer Reiter: Ukraine-Krieg, COVID, Energiekrisen, Krankheiten und Klimawandel. Mögliche agrarrechtliche Gegenstrategien wie Sicherheitsnetze und landwirtschaftliche Reserven, Interventionen, obligatorische Vorratshaltung oder Versicherungen klangen demgegenüber unauffällig und technisch. Ob das wirklich so zutrifft, damit setzten sich 8 Landesberichte und 2 Individualberichte auseinander.

In Kommission II stand unter dem Titel „Kohlenstoff, Biodiversität und Nährstoffe: Neue Überlegungen zur Landnutzung" mit dem Naturkapital unser aller Lebensgrundlage im Mittelpunkt der Beratungen. Die Erörterung verschiedener Modelle in Bezug auf Kohlenstoff, Biodiversität, Nährstoffe und Landnutzung in verschiedenen Rechtsordnungen sowie Chancen und Gefahren boten Gelegenheit ein wichtiges, aber zumindest juristisch meist vernachlässigtes Themengebiet zu analysieren. Pestizide,

---

3 Insbesondere XIV. Kongress, Kommission II „Old and new legal techniques for market regulation", Salzburg 1987; XX. Kongress, Kommission I „AGENDA 2000 – Market and price policy", Amsterdam 1999; XXI. Kongress, Kommission I „Legal instruments of the agricultural products market", Helsinki 2001.

4 Insbesondere XIV. Kongress, Kommission I „The law of agriculture and forestry and environmental problems", Salzburg 1987; XVIII. Kongress, Kommission I „The penetration of environmental law in the field of rural law", Oxford 1995; XXVIII. Kongress, Kommission II „Legal framework of environmental law for agricultural production" Luzern 2013. Siehe auch III. Symposium „Environmental pollution and agriculture", Plymouth 1986.

5 XXX. Kongress, Kommission I „Food Sovereignity and food security: concepts and legal framework", Kommission II „Protection of Cultivated Land: Rural Planning Law and Agricultural property and Real Estate Law", Poznań 2019.

Düngemittel und Futtermittel sowie der Einsatz von Kohlenstoff, Nitrat, Phosphor, Glyphosat und Neonicotinoide einschließlich Ausbringungsvorschriften und Ausbringungsverboten stehen derzeit in der Kritik, können aber zu einer krisenresistenteren Landwirtschaft und damit Nahrungsmittelproduktion beitragen. Themen wie Nährstoffhandel, Landbewirtschaftungspolitik und Gewässerschutz boten sich genauso an wie die Genehmigungsregime und das Korrektiv der Beschwerderechte von Umweltverbänden. Hier wurden 7 Landesberichte und 1 Individualbericht erstattet.

Die Kommission III widmete sich wie seit dem Cambridge-Kongress 2009 üblich dem Thema „Bedeutende aktuelle Entwicklungen im Recht des ländlichen Raums international, in der EU sowie in den Staaten und Regionen". Dabei ging es um bemerkenswerte nationale Rechtsentwicklungen in den einzelnen Ländern der Berichterstatter, aber auch um Bezug zum und Nachvollzug des europäischen Rechts sowie allgemeine Trends. Die im Fragebogen vorgeschlagenen Themen wie Nitratrichtlinie, Hochwasserschutz und Renaturierung, Bewässerung, Klimawandel und Landwirtschaft dienten wieder als Bezugsgrößen, die beliebig ergänzt und erweitert werden konnten. Aus dem EU-Recht konnte ein Schwerpunkt auf die zahlreichen Aktionspläne und Strategien im Rahmen des Green Deal ebenso gelegt werden wie die Umsetzung der neuen GAP ins nationale Recht oder die zu beobachtende Integration mit dem Lebensmittelrecht („farm to fork"). Schließlich konnte das Themenfeld ausgeweitet werden hin zu internationalen Abkommen (insbesondere CETA, TTIP), landwirtschaftliche Kataster, Arbeitsrecht (Saisonarbeitskräfte) oder das in vielen Staaten drängende Problem von Wölfen und Weidemanagement. 11 Landesberichte und 1 Individualbericht wurden hier eingereicht.

Die Fragebögen, die von den Generalberichterstattern in Absprache mit dem Generaldelegierten erstellt worden waren, bildeten die Basis der Landesberichte und damit der Kommissionsarbeit. Gleichzeitig bestand genügend Freiraum eigenen Schwerpunktsetzungen und Strukturen zu folgen und dennoch die Vergleichbarkeit sicherzustellen. Die Debatten flossen dann auch in die Generalberichte und Schlussfolgerungen der einzelnen Kommissionen ein.

Das Kolloquium „Public Money for Public Goods: Nachhaltige Landwirtschaft. Die neue GAP und die Agrarpolitik des Vereinigten Königreichs" war speziell auf den Veranstalter zugeschnitten und befasste sich neben der neuen Gemeinsamen Agrarpolitik der EU insbesondere mit der künftigen Agrarpolitik von England, Wales, Schottland und Nordirland post-Brexit. Ein Einblick in die Konzepte und deren Umsetzung, insbesondere in der EU in die nationalen Strategiepläne und in den UK „Four Nations“ in Agriculture Act 2020 und Agriculture (Wales) Bill 2022 versprach eine interessante Horizonterweiterung. Dies für die EU-Mitgliedstaaten entweder als Inspiration wie eine renationalisierte europäische Agrarpolitik gestaltet werden könnte, oder als Bestärkung beim „gemeinsam“ zu bleiben.[6] Ein solch von allen Teilnehmenden gleichsam außer Programm gemeinsam besuchter Themenblock wurde erst zum zweiten Mal[7] durchgeführt und bewährte sich abermals glänzend. Damit dürfte sich das Format als Ergänzung zur Kommissionsarbeit endgültig etabliert haben.

III. Kommission I

Die im Fragebogen zur Kommission angesprochenen multiplen Krisen sind Realität und stellen uns vor besondere Herausforderungen. Das hier zu bearbeitende Thema zielte dabei auf mögliche Antworten. Aber gibt es solche überhaupt, insbesondere solche im Agrarrecht?

A. Ernährungssicherheit

In ihrer im Fragebogen angesprochenen Mitteilung vom 23. März 2022 betreffend Gewährleistung der Ernährungssicherheit und Stärkung der Widerstandsfähigkeit der Lebensmittelsysteme[8] konstatiert die Europäische Kommission eine weitere Destabilisierung der ohnehin anfälligen Agrar-

6 Vgl. *Bianchi*, Y a-t-il encore quelque chose de « commun » dans la nouvelle Politique agricole commune?, RTDE 2005, S. 623 ff.; *Gilsdorf*, Der Grundsatz der Subsidiarität und die gemeinsame Agrarpolitik, GS Grabitz (1995), S. 77 ff.; *Priebe*, Wie „subsidiär“ kann die Gemeinsame Agrarpolitik sein?, EuZW 1993, S. 425; *ders.*, Differenzierung und Dezentralisierung in der gemeinsamen Agrarpolitik, FS Steinberger (2002), S. 1347; *Seidel*, Rückführung der Landwirtschaftspolitik in die Verantwortung der Mitgliedstaaten? – Rechts- und Verfassungsfragen des Gemeinschaftsrechts, AgrarR 2000, S. 381.

7 Vgl. das Kolloquium „Die Reform der GAP“ am Kongress in Poznań 2019; siehe CEDR (Hrsg.), Food sovereignty, food security and the contribution of agricultural law (2023), S. 375 ff.

8 Mitteilung der Kommission an das Europäische Parlament, den Europäischen Rat, den Rat, den europäischen Wirtschafts- und Sozialausschuss und den Ausschuss der Regionen, „Gewährleistung der Ernährungssicherheit und Stärkung der Widerstandsfähigkeit der Lebensmittelsysteme“ vom 23. März 2022, COM(2022) 133 final.

märkte durch die Ukraine-Invasion. Aufgrund der COVID-19-Pandemie und des Klimawandels stehe die Landwirtschaft weltweit unter Druck. Die Ernährungssicherheit sei schon jetzt durch Dürren, Überschwemmungen und Hitzewellen sowie den Anstieg des Meeresspiegels bedroht und diese Bedrohungen würden aufgrund der Erderwärmung noch weiter zunehmen und insbesondere anfällige Regionen treffen. Auch wenn die Lebensmittelversorgung in der EU derzeit nicht gefährdet sei, die Invasion der Ukraine und eine weltweite Explosion der Rohstoffpreise würden die Preise auf den Märkten für Agrar- und Meereserzeugnisse in die Höhe treiben und die Schwachstellen des Lebensmittelsystems deutlich machen, nämlich die Abhängigkeit von u.a. Energie-, Düngemittel- und Futtermitteleinfuhren. In diesen Ausführungen ist eine gewisse Trostlosigkeit zu spüren, aber auch der alle Klagen verbindende agrarische Blickwinkel wird klar: einmal mehr geht es im Agrarrecht um Ernährungssicherheit und Lebensmittelversorgung. Und die Antworten – internationaler, supranationaler und nationaler Natur – die in der Kommission I vorgestellt und diskutiert worden sind, sind denn auch vornehmlich solche wirtschaftsrechtlichen Charakters.

B. Instrumente

Die genannten Instrumente wie Arbeitskraftregelungen, COVID-Hilfen, Liquiditätssicherung, Ausfuhrbeschränkungen, Begrenzung von Spekulationsgeschäften, Inanspruchnahme der EU-Agrarreserve u.v.m.[9] sind zahlreich, zum Teil sehr differenziert und vermutlich unterschiedlich erfolgreich. Damit scheint auf diesem Weg ein ganzes Instrumentarium zurückzukommen, das sich mit Marktregulierung nur unzutreffend umschreiben lässt. Schlagworte wie Sicherheitsnetze und landwirtschaftliche Reserven, Intervention, Pflichtteillager und Versicherungslösungen klingen nach einer (ohne Not) verlorenen präliberalen Zeit.

Eine dieser längsten und mächtigsten Krisen sind jedoch Klimawandel und Biodiversitätsverlust. Diese Themen, originär Gegenstand des Klimaschutz- und Umweltrechts, sind längst in das Agrarrecht integriert worden[10], noch einmal wesentlich akzentuiert mit der jüngsten GAP-Reform.

9 Landesbericht Deutschland (Kommission I).

10 U.a. *Mögele*, The Integration of Environmental and Climate Protection into the Common Agricultural Policy – Legal Concepts and Developments, EurUP 4/2018, S. 405 ff.; *Norer*, Saving the world under agricultural law or overtaxing it? – On the

Interessanterweise war nun im Krisenmodus zu beobachten, wie auftretenden Interessenskonflikten mittels zeitweiser Aussetzung solcher Regelungen zugunsten der Nahrungsmittelproduktion begegnet wurde.[11] Unweigerlich muss die Frage erlaubt sein, ob sich damit die agrarumwelt- und agrarnaturschutzrechtlichen Regelungen nicht doch als zu ambitioniert und zu wenig ausgewogen erwiesen haben. Ein umweltpolitisches Primat in der Agrarpolitik, das dem eigentlich gleichrangigen Ziel der Ernährungssicherheit nicht ausreichend Rechnung trägt, ist zu hinterfragen. Exemplarisch hat sich das zuletzt in den Diskussionen um das EU-Gesetz zu Wiederherstellung der Natur (EU Nature Restoration Law) im Europäischen Parlament gezeigt.

Den nationalen Gesetzgebern verbleibt hier kaum Spielraum. So wurde zwar in Deutschland die Land- und Ernährungswirtschaft als systemrelevante Infrastruktur anerkannt, wobei die damit verbundenen Rechtswirkungen überschaubar sein dürften.[12] Darüberhinaus zählt dort die „Gewährleistung einer leistungsfähigen Landwirtschaft" verfassungsrechtlich abgesichert zu den anerkannten öffentlichen Interessen.[13] In den Landesberichten finden sich Hinweise auf einfachgesetzliche Legislativakte wie Krisensicherheitsgesetze, Lebensmittelbewirtschaftungs- und Versorgungssicherheitsgesetze sowie finanzielle Unterstützungen zur Krisenbewältigung.[14] Aber auch staatliche Leistungen an Ernteversicherungen und Solidaritätsfonds[15] oder das Schrauben an Zolltarifen[16] sind ein Thema.

---

methodology of integration non-agricultural claims into European agricultural law, CEDR-JRL 1/2022, S. 28 ff.

11 Z.B. Durchführungsbeschluss (EU) 2022/484 zur Ermöglichung von Ausnahmeregelungen von der VO (EU) Nr 1307/2013 und der Delegierten VO (EU) Nr 639/2014 hinsichtlich der Anwendung bestimmter Bedingungen im Zusammenhang mit der Ökologisierungszahlung für das Antragsjahr 2022, ABl. L 98/105; Durchführungsverordnung (EU) 2022/1317 zur Ermöglichung von Ausnahmeregelungen von der VO (EU) 2021/2115 hinsichtlich der Anwendung der Standards für den guten landwirtschaftlichen und ökologischen Zustand (GLÖZ-Standards) 7 und 8 für das Antragsjahr 2023, ABl. L 199/1. Damit sollen verfügbare Flächen so weit wie möglich zur Erzeugung von Lebens- und Futtermitteln genutzt werden können.

12 Landesbericht Deutschland (Kommission I).

13 Landesbericht Deutschland (Kommission I).

14 Landesbericht Österreich (Kommission I); Landesbericht Deutschland (Kommission I); Landesbericht Polen (Kommission I), Unterstützung für die Herstellung von Mineraldünger; Landesbericht Spanien (Kommission I).

15 Landesbericht Österreich (Kommission I); Landesbericht Italien (Kommission I); Landesbericht Polen (Kommission I).

16 Individualbericht Plazas (Kommission I); Landesbericht Frankreich (Kommission I).

In Frankreich und Italien wurde sogar die Ministeriumsbezeichnung geändert[17], in Italien ein neuer Food Sovereignty Fund geschaffen[18], in Polen gibt es zahlreiche auf die Ukraine bezogene Regelungen[19] und in Spanien wurde der nationale GAP-Strategieplan angepasst[20]. Die Beispiele ließen sich fortsetzen.

Im Ringen um einen Interessenausgleich ist die Ausgangslage mitunter prekär. Klima- und umweltschutzrechtliche Interessen kommen sowohl im Klima- und Umweltschutzrecht als auch – in thematisch fokussierter Form – im GAP-Recht zum Ausdruck. Im Gegensatz dazu finden sich die Interessen der Versorgungssicherheit nahezu ausschließlich im Agrarrecht verankert. Mögen auch beide Interessen formal gleichrangig zu beurteilen sein, was mit Art. 39 und Art. 191 AEUV sogar im Primärrecht der Fall ist, so hat sich der bereits seit Jahrzehnten zu beobachtende Prozess der Ökologisierung des Agrarrechts in letzter Zeit noch einmal deutlich akzentuiert. Der Druck zulasten der Erzeugung kommt also systematisch betrachtet zweifach, von außen (Umweltrecht) und innen (Agrarrecht), während die Versorgungsinteressen nur einfach (Agrarrecht) gestützt werden.

Insgesamt scheint, und das haben die Arbeiten in Kommission I m.E. deutlich gezeigt, den vielfältig sich beeinflußenden multiplen Krisen kein juristisches Gesamtkonzept gegenüberzustehen. Ein kleinteiliger wirtschaftsrechtlicher Werkzeugkasten bis hin zur befristeten Aussetzung (ansonsten aber unbehelligt gelassener) agrarrechtlicher Ökoregelungen mag kurzfristig Antworten ermöglichen, erscheint aber nicht ausreichend geeignet, sich für künftige Krisen in geeigneter Weise zu wappnen. Die größte Herausforderung wird denn auch die Koordination der Aktivitäten auf EU-Ebene sein, unter Berücksichtigung der ökonomischen, sozialen und legislativen Unterschiede in den verschiedenen Ländern.[21]

---

17 In Frankreich seit 2022 „Ministère de l'Agriculture et de la Souveraineté Alimentaire"; Landesbericht Frankreich (Kommission I). Siehe dort auch zur Initiative „Food and Agriculture Resilience Mission (FARM)". In Italien seit 2022 „Ministry of Agriculture, Food Sovereignty and Forests"; Landesbericht Italien (Kommission III).

18 Landesbericht Italien (Kommission I).

19 Landesbericht Polen (Kommission I).

20 Landesbericht Spanien (Kommission I).

21 Landesbericht Polen (Kommission I).

C. Resümee

Mögliche Antworten des Agrarrechts auf die gegenwärtigen multiplen Krisen präsentieren sich wie erwartet vielfältig und kleinteilig. Da wird ein Umweltstandard befristet ausgesetzt, hier eine Liquiditätshilfe gesprochen und dort eine Versicherungsunterstützung propagiert. Was fehlt ist ein übergeordnetes und systematisiertes Gesamtkonzept mit dem Ziel einer ganzheitlichen Sicherstellung von Ernährungssicherheit und Resilienz im Agrar- und Lebensmittelsektor und dessen Durchsetzung, notfalls auch gegen entgegenstehende (Umwelt)Interessen.

IV. Kommission II

Die in Kommission II behandelten Überlegungen zu einer neuen Landnutzung unter dem Aspekt von Kohlenstoff, Biodiversität und Nährstoffen sind von grundlegender Bedeutung. Wie im Fragebogen ausgeführt finden ganze 38 % der weltweiten Landnutzung auf landwirtschaftlichen Flächen statt, was diese und damit die Gemeinsame Agrarpolitik und das GAP-Recht und ihren Umgang mit dem Naturkapital in den Fokus rückt. Am augenfälligsten und deshalb auch am häufigsten behandelt wird die Problematik beim Umgang mit Pflanzenschutzmitteln und Düngemitteln.

A. Rechtstitel

Der Verdienst dieser besonders anspruchsvollen Kommission besteht darin, sich auch einmal der Nutzerseite zu widmen, also insbesondere nach den Rechtstiteln der Nutzenden sowie der Bewertung, dem Handel und der Besteuerung zu fragen.

- Was die Nutzungstitel betrifft, so ist zwischen allen Formen des Eigentums[22] – alleiniges oder geteiltes, privates und öffentliches[23] – und für ge-

22 Vgl. den Vorschlag für eine neue Kategorie von „public goods" in Italien; Landesbericht Italien (Kommission II). Eine Definition findet sich im Gesetzentwurf der Rodotà-Kommission, wonach Gemeingüter „Dinge sind, die funktionale Nutzen für die Ausübung der Grundrechte und Freiheiten des Menschen haben" (*Rodota*, Verso i beni comuni, Riv. Crit. Dir. Priv. 2017, S. 495 ff.). Dort auch zum Spezifikum der sog. Land-Banks.

23 Landesbericht Spanien (Kommission II).

wöhnlich der Pacht zu unterscheiden. Damit wird ein traditionell nationaler Rechtsbereich angesprochen, der sich in verfassungsrechtlichen Eigentumsrechten und deren Einschränkung[24] sowie diversen Landpachtrechten[25] manifestiert. Das sind oft sehr alte Rechte wie gerade hier im Vereinigten Königreich oder man denke nur an die commons[26], die vielleicht Hinweise auf nachhaltigere Nutzungsformen bieten können. Das müsste jedoch Gegenstand eines der kommenden Agrarrechtskongresse sein.

- Was Bewertung, Handel und Besteuerung betrifft, zeigt sich in den einzelnen nationalen Rechtsordnungen ein differenziertes Bild.[27] Bonitierungsvorgaben, grüner Grund(stücks)verkehr, Wasser- und Holznutzungsrechte sowie das Steuerrecht unterscheiden durchaus nach Boden, Wasser oder Wald. Ihr Einfluss auf die Thematik ist bisher deutlich hinter jenen ökologischer Regelungen zurückgetreten und ist es wert eingehender untersucht zu werden.

B. Stoffeinträge

Am augenfälligsten wird die Problematik der in Kommission II behandelten Themen beim Umgang mit Pflanzenschutz- und Düngemitteln. Die Diskussionen um insbesondere Glyphosat und Neonicotinoide werden in der Öffentlichkeit leidenschaftlich geführt und haben auch zu bemerkenswerten legislativen Ergebnissen geführt.

So etwa in Deutschland, wo der Einsatz von Pflanzenschutzmitteln in für den Naturschutz bedeutenden Gebieten und an Gewässern unter-

---

24 Insbesondere zur Problematik der Kumulation von Eigentumseingriffen ins agrarische Grundeigentum siehe *Kreuzer*, Mehrfachverplanung von landwirtschaftlichen Nutzflächen, AgrarR 1979, S. 183 und 185; *Schulze-Hagen*, Ausgleich von Mehrfachbelastungen von hoher Hand – DGAR-Ausschuss „Enteignungsrecht" zu Mehrfachbelastungen, AgrarR 1991, S. 188; *Norer*, Land- und forstwirtschaftliches Eigentum – Aktuelle Rechtsfragen, in: Norer/Reinl (Hrsg.), Land- und forstwirtschaftliches Eigentum – aktuelle Rechtsfragen (2004), S. 52 ff.; zuletzt *Holzer/Lienbacher*, Agrarisches Eigentum und seine Beschränkungen (2024), S. 73 ff.

25 Insbesondere Landesbericht Vereinigtes Königreich (Kommission II).

26 *Ostrom*, Governing the commons: The evolution of institutions for collective action (1990); *Elliott/Boland*, Handbook of Research on Cooperatives and Mutuals (2023). Siehe bspw. *Haller/Liechti/Stuber/Viallon/Wunderli*, Balancing the Commons in Switzerland (2021).

27 Vgl. nur Landesbericht Deutschland (Kommission II); Landesbericht Italien (Kommission II); Landesbericht Spanien (Kommission II).

sagt wurde und speziell von Glyphosat im Haus- und Kleingartenbereich und auf Flächen, die von der Allgemeinheit genutzt werden, verboten wurde.[28] Mehr Kreativität bewies dabei der österreichische Gesetzgeber, der – nachdem ein bereits im Parlament beschlossenes generelles Verbot als formal unzulässig von der Europäischen Kommission zurückgewiesen worden war[29] – das Inverkehrbringen von Pflanzenschutzmitteln mit dem Wirkstoff Glyphosat für öffentlich zugängliche Sport- und Freizeitplätze, Schwimmbäder, Kinderbetreuungseinrichtungen, Bildungseinrichtungen, Kinderspielplätze, Park- und Gartenanlagen, Friedhöfe, Einrichtungen der Behindertenhilfe, Einrichtungen der Altenbetreuung, und Gesundheits- und Pflegeeinrichtungen, für den Haus- und Kleingartenbereich sowie für die nicht-berufliche Verwendung, sofern kein Sachkundenachweis vorliegt, verbot.[30] In der Schweiz weckte das Thema den direktdemokratischen Geist, wobei 2021 gleich zwei Volksinitiativen an der Urne deutlich abgelehnt wurden. So forderte die sog. Trinkwasserinitiative[31], dass nur noch diejenigen Landwirtschaftsbetriebe mit Direktzahlungen oder Subventionen unterstützt werden sollen, die u.a. keine Pestizide einsetzen. Die sog. Pestizidinitiative[32] wollte den Einsatz synthetischer Pestizide in der

---

28 §§ 4, 4a Verordnung über Anwendungsverbote für Pflanzenschutzmittel (Pflanzenschutz-Anwendungsverordnung) vom 10. November 1992 (BGBl. I S. 1887). Im Landesbericht Deutschland auch zur Ausweisung von „roten Gebieten“ (Nitratbelastung) und „gelben Gebieten“ (Phosphorbelastung) gemäß Grundwasserverordnung.

29 Dazu *Holzer*, Glyphosatverbot im Spannungsfeld von Unionsrecht und nationalem Recht, in: Norer/ders. (Hrsg.), Agrarrecht Jahrbuch 2020 (2020), S. 246 ff.

30 Art. 3 Abs. 4 Pflanzenschutzmittelgesetz 2011, BGBl. I 2011/10.

31 Die Initiative *„Für sauberes Trinkwasser und gesunde Nahrung – Keine Subventionen für den Pestizid- und den prophylaktischen Antibiotika-Einsatz“* des Vereins „Sauberes Wasser für alle“ beabsichtigte, mit Art. 104 BV den Landwirtschaftsartikel der Bundesverfassung so zu modifizieren, dass die sichere Versorgung der Bevölkerung mit gesunden Lebensmitteln und sauberem Trinkwasser sichergestellt werden soll. Das sollte dadurch erreicht werden, dass nur noch diejenigen Landwirtschaftsbetriebe mit Direktzahlungen oder Subventionen unterstützt werden sollten, die keine Pestizide einsetzen, in ihrer Tierhaltung keinen prophylaktischen Antibiotikaeinsatz betreiben und nur so viele Tiere halten, wie sie ohne Futtermittelimporte ernähren können. Das eidgenössische Parlament empfahl die Initiative zur Ablehnung. Die Initiative wurde schliesslich mit einem deutlichen Mehr von Volk und Ständen in der Abstimmung am 13. Juni 2021 abgelehnt.

32 In dieselbe Kerbe schlug die Eidgenössische Volksinitiative *„Für eine Schweiz ohne synthetische Pestizide“*. Diese Initiative verlangte eine Anpassung von Art. 74 BV betreffend den Umweltschutz, wonach der Einsatz synthetischer Pestizide in der landwirtschaftlichen Produktion, in der Verarbeitung landwirtschaftlicher Erzeugnisse und in der Boden- und Landschaftspflege, wie auch die Einfuhr von Lebensmitteln, die synthetische Pestizide enthalten oder mithilfe solcher hergestellt wurden, generell

landwirtschaftlichen Produktion, in der Verarbeitung landwirtschaftlicher Erzeugnisse und in der Boden- und Landschaftspflege, wie auch die Einfuhr von Lebensmitteln, die synthetische Pestizide enthalten oder mithilfe solcher hergestellt wurden, generell verbieten. Aber auch in anderen Landesberichten wird der – rechtlich zulässige – Einsatz bestimmter Wirkstoffe als umstritten beschrieben.[33]

C. Anreize

Neben dem Ordnungsrecht[34] werden häufig finanzielle Anreize zum Schutz von Naturkapital in der Landwirtschaft gesetzt, vornehmlich durch angebotene Finanzierungen der 1. sowie 2. Säule der GAP in der EU[35] oder in Drittstaaten mittels nationaler Förderungen[36].

Aktuell werden dabei insbesondere die Direktzahlungen als Einfallspforte sichtbar.[37] Diese bieten sich für die hier untersuchten Zwecke unmittelbar an und sind aus Sicht des Umweltschutzes geradezu ideal, weil der Bezug von Direktzahlungen

- für die Landwirte de facto unverzichtbar ist;
- weitgehend flächendeckend erfolgt und damit rasch breite Wirkung in der Fläche erzielt werden kann;
- rechtlich weitgehend problemlos verschärft werden kann (da sich in der Regel keine eigentumsrechtlichen Probleme stellen);

---

verboten werden sollte. Die Initiative und der von der Kommission eingereichte Gegenvorschlag sollten eigentlich zusammen mit der neuen Agrarpolitik (AP22+) behandelt werden. Aufgrund der Sistierung der AP22+ wurde über die Initiative jedoch bereits am 13. Juni 2021 abgestimmt. Volk und Stände folgten der Empfehlung der Bundesversammlung und lehnten die Initiative deutlich ab.

33 So Landesbericht Italien (Kommission II); Landesbericht Spanien (Kommission II), dort auch zur Umsetzung der Nitratrichtlinie 91/676/EWG zum Schutz der Gewässer vor Verunreinigung durch Nitrat aus landwirtschaftlichen Quellen, ABl. L 375/1.

34 Siehe insbesondere den gesetzlich verankerten sog. Absenkpfad in der Schweiz; Landesbericht Schweiz (Kommission II).

35 Landesbericht Frankreich (Kommission II), dort auch zum Labelling; Landesbericht Deutschland (Kommission II); Landesbericht Italien (Kommission II), dort auch zu den Hindernissen der nationalen Implementierung von *payments for ecosystem services (PES)*; Landesbericht Spanien (Kommission II).

36 Landesbericht Schweiz (Kommission II).

37 So *Norer*, Gewässerschutz und Landwirtschaft im Recht: Nutztierhaltung, Produktionsmittel und Verunreinigungsverbot, in: ders. (Hrsg.), Landwirtschaft und Wasser – Gewäserreinhaltung, Gewässerräume und Bewässerung in rechtlicher Perspektive (2023), S. 32 f.

- durch einen effizienten Agrarfördervollzug kontrolliert wird (im Gegensatz zum teilweise wenig effizienten Umweltrechtsvollzug);
- aus dem Agrarbudget erfolgt.

Hier zeigt sich einmal mehr die bereits des Öfteren beobachtete Tendenz des Vollzugs des Umweltrechts durch das Agrarrecht[38], ausgeweitet nunmehr auch auf das Klimaschutzrecht sowie mit der sozialen Konditionalität[39] auf das Arbeits- und Sozialrecht.

D. Verfahrensrechte

Ein wichtiger Punkt kommt hier auch den Verfahrensrechten zu, wo die Rechtsentwicklung aktuell auf zwei verschiedenen Schienen verläuft. Zum einen im klassischen Verfahrensrecht und – erweitert – in der Frage der Justiziabilität von Naturkapitalwerten. Zum anderen und dem vorausgesetzt in der Diskussion über subjektive Rechte der Natur.

- Was das klassische Verfahrensrecht betrifft, ist exemplarisch auf die europäische als auch nationale Rechtsprechung zum Verbandsbeschwerderecht bei der Zulassung von Pflanzenschutzmitteln hinzuweisen. So haben auf supranationaler Ebene die europäischen Gerichte wiederholt den Zulassungsverfahren von Pflanzenschutzmitteln zugrundeliegende Dokumente als Umweltinformationen eingestuft und die damit verbundenen Zugangsrechte von NGOs bejaht.[40] Als Beispiel für einen Nicht-EU-Mitgliedstaat haben etwa in der Schweiz die Höchstgerichte das Verbandsbeschwerderecht im Verfahren des Bundesamts für Landwirtschaft zur gezielten Überprüfung von bewilligten Pflanzenschutzmitteln

---

38 So bereits *Hofer*, Das neue Landwirtschaftsgesetz und dessen Entstehung, BlAR 2/1996, S. 71; kritisch *Norer*, Lebendiges Agrarrecht. Entwicklungslinien und Perspektiven des Rechts im ländlichen Raum (2005), S. 348.

39 Art. 14 VO (EU) 2021/2115 mit Vorschriften für die Unterstützung der von den Mitgliedstaaten im Rahmen der Gemeinsamen Agrarpolitik zu erstellenden und durch den Europäischen Garantiefonds für die Landwirtschaft (EGFL) und den Europäischen Landwirtschaftsfonds für die Entwicklung des ländlichen Raums (ELER) zu finanzierenden Strategiepläne (GAP-Strategiepläne), ABl L 435/1.

40 EuGH Rs. C-442/14 vom 23. November 2016; aber Rs. C-673/13 P vom 23. November 2016. EuG Rs. T-545/11 RENV vom 21. November 2018; Rs. T-716/14 vom 7. März 2019; Rs. T-329/17 vom 7. März 2019, aber Rs. T -725/15 vom 14. Dezember 2018. Siehe auch *Buonsante/Friel*, What is Information Relating to Emissions into the Environment?, EJRR 2017, S. 453 ff.

zugelassen.[41] Beide Rechtsprechungen stehen im Zusammenhang mit der Aarhus-Konvention[42], die einerseits den Zugang zu verwaltungsbehördlichen Verfahren vorschreibt, um die von Privatpersonen und Behörden vorgenommenen Handlungen, die gegen umweltbezogene Bestimmungen verstossen, anfechten zu können (Art. 9 Abs. 3), andererseits die Zurverfügungstellung von Umweltinformationen für die Öffentlichkeit durch die Behörden verlangt (Art. 4 Abs. 1).

Ein zweites und bekannteres Beispiel sind die zahlreichen Klimaklagen.[43] Während derzeit aller Augen auf den EGMR gerichtet sind, hat von den nationalen Urteilen besonders der Klimabeschluss des deutschen Bundesverfassungsgerichts[44] für Aufsehen gesorgt. Zwar wird dort eine Beschwerdebefugnis von Umweltverbänden für Verfassungsbeschwerden abgelehnt und eine Verletzung der Eigentumsgarantie verneint, jedoch wird eine grundsätzliche Schutzpflicht des Staates hinsichtlich des Eigentums in Bezug auf Gefahren des Klimawandels bejaht.

- Was subjektive Rechte der Natur betrifft, so werden diese Fragen seit Jahrzehnten diskutiert, ohne freilich – so zumindest mein Eindruck – zu einem wesentlichen Fortschritt gekommen zu sein.[45] Trotz Forderungen nach einem weitgehenden Einbezug von Naturentitäten und somit etwa auch von Wäldern oder Gewässern (man denke nur an die Salzwasserlagune Mar Menor in Spanien)[46], fokussiert sich die Diskussion derzeit

---

41 Bundesgericht: BGer 1C_312/2017 vom 12. Februar 2018. Siehe auch *Thurnherr*, Anmerkung der Redaktion, URP 2018, S. 214 ff.
Bundesverwaltungsgericht: BVGer, Urteil B-64/2016 vom 25. April 2017; Urteile B-662/2016, B-663/2016, B-665/2016 und B-666/2016 vom 3. April 2019; Urteile B-532/2019, B-535/2019 und B-556/2019 vom 25. Oktober 2019. Siehe auch *Seferovic*, Ideelle Verbandsbeschwerde im Zulassungsverfahren für Pflanzenschutzmittel? – Ein Beitrag zum Begriff der Bundesaufgabe nach Art. 2 NHG, URP 2017, S. 418 ff.

42 Übereinkommen über den Zugang zu Informationen, die Öffentlichkeitsbeteiligung an Entscheidungsverfahren und den Zugang zu Gerichten in Umweltangelegenheiten (Aarhus-Konvention) vom 25. Juni 1998.

43 Landesbericht Deutschland (Kommission II).

44 BVerfG, Beschluss des Ersten Senats vom 24. März 2021 – 1 BvR 2656/18. Siehe Landesbericht Deutschland (Kommission II und III).

45 Landesbericht Deutschland (Kommission II) betreffend die bayerische Initiative „Rechte der Natur", welche über einen Volksentscheid einen Art. 101 in die Bayerische Verfassung aufnehmen möchte.

46 Landesbericht Spanien (Kommission II). Zu den Naturklagen insbesondere *„Seehunde in der Nordsee"*, VG Hamburg, Beschluss vom 22.09.1988 – 7 VG 2499/88; *„Massentötung von Rindern"*, VG Frankfurt a.M., Beschluß vom 01.03. 2001 – 1 G 429/01; *„Kivalina"*, Native Village of Kivalina v. ExxonMobil Corp., 696 F.3d 849 (2012); *„Ganges und Yamuna"*, High Court of Uttarakhand at Nainital, 126/2014, Order v.

auf die Tierrechte und damit auch auf die Kritik an der landwirtschaftlichen Nutztierhaltung[47]. Ein Wandel unseres letztlich anthropozentrisch ausgerichteten Rechtssystems hin zu einem ökozentrischen Modell wird in Rechtswissenschaft und Rechtsphilosophie zum Teil kontrovers diskutiert.[48]

E. Resümee

Überlegungen zu neuen Formen der Landnutzung und insbesondere Fragen von Bewertung, Handel und Besteuerung von Naturkapital werden selten grundlegend gestellt. Rechtlich betrachtet greifen hier supranationale und nationale Regelungen mitunter besonders eng ineinander und sorgen für eine der Rechtsanwendung wenig förderliche und unangenehme Kompilation. Die Palette landwirtschaftlicher Produktionsmittel erweitert sich wegen des wissenschaftlichen Fortschritts in manchen Bereichen bedeutend, man denke nur an die neuen Pflanzenzüchtungen (NGT), der rechtliche Rahmen wird im Gegensatz dazu immer enger. Juristische Kleinkriege zwischen EU-Recht und nationalem Recht, wie bei Glyphosat zu beobachten, bringen wenig und erschweren die Einsicht, dass auch die technisierte moderne Landwirtschaft auf Dünge- und Futtermittel, Pflanzenschutzmittel und Saatgut angewiesen ist, wenn sie die Ernährungssicherheit garantieren soll. Das gilt auch, wenn man die Aarhus-Konvention weit interpretiert oder Naturentitäten subjektive Rechte zuweist.

V. Kommission III

Der Fragebogen zu Kommission III wurde dieses Mal besonders ausführlich erstellt, da darin relevante Themenfelder ziemlich abschließend abgefragt wurden. Daher ist es nicht verwunderlich, dass auch die Antworten

---

20.03.2017 – Supreme Court of India, 07.07.2017; „*Urgenda*", The Hague District Court C/09/456689/HA ZA 13-1396 (2015), Urgenda Foundation v. The State of the Netherlands; „Huaraz", OLG Hamm, seit 2018 anhängiges Berufungsverfahren I-5 U 15/17, Saúl Luciano Lliuya/RWE.

47 Statt vieler *Stucki*, Grundrechte für Tiere: Eine Kritik des geltenden Tierschutzrechts und rechtstheoretische Grundlegung von Tierrechten im Rahmen einer Neupositionierung des Tieres als Rechtssubjekt (2018).

48 Landesbericht Deutschland (Kommission II) m.w.N.

teilweise sehr umfassend ausgefallen sind. Landesberichte von teilweise mehr als 60 Seiten haben mich sehr beeindruckt.[49] Es ist unmöglich, dieser präsentierten Breite hier auch nur annähernd gerecht werden zu können. Deshalb seien hier nur ein paar wenige Punkte herausgegriffen.

A. Strategien statt Normen

Der Europäischen Kommission und überhaupt den europäischen Gesetzgebern stehen bekanntlich die Handlungsformen des Art. 289 AEUV zur Verfügung, also Verordnungen, Richtlinien, Beschlüsse usw. Aktionspläne und Strategien hingegen finden sich dort nicht aufgeführt. Gleichwohl wird man derzeit mit einer Vielzahl solch rechtlich unverbindlicher Absichtserklärungen überflutet: Green Deal, Farm to Fork Strategie, Biodiversitätsstrategie, ökologischer Landbau, ländlicher Raum, Bodenstrategie oder „Fit for 55". Visionen folgen Strategien und Aktionspläne, Strategien und Aktionsplänen folgen Leitlinien und Leitlinien folgen Legislativvorschläge. D.h. nicht, dass dem keine „harten" Regularien folgen können, wie z.B. das bereits erwähnte Gesetz zur Wiederherstellung der Natur (EU Nature Restoration Law) bewiesen hat. Gleichwohl entsteht der Eindruck, dass die Umsetzung dieser Themenfelder einen breiten und unübersichtlichen Mix neuer supranationaler und nationaler Regelungen hervorbringen wird.[50] Polen hat sogar eine Beschwerde beim EuGH eingebracht.[51]

Das Gegenprogramm scheint es in den USA zu geben, wo die zentralen Farm Bills wichtige agrar- und ernährungspolitische Maßnahmen festlegen, die viele Aspekte des ländlichen Rechts in den Vereinigten Staaten regeln.[52]

B. GAP-Umsetzung

In den Antworten der Landesberichte zum Thema der Umsetzung der neuen GAP-Strategiepläne zeigt sich in beeindruckender Weise die damit verbundene Renationalisierung der vorgeblich „Gemeinsamen" Agrarpolitik. Die Entscheidungsspielräume werden in aller Breite genutzt und die

49 Vgl. Landesbericht Polen (Kommmission III) als Gemeinschaftswerk.
50 Vgl. Individualbericht Perteguer Prieto (Kommission III) in Bezug auf die spanischen Landregister.
51 In Bezug auf „Fit for 55"; Landesbericht Polen (Kommission III).
52 Landesbericht USA (Kommission III).

Fülle an national unterschiedlichen Angeboten scheint verwirrend. Ebenso die dadurch hervorgerufene Normsetzungstätigkeit der Mitgliedstaaten, die der Genehmigung der einzelnen Strategiepläne folgt.[53] Diese erfolgt in der Regel sehr detailliert.[54]

Dass sich dabei Umsetzungsprobleme stellen, ist wohl unvermeidbar. Diese reichen von der gar nicht so simplen Frage nach der Rechtsnatur der Strategiepläne[55] und bis hin zu inhaltlichen Fragen[56].

C. Wertschöpfungskette

Was die Stärkung der Stellung der Landwirte in der Wertschöpfungskette betrifft, so haben dazu verschiedene Mitgliedstaaten in Umsetzung der UTP-Richtlinie[57] nationale Legislativakte erlassen.[58] Nicht-EU-Mitgliedstaaten wie die Schweiz kennen keine vergleichbaren Regelungen.[59]

So etwa Deutschland mit einem Gesetz zur Stärkung der Organisationen und Lieferketten im Agrarbereich, das Anerkennung und kartellrechtliche Freistellung von Agrarorganisationen und Verbote unlauterer Handelsprak-

53 Landesbericht Frankreich (Kommsion III); Landesbericht Deutschland (Kommission III) auf Bundes- und Landesebene; Landesbericht Slowenien (Kommission III); Landesbericht Spanien (Kommission III).

54 Vgl. nur bspw. die zahlreichen Begriffsbestimmungen in den deutschen Umsetzungsakten; Landesbericht Deutschland (Kommission III). In Italien umfasst bereits der Nationale Strategieplan mehr als 4000 Seiten; Landesbericht Italien (Kommission III).

55 Siehe *Holzer*, Grundsätzliches zur Umsetzung der GAP-Reform 2023-2027 in Österreich, in: Norer/ders. (Hrsg.), Agrarrecht Jahrbuch 2023 (2023), S. 173 ff. Diese Frage ist aufgrund der bisher geübten Umsetzung der GAP in Österreich sowohl im öffentlichen als auch im Privatrecht von großer Bedeutung.

56 Landesbericht Deutschland (Kommission III).

57 RL (EU) 2019/633 über unlautere Handelspraktiken in den Geschäftsbeziehungen zwischen Unternehmen in der Agrar- und Lebensmittelversorgungskette, ABl. L 111/59.

58 Siehe *Paredis/Keirsbilck/Terryn/Verdonk*, Unfair Trading Practices in the Agricultural and Food Supply Chain. Implementation of Directive (EU) 2019/663 in the EU-27 (2024); *Mögele/Sitar*, in: Montag/Säcker/Bien/Meier-Beck, Münchener Kommentar zum Wettbewerbsrecht, 4. Aufl. (2022), C. Landwirtschaft, Rn. 482 ff.; *Daskalova*, Regulating Unfair Trading Practices in the EU Food Supply Chain, in: Lianos/Ivanov/Davis, Global Food Value Chains and Competition Law (2022), S. 373 ff.

59 Landesbericht Schweiz (Kommission III).

tiken regelt.[60] In Polen, Slowenien und Spanien wurde eine bereits bestehende nationale Regelung entsprechenden Anpassungen unterzogen.[61] Andere Länder setzen daneben auf steuerliche Erleichterungen[62] oder Kapitalzuschüsse und zinsverbilligte Darlehen an Unternehmen der Agrar- und Ernährungswirtschaft.[63]

D. Mehr Pflichten oder Rechte?

Insgesamt könnte man sich nach der Lektüre der Berichte und den Diskussionen in Kommission III die Frage stellen, ob denn unter dem Strich insgesamt mehr Pflichten oder mehr Rechte für die Landwirte geschaffen wurden.

Abgesehen vom Langzeitprojekt der Vereinfachung der GAP[64] ist die Frage wohl nicht eindeutig zu beantworten. Einerseits finden sich Bewertungen insbesondere zum Bereich Organisation und Durchführung der landwirtschaftlichen Tätigkeit, wonach ein legislativ bedingter erhöhter Aufwand zulasten der Betriebe ausgemacht wird.[65] Diese gestiegenen Verpflichtungen können aber wohl nicht nur dem Europarecht angelastet werden, sondern gehen oft auch auf nationale Gesetzgebung oder Rechtsprechung zurück.[66] Andererseits lassen sich auch – zart, aber doch – so etwas wie Entlastungen oder zumindest versuchte Entlastungen ausmachen.

60 Agrarorganisationen-und-Lieferketten-Gesetz (AgrarOLkG) vom 24. August 2021 (BGBl. I S. 4036); Landesbericht Deutschland (Kommission III). Siehe auch Landesbericht Italien (Kommission III).

61 Landesbericht Polen (Kommission III); Landesbericht Slowenien (Kommission III), siehe den sog. Food Supply Chain Relationships Ombudsman; Landesbericht Spanien (Kommission III), siehe die sog. standard agri-food contracts.

62 Landesbericht Frankreich (Kommission III); Landesbericht Polen (Kommission III).

63 Sog. Supply Chain Contracts and District; Landesbericht Italien (Kommission III).

64 Siehe *Norer/Bloch*, G. Agrarrecht, in: Dauses (Hrsg.), Handbuch des EU-Wirtschaftsrechts, Bd. 1 (29. Ergänzungslieferung 2011), Rz. 268 ff. m.w.N. Vgl. auch Simplification of the EU's Common Agricultural Policy (CAP), https://www.consilium.europa.eu/en/policies/cap-simplification/.

65 Landesbericht Deutschland (Kommission III).

66 Bspw. in Deutschland auf nationale Gesetzgebung (Änderungen bei Agrarstatistik, Umsatzsteuerpauschalierung und Aufzeichnungsvorgaben für Tierhalter, strengeren Vorgaben zum Pflanzenschutz und Schutz von Insekten im Bundesnaturschutzgesetz) und auf Rechtsprechung (Vorgaben des Bundesverwaltungsgerichts betreffend das Verbot von männlichen Hühner-Küken); Landesbericht Deutschland (Kommission III).

So wurde in den Niederlanden ein neues Umwelt- und Planungsgesetz erlassen, das 26 Gesetze, 60 Regierungsverordnungen und 75 Ministerialverordnungen ersetzt.[67] Auch bereits die bloße Beibehaltung bewährter Regelungen kann vielleicht darunter gezählt werden.[68]

E. Resümee

Das Resümee dieser Kommission vom letzten Kongress[69] kann, wenngleich vier Jahre her, ungeschaut übernommen werden. Angesichts vergleichbarer Problemlagen und der für die meisten Berichte einigenden Klammer der GAP erstaunt immer wieder die Vielfalt an berichteten Themen, Akzenten und Formen. Mag man der EU im Kreativitätsrausch des Green Deal zwischen all den Visionen, Strategien, Aktionsplänen und Legislativvorschlägen eine ordnende Hand absprechen, so muss das auch für die nationalen Gesetzgeber gelten. Eifrig wird an der Umsetzung der europarechtlichen Vorgaben gewerkt, der möglichst idealen Einpassung in die bestehende nationale Rechtslandschaft und als wenn das nicht genug wäre, noch zusätzlich an der Anreicherung um nationale Erweiterungen (Gold-plating[70]). Das wird in den wenigsten Fällen geeignet sein zu einer Reduktion von Pflichten und Administrativlasten der praktizierenden Landwirtschaft beizutragen.

---

67 Der Zweck dieses Gesetzes ist es, verschiedene Gesetze und Vorschriften in den Bereichen Bauwesen, Umwelt, Wasser, Raumplanung und Natur zusammenzufassen, um die Vorschriften für Raumordnungsprojekte und das Lebensumfeld zu vereinfachen. Auch der Agrarsektor und auf Agrarrecht spezialisierte Juristen sind von diesem Gesetz betroffen, da es Vorschriften zum Grundbesitz und zur Landnutzung in Randgebieten enthält; Landesbericht Niederlande (Kommission III).

68 Landesbericht Schweiz (Kommission III).

69 *Norer*, Synthesebericht, in: CEDR (Hrsg.), Food sovereignty, food security and the contribution of agricultural law (2023), S. 493.

70 https://en.wikipedia.org/wiki/Gold-plating_(EU_law).

VI. Kolloquium[71]

Schließlich zeigt das Kolloquium, dass es viel zu verlieren gibt. Es geht gerade auch um die Leistungen, die die Landwirtschaft im bewährten multifunktionalen Konzept erbringt. Diese sind mit der Landwirtschaft verbunden – entweder direkt, weil sie gleichsam als Nebenprodukt im „Kielwasser"[72] landwirtschaftlicher Bewirtschaftung (oder bei ökologischen Ausgleichsflächen auch Nicht-Bewirtschaftung) anfallen, oder indirekt, weil es sich um Leistungen handelt, die sich von klassischer agrarischer Tätigkeit entfernt haben. Der Versuch, solche multifunktionalen Leistungen zu definieren und sie mittels Internalisierung externer Kosten in Wert zu setzen, hat das Agrarrecht teilweise intensiv beschäftigt.[73]

Irgendwie erinnert die aktuelle Debatte um „Public money for public goods" an diese uns wohlbekannten Entwicklungen. In einem ersten Schritt muss ein solches „öffentliches Gut" gefunden und definiert werden,[74] in einem zweiten Schritt muss jemand – hier wohl die Politik, vielleicht sogar die öffentliche Meinung widerspiegelnd – diese Leistung auch als öffentliches Gut anerkennen und bereit sein, dafür öffentliche Gelder zu verwenden. Der einzige Unterschied zum Multifunktionalitätskonzept, darauf hat *Mögele* in seinem Statement hingewiesen, dürfte darin bestehen, dass diese abgeltbaren Leistungen bisher als „Nebenleistungen" zur Landwirtschaft verstanden wurden – immerhin geht es ja hier um Agrarpolitik –, während sich im „Public money for public goods"-Konzept diese Nebenleistungen zu verselbständigen drohen und sich zur Hauptleistung aufschwingen wollen, womit sie aber m.E. endgültig die kompetenzrechtlich ohnehin sehr großzügige GAP zu verlassen scheinen.

Beispiele wurden viele genannt. Die umwelt-, natur- und klimaschutzrechtlichen öffentlichen Güter sind allgemein bekannt, Landschaftsschutz oder Schutz vor Naturgefahren müssen diskutiert werden, ebenso wie Ver-

71 Siehe auch *Busse/Mögele/Petetin*, Das Kolloquium „Public money for public goods" im Rahmen des XXXI. Europäischen Agrarrechtskongresses des CEDR in Cardiff, AUR 2024, S. 2 ff.

72 Die heute nicht mehr vertretene „Kielwassertheorie" besagt, dass die meisten gesellschaftsnützlichen Funktionen kostenlos im Kielwasser der land- und forstwirtschaftlichen Produktion folgen. Vgl. *Glück*, Das Elend der Kielwassertheorie, Internationaler Holzmarkt 5/1982, S. 15 ff.

73 Vgl. *Norer* (Hrsg.), Agrarische Diversifikation – rechtliche Aspekte von Agrotourismus bis Energieerzeugung (2013).

74 Grundlegend *Vanni*, Agriculture and Public Goods. The Role of Collective Action (2014).

sorgungssicherheit und Besiedlung peripherer Gebiete. Egal wie man nun die öffentlichen Güter theoretisch positioniert – und da spricht viel dafür sie „öffentlichen Interessen" gleichzuhalten – hilft es, wenn der Gesetzgeber diese bereits als von öffentlichem Interesse bzw. als Rechtsgut normativ verankert hat.

Um ein Beispiel zu geben: Im Zusammenhang mit der Wolfsproblematik und deren Auswirkung auf die Weidehaltung in den Alpen musste ich mit den öffentlichen Interessen, die für eine Almbewirtschaftung sprechen, auseinandersetzen. Die Bestoßung mit Nutztieren während der Sommermonate bringt überraschend viele Effekte mit sich, die alle für sich von öffentlichem Interesse sind. Ohne allzu sehr ins Detail zu gehen: Die Almbewirtschaftung

1. hält die Landschaft offen (andernfalls würden die freien Bergwiesen allmählich zuwachsen), was insbesondere für den Tourismus von Bedeutung ist;
2. erhält die alpine Biodiversität (der Artenreichtum ist auf bestoßenen Bergmähdern ein Vielfaches höher als auf nicht gepflegten oder eben zugewachsenen Flächen);
3. schützt vor Naturgefahren (insbesondere Schutz vor Erosion und Lawinen);
4. erhält traditionelle Bewirtschaftungsformen und pflegt das kulturelle Erbe;
5. entlastet die Landwirtschaftsbetriebe vom Zukauf (importierter) Futtermittel in den Talbetrieben;
6. steigert die Qualität der landwirtschaftlichen Produkte und kann mit entsprechendem Labelling („Alpkennzeichnung") mehr Wertschöpfung erzielen;

   usw.

Was dabei erstaunt: Nahezu jeder dieser multifunktionalen Effekte findet sich auch in entsprechenden Normen als von öffentlichem Interesse verankert. Hier in diesem Beispiel etwa im Völkerrecht (UNESCO Übereinkommen zur Erhaltung des immateriellen Kulturerbes, Alpenkonvention), im Europarecht (2. Säule der GAP mit Agrarumweltmaßnahmen, FFH-Richtlinie) oder im nationalen Recht auf Bundesebene (bspw. auf Verfassungsstufe in Österreich die Versorgungssicherheit im BVG Nachhaltigkeit[75]) oder regionaler und lokaler Ebene (bspw. in Österreich die Almschutzgesetze diverser Bundesländer).

Wir müssen folglich unseren Fokus über das Agrarrecht hinaus richten und für die Frage der Anerkennung und Inwertsetzung bestimmter öffentlicher Güter solche normativen Verankerungen in die Diskussion werfen bzw. solche schaffen. Damit werden sie zu sichtbaren, normativ verankerten Interessen, die bei der gesellschaftlichen Aushandlung von „public goods" nicht ohne weiteres übersehen werden können.[76]

VII. Abschluss

Zum Schluss eine kurze Bilanz dieses Kongresses. 11 Stunden Kommissionsarbeit, 2 Stunden Kolloquium, 9 Stunden Essen. Ich liebe walisische Kekse. Ich glaube, Hog Roast kann man in Zukunft nur noch in walisischen Heckenreihen genießen. Walisischer Whiskey ist großartig. Walisisch zu lernen ist wahrscheinlich weniger kompliziert als die agrarpolitischen Visionen der vier Nationen des Vereinigten Königreichs zu verstehen. Ich werde meine Gartenhecke in Zukunft nur noch mit einem Viehtransporter schneiden. Vielleicht können Sie einigen meiner Eindrücke zustimmen.

Die Kommissionen I und II haben den Krisen getrotzt und gezeigt, dass insbesondere ein krisenfesteres Agrarumweltrecht notwendig ist, das auch die Ernährungssicherheit ausreichend berücksichtigt. Darüber hinaus müssen neue Formen der Flächennutzung auf umfassenden Überlegungen beruhen, die nicht nur den Stoffeintrag, sondern auch die Rahmenbedingungen der Nutzung, des Handels und der Besteuerung einbeziehen.

Angesichts der derzeit grassierenden Brüsseler „Strategie" und einer stärker renationalisierten neuen GAP hat die Kommission III dem nationalen Gesetzgeber einen größeren Spielraum eröffnet, der möglichst nicht zu mehr Verpflichtungen für die Landwirte führen sollte.

---

75 Bundesverfassungsgesetz über die Nachhaltigkeit, den Tierschutz, den umfassenden Umweltschutz, die Sicherstellung der Wasser- und Lebensmittelversorgung und die Forschung, BGBl. I 2013/111.

76 Damit kann der Boden bereitet werden für die wichtige, aber nicht mehr juristische Frage der monetären Bewertung solcher Leistungen. Was die Ökosystemleistungen betrifft, ist man meinem Eindruck nach schon sehr weit, während die Bewertung von etwa Landschaftsbildern oder Erholungswirkungen erst angedacht worden ist.

Schließlich zeigte das Kolloquium die Verhandlung des Ansatzes „public money for public goods“ auf und belegte die Bedeutung einer rechtlichen Verankerung originärer agrar- und ernährungsrechtlicher Interessen.

Allerdings: Letztlich bleibt auf ewig eine Lücke in der zweijährigen Abfolge unserer Kongresse, 2017 Lille, 2019 Poznań, 2023 Cardiff. 2021? Das war vielleicht der intime Kongress mit uns selbst und dem Stemmen gegen die Krisen. Der Kongress, der nur in unseren Gedanken und Herzen stattgefunden hat, an einem jeden für uns an einem anderen Ort, zu unterschiedlichen Zeiten und Themenschwerpunkten. Unsere Arbeit hier hat bewiesen, dass das Agrarrecht einen bedeutenden Beitrag zur Bewältigung von vielfältigen, mutiplen Krisen zu leisten imstande ist. Da müssen wir weitermachen. Denn wir wollen keine weitere Lücke in der Agenda. Wir wollen uns 2025 wieder treffen, wo hoffentlich manche der Krisen bewältigt oder zumindest eingedämmt sind. Vielleicht auch gerade wegen des Agrarrechts. Um den Kreis zu schließen: Hoffentlich haben wir gelernt, unsere Drachen zu zähmen.

Danke für Ihre Aufmerksamkeit!

VII.
Liste des Rapports nationaux – List of National Reports – Liste der Landesberichte

Liste des Rapports nationaux – List of National Reports – Liste der Landesberichte

Les rapports nationaux suivants ont été présentés au XXXIe Congrès et Colloque Européen de Droit Rural. Ils sont accessibles sur le site Internet du C.E.D.R, cf. www.cedr.org.

Country	Commission I	Commission II	Commission III
President			
	Rudy **Gotzen**	Alex Carson **Taylor**	Franci **Avsec**
General Reporter			
	Alicia **Epstein**	Catherine **Taskis**	Aneta **Suchoń**
National Reports			
Austria	David **Sams**		
France	Bernard **Valluis** Jean-Baptiste **Millard**	Luc **Bodiguel**	Christine **Lebel** Manon **Sahut**
Germany	Anna **Kiermeier**	Friederike **Heise** Cara **von Nolting**	Hendrik **Kurth** Anna-Lena **Poppe**
Hungary	István **Olajos** Tamás **Andréka**	Anikó **Raisz**	Anikó **Raisz** Zsófia **Hornyák** János Ede **Szilágyi**
Italy	Laura **Costantino**	Mario **Mauro**	Margherita **Brunori**
Netherlands			Jeroen **Rheinfeld**
Poland	Dorota **Łobos-Kotowska** Jerzy **Bieluk** Katarzyna **Leśkiewicz** Izabela **Lipińska** Aneta **Suchoń** Paweł **Gała** Joanna **Mikołajczyk** Monika **Łata** Marek **Stańko** Tomasz **Marzec**		Paweł **Blajer** Monika A. **Król** Przemyslaw **Litwiniuk** Konrad **Marciniuk** Agata **Niewiadomska** Adam **Niewiadomski** Jakub **Pietrzak** Paweł **Wojciechowski**
Slovenia			Franci **Avsec**

Spain	Esther **Muñiz Espada** Teresa **Rodríguez-Cachón**	María José **Cazorla Gonzáles** Fernando **del Moral Torres**	Pablo **Amat-Llombart** Juan Manuel **López Torre**
Switzerland		Stephanie **Hug**	Paul **Richli**
UK		Mike **Holland**	Mike **Holland**
USA			Margaret **Rosso Grossman**
Individual	María **Aránzazu Calzadilla Medina**	Christopher **Rodger**	Rocío **Perteguer Prieto**
	Nelson **Plazas**		